The Dragon of Lochlan Hall

Highlander: The Legends, Volume 9

Rebecca Ruger

Published by Rebecca Ruger, 2024.

ISBN: 9798333588166

Written by Rebecca Ruger

Chapter One

Summer 1307
Saunt Ceerus, Scotland

SHE HADN'T TRAVELED far or often in her life, but she had yet to find a place as dramatic or as magnificent as home. The landscape surrounding Lochlan Hall swept along the sandy shore of the Aberdeenshire coast, just north of Montrose. With towering sea cliffs and swathes of beautiful beaches, the fortress was surrounded by an ever-changing view of the sea, a rich colony of sand dunes and flower-rich meadows, the vista never less than stunning.

Wildflowers thrived in the inland grasslands, sheltered from the sea by the cliffs and dunes. Now, at the height of summer, they were a riot of color—the deep violet of clustered bellflower, the vivid red of the delicate maiden pink plant, and the pale purple of the knapweed.

The cliffs themselves were home to hardier species, able to cope with the thin soil. Sea pink, or thrift, filled the crevices while her favorite, the cascading white sea campion dripped graciously down the cliff face. Gray and white fulmars nested in sheltered nooks at the top of the cliffs and less often, peregrine falcons might be spotted as well.

The beach directly below Lochlan Hall stretched for more than a mile, the shore flat and the beach wide. Sand dunes mounded at both the north and south ends and only a few plants were able to survive there, marram grass and the gray-green sea-lyme grass. In the spring there might be purple vetch and blue forget-me-nots, but their color had months ago faded.

The beach was rarely vacant or without industry. Unless one ventured beyond the northern bend, around a rocky outcropping where the sea could sometimes dash a person against the bare-faced rock, it was rare to find sanctuary or solitude on the beach.

Raina MacQueen sat, as she did once a week, upon a chair and at a table planted in the sand, surveying the scene. Lochlan Hall's fishing industry was alive here at the edge of the sea.

Nets, dark and heavy with recent use, were stretched out over wooden frames, drying in the sun. A row of simple fish weirs, constructed from wooden stakes and woven branches, jutted into the tidal waters, guiding fish into traps with the rhythmic push of the waves. Currachs, the small, rounded lightweight boats, bobbed gently at the water's edge, ready for the next outing.

Nearby, a series of wooden racks held the day's catch, salmon and other fish glistening in the sunlight as they dried. Smoke curled from a few low huts, the rich scent of smoking fish punctuating the tangy sea air. Inside, rows of salmon hung from hooks, curing slowly over smoldering fires.

Workers stood at cleaning stations, their hands swift and efficient as they gutted and cleaned the fish. The offal was collected in wooden basins, soon to be discarded or repurposed as bait.

Barrels of salt were lined up under a makeshift shelter, ready to preserve the next batch of the harvest.

Raina's gaze shifted to the storage area where barrels and baskets of processed salmon were neatly stacked, awaiting transport. Nearby, a group of men loaded the packed fish into a sturdy knarr, Lochlan's lone cargo ship, its hull wider and deeper than the currachs, built for greater voyages, ready to carry the cargo forty miles to Aberdeen.

More than twenty people were busy upon the beach on the weekly shipping day, but none spoke to her. Even when they lined up to receive their benefit, the coins Raina would record and disperse, they would scarcely deign to speak to her. At best, they were cool, only woodenly polite, as if they expected her wrath if they were not. At worst, they sneered and scowled at her, hardly bothering to conceal their disdain.

She was Lady Raina in their eyes, entitled daughter of an unkind lord.

Suspected witch as well, she was too often compelled to acknowledge, or meanly reminded. Though it took great effort, she preferred not to think about that unjust, unwarranted accusation.

Recently returned from her aunt's house near Glasgow, where she'd spent the last three years in search of a suitable match—her father's hope and definitely not hers—she had also become known, to her everlasting chagrin, as the *Killer of Men*.

Rubbish, all of it. As if she'd had a hand in the death of her betrothed.

Any of them.

All three of them.

She'd had no say in the choice or in the bargaining, had held her head high as her aunt paraded her hither and yon, to this manor house and that keep, primarily in and around Glasgow where wealthy families abounded apparently. The meetings were arranged by her father, the introductions managed by her surly aunt. Raina thought her father must have offered his sister a reward; she could imagine no other incentive, as the woman was as cheerless in those endeavors as she was to Raina herself.

William MacLeod, her final suitor, she had mourned to some degree, as she had been fond of him. Fond mayhap was too strong; she had appreciated that he wasn't ancient, crooked, blind in one eye, or the owner of a grotesque lecherous stare, traits known by her two previous suitors-cum-betrothed. Raina had viewed him as the lesser of all evils presented to her as a possible lifelong mate. However, he was known to have a bit of a temper and that—and not any wish or witchcraft of Raina—had been what killed him. Known as well for his fondness for drink, MacLeod got into a violent altercation at a tavern. The brawl escalated, and he was fatally wounded by a knife thrust. His death was swift, ending his betrothal to Raina and sparking a brief investigation that concluded with little fanfare.

Her first betrothed, Sir Andrew Carmichael—the one-eyed, bent baron from Barrhead—was four years older than Raina's own father, who'd been in the autumn of his years when Raina was born twenty-four years ago. She'd been forced to shout simply to have conversation with the baron. He'd smelled of stale sweat and sour wine, and his skin was pallid and liver-spotted, hanging loosely from his gaunt frame.

She'd cried into her pillow for three nights straight when the contracts had been signed and the wedding date set, unable to rouse a smile in any hour of any day until the news came, three weeks before they would have wed, that he'd died in his sleep.

Naught but a scandalous four months later, she'd become the intended of Baron Whitehall, a man notorious for his unsavory reputation. A corpulent and greasy merchant from Dundee, the baron had an unsettling habit of invading her personal space, standing too close, his breath hot and smelling faintly of onions and ale. His hands, pudgy and damp, would often find excuses to brush against her, the touch lingering far too long. His laughter, a high-pitched, wheezing cackle, had grated on her nerves, having become the content of more than one nightmare.

The baron had succumbed to a sudden and severe illness that swept through Dundee. Despite the efforts of the best healers and herbalists, he deteriorated rapidly, his body unable to withstand the fever that ravaged him. His death, while tragic, was viewed by Raina as a merciful release.

With each death, the whispers grew louder. The once-bright prospect of marriage now seemed a grim impossibility, tainted by loss and rumor. She'd been brought home—still unwed, in mortifying humiliation, she was quite well aware—to attend her father, as he himself had been laid low by a grave illness.

He lay up there now, inside the vast fortress, all his never-ending schemes, for wealth, for power, for accolades, seeming only wasted endeavors when he'd failed in so many other areas, as a husband, a father, and a man.

Laird Malcolm MacQueen had never been a kind man, or rather he'd been kind and generous only to his ambition, which knew no bounds, He'd been ruthless in his pursuit of status and riches, often at the expense of those closest to him. To him, family was merely a means to an end, each person a tool to be used in his relentless climb to prominence.

As a husband, he had been distant and cold, more concerned with alliances and dowries than with love or companionship. Raina's mother had spent her days in lonely isolation, her spirit gradually eroded by Malcolm's indifference and harshness. When Lisbeth MacQueen passed eleven years ago, Raina felt as if she were the only one who mourned.

As a father, Malcolm had shown little affection or warmth towards Raina. She was naught but a pawn in his intricate game of power, her worth measured by the suitors she could attract and the alliances she could secure. Only the war with England and her father's part in it had saved her from an earlier marriage. Each betrothal he arranged was calculated to enhance his standing, with no regard for her feelings or happiness. Her fears and aspirations were dismissed as inconsequential, her dreams crushed under the weight of his expectations. Malcolm's iron-fisted rule over Lochlan Hall was mirrored in his dealings with his daughter. His words were often sharp, laced with criticism and disappointment; often he spoke with his fists or an open hand. He demanded perfection yet offered no guidance or support. Any show of weakness was met with scorn, any plea for understanding ignored.

Her brother had scarcely received either more notice or affection, despite being Malcolm's heir. More than a year had passed since Donald had been lost to the war. Once Raina and Donald had been close, once she had adored her older brother, had cherished him. However, a chasm had grown between them, forged by their father's frequent habit of pitting them against one another—as if they might battle for affection that was never shown—and when word came of Donald's passing, Raina had been left with a quiet void rather than a sharp pain. Donald's death brought him release from their father's harsh expectations, and it left Raina at times with the bitter resentment that she'd not been allowed the same.

She swept her gaze again over the beach and the bustle of activity, knowing the fisherman and women wouldn't begin to approach her for a while yet to claim their wages, not until the day's work was done. The familiar and unkind melancholy, which she loathed but was at a loss to rectify, sat heavily upon her. Her sweet mother had filled her with ideas and visions of a bright future, but now those dreams seemed distant and unattainable. Her mother had instilled in Raina a belief in a future that transcended her father's cold ambition and lack of affection, urging her to seek a life where kindness, compassion, and personal fulfillment were paramount. She had painted a future where Raina's strength and intelligence would be celebrated, where she could lead and inspire, where her voice would be heard, ringing with authority and kindness.

Yet, here she was, trapped by duty and expectation, her spirit tethered to a life that was as different from her mother's benevolent ambitions as was the sea from the sky.

She sighed and put her hand over the small rock covering the open ledger, pressing it down as a strong gust of sea air threatened to scatter the pages. With her other hand she clasped at the inkwell and quill. The basket in which she carried all her supplies, the ledger, the ink, the leather pouch of coins, wobbled and tapped against her leg beneath the table. The small money bag now sat upon the table as well but was unlikely to be moved by the wind, owing to the weight of it.

Seòras, Lochlan's steward, was expected to join her, as was his custom. He usually sat stoically and silently at her side, a figure of quiet authority. While Seòras maintained an aloof and taciturn demeanor, was not warm and engaging, Raina didn't mind his presence. He possessed a deep understanding of the estate's workings, effortlessly fielding questions and resolving issues that arose among the workers—matters Raina herself had yet to fully grasp, having been gone three years until this spring and prior to that, having been discouraged from learning anything useful.

The steward's timing was impeccable, often appearing just as the fishermen and women began to gather, forming a queue before Raina. She, on the other hand, never wanted that the workers should have to wait for their pay, always ensuring she arrived early to attend to their needs. Time spent on the beach didn't bother her; in fact, she embraced these moments. Any time at the seaside was well spent, she believed. The sound of crashing waves and the cries of gulls filled her ears, a calming backdrop to her thoughts. She glanced up at the turbulent sky, where dark clouds raced overhead, hoping the rain held off until her small task here was complete.

Her brief inattention allowed another rogue gust of wind to sweep the quill from the table. Raina stood from her small stool to fetch it, having to chase it a bit along the bottom of the cliffs as the wind carried it along. She caught up with it at the same time a hushed murmur swept through the workers. Pausing, a flush rising, she expected that they were laughing at her ungainly attempts to retrieve the feather.

No hostile gazes were settled on her though, but all cast overhead. Fingers pointed urgently toward the cliff and above, at Lochlan Hall. Raina followed their anxious gazes, her heart lurching in her chest. High on the cliff, a chilling sight met her eyes.

An army, hundreds strong, clad in green tartan, descended the steep slope with chilling precision. Banners emblazoned with fierce dragons whipped in the wind, their colors stark against the gray stone fortress. The rhythmic thud of their boots echoed ominously, drowning out the gentle lapping of the waves below. Their formation stretched across the cliff's edge, a formidable wall of warriors poised to descend upon the beach.

The glint of polished armor and the flash of deadly weapons caught the pale daylight, casting a sinister quality over the once serene landscape. Fright rose inside her, and among the workers as well as they watched the army advance.

Frozen in bewildered horror, Raina noted how the invaders negotiated the descent from Lochlan Hall's formidable cliff. The cliff face, while imposing, revealed pockets of gradual decline—narrow paths worn into the rugged terrain by centuries of use, the same pathways Raina and Lochlan's hardy fishermen used.

Where grass and rock met in a patchwork of earthy hues, a faint trail wound its way down. Here and there, tufts of resistant grasses clung stubbornly to the cliff's edge, providing precarious footing for those daring enough to descend.

As they progressed, their disciplined formation remained intact, each warrior navigating the natural obstacles with agility. The path, though treacherous in places, became easier after the initial rough go, offering the invaders a clear route to the beach below, weaving through patches of scrub and clusters of wind-sculpted dunes. About midway down, twenty feet above the shore, the remnants of steps carved into the stone were still visible and navigable. 'Twas a narrow stair, cleaved into the cliff face and battered sometimes by the sea, but sturdy yet, allowing the coming army to dash quickly two by two.

As the horde descended, Raina began to back up, slowly, confounded by so alarming and unexpected a sight. The table, the ledger, and the leather pouch were all forgotten as fright creeped along her spine.

Movement to the north caught her eye and her mouth formed a small *o* of horror, finding another horde rushing toward them from the lower cliffs there, obviously having found the hidden path a tenth mile further, a natural slope that allowed for a quicker descent. A clamor of noise came with them, louder and louder as they neared, their urgent shouts and the clatter of armor drowning out the soothing roar of the sea.

"To the boats!" Someone shouted. "To the boats!"

Seized by awareness and a greater fright, Raina turned and picked up her skirts, sprinting toward the sea. Her heart pounded as she ran through the sand and plunged into the water, splashing through the shallows, her stride desperate, her gaze on the nearest boat, the hide-covered currach.

The villagers, panicked and fearful, surged around her, scrambling into the boats in a frantic bid to escape the approaching army. She was jostled and shoved and once sent sprawling face first into the knee-high water, and then bumped again as she tried to find her feet. The skirt of her léine was caught beneath her knee and a crashing wave rolled and submerged her, the world around her reduced to a blur of churning water and muted sounds. She flailed, trying to regain her footing, but her soaked dress clung to her like a leaden weight, dragging her down. Finally, she emerged, spitting out water, and fought hard to put her feet beneath her, her hair plastered to her face.

Before she could reach the safety of the boat, rough hands seized her, yanking her back towards the shore. She struggled, her breath coming in ragged gasps, but the grip was unyielding. As she was dragged through the surf, she slipped, her feet losing purchase on the slick, uneven seabed. For half a second, the hands of the enemy left her, only to return, closer and more relentless, wrapping around her waist, lifting her off her feet.

Helpless and disoriented, Raina was carried back to the beach, her back pressed against her captor's chest. She strained against his hold, clawing at the arm around her middle, kicking her legs, but his grasp remained unyielding.

Others—all of them—suffered the same fate. A score of Lochlan's own was recovered before any boat had made good its escape, the invaders having quickly boarded the knarr and the currachs, forcing people into the water and toward the beach.

Never in her life had she experienced anything so harrowing, so blood-curdling.

Upon the sand, Raina was dropped to her feet, and dragged by her wrist to where the fisherfolk were being herded into one group, penned in by sword-wielding, mean-faced warriors. She was shoved so roughly that she crashed into Duncan, a brawny, miserable man. He shot her a venomous glare, his eyes narrowing into a snarl of disdain, and thrust her away.

Her hair, once neatly beribboned, was now a tangled, sodden mass plastered to her head and face. Saltwater streamed from her, trickling down her cheeks and dripping from her chin. Her léine, a rich plum velvet, and her kirtle underneath, hung heavily on her small frame, the fabric clinging to her like a second skin. Her teeth chattered, both from the cold and from fear, and her limbs trembled with exhaustion. Dimly, she realized she still held the feathered quill in her hand, the delicate plumed barbs clumped together.

Raina realized a fleeting surprise that there had been no resistance; the fisherman had not fought. But then she needed only a moment to understand why they'd chosen—attempted—to flee and not to fight: the overwhelming number of invaders and the disparity in weaponry. The enemy force was vast, outnumbering the villagers by hundreds, which would have made any attempt at resistance futile and likely to result in swift and brutal reprisal. And while the fishermen were skilled with their skinning knives, these were tools meant for their trade, not for combat against armed soldiers clad in armor and wielding swords and spears. Faced with such overwhelming odds and armed with only small knives, their instinct for survival prevailed, prompting them to flee rather than confront the invaders head-on.

As Raina and the fisherfolk stood huddled together, uncertain of their fate, the sea of warriors slowly began to step aside. A figure emerged, commanding attention with his terrifying presence as he strode forward through the ranks of men.

The only other woman among the group, Nell, a squat and pale lass of no more than twenty, stood next to Raina and crossed herself, beseeching the Blessed Mother to save her.

The man walking through the parting soldiers appeared to be nearing forty, his close-cropped hair mostly gray, accentuating his weathered features and the lines etched into his stern countenance. Unlike the rugged and disheveled men around him, this man appeared fresh and unruffled, his attire meticulously maintained. Pale sunlight glinted off the shiny steel of his sword and the polished metal of the brooch securing his breacan, casting occasional flashes that caught the eye.

He exuded an aura of menace and authority that chilled the air, commanding attention without effort. His posture was upright, every movement deliberate and controlled, giving the impression of a predator confidently stalking its prey, each step calculated to instill fear.

As he approached, his gaze swept over the captive fisherfolk with cold intensity, his hard blue eyes piercing through the chaotic scene with chilling clarity. His stare seemed to strip away any pretense of hope, leaving only a stark realization of their vulnerability.

Raina shuddered at what seemed a deliberate cold-heartedness and shrunk a bit behind all those who stood in front of her.

No one spoke, no one whispered. The only sound that filled the tense silence was the roar of the sea, suddenly as angry as the man approaching, it seemed.

As the man neared the herded and cowering peasants, he called out in a deep voice, "Raina MacQueen, daughter of a traitorous lord, come forth!"

Raina gasped quietly while her eyes widened dramatically.

The invading commander stood waiting, his eyes cold and assessing, looking at each face in the crowd.

Later, she would generously suppose that no one *meant* to betray her, but aye, enough glances were aimed at her, that the man with the icy eyes had only to say, "Seize her," before several soldiers pushed through the throng of frightened peasants and took her by the arms, bringing her roughly forward.

Raina was pushed to her knees before him, her breath coming in harsh, uneven gasps. Though she did not rise, she lifted her head, meeting his gaze with as much defiance as she could muster. Strands of wet hair again stuck to her face, partially obscuring her vision. She clenched her teeth to keep her lips from trembling. Water dripped from every inch of her, pooling around her knees in the sand. She knelt before him a bedraggled wreck, not much grander than a drowned rat, and knew this was not the way she wanted to die.

Grimly, on limbs of pudding, she forced herself to stand.

He surveyed her thoroughly for many long seconds without uttering a word, his lips thinned with displeasure.

A cold hand clutched at her heart for the assault of his stare.

Though she raised her chin defiantly, her insides quaked, fear coursing through her.

"I am Raina MacQueen," she acknowledged, amazed that she spoke firmly, that she hadn't croaked these words.

"Ye dinna look so much the *Killer of Men* now," he said after an excruciating length of time. His voice was deep, inexplicably smooth for one who owned so ominous a glare, a voice of absolute authority.

Despite her best efforts, her lips quivered anyway. Courage melted under the hot menace of his stare and with his mention of the horrid name that had followed her home to Lochlan Hall.

He knew her?

"I am Torsten de Graham, mormaer of Glenbarra Brae, knight of the realm, dispatched by King Robert Bruce to take Lochlan Hall for the cause of freedom," he declared with notable arrogance. His voice dripped with disdain as he continued, "And aye, ye are Raina MacQueen, title holder of the unfortunate epithet, *Killer of Men*, of which I will now relieve ye." He narrowed his cold blue eyes. "Is it *any* betrothal itself that ye despise? Or was it those men put forth as yer intended? Three, was it? Three men ye've been promised to and three men have died by means foul and brow-raising, ere any wedding could take place?"

Confusion briefly overtook her fear. "Relieve me of...?" Completely at a loss, it didn't occur to Raina to deny the awful label that had been so cruelly attached to her, but rather she confirmed it by asking, without a shred of wit, as if this was her only concern, "How do you expect to relieve me of...?"

He smiled darkly.

"I simply willna give ye time to kill me or have me killed," he said, his voice a pool of ice. "We will forgo the betrothal and be wed today."

Chapter Two

He studied her, eminently curious about the woman who would become his wife.

Torsten's gaze swept over the disheveled woman before him, noting every detail with a soldier's precision. He thought she might be vibrant under different circumstances, but he could not be sure. Certainly, she was not at the moment.

Her pale porcelain skin, though nearly flawless, was drained of color. A scar the size of a small coin marred her cheek, just beneath her right eye. It was a slanted rectangle of raised skin, smooth but unmistakable. The years had softened its edges, yet it remained, a vivid reminder of some long-forgotten injury. Her rosy lips trembled, outlined in blue, highlighting her cold fear. Eyes of rich amber, fringed by dusky lashes, were slanted upward at the outer corners, giving her a cat-like appearance. But those eyes, so striking and stark against her bloodless cheeks, were now frozen and unblinking, locked in a wide-eyed stare that betrayed her tremendous fright. Her soaked locks were attached to her face and neck in tangled strands, and her dress, heavy with water, adhered to her slender frame, emphasizing her fragility.

There was little, he decided, to recommend her as a mate; even had the setting been less harrowing, he felt confident that he would not have given her a second glance. She was beyond the blush of youth, well-beyond those years, he imagined, guessing her to be at least half a decade more than twenty.

The *Killer of Men*? Looking at her now, she appeared more a rain-soaked sparrow caught in a sudden squall than an indiscriminate executioner of suitors.

He raised a brow at her, awaiting some response to his surely startling statement.

Those cold blue lips moved for a moment before any words were uttered.

"No. I will not." She shook her head. The wet clumps of hair clinging to her neck maintained their hold, only sliding back and forth against her flesh. "I choose death."

Torsten rolled his eyes with impatience at such theatre, or rather what he supposed was expected to be her valiant resistance.

"'Tis nae an option," he clipped. "Nae yers, at any rate." He stepped closed to her and said in a voice dangerously quiet, "Let me make this clear. Ye will wed, or I will slay a man a day, each and every day, for as long as ye refuse." He shrugged, unmoved by her swiftly expanded fright or the gasps and murmurs evoked from the crowd of people hemmed in behind Raina MacQueen. "I imagine eventually," he continued, "I get through the men and begin with the women and bairns. Dinna matter to me."

"But you cannot—" she tried to challenge.

"Aye, I can." He waved his hand behind him, where more than half his army stood at the ready. "Clearly, ye can see that I can."

'Twas then an easy choice.

Or rather, it should have been.

Torsten's marginal interest in his new bride-to-be grew tenfold in that moment, watching as she seemed to contemplate his words, as if she might actually allow him to carry out his threat against innocents. She didn't take her gaze from him but seemed to stare through him for a moment, her mahogany eyes brightened with possibilities, it seemed.

So long did she take to consider her choices that murmurs of discontent rose from the very group of people he'd just threatened.

She shook herself again, harshly, as if to dispel some notion that she might have taken leave of her senses, that she did have options.

"Very well," she said woodenly, nodding stiffly.

Supposing that the tears that rose and glistened in her eyes now might actually be manufactured, Torsten's lip curled with disdain for these perceived theatrics.

Having concluded what he'd set out to do for the moment, he pivoted on his heel, advising his men, "Bring them up, all of them," easily and purposefully dismissing his bride.

He climbed through the dunes and then ascended the ancient set of stone steps, navigating the steep cliff at the top where there was scarcely a safe path. At the summit, he glanced downward, taking a closer look than before, noting that the cliff dropped no more than twenty yards in total, from the base of the keep at the edge of the crag to the flat sand of the beach below. He caught a glimpse of Raina MacQueen, escorted by Uilleam, his hand firm upon her arm despite her grim-faced efforts to shake him off.

Turning, Torsten continued on toward the keep, debating if he would enlist masons to begin work on a curtain wall. Mac-

Queen had built no palisade around the keep or any of the outbuildings. Mayhap he believed there was no need, for the cliffs at their back made attack nearly impossible, and all the land in front of Lochlan Hall was flat grasslands as far as the eye could see, preventing any surprise attack, and making defense rather easy if enough skilled archers were employed. Mayhap the old man was only arrogant, supposing his English loyalties and vast wealth would protect him.

The de Graham's approach—Torsten backed by an army of four hundred—had certainly not gone unnoticed. It had, however, hardly been contested. They'd met resistance by the castle guard, since learned to number thirty-seven, scarcely enough to protect so rich and vast an estate, certainly not when a third of them, they'd also learned, also acted as fishermen and were upon the beach in that capacity rather than defending their home.

Perhaps he was arrogant himself now, assuming that his large army rather precluded the need for a curtain wall.

They'd arrived only thirty minutes ago, had secured the castle and village with naught but two injuries to their own and hardly a scratch to the MacQueen people, who'd thrown down their weapons with contemptuous haste. Torsten had expected to wait in the hall for Raina MacQueen to be brought to him—since Malcolm MacQueen was too incapacitated to leave his bed, he'd discovered a quarter hour ago—only to be informed by Lochlan's steward that Lady Raina was not inside the keep but upon the beach.

He found the steward where he'd left him, seated at the end of the high table in the cavernous great hall, which was about as clean as any Torsten had ever visited. For being the center of life at Lochlan Hall, it should have shown signs of frequent use, but instead the stone floor was devoid of rushes, seeming to be free of stains; the numerous candles set in iron rings and suspended high above were tall and unused, both the candles and the frame in which they sat lacking even a single drop of old, hardened wax. The hearth, which encompassed half of one entire wall, was not blackened with soot and grease but rather the stones might have been recently laid, so unblemished were they—indeed, the fire pit inside was empty, nary a bit of kindling or peat to be found, nor any evidence that a fire had ever been laid there.

Torsten approached the steward and the table, the latter which gleamed as if freshly scoured and polished, or like the hearth, never used. He had questions about this, but they could wait.

"Lady Raina has agreed to be my wife," he shocked the steward by saying. "Call forth the priest, if one abides, or send for the closest one—"

"You do not have Lord Malcolm's consent," the steward argued, his thick brows knitting. "And he will not give it, I assure you."

"I dinna need his consent," Torsten informed him just as his men began ushering the fisherfolk and as expected, his bride, into the hall. From his tunic, he withdrew a scroll, which he tossed down onto the table. "I have the king's consent and the bishop's dispensation to wed Raina MacQueen."

"This is—"

"Nae any of yer concern," Torsten advised the thin man pointedly, his tone curt. "Remember that for future reference regarding anything I do or say, or any action I take going forward as laird and commander of Lochlan Hall."

The reedy man gasped with affront and sent the sealed scroll rolling across the table with a flick of his fingers before crossing his arms over his chest.

Allowing a snort of amusement to erupt for the steward's childish manner, Torsten turned and summoned one of his officers. "Thomas," he said when the young man arrived at his side, "find a suitable cage, cell, or gaol—whatever ye manage—in which to house Lochlan's steward for the immediate future." He glanced back at the man, who'd previously and reluctantly identified himself at Seòras, and whose gray eyes were now round with shock. "He'll need time to accept how things will work and proceed here at Lochlan Hall."

"Aye, laird," replied Thomas with a biddable nod before collecting the steward and dragging him away from the table.

With that, Torsten turned to face the score of persons being bustled into the hall, his gaze easily finding Raina MacQueen, as she was at the head of the captives, being led still by Uilleam. She didn't resist forcibly so much as she dragged her feet, so that the lad was compelled to yank her forward with less gentleness than was advisable.

When she realized the steward's apprehension and removal from the hall, she adjusted her manner, now marching forward willingly and with a sudden fire in her amber eyes.

"Where is Seòras being taken? You have no right—"

"*Ye* have no rights," Torsten cut in, meaning to forestall this argument and others with his uncompromising tone. "Ye are the captured, the vanquished, the imprisoned. *I* have every right and I will utilize all of them. Who is Lochlan's priest and where might he be found?"

"I will not—"

"Bluidy hell, woman," he growled impatiently. "Niall! Bring me the other lass," he called out, his countenance severe as it remained fixed on Raina MacQueen, "the fisherwoman."

A short yip of fright was followed by footsteps approaching, one set marching, one set scraping.

Torsten turned as they neared and said harshly to Niall. "Strike her with closed fist if Lady Raina fails to answer my questions. If she refuses still to answer, cleave that one's hand from her wrist with yer sword."

"Aye, laird," came the obedient reply at the same time disgruntled murmuring erupted from the crowd of onlookers.

Facing Raina again, he caught sight of her open-mouthed astonishment before she clamped her lips closed.

She didn't look at him, however, didn't visit upon him any fright and dread, but exchanged a wordless stare with the fisherwoman. Torsten was briefly surprised to find that both woman's gazes were ablaze with some undercurrent of animosity.

Curious, he mused, and repeated, " Who is Lochlan's priest and where might he be found?"

While she kept her hostile gaze fixed on the other woman, Raina MacQueen swallowed and answered, "Father Walter, and if he was not found within the keep, inside the chapel, he will be at the kirk in the village."

"The kirk was empty," Torsten advised her.

Raina transferred her gaze to him. Her eyes, now vivid with a stubborn defiance, bored into his. Her jaw set, she squared her shoulders, alive with a mulish resistance that belied her earlier bloodless terror. "I am not his keeper," she said imperiously.

Torsten studied her, intrigued—though no less annoyed—by this shift in demeanor. Meaning to turn and instruct his men to find and bring forth the priest, he pivoted just in time to witness a dozen de Graham soldiers entering the hall, escorting more peasants who appeared to have been rounded up from the village. The hall, spacious though it was, had its capacity only just beginning to be stretched as the crowd inside doubled in size.

Among those entering now was a man who must surely be Father Walter, garbed in a soft gray cleric's robes, his face wreathed in remnants of white hair, a few long strands attached to his crown. He wore a solemn but composed expression, his eyes scanning the scene inside the hall with a concern that did not appear altogether anxious.

"Ask and ye shall receive," Torsten quipped without humor.

The cleric was elderly, possibly being moved at speeds greater than he was accustomed to, but unlikely to stumble with heavy de Graham hands on each of his arms.

When the priest was brought before him, his brow furrowing as he met Raina's gaze, Torsten introduced himself. "Father Walter," he began, "I am Torsten de Graham, mormaer of Glenbarra Brae, dispatched by King Robert Bruce. By royal decree and at my command, you are instructed to perform the marriage ceremony between Lady Raina MacQueen and myself."

Father Walter's gaze flickered with apprehension, but he maintained his composure. "My lord," he started, his voice steady but tinged with unease, "I am bound by the laws of God and man. I cannot—"

"Aye, the laws of man as well as God. In this case, that would be King Robert and myself," he declared, his words sharp. "You will marry us, or you will face the consequences of your defiance."

That, apparently, was the meek end of said defiance.

Father Walter bowed his head briefly. "Very well, my lord," he acquiesced solemnly. "I will perform the ceremony."

Torsten's lips curled in a satisfied smirk, his gaze unwavering. "Proceed then, if ye will."

The priest's eyes widened. "Now? But I haven't the proper vestment, haven't my missal—"

Torsten leaned forward, suggesting coolly, "I'm sure ye can muddle through it, guid man."

Father Walter bobbed his head repeatedly in an artless nod before his gaze flickered again to Raina.

Torsten moved to her side, and briefly frowned at Niall, inclining his head harshly until the fisherwoman whom he'd threatened was returned to the crowd of peasants.

Torsten's closest advisors, Gilles, Rory, and Aonghas, came to stand at his side.

"My father should be present—" Raina began to protest.

"We will speak with him later," Torsten clipped, standing tall at her side, his left palm laid over the back of his right hand in front of him. "I hear he is nae long for this world; I am as eager as ye are to introduce to him yer bridegroom, the new lord of Lochlan Hall."

Despite his initial hesitation and lack of preparedness, Father Walter stumbled through the ceremony. His voice trembled slightly as he spoke the traditional vows, and his knuckles were white as he clasped his hands before the couple.

Raina's responses were barely audible, her voice wooden and small. She repeated her vows mechanically, her eyes fixed stoically on some point across the hall. Torsten sensed little fear now, only a resigned acceptance of her fate.

The satisfaction he knew for how easily his mission had been accomplished notwithstanding, Torsten's expression was unreadable as the ceremony concluded with a perfunctory blessing from Father Walter.

The air was heavy with tension, the makeshift ceremony lacking any semblance of joy. As the peasants looked on in silence, Torsten and Raina were bound together in a union that neither desired nor celebrated, but one that had just altered the trajectory of their lives.

With barely a glance at Raina, who remained frozen and pale in front of the high table, Torsten stepped around the cleric, his gaze sweeping over the assembled peasants and fisherfolk who had been forced to gather in the hall, their expressions ranging from bewilderment to fear.

"People of Lochlan Hall," he began, his voice carrying a commanding edge that demanded attention. "I am Torsten de Graham, dispatched by King Robert Bruce to bring this fortress rightfully under his banner. Ye now find yourselves under my rule, and I come nae as a tyrant but as a steward of justice and order." He paused, his gaze skimming the stupefied faces of the crowd, before continuing with a firm tone, "Yer livelihoods will continue as before. Those who toil in the fields and ply the waters shall do so under my protection. But make nae mistake, there will be changes. Yer allegiance now lies with me and King Robert Bruce, and the laws of this land, however they were practiced before, are now superseded by my commands." His eyes narrowed slightly as he emphasized the next point, "Any disputes among ye will be settled under my jurisdiction. I expect loyalty and obedience, and those who uphold the peace shall be rewarded." Torsten's voice softened slightly as he concluded, "I do nae seek unnecessary hardship, but ken that any defiance or resistance will be met with swift and severe consequences. Together, we shall build a future where Lochlan Hall prospers at the same time it supports the reign of Robert Bruce, our rightful king." He paused briefly, returning to Raina's side, who looked as if she hadn't blinked and might be holding her breath. "And now ye will cheer and wish yer lady well," he commanded the bleak crowd.

Feet were shuffled and eyes averted from both Lady Raina and their new laird. Not a word was spoken, and no hands were joined and clapping.

Torsten narrowed his eyes, considering the crowd. Most often, governed by fear, a subjugated throng would obey swiftly, if not enthusiastically. But when he discovered more than one darting glance, aimed with precision and what he imagined was extreme censure at Raina, he began to believe that all was not rosy and sweet under the roof of Lochlan Hall.

He lowered his head toward her hair, still damp and disheveled and emitting a scent of lavender. "They dinna seem to like ye," he taunted her, "nae more than me."

"I will happily yield the popularity contest to you, sir," she said acerbically, if quietly, lifting her chin. "You *and* they can go to hell."

Though he cared little for the machinations of Lochlan Hall, much less for melodrama, he could not allow his command to go unanswered. Mayhap his new wife was more shrew than actually a killer of men, mayhap these people took umbrage at how long it had taken her to spare their lives by agreeing to wed him, mayhap both parties were to blame for what was apparently a contentious relationship between lady and peasants. Whatever the case, he didn't care, save that he needed to exert his authority and they needed to understand what he expected of them.

"And now," he repeated through clenched teeth, "ye will cheer and wish yer lady well."

Lackluster was their response, and that was painting it with a generous brush, but they did applaud the newly-wedded couple.

On his left side, Gilles muttered under his breath, "Bluidy half-wits."

"Come, bride," Torsten said next, putting his hand to Raina's elbow, at which she flinched, "let us bring fair tidings of our nuptials to yer sire."

RAINA'S THOUGHTS SWIRLED in a blur of chaotic images and emotions. Everything had happened so quickly—in truth, the nuptials had been a haze, a ceremony she barely comprehended as her mind raced with fear with what she could have or should have done differently to have escaped this fate.

Honest to God, a fleeting thought had circled round her brain down at the beach when Torsten de Graham had initially threatened to harm others if she did not consent to wed him. *What do I care?* She'd contemplated then. *They hate me. I owe them nothing.* From the day she'd returned to Lochlan Hall at the beginning of the year, they'd shown her neither respect nor kindness, naught but contempt at the worst and indifference at the least. In truth, it was fleeting, the feelings behind her hesitation, and she did know an instant remorse for her own cold-hearted thoughts, but there it was, however briefly it had been alive in her.

She swallowed, the air catching in her throat, knowing that she wouldn't have actually allowed another to die for her—or apparently be injured, as in the case of the wretch, Nell, who possibly and regularly exhibited the most overt disrespect.

Instead Raina rather expected that she might have signed her own death warrant when she nodded, agreeing to wed the man who appeared as if he might be the type to wish she would refuse so that he *could* satisfy his bloodlust. He would have to settle for tormenting and torturing her as his wife, she guessed.

Surely, the man breathed fire, so hostile was his manner. The dragon emblem on his banner was fitting then, so symbolic of the ferocity and fear he inspired in all who dared cross his path.

Now, as she was followed by Torsten up the wide staircase at the end of the hall, she was angry with herself for her own powerlessness, for how quickly and easily she'd succumbed, and was gnawed at by a dreaded uncertainty about what lay ahead.

Torsten de Graham—God help her, her *husband* now!—was imbued with a severe and icy demeanor, with no care for his new bride beyond the orders he carried from Robert Bruce. He was here to claim the castle for the patriots of the war, and Raina was just another piece of that conquest.

Taking a deep breath, Raina squared her shoulders and turned left at the top of the stairs, walking down the corridor to the stairwell at the southeast corner and climbing up to the third floor and the family chambers.

As she pushed open the door to her father's chambers, Raina steeled herself for the confrontation ahead. Her father, frail and ailing, was a shadow of his former self, but his sharp tongue and cold eyes could still pierce her deeply. Actually, his sharp tongue no more, since her father had struggled to speak in the last week, his words mere sounds, indecipherable but always harshly given. She anticipated his contempt, certain he would scorn her for having wed de Graham instead of sacrificing herself to salvage the MacQueen pride. Silently, she prayed for the strength to endure whatever fate awaited her, her hatred for both her father and her new husband burning fiercely within her. In fact, no; she didn't hate her father. When she wasn't afraid of him, she simply felt nothing at all.

Raina stepped into the dimly lit chamber, her eyes quickly adjusting to the gloom. Her father lay in a large, canopied bed, draped in rich, dark fabrics embroidered with the MacQueen crest, depicting a fierce eagle with wings outstretched and talons ready, symbolizing strength and defiance. The room was filled with the scent of medicinal herbs, and the air felt heavy with decay.

Her father, once a robust figure, now seemed shrunken and small against the grand bed. Though his skin was pasty white and his frame frail, his eyes, though dimmed by age and illness, still held a glint of sharpness and malice. His long, thin white hair spread across the pillow, and his breathing was labored, indicating the harsh decline of the last few weeks.

Beside the bed stood a nurse and a male attendant, both of whom stared at Torsten de Graham, their expressions clouded with either dread or fear.

Without a word, Torsten dismissed them with a curt wave of his hand. They scurried from the room, leaving Raina alone with her father and the imposing figure of her new husband. The heavy door closed behind them with a foreboding thud, sealing Raina in the room with the two men who had so deeply shaped her fate, neither to her benefit by her reckoning.

Upon the large bed, his frail form propped up by numerous pillows, Malcolm MacQueen's eyes were fixed intently on Torsten. His lips quivered as if he wanted to speak, but no words came out. His agitation was palpable, his thin, bony hands clutching the bedclothes tightly, betraying his frustration and helplessness against the grip of his illness.

Grudgingly, sensing she had some responsibility here and now, Raina said, "Father, this is—"

"We've met already," Torsten de Graham coldly informed her, cutting her off without glancing at her. "I visited earlier, ere we ventured down to the beach. I advised Sir Malcolm that his keep belongs to me now."

He stared with what seemed a sinister delight at the frail man, suddenly appearing larger and more dynamic, indeed more powerful, when compared to the shriveled man that was her father.

"But I dinna say much more than that," he said, his gaze fixed on Malcolm MacQueen, "dinna tell him that I intended to wed ye. But I'm pleased to tell him that the deed is now done."

Raina stood opposite Torsten, her gaze moving from his ruthless visage to her father's, who croaked and squeaked his helpless distress.

"Your son is dead," Torsten declared, a cruel edge to his voice, "and your daughter is now mine, a de Graham. Your bloodline will die with ye. I'll nae kill ye to spare ye. I want ye to lie here and ken what is happening all around ye, in your own keep. And I want ye to recall what atrocities ye visited upon so many places—Dunkeld, Selkirk, Alderlea among others. Ye did that, allowed the rape and plunder of those places, nae only allowed it but contributed to the villainy. Had nae anything to do with war, 'twas naught but evil. And now I've avenged those souls put under your blade and surely countless others upon whom ye visited the same carnage. I've taken everything away from ye."

Stunned, her mouth agape, Raina watched as her new husband turned on his heel and strode from the chamber.

Chapter Three

Upon the precipice, the toes of his boots creeping over the edge of the crag, Torsten stood with his hands on his hips gazing down at the beach below. A dozen of his men were there, having returned with five fisherman, meaning to attend the fish that had been caught but not processed. There was no need for waste. They were ordered simply to process the fish as they would and store them in the ice house, one of two maintained by Lochlan Hall, he'd learned, the furthest one being at the north end near the donkey track that nearly half his army had used to approach the beach hours ago.

The sea was curiously calm under a sky that continued to threaten but thus far failed to produce any rain. The transport boat and the smaller currachs bobbed listlessly in the water, moored by anchors dropped to the sea floor.

Torsten's gaze fell on the table and overturned chair almost directly below him. He hadn't known it was her at the time, but that's where he had first seen Raina MacQueen, moments before he and his army had descended. He hadn't yet figured out what she'd been doing there—simply sitting and observing? Was she the MacQueen taskmaster, there to ensure the work was done efficiently and without theft, grumbling, or waste?

He sighed gustily, and then filled his lungs with tangy sea air, his mind briefly recalled to an image of Meera Agnew, his betrothed, one of Malcolm MacQueen's victims.

He only recently discovered who was responsible for the craven attack at Alderlea that was now three years old. News hadn't caught up to Torsten in the field until almost a year had passed. Having returned to Alderlea at the first opportunity allowed by the war just this past winter, he'd spoken to her mother, who had wept through the entire tale, cursing her own inability to have stopped it, bemoaning the fact that she lived while her daughter was cold in the ground. The woman had lost her husband, daughter, and countless others in their clan on that day that MacQueen had passed through, vowing that he needed only grain and ale for his soldiers, and would take no more.

Torsten knew he hadn't been in love—though Meera Agnew had been breathtaking to look upon, she was occasionally petty and talked entirely too much—but he had accepted the decision of his elders, the mormaers out on Skye; it was time that he wed and ensured the de Graham name prevailed. He'd thought she'd have made a fine mistress to Glenbarra Brae. She'd been of a good family with strong ties to several other noble families, Carricks, Frasers, and Morays included. 'Twas a good match.

Or it would have been.

He'd wanted to kill MacQueen, that had been his intent when he beseeched Robert Bruce to give him the task of sacking Lochlan Hall and not any other capable knight. He'd dreamed of how he might do it, what method to employ, if he would make it slow or quick. But one look at the man this afternoon, before he'd taken his army down to the beach, had advised that a full and gratifying revenge would not be his. Putting the man out of his misery for whatever ailment had debilitated him, reducing him to a drooling mess, would have been an act of mercy, and Torsten would show none to any MacQueen. Ah, but Malcolm MacQueen's mind was still sharp, Torsten had gleaned that in his rheumy but fervid gaze. Malcolm MacQueen recalled his own wickedness, had recognized the places where he had wrought devastation; Torsten had seen the acknowledgement in his eyes. That had brought Torsten some degree of satisfaction, to let him know that it was his pleasure to have seized his castle and wed his daughter while he lay helpless, unable to do anything about it.

And yet, Torsten was brutally dissatisfied. He was now possessed of a vast keep upon the edge of the sea, had essentially vanquished his enemy without lifting a finger, had more than doubled his wealth for the income of Lochlan Hall, and he felt there was scarcely cause to rejoice. He'd also acquired bitter and suspect serfs; there was no farming, naught but selling beef and hides from the extensive cattle operation, and exporting fish, neither industry being familiar to Torsten at all; his enemy lay dying but not by his own hand; and he was now possessed of a wife who bore the name and shared blood with the man he hated almost most in the world; he would be tied to her until either he died or she died, a woman for whom he felt only disdain, for whatever role she'd played in her sire's nefarious deeds, here or afar.

Aye, it didn't quite quench his want of vengeance, felt utterly inadequate, and he feared he might live forever with regret and remorse and this tremendous fury, which on some days he believed might consume him from the inside out.

He debated returning to war, leaving a third of his own army here to build a palisade, to defend that which was now his, but knew that he could not yet. Robert Bruce had designs on Lochlan hall not only to have thwarted the intentions and enterprise of a treacherous Scotsman, but to appropriate for the duration of the war half of Lochlan Hall's cattle and fish to feed his growing Scots army. Torsten would abide for a while, at the king's command, to ascertain whether or not it was feasible. While King Robert didn't mind taking from the treacherous MacQueen, he dithered a wee bit about stealing earnings from innocent serfs or food out of their mouths. If it were discovered that Lochlan Hall could afford to contribute to provisions of the Scots army and feed its people, Torsten might then put people in place to manage it and get back to war, as he preferred.

Another sigh emerged before he turned from the cliff's edge and returned to the keep. He did not relish the task ahead, confronting his bride in her chamber, which he would now make his own.

Raina MacQueen's initial fright had given way to a meager defiance, easily quelled by threats to others, apparently even a fisherwoman she despised. Confronting her alone, as he would, might allow for greater boldness, with no one about to threaten to provoke either meekness or compliance.

Yet, while he didn't relish the encounter, he wanted it done, wanted rules laid down and expectations clearly outlined, leaving no room for rebellion.

Gilles was inside the hall when Torsten arrived, frowning down at the young lad to whom he was speaking. Several other de Graham officers milled about, waiting either for instructions or to give reports.

Torsten approached Gilles and the lad first, curious about the scowl on his captain's face.

"I'm wanting to ken where the trestle tables are," Gilles explained to Torsten, "and the lad tells me—he's Crispin, by the by— there are none. They dinna have meals in the hall. No one comes from the village to sup in the hall."

And now Torsten was frowning, staring down at the scruffy lad for an explanation.

"The lady takes her—" the lad began, addressing these comments to Torsten.

"Lady Raina," Torsten corrected automatically, crossing his arms over his chest.

"Aye, Lady Raina takes her meals in the little hall," said the lad, pointing a bony finger to the ceiling. "Abovestairs. milord, as mi—Lord Malcolm—did as well, at one time, before he fell ill."

"Someone poison the auld bastard?" Gilles asked with a harrumph.

Expecting that the scrawny lad with a mop of shaggy brown hair would have denied this anon, Torsten lifted a brow when the lad only shrugged, seemingly unconcerned.

"Are there none in need?" Torsten inquired. Glenbarra Brae was a healthy, thriving estate and still the folks in the village took their supper with their laird in the great hall so that they were not burdened with providing meals for their family, naught but their first meal of the day.

Again, the lad shrugged.

"Ye look as if ye could use a guid meal," Gilles remarked. "Ye work here, inside the hall?"

"Aye, sir. I tend the hearths and scrub the floors," the lad answered. "My brother, Nicol, works in the scullery, and my cousin, Arthur, serves the meals. Patrick, the wainwright's son, cleans the garderobe."

Torsten and Gilles's brows knitted again, at the same time.

"All lads?" Gilles questioned. "Nae lasses?"

The lad swiped at his nose with the knuckle of his forefinger. "Nae, sir."

"Why nae?"

Again, the narrow shoulders lifted and dropped. "I dinna ken, sir."

"Lady Raina has maids, though," Torsten assumed.

"Nae, sir."

"The kitchen staff?" Gilles persisted.

"Fergus, Simon, Nicol, Arthur, and aye, sometimes I have chores there."

Torsten and Gilles exchanged curious glances.

"At what hour does Lady Raina take her supper in the little hall?" Torsten asked.

"Seven, sir."

"And she takes dinner at midday?"

"Nae, sir."

More befuddled than concerned, Torsten excused the lad. He would learn more, possibly, from his wife.

"Half-arse backwards," was Gilles opinion, given as he watched the lad scurry away, his soft leather shoes silent upon the timber floor. "Those lads would be better served learning a trade, or down at the beach, fishing, boatin'."

"And where, I wonder," Torsten mused, "are they keeping all the lasses?"

"'Course, we'll need to bring in more for the kitchen," Gilles suggested. "We've got four hundred hungry lads. I expect there'll be some shuffling, getting the kitchen set up to feed them."

"I'll speak to the daughter this evening," Torsten said, adding that to his mental list of things to discuss.

"The daughter?" Gilles challenged. "Ye mean yer bride, dinya?"

"One and the same, Gilles," Torsten remarked curtly.

He then received a report from Gilles about the attitude of the villagers, including the fishermen, as perceived by the de Graham units who'd escorted them the half mile away to their homes.

"Sullen, confounded," Gilles related, "but nae yet any talk of resistance. We'll keep an eye on it."

Next, another soldier approached, giving an inventory of existing weaponry and armor stores.

For the next two hours, Torsten received report after report, demanding a comprehensive accounting of everything that comprised the MacQueen lands: the extent of the demesne, boundaries and percentage of forest, the number of structures and homes, the number of lochs and rivers, and even the irrigation methods already in place.

He would meet with the steward, Seòras, in the morning—provided the man had learned a bit of humble obedience before then—to discuss greater details, such as the livestock counts and conditions, trade routes and partnerships, and tax records and revenue streams. He wanted to know everything.

Later, when the deep, resonant toll of the castle bell echoed through the halls, marking the nineteenth hour of the day, Torsten excused his men, advising they were released for the day, those not on watch duty, and should seek food and ale in the camp.

Torsten ascended the stone steps to the second floor, and searched three different chambers ere he discovered the 'little hall'. Unlike the expansive and austere great hall on the ground floor, this chamber exuded a sense of intimate luxury.

Richly woven tapestries adorned the walls, depicting scenes of Saunt Ceerus life and ancient battles, their vibrant colors contrasting with the dark wood paneling—an enormous expense seen rarely outside of large or foreign cities. A large, intricately carved fireplace dominated one wall, its mantel decorated with fine silver candlesticks and a few delicate trinkets, evidence of the MacQueen's wealth. The room was warmly lit by several different groupings of candles, in trays and tabletop candelabras, shining softly upon the polished oak table that stood in the center.

Plush, high-backed chairs upholstered in deep burgundy velvet were arranged around the table, their cushions inviting and comfortable. The floor was covered with a thick, woolen rug, its colorful pattern adding to the sense of opulence. At the outer wall, heavy drapes of a coordinating burgundy fabric framed narrow windows, through which the fading light of evening streamed.

Torsten took in the luxurious surroundings, so ridiculously opposite the spartan conditions he and his men endured in the field.

Raina had not yet come—he wondered if indeed, she would at all.

He moved to a window, where the heavy drapes were pulled back by tassels of gold cord, allowing a clear view of the grounds below, from which the de Graham's had approached today. Presently, his army's tents were spread out in neat rows of tens across the flat grasslands. The men were busy with their evening preparations, setting up small fires and cooking their meals. Smoke from the fires curled into the twilight sky. The orderly arrangement of tents and the disciplined movements of his soldiers spoke to the rigor and efficiency he demanded.

As Torsten's army had advanced on Lochlan Hall, they had not done so without careful consideration of their sustenance. While there were no dedicated cooks among his men, the strategy for feeding the force was well-practiced. Foraging parties had been dispatched to gather food from the surrounding countryside along the way, returning with livestock, grains, and whatever provisions could be spared by the local peasantry, or stolen from any enemy or supporters of their enemy they happened upon. They would survive a few more days dining as if they marched still, until the kitchens could be staffed to feed his large entourage.

At the sound of the door creaking, Torsten turned from the window, nearly amused by a fantastic thought that flashed in his mind, of his new bride lunging at his back with dagger in hand.

Clearly, she was startled by his presence, was his first observation, her slender figure and face arrested near the door, as if she debated whether to enter fully or quietly back away.

Next, he noticed the irrefutable change in her appearance.

Gone was the disheveled woman from the beach, replaced by a vision of quiet grace. She had changed into a fresh léine and kirtle, the fabric a deep, rich blue that complemented her fair skin. Her auburn hair was nearly dry and pulled back neatly from her face in a loose queue, the tail of it draped over one shoulder, gleaming like burnished copper in the soft light of the chamber.

Her amber eyes, though wary yet, were no longer frozen with dread; the dark fringe of lashes accentuated their feline slant. A subtle flush to her cheeks heightened her color, and her lips, no longer blue with cold or trembling with fear, were parted slightly, their shape softened and clarified, being rosy and full and shaped as a bow.

There wasn't anything done specifically, not that he could see, to enhance her features, no cheek or lip powder, no perfume, no elaborate hair style, and yet....

Torsten's gaze swept over her, taking in every detail. She was undeniably lovely, her beauty enhanced by the air of defiance that still clung to her. Despite the circumstances, she stood with a quiet dignity as she met his gaze and for a moment, Torsten felt a spark of something he couldn't quite name. Admiration, mayhap, respect for her tenacity possibly, or perhaps naught but a joy that she wasn't howling and weeping. But whatever it was, as quickly as it came, he pushed it aside, reminding himself of his purpose and the orders he was bound to fulfill.

Torsten cleared his throat.

"Come, bride," He invited in a level tone before she might have escaped. "We shall dine together and begin to learn about each other."

Though she did step further in to the large chamber, she favored him with a pointed glare. "I'm expected to believe you have interest in me as a person?" When he cocked his brow at her, she furthered, "That I'm not actually to remain but a pawn in your little scheme of revenge? Or worse, perhaps," she proposed. "With my father dying, I assume little joy would be known in killing him, and thus, you've decided that I will pay for his sins."

"Your father may deal dishonorably but I do nae." He paused and withdrew the chair at one end of the table. "I do nae kill or torment innocents—though your culpability in his numerous crimes remains to be seen. The denizens of Lochlan Hall dinna ken too highly of ye and I'm wondering why."

Ignoring what was nearly a question, and without advancing further, she challenged his statement. "Is it honorable to force a marriage upon a stranger, one you plan to harass and...and God knows what else?"

"Ye mistake me," he said through clenched teeth. "Wed we are by the king's command and nae by my choosing." –this wasn't precisely true, but in theory it was. He had requested the assignment.

She raked her gaze over him boldly, and with a surge of disbelief. "I'm expected to believe you are a pawn? I think not."

"Will ye sit, or shall we dine standing?" He wondered.

Her gaze darted around the chamber, as if she wished the table were longer and the chairs placed further apart, mayhap his in another room. With a huff and a tight jaw, she flounced into the chair he held for her.

Torsten took the seat opposite her, almost a dozen feet away. He expected that this would be one of the few, if not the only time he and she would dine privately as such, here in this little hall. He intended that the great hall should be open to his army daily—a huge undertaking but one that he would take pains to implement—as he would much prefer to sup in the company of his men, rather than his bride.

"Where is your father's army now?" He asked. "Who leads them?"

She shrugged. "I have no idea. My brother led them of course, but as you already know, he is presumed dead—"

"Presumed?"

"He was reportedly felled at Methven, but we have received neither remains nor effects."

"'Twas a vast field of battle, stretched over many miles," he allowed. "His body likely was never recovered, is ash upon the earth if nae already food for scavengers." He frowned. "And since then, your father's army has not returned, not at all?"

"Not that I am aware of. I only returned to Lochlan Hall this past winter. I'd been gone—"

"Ah, yes, collecting bridegrooms and then condolences when they met their ends."

Stiffening in her seat, Raina glared at him. "Why do you hate someone you've never met before today? Are you so simple of mind that you believe all the sordid rumors you hear?" She tipped her head a bit to the right and goaded him yet more. "Are you so backwards in your thinking that you would hold against me the sins of my father?"

Torsten's lips curled into a smile that hinted at both restraint and menace, his eyes narrowing slightly as he regarded her with a mix of scarce amusement and something darker beneath the surface.

"I will advise ye, wife," he said slowly, "that going forward, ye never again take that tone with me."

"And I will advise you, husband," she responded without hesitation, "that until you refrain from treating me with such open hostility, you should expect the same."

He scoffed mildly at her reprimand and subjected her to a lengthy and thorough perusal, quite pleased when she wilted a bit under his scrutiny. She was bonny, he could not deny, so much so that it was no surprise that she'd managed to rack up one suitor after another. "What was your scheme, by the way?"

He asked with seeming indifference. "Were ye being sold? Your sire collecting coin, selling ye to the highest bidder? They were men of means, your intended. Were ye sent to town to entrap them, tease them, entice them, until they were throwing money at your father? Until they met their verra convenient ends?"

Raina gasped, stricken by what he insinuated, the slight color in her high cheeks flushing red.

Torsten's brow lifted. "Struck a nerve, have I? Hit too close to the mark? The game is played and done, Raina. Nae more fools to be swindled, nae more coin to earn."

"Again, you don't truly intend to get to know me," she said haughtily. "You only mean to denigrate and harass me."

She pushed back her chair and made to stand.

"Ye may nae take yer leave," he told her.

Proud and angry, she rose to her feet, clearly about to challenge him.

At that precise moment, the heavy oak door swung open with a creak, admitting two skinny lads. They entered the room, each balancing a covered tray laden with food, which they promptly brought to the table.

The two lads approached the table with careful steps, their eyes cast down in deference—or with a desire not to trip— and placed the covered trays on the bare table. With a synchronized motion, they lifted the lids from the platters. On one tray, steaming venison pie enclosed in a golden crust, its savory aroma wafting through the room. Beside it, a bowl of roasted vegetables, still glistening with butter. On the other tray, a selection of freshly baked bread, warm and fragrant, accompanied by a bowl of butter and a variety of cheeses, their rich scents mingling enticingly.

"Good evening, sir," Raina said, a glint of superiority in her gaze as she used the presence of the lads to escape him.

And while the lads' bewildered gazes darted between Torsten and Raina, she slipped quietly from the chamber.

"Thank ye, lads," he said politely, his jaw clenched, dismissing them, deciding that he much preferred to dine alone.

Chapter Four

She'd escaped just in time, her eyes bulging wide. She clamped her hand over her mouth to contain the squeal of dismay that threatened to erupt and scurried down the corridor, mounting the twisting stairs. She bypassed the third floor and her own chamber and climbed to the fourth floor, where she might be assured of privacy. Not that she imagined for one moment that Torsten de Graham would bemoan her departure or give chase—unless he meant only to exert his authority over her.

Actually, upon further reflection, she guessed that he might do just that, simply to prove that he could, that he controlled her, that he could bend her will to his own, regardless of her wishes or intentions.

Softly opening the door of a chamber used primarily for storage, she slipped inside among old, covered furniture and stacked chests, the chamber gloomy and gray, the shutters closed over the lone window. She sank against the back of the door, her mind swirling with Torsten's unsettling words.

He was utterly repulsive, deliberately provocative, and frankly made her former suitors seem saintly by comparison. But that, strangely enough, was not why she'd wanted so badly to escape the little hall.

For the first time, Raina found herself entertaining a chilling thought: could her father have been involved in the deaths of her previous suitors? Torsten's words cut deep, stirring doubts that gnawed at the edges of her consciousness.

Were ye being sold? Your sire collecting coin, selling ye to the highest bidder? They were men of means, your intended. Were ye sent to town to entrap them, tease them, entice them, until they were throwing money at your father? Until they met their verra convenient ends?

But...no, it wasn't possible.

Was it?

Sweet Mother of God, had her father anything to do with the death of three men to whom he'd betrothed her? Men from whom he had indeed collected land, gold, and cattle, promising the title to Lochlan Hall upon their wedding?

How had she never imagined this before? She was fully aware how cold and calculating her father could be, how his ambition for wealth and status overshadowed any idea of impropriety—but murder? The thought that he might have orchestrated the deaths of her suitors for his own gain seemed beyond comprehension. But no, one had died in his sleep, his advanced years and surely not the hand of her father at work. Another had perished along with many others inside Dundee when some diseased fever had stricken the town, though in truth, it was known that many more had battled the fever and survived. Raina supposed that the pieces could be made to fit neatly together to support either scenario, three men dying by various causes without assistance from another living soul or three men hastened to their deaths at the behest of one man, her father. The very idea of the latter left her with a sickening sense of doubt and betrayal.

Horrifically, there was more, Torsten's other accusations against her father.

I want ye to recall what atrocities ye visited upon so many places—Dunkeld, Selkirk, Alderlea among others. Ye did that, allowed the rape and plunder of those places, nae only allowed it but contributed to the villainy.

She swallowed hard, scarcely able to believe that, despite knowing her father's wickedness, her understanding of his *known* faults and crimes might have barely scratched the surface of the evil he'd actually perpetrated.

Briefly, Raina considered whether asking her sire directly would uncover the truth. He was dying and presently uncommunicative, but might the truth be revealed in his still-sharp gaze?

Drained by these unsettling thoughts, Raina succumbed to exhaustion and dropped into the nearest covered chair, a cloud of dust briefly swirling around her. The entire day had been a tumultuous series of harrowing events, unsettling revelations, and unwelcome surprises—not least of which was her marriage to such an unyielding, unkind, and cold man who apparently intended that his role as husband should in part be played with an aim to torment her.

Staring blindly at a pile of rolled and forgotten tapestries, likely decades older than she was, Raina covered her cheeks with her hand and wondered what would become of her, and of Lochlan Hall under the grip of so formidable a man. Mayhap naught would change, she supposed after some thought on the matter; her father ruled with an iron fist and had for many years. Perhaps Torsten de Graham would only continue to lord over Lochlan Hall and its people as Malcolm MacQueen had, with the same oppressive authority, the same unyielding governance, and little regard for the health and happiness of his people. Or his daughter.

Her mind buzzed with what that would mean for her. In truth, and though she resented what it said about her, with her father's failing health—and his expected death—she had been looking forward to freedom from oppression. How sad, though, that she'd actually anticipated her father's demise, longing for the day when she might be free of his iron rule.

Nothing to look forward to now.

Now, with Torsten de Graham as her husband, she feared she had traded one tyrant for another. The hope she had clung to seemed more distant than ever, overshadowed by the presence of a man who frightened her to her core.

It's not supposed to be like this, she thought with bitter melancholy. Swiftly, she chastised herself for such selfishness. True, her life was joyless, but she lived and breathed yet while so many others did not, lost to war, disease, accidents, and aye, even murder. Annoyed at her own despondency, she was reminded of something her mother had said to her, more than once: *Forge your own path; create—don't wait—for your heart's desire.*

She had tried, truly she had. Yet, every attempt to carve out a life of her own had been thwarted, leaving her feeling more imprisoned than ever. Her father's ruthless schemes, the untimely—and now suspect— deaths of her betrotheds, and now this forced marriage to Torsten de Graham, each step she took toward freedom seemed to bring her back to the same cage. Perhaps she'd been too vague in her ambitions. She'd not ever defined her *heart's desire,* had never imagined a certain wish or idea, had only ever known that she didn't want *this,* her life.

Emotionally drained and lulled by the quiet solitude of the storage chamber, Raina soon fell asleep there in the dusty, shrouded chair.

She stirred awake, momentarily confused by the sudden intrusion of light, until she recalled her location and understood that someone had come into the chamber holding a candle. Groggy, blinking rapidly, fright enveloped her instantly and was not relieved when she realized Torsten de Graham had come. He held in his hand a simple metal candlestick, the wide base of the holder catching the drips from the tallow candle. The candle had burned low, and she was caused to wonder if he'd searched at length for her, or if he'd stood watching her sleep for some time.

The flickering candle held waist high cast an eerie glow, illuminating his broad figure. Shadows danced across his angular features, accentuating the sharp lines of his jaw and deepening the hollows of his cheekbones. His furrowed brow indicated his current mood, or again his displeasure.

Having been slouched in sleep, Raina put her elbows on the arm of the chair and straightened a bit, watching him warily.

"'Tis late," he said, his voice surprisingly soft and low, without the hard edge to which she'd already grown accustomed. "We should find our chamber."

Raina blanched. The implications of his words hit her with a cold, visceral horror. This man, whose existence she had only just learned of today, was now her husband by the decree of fate and war. The expectation that their union would be consummated tonight sent a shiver of revulsion down her spine. She felt exposed and vulnerable in the dim light of the candle, her gaze darting between his face and the dancing shadows that seemed to mock her fear.

Her knuckles turned white as she gripped the chair's arms. Though she shriveled inside, she pushed herself to her feet and without meeting his gaze, walked around him and out of the chamber. His presence loomed heavy and oppressive behind her as he followed, his footsteps echoing ominously along the corridor and down the winding spiral stairs.

Her chamber was situated a considerable distance from her father's bedchamber, located at the opposite end of the second floor. At the door, she paused and drew in a deep, fortifying breath before pushing it open and stepping inside.

Going directly to a small bedside table, Raina brought to life a flame in a candle there, her motions slow and stiff. When she could delay it no more, she turned and faced her husband, finding that he was not looking at her but taking stock of her bedchamber.

The walls were stone, softened by hangings of fine cloth in deep hues of burgundy and gold. A substantial, finely detailed pine bed dominated the room, draped with sumptuous furs and embroidered linens. Heavy velvet curtains framed the window overlooking the North Sea, now shrouded in darkness, its distant roar barely audible through the thick stone walls. A long chest sat at the end of the bed and a tall closet stood against an interior wall, both of which stored her clothing, linens, and small personal items, mostly mementos of her mother. A wooden table, adorned with a plain white cloth, held a small mirror, her combs, and other toiletries. In front of the hearth, two overstuffed cushioned chairs sat, angled toward each other, rarely employed, atop a thick wool rug exactly the color of dark wine.

Fleetingly, Raina stared longingly just beyond where Torsten stood, at the closed door.

When he was done perusing the chamber, he turned his gaze to her.

"I won't lie with you," she said, stiffening her spine. Her heart thudded in her chest. "Husband or no, you've shown me no—"

"I have nae interest in beddin' ye," he said frostily, "but we will share a chamber for a while."

Relief was confounded by the inexplicable offense taken at his cruel dismissal.

Though he apparently desired nothing from her, she yearned for clarification. "No interest on this night?" She questioned in a brittle manner. "Or do you intend that our marriage never be consummated?"

He'd walked forward, setting down the candle holder on the small, cloth-covered table, extinguishing the flame with his thumb and forefinger. When he turned, his rigid countenance was inscrutable.

From across the bed, he began to remove his belt, on which his scabbard and sword hung.

Raina swallowed thickly.

His eyes narrowed, he remarked, "Ye just expressed your own unwillingness. Why do ye question mine?"

"I don't," she was quick to assure him, her frown swift. "It's just that I would rather—I don't want to live with... with that hanging over my head."

He didn't say it, but she imagined that pride compelled him to sleep in her chamber. Certainly, the tyrant wouldn't want his troops supposing he hadn't the stomach for rape.

Steeling herself, she dared to ask, "What else should I know about... your expectations? About this sham of a marriage. Will I be a prisoner? What is allowed or prohibited?"

He sighed as he looped the belt around the post at the head of the bed, which apparently would be his side going forward, or *for a while.*

"Maintain the keep as ye have," he said brusquely. "Dinna leave the keep or bailey without permission from either myself, or Gilles, or Rory."

"I don't know who either Gilles or—"

"Ye will meet them soon enough."

"The peasants have their freedom and yet I am a prisoner?"

"Ye are free inside the keep to carry on as ye have, as chatelaine—"

"But I—"

"Do whatever it is that occupies your time," he said dismissively, unpinning the dragon's head brooch from his chest, laying it upon the bedside table. Next, he doffed his plaid, his long fingers gripping the gathered section at his shoulder and drawing it down and away.

Raina watched, her eyes affixed to his hands. Thoughts raced through her mind like startled birds. She noticed the scars etched into the weathered skin of his hands, evidence of battles fought and hardships endured. Strong and tanned, his hands deftly removed layers of armor and clothing as though shedding the weight of his responsibilities. She sensed a chilling reminder of his power—those hands, she presumed, wielded a sword that had often brought death, mayhap meted out justice with ruthless efficiency, or committed sins she dared not imagine.

Recalling their conversation, she stammered, "I don't... that is, there is nothing to occupy my time."

"Ye fancy yerself above manual labor?"

"I do not. I simply haven't—"

"Ye *will* labor," he assured her darkly, "nae less than any man or woman inside Lochlan. Dinna ken ye are above it."

Rather than explain to him that she hadn't been allowed a significant role in running the household as should have been expected of the daughter of the house, that her efforts had for months been met with inflexible resistance and icy resentment, Raina took issue with Torsten de Graham's method of communication. "Is this how it will be? I will rarely be allowed to actually finish a sentence or question?"

"I dinna suffer idle, pointless chatter," he said, "and nor do I plan to entertain haivering or demands."

"You are so quick to judge," she remarked with annoyance, "but don't allow a person to challenge your erroneous beliefs or views."

He shrugged as if he were scarcely bothered by his own error or her opinion of it.

Raina gave up. Not entirely out of fear or the threat of his chilling attitude, but rather out of sheer exasperation. He embodied something beyond arrogance—something higher, greater, more damaging, and altogether uglier. A sinking realization crept over her: he was a man who did not care to understand, who had already decided she was beneath his regard. Faced with such obstinacy, she knew any attempt to reason with him would be futile, leaving her feeling adrift in the riotous sea that was, sadly, her marriage and her future.

But then she hated herself for how meekly she'd gone along with everything thus far. Her resolve strengthened as she faced Torsten across the dimly lit chamber, her eyes blazing. "I will not share a bed with you," she declared, her voice wavering only slightly. "I've endured enough intrusion today."

Torsten's eyes narrowed, his features darkening with displeasure. "Do ye think yer defiance will change anything?"

"I don't even know you!" She challenged. "You are a stranger to me."

"I *could* bed ye now," he growled, his voice low and threatening. "I promise we'd nae be strangers by the time I was done."

Her jaw clenched at the same time her stomach flipped and she had to fight hard to resist the urge to flinch under his gaze. "I won't," she stated firmly, her hands balling into fists at her sides.

"Aye, ye will share this bed," he said, his tone infuriating for how certain and sure he sounded. He paused at the far side of the bed, his hands on the hem of his tunic. "Ken this, bride," he said, "I care nae more for ye than I do for a speck of dust on the hearth. What frightens ye, pleases ye, riles ye, it dinna matter to me. Whether ye ken joy or sorrow, I dinna care."

His response came as no surprise, not really, not after what she'd been shown of his character today.

Her eyes narrowed with her own contempt. Her chin quivered and her chest expanded with hatred, and she allowed it to rise and blossom and engulf her, so easily done—

—and then so swiftly dispersed and deflated, forgotten, hatred gone in a flash as her husband of half a day lifted his linen tunic over his head, exposing his naked torso.

Raina had all she could do to keep her eyes from widening.

She hadn't thought about it, about him half naked, but she supposed now that if she had, she might have expected that beneath the immaculate clothes, and the quilted leather brigandine and proud tartan, he would appear smaller, weaker, as if stripped of the imposing armor, he was not half the man his outer appearance suggested.

Not so. Despite being well into his third decade as she believed, Torsten de Graham was incredibly fit.

More than that, actually.

Despite the flush that crawled up her neck and warmed her cheeks, she couldn't drag her gaze away from him. Broad shouldered and with flesh taut with what seemed a youthful vigor, he was perfectly sculpted, his skin bronzed like the fishermen who often labored shirtless upon the beach and in the boats. A smattering of black and silver hair covered his chest, short and silky in the glow of the candle. The muscles of his arms were defined with great detail, bunched, corded, veined, rippling even with the simple task of folding his tunic.

There was nothing soft about him, which was fitting, she supposed; his chiseled torso was equally matched to his severe demeanor, both unyielding.

Uncharitably, she imagined that pillaging, plunder, and murder kept him in fine physical form.

Sadly, it did not occur to her to avert her gaze until *after* he'd caught her staring.

Her cheeks flamed brighter and hotter at the slowly evolving, knowing smirk he showed her, a silent acknowledgment of her observation.

Raising a brow, he began to untie the laces at the waistband of his breeches.

Horrified—both with her own mortification and for what might come next—Raina promptly spun around, presenting him with her back.

A softly uttered snort of derision answered, and Raina closed her eyes against...everything: him, his sneering contempt, the fact that she was married to him, her life, this humiliating moment, everything. Her head dropped to her chest while she composed herself.

Drawing in a deep breath, bemoaning the fact that there was no privacy screen in her chamber, and neither was there a small, connected anteroom in which she might change, Raina snuffed out the candle on the table beside what she now considered her side of the bed. Her fingers trembled slightly as she began to disrobe, bending to doff her short boots and hose and peeling off her léine. Thankfully, as she'd been denied a maid at Lochlan Hall, she was accustomed to undressing without assistance.

Reminding herself that her new husband hated her and that he had no designs on her as a mate, she didn't fret overmuch about the gray light of the darkened room, which might be enough for him to see her outline, but naught much else before she slipped under the sumptuous covers garbed in her shift.

Her bed at her aunt's house near Glasgow had been a short and narrow fixture, not quite large enough for even her small frame. She supposed she should be grateful for the breadth of her bed here at Lochlan Hall, for the fact that it was large enough that there was no reason that any part of her should ever come into contact with any part of him.

Still, this was the first time she had ever shared a bed—with anyone. She couldn't even recall that her mother had ever snuggled beside her when tucking her in or while comforting her after a night terror. Her nerves were frayed, and anxiety gnawed at her, increasing dramatically when she held her breath, wondering if he were completely naked now. Though they lay on opposite sides of the bed, the vast expanse offered little comfort. Her heart pounded, the unfamiliarity of it all unsettling her deeply.

For a long moment as she lay there, frozen, Raina reflected with growing self-contempt on her acquiescence throughout the day. How easily she'd gone along with everything! True, she'd shown some defiance at each astonishing event—the invasion, her wedding, sharing a table and now a bed with this stranger—but overall, she had failed miserably, too effortlessly beaten into submission each time.

Perhaps what she considered her own stalwart courage was an illusion. Over the years, she had perfected the art of playing a stoic role, never revealing emotions, which had in the last decade mostly been negative. She'd become adept at nodding in compliance to her father while keeping her chin high and her opposition to herself, having learned that it was simply easier to go along with his disagreeable plans.

Distractedly, she touched her forefinger to the scar on her cheek, a remnant from long ago of what her opposition could earn her. What she had once possessed in great quantities—courage and boldness—had been reduced over the years. All that remained, she feared, was a dispirited expression coupled with an embarrassingly small willingness to resist.

A spare glance to her left showed the outline of her husband's bare shoulder above the bedcoverings. He'd turned on his side, his back to her.

Raina tried to steady her heart rate and her breathing.

After an anxious quarter hour, where she lay stiffly on her back, having not moved a muscle, Torsten jerked around and spoke, his voice cutting through the silence, "Bluidy hell, woman. I trow I can hear your nerves splintering. Settle now, for Chrissakes, so that I might ken some peace."

He wanted peace?

He wanted peace!

Mayhap he also heard her teeth grinding with her renewed rage.

"And dinna think to escape this bed," he continued, his sharp tone lessened, but only minimally. "I may nae have designs on ye tonight, but we are bound together, like it or nae. Ye'd best accept it and learn to live with it."

"Go to hell," she muttered, summoning a wee bit of that neglected courage for how callous he was. "Or perhaps consider sleeping with one eye open, lest the *Killer of Men* strikes again."

He laughed at this, the sound unpleasant, sneering. "I ken ye're neither brave enough nor strong enough to see it done," he said and turned his back to her as if to prove he feared no reprisal from her.

Raina squeezed her eyes shut, the sorrowful truth of his words settling heavily in her mind.

She'd been brought low before—often—in her life but never had she felt so utterly adrift and alone.

I need to fix this. I can't live like this for the rest of my life.

This can't be it.

Chapter Five

Not surprisingly, what little sleep she had was neither deep nor restful. She was awake when the sun rose, watching the chamber evolve slowly from blackness to pre-dawn gray before the sun, rising in the east outside her window, casting its soft and pale light throughout the room.

She was fairly certain her new husband hadn't moved at all through the night, being yet on his side, one broad shoulder and arm visible above the blankets. A long scar of mottled red and white made a jagged line along his arm, from the back of his shoulder almost to his elbow. It sat like a rope upon his flesh, appearing to have either been gruesome in origin or poorly stitched, one portion of it as thick as her thumb.

She moved her head slowly on the pillow and stared at the back of his head, more than only a little curious about how short he kept his hair. The line of hair along his neck was perfectly straight, showcasing the precision of the cut. The hair at the nape of his neck was mostly black, clipped extremely close to the skin, the same way it was around his ears. Higher up on his head, the gray hair took over, growing in thick locks that were kept just a touch longer. Raina wasn't sure why she expected that his hair would have been or should have been coarse and wiry—save that it would match his demeanor—but it appeared silky and soft.

A curiosity, at any rate, as she knew few men who kept their hair shorn so close to their heads.

She was advised of his waking by the way he stretched his bare arm toward the ceiling, luxuriating in a lengthy morning stretch. Her lips parted, fascinated by the play of muscles in his upper arm and forearm, as they shifted and danced and stiffened as he flexed. Naught but a moment later, he threw back the furs and blankets and sat up, putting his feet on the floor. For a moment, he only sat, his face turned toward the end of the bed and beyond, unmoving as he stared out the window.

Raina's gaze traveled over the expanse of his broad back, noting the powerful muscles rippling beneath his skin as he lifted his left arm to scratch the skin over his left shoulder. His shoulders were wide and strong, leading to a well-defined back that tapered down to a narrow waist. The morning light highlighted the ridges and valleys of his toned body, giving him a statuesque appearance. Scattered across his back were other unmistakable marks of battle—old scars from sword slashes and arrow wounds, some pale and faded with time, others newer and still slightly pink. Raina found herself reluctantly entranced by the sheer strength and masculinity radiating from him, every inch of his frame exuding a raw, primal power.

Unbidden, her mind drifted into a hazy reverie, imagining what it would be like to be shielded by such a powerful and imposing figure. To be under his care, enveloped in his strength and protection, rather than under his thumb and regarded with disdain.

Shaking herself mentally against any pointless hope or wish, she thought again of what he'd said yesterday, what he'd accused her father of, horrific assaults and depraved murder. As shocking as it had been, Raina hadn't been able to muster an instant and certain denial—she had some idea, improving daily, of what her father was capable of.

Hadn't she always imagined how brutal her father would be in war? Hadn't she known pity for any man, woman, village, or army that was unfortunate enough to cross his path?

Understanding that she, now wed to this angry man, would likely pay for her father's sins, Raina was rather surprised that she hadn't been mistreated or abused thus far. But she hadn't time to dwell upon Torsten de Graham's character, what had prevented him from doing so. He stood then, revealing that he hadn't slept naked beside her but wore his braies yet, and before Raina could wrench her gaze away and close her eyes to feign sleep, he turned, his dark-eyed gaze locking onto hers with an intensity that made her heart skip a beat.

Apparently, yesterday's gruff and severe countenance was not only the result of the siege, confronting his enemy, and being compelled by the king to wed a woman he obviously loathed; but instead the cold indifference and unyielding resolve were simply facets of his natural demeanor. Raina shuddered despite the weight and warmth of the bedcoverings.

Of course there was no morning greeting.

"Rise, wife," he said, moving the neatly piled stack of his clothing onto the bed. "We shall break our fast together, and with the steward. I aim to learn more about the administration of Lochlan Hall." He shook out his tunic and lifted it over his head, pulling it down around over his shoulders and torso, concealing all the glory of his bare chest and lean abdomen.

Teeth clenched, Raina nodded. And while he dressed there at the side of the bed, Raina slipped out from beneath the blankets, her cheeks pinkening instantly as she imagined his seething gaze fixed on her back as she approached the tall, two door cupboard. Not meaning to dally, she plucked out the first léine her hands touched, a simple bliaut of light green wool, the narrow sleeves richly embroidered. With her back to the chamber and Torsten de Graham, she pulled that over her head and took her time lacing up the darker green silk ribbons at each side.

A knock sounded at the door, startling Raina despite the fact that the same tentative rap came at this time every morning. She waited, since the lad Crispin normally entered soon after knocking, though today he did not.

"Enter," called Torsten.

The door was pushed open with a narrow foot, the lad's hands filled with an ewer of water, which he brought every morning. 'Twas the only service Raina was allowed, an edict of her father which Seòras had asserted should remain. Crispin delivered water to rinse her face and teeth. Sometime later in the day, he would empty the chamber pot, though Raina rarely employed it, preferring to use the garderobe at the end of the hall.

She turned but briefly to acknowledge the lad's presence, inclining her head. She tried to imagine what he saw or thought—the newly wedded couple risen and dressing, not a word exchanged. Raina's movements were careful and deliberate, as if any sudden action might shatter the fragile silence she much preferred. Surely, the lad could not be oblivious to the tension in the air, the palpable strain that hung over the chamber like a dark cloud.

The stain of a blush remained on her cheeks, guessing that any person she encountered today might regard her differently, imagining that her new husband had asserted his rights in the marriage bed last night.

"Thank you, Crispin," she said as the lad scurried to exit the chamber. Another fleeting glance showed him backing out, pulling the door closed, his gaze darting curiously between husband and wife.

To her relief, Torsten departed only a moment later, saying naught but that she should not tarry.

When he was gone, she drooped a bit, relaxing her shoulders, the anxious rigidity difficult to maintain. Dropping her head to her chest, she prayed for strength and peace.

She made quick work of her morning toilette, washing her face and hands and scrubbing her teeth before combing out her hair. Although she didn't miss the matronly and unfriendly maids at her aunt's house, who barely let her do anything for herself, since returning home, she faced the challenge of managing her own hair. It was thick and long, and combing through the tangles was quite a chore. With few duties inside Lochlan Hall, Raina usually had the luxury of taking her time. However, today she feared that she should not keep her husband waiting too long. Finding a green silk ribbon that matched the laces of her bliaut, she gathered her long, thick hair and secured it neatly at her nape, allowing the length of it to cascade down her back.

When she was done, she walked down the passageway to the little hall, surprised to enter and find it empty, devoid of even the lone setting that normally sat at one end of the table. With her hand on the door, she stared for a moment, nonplussed, until she became aware of noise drifting upward from below.

She approached the open gallery on the second floor, peering over the edge to survey the scene below. The great hall stretched out beneath her, the space presently filled with bustling activity, as she'd never seen it before.

Straightaway, her eyes found Torsten, seated in her father's chair, and surrounded by several de Graham soldiers, some also sitting at the table, others standing before it. Voices overlapped in serious discussion, the sound easily carrying in so cavernous a chamber.

She hesitated at the gallery's edge, biting her lip, wanting very badly to run the other way. Gathering her courage, she descended the stairs, her heart pounding in her chest with each step. As she reached the ground floor, her steps slowed, and she swallowed hard before crossing the length of the hall.

Torsten's gaze met hers when she was halfway across, his expression unreadable. He nodded at whatever the man directly in front of him was saying, the man using his hands often and animatedly in his speech.

Approaching nervously, she moved towards the high table, and then around to the back side. Slowly, conversations ceased or were abandoned, her presence gradually drawing attention, and she felt the eyes of many upon her.

She tried to smile at the group in general but feared it came off as naught but a stiff grimace.

Torsten stood and held out the chair next to his, in which Raina had never once sat, the chair having been vacant since her mother had passed. Having received scant courtesy from him thus far, the kindness rather surprised her, but she did not acknowledge it in any way. She was here because he'd said that she should be; if he'd not requested her presence—it hadn't quite been an imperious command, she allowed—she would have made herself scarce, unavailable, mayhap all day long.

Though he returned to the front of his chair, he did not immediately sit beside her.

"Lady Raina," he said, "allow me to introduce to you the officers of my army." He pointed first to the man at her right, a man as unkempt as Torsten de Graham was tidy, quite a bit older than Torsten himself, with flowing chestnut hair, liberally streaked with white, and what seemed kind green eyes. "Gilles MacPherson, captain of the de Graham militia and master-at-arms."

"How do you do?" She greeted him.

"Well enough," said the man. "And pleased to ken ye, lass."

As his smile seemed genuine, Raina found herself returning it easily, appreciating the warmth in his demeanor.

"This is Aonghas MacCoinnich," Torsten gestured to the man on his left, who stood with an air of authority and readiness, "our logistics officer. He ensures our supplies are well-managed and our troops well-fed."

Eòghann nodded at Raina, his expression serious yet respectful.

Torsten moved along, introducing each man: Rory MacLeod and a very young man named Thomas were the army's scouts; Eòghann Cameron, a stout man with a thick beard and a serious expression, was de Graham's engineer; Uilleam Stewart, tall and lean, with sharp features and a meticulous air about him—the young man who had hurried her along from the beach to her wedding yesterday—was the quartermaster; and James MacGilchrist, of average height, with striking blue eyes that seemed to miss nothing and an anxious air about him, held two roles, intelligence and intendance officer—Raina might imagine what the former was, but she hadn't any idea about the latter role.

Each man nodded politely at her. Thomas, possibly the youngest of the officers, repeated Gilles's greeting, saying he was pleased to meet her.

"I am woefully ignorant of all the necessary duties inside an army," she said, her gaze moving around the group of men, "but I imagine I will begin to understand more as time goes on."

As was her husband, these men should be counted as her enemy, but as none of them had yet to exhibit any of their commander's hostility, she had no cause to be rude or cool to them. She meant to give them the benefit of the doubt, hoping none would prove to be as cold as Torsten de Graham.

Torsten finally sat, and just now Raina realized that several platters of food sat before the new laird of Lochlan Hall. It seemed a grander selection than she'd ever been served.

The spread included fresh-baked bread with butter and preserves and honey, slices of cured ham and smoked fish, and a selection of cheeses. A bowl of berries soaked in cream and pitchers of ale accompanied the meal. Used trenchers, earthenware bowls, and wooden cups were scattered about the table, hardly having any remains.

Talk resumed around her while Raina stared with curiosity at the elaborate fare—elaborate by Lochlan's previous standards for the morning meal—but soon enough her attention was drawn to the conversation around her.

"Twenty-eight fishermen," James MacGilchrist was saying, "but three nae able-bodied at this time, and two to three who only work as needed. One lass involved there. They work four or five days a week, dependent upon the weather, the sea, and the bounty."

Torsten frowned at Raina. "Why does the lass partake in the fishing?"

Raina cleared her throat. "Nell's husband died, and she was allowed to take his place in the fishery. She...she has small children and no other kin to speak of." She shrugged, having divulged all that she knew about Nell's circumstance.

Torsten's gaze remained fixed on her, his brow furrowed. "And what were you doing yesterday down at the beach with the ledger and coins?"

"I oversee the distribution of wages," Raina replied evenly. "Each week, the fishermen and Nell receive payment for their catch. It's my responsibility to calculate their earnings based on the weight of the fish caught and a share of that divided by the hours worked," she said, finding it difficult to meet his gaze steadily. Several times, her gaze darted away from him, so unnerved by the probing quality of his stare. "This ensures they receive fair compensation for their labor, consistently."

This responsibility was Raina's sole domain, her only opportunity to contribute, granted solely because of her skill with numbers. Also though, her father had insisted that only a MacQueen should handle wage disbursement, a tactic to foster loyalty and gratitude among the workers—"so that they know to whom they owe their allegiance and to whom they are indebted," her father had once said. Despite appreciating Seòras's support beside her, Raina often felt his presence was more about her father's distrust, as if she might be suspected of mishandling or pilfering funds if left unattended.

Torsten's scowl deepened. "And what happens in winter or during bad weather? Are they not compensated fairly for their time, even if the fish catch is low?"

Understanding his concern, Raina explained patiently, "There is a minimum wage based on hours worked, ensuring they have some income even during lean weeks. A good haul adds to their earnings, while a poor week still guarantees them compensation, albeit less generously." She couldn't deny, however, that the minimum amount was often insufficient for the fisherfolk, many of whom struggled to support their families.

With that explained and presumably comprehended, Torsten introduced another subject, asking James what he'd learned about the trade network in place in Aberdeen.

"Excuse me," Raina cut in quietly. "I'm sorry," she said when Torsten turned yet another implacable scowl her way. "But might I be allowed to continue? I mean, I did not have a chance to begin paying the wages yesterday...and I, well, I imagine they will need their income."

"Aye," Torsten allowed after only a moment's hesitation. "Gilles and Rory will escort ye down there this morn."

Again he tried to instigate the next matter of business.

Raina held up her hand to forestall him. This he did not like at all, as evidenced by the tension that tightened his jaw and the impatient flicker in his eyes. His posture grew more rigid, and he drew in a sharp breath, clearly signaling his disapproval of being halted once more. Despite his silent rebuke, Raina pressed on, rather pleased by the sudden boldness that helped her do so.

"Apologies, but it is Seòras's practice to accompany me—"

"The steward?" Torsten clarified, and one of his men chuckled. "Nae. He'll nae be going anywhere until he adheres his loyalties to de Graham and Robert Bruce."

"Oh," she said, not knowing at this moment how she felt about that, either Torsten's rigidity or Seòras's apparent stubbornness. "And what has happened to the pouch of coins and the ledger that I had brought down to the beach yesterday?" she asked. "I assume you have...claimed the coins?"

"Lochlan Hall belongs to me," he said coolly, "and thus the coin is mine, attained by the king's command and nae stolen. But aye, the purse was put into safekeeping. Gilles will present it when ye're ready to trek down to the beach."

Though his response felt like a rebuke, Raina nodded and murmured, "Thank you."

That was all she wanted for now.

For the next hour, she listened without speaking, more interested in how Torsten de Graham communicated with his officers and how he reacted to items that were presented as concerns rather than the issues themselves, some of which detailed the inner workings of Lochlan but which she knew very little about.

For a while she stared with longing at the plentiful fare sitting before her, her stomach gnawing at her because she'd walked out on supper last night. There were no clean bowls or unused trenchers on the table, and it took her many minutes to work up the courage to reach for a crust of bread, shrinking back into the oversized chair to nibble upon it. When neither Torsten nor any of his men took issue with this, Raina helped herself to a generous slice of cured ham.

Mostly, she stared straight ahead, over the heads of Rory and Uilleam who stood directly in front of the table and was revisited by a series of thoughts she'd had before.

She kept waiting for things to get better, kept hope alive even as it was foiled again and again. Her mother died, and she'd thought she'd grow closer to her father, believing he might find solace in their shared grief. Instead, he became even harsher and grew more distant.

When she was sent to her aunt's house, she thought it would be an improvement over Lochlan Hall, hoping her aunt might be warm and nurturing like her mother. But her father's sister was as cold and indifferent as her brother, her keep more an austere tomb than home.

Upon returning to Lochlan, she expected the peasants' dislike of her to have lessened, imagining they'd have forgotten about the implausible reasons behind their hatred. But their disdain was as sharp as ever, and her father's illness had only made him more tyrannical before he'd lost the ability to speak, had not softened him as she had hoped.

Hope was ridiculous, she decided. She refused to entertain it any more. This was her life now, married to this cold-blooded man, stuck at Lochlan Hall all her days. Mayhap Torsten was right; she'd better get used to it. Every glimmer of hope she had clung to had been snuffed out, leaving her with nothing but the harsh reality of this new and dreadful situation.

Gilles interrupted her reverie, his words advising her that their meeting had concluded.

"I've a bit of time to spare now, lass," he said. "Let's take care of yer chore on the beach."

Chapter Six

After Gilles had brought forth the coins, he, Raina, and Rory then proceeded down to the beach, where the fishery bustled same as it had yesterday, as if no great calamity had occurred less than twenty-four hours ago in the sand.

The table and chair were still there, both tipped over and separated by twenty feet. Raina righted them, not sure if the siege had toppled them or if the sea had. She dragged the table back to where it had sat yesterday, and Gilles set down the coins. Rory laid the ledger on the table.

While Raina dragged the chair through the sand, Gilles moved the table further back, close to the cliff.

"Dinna mind me, lass," he said. "These auld knees will give me grief if I stand too long."

He'd positioned the crude and lightweight table at the base of the cliff, where a shelf of red sandstone made a suitable seat, and promptly sat down.

"And where does this come from anyhow?" Gilles asked of the table, tapping his palm against it.

"It's kept in storage in a chamber near the kitchen," she replied.

"And how does it come down? Goes up and down every week?"

Raina nodded. "I carry it."

Gilles's frown was swift and severe. "Do ye jest? Ye carry it, haul it down that treacherous decline?"

Raina glanced at Rory, who was frowning as well. "Yes. It's...not very difficult." But then, it wasn't exactly easy. "I cannot sit in the sand nor stand while—"

"And ye go back up and bring down the chair?" Gilles was astounded.

Raina nodded but didn't tell him that she had to trek up and down a third time, every week, to bring down the ledger and coins.

"Nae. Nae," Gilles protested. "And ye're done with that. Going forward, they'll come to the hall and ye'll—"

"But... I like being at the beach," Raina informed him. She couldn't have this taken away from her. It was one of the few solaces she knew at Lochlan, the sea itself a reminder of the world's vastness and the freedom that lay just beyond her reach.

Mayhap Gilles read her anxious mien. His face twisted with a bit of displeasure, but he did relent.

"Fine, but ye're nae to be dragging this around nae more," he said sternly, tapping his forefinger on the table. "I'll assign a few lads to carry the table and chair each week."

Raina smiled with delight. "Thank you."

She sat down then and looked out beyond the sand, drawing in a deep breath of salty air. The North Sea stretched out before her, a vast expanse of churning, steel-gray water under a sky dappled with clouds. Small waves crashed against the shore in a rhythmic, almost hypnotic pattern, their frothy crests glinting in the pale sunlight. Seabirds wheeled overhead, their cries mingling with the sound of the surf, and a cool breeze carried the scent of salt and seaweed.

The knarr and currachs bobbed gently in the shallows, their black water-stained hulls contrasting with the muted tones of the sea and sky. The fisherfolk moved about, tending to their nets and gear, half of them preparing to take out the currachs, their voices carried to her ears by the wind.

"And what now?" Gilles asked, drawing her gaze to him. "Why are they nae coming?"

"Oh," Raina responded. "Well, I normally don't arrive this early. I like to come at the end of the day, and I wait for them to conclude their work day."

"Wait? Nae, we willna be doing that either," he said. He waved an impatient hand at Rory. "Round 'em up. If they want to be paid, they best get it now or they'll go without."

Rory went off immediately while Raina tried to protest this. "But I—"

"Nae buts," he said. The ledge upon which he sat was a little higher than her chair, which had sunk into the sand when she sat. He put both palms onto the table and leaned down toward her, his gaze sharp. "Ye are Lady Raina, wife now to Torsten de Graham, and they," he said, pointing one hand toward the people on the beach, "owe their livelihood to ye and Lochlan. They might wait on ye, but ye dinna wait on them. Remember that."

Raina nodded obediently.

The sea's salty breeze tugged at her hair and skirts as the fisherfolk began to form a queue, their faces stern, likely displeased to have been called from their labors. Raina greeted the first fisherman with a curt nod, her expression impassive as she collected a small scrap of paper from him.

"Robert," she acknowledged, perusing the paper and the scratch upon it.

"Mm," the man replied indifferently.

"And what's that?" Gilles wanted to know.

Raina tipped the piece of vellum toward him, so that he could see it contained only a name and a number. "Their supervisor, Kenneth, keeps track of their hours. They would have been given this the night before last."

Gilles nodded, and Raina carried on, recording Robert's hours in the ledger and using a separate sheet of vellum to calculate his wages based on the numbers she already had regarding how many pounds of fish they'd hauled in the week prior.

Raina dipped the quill into the ink once more and recorded his name and the amount due in the ledger, then counted out the appropriate coins. "Here you are," she said, handing him the money without further acknowledgment.

Gilles stood nearby, his keen eyes observing the proceedings. After a few more fishermen had come and gone, he cleared his throat and addressed the queue.

"From now on, each of ye state yer name as ye approach," he commanded, his voice carrying over the sound of the waves. "I want to ken who's who."

The next fisherman, a stocky man with a bushy beard, stepped forward and did as instructed, announcing his name. "Wedast."

Raina recorded the name in the ledger and handed him his pay, her demeanor unchanged. "Thank you," she said mechanically.

As the queue continued to move, Raina fell into the usual rhythm of the task. Each fisherman stepped up, stated his name, received his pay, and exchanged minimal or no words with her. The atmosphere was tense, the fisherfolk's resentment palpable.

Gilles observed quietly, occasionally nodding in approval but mostly silent.

"Charles," said the next man, a tall, lanky fellow who barely glanced at her.

Raina made the entry and gave him his coins, her smile forced. "Good day."

The process continued, Nell being the next in line. She and all the fishermen maintained a cold distance, and Raina reciprocated in kind. Gilles, true to his word, made an effort to remember each name and face, occasionally asking a question or two, his tone congenial.

"How's the catch been this week, Duncan?" he asked one of the men, a broad-shouldered fisherman with a sullen expression.

"Better than last, sir," Duncan replied tersely. "The herring are plentiful."

Gilles nodded, his approval muted. "Guid."

Duncan stared down at Raina then, a sneer turning his mouth down. "Hope ye got what ye deserve in the marriage bed last night."

Gilles pulled himself up off the shelf of the cliff and approached the man. With his hand on the hilt of his sword, he asked in a low growl, "What did ye say?"

Instilled with neither fear nor shame, Duncan stood eye to eye with Gilles and repeated his lewd remark, this time brazenly enunciating each word.

Raina's brow knit when Gilles tossed back his head and roared with laughter. Her heart dropped from her chest to her belly. Duncan chortled along with him, and several others joined in as well. She clamped her trembling lips together, feeling the sting of humiliation and isolation. Though she forced herself to remain composed, her face flushed with anger and embarrassment.

In the next moment and without warning, Gilles's laughter stopped unexpectedly, and his fist shot out, connecting solidly with Duncan's jaw. The force of the blow sent Duncan staggering back, his sneering chortle abruptly silenced. The other men fell quiet, the echo of the impact lingering in the air.

"Never—ever—speak to her in that manner again," Gilles growled, his eyes blazing with anger. "I'll tolerate nae disrespect—that's yer laird's wife, Lady Raina to ye." He straightened and addressed the people still in line. "Any of ye imagine ye can cross that line and nae suffer for it, be warned 'tis nae so. Ye'll be dealing with me."

Duncan rubbed his jaw and glared at Gilles.

"And I'm waiting on ye to acknowledge this and make yer apology to Lady Raina," Gilles instructed, his voice as cold as ice.

Getting to his feet, showing more embarrassment to have been knocked down by a man almost twice his age, Duncan nodded at Gilles and muttered a grudging and lackluster, "My apologies," to Raina.

Gilles nodded once, then turned back to Raina. "Continue," he said, his voice softer now, "but cut his pay in half and continue to do so until ye hear from me that he's discovered half a brain and has learned how to conduct himself in yer presence."

Raina, though shaken, gave a tight nod, her eyes avoiding Duncan's. She resumed her task, her hands shaking slightly as she recorded the reduced disbursement in the ledger.

After that, Gilles stood protectively in front of the table now, arms crossed over his chest and glaring at each man who approached. Rory had moved closer from the end of the line, wearing an equally unpleasant expression.

When all was done and the last man had been paid, Gilles narrowed his eyes at Raina. "I kent ye said ye favored the beach," he clipped.

Raising her chin, Raina defended her remark. "I very much enjoy the beach and the sea, but much less so the people."

Rory stepped closer to the table, his frown as harsh as Gilles's. "Why dinna they like ye?"

Raina moved the ribbon to the center of the ledger and closed the book. "Haven't you heard?" She questioned Rory with an infuriated smirk. "I've killed three men, have I not?"

There was more to it, she knew, so much more to their hatred. More rubbish, more maddening for the origins of it.

It began with a dreadful storm that struck the village six years ago, shortly after her mother had died. Lightning had struck the thatched roof of the cattle barns, causing a fire that decimated half their stock and razed half the homes nearby. In the chaos, a young girl, Clara, had gone missing, and despite exhaustive searches, no trace of the girl was ever found.

Some villagers, in their grief and desperation, began whispering about seeing Raina lingering near the outskirts of the village that very night. They claimed she was chanting softly to herself, her eyes glinting eerily in the flickering light of the burning hall. Others swore they saw her clutching a peculiar talisman, muttering words they couldn't comprehend.

Despite Raina's protestations and the fact that she was abed all that night—sadly, with none to support her alibi— the suspicion took root. Clara's disappearance became linked to Raina's presence, and soon, accusations of witchcraft spread like wildfire through the village. Even now, years later, the memory of that tragic night continued to fuel the villagers' animosity towards her, painting her as a witch responsible for their misfortunes, those on that night and any since.

The death of three suitors certainly had not endeared her to them, had only fueled the gross supposition that she was indeed a witch.

Regarding those most recent rumors, she informed them, "Your laird believes it and I'm sure he plans to hold it against me, among other crimes for which I am not responsible."

"Bluidy hell," Gilles grumbled. Heaving a large sigh, he instructed Rory to take the table back up to the keep.

While Raina packed into the basket the much lighter purse of coins, the journal, ink, and quill, Gilles watched her through narrowed eyes. Rory lifted the table over his head when it was empty and marched away, making the chore look easy.

Gilles picked up the chair, meaning to lug it back to the keep, but didn't move immediately.

Measuring her with a probing stare, his green eyes darkened with intention, he said to her, "Aye, and take it from someone who kens yer new husband, lass, better and longer than any. Ye stand yer ground with him," he counseled. "He's nae without honor, nae without fairness. But aye, he'll walk all over ye if ye show weakness. He has nae respect for that."

"Ye want me to adjust my character to soothe my new husband?" Raina challenged. "The one I didn't want?"

He harrumphed at this, not unpleasantly, but as if to convey that he took her point.

"Ye endured quite a few shocks yesterday, lass, by my reckoning. Suffered a mighty army overtaking yer home. Unexpectedly wed—to *one ye dinna want*—and mayhap ye learned a thing or two about yer sire ye'd rather nae have kent. Ah, but ye dinna weep. Ye went resolutely toward what ye imagine is yer doom—the wedding. All day long, nae blatting, nae bawling. So aye, I dinna ken I'm suggesting ye become a different person. I only suggest that ye needn't be afraid to be who ye are." He raised a brow at her, seeming to hope she understood. And then he hoisted the chair over his shoulder, using only one hand to secure it. "Och, he looks like he'll bite—yer husband, that is—but I promise ye he willna. Breathe fire, he will, he is the dragon after all. But he willna bite his wife. He's nae made like that."

Only because he seemed so compassionate, almost as she expected a father might behave—but what did she know about kindhearted fathers?—she almost dared to ask if she behaved so, more resolutely, toward the peasants and the fisherfolk, if she might generate less animosity. But she knew the answer already. She'd attempted many times over the years to sway their unfair beliefs about her: ignoring them, reasoning with them, growing imperious, and becoming resigned. Their opinions had never changed. She remained, since returning to Lochlan Hall, merely resigned.

Gilles narrowed his eyes at her, measuring her thoughtfully. "Peacekeeper, are ye? Never wanting to stir the pot or make waves? Ye'd rather mend fences than swing axes," he guessed.

She nodded stiffly, knowing she disliked confrontation and all manner of conflict, that she'd learned that any and all machinations to change what was thrust upon her went unnoticed, unheeded.

"Make the waves, lass," Gilles sagely advised, "lest ye drown in someone else's sea."

With that, he turned and began the climb toward the keep.

Raina followed, a wee bemused by Gilles's perception, no less than she was touched by his consideration.

Make waves lest she drown in someone else's sea, she mused.

SHE'D KEPT A LOW PROFILE throughout the afternoon, partly driven by an unconscious desire to avoid her husband. With no official duties within the keep, Raina often found herself slipping away. Today, after returning from the beach with a slight but noticeable spring in her step—thanks to the unexpected kindness from Gilles and, to some extent, Rory—she paid a visit to her father. Though he could no longer speak, his disdain for her was palpable, likely a delayed reaction to her being forced to wed Torsten de Graham. She refused to let his scorn affect her.

Sadly, though buoyed by her improved mood, she found herself at a loss for how to channel her energy. Eventually, she did what she knew best: she sought refuge within the keep, retreating to her mother's former solar. There, she spent the day engrossed in an embroidery panel, meticulously stitching a scene of gulls soaring over the tumultuous sea.

Supposing that she was expected, and because her stomach had not met a substantial meal in almost thirty-six hours, Raina arrived in the little hall just before seven that evening. Torsten was already there, his back to the chamber, staring out the northern window.

"I would offer ye a chair," he said, "but I willna bother if ye mean again to leap from it and flee." His tone was edged with sarcasm, a reminder of the previous night's tension.

Raina stiffened, her hands clenching at her sides. "I did not flee," she replied, her voice cool. "I merely sought a more congenial atmosphere." Forcing and air of nonchalance, which she hoped masked the thudding of her heart and the quickening of her breath that his enigmatic presence provoked, she said lightly, "Perhaps you will resist provoking me, and we might be allowed to sup in relative peace."

Sweet Jesus, but she hoped that Gilles had not led her falsely.

He gave a short, humorless laugh. "Anything is possible, I suppose. Sit, then. Let us attempt to get through this meal with some semblance of civility."

Raina moved to the table and took her seat, keenly aware of his eyes on her. As she settled into the chair, she forced herself to meet his gaze, determined not to show any sign of weakness.

She hated that she felt like a child playing dress-up in his presence, hated that in the company of his imposing demeanor she felt wholly inadequate, as if there was reason for him to look down on her. His piercing eyes, dark and intense, seemed to see through her pretense of calmness, making her feel vulnerable and exposed.

More than anything, she despised herself for her inability to deny his indisputable handsomeness. His strong jaw, high cheekbones, and firm mouth all suggested a man accustomed to command and control, forming a striking façade. Though loath to admit it, the more she saw of him, the more handsome he appeared. How could she find anything appealing in a man who had laid siege to her home, forcing her into this unwanted union by the king's decree? She despised him for what he had done, for the way he had disrupted her life. And yet, his presence was impossible to ignore, a blend of raw power and an enigmatic aura that both repelled and fascinated her.

Fairly quickly, she decided that she might almost enjoy sharing the boards with him. If he would say nothing, keep all his noxious and self-serving opinions to himself, if he would remain completely silent, she might actually enjoy simply being able to stare at him.

Crispin and Arthur arrived shortly after Torsten and Raina had seated themselves, the lads looking no more comfortable today than they had yesterday. Supper was laid before them, individual platters of the same fare presented to both ends of the table. Arthur removed the trays when they were done and Crispin remained a moment more, pouring wine from a pewter flagon into each of their goblets before he set the carafe in front of Torsten and took his leave.

"Why is the household staff made up entirely of lads?" Torsten asked when the door closed behind Crispin. "Why are there nae lasses? I've seen several in the village who could take on roles here inside the keep."

"I...I'm not sure," she said hesitantly, made nervous by the query. "It's been this way for years."

"Your father's edict?"

"I suppose so."

She did have an inkling, though, of what had prompted the removal of females from the keep. She remembered her father raging at her brother about his treatment of a young girl named Lori. There was another incident, shortly after her mother had passed, when a village lass, Barbara, had been brought into the hall, her face bruised, her lip bloody, and her father's hand heavy on her shoulder as he confronted Malcolm MacQueen. Barbara's father had accused Raina's brother, Donald, of assaulting his daughter and had demanded recompense that stormy night. Raina, barely more than a child herself, hadn't understood the true nature of the accusations. She had assumed it was a mere scuffle, a fight with fists provoked by either Donald's want to bully or Barbara's known barbed tongue, but not anything more sinister.

Within weeks of that incident, Barbara's father, Roland Pender, had left Lochlan Hall to join the MacQueen army. A few months later, the girl Clara, had gone missing.

Barbara had moved to Montrose, taking a position inside an inn.

Shortly after that, Donald had been sent away from Lochlan, accompanied by a dozen soldiers, part of the Hall's home guard. He'd been brought to his father's side, made to fight in the war against England.

Raina never allowed her thoughts on the matter to progress further than that, would not allow herself to put two and two together. Her brother, Donald, was not kind, not always pleasant, but he wasn't capable of pure evil. The idea that he could be responsible for such heinous acts was too abhorrent to entertain.

Whenever her mind began to wander down that dark path, she would immediately halt it, redirecting her focus to more palatable thoughts. It was easier to believe that the accusations were baseless, the result of misunderstandings or even malice. The villagers' gossip was just that—idle talk born of jealousy or spite. And the disappearance of Clara? Surely it had to be a coincidence, a tragic but unrelated event.

Raina had not seen Donald since he'd left to take part in the war many years ago. She'd been informed by her aunt that he was in residence at Lochlan almost two years ago, but Raina had not been permitted to return home to see him, and his stay had been brief, she'd learned.

"The lads need to be laboring in the fishery, learning that trade," Torsten said now, "and nae serving meals and scrubbing chamber pots. Some mayhap will be chosen to take up arms and will need to be trained in that regard." After another lengthy perusal in which she felt both undressed and lacking, he said, "I will leave it in your hands to correct this backward arrangement. Bring up lasses from the village to replace the lads. I'll allow a week for this to be implemented before the lads are removed from the keep."

Her reaction to this was, admittedly, conflicted.

She liked the idea of having, finally, something to do. But she disliked his authoritative manner, his want to disrupt the household and the methods that had been in place for years and seemed to work well.

"And get yourself a maid," Torsten said, spearing a hunk of venison with his eating knife. "Why have ye not?" He plopped the meat into his mouth and chewed thoughtfully, awaiting her reply.

"I did not imagine any of the lads would have made a good candidate," she said. "And mayhap you've surmised already, but my father was—is," she corrected, since he lived yet, "frugal." An understatement, that, since Malcolm MacQueen was in fact miserly to a fault, and to the detriment of many.

Torsten scowled at this, his mien suggesting his disbelief. "Aside from the austerity of the great hall, the keep is well appointed." He waved his free hand around the little hall. "Plenty of coin spent here and in yer chamber. Yer léines were nae made locally, my guess, but are pricey imports." Tipping his knife to the flagon of wine. "Flemish? Or from Gascony?"

Though she bristled at his insinuation that she lied, she understood why the discrepancy may have advised him to believe as much. "Any precious and costly décor inside Lochlan are simply remnants from when my mother lived, and from a time when Lochlan Hall saw many important visitors. My léines—all of my wardrobe— were purchased, begrudgingly I'm sure, for my time in Glasgow."

"Ah, meant to snare a husband," he said. "And why do ye nae sup or use at all the great hall? Why does Lochlan nae open its doors to the peasants, at least to those in need?"

"That would be a costly endeavor, would require peat and kindling for the fires, someone to fetch it, would need a great many more servants, and more food and staples than my father would allow to be kept on hand. When my mother passed, many...gentler traditions passed with her."

"They labor for ye, those peasants, put coin in yer coffers to afford yer fine garb," he said. "Turn it around now. Bring in what ye need to host suppers for all. I've got an army of nearly four hundred, and they will need to be fed."

"I don't know—"

"Figure it out," he said coolly.

Raina glared at him. She'd wanted to convey to him several things. First, 'twas unlikely the peasants in the village would choose to willingly work inside the keep, certainly not under her direction. And next, she didn't believe for one second that they would choose to sup in the great hall.

"I will make that my life's mission," she said bitingly, spearing a morsel of beef onto her knife.

Torsten tilted his face at her from across the table, one brow raised presumably with some surprise at her tartness. A snort of a chuckle burst from him, the sound unpleasant. The smile that accompanied it, however, and though it was meanly given, was quite striking, making him appear more approachable, nearly human. But Raina didn't know if that were a good thing or not.

Chapter Seven

"Lochlan ain't right. Nae one thing 'tis as expected. Forget the auld man dying in the bed, with eyes that see and ken but with nae voice—ghost in the making is what he is."

That had been Gilles's impression more than an hour ago, ere Torsten had come to the bedchamber.

"Ye should ken," Gilles had continued, "they hate her. The fishermen, that is. I had to shut one up with my fist—*Jesu*, the way they glare at her, and the bile spewed from that one's mouth. She barely says two words, and what's she done to earn their enmity? Says they believe she personally kilt those men, the ones she was meant to marry." He snorted his disbelief. "Dinna let anything happen to ye—they'll have her tied to a stake and torches lit ere ye're cold and nae because they like *ye*."

Just as Torsten had been wondering why Gilles thought he might care, his captain had begun to tick off on his fingers other things at Lochlan that disturbed him.

"The keep is a tomb," he'd said. "Those scrawny lads serving and scrubbing is nae right, nae natural. Kitchen's a mess—have ye seen it? Supplies are haphazardly stored, half of them going bad before they're used, is my understanding. Garden plot too small for so large a keep, and nae maintained properly. The stables are nae better, everything in disarray, horses gaunt, stalls unclean—I wouldna put my auld wife in one of them and ye ken she and I ne'er did see eye to eye." He tapped his thumb lastly. "And dinna get me started on how they treat her—and what do I ken? here but two days—but it inna right, I can assure ye that."

"As ye seem to be so concerned for her well-being and how she's received, I'll put ye in charge of her. If the peasants despise her as ye say, she'll need an escort as she attempts to staff the keep properly. Make sure—bluidy hell, dinna shake yer head. I've just given ye—"

"Ye want to make changes and aye, that's reasonable, but she'll need to do that herself. I'll set a pair of lads on her, aye, but they'll keep their distance. She needs to do this herself. Ye dinna want a wife who canna—"

"I dinna want a wife at all," Torsten had reminded him, maddened by Gilles's concern for Raina. "And I dinna care how she gets on or that her day might be comprised of petty squabbles."

"*Jesu*, ye're a cold-hearted bastard."

He'd have punished severely any other person who had dared to speak to him in that manner.

"And ye're getting soft in yer auld age," Torsten had returned. "This is nae home, nae where we're meant to be. I've a duty to the king, half of it accomplished already. As soon as I ken everything I need to about Lochlan, we'll be gone."

"And what? Ye're going to abandon her? Ride off to war, ne'er see her again?"

"What do I owe her?"

"Bluidy hell, lad, ye took vows with her."

"At the king's command!" Torsten had reminded him heatedly.

Gilles had stood down, his shoulders sinking a bit as his expression became one of gape-jawed, scornful wonder. "Ye canna be so dense, can ye? She's young, and just committed the rest of her life to ye—nae of *her* own will, either!—and ye want to abandon her, and what's she got all her life? Nae husband, nae bairns—'cause I ken ye've nae bedded her; she's nae wearing a look of horror—nae anything but this wretched place and the scorn of many."

"God's bluid, but I'll nae be making bairns with the daughter of—"

"Christ Almighty, ye're..." he stopped, shaking his head. After exhaling a huge sigh, he waved his hand. "Mayhap it dinna matter. War'll kill ye soon enough—surprised it hasn't gotten ye yet. She'll be free, a widow then, mayhap allowed to make her own choices."

"Why the bluidy hell do ye care so much what becomes of her?"

"Because ye dinna!" Gilles had hissed. "Nae one does, by the looks of things. Talk to the fishermen, listen to their enmity. Speak with the herders and the folks in the village—Aonghas did. She is universally hated and ye're gonna tell me that's warranted? They call her a witch but dinna give a reason for it. Ye look at those calf eyes of hers, see how she startles at almost every noise, how bluidy meek she has made herself, her courage so swiftly wrecked in the face of fury, and ye ken the hatred is merited? I kent we protected the innocent, womenfolk and bairns."

"*Jesu*," Torsten had seethed, "she's nae Deirdre."

"Ye leave my daughter out of this. It's got nae anything to do with her."

"Are ye sure?" Torsten had pressed, knowing full well that Gilles lived with it, mountains of guilt and remorse, for not having been there when Deirdre had been slain by the farrier's son after she'd rejected his suit.

Torsten sat now in the bedchamber he shared with Raina, settled in one of the overstuffed chairs near the hearth, where he'd built a small fire as there had been none—evidence of Malcolm MacQueen's lasting influence and obsessive frugality? His pulse still pounded with annoyance for his conversation with Gilles, and his captain's misplaced concern for Raina MacQueen.

Raina de Graham, he reminded himself.

Killer of Men.

Suspected witch as well, it seemed.

To be fair, he did agree with Gilles in one regard, that as his wife, she should be accorded respect, no matter what the peasants thought of her. He would keep an eye on that matter, be a little more attuned to the nuances of lady and peasants but didn't imagine he would do anything about it. He simply didn't care enough.

He didn't mind watching her from across the chamber now as she slept, but he wouldn't let himself care. Not for Malcolm MacQueen's daughter. She was a complication he hadn't wanted, a forced alliance he resented. Yet, as he continued to observe her, he couldn't deny a growing fascination, a reluctant interest stirred against his better judgment.

Her face, serene in slumber, was highlighted by the small but mean scar high on her cheekbone, the soft firelight casting subtle shadows that emphasized its jagged edges, making the mark all the more intriguing. He had a mild curiosity about its origin, a tale he hadn't yet uncovered.

Her delicate features contrasted sharply with the defiance he had witnessed in her eyes. Little of it had come to life, however. As Gilles had said, she put forth only brief instances, quickly frustrated, of courage. The fragility of her appearance was neither a scheme nor emphasized to evoke pity; she was simply weak. Frightened and cowed, every emotion visible on her frequently bloodless face, every ambition of defiance readily thwarted by his threats and her fear.

His jaw tight, he noted the gentle rise and fall of her chest as she breathed, her face devoid of any sorrow or fright, soft and unguarded in sleep.

He didn't want to be attracted to his wife but could not deny what was obvious: she *was* bonny.

She did not braid her hair as he was aware many women did overnight, did not employ any head covering to keep her locks free of tangles. 'Twas a glorious mane of hair, loose and unrestrained, spilling over the pillow, glinting with gold in the firelight.

Her lips garnered much of his attention, soft and slightly parted, hinting at the vulnerability she hadn't yet hid from him. Full and inviting, the shape delicate and perfectly curved, Torsten allowed himself to imagine they would be warm and supple to the touch, yielding under his kiss. There was an innocence there, an untouched quality that seemed at odds with a woman who in her waking hours was known as the *Killer of Men*.

Beguiled by her presently, and infuriated that he allowed himself to be so, he focused on her traits that he found unappealing. Though her physical appearance was undeniably tempting, he couldn't ignore her meek acceptance of her fate, which troubled him. Had he been given a choice, he'd have selected a wife who matched his courage, honor, and authority—a partner better suited to govern two houses alongside him.

He would do best to avoid her, steer clear of any temptation. Another week or so, he could abandon this chamber and claim his own. By rights, that should be the one in which her father lay dying. Despite what he portrayed and what many believed, he was not so heartless as to cast her father from either his bed or his chamber before he succumbed to whatever was killing him. However, Torsten understood another truth, that if Raina MacQueen were not in residence, he would not have hesitated to have Malcolm MacQueen removed from the keep.

Or hastened to his grave.

PEIGI MACGREGOR WAS a tall woman with a robust build refined by years of hard work. Born and raised in Lochlan's village, she was the daughter of a fisherman and a seamstress, having learned the trade of both parents from an early age. Her mother had died when she was young, leaving Peigi to help raise her three younger siblings, the youthful responsibility—Raina's mother had long ago said—having been the foundation for Peigi's resiliency and fierce independence.

With hair the color of golden straw that was ever tied back with a leather thong and eyes that didn't know if they wanted to be blue or green but were always sharp, her face was strong and weathered by the sea and sun. Raina guessed her to be of an age with her mother, though the freckles across her nose and cheeks sometimes made her appear younger. A few small scars dotted and carved her complexion, remnants of various mishaps over the years. Despite what was a rugged appearance, there was a certain warmth to Peigi MacGregor, frequent hints of softness in her broad, gap-toothed smile. She'd married young, to

Hamish MacGregor and gave him three sons, the oldest nearly two decades ago, all of which labored in Lochlan's livestock farming and tannery operations. A daughter, born years ago, had succumbed to childbed fever; Raina's mother had said she'd buried her daughter in the morning and had carried on that day with all her chores, burying her grief in her labors.

Known for her blunt honesty and practical outlook on life, Peigi didn't mince words and had little patience for deceit or pretense. Certainly her straightforwardness often came across as brutal—Raina herself had winced a time or two in Peigi's company for her sometimes pitiless clarity—but those who knew her understood that she meant well and that her honesty came from a place of care and concern, and to a lesser degree, from her conviction that she knew better than most.

She was, in many regards, Raina's ideal, what she often imagined she might have been if she'd not been born the daughter of Malcolm MacQueen, and what she sometimes imagined there was still time to be—fierce and unrepentant.

She valued Peigi as a person not only for her pragmatic mindset and for how deeply she cared for her family, but also because despite the general disdain for Raina in the village, Peigi accepted her without judgment. She was one of the few who did so, having little tolerance, she'd said, for superstitious rubbish. Instead, she had always treated Raina with a level of respect and kindness that was otherwise unknown to Lochlan.

"I choose to form my opinions based on fact and by what I see for myself," Peigi had said to Raina several months ago, "and nae any wild imaginings."

Replaying in her head the words she'd imagined were needed to request Peigi's help, Raina hesitated as she approached Peigi at the narrow stretch of river where the waters flowed towards the sea, where the woman was busy laundering her family's clothes.

A dozen articles of clothing were draped over thistle and rock along the riverbank, and a large unwashed pile remained next to Peigi, where she sat on her knees, scrubbing what appeared to be one of her own kirtles with practiced efficiency. The river's clear waters swirled around smooth stones, its surface shimmering with hints of silver as they reflected the sunlight filtering through the sparse clouds.

The silhouette of the keep was behind Raina, and to her left, beyond the estuary of brackish water, where the freshwater met the saltwater, the vast expanse of the North Sea stretched to the horizon, its waves rolling in with a steady rhythm that was only slightly muted at this distance.

Peigi glanced up as Raina approached, her expression not so much softening as fixing on Raina with an acute curiosity. Her face scrunched up, which effectively bared her teeth. Hands roughened by decades of hard work, she continued scrubbing as she greeted Raina.

"Och, the new bride," she said, her voice slightly raspy—from years of sea air and stern words, Raina had always imagined. "Ye dinna look nae worse for wear."

Raina couldn't help the small wince that came, reminded of the greatest turmoil in her life presently.

"Might I trouble you for a moment of your time?" Raina asked.

Peigi paused in her scrubbing, sighing, possibly with some irritation at being interrupted. Leaving the kirtle to sit among the rocks in the shallows, Peigi sat back on her heels and wiped her hands in the lap of her apron.

"Aye, and what brings ye out today?"

"I need your guidance," she began, choosing her words carefully. "Torsten has asked—my husband, that is... has made it clear that the lads working inside the keep are not being employed to the best of their ability. He requests not only that they be replaced—they will fill other roles, he assures me—but that Lochlan Hall be properly staffed." Expecting Peigi to be as befuddled as she was, Raina added with no small amount of incredulity, "He wants the hall open each evening, so that all of Lochlan might sup together, any who would desire to, or need to."

Peigi's brow furrowed slightly, but she showed no other reaction. "Aye, and that's a long time coming, eh, lass? "'Boot time ye took yer place as mistress of Lochlan." She snorted a small laugh. "Mayhap marriage agrees with ye, even if the dragon does nae." She laughed at her own words, slapping her thigh once.

The dragon, Raina assumed, was Torsten de Graham, whose banners and crest were emblazoned with several depictions of the dreaded beast.

Peigi climbed to her feet and brushed off her skirts a bit. "And what guidance do ye need?" She shrugged. "Plenty of lasses with ample idle time but nae occupation."

"Yes, I imagine there are," Raina acknowledged. "However I would expect a cool reception, if any door were not slammed outright in my face if I merely went round seeking a substantial workforce for inside the keep."

Peigi nodded. "I imagine the same. And if ye're asking me to do yer bidding, take time away from my own work to make sure yers is suitably—"

"No, no, not that," Raina protested, shaking her head. "I only ask if you can imagine a better way to go about it. I thought to post something, listing the positions that would need filling—which would be, as you must imagine, everything from the housekeeper, a lady's maid, right down to scullery and bedchamber maids. But then I...I'm not sure anyone outside the keep can read."

"Nae, I'm sure they canna. But housekeeper, ye say?"

Raina nodded. There was none, hadn't been one since Margaret Thwally had departed shortly after Raina's mother had died, refusing to work in Malcolm Macqueen's household, with his new austerity rules, and no Lisbeth MacQueen to serve as buffer as she had for years.

Raina was reminded that everything had changed, everything had fallen apart after her mother had died.

"Making all the rules? All the decisions?" Peigi questioned further. "The housekeeper?"

"Within reason, yes," Raina supposed. "I expect that...my husband will want that I take on a leadership role."

"Fine, and I'll do it," Peigi announced, swinging her gaze around to her laundry, items cleaned, those still drying, and all that had yet to be washed.

"You'll do...what?" Raina wondered, hoping she meant to assist in finding candidates to fill the roles but curious as to how she might go about it. Strongarm them, was Raina's guess.

"Take the job," Peigi said, frowning at Raina as if she'd been perfectly clear.

"Take the job? Which job?"

"Housekeeper," Peigi said tartly, her gaze extending beyond Raina, scanning the trees that flanked the river.

Raina's eyes widened. Never had she imagined, not for one second had such a fantastic idea entered her mind, that Peigi herself might assume a role.

"You want to be Lochlan's housekeeper?"

"Lass, are we nae having the same conversation? Ye come asking for help and I'm saying I'm agreeable—"

"Peigi, I'm thrilled," Raina cut in before the woman's dander got up. "I just never imagined that you would be interested. I've never seen you but when you're working, always about some chore taking care of your house and your sons—"

"Aye, and make nae mistake, I'll be taking advantage of it," Peigi freely admitted. "Sure and the work'll get done, but I'll be adding my house's laundry to the keep's weekly washing, and I'll be bringing my hungry lads round each night to sup in the hall. And dinna ken I'll allow ye to sit back and only watch. Past time, I'm sure, ye learned how to maintain the keep."

Smiling, her shock and gladness huge, Raina lifted her hands and clapped them together. "I cannot believe this. This is perfect. They'll come work for you—they'll come by the—"

"Nae," Peigi cut in, pointing her finger at Raina. "They'll work for ye, and be paid by ye, by Lochlan. Ye'll be the queen and I yer general," She smiled large, revealing once more the vast gap between her two front teeth.

"I cannot thank you enough, Peigi. This is...this is everything. So generous of you."

"'Tis nae strictly for ye, lass, though I ken ye canna do it without me. My bones are creakin', my lads nae help to their auld mam. I'm looking to make my life kinder. Ye ken I'm a hard worker but I'll nae mind having a few hours each week meeting with the lady of the keep," she said, winking boldly at Raina, "discussing menus or some such things, mayhap with our feet up."

Raina laughed outright at Peigi's boldness, and covered her mouth with her hands, so tickled with her sudden good fortune. Oh, what she could learn from her! And to have a friend, such as she was, inside the walls of Lochlan!

"Christ, and a lady's maid for ye—that'll be Helen," Peigi said next, already considering others who might join them. "She's too young, of course, but biddable yet, trainable even, and her mam dinna put much stock into the rumors of yer witchcraft so she'll allow it. We'll get her out from under her da's heavy hand. Paying guid wages? Dinna tell me ye're offering naught but room and a day's meal; we've got that already."

"I'm not sure, actually. Torsten only said to hire servants. I might suppose *hire* means paid." She shrugged. "And why should they not be? If the fisherfolk and those involved in the beef production and the leather trade are compensated, why should the household servants not be?"

"That's right, and ye tell him that when he balks about it," Peigi agreed. She squinted against the sun, one eye nearly closed, and considered Raina. "What's he like? Ye're nae dead, nae bruised, nae running and crying. Decent sort, is he?"

Her unexpected query gave Raina pause. She'd learned one steadfast lesson from her mother, a principle she often pondered, wondering how her mother had pulled it off: Lisbeth MacQueen never uttered a disparaging word about her husband, not to anyone, not ever. Despite Raina's certainty that her mother harbored disdain for Malcolm MacQueen, demonstrated by countless heated arguments within the keep, her mother remained steadfastly silent on the matter of her husband.

"My frame of reference is shallow and narrow, Peigi," she said after a moment. "I will let you form your own opinion."

"Hmm," Peigi murmured, narrowing her eyes a bit. "Aye, for the best. Ye're too sheltered to ken a true dragon from a pretender." She glanced around again, squinting once more into the trees beyond Raina. "Ye ken ye're being followed—dinna turn around, ye daft girl," she chastised sharply when Raina nearly did just that. "Aye, at least two, mayhap more. Dragon's minions, my guess. I hear he's got plenty to spare. But now I wonder, does he distrust ye or does he protect ye?"

It was Raina's turn to snort. "Your guess, Peigi, is likely more astute than mine."

"Aye, and we'll find out. C'mon, then," she said, beckoning Raina forward. "Help me get these back to the house and we'll make the rounds, collecting lasses as we go."

Unable to recall the last time she'd been imbued with so much hope and what seemed like actual good fortune, Raina happily began folding and stacking all the MacGregor garments left out to dry while Peigi wrung out the water from the kirtle and picked up the unwashed pile of clothes.

They spent the next hour going from cottage to cottage, Peigi knowing the names of every person in the village, and how many able and age-appropriate daughters they had.

If they resisted, Peigi would either nudge them gently or outright shame them.

"Ye want yer lass to learn to provide for herself, do you nae?" She said to one anxious mother.

"Lady Raina insists that we give instruction weekly," she invented for the benefit of another. "All these girls will learn the seamstress trade, and ye ken there's nae better than me to teach them."

"What?" She'd frowned brutally at another parent, who was busy eyeing Raina nervously. "Ye want yer daughter to continue with her slovenly ways, nae help to ye—aye, I've seen her, watching ye work dawn till dusk, and she nae lifting a finger. If she were mine, I've have tanned her hide long ago, but this'll do just as well, a little humility forced down her throat, answering to me now and ye ken I'll get the work out of her."

In fairly short order, they'd culled seven young women from the village to begin working at the keep. As they moved on to another cottage, Raina marveled to Peigi, "I can't believe they are all so agreeable. Or rather, how adept you are at refuting their reservations."

"Forthright is what it needs," Peigi said blithely, seemingly to enjoy herself. "Ye canna dance around unpleasant truths."

"I am not...I am not strong, not like that." She was pretty sure *strong* was the word she wanted. *Forceful* would have been too harsh.

"Ye are nae," Peigi agreed swiftly enough to cause offense. "Or rather ye might be, if ye're yer mother's daughter, but aye, I guess he beat it outta ye, dinna he?"

He, Raina imagined, was her father. And yes, it had proven difficult, nearly impossible at times to challenge her father's authority and edicts. Absently, she touched the thumb size scar on her cheek, which she'd worn for almost ten years now, one of several reminders of a time she'd done just that, tried to stand up to her father.

As they exited the small and tidy home of Johann, who had just committed her daughter, Lorna, to a position inside the keep, they were advised of riders coming, the clomp of shod hooves sounding down the lane.

Raina's heart skipped a beat as she saw Torsten de Graham leading a small group of soldiers through the village. She couldn't deny how magnificent he looked atop his large destrier. His powerful frame sat with effortless command, his broad shoulders and straight posture remarkable, while his chiseled features were set grimly. The sun glinted off the gray hair of his bare head, and his cloak billowed behind him, adding to the striking image.

Raina's breath caught when his piercing blue gaze found her, immobilizing her with the intensity of his stare.

"The dragon comes," Peigi murmured softly as she and Raina stopped.

Reining in upon the lane, a dozen feet between them, Torsten inclined his head at Raina.

"Good day, sir," she said. "This is Peigi MacGregor," she introduced. "She has agreed to assume the role of housekeeper inside the keep."

Torsten pulled his gaze from Raina and turned it upon Peigi. Recalling how she'd withered under the fierce scrutiny of that blue-eyed gaze at their first meeting, Raina turned to see how Peigi fared.

No withering here; Peigi was a fine match to Torsten, fearlessly subjecting him to the same thorough examination as he did her.

"The new laird," Peigi mused. "Here's hoping ye're some improvement over the auld one."

Torsten's rigid expression did not lessen, though he did purse his lips a bit while he continued to measure her. "And we'll hope as well that ye ken what yer about, managing a keep the size of Lochlan."

"Can only be an improvement," Peigi shrugged indifferently, "since the position's been vacant for nigh on a decade."

"Hm," was Torsten's response, his eyes narrowing a bit before he nodded at the pair and said, "I'll leave ye to it."

"Nae one for small talk, is he?" Peigi said to Raina when Torsten and his retinue had moved on. "At least he's easy on the eyes." She turned to Raina, elbowing her lightly and grinning. "I wager that made the bedding a bit more palatable."

Raina averted her eyes while her cheeks pinkened.

"*Jesu*, he's nae bedded ye?" Peigi guessed.

"No," Raina reluctantly admitted, her voice steady. "He said he wasn't interested."

Fisting her hands on her hips, Peigi looked Raina up and down. "Aye, that dinna surprise me after all. Bonny ye are, lass, but all that simpering and downcast gazing willna win his interest. And it does remain, wife or nae, ye are the enemy."

Raina's eyes widened. "I don't want his interest," she blurted, nearly aghast, before she thought better of it.

Peigi dropped her hands and took a step closer to Raina. "Aye, ye do, lass," she assured Raina gravely. "Ye need it. He'll nae be here long—the stench of war is all around him. He revels in it, loves it, will seek it out. And if ye dinna give him a bairn, he'll nae ever have cause to return. If ye dinna have a bairn," she repeated, pointing a finger to highlight her speech, "before the war makes him dead—and it will; it takes everyone—ye'll be cast out by whomever Robert Bruce next sends to Lochlan. Secure yer place by giving him a son, who'll one day be laird of Lochlan."

"I don't think I can—"

"Ye can and ye must. Bringing him round will be the easy part," she said and then turned, directing her gaze to the group of riders moving away. "Nae, mayhap the easy part will be making the bairns. He's got the look about him, one who kens his way around a woman's body. Ten marks—which ye ken I've no business wagering—says he'll make ye very happy in the bedchamber."

Raina's eyes somehow widened more, both dismayed and rapt with curiosity by the very idea.

"Bring him around? How? He can scarcely stand to look at me."

"Possibly, but that's got nothing to do with ye. Mayhap he's peeved about the edict from the king that forced him to wed ye, mayhap for whose daughter ye are, but I guarantee ye, lass, he'll change his tune if ye change yers. He'll nae find a bonnier lass within a score of miles of Lochlan, that much I ken. We'll get yer hands dirty," she said with a laugh, "taking care of that big house, and we'll get yer mind dirty as well, taking care of that big man."

Chapter Eight

Little escaped Torsten's notice. As commander of a large army, one who led men into war, it had become second nature to observe everything, to be attuned to the smallest details that might affect the order and efficiency of his domain. Thus, over the next few days, he was aware of even minute changes within Lochlan Hall. The great hall began to fill with trestles, boards, and benches, fires were laid daily in the hearths, and the corridors were lit with small torches affixed inside iron rings in the stone walls. He'd entered their bedchamber midday yesterday, needing a change of clothes, only to find the large bed stripped of all linens; in the bailey, he'd noticed half a dozen young women, Raina included, tending to the laundry over a large steaming cauldron; where before only lads were known as servants, rarely seen but at meal time, now a bevy of young lasses scampered about the keep at all hours of the day.

He was aware as well of Raina's busyness and her hand in these changes, and silently applauded how she'd embraced the task with such determination. He gave praise easily to his men, a high morale constantly needing to be upheld, but wasn't sure he needed to afford any similar appreciation to Raina for simply tackling a role that she should have assumed years ago. Still, he did know a grudging respect—and admittedly, a wee bit of surprise—for how she'd leapt in with both feet, taking on the role of chatelaine with what seemed an eagerness.

If he encountered his wife during the day lately, she was most often garbed in an apron and wore a kerchief over her hair. He thought she appeared more animated even, much less the timid little mouse he married. He couldn't be entirely sure, however, having spent little time in her company over the last two days. She'd sent a message to him last night and the night before, by way of the lad, Crispin, advising she would not be supping in the little hall, having too much work left in her day. And as he'd made a point to only seek their shared chamber late at night when he felt certain she should be asleep already and because he rose and was gone before she woke, Torsten scarcely saw her at all. When he did it was from a distance or in passing.

While Raina busied herself with her newfound duties, Torsten familiarized himself with Lochlan's cattle and fishing operations. He spent his mornings inspecting the herds, noting their condition and the methods employed by the herdsmen. The cattle were well-kept, evidence that while MacQueen practiced frugality elsewhere as if he believed he might be smote by lightning if he did not, he'd shrewdly invested in and cared for that which made him money.

In the afternoons, Torsten turned his attention to the fishing operations. He visited the beach, observing the fishermen as they brought in their daily catch. The process was efficient, the men experienced and hardworking. He visited the docks, built south of the beach where the River North Esk met the sea, noting some areas that were in need of repairs and imagining ways to expand the harbor if he should desire one day to expand the fishing trade.

Torsten's presence was met with a mix of curiosity and caution by the peasants of Lochlan. Though he offered a nod here and a word there and frequently spoke at length to those in charge of the cattle and the fishery, he made no effort to engage with others, expecting that he would soon be gone.

He'd dispersed his army round Lochlan, both to ensure defense and maintain order. Small contingents patrolled the village and the surrounding headlands. Others guarded the perimeters of Lochlan Hall, fortifying the stronghold against any potential threats, their presence a stark visual representing the new power overseeing the region. The blooming heath at the approach of Lochlan Hall was now a sea of tents, wagons, and horses. The officers made house in Lochlan's barracks and soldiers drilled rigorously upon the training grounds, a section of land appropriated between the grassland and the pasture.

On the fourth night as a newly wed man, he arrived at Raina's bedchamber close to midnight, expecting as had been the case the last two nights, that his bride would be fast asleep. Instead, he found that she was not, but seated at the small stool in front of the dressing table, combing out her long hair. Her hand went still when he entered, only for a moment, before she resumed the strokes down the vast wealth of dark hair.

Torsten paused at the threshold, captivated by the sight of her profile illuminated by the soft glow of a single candle. She wore only her shift, her bare feet tucked under the stool, which she now subtly shifted in response to his presence. Slowly, he closed the door behind him, his gaze lingering on her as she performed such a quintessentially feminine task.

Often obscured beneath layers of dread and timidity, Raina's beauty shone now in the intimate solitude of the bedchamber.

Her dark hair, draped over one shoulder as she combed through the locks, gleamed like silk as candlelight was caught in its depths. Even the hint of rigidity in her features, wrought by his arrival no doubt, could not harden the delicacy of her face.

Neither said a word.

Torsten crossed the room and began to doff the many layers of clothes. Keenly aware of her in his periphery, he knew when she tied the length of her hair with a ribbon and rose from the stool, padding across the floor on bare feet. She extinguished the candle on the table flanking her side of the bed with a sharp puff of air before slipping beneath the covers. A brief glance over his shoulder showed that she lay on her side, her back to him.

Though he was seldom troubled by any need to fill awkward silences, he was plagued now by some sense that he should exchange *some* words with his wife. However, no ideas came to him regarding what he might say. He continued to undress, unsure how to break the quiet that enveloped them and soon enough a frown lowered his brows, wondering why he should want to. Shaking off so uncharacteristic an urge, he snuffed the candle on the table closest to him and climbed into bed.

He lay on his back, his eyes adjusting to the charcoal gray light, and stared at the timber ceiling inside the chamber. Fairly quickly, he pushed off the heavier furs as covers. Through the open shutters of the lone window, the unusually warm night air drifted in, bringing with it the faint scent of the sea. Waves breaking against the shore easily relaxed him. He'd already decided he enjoyed the soothing sound of the sea in the night. Honestly, he believed he slept better here at Lochlan than he had anywhere else, at any time.

When he felt Raina shift next to him, he turned his head on the pillow to face her.

She was still on her side, facing away.

"I expect that tomorrow," she said over her shoulder, her voice quiet and sweet, "we will be ready to open the great hall for supper."

"Verra guid," he said, for lack of any other idea as a response. Truth be told, though, this was much sooner than he'd anticipated. 'Twould not be easy to feed so large an army, and the villagers, too, if they should come. "That'll need more tables and benches that what's there now," he said then, as that occurred to him.

"Those were recovered from the cellars," she told him. "The carpenter, Bernard, said he'd have half a dozen finished by tomorrow—apparently several of your soldiers are lending a hand there—and twice that by next week."

"Hm, verra guid indeed." He scratched his hand back and forth on his naked chest.

"With so large a number to feed," Raina went on, "it will require that we stagger the seating, if you will. I asked Rory to assign the first hour to half your men and the second hour to the others."

He nodded and then realized she couldn't see that. "A guid idea." And even more remarkable, that she'd taken it upon herself to approach Rory to set the schedule with him.

After a moment of silence, he felt her settle again, her face no longer angled toward him.

Again, for reasons yet unknown, he searched his brain for something to say.

"Ye've been industrious these last few days," he finally managed, his tone awkward with what he believed a feeble attempt at conversation.

Raina didn't move when she responded. "Yes. It's been good for me. And for Lochlan, of course."

He found himself unexpectedly drawn to the gentle cadence of her voice—whispered honey, he thought, giving rare life to a wee bit of fancy. Small talk, however, was most certainly not his forte, and he could imagine no other conversation to engage her. Probably for the best, he decided, puzzled by whatever bug had bit him that made him suddenly want to talk with his wife.

A moment later, Torsten heard a soft, whispering flutter near the window, followed by what seemed a more frantic swish and a knock against the shutters. Instinctively, he turned, reaching for the hilt of his sword at the side of the bed, muscles tensing with readiness. His hand hovered over the weapon, poised to defend against any intruder that dared enter their chamber, even as he imagined the likelihood impossible for the window being so high upon the wall.

The fluttering sound grew louder, more urgent, and Torsten's grip tightened on the sword as a black silhouette tore through the air, flying into the chamber.

"Good gracious, what is it?" Raina asked, sitting up in the bed.

"A bat," he answered calmly, knowing his sword would be of little use to either kill or capture the uninvited visitor.

Raina yelped and ducked under the blankets when the bat flew by her head.

Disoriented, the bat darted all around, back and forth across the room, though never so fortunate as to go near the open window. It was fast, but only a grim shadow darting, the swish of its wings frantic. Torsten ducked at the same time he swung out his hand as the bat came right at him.

He hurried to relight the candle and smacked at the creature when it zig-zagged over the bed again, seeming to be aiming specifically at Raina. Wisely, she tossed the heavy furs at the panicked creature just before she scrambled and scooted across the bed, hopping off near Torsten. The fur had missed, and the bat continued to circle the room erratically.

While Torsten surveyed the chamber, wondering what he might use to capture the bat or how he might steer it toward the window to exit, Raina sidled behind him, gripping his arm and yipping again when it flew too close, the swish of its wings loud as it neared. Torsten backhanded the flying creature, knocking it to the floor. Dazed, the bat flipped and flopped and Raina panicked, wanting to be far away from it. At the same time as she began to back away from it, distancing herself from Torsten even, the bat found its wings again. Raina yipped again and turned to run. Torsten pivoted and wrapped a steely arm around her waist, hauling her back against his chest just as the bat gained altitude; if he'd not stopped her, she'd have collided with the bat.

When he set her on her feet, she turned instinctively into his chest, burrowing in fright. He wrapped his arms around her, covering her head while the bat continued to flit around the chamber.

"Dinna move," he said, his breath against her hair. "It'll land eventually if it perceives nae threat." He would deal with it then, and more easily than he could while it was flitting around in a panic. "Wait, lass."

Raina went still in his arms, her hands tucked between them, pressed against his chest as was her face. She turned, laying her cheek against his chest and arm, likely wanting to keep track of the flying menace as Torsten studiously did.

Despite his concentration on the flight of the bat, in no time Torsten became acutely aware of the feel of Raina in his arms. Her warmth pressed against him and her soft breath brushed his bicep as she clung to him. The bat's frantic fluttering faded into the periphery of his awareness as he focused on the delicate curve of her body and the subtle rise and fall of her breathing. He tightened his hold on her as the bat flew close once more, wanting to shield her, and in doing so found himself more attuned to *her* than the chaotic movements of the bat.

Though she was of average height, she was slender, amazingly soft, he knew now, and damn if she didn't fit perfectly in his arms. And *Jesu*, she smelled good. Lavender? Roses? He wasn't sure. Beguiling though, that much he knew for certain.

"Daft wee goblin," Raina murmured with annoyance, her voice muffled.

Seized by an unexpected amusement, Torsten chuckled at her name-calling. "Aye, but he's slowing down, seems less frantic now, aye?"

"Dead or gone would be so much better than less frantic," she reasoned.

Another chuckle rumbled along his chest. "We agree on that."

They were made to stand like that for several long minutes, the bat mostly avoiding them now, the candle's light beside them likely keeping it at bay. His arm held prisoner the tail of her hair, his hand reaching the far side of her back. He inhaled deeply, his chin just atop her hair, drawing in again the fresh and delicate scent. Suddenly ungovernable, his body responded, heat quickening in his groin.

Bluidy hell.

Torsten recognized the exact moment when Raina's apprehension about the bat shifted to an awareness of him and the sensation of being held in his arms. She stiffened and didn't move a muscle for an entire minute before slowly lifting her face from where it had been pressed against his arm. Gradually backing away in his arms, she removed her hands from his chest.

Torsten glanced down at her, at her downward face. Her lashes were long, swept against her cheeks, very noticeable now. It took her a moment but eventually she raised her face to him, her eyes wide with some heretofore unknown anxiety over the intimacy of their embrace, he bare-chested and she garbed in only her shift.

"Sorry," she murmured, the still-flitting bat apparently forgotten. Lifting a furtive hand, she brushed a lock of disheveled hair from her cheek.

"I only meant..." he began.

"No, it's..." she started and stopped, then started again. "It's fine. I think... we're safe now. He's definitely less agitated."

Torsten cleared his throat, straightening fully. His hands slid away from her. He wore a ferocious scowl. "Aye."

Still, it seemed there were two bats inside the chamber—the actual creature and the sinister shadow of it that raced all about the walls and ceiling. It was another few minutes before the bat finally landed, choosing to wedge itself into a darkened corner, where the timber ceiling met the stone wall.

"Perfect," he said, stepping around Raina and retrieving his plaid.

It wasn't perfect, though, not really. The walls were long and the ceiling high.

"Perhaps use the stool to stand on," Raina suggested, possibly understanding that he meant to use the plaid as a net, trapping the creature inside.

"That'll nae hold my weight."

"I sit on it every night," she said even as he moved toward the larger chairs before the hearth. "It holds me."

"Ye dinna weigh half what I do," he guessed. He considered the height of the upholstered chair's seat and then the position of the bat, judging that he should be able to reach.

Tossing the breacan onto the chair, he lifted the hefty piece of furniture and slowly walked it over to the corner, not wishing to startle the bat into another crazed flight around the chamber.

"Be careful," Raina cautioned nervously as he slowly stepped up onto the chair.

"Mayhap take cover, lass," he suggested, steadily raising himself upward from a crouch.

When he was standing straight, and the bat was still another two feet above his head, he unfolded the plaid a bit and positioned it in two hands and lifted his arms. Just as he stretched to capture the bat in the wool, the creature startled, and his wings flapped. At the same time Torsten thrust his arms upward he heard a loud crack. He'd just trapped the bat against the corner when the chair gave way beneath him. He cursed foully as he tumbled to the floor atop a heap of splintered wood and unmoored cushion. Raina squeaked as the bat darted around the chamber in a renewed frenzy.

Grimacing, rolling off the broken chair, Torsten saw Raina running across the chamber, shrieking, covering her head with her arms as she ran to the door. She flung it open and concealed herself behind it, and it struck Torsten as absurd when she called out from her hiding place, "Are you all right?"

Grumbling something unintelligible, he flopped onto his back and took a deep breath, watching with annoyance as the damn bat continued to spin about the room.

And then, as if she'd planned it, and had not only thought to shield herself, the bat proceeded to fly straight out of the chamber via the door Raina had opened.

"Is it gone?" She asked. "Did it just fly away?"

"Aye. Close the door."

She did so promptly, dropping the latch in place. As if the *daft wee goblin* might know how to unlock doors.

A second later, she was standing over him, her bonny face etched with concern.

"Torsten?"

"Aye, I'm fine," he said. He heaved in a great big breath and brought himself upright to a sitting position.

Raina glanced at the pieces of the broken chair and bit her lip, her gaze returned to him.

"I would advise," he growled, "that ye make nae remark that the stool would nae have broken."

And the most amazing thing happened in response to his very serious and very dangerously uttered warning.

Raina fought against it at first but lost the battle eventually. A smile blossomed on her face, hesitant at first, before it evolved, becoming genuine and radiant, if a wee shy. It lit up her features, transforming her usual reserved expression into something truly captivating. Torsten forgot about the bat, the broken chair, and the ache in his back from where he'd landed on one of its legs. All he knew at that moment was Raina's smile, the first he had ever seen from her. He was both startled and shockingly enchanted.

As quickly as the enchantment had settled in, he forced it away, replacing it with frustration. Grumbling under his breath, he pushed himself to his feet, brushing away Raina's hands as she tried to help.

"The mess can wait until morning," he said gruffly, avoiding her eyes as he dusted himself off.

Raina's smile faltered and she stepped back, allowing him space.

"Of course," she replied.

Torsten turned away, trying to ignore the pull he felt toward her, trying to focus on anything but the way her smile had made him feel.

"Let's get some rest," he muttered, more to himself than to her, as he moved back to the bed, his mood still darkened by the unexpected attraction he'd felt.

Raina followed, quietly slipping into bed beside him.

Torsten snuffed out the candle once more.

Staring at the ceiling again, he understood he was hardly humiliated by the fall and his inability to capture the nuisance bat. What did he know of wrangling a demon? Nae, his current frustration had everything to do with his sudden awareness—stark and overwhelming—of his wife.

He tried, he really did, to put the entire episode from his mind. He didn't dwell on what he'd felt, how it affected him, that she'd initially run toward him, her husband, seeking the shelter of his arms. Clearly, he wasn't foolish enough to reimagine the *feel* of her in his arms, the way his body had responded to her.

He'd felt fairly sure then—was fairly certain still—that he was fiercely attracted to his young wife.

RAINA AND PEIGI HAD spent quite a busy week together. They conducted interviews with each girl brought into service, afterward deciding where best to place them in the household. They agreed to keep on only Cook and one lad, the youngest, making him the charboy. When he was old enough to assume other duties, he'd be replaced by his younger brother. They visited the granary and the smokehouse, the cellars, pantry, and larder, taking stock of Lochlan's provisions, trying to imagine how they would feed an army. They deduced they needed no less than ten in the kitchen—subject to change, they knew—and invited Nell to join the staff after Peigi said she had no business working as one of the fishers. Nell had laughed in Raina's face, saying she'd rather go hungry than step foot inside Lochlan Hall.

Seòras had since been released from his confinement and returned to his duties, but was scarcely helpful, seeming to hold a grudge against Torsten and every de Graham, and now even Raina. And then one day, shortly after his release, he simply disappeared. Rory said to Raina that the steward was seen walking away from Lochlan Hall with a satchel under his arm.

"And guid riddance to him, the mean auld goat," was Peigi's thought on the matter.

The morning after the incident with the bat, Raina could think of little else—not the bat actually, but of Torsten's brawny arms around her, how safe and cherished she'd felt in those moments. She was ridiculous, of course, to imagine herself cherished, but she allowed the fantasy to persist throughout the day.

She was certain of one thing, though, and it was not imagined: she lost a little bit of her fear of Torsten. She wholly believed a man who held her as tenderly, as protectively as he had would not ever harm her.

At length, she thought about what Peigi had said, about needing her husband to consummate their marriage so that she might have children and secure her place at Lochlan for the rest of her life. Twenty-four years she was and should by now have been wed and already gladdened by several children. Little did she know about what the actual bedding required or entailed. But she knew this: whatever dread and fear she'd imagined initially was nowhere to be found. If coupling proved as titillating as simply being held in his arms, she rather thought she might insist that Torsten make her his wife in truth.

Her spirits improved dramatically, and not only with any recollection of Torsten's arms around her. She had a friend to talk to now, to share thoughts and anecdotes with, telling Peigi of the adventure inside her bedchamber with the bat.

After Peigi's initial astonishment about the bat and the broken chair, Lochlan's new housekeeper took Raina to task, disgruntled that she hadn't used any part of the incident to her advantage, to steal a kiss or provoke a kiss.

"Laughter, ye ken, is an aphrodisiac."

"I did not know—how was I supposed to...work a kiss into that scenario?"

"Ye should have leapt upon him when he fell," Peigi said impatiently, as if that should have been obvious, "gushing with concern over him, whether he was injured or not. At the very least, ye could have enjoyed a feel, touching those meaty arms under the guise of looking for injuries—men do it all the time."

"I don't...this isn't making sense to me, Peigi."

Peigi sighed. "Aye, I can see that, can tell by the look of confusion befuddling yer face. Aye, mayhap we'll have to put all our hopes in him, hoping night after night lying next to a bonny lass—his wife, nae less—will cause him to finally act on it, when he can stand it nae more. He's nae the marauding kind, hasn't plowed his way through any and every willing and available lass at Lochlan—and mark my words, there'd be more than only a few. So aye, he's got to get it somewhere eventually. My guess: he soon turns to ye."

Raina nodded as if she understood, but she was in fact a little hazy on the details of Peigi's argument.

Her improved disposition was only briefly challenged that same morning after the bat had entered her chamber. She'd visited her father, as she had not in days. While he watched her with sharp but hooded eyes, she'd said, "I...I know that you're dying and I'm sorry for that—for you—but I hope you know some relief. Aye, Donald is gone, but I'm still here and a MacQueen will remain at Lochlan Hall. I'm fairly certain, Father, that my marriage to Torsten de Graham will not be in vain. I almost begin to believe it will...that something good might come of it."

Wishful thinking, of course. But truth be told, it had been so long since she'd found anything to which she might attach hope, so that she rather seized on her marriage and Torsten's first demonstration of kindness as something worthy of optimism.

Her father, however, disagreed. He hadn't spoken in weeks but managed to mouth one word at that moment.

"Whore."

Raina's heart clenched at the cruelty of the word, but she refused to let it shatter the possibility of a brighter future.

Chapter Nine

"It wasna fully awful," Peigi said.

Raina sent her an incredulous look. "Wasn't it?"

They sat at the high table with one empty chair between them. While Raina had her elbows on the table and her chin in her hand, Peigi was draped wearily in her chair, bleary-eyed and limp.

It was late in the evening, the hall vacant and dimly lit. Less than half of the candles in the overhead chandeliers still burned, the others having been reduced to dark stubs, some having gone out hours ago. Trestle tables sat in disarray, benches were scattered, one turned on its side. The floor was an unholy mess, littered with dropped food and spilled ale. Even hours later, the chamber smelled atrocious, of grease and smoke and the stench of too many bodies crammed into the large space.

In Raina's mind, the first night of supper inside the great hall had been an unmitigated disaster. Despite their best efforts and staggering the de Graham army's arrival, the hall simply wasn't fully prepared to host so large a number of people. The overcrowding and lack of plentiful benches made it difficult for all to find a seat, which had led to confusion and frustration. In spite of what seemed thorough planning with Cook's assistance, the amount of food prepared had been insufficient and those assigned to the second hour had received significantly less, prompting a bit of justified grumbling. The kitchen staff had been overwhelmed by the sheer volume of food to prepare, causing delays, sending out several dishes either burnt or cold. Though the lads previously employed by Lochlan were still in service for another few days, many of the new servers, the lasses from the village, were terribly inexperienced, spilling food and ale and contributing to the disarray. One of the lasses, while pouring ale from a pitcher, had knocked over a tabletop candle, which had met with grease on the table, causing a small and brief fire in the center of the hall, which had only added to the chaos.

Raina sighed now, overwhelmed by the scale of the event and all the issues that had risen.

Peigi chuckled lazily. "Guid news though, lass. It can only get better."

Lochlan's new housekeeper was far less troubled than Raina for how inept had been their first endeavor.

"God willing," Raina said. After a sigh, she imagined, "I suppose just as we sat and hammered out all these details, we only need to do so again, now better prepared, having an understanding about what to expect and what is required to serve so many."

Peigi nodded. "Saint's be weeping, lass, but that was a lot of food."

"But not enough."

"Aye, we'll make a list, what more we need," Peigi said.

"We need more of everything," Raina presumed. "Servers, kitchen staff, supplies—we need more kettles and cauldrons, and almost every other kitchen utensil." She grimaced and turned her face toward Peigi again. "Are you already regretting taking on the role?"

"Nae one bit," Peigi said without hesitation. "I love a guid challenge."

Smiling wearily, Raina realized she did, too. There was plenty of room for improvement, a better way to do it, she knew. Change would not come overnight, she understood, but she looked forward to proving to herself that she was capable. Scarcely had she been given any role or task, and she was determined not to fail at this one. If she intended to break free from the meaningless life she lived and pursue something better, she knew she had to give it her all.

A moment later, the door to the hall opened and half a dozen men stepped inside. Raina's gaze fixed on Torsten straight away as he stepped into the hall with Gilles, Aonghas, and a few others.

Torsten, normally so immaculate in appearance was unaccountably...unkempt. His breacan was nowhere to be seen; he wore only a tunic and breeches, the shirt billowing and full around him, not confined by either his plaid or his belt, the latter which he held in his hand, the scabbard and sword gleaming a bit in the soft light. His boots were caked in mud, the dirt crusted well above his ankles.

It was the first time she had ever seen him so ragged and untidy.

The men with him, which included two MacQueen men, Colin and Dugald, were just as disheveled. Gilles looked as if he'd swum in mud, his breeches and tunic stained quite liberally. Only their hands were clean, leaving Raina to assume they'd washed at the well in the bailey.

He and the others paused just inside the door, taking in the cluttered but vacant hall.

Raina's annoyance flared as they crossed the hall. All evening she'd watched the door for Torsten's expected arrival. She'd given him notice that supper would be served tonight. She'd fully expected that as laird, he should have bothered to come.

"Och and we missed it," Gilles said. "But mayhap the mistress is benevolent, and the kitchens might still offer some scraps."

Peigi snorted. "Mistress is benevolent, aye," she said, "but she's nae sorceress, canna snap her fingers and make a feast rise from the crumbs that remain, canna raise even a paltry dry trencher at this hour."

Several brows lifted at this pronouncement, that there was no food.

Understanding they would find no sustenance here at this hour, Colin and Dugald turned and took their leave.

Torsten and his men continued forward.

"It would have been nice if you'd been here," Raina announced to Torsten.

Torsten paused in front of the table where Peigi and Raina sat so wearily. His brows slanted downward. "One of the rivers was blocked, the storm three days past having downed several trees. There was nae water getting to the pasture—"

"And that will still be there tomorrow," she interrupted. "You should have been *here* tonight. These are your people now. They needed to see you, to hear from you."

His jaw tightened, and he met her gaze with a steely one of his own. "What would ye have me do, Raina? Stand here and give a speech while the cattle thirst?"

"Bah," she scoffed. "Hardly would they have perished overnight, I suspect. That issue could have waited. These people have been through enough upheaval. They need reassurance, a sense of stability. You should have stood before them and spoken of your new rule and the future of Lochlan, to put their minds at ease."

His eyes narrowed, and he took a step closer to her, his voice low and commanding. "I am the laird, and I will lead as I see fit. The livestock are part of Lochlan's livelihood, and without them, there is nae future for anyone here."

She met his intensity with her own, refusing to back down. "You are their laird, yes. But leadership is sometimes about delegating, is it not? Others could have been addressing the trouble at the river while you showed *your* people that you care, that you are here for them in times of peace as well as crisis. Tonight was about unity, about forging a bond between the MacQueens and the de Grahams."

Torsten's expression remained hard. "I will nae be lectured on leadership, especially nae by ye."

Though she was pleased to have spoken her peace, she sighed with resignation. "I didn't imagine you would be." She rose from the table and exited the hall, going to the kitchens, where no doubt there remained plenty of work to do.

The last face she saw belonged to Gilles. He winked boldly at her, she imagined with some pride for how she'd called out Torsten for what she perceived as his wrongdoing.

RAINA USED TO VISIT the weekly market in Montrose with her mother, a practice she enjoyed then and recalled with fondness now. After her mother was gone and before being sent to live with her aunt, she occasionally ventured there alone. Those solitary trips lacked the joy of wandering High Street with a companion, but they were still a welcome escape. Upon returning from her aunt's house, she resumed her visits almost every week, relishing the opportunity to leave Lochlan behind for a while—not so much the house itself, but the people in and around it.

Having driven Lochlan Hall's wagon many times, Raina asked the stablemaster to hitch up a team. Today, she was looking forward to the market with company once again, as Peigi, her new maid Helen, and Anne, who now worked in the kitchen as well, all intended to accompany her.

Josias, the stablemaster, shook his head at her request, and frankly, looked quite pleased to thwart her plans.

"Nae, milady," he said, his wild hair and perpetual scowl giving him an air of disgruntlement, which he was often pleased to visit upon Raina. "I dinna ken the laird would allow it."

Instantly bristling with annoyance—Josias regularly spouted some reason or another, almost weekly, as excuses why he wasn't sure he would or could ready the wagon for her—Raina managed to bite back the response that screamed in her head. She believed the surly stablemaster was either consumed with loathing for her or possessed an extreme inclination towards laziness. More than likely, both were the cause of his frequent opposition. Raina was regularly compelled to assert her dominance over the man.

"Josias, I will let you know when what *you* think eclipses what *I* know," she said, employing a firm tone. "Recall your station, sir," she reminded him tartly.

As was most often the case, he first subjected her to a lengthy and ugly perusal before shrugging, as if it meant no difference to him after all, before he ambled off deeper in the stables.

Rolling her eyes at the man, Raina exited the stables, finding Aonghas propped up against the rail overlooking the first stall and Torsten de Graham's large destrier.

"Fine man, that one," Aonghas quipped.

"Isn't he, though?" Raina returned, still annoyed.

"Where ye off to, Lady Raina?" He asked.

Raina was given pause, having some idea that he only pretended a particular nonchalance, but that he was actually, though mayhap not directed to, spying on her for his laird.

Drawing in a breath of fortitude, she told him, "Headed to the market in Montrose, sir, as I do regularly." She didn't tell him—didn't think he needed to know—that on this day, she had an actual purpose. Whereas her previous trips to Montrose were mostly made to escape Lochlan, she and Peigi had discussed purchasing more kitchen supplies, cauldrons and kettles, and baskets and porcelain ware, things that were not made by anyone within Lochlan.

"But ye canna go alone," Aonghas said, a bit of a question in his voice.

"I am not. Three will accompany me." She wasn't sure why Aonghas should concern himself with who she traveled with, or even if she made the short journey alone.

When he nodded, seeming satisfied with this, Raina nodded as well and returned to the keep to collect her cloak and her coin purse, and Peigi and the lasses from where they were bustling in the kitchen, trying to finish a certain amount of work ere they departed.

It was another thirty minutes before she and the others were ready, but thankfully they found the wagon and a pair of docile palfreys waiting them in front of the stables. The courtyard was otherwise empty, neither Josias nor Aonghas having hung around.

Peigi sat beside Raina on the wagon seat, her robust frame taking up a little more than half the smooth wooden board. Helen and the lass, Anne, sat in the bed of the wagon. As one was more timid and quiet than the other, Raina didn't suppose she'd struggle too much to hear anything that might be said by either of them, expecting they wouldn't say too much to begin with. Peigi, no doubt, would direct and compose most of their conversation, as she normally did.

However, Helen did ask what the market was like, confessing she'd never been to Montrose.

"Used to be," Peigi said as they set off from Lochlan Hall, directing her conversation sideways so the lasses could hear her response, "the market was kent as spirited theatre. 'Twas occasionally a wild place to be. Vendors shouting their wares from every corner, street performers hollering out scenes, and och, the birds! Come from all around, screeching overhead, diving to steal scraps. 'Tis verra noisy. I expect we'll see everything from fresh produce to livestock, fabrics, and trinkets. Though it's nae only the goods that make it memorable. The people, aye, are oft a sight to behold. Farmers, merchants, travelers, plenty of monied folks in their finest garb—all gathered in one noisy, overcrowded, smelly spot."

Intrigued by Peigi's description, Anne and Helen came closer in the bed of the wagon, kneeling behind the bench seat, their hands on the wooden slats.

"It can get rowdy, though, and ye two stay close, eh?" Peigi continued, always and easily encouraged by an eager audience. "Fights are nae uncommon, and over the smallest of things—a slighted bargain, a stolen glance, the jostling. I've seen more than one man leave the market with a bloodied nose or a blackened eye. Sure and the constables're kept busy. But it's nae only the menfolk; I remember a time when two clacking hens nearly tore each other's hair out over a bolt of cloth. The market has a way of bringing out the best and worst in folks."

Raina, too, was familiar with how entertaining the market could be. She assured Helen and Anne, "There's still a great charm to it, a pulse of life that you won't see at Lochlan, that you can feel in your bones."

Anne grinned, her excitement palpable, not diminished by Peigi's cautionary speech. "'Tis said the pastries at the market are unlike any others. Is it true?"

Raina smiled. "Aye, they are. We'll make sure to get some."

Peigi chuckled. "Tell milady how fair and bonny she looks today and mayhap she'd put out the coin for ye."

Raina laughed at this along with the girls.

They drove along a fairly well-traveled road, the fields and woods flanking the familiar path, alive now with summer's bounty, green and vibrant.

It wasn't long before their journey was abruptly interrupted. The sound of hooves thundering up behind them made Raina turn. Torsten and several of his men were approaching at a gallop, their expressions grim.

Torsten pulled his horse up alongside the wagon. The lines around his mouth and the furrow of his brow made his displeasure unmistakable.

"What in God's name do ye think ye're doing, Raina?" he demanded gruffly.

Raina's heart sank. "We're... going to the market in Montrose." Was it only two nights ago that his gaze had sat softly upon her during and after the incident with the bat in their chamber? A fleeting moment, aye, but she could have sworn she'd glimpsed something other than this anger and distance in his blue eyes.

"With nae outriders?" He snapped. "With nae notice to anyone? There's a war on, woman. The roads are dangerous. Ye cannae just take off like this."

She straightened her back, meeting his glare with a steady gaze. "I've driven this wagon on this route many times before." She glared at Aonghas, next to Torsten. "And I *did* mention where I was going."

"Ye said ye had a guard, lass," Aonghas stated.

Raina gasped. "I said three others were going with me," she reminded him. It wasn't her fault he'd misunderstood her. "And here they are."

Torsten's eyes flashed with anger. "Turn the wagon around, now."

Raina bit her lip, frustration and defiance warring within her. "We're almost halfway there," she protested.

"Halfway to danger," Torsten retorted. "Turn around."

Unwilling to give in—an improved supper depended on it—she challenged further, "I'm not...anyone of import. Why would I be in danger?"

"Ye are someone," Torsten said furiously. "Ye are *my* wife! *Jesu*, never mind that ye're four bluidy females traipsing around the coast with nae one to protect ye, but my wife does nae take out the wayn, driving it herself for Chrissakes and blithely tramping across the moor."

"But I regularly go to market—"

"Nae more. Nae without an escort. Do ye understand me, wife?"

She conceded internally that Torsten possibly had a point, but the way he was speaking to her made her bristle. "I do not understand, husband. You're overreacting. *And* you're being boorish."

Impossibly, Torsten's face darkened even further, his fury no longer boiling only just beneath the surface. His anger was so fierce it seemed to ripple off him, charging the air around them with furious heat.

"Boorish?" he repeated, his voice dropping to a low, foreboding tone. "Ye think this is me being boorish?" His anger was so intense it was almost tangible as a mist, the quietness of his tone somehow more terrifying than if he had shouted. "Nae, wife," he continued. "Ye have yet to see me boorish. Turn the wagon around, now, or I will do it myself."

While he boiled and seethed, possibly trying to prevent himself from erupting further, and though she was taken aback by the intensity of his reaction, Raina dared to point out, "You're here now, and with a retinue. Mayhap you should accompany us to the market."

Appearing somewhat incredulous that she dared to defy him still, he ground out, "We dinna have time to—"

"And *we* won't have the kitchen in order nor be able to feed *your* army," Raina pressed on through clenched teeth, "unless we purchase more equipment and contract extra servants. And right now, you are wasting our time, of which *we* haven't much to spare."

Torsten's jaw worked as he glared at her, and Raina suspected his pride warred with the practical sense of her argument. The muscle in his cheek twitched as he struggled to keep his temper in check.

For a moment, it seemed he might again order her to turn back. But then, with a sharp intake of breath, he gave a curt nod. "Fine," he conceded through gritted teeth, his tone laced with barely contained frustration. "We'll accompany ye. But we've one hour to give and nae more."

Raina nodded, a large dose of relief mixed with a small sense of triumph. Torsten's eyes still flashed with anger, but she considered his concession, though begrudging, a small victory of sorts.

"Thank you, husband," she said softly, not daring to push her luck further. Certainly, she didn't advise him that the drive to Montrose, what remained in this direction and what would be needed to return home, would likely consume an hour all by itself.

TORSTEN RODE GRIMLY at the head of the small party, his blood still boiling from how he'd been manipulated by his wife. The audacity of her defiance, the way she'd stood up to him without lowering her gaze once, played over in his mind. Raina was recently fiery when she believed herself in the right, and though it infuriated him, it also intrigued him. He felt a reluctant respect for her boldness.

The trip to Montrose was tense, but possibly only for Torsten. While he and his men maintained a vigilance as they journeyed, Raina, Peigi, and two very young lasses in the back of the wagon, kept up a steady stream of conversation. The young girls, who Raina at one point addressed as Helen and Anne, talked about everything from the market itself, their necessary purchases, with Peigi announcing she had a firm mental list, and even the clear sky and mild air.

When they arrived at Montrose, the main road bustled with activity, the morning hours at a weekly market always busier than the afternoon, by Torsten's understanding, no matter where the venue. Stalls lined the High Street, vendors calling out their wares, and the air was filled with the scents of fresh bread, roasted meats, and the briny tang of the nearby sea. High Street was a crush of people, nearly every color of the rainbow represented in their garb. The vibrant atmosphere differed sharply with the grim mood that had followed Torsten from Lochlan Hall since Aonghas had approached him, asking Torsten whom he'd tasked to escort Raina to Montrose.

Raina, on the other hand, seemed to come alive inside the bustling market, as if she fed off the energy and cheer. Outside the walls of Lochlan Hall, where no one knew her and didn't harbor any ill will towards her, she was much less guarded. She and Peigi and the young lasses laughed often as they moved from stall to stall. Raina pointed out scenes and stalls and items that she didn't want either Helen or Anne to miss.

Torsten watched her, almost constantly, his anger over such an inexplicable indulgence slowly giving way to grudging admiration—and admittedly, a fascination with so many smiles, so freely come to life.

Walking along High Street with his men in tow, several paces behind Raina and her party, he watched as his wife alerted a woman, a stranger, to something attached to and following the woman's every move—a long strip of soiled fabric dragging under the hem of the woman's léine, likely torn from a stall or picked up in the street and attached to her shoe. Raina's gentle laugh and the woman's surprised reaction, slapping a hand to her cheek as a blush surfaced, roused a greater curiosity in him. There wasn't any need for Raina to have pointed out the fouled piece of fabric that trailed behind the woman.

The woman, who appeared to be a fishmonger's wife, looked initially perplexed and then embarrassed, possibly wondering how long she'd dragged that piece around. Quickly enough, she expressed her gratefulness to Raina, who helped her detach the fabric. It was an unexpected and unnecessary kindness, one that took him by surprise. The warmth of Raina's interaction, the genuine care she showed to a stranger, was something he hadn't expected to see from someone so bitterly rebuffed at Lochlan.

Against his will, seemingly unable to resist, he continued to watch Raina as she moved through the market with a grace and confidence he hadn't seen before. She interacted with her companions, the vendors, and other market-goers easily, her smile genuine and seen frequently. It was a noticeable departure from the wary, guarded woman who lived within the walls of Lochlan Hall. Undeniably, Torsten's frustration for having been coerced to accompany her to Montrose ebbed slightly as he observed her. He still didn't fully trust her, and his anger was far from gone, but he realized now that his wife was more complex than he'd given her credit for, a complexity that he found fascinating.

As they continued through the market, Torsten expected that his men remained watchful, their eyes scanning the crowd for any potential threats, since he, again and again, found his gaze drifting back to Raina, intrigued by this lively woman with the easy smile.

ANY FOOL COULD SEE that the dragon from Lochlan Hall was enchanted by his wife.

Several people, including more than one fool, were indeed watching. One of them was a figure obscured by shadows, keeping beneath the overhang of a market stall's thatched canopy. The hood of his cloak covered his head, concealing watchful brown eyes.

Eyes narrowed with growing derision, Donald MacQueen had been shocked to discover his own sister among the crowd at Montrose's market. More astonishing still, to realize that she was accompanied by Torsten de Graham himself.

Her husband, Donald had learned in the last few days.

News flowed like ale at a tavern inside a market town, he'd learned long ago. Merchants and travelers, drawn to Montrose by its commerce and strategic location, brought tidings from distant lands and neighboring villages. Facts and rumors swirled through the air, whispered in hushed tones over barrels of salted fish or proclaimed with authority over bolts of wool.

But Donald hadn't learned anything here in Montrose that he hadn't discovered for himself in the last few days, since he'd returned home, or rather had attempted and expected to return home.

Having been unsure of what he might find at Lochlan after so long an absence, he'd been compelled to send ahead a few scouts when he'd reached Saunt Ceerus. They'd been gone for an infuriating number of hours, and Donald's impatience had quickly evolved to boiling rage when he'd been told that only two days prior, Torsten de Graham and his massive army had taken Lochlan Hall—quite effortlessly, not one life lost.

And worse, while his father lay dying in the same house, his sister had been compelled to wed Torsten de Graham.

Refusing to blame himself for the seizure of Lochlan or his sister, Donald did not dwell too long on the truth, that he might have found his way home sooner, months ago in fact, plenty of time to have prevented the capture of Lochlan. Ah, but that the young lasses in and around Newmiln, where he'd spent some time recovering from wounds at Methven, had proven far and above his ability to resist.

Och, but that had been the other surprise, delivered by the scouts who'd happened upon a pair of cowherds chasing down an errant bull outside one of the MacQueen pastures: Donald MacQueen was presumed dead, lost at the battle of Methven. He didn't wonder how that might have happened. He had lay dying after the devastation of Methven and only his men, returned and searching for MacQueen bodies to bury, had saved him.

His army, or the bulk of it, had been assumed under Acheson's banner, as commanded by Edward I. Donald had only recently regained them, or what had remained of them. He'd been well aware that neither Longshanks nor his commanders had much use for Donald MacQueen, save that they were pleased to add several hundred hungry fighters to their rosters. But now, with the death of Longshanks, Donald had begun to ingratiate himself to his son, supporting the young Edward's outrageous reliance upon Piers Gaveston, even going so far as to suggest to the new king that he make Gaveston an earl. While Gaveston was a monstrous bone of contention between Edward II and England's nobles and subjects, Edward had desperately seized upon Donald's support as if it mattered what a Scottish landholder might think.

And it had been enough to return the MacQueen army to him.

Sadly, the army was not large enough to defeat de Grahams greater force.

He needed another way to retake Lochlan Hall.

Now, hidden in Montrose, he clenched his fists in simmering anger as he observed his sister, Raina. Far from abused or terrified, she appeared at ease, happy even as she wandered from stall to stall with three other females, one of whom he recognized as Peigi MacGregor.

True, the newly married couple did not speak to each other, not that Donald observed, but damn if there was not a surfeit of covert glances directed at the other.

It enraged Donald to see his sister steal glances at Torsten de Graham, her demeanor cautious yet curious, not filled with even a hint of dread or fright. He stood at quite a distance, but Donald would have sworn that his sister's expression softened each time it settled on de Graham.

Raina's fair complexion flushed slightly on a few occasions when she found her husband's gaze already upon her. Wedded to the enemy, it appeared she had forgotten their family's honor, or simply didn't care that she belittled it.

Considering her more closely, as he'd not seen her in years, Donald supposed that she was fetching, beyond that mayhap. While he recalled a wide-eyed young girl with only passable looks—those oddly slanted eyes!—and entirely too much confidence in her own limited abilities, she appeared now to have caught up with herself, maturing into a woman with undeniable grace and uncommon beauty. Donald and Torsten de Graham were not the only ones staring at her.

Her auburn hair caught in a gentle breeze that played with the strands around her face. She wore a simple linen gown, the color of heather, cinched at the waist with a braided leather belt. Donald watched, his lip curling, as Torsten de Graham at one point very noticeably examined the sway of Raina's hips as she moved.

Seeing Torsten's gaze return again and again to Raina, Donald's anger soared at the same time it dawned on him that de Graham was smitten with Raina.

Ah, and here was the means by which to retake Lochlan Hall, he mused, his mood improving drastically.

Raina was Torsten's weakness. Donald was certain of it, and he would use it to reclaim what was rightfully his.

Chapter Ten

Though she had embraced her new duties as chatelaine of Lochlan, Raina sometimes found that she nearly resented how little time she had for escape, to be outdoors. Today, she happily volunteered to collect some herbs and plants needed by the kitchen—wild garlic, sea beet, and occasionally sea fennel, all of which could be found along the north side of the beach.

The slope there was more gradual than the cliff directly behind the keep, making the descent easier and less treacherous. She navigated a winding path that led her through a series of undulating sand dunes, their golden peaks dotted with tufts of hardy grasses swaying in the sea breeze. Sand shifted under her feet, sometimes causing her to stumble slightly, but she pressed on, enjoying the sensation of the soft grains beneath her leather boots. If the weather were less inclement—it appeared as if a storm considered brewing, the clouds overhead dark and suspect—she'd have removed her boots and hose and luxuriated in the feel of the sand between her toes. Wind rifled through her hair, pulling long strands from the blue ribbon. She tucked them behind her ears only to have them quickly and repeatedly disturbed, floating and swaying around her face so that she gave up trying to control her hair. There was some joy, some sense of unfettered freedom that came with this, allowing her hair to escape its confines, same as she had escaped hers.

There was something about being outdoors, surrounded by nature, her senses invigorated, that spoke to her soul. 'Twas rare that she embarked upon any such outing without recalling that she had often explored the woods and fields and beaches with her mother, learning about the various plants and their uses.

As she continued downward, the dunes gradually flattened out onto the beach proper, where scattered shells and bits of driftwood were half-buried in the sand. The wrack line, the furthest the tide had reached and had deposited bits of sea debris, curved along the flat sand of the shoreline.

She walked along, heading further north, far back upon the sand, where the wild-growing plants thrived, generally safe from the encroaching sea. The sea beet's vibrant green leaves, the pungent wild garlic, and the crisp, fleshy stems of sea fennel grew in abundance here, usually untouched by the salty spray of the waves. This secluded spot, shielded by the dunes now above her and a portion of rock and cliff that jutted out into the sea, obscuring the fishing industry on the beach further south, felt like a hidden sanctuary. She was glad to avoid the other beach where the fisherfolk were busy with their work. They had yet to warm up to her as the household staff gradually—very gradually—were. She was both soothed by the sound of the waves crashing in the distance and invigorated by the salty sea air as she made her way along the wild blooming plants, basket in hand.

Bending down, she carefully plucked at the leaves of the sea beet, their slightly salty taste a perfect addition to many recipes. Next, she moved on to the wild garlic, its pungent aroma filling the air as she gently tugged and twisted at the plants, ensuring she didn't damage the roots. The sea fennel was further ahead, the yellow-green flowers of the hardy perennial easy to spot, its salty citrus flavor making it perfect for pickling. She gathered several generous handfuls, knowing Cook would be pleased.

When her basket was nearly full, Raina took a moment to perch on a large, smooth rock, happy to sit idly and gaze out at the sea. The horizon stretched endlessly before her, the white-capped waves shimmering despite the overcast sky. The wind picked up slightly, rustling the dunes and carrying the scent of the sea to her. She closed her eyes and took a deep breath, savoring the moment and her solitude. Until recently, as in the last week when she felt as if she'd made some headway in regard to developing respectful if not entirely friendly relationships with others, this was one of her few joys.

Nothing good ever lasts, she was reminded a few moments later as a fat raindrop pelted her cheek. Opening her eyes, she discovered that clouds that moments ago had been rolling slowly overhead now churned with alarming speed. The sky darkened ominously, and the wind's gentle rustle turned into a fierce howl, whipping her hair around her face and sending the dunes into a swirling frenzy of sand and reeling grasses. The sea was suddenly a roiling expanse of dark, menacing waves crashing violently against the shore.

Another raindrop hit her, followed by several more in quick succession. Within moments, the drizzle turned into a heavy downpour. The storm had come upon her with frightening swiftness, not uncharacteristic of the sea's temperament but still unexpected. Raina quickly gathered her basket and stood, ducking her face away from the hard onslaught of rain, her heart pounding with an urgency to return to the keep before the storm fully unleashed its fury, afraid this might not yet be it.

Her skirts were plastered against her bottom and between her legs, making each step a struggle as she was driven along by the strong gale. Turning her back to the water and heading up into the dunes, her skirts billowed out in front of her, her hair whipping wildly around her face. The basket she carried was jerked upward and then down by the wind, losing half its contents. Raina was shoved forward several times, forced to put her hand out to keep from stumbling as she climbed. Desperately clambering, already soaked by the rain, she knew that if she could just make it beyond the dunes, she could find shelter in the trees.

Her hair, though drenched, was not plastered flat against her but rather flapped heavily with water, slapping and stinging her eyes, cheeks, and neck. "Lord love a sinner," she grumbled, spitting strands of hair from her mouth.

She paused briefly halfway up the dunes to glance back at the sea, her eyes widening at how quickly the roaring waves were advancing up the beach. Resuming her climb, she prayed that none of the fishermen were out in their currachs at this moment.

As much as she dearly loved nature, she knew a growing sense of unease and a twinge of fear as the storm intensified around her, the raw power of it both awe-inspiring and intimidating. The wind howled with actual sound, and the rain stung her skin like icy needles. A bolt of lightning was followed swiftly by a loud crack of thunder.

She grabbed hold of the marram grass in the dunes, using it as an anchor to pull herself up the slope. The cold, wet blades slipped through her fingers, nearly causing her to tumble backward. Desperately, she launched herself sideways to avoid falling back down the slope, landing hard on her arm. Having fallen into a hollow between the gentle mounds of the sand dunes, Raina lay still for a moment. Though the rain continued to drench her, the recess provided some shelter from the harshest winds. More lightning flashed, followed by booming thunder.

Already her chest heaved from her exertion. But after adjusting her grip on the handle of the basket, she forced herself to her feet once more and with her head tucked against her chest, trudged on up the incline.

"Ye little fool!"

Raina lifted her gaze, squinting hard against the elements, surprised to see Torsten approaching from the crest of the slope. Though he seemed much less perturbed and manipulated by the storm, his teeth were bared, and muscles flexed in his neck and forearms as he pushed through the wild wind and heavy rain toward her.

With renewed vigor, Raina surged forward. When he was close, making quick, seemingly effortless work of the distance between them, Raina reached out her hand at the same time he did. He did not take her hand, though, but clamped his fingers around her upper arm and turned, marching her uphill. With his other hand, he took control of the basket.

At the crest of the slope, he guided her toward the cover of the birch and oak trees in the large, wooded vale, maneuvering her to stand with her back against the wide trunk of a relatively small hazel tree. He stood directly in front of her, close enough that his thighs brushed her legs, and she was served an untimely, wayward reminder of how he'd held her in his arms the other night. Both his hands gripped both her arms, presumably to keep her safe and in place.

But then he began hollering at her, having to shout to be heard above the bellowing wind and the deafening sound of the sea, and though she wasn't necessarily fearful of his wrath, she did shrink a bit in the fury of it, for being so close and unable to escape it.

"Are ye bluidy daft? What the hell were ye doing? Ye could've gotten yerself kilt! Did ye nae ken the storm was coming?"

"Did *you*?" Raina asked, her frown as severe as his, as a response to being treated like a simpleton. "Did anyone? 'Twas naught but a harmless gray sky and light winds ten minutes ago."

"Ye've lived here all yer life, have ye nae? Dinna ye ken when a storm's brewing?"

"I have lived here *most* all my life," she acknowledged, "and I know more than you that the sea and sky can change in a heartbeat, cannot at all be counted upon to act as one might expect it will."

His scowl did not lessen. "Do ye have to argue and contradict and challenge every bluidy thing I say?"

"When you're wrong," she replied without hesitation, "I most certainly will."

His mouth twisted with displeasure, whether at her remark or for the audacity of challenging him. His entire face contorted with grim determination, eyes mirroring the stormy sea's ferocity, as he drew her forcefully against him. Raina collided with the muscled wall of his body with an 'oomph,' before he lowered his head and covered her mouth with his own. Instinctively, she lifted her hand to push him away, but he responded swiftly, releasing her upper arm and gripping her wrist, holding her hand to the side.

It needed only a second and the barest movement of his lips against her for Raina to understand that she was being kissed. Even as her lips were joined to his, though unmoving, unknowing, her brows lifted in wonder and confusion.

Her fingers curled into the linen of his tunic, any resistance quickly fading. Unbeknownst to her, her shoulders relaxed, her entire body seeming to melt against his.

His kiss was equal to the hardness and unyielding nature of the man himself, his mouth initially brutal and punishing—until Raina tentatively responded. Uncertain of her own actions, she had only a fleeting moment of his dominance to guide her, yet a frantic, swirling sensation in her belly urged her to kiss him back. She tugged at his tunic, mimicking his movements with her mouth and lips. Torsten emitted a guttural sound of approval, which began deep in his chest and rumbled up his throat. He parted his lips, and Raina reciprocated, which seemed to serve as an invitation, beckoning his tongue. He brushed his tongue against her lips before delving deeper, meeting her tongue with his own. She gasped in response, feeling her heart race, pounding in her ears.

Slanting his head, Torsten molded his body against her, pressing her further against the tree. His lips were warm and firm, his tongue probing and delightful. Raina exhaled a breathy sigh into the kiss, wanting it to go on and on and on.

As suddenly as he'd kissed her, he abruptly halted. He pulled back, almost jerking away from her. His breath was heavy, and his gaze bore into her as though she had forced the kiss upon him, rather than the other way around. Anger flashed in his eyes as he wiped rain and, she presumed, the taste of her kiss from his mouth.

The storm had not subsided, yet neither was conscious now of its fury, consumed instead by the intensity of their own emotions.

Having dealt for years with men who blamed her for their own shortcomings—most especially her father and at times her brother—men who visited anger upon her for their failings, Raina sensed that Torsten's anger was a reflection of his own internal struggle. It was a defensive reaction, she was certain, though the particulars of it escaped her at the moment.

He was gorgeous despite his fury, his lashes spiky with rainwater, his blue eyes sharp and bright, alive with fervor. His cheekbones were pronounced, the hollows beneath shadowed with a day's growth of black and silver whiskers. His lips were closed, thinned, while his nostrils flared with his sharp breaths.

Calmly, though her heart raced yet, Raina responded to his unrest. "You kissed me, Torsten," she said with resolve, having to raise her voice to be heard. "And I kissed you back as, I suspect, a... a wife might do."

She didn't ask, but wondered, *What is he afraid of?*

It came to her suddenly.

Ah, the loss of control, that was it. She'd wager Lochlan's last coin he despised having lost control.

"That was ill-advised. I dinna intend..." was all he said, his statement unfinished.

Boldly—as bold as she'd ever been—Raina stated with conviction, "I rather liked it."

This caused his jaw to tighten even more, raising a vein in the rugged column of his neck.

Torsten bent and scooped up the basket he'd dropped at some point.

"Take yer damn basket," he said, shoving the nearly empty willow vessel at her. "Let's get back to Lochlan."

When it was in her hand, he turned and continued on, toward the keep.

If he had stalked ahead of her, unconcerned whether she followed or not, she'd have been a wee bit troubled.

But he took her hand, her safety still a priority to him, stomping through the trees, pulling her along.

Raina bit back a decidedly feminine, very pleased smile.

Though she'd never been afraid of storms, she understood that this one was brutal, the wind and rain destructive. Going forward though, it was unlikely that she would equate violent storms with anything other than Torsten's scorching kiss.

THE NEXT MORNING, WHEN time allowed, Raina nervously related to Peigi that Torsten had kissed her.

"It was, well, unexpected, but I cannot say—"

"Saints awaiting, lass," Peigi gasped and scowled, "but he only just now kissed ye? Yesterday?" She paused, standing inside the enclosure of the kitchen garden, one hand filled with the sage she'd collected. Her mouth hung open for a moment before she used it again. "Och, this is going to take longer than I imagined. Here's hoping ye're still in yer child-bearing years by the time ye and him finally get around to making them bairns." Shaking her head, she moved on to the marjoram, her fingers deftly plucking at the leaves of the plants.

A wee bit embarrassed, feeling as if she had failed in some regard, Raina moved her toe and her gaze along the bottom of the wattle-and-daub fencing that surrounded the sizeable garden. Swallowing, she pushed onward. "But Peigi, what's next? Torsten kissed me but...but no more than that. He did not come to bed last night until after I was asleep and thus I did not have an opportunity to...um, seek another kiss."

With a heavy sigh, Peigi straightened and considered Raina, her expression weary in the manner of one who cannot believe they have to give instruction about something that should already be known.

Raina's cheeks filled with heat, a larger humiliation suffusing her. Waving her hands dismissively, she rushed out, "Sorry. Forget it. I shouldn't have—I mean, of course it's not for you—"

"Now hang on a minute, milady," Peigi cut her off. She motioned with her hand, the one that held the sage, repeatedly pushing it downward as if to ask for calm. "Gimme a moment, will ye? I'm still trying to comprehend how ye could have reached this age and nae ken what goes on between a man and woman—what are ye, anyway? Two and twenty? More?"

Clearing her throat, Raina answered, "Four and twenty."

Peigi's eyes widened. "Mary's tears, but how can ye...?" She waved her hand again. "Never ye mind. Done is done and here we are. Ye dinna ken, but ye want to." Planting her hands on her hips, twisting her mouth, she said, "All right, let me hunt inside my brain a moment."

Raina bit her lip, watching the process. Peigi's eyes narrowed as she seemed to gaze at some invisible spot in the air before her. Her lips pursed, then twisted, then pursed again. One hand came up to tap her chin thoughtfully, the sage leaves scraping her face and neck. She muttered to herself, a barely audible string of words that included "that'll ne'er do" and "by the holy rood." Her brows furrowed deeply, and she scratched her head in a manner that suggested she was sifting through a particularly tangled thicket of thoughts.

Thinking that she should add—and wincing as she did so—Raina said, "He ah, that is, he didn't seem very happy about having kissed me. But I'm not sure—well, I have an idea that he does not like the unexpected, and that he was angry with himself for having given in to... I guess it would be... *desire*?"

"By the bones of Saint Andrew," Peigi breathed, "but ye really are... ignorant of...shite, everything. Ne'er been kissed? Ne'er been groped? Haven't seen that look that comes in their eyes, like he's a starving ploughman and ye're a worthy feast?"

Raina shook her head, but then recalled the ravenous look that had darkened Torsten's countenance yesterday. "Maybe that's what I saw yesterday. He stared at my mouth for quite a moment, as if..." she didn't know what to compare it to.

Peigi did. "As if he wanted to be attached to it?" She asked, snorting out a chuckle.

"I...I suppose."

Eyes now bright with determination, Peigi announced, "All right, lass. I've sorted it out. Ye've got to be bold, but subtle. Ye need to—och, how to say it—make him *want* to kiss ye again, despite his internal objections, whatever those're about. So, aye, a man likes to see a bit of flesh, can hardly resist it when it's close. Ye'll set yer bath up in the chamber and time it so that ye're bare as the day ye were born inside the tub when he comes up at night."

"And have him discover me naked?" The very idea reddened her cheeks even more.

Peigi rolled her eyes. "Ye ken there'll have to be some degree of bareness to get the deed done, do you nae?"

"Quite frankly, that is not—I cannot imagine myself being so bold as to—"

"Sure and there's yer problem," Peigi announced.

Raina nodded, conceding some truth there. "Very well, but I—do I have to go to such drastic lengths? Isn't there something I can simply *say*?"

"While we women hear and feel, men see and crave touch. Mere words simply winna do." She paused and narrowed her eyes at Raina, measuring her. "Least any words that would entice him are unlikely to be uttered by ye. That would need more boldness than ye possess. We dinna ken why he dinna want to bed ye or hasna yet, so ye make yerself irresistible and that'll take care of itself."

Raina blinked, half-amused and half-terrified by Peigi's intensity. "Irresistible?"

"Aye, irresistible. Ye've got the looks, milady, and a nice young body. Ye just need to use them. Smile at him, touch his arm when ye speak—och, dinna be afraid to let yer breast rub against his arm. Let him see ye're interested, but dinna throw yerself at him like a desperate maid. Men like to do the chasing, ye ken."

Raina nodded slowly, absorbing Peigi's advice, internally dismissing half of it. Good gracious, rub her breast against his arm! "And if he doesn't respond?" She pressed.

Peigi snorted. "Oh, he'll respond, lass. A man can only resist for so long. Trust me on that." She lifted the sage-crowded hand again, pointing her forefinger toward the heavens, seemingly struck by inspiration. "Ye could always take a wee tumble, milady. That's a fully-clothed idea," she said, her eyes twinkling.

Raina blinked. "A tumble?"

"Aye. Pretend ye've sprained yer ankle. Make it look convincing. He'll have to carry ye, winna he? And a man carrying a woman, well, it's improbable that he winna feel *something.* Put yer arms around him, lean yer head on him like he's yer savior—again, dinna overdo it. But aye, proximity can work a few miracles."

Raina laughed nervously. "You're serious?"

"As serious as yesterday's storm," Peigi replied, her grin widening. "Sometimes, lass, ye need to give fate a little nudge. Mind ye, though, dinna actually hurt yerself in a tumble if ye decide to try it." Her face softened a bit, a sweetness entering her gaze. "Picture yerself holding yer bairns, lass, one after another, year after year. That'll help ye set aside any unease about using bold methods."

Nodding, Raina thanked Peigi for her wisdom, over which she would mull for several hours she was sure.

She left the housekeeper in the garden, and though she wasn't ready yet to seek out her husband and put either of Peigi's wild ideas to the test, Raina did give considerable thought to Peigi's parting words.

Picture yerself holding bairns.

The thought of having a baby had always been a tender, cherished dream. It was the one thing that had made her agreeable to the less-than-ideal matches proposed to her before. In those previous instances, the idea of a child to love and be loved by was all that had kept her sane and willing to entertain those unsuitable suitors.

With Torsten, the idea took on a new, more vivid dimension. She imagined a child with his strong features, perhaps his determined eyes and his unyielding spirit. Frankly, she wouldn't mind a son who one day grew into the image of his father—in every manner save for the cold, dark side of him. And the prospect of being a mother, of holding a small life she had created, and nurturing it with all the love she had but had so rarely been used, filled her with a warmth and longing that was impossible to ignore.

She envisioned the tiny fingers grasping hers, soft coos and wee giggles, the first steps, and the joy of seeing her child—many bairns perhaps—grow and thrive. This vision of love and connection was what she yearned for, something that did not necessarily require any input from Torsten once the making of the bairns was done.

Maybe Peigi was right. Maybe she did need to give fate a little nudge to have what she wanted, the chance to hold her own bairn in her arms.

Chapter Eleven

In truth, her own nerves may have delayed her putting into action one of Peigi's mad suggestions. But it was also true that Raina simply did not encounter quite the right circumstance.

Peigi's brazen idea that she should bathe inside her chamber, waiting for Torsten to happen upon her, was not only outside the limit of what lengths she was willing to go—just yet—but also seemed a bit obvious, and thus was fairly quickly discarded as a possibility. Torsten usually came to their chamber late at night, and what might be her reason for having a bath so close to midnight? In theory, Raina judged it implausible, likely to be seen through. Additionally, she had to consider that option would require help—unwilling accomplices, she deemed them, any and all of the household staff that would be asked to bring and fill the heavy tub. And she couldn't imagine herself being so selfish as to demand that they, too, keep late hours merely to satisfy her errant plot.

For lack of any of her own ideas to compel Torsten's awareness and hopefully another kiss and more, the scheme to feign a stumble and a sore ankle won out.

But then Raina struggled with a wee dread, having no idea what she was actually asking for. She hadn't the courage to ask Peigi what she should expect. If her plan worked, if Torsten could be made to kiss her again...then what? Her knowledge of intimacy was limited to the ways of animals, and she was hardly enthusiastic about experiencing what bulls did to cows. She slapped her hands over her face, bemoaning the fact that she was so uneducated, so unworldly. There, she believed—and only there—her mother had certainly failed her. In her defense, however, Lisbeth MacQueen in all probability imagined that she had many more years yet, decades even, with her daughter.

It wasn't until two days later that she finally found an opportune moment to set her wobbly plan in motion, catching Torsten outdoors. It wasn't ideal, as he was surrounded by a dozen of his men and all their large destriers, having just returned. But then she imagined she might use the crowd to her advantage—the horses, specifically.

Heart pounding, knowing she had never before invented or purposefully created such a ruse, Raina strode across the cobbles, appearing to any onlooker as if she were approaching her husband. At the hindquarters of the first horse she encountered, she gritted her teeth, thinking *now or never*, and let out a little yelp before dropping to the ground.

Mayhap they would believe she had been bumped or kicked by the large destrier.

Her fall, she judged, was convincingly clumsy, though sadly not entirely intentional. Having never faked a fall before, the gasp that escaped her was real, and her hands flailed dramatically before she landed heavily on her knees.

She hadn't thought it through; from her vantage point, she could not see Torsten's reaction, or even if he had seen her at all. Still, the wince she gave as she pivoted onto her bottom was genuine, realizing she had landed wrong on her hand; her ankle did not hurt in the least, but her wrist was sore. The horse's tail swished as its rider urged it forward, away from her, muttering a surprised and sincere apology. The dusty ends of the tail brushed across her face.

"Raina!" Torsten's voice rang out, infused with genuine concern, which she was happy to hear.

Ah, success.

The throng of horses and men parted in front of her, revealing Torsten hastening toward her, his brow furrowed.

There was little need to feign embarrassment for her mishap—the embarrassment was real. The courtyard had fallen silent, with whispers of concern and even a titter of laughter, the latter perhaps provoked from someone in the group of peasants near the well. Raina glanced up at Torsten as he crouched at her side.

Torsten's footsteps halted beside her, his tall, broad-shouldered figure casting a shadow over her and the cobbles. His expression, chiseled and severe as always, betrayed no hint of softness. Lowering himself onto his haunches at her side, he asked in a voice as sharp as his gaze, "Dinna ye ken nae to walk behind a horse?"

Raina blanched a bit, suffering a mild surprise at his reaction, reproach rather than concern. Just as quickly, she realized she shouldn't have been surprised. Clearly she hadn't expected warmth, but this cold severity cut deeper than she anticipated.

"It was my fault," she managed, her tone aggrieved. "I didn't...." she left that unsaid, supposing her plot was effectively thwarted by his cool indifference. She rubbed her sore wrist in dejection. It wasn't like she could stumble and fall every day until he cared.

"Are ye hurt?"

Raina glanced up, recognizing an opening. A glimmer of hope spiraled inside her.

"My ankle," she said automatically.

"Yer ankle? But ye're rubbing yer wrist."

"Yes, um, that's sore as well."

Torsten flipped back the hem of her skirt, exposing her hose-clad ankles and short boots but not much more. With more gentleness than she'd have suspected him capable of, he assessed one ankle, moving his finger and palm over the hose.

Raina's breath caught in her throat. It dawned on her then that if her ankle were truly sore, she should probably have some reaction. When he examined the second ankle in the same manner, she stiffened and drew in a breath, believing that had been well done indeed, that it had come across as very authentic.

"Mayhap it's only sprained," he said. While his fingers remained wrapped lightly around her ankle, Torsten faced Raina. "Can ye move it at all?"

"Yes, I think so," she said and did so, pivoting her ankle just a wee bit. She grimaced again for good measure since he was regarding her so closely.

"Nae broken then," he surmised, "or the pain would be unbearable."

"Oh, no," she was quick to say, "it's not broken. I mean, I don't think it is. I just don't know if I can stand on it."

Why wasn't her big, strong, impatient husband simply lifting her into his arms? Was he afraid of touching her?

"I think it'll be all right," she said, attempting to get to her feet.

Torsten stood quickly and assisted, his strong hands on her arms.

Committed now to her ruse, Raina pretended that putting weight on her ankle was painful, immediately shifting her weight to her other leg.

Grumbling something unintelligible but clearly annoyed, Torsten finally scooped her into his arms. Raina rolled her lips inward to prevent a satisfied smile from coming. As he bore her into the keep, Raina recalled Peigi's suggestion and lifted her arms, wrapping her hands around his neck, her fingers connecting with rigid cords. Laying her head against his chest was not so easy in this position and Raina abandoned that notion, and then was alarmed when it seemed his intent was to deliver her to a chair at the high table in the hall.

"Oh no, I—I would rather, that is, I think I should be brought to my—our—bedchamber. Do you suppose I should elevate my foot?"

Whether he did or not wasn't made known, but Torsten changed direction, and carried her up the stairs at the opposite end of the hall and down the corridor, hardly slowed at all by her weight.

Raina snuggled as close as she could to him, inhaling his scent, horse, leather, man, not at all unpleasant. His arms were strong beneath her, muscles rigid at her back and under her legs.

He mounted the far staircase and kicked the door open with his foot and was careful to turn a bit as he entered so that her head was not banged. Inside, he strode straight to the bed.

She was a bundle of nerves by this point, expecting she still needed to provoke a kiss though she'd yet to imagine how. Raina simply hung on when he set her down on the soft mattress, her hands still gripping his neck, so that he couldn't just pull back and straighten away from her.

He tried to, though. But Raina held on and tipped her face up to his, closing her eyes, waiting.

There was a moment, just a moment, when he did not move, and Raina waited, expecting his lips to touch hers. Her pulse raced with anticipation.

Then his fingers circled her wrists and drew her hands away from his neck, his grip firm.

"Bluidy hell, Raina," he growled. "What are ye about?"

His anger caused her eyes to snap open. His blue eyes were set harshly upon her, his dark brows slashed downward.

Flustered and disappointed, she stuttered a disjointed response. "I thought...you seemed so—don't you want to kiss me?"

"What the—" he began and then stopped, his lip curled as he did now straighten away from her. "Are ye even injured?"

She gasped in outrage, though she couldn't bring herself to refute it verbally, which would have her lying outright.

"I've said to ye, have I nae, a marriage in name only suits me just fine. I'm nae interested in furthering the union."

"But...you kissed me during the storm—"

He glared at her. "Aye, and I've said I should nae have. A momentary lapse of judgment. It will nae happen again."

Angry and unaccountably wounded by his swift and severe rejection, but overcome by a need to understand this enigmatic man, she asked, "Then why did you?" She put her hands behind her on the mattress, wincing a bit as her wrist really was sore.

He didn't like being questioned. His jaw tightened as he stared down at her, a muscle ticking at the corner as if he were physically restraining himself from responding. His eyes, that stormy blue, darkened further, a clear sign of his mounting irritation.

She bristled at his refusal to answer, her own ire stirred. Tight-lipped, she suggested, "In that case, an annulment should be easy to obtain, given the circumstances. Wed by force under threats of violence, to which there were plenty of witnesses. And the union unconsummated, meaning it's not really a marriage at all—"

"There will be nae annulment," he ground out.

"Then mayhap I will simply leave."

"Ye will nae. Christ, dinna ye understand how war and the spoils of it work?"

"I do understand," she shot back, hating the weakness that caused wretched tears to rise. "You claim the spoils and to hell with any person who happens to have her life ruined by—"

"What do ye want, Raina?" He clipped impatiently. "What are ye after?"

"I want a child," she answered bluntly, holding her breath, hardly able to credit the boldness that possessed her.

Torsten was speechless. His frown darkened and his lips thinned but he said nothing.

"And if you are not willing to give me that," she continued heatedly, "what right do you have to prevent me from marrying someone who can or will? It's not fair. It's selfish and arrogant, that you don't—haven't once!—considered me and what I—"

"God's fury, lass," he seethed. "There's a war going on! All of us will sacrifice, as we have and as we will. Ye are nae made special that any singular accommodation is granted ye, for what ye willna have because of war."

"That's rubbish," she challenged, lunging to her feet, uncaring that she might seem miraculously cured. "What a piss poor excuse," she furthered, using one of her father's vulgar expressions. "By my understanding, people continue, every day, to wed and to conceive. War indeed, but life goes on."

"It dinna matter," he said, his jaw tight. "It remains that I haven't any interest in consummating this marriage—"

"Is it me personally? Or are you against marriage in general?" She interjected.

"—certainly nae with the daughter of Malcolm MacQueen," he finished.

Raina stared, horrified. *Sweet Jesus*. He loathed her. Simply because she was her father's daughter.

Her heart twisted inside her chest, hope cruelly stomped and crushed under the boot of his hatred.

She returned his furious glare, absurdly annoyed for how ridiculously handsome he was. Childishly, she thought that was unfair as well. If he'd been crafted as homely, or was unkempt, or carried a foul scent, or possessed eyes that didn't pierce her so, she would in all probability be thrilled that he didn't want to touch her. Truth was, however, that he was striking, and he had shown tenderness, more than once, and she was...well, part of her was smitten, anyway.

Had been smitten. He'd just killed whatever had blossomed and lived so hopefully inside her.

Mayhap she'd only been smitten with his kiss, though. And his arms around her when he was half-clothed. She did not particularly care for his regularly brusque demeanor.

"You've made yourself known, as have I," she said at length, her tone wooden. "Don't be surprised if one day you find—"

"Dinna even think to leave Lochlan," he warned her dangerously.

"I have no intention of abandoning my home," she said, though she wasn't certain that was true.

When he seemed to have nothing further to add, she turned on her heel and left him, a sigh erupting as she exited the chamber. Sure, she'd trembled inside her shoes in the face of his fury and for how awful was the truth now known, but at least she knew for certain where she stood.

Not only had the kiss meant nothing, but he actually despised her, she now understood.

Raina was gutted by heartache. This was the closest she'd ever gotten to having a child of her own—close but still so far. She'd worked herself into a fine frenzy of hope over the last few days, since he'd kissed her, since she'd begun to imagine holding a bairn in her arms.

As she marched down to the kitchens, her blood boiling at the injustice of it all, she considered that seeking an annulment would mean that she would likely be forced to leave Lochlan Hall. And then were would she go?

She wondered what was worse: remaining at Lochlan, with her indifferent husband—as hurtful as had been her tyrannical father, but in a different manner—or returning to her aunt's house and living there, attempting again to find a husband, but this time without the benefit of her father's influence and whatever false promises he'd made to her previous intended bridegrooms, and now known as the *Killer of Men*.

Inside the kitchen, she seized upon the first bit of busy work she found, needing to occupy her mind. A basket of cabbages sat beside the long wooden counter in the middle of the kitchen. Running her hand over the end of the board, Raina judged it clean, claimed a chopping knife, and began hacking away at the poor vegetable.

The constant thud of the knife against the cutting board was soothing, a fine way to channel her frustration. She was so engrossed in her task that she didn't immediately notice the kitchen maid, Lorna, standing off to the side, wringing her hands nervously.

"Milady, that's my chore," Lorna said when Raina finally noticed her presence.

Raina paused, looking at the young maid and then at the half-chopped cabbage. "I needed something to do," she said, nearly breathless, her efforts neither slow nor without a fair amount of violence.

Lorna bobbed an agreeable nod. "Aye, milady. I'll, um, see to the bread then."

Raina gave a grateful nod and returned to her task, the repetitive motion and the physical exertion helping to work off some of her steam. But her thoughts were still a whirl of anger and confusion, and she found it difficult to focus on anything else.

After almost thirty minutes, every head of cabbage in the large basket was chopped and Raina was feeling somewhat calmer. She set the knife down and wiped her hands on her apron. She made her way to the rear lower passageway, hoping a breath of fresh sea air outside the back door might help clear her mind further.

Just as she stepped outside, a young lad from the village came running up to her, breathless and wide-eyed. "Milady, ye must come quickly," he panted.

Alarm shot through her. "What is it, Geoffrey?" She asked, recognizing the bailiff's son.

"The laird," he gasped, his large eyes wide with fright, "fell from his horse, he did. He's asking for ye."

Raina's heart lurched. Without another word, she gathered her skirts and hurried after the boy, all thoughts of her earlier frustration with Torsten forgotten in her rush to reach him.

As she followed Geoffrey, her mind raced with questions and fears. Torsten's brusque rejection and the argument that wasn't yet an hour old churned in her mind. She wondered if Torsten had been thrown, his destrier spooked by something; she didn't know for sure but had to imagine he was an accomplished rider. Weren't his soldiers with him? He rarely went anywhere about Lochlan without at least one other person, always in discussion about something, so much as she'd noticed. Her heart thudded with fright, imagining her magnificent and seemingly invincible husband broken and bloody, imagining all sorts of scenarios that might have compelled him to ask for her.

Why *would* he ask for her now, after making it clear he wanted no real marriage with her? That she was his enemy still? Was his injury so grave that he meant to make an apology to her ere he succumbed to his wounds?

They followed the narrow shelf along the edge of the cliff that overlooked the sea, the path winding far to the north where it became a woodland—the very spot where Torsten had kissed her. The memory of that kiss, a rare moment of vulnerability from him and an unexpected delight for her clutched at her heart now but served to spur her on.

"Just over here," as the lad had said more than once, seemed to be ever further ahead.

"Geoffrey! Wait!"

The lad was far ahead now, swift and agile darting through the trees. Raina struggled to follow the sparse and fleeting glimpses of the boy as he raced forward.

As she sprinted through the trees, she supposed that any of these gnarled and protruding roots might have caused Torsten's steed to stumble. Had he pitched his rider over his head? Sweet Mother Mary, but had Torsten broken his neck or back?

"Here!" Geoffrey shouted, sounding closer.

Finally, Raina became aware of a group of mounted men milling about, their figures seen through the boughs and leaves as she approached. It did not register immediately that none of the mounted men were de Graham men.

Nonplused, she surveyed the ground, expecting to find Torsten there.

But none of these men were Torsten and no one lay on the ground, injured.

Her chest heaving, she lifted her face to the men on horseback, some of them slowly moving to surround her. The lad, after a quick nod to a man wearing a cowl so tightly drawn that his face was unseen, sprinted away, swiftly lost inside the woodland.

"Where is...?" She began, just now comprehending fully these were not de Graham men; not one of them wore the familiar green tartan. And these were not even villagers; though many wore kerchiefs, the faces that were visible were unknown to her. "I don't understand."

"Take her," was all that was said, and reality crashed upon her.

They intended to abduct her.

Raina turned, meaning to flee, to run as fast as she could, but was caught almost immediately by a lanky lad leaping from the saddle and upon her, knocking her to the ground.

"Bleedin' sinners! *Take* her, ye eejit! Dinna maim her!"

With little hope and likely only one chance, Raina stopped fighting, pausing to draw in breath as she was hauled to her feet. When she was standing and rather than question what was happening and why, she tipped her face to the sky and let out a bloodcurdling scream.

It was, sadly, cut short rather swiftly. A man rushed her again, tackling her once more to the ground, his hand on the back of her head, shoving her cheek into the dirt. This one was neither lean nor lanky, the knee upon her back heavy and strong. She struggled with every ounce of strength she had, but his grip tightened, and the weight of his knee pressed harder against her back, forcing the air from her lungs. As his hand pushed her head further into the dirt, a finger came dangerously close to her mouth. In a desperate bid, she opened her mouth and bit down on his finger with all her might, tasting blood as she did so.

"Bluidy hell!" the man shouted, jerking his hand back in pain.

Raina spat out the blood and dirt, trying to scramble to her feet, but another man was already upon her, grabbing her arms and pulling her up roughly. She kicked and thrashed, refusing to go quietly.

"Ye'll pay for that, lass," the injured man growled, nursing his bleeding finger as he glared at her.

"Let go of me!" Raina screamed, but her captors were relentless, their grips like iron.

The man with the cowl urged his steed forward, his voice cold and commanding. "Enough of this. Gag her if you must, but we need to move quickly."

Fear and defiance warred within her as she continued to struggle, but the truth was the infidels easily overpowered her, binding her hands and placing a gag over her mouth. Helpless, furious, and beyond frightened, Raina was hoisted onto one of the horses and taken further away from Lochlan Hall.

Chapter Twelve

Several trees had been felled and hauled from the nearby woods, their trunks stripped of all bark and any useless branches. The great logs lay in the grasslands, arranged in neat rows that ran parallel to the army's tents. This open space, teeming with activity today, separated the army's encampment from the keep and its outbuildings. The perimeter of the planned fortifications had been carefully marked off with ropes, tracing the boundary where the wooden palisade would soon stand.

Men of the de Graham army moved with purpose, some wielding axes to shape the logs into uniform lengths while others dug deep post holes into the earth. The sounds of sawing, chopping, and the thud of mallets echoed through the air. Horses, straining against their harnesses, pulled the logs into position, while carts loaded with tools and supplies creaked under their weight.

A palisade would not long stand a large siege—the de Graham army would have made quick work of it—but it would have some use, defining and controlling the area, and more crucially, it would serve as an initial barrier, slowing down an enemy, preventing a cavalry charge, and allowing defending archers to wreak havoc on a stalled attack.

Returned from the keep and his encounter with Raina, Torsten worked alongside his men, happy to take out his frustration with an axe, splintering the end of the long logs until they were spears and could be struck into the ground as the skeletal framework. He was still furious with Raina for placing demands on him, for expecting him to care. At the same time, he was furious with himself also, for some small but persistent voice inside him that nagged, suggesting mayhap he didn't only want their union to be in name only. Having teased himself with one taste of her sweetly innocent kiss, could he live all the rest of his life without seeking another?

He was mid-swing when a scream drifted toward him. 'Twas not overly loud, was distant and ended so abruptly that he wondered if he'd heard it, or if the sound of the sea, ever present as a background noise, only played tricks on him. But then he noticed that others had paused as well. Men turned toward the north, their brows uniformly knitted before they looked between themselves, asking with their expressions but not any words if anyone else had heard that abbreviated shriek as well.

He swung once more before an uneasy feeling inside him and his steadfast sense of responsibility pushed him to investigate the sound, knowing that dangers lurked everywhere. It was only ten days ago that he and his army had ridden unchecked into Lochlan. Who was to say that another army did not now attempt the same?

Striking the axe into the trunk on which he'd been working to trim, Torsten collected the tunic he's stripped off and returned his belt and sword to his waist. As he strode across the tall grass toward the stables close to the keep, he spied Peigi emerging from the door to the hall. She appeared anxious, her hands wringing in her apron even as she glanced around urgently and stumbled forward.

She changed direction when she noticed Torsten, heading straight for him.

"Have ye seen Lady Raina?" She asked with some urgency.

Instantly his hackles rose, and Torsten quickly closed the distance between himself and Lochlan's housekeeper. "Nae for almost an hour. Where did—?"

"I just heard someone scream—I trow that was a woman's scream," she fretted. "And Helen said she saw the mistress leave out the back door, following the lad, Geoffrey, out along the cliffs."

His blood curdled. "How long ago was this?" He asked, moving again, striding with purpose toward the stables now.

"Quarter hour ago, mayhap more," Peigi answered, struggling to keep up with his long strides.

He paused just outside the entrance to the shadowy stables and turned, hollering out for Aonghas and James to come.

"Bring an entire unit!" he shouted. "Now!" Without waiting for them, he stepped inside and approached the first stall, where his destrier was housed. Hurriedly, he proceeded to saddle the big black.

He wasn't sure why Peigi had followed him, but thought to say, "She's angry with me. Any chance she simply went out to clear her head, or expend energy?"

Peigi snorted. "Aye, I ken something got under her skin. Should've figured it was ye."

Torsten paused only long enough to turn a nasty scowl onto the housekeeper.

"But nae, she took out all her frustration on the wee cabbages, chopping away with that knife as if they were someone's head. She'd settled down though before she left the kitchens."

Torsten rolled his eyes at this—at Peigi's cheekiness, not at Raina wanting to work out her frustration, since he'd been doing the same.

"Did ye check the beach?" He asked, knowing the cliff's edge was only ten yards from the entrance to the kitchen at the back of the keep, and that the door on fine days was mostly kept open.

"I did," she said, just as Aonghas and James arrived, jogging into the stables. "Nae one there. Even the fishermen are gone for the day."

"My wife seems to have been going with or chasing some lad along the beach," Torsten informed his men, "without reason as we ken. Let's investigate that scream—if that is indeed what we heard."

Aonghas turned and gave the same information to the men coming in his wake, sending them back to the horse line to retrieve their own steeds, as only the officers' horses were kept in the stable.

Just as Aonghas and James began to saddle their steeds, Torsten walked his destrier outside the stables and vaulted into the saddle. "Search the entire keep," Torsten advised Peigi, who was yet close on his heels, "lest Lady Raina was merely overlooked inside." With that, he kneed the destrier into motion and took off in search of his wife, skirting first around all the debris and supplies related to the palisade's construction before he gave his horse his legs.

He rode fast but not at a breakneck speed, imagining plenty of plausible reasons for Raina to have followed the lad, and for the scream itself. Peigi had said the beach was clear, vacant, so the idea that someone, even Raina, had fallen over the edge was unlikely. The scream had come from the north, where the path and slope were gentler. A fall there would land someone in a sand dune. At most they'd be scratched.

Christ, if this was Raina pretending again to have injured herself simply to garner sympathy and another kiss, he'd wring her neck for the fright she'd roused.

His men had just caught up to him, more than fifteen of them grouped together with a few more stragglers galloping to catch up, when he entered the woodland that overlooked the lower cliffs at this location. Naturally, his mind returned to the scene here a few days ago, that most stunning kiss.

He recalled the way she'd responded, at first with some stiffness, as shocked as he was by his kiss. But *Jesu*, how swiftly and sweetly she'd melted into him, clinging to him, eager and astonishingly innocent. He shook his head to clear the memories, refocusing on the task at hand. The shadows of the trees danced around him as he guided his destrier along the narrow, twisting path inside the woods.

They rode for half a mile before the trees cleared, opening up onto another vast expanse of meadow. While inland the landscape was flat and unchanged as far as the eye could see, the ridgeline along the cliffs rose and fell, was sandy and soft and then jagged with rock. He spied a group of riders galloping hard, cresting a knoll and then disappearing as the terrain dipped low. They were at a great distance, far enough that they appeared only specks on the northern horizon, but Torsten's instincts warned that they were somehow related to that scream.

"There!" He called out, pointing to the riders. "Spread out!" He couldn't be sure at this distance but thought there weren't more than eight or ten riders.

He and his men gave chase. The wind whipped at his face, and he leaned low over the horse's neck, his fury and curiosity aroused. Just as he wondered who these men were and what their business inside Lochlan might be—nefarious was his guess, based on their swift ride—he realized that one of those fleeing horses held two people and that one of them was garbed in dark wine garments, the skirt of which billowed alongside the horse as it ran.

At the same time Torsten's heart dropped to the pit of his stomach, recognizing the color of the léine Raina had worn today, Aonghas shouted above the thunder of galloping hooves.

"'Tis Lady Raina!"

Torsten's muscles tensed and his fists clenched tighter on the reins, as angry as he could ever recall being.

The destriers were no match to the speed of the sleek chargers being ridden by Raina's captors; in the open field, the chargers would outrun the destriers all day long. Yet, while the chargers excelled in speed and agility over relatively flat terrain, the mighty de Graham destriers had been trained for war and compensated for their slightly slower speed with their strength and endurance in rugged, challenging landscapes. Torsten hollered and pushed his steed to give more, to go faster, to get to her. Giving up was not an option; he would ride the horse dead before he abandoned his pursuit.

Still, the pursuit went on for miles and gaining ground was slow, and truth be told, if not for Raina's help, they might have ridden for hours and eventually lost ground, as the destriers' disadvantage was that they were capable of endurance over short distances and intense engagements, of which war was mainly comprised.

But either out of sheer will to escape or because she realized Torsten's pursuit and meant to assist in her own rescue, Raina struggled fiercely with her captor. Several times, the horse upon which she rode veered or jerked suddenly, signifying an upset in its riders. Torsten saw her bound hands swinging wildly at one point, resisting her captor's attempt to subdue her. She kept fighting and soon enough, went tumbling from the saddle.

Not all of the kidnappers stopped, but half of them did—there were eight, Torsten was close enough to count now.

"Keep fighting, lass," he growled between his clenched teeth as he raced toward her.

And she did. Though two men, including the one with whom she'd ridden, had dismounted to recapture her, she jumped to her feet and stumbled wisely inland and not toward the sea cliff, where there was nowhere to run. It was only seconds before hands seized her again, but she did not crumble with defeat, but continued fighting, kicking her legs and punching blindly with her trussed hands.

As Torsten and his men were nearly upon them, the two mounted men took off and one of the men trying to control Raina glanced at the coming fury and decided to save himself, leaping onto his horse's back and galloping away. It took the last man another second to decide to give up the hostage to save his life. But he'd hesitated too long and another few seconds and more ground were gained as his horse was spooked by the frothing, charging destriers, dancing away as the man tried to mount. He did eventually gain the saddle and made haste to depart.

Torsten thundered past Raina for the moment, as did his men, intent on catching those who had abducted her. When he was close enough to the last man to touch her, Torsten launched himself from the saddle at the man. They tumbled off the far side of the running horses, smacking hard on the ground and rolling several times with the momentum of Torsten's attack. The man fought uncontrollably, with flailing arms and by bucking his body as Torsten obtained the upper hand, rising over him. He struck the man across his face, and then again from the opposite side with his left hand.

"Nae one takes what belongs to me," he roared, his eyes blazing with the intensity of his righteous fury. "She is mine," he growled as he swung his fist again. "And I protect what is mine with blood and steel." With the man pinned beneath him, it was not difficult to pull his dagger from his belt and sink it into the man's chest. His lip curled, Torsten spared only a moment to watch the life ebb from the man's desperate gaze before he pushed himself off the body and went to Raina.

He landed hard on his knees at her side, where she'd last fallen and lay still, carefully turning her over. "Raina?"

Her eyes were wide with fright above a grimy rag that had been shoved into her mouth, attached with a kerchief around her face, her mouth forced open, the binding tight. Lifting himself on one knee, he reached over the back of her, frantically addressing the knot at the back of her head while she collapsed against him, the crown of her head meeting with the top of his chest. She clutched at his tunic, one hand grabbing his flesh as well. Her fingers trembled against him.

"'Tis done," he said, his voice thick with emotion. "'Tis done, lass. Ye're safe. All guid." He kept talking, meaning to assure her. "Let me get this bluidy knot out." Her hair was tousled and tangled around the binding. "There," he said, and gently pulled the soiled fabric from her. Taking her by the shoulders, he pushed slowly until there was some space between them. At the same time, Raina reached up with a shaking hand just as Torsten gently pulled the gag from her mouth, tossing it aside.

"*Jesu,* lass," he breathed. "Who were they? What did they want with ye?"

Tears fell. She shook her head. "I don't know. Th-they didn't say. They hardly spoke. One man just said, 'take her.'"

"But what brought ye out to them?"

"Geoffrey, the bailiff's lad, came to the keep. He said you had fallen from your steed," she whimpered. "He said ye asked for me. I...I thought ye were gravely...I didn't think. I just ran. I followed Geoffrey, imagining the worst."

Christ, they'd laid a trap using him as the bait, or his name as pretense.

"Yer mouth is bleeding," he said, livid now for the fright gleaned in her gaze. "If they struck ye, I'll— "

Shaking her head again, Raina admitted, "I bit him, before he put the gag in my mouth."

Enough to draw blood, obviously. "Well done, lass. And the scream that tore from yer throat. We'd nae have...." He let that trail off, unable to even conceive what might have become of her if she'd not managed to scream.

Gazing up at him with tear-stained eyes and cheeks scratched and dirty, she asked, "Is he dead?"

Torsten nodded, a wee offended she might imagine he would allow the man to live.

"Are...are they all dead?"

Torsten glanced around. Only a few de Grahams surrounded them, their gazes sharp on Raina. James grimaced as if he felt Raina's fear and was troubled by it.

"If they're nae, they will be. The lads'll nae give up until they're caught, each one of them."

He thought now, belatedly, he should have advised that at least one remain alive; he would have liked answers to the questions of who was behind the abduction and why.

Raina dropped her head to her chest and wept, keening softly, her shoulders drooping. Whether she cried for the fact that the brigands were dead or merely in relief that her ordeal was over, Torsten did not know.

Holding her shoulder lest she fall without him to lean against, Torsten stood and easily took Raina into his arms, carrying her to his steed. Over the top of her head, buried limply against his chest, he inclined his head at Aonghas, one of several to have since returned from chasing the other kidnappers. "Find the lad, this Geoffrey. Bring him to the keep."

Aonghas mounted and departed, instructing the others to stay with their laird.

"Double the guard as soon as we get back," he said to James, who walked with him, his concerned gaze on Raina.

"Aye. I'll set 'em up at the beach and in these woods."

"And put a unit on the road from Montrose," Torsten ordered, since that was the largest, closest burgh. Whoever had attempted to abduct Raina might have originated from or convened there.

James held the destrier's harness while Torsten set Raina in the saddle and then climbed up behind her. Raina collapsed against him as soon as he sat. James handed him the reins and Torsten urged the horse into a light cantor, eager to get her home.

"What do ye ken of the bailiff?" He thought to ask as they rode, partly to distract her from any residual fright.

"Very little," she answered. She straightened a bit, losing a bit of what had been a shrinking fear and what had seemed a vast dreadfulness. "Ronald, he is, the bailiff," she said, her voice less halting. "He was retained or elevated while I was in Glasgow. He mostly oversees the cattle outfit. I have little interaction with him."

Torsten did not press her for more and they continued on in silence.

He was acutely aware of Raina's presence in his arms, of her slight frame pressed against his chest. The steady rise and fall of her breath was felt along his forearm wrapped around her middle. Her hair, soft and fragrant, brushed against his chin. He inhaled deeply, savoring the scent of lavender and the subtle sweetness that he'd learned was uniquely hers. 'Twas an intimate closeness he'd not anticipated, and despite or mayhap because of the gravity of the situation, it stirred something deep within him. While the cadenced motion of the destrier had some part in soothing his frayed nerves, he understood that Raina nestled in his arms brought him a larger relief. She was here, with him, shaken but ultimately unharmed. The terror he'd felt, the wild fear that had gripped his heart when he had witnessed her being abducted, slowly ebbed away.

Rather than dwell on what fear he had known—and the reasons behind the depths of it—Torsten focused on what his response to such a vile and daring, if incomprehensible, plot would be. Doubling the guard would only be the beginning, he guessed; more measures might be employed to protect Raina and Lochlan after he'd spoken to the lad, Geoffrey. Having no idea what he was up against, he couldn't afford to take any chances, and yet visions of watchtowers manned with skilled archers and equipped with signaling devices for rapid communication floated around his mind. He considered the importance of alliances and thought he might seek to create ties with neighboring clans, negotiating mutual defense pacts as the de Grahams had done for centuries around Glenbarra Brae. There, they'd enlisted the locals as informants, and they were rewarded for their loyalty and vigilance in reporting any threats.

As Aonghas had preceded them, by the time Torsten and Raina rode up to Lochlan Hall, the work of several dozen on the palisade had stopped and they had quite an audience.

The post-hole diggers and tree-cutters stood grouped together around Aonghas, who had yet to dismount. To a man, their faces were etched with the hard lines of experience and the grit of countless battles. They were men who thrived in the chaos of combat but whose eyes now softened slightly, wearing expressions of deep concern and fierce protectiveness. While he didn't imagine their concern was entirely personal, they had embraced Raina as one of their own, and her tribulation was perceived as a threat against a de Graham, which she now was. The bond of loyalty they felt for Torsten extended naturally to his wife, and her safety would be a matter of honor for them, the lack thereof an affront to every fighting de Graham man.

Raina stiffened a bit, giving Torsten some sense that she abhorred so much blatant attention focused on her. When she drew herself up further in the saddle, he supposed she also disliked being viewed as a victim. Though she'd just endured a harrowing ordeal, she didn't want to be pitied or coddled, he guessed. She held her head high, her gaze fixed on the men as they passed, no doubt silently proclaiming to any watching that she was not broken.

Peigi awaited them in front of the keep, flanked by several of the newly hired household lasses, these ones with a more personal concern for their mistress. Though the housekeeper had cried no tears, it was clear she'd been worried, approaching the horse and riders before Torsten had reined in the big black, her large eyes shining with relief as they fixed on Raina.

Torsten wasn't needed to aid Raina in dismounting; Peigi's take-charge nature took over immediately, her movements brisk and purposeful. She reached up, her strong hands ready to assist Raina down from the saddle, her garrulous demeanor scarcely subdued by the gravity of the situation.

"Ah, lass, there ye are," Peigi exclaimed, her voice a mix of exasperation and relief. The gap between her front teeth became more pronounced as she smiled—the smiled was both forced and pained, by Torsten's assessment. "Gave us quite a scare, ye did. Abducted? And by whose orders, I'll be wanting to ken," she said fiercely. "And just ye wait until I get my hands on the lad, Geoffrey." She paused as Raina set her feet on the ground. "Come here, see. Let's have a look at ye. No worse for wear, I hope." She brushed a lock of hair away from Raina's face. "Dinna cry nae more, lass," Peigi said, looking as if she might now join Raina in tears. She glanced up at Torsten, giving him a quick nod of acknowledgment before she returned her steady regard to Raina. "Yer husband recovered ye, and nae surprise there. All that fierceness, all that meanness probably put to guid use against them villains." With an arm around Raina's shoulder, Peigi steered her toward the keep, calling for the lasses to follow. "Come along, girls. A hot bath and a warm meal are just what she needs now." Though she kept walking forward, Peigi called over her shoulder to Torsten, "And dinna ye worry about a thing, we'll have her right as rain in nae time."

Torsten nodded.

Peigi's deep concern shone through every word and gesture, and Torsten was grateful—for Raina's sake—for the housekeeper's unflinching attachment and her nurturing care, which were exactly what Raina needed now.

Torsten dismounted and in short order, convened his officers inside the hall, which was vacant now as it was still hours before supper. He alerted those that hadn't heard, Gilles and Rory included, about what had nearly befallen Raina.

A collective gasp rippled through his men, and the officers exchanged alarmed glances.

Gilles was the first to respond vocally. "Abducted? But...why? *Jesu,* was the lass harmed?"

"She's shaken but unhurt," Torsten replied, his eyes flickering with his persistent anger. "We were able to intercept them ere they got too far. Peigi has her abovestairs, she's in guid hands."

Rory MacLeod was equally stunned. "We have patrols and lookouts. How did this happen?"

At the same time, Eòghann wanted to know, "How many?"

"Was it locals?" Uilleam inquired.

Torsten raised a hand to calm the rising tide of questions. "We ken verra little, save that Lady Raina was cajoled out of doors, away from the keep, by a local lad name Geoffrey. It appears they knew precisely when to act. They were only a group of eight."

James spoke up. "They're dead now, of course. I dinna recognize any man." He paused and looked at Uilleam, who'd been there as well. "Ye neither? Nae, they were nae locals."

Uilleam suggested, "Mayhap have a few from the village brought out to where those bodies are, they might be able to identify them."

Torsten agreed. "Uilleam, you and Rory take care of that. Gilles, make sure every de Graham man is told what nearly happened. I want them vigilant. And I want ten men in Lady Raina's shadow any time she leaves the keep." He would, naturally, dissuade her from doing so until more was known. "Aonghas is taking a unit to the village to search for the lad, Geoffrey."

James looked particularly troubled. "We dinna ken who's behind it. We dinna ken if those eight were part of a larger group."

Torsten's jaw tightened. "Nae, we dinna."

Gilles was troubled by the motive. "Why abduct the lass? Aye, the peasants dinna care for her, but...Christ, did they mean to commit murder?"

James discounted this possibly. "Why ride off with her, rather than simply strike her down where they'd met her?"

Torsten knew a primeval reaction to James's words. The very idea of Raina being struck down, the light gone from her eyes, filled him with a rage so intense it was almost blinding. He took a deep breath, forcing himself to remain composed. "I dinna ken," he said, though his voice was strained. "This is about taking her alive. They have a purpose for her—one we need to uncover."

"If they had want her alive," Aonghas remarked, "then she is a pawn in a larger game."

"Ransom?" Rory suggested, the idea not unheard of.

"If so," Gilles said thoughtfully, his brow furrowed, "then he's the target." He pointed at Torsten. "And what do ye have that they might want?"

"Lochlan, I imagine," Torsten answered.

The discussion lasted for another quarter hour, but too little was known, rendering the majority of their thoughts and words as naught but speculation.

When they dispersed from the hall, each man had been assigned some task or chore. Torsten exited the keep, returning to his destrier, taking a party of forty men with him, intent on surveying the vast expanse of Lochlan for himself.

He was about this for many hours, until the late night summer sun had dipped below the western horizon. After he'd stabled his destrier for the night, he was met by Peigi in the once-more vacant hall, the supper hours having come and gone.

"Go on. Sit right there," she said, pointing to the bare high table. "I'll bring ye a trencher and a horn of ale."

"How is Ra—my wife?" He wanted to know.

"She's scared and who would nae be?"

Torsten sighed and nodded as Peigi strode on toward the kitchen. He stepped up on the dais and sat, lifting his sword and scabbard as he did so before letting it rest on the ground. He rubbed the heel of his hand between his eyes, trying to ease the scowl that hadn't ceased in hours.

Peigi returned after only a moment, laying a full trencher of meat stew in front of him, along with a horn of ale as promised and a pitcher of more.

Torsten gave her his thanks and dug in, tearing off a portion of the bread plate before he realized the housekeeper still hovered at his shoulder. The scowl returned and he turned it upon Peigi.

"Dinna tarry," she said, boldly but quietly. "Ye put aside whatever ye feel about Lady Raina, put aside whatever hatred ye harbor for any MacQueen and Lochlan. Yer wife'll be frightened, will have nightmares nae doubt. Go on then, soon as yer done here, get up there. Dinna leave her alone, stewing and reliving it all in her head. Hold her and tell her everything will be all right, that ye'll make it so."

Maddened by her audacity, he growled at her, "I dinna need ye to tell me—"

"Aye, ye do, by my understanding," she interjected impudently. "Ye've got a fine army; they ken how to hold a sword and ride those big beasts, and they march in a straight line. But will ye teach them to be guid men and guid husbands? Sure and how might that be accomplished when ye are nae yerself?" She fixed Torsten with a steady gaze, her voice ringing with the weight of her conviction. "Ye ken leadership is about setting an example, showing kindness and understanding. Yer men look to you, sir, nae just for orders but for how to live and behave. If ye show nae regard for Lady Raina's feelings, how can ye expect them to respect the feelings of their own wives, their families? A man who commands respect must first be worthy of it himself."

Torsten's jaw tightened, enraged at being admonished—indeed, lectured!—by the woman. He tossed down the chunk of bread, causing a bit of juice to splash onto the table. "I'm warning ye," he said, his voice dangerously low, "ye're about three seconds away from—"

"And I'm warning ye," she shot back with the most astounding lack of fear. "I'm nae afraid of ye. A man too scared to kiss his own wife is nae threat to me."

His mouth twisted into an ugly sneer but before he might have taken her to task or had her thrown in the dungeon simply to appease his mounting ire, Peigi whirled around and strode away.

Chapter Thirteen

Raina marveled over how *un*afraid she was in the wake of what had been a decidedly terrifying ordeal.

True, it was many hours later, but she'd rather expected to be still a quivering puddle of nerves.

But she was not.

Instead, she was possessed of what was likely an unhealthy dose of anger, maddened by having too many questions and scarcely any answers. *Why* had she been taken? *Who* was behind the plot? What might have become of her if not for Torsten's rescue?

She reviewed again the faces of the men in the party, still quite sure she recognized no one.

She pressed her forefinger and middle finger to the skin between her brows, massaging and smoothing the flesh, quite sure she'd wind up like Torsten, with those permanent vertical marks if she didn't do something to counteract her persistently knitted brow.

Considering Geoffrey's role in the scheme, Raina was forced to imagine the plot was conceived by some of Lochlan's own. But why? They'd hated and feared her for years; why now? Did they hold her responsible for the de Grahams having overtaken Lochlan?

And why use the ruse of Torsten having been injured and calling for her?

She was compelled to examine that as well, her inexplicable response at that time, upon being told that Torsten was injured, gravely she'd assumed since she'd been told he'd asked for her. Why had her heart skipped a beat in fear? Why had she followed the lad without question, simply to reach Torsten in time, all the while fearing she might not?

Maddening, all of it, the confusion, the lack of answers.

Tucked into her bed, her hair yet damp upon the pillows, she sighed with frustration, knowing sleep might well be impossible.

Mayhap though, she had at least one answer, though she resisted it mightily.

But...*did* she care for Torsten?

But how could she? What had he done to earn even the smallest scrap of interest—or...affection?—from her?

He'd let it be known this very day that he viewed her as the enemy, had effectively said he wanted nothing to do with her!

Having not once harmed her, despite the origins of their association, did not a cause for affection make!

Could it be that her own response to his oft-probing and sometimes scorching gaze influenced her emotions? But no, the way his fierce eyes sometimes curled her toes and ignited a blush was surely not a cause for fondness.

And his kiss, though delicious in a dangerously fascinating way, could not rouse warmth and want, certainly not of the heart.

No, she had no affection for Torsten, she assured herself. In all probability, she'd have reacted in a similar manner no matter what name Geoffrey had used. He might have said that Nell or Rory—or any other person—lay broken and dying, asking for her, and she'd have sprinted to the scene all the same, propelled by human decency and a sense of duty.

She knew now—had been heartbreaking reminded!— that Torsten viewed her not as his wife, but still as his enemy, that daughter of the man who had betrayed Scotland, an enemy for taking a side that was not his own. Truth was, Raina didn't trust *him*. She didn't trust a man who frequently stared at her with such avid displeasure but then forced a kiss on her. Didn't one have to at least *like* a person in order for the idea of a kiss to enter one's awareness? She didn't trust a man who insisted in one moment he had no intention of having a real marriage with his own wife and naught but an hour later, looked as pale as a ghost when he recovered her from fiends intent on kidnapping her. Allowing herself to read anything into either the kiss or what seemed a bloodless fright earlier at her near-abduction—allowing herself to hope, essentially—seemed to be only a swift and sure path to heartbreak, she was somehow certain.

And yet, she could not discount either his striking good looks or his enthralling kiss as grounds for affection. And then there was the feeling, the grand and unmatched sensation, of being in his arms, so safe and protected, a sensation she hadn't known in years. Since her mother died more than a decade ago, affection had been a rare commodity in Raina's life. In Torsten's arms, she felt a flicker of something long buried, a sense of belonging and yearning she scarcely remembered.

And in light of his cruel remarks this morning, she hated herself for it.

No. No! She shook her head, furious with herself for allowing this stream of thought.

'Tis a dangerous path, she warned herself, bound to wind up in heartache.

Though it was true that he seemed furious when he came to her rescue, his rage had likely been driven by his possessive and territorial nature rather than any genuine concern for her.

No one takes what belongs to me, he had said.

It wasn't about her specifically; it was about his rage and his need to defend what he saw as his territory. He might have been defending Lochlan or Glenbarra Brae. His fury was not a sign of affection, but rather a manifestation of his desire to protect his domain and maintain control.

I protect what is mine, he'd uttered in that terrible voice. She was a *what*, not even a *who*.

By the time the door creaked open to admit her husband, Raina had turned on her side, seriously courting sleep but, sadly, still awake. She listened to him move about the chamber, recognizing the sounds he made as he readied himself for bed: the metallic clink of his belt being unbuckled, the soft thud of the scabbard and sword as he set them aside, the rustle of fabric as he doffed his tunic, and the splash of water as he washed his face at the short cupboard with what remained in the basin. Each noise, familiar after less than a fortnight, from the subtle creak of the floorboards to the gentle clatter of his belongings, painted a picture of his nightly routine.

The bed shifted when he climbed into it, and Raina had all she could do to remain still when she felt him moving closer to her. With her back to him, her eyes widened a bit when his strong hand landed softly on the curve of her hip.

Even now riled with frustration, Raina was not inclined to playact. She turned toward him, showing him her face in the soft gray light.

"I'm awake," she said, assuming he meant to gauge her recovery for himself, which was possibly why he'd touched her, so gently or at all. She assured him, "I'm fine."

A rare breath of quiet laughter erupted from him. "But I dinna ken if I am."

She smiled a bit at this, his attempt to pretend he'd been scared, but the smile was tempered by an aloof sadness.

"I have a suspicion you will be all right."

"Aye, I will," he said thoughtfully after a moment, in which time Raina was sure he was trying to discern her mood, or mayhap the reason for her remoteness. "But turn over here and I will—do ye want me to...hold ye...or...?"

The smile that answered this was bittersweet, touched by his boyish stammering and his seeming desire to console her. Despite herself, she wasn't immune to the charm of his awkward tenderness, a stark contrast to his mostly brusque demeanor. Frankly, his attempt at gentleness now left her conflicted, part of her longing for the warmth he offered and the sensible side of her wary of his unpredictable nature. It seemed every day he would have her second-guessing what she'd thought about him only the day before, and what she expected of his behavior going forward.

He'd kissed her and had been angry.

She'd provoked him, meaning to have more than only a kiss, only to be ruthlessly denied.

He'd saved her, had come to her rescue, and now wanted to play doting husband?

Raina didn't know if she were coming or going, every day another encounter, another mood, another position in regard to their marriage. Honestly, she was not so sure that she was as naïve as he was confounded by his own emotions and desires.

Torsten de Graham didn't know what he wanted, was all she could imagine.

But damn, if she'd let him toy with her, pulling her close and pushing her away by turns, while he made up his mind.

"I don't...I don't need coddling," she told him coolly. "I am beyond grateful for your help, for recovering me, but I need nothing from you."

His brow furrowed once more, a flicker of confusion crossing his face. His eyes, dark and searching through the bare light, reflected a hint of something else unfathomable, but that Raina supposed must be annoyance.

"Ye are my wife," he reminded her.

Raina turned fully onto her back, showing him a small but bitter smile. "I am not. I am no more your wife than Peigi or Helen or...or Gilles, for that matter. I am naught but the name put to paper next to yours, in a wedding contract, but this is not a marriage. We inhabit the same house and share this bed, a thousand miles apart despite the close proximity."

"This is a far cry from what ye said only this morning to me, what ye expressed as yer desire for this marriage?"

"And what? My near-kidnapping has changed your mind on the matter? I'm sure it has not." She would guess that heaven and hell would have to move and shake to change this man's mind. When he seemed befuddled, angrily so, Raina pressed on. "Am I not your enemy still? Will you make this marriage real? Or will you allow me to pursue an annulment? Will you be so generous as to grant me a divorce? Will you perish in battle? No, you will not. And thus, I will be all my life attached to you, without means of escape. And without the benefits of marriage, namely children."

"This is simply a continuation of the same discussion we had this morn," he presumed.

"I'm simply letting you know you can't one day be cold and the next hot and expect me to ride each high wave and then sink beneath the surface with you. You don't want a marriage with me so why waste your time with this false concern now? You have denied me...everything. Everything save security, and for that I am grateful. But otherwise, I am naught but a name on paper, a means to an end, nothing more. Let's not pretend otherwise."

HE KNEW HE WOULDN'T be able to sleep unless he could somehow manage to stop grinding his teeth.

He remained as he was, leaning on his elbow in the middle of the bed, while Raina had again turned her back to him, dismissing him and what was actually a genuine concern.

This—this!—was half the reason he didn't want a wife, or a proper union with the one he was compelled to take. Drama, nagging, demands, all the things he'd seen too often in men wretchedly joined in marriage and of which he wanted no part.

Sighing, he rolled onto his back, tapping his fingers impatiently upon his bare chest.

Aside from the very powerful truth that she was his enemy, Torsten's internal struggle with the idea of a full marriage to Raina, rather than just a tool of war or an edict by his king, was deeply rooted in his personal convictions and the rigid framework of his life. He prided himself on the complete lack of emotional connections, his demand for perfection, and his absolute authority. Control was paramount to him, a bulwark against the unpredictable tide of emotions, most especially love, which he viewed as disruptive and dangerous.

He hadn't loved Meera but damn how her savage death had haunted him. He didn't ever want to be incapable of control, as he'd been for some time after being informed of Meera's death, so frantic with rage for so long.

Nonetheless, Torsten couldn't deny that Raina had stirred something within him. Her abduction had shaken him profoundly, revealing a vulnerability he hadn't felt in years, a fear that had been so deeply and frighteningly personal. He'd reveled in their lone kiss, had nearly melted for how innocent but eager had been her response; but more than that, more than only the physical delight, he'd been tempted by the possibility of a connection with her, which in truth had scared the devil out of him as much as it had perplexed him—why her? Why now?

She was the enemy, he reminded himself over and over.

And yet she was not, he knew. He knew this. She'd once questioned whether he was so narrow-minded as to hold her father's sins against her. He did, or he had, but he knew it wasn't right, wasn't fair. She was as innocent of her father's crimes as Torsten himself was. She was kind and considerate, was never without fear but was always brave, was hard-working and possessed a keen intellect and sharp wit. And what she lacked in confidence, she more than made up for with bravado. And she felt like heaven in his arms.

When she'd...well, she'd propositioned him, had thought to seduce him—that's what had happened this morning when he'd brought her, supposedly injured, to this chamber—he'd been forced to cull the depths of inner strength as he'd rarely been caused to do, simply to resist her. Christ, how sweet she'd been, how bluidy hopeful.

Torsten contemplated the consequences of giving in to those desires. Could he maintain his disciplined life if he embraced his role as a husband? Say he did give in, and his body clearly wanted to—his mind and other organs were leaning in that direction as well—what was the worst that could happen? Would allowing emotions to flourish jeopardize the iron control he prized? The prospect both intrigued and unsettled him, challenging his belief that a life devoted to war and duty was the only path worth pursuing.

As he grappled with these thoughts, Torsten found himself torn between duty and desire, control and passion.

He had little choice but to admit that Raina had not misspoken— *one day be cold and the next hot*. As much as it shamed him, he knew that what seemed to her a mercurial mood was in fact evidence of his attempt to distance himself, or to maintain a distance, at which he—obviously and repeatedly—failed.

Roughly rubbing his brow, he wondered if he was overthinking the whole bloody thing. In truth, he'd long suspected he was incapable of love or any softer emotion. Could he fulfill his duties as a husband without fear of losing control to passion, or losing himself to any other useless tender sentiment?

At length, he did sleep but his rest was fitful, and he woke at dawn, dressing quietly before he slipped from the chamber. He availed himself of a bruising morning ride atop his destrier and upon his return, saw to the stabling and brushing of his steed himself. He made a mental note at that time that Lochlan's stables needed further attention; rarely had he come and found either the stablemaster or any lad available to ready his horse or tend to its needs upon his return.

Upon exiting the stables, he was met by Gilles, Aonghas, Thomas, and Rory.

Torsten inclined his head, expecting they brought news.

"James, Eòghann, and Uilleam are bringing in the lad," Gilles announced as he approached. "Found 'im inside a cottage that is nae his own, being hidden by others."

"I'll want them brought up as well, those cottagers," Torsten directed. "His father? The bailiff?"

"Nea yet," Gilles relayed. "But he might be heading north, by some accounts, has a sister outside Montrose."

Torsten had more questions, but knew they would likely, and better, be answered by the bailiff and his lad, Geoffrey when they arrived.

"How's the lass?" Aonghas inquired.

Torsten shrugged, his jaw tightening. "Says she's fine." And rather with some lingering annoyance, he added, "Says she dinna need me to coddle her."

A blanket of silence fell over the group for one, two, three seconds. Until Gilles cleared his throat and asked, his tone halting, "Ye...meant to coddle her? *Ye* did?"

"Not coddle," Torsten replied impatiently, "but embrace, enfold, what have ye. I kent she might have had some lingering fear," he clipped defensively.

"And she...refused ye?"

Torsten drew in a deep breath, wondering if he wanted to have this conversation with these men at this time. What could they possibly know, more than he did, about women and wives?

In an unprecedented move—a sign of his own turmoil—he disclosed, "She dinna want the marriage, as ye ken, but then she dinna want a childless union either and is...perturbed with me because I have nae desire to sleep with the enemy."

Again, his statement was met by what seemed an incredulous silence.

Until Aonghas broke it, not bothering to hide a broad smirk. "Ye're...ye're jesting, eh? Ye're wife—the one who looks like she'd make fine work of haunting a man's dreams—wants ye to consummate the marriage and ye refused?"

Testily, very sorry he'd brought it up after all—he had never revealed so personal a matter as this to his men— Torsten growled, "I wed by order of my king. Ye ken fully that I have nae intention of staying here. The war will—what the bluidy hell is so funny, Gilles?"

Gilles reigned in his obnoxious laughter swiftly enough that Torsten thought it might have been forced. "Shite, for years I believed ye were the smartest man around, more clever than most other gowks at any rate. I kent ye were leagues beyond the rest of us, but ye're...*Jesu*, ye're as thick as bricks, inna ye?" His brows shot up into his forehead, as if he expected a reply. "What's the point of all this?" He lifted his arms widely. "War, death, destruction—what's any of it mean, if there's nae one to go home to?" He shook his head and harrumphed another snort of laughter. "Would it be so bad to seek—to desire for yerself—a solid union with the lass?"

"Certainly if she seems to desire it herself," Aonghas added logically.

Annoyed by the interference, regretting that he'd nearly invited it, Torsten asked, "And what the bluidy hell do any of ye ken about being married?"

Gilles's answering scowl mirrored Torsten's. "Ye ken damn well I was wed, for more than a decade. And for more'n half of that, I actually liked the bluidy woman!"

Aonghas frowned. "Ye're nae the first of us to wed, more rather nearly the last. Lost my Beth almost a decade ago, 'twas Sunday the first of June. Nae a day goes by I dinna ken on her, what might have been."

Rory spoke up. "I've mentioned Liosa to ye—many times. Christ, been married for nigh on three years." He narrowed his eyes at his laird, seemingly offended that Torsten hadn't recalled, or hadn't paid attention in the first place. "She awaits me at Glenbarra Brae. Going home to her is what keeps me going, I'm fairly certain the idea of her is what's kept me alive, saved me more than once."

Torsten stared, dumbfounded, having no idea that Aonghas had been wed or that Rory still was. Or...mayhap he had known this. Certainly he recalled that Gilles had been wed. It returned to him now, a recollection of Rory's festive nuptials at Glenbarra Brae, and another memory, burying Aonghas's wife, Beth, just before they'd departed and had ridden to meet William Wallace at Falkirk.

He frowned at Thomas, wondering if he, too, was wed.

The lad held up his hands, admitting, "I've got nae one, but I'll take the first one that'll have me."

"All ye ken is war and fighting," Gilles continued, putting into words what Torsten had thought only a second ago, "and aye that makes ye clever in the field, but lad, what're ye going to do when we're nae more in the field? Ye ken this war'll nae last forever? Ye want to be auld and gray like me—er, grayer—with nae one at yer side?"

Rory wondered, with furrowed brow, "Why do ye fight at all? My da' said to point my sword in front of me to protect those I loved who stood behind me. But ye...why do ye fight?"

"I fight for many reasons," he began, hardly able to believe he had to list the numerous motives. "I fight for loyalty to my king, who commands my allegiance. I fight for the honor of my clan, to protect the lands and people who depend on me. I fight to reclaim what was stolen from us, to right the wrongs done to Scotland and its crown. I fight for the freedom of our land, to push back against those who seek to subjugate us." He paused, his jaw clenching. "I fight because it's all I've ever known, all I've been trained to do."

"All noble and true, and there's nae one better at it than ye, lad," Gilles said. "But ye left out the greatest cause."

Incensed and yet still curious, Torsten planted his hands on his hips and waited.

"Ye fight for the future, do ye nae?" Gilles asked.

Torsten held Gilles's earnest gaze, his words piercing Torsten's armor of pride and duty.

And now Torsten glared at them, his annoyance tempered by a vulnerability he was unaccustomed to, and for which he did not particularly care. Reacting intuitively, defensively, his glare darkened. "Christ, I'm surrounded by softlings, downy chicks with stars in their eyes over worthless emotions."

Failing to heed the warning of Torsten's rising anger, Gilles chortled again. "Says the man who's ne'er been in love."

"That's enough," Torsten barked, which effectively shuttered Aonghas and Rory's expressions, though not that of his captain. "When does the lad come?"

"Any minute now," Gilles answered. "And what are ye're plans for 'im?"

Torsten sneered at Gilles, "What the hell do ye ken I'm planning? I want answers, and if he dinna give them to me, he'll suffer greater consequences than he will for what role he played."

"Ye canna flog 'im or—"

"Christ, and what?" Torsten exploded. "Ye want me to feast the lad, lay a bounty before him and ask him nicely if he'll give me the answers I need?"

Shrugging as if he didn't care either way, Gilles argued mildly, "Provoke a revolt, ye will, ye whip that lad. Lock 'im up for a few days, see what he kens, but ye canna lay open his back. He's nae more than ten and two."

"Auld enough to ken better, I should imagine," Torsten grumbled, and spun on his heel, returning to the keep.

The lad, Geoffrey, never was brought before him.

"Slipped through their fingers, chased 'im all the way down to the sea, where he disappeared, has nae surfaced yet, and nae body washed up," was reported to Torsten late in the morning, over which he was beyond furious.

NO MATTER HOW HE TRIED, Torsten could not escape the echo of Gilles, Aonghas, and Rory's words. They lingered in his mind, clinging like burrs to his thoughts. And to his great annoyance, when eventually his anger began to fade, the bloody idea began to grow on him.

At first, he tried to dismiss it, attributing the notion to merely a want of coupling—it had been months since he'd lain with a woman. But the more he pondered, the more the idea took root.

The idea began to shift from an abstract concept to a tantalizing possibility. He imagined Raina laughing at something he said, her eyes bright with amusement rather than wariness. He counted as other enticing prospects another kiss, more kisses, and joining his body to hers. He thought of the trust that might grow between them, and wondered if respect and affection could possibly follow.

Fairly quickly, Torsten found himself unexpectedly wrestling with desires he had long buried beneath the mantle of duty and discipline, and finally admitting what he knew to be true: Raina's presence had unsettled his carefully constructed world, stirring emotions he had for most his life deemed unnecessary and inconvenient.

But his newfound realization came with complications. Raina, understandably, didn't trust him. His past actions—his bluidy waffling, his inability to resist her completely, his reactive iciness when he was angered by his own desire for her—had created a rift between them. He chuckled humorlessly, considering the odds of Raina believing he'd had a sudden change of heart. Torsten pondered how to bridge this divide, how to convince her of his sincerity and his newfound desire for a genuine partnership, all this when the idea was yet so new to him and not entirely welcome.

He was adept at warfare and strategy, skilled in the art of command and battle tactics. Yet, when it came to matters of the heart and wooing a woman like Raina, he felt utterly out of his depth.

He thought about it the next few nights, rather waiting for the extraordinary feeling to pass, firmly believing that it would.

But it did not.

And he became more disturbed than he cared to admit by Raina's continued indifference. He wasn't sure that she was asleep each night when he came to bed or if she only pretended that she was. And he scowled when he realized that he missed having any interaction at all with her, and he almost wished now a bat would fly into the chamber or that she would turn to him to announce her plans for the morrow, making small talk, or even imperiously request that he escort her again to the market.

He considered what was at stake, picturing Raina standing over him when the chair had collapsed beneath him after his unsuccessful attempt to trap the bat, showing her first smile to him, that dazzling smile that had transformed her. That might have been the first occasion, honestly, that he'd been aware of her as a woman, his woman, and not merely a pawn, his unwanted wife.

Almost daily, even before now, he was visited by the image of her after he'd kissed her in the rain, her hair matted around her head, her garb soggy, her cheeks flushed charmingly, and her bright eyes fixed on him, when she'd challenged his want to take it back. *I rather liked it*, she'd boldly proclaimed.

He recalled her enthusiasm at the Montrose market, how blithe and carefree she'd been, that woman who was brave enough to drive a wayn about the coast as if she feared nothing. She'd smiled more than she had not on that day, and Torsten could not recall in all his life a time when he'd been more taken with a woman's beauty and spirit.

Those memories, a gnawing desire for more, was at stake, he supposed.

Ye fight for a future, do ye nae?

Chapter Fourteen

She considered all the emotions she'd known in her twenty-four years: joy and sorrow, melancholy and anger, anticipation and dread, among a host of others. Fear, she realized, had only been known in small doses, and those occasions had mostly been known in the face of her father's fury and weeks ago, in the moment of and in those first few days of Torsten de Graham's arrival.

But now and despite the curious lack of fear in the initial hours after her abduction, it was with her every hour of the day. Never in her life had she turned her head over her shoulder so much, never had she jumped and startled with every little noise, never had she gazed with so much suspicion upon the people of Lochlan. The fear was a constant, gnawing presence, an uninvited guest that shadowed her every step. Each day was a battle against the rising tide of anxiety that came with some nagging dread that she was being watched, her movements tracked by unseen eyes. The sense of being hunted, like prey in a predator's sights, was disconcerting.

Only sleep offered respite, there in the bedchamber with Torsten at her side. There, and only then did she feel safe.

Soon enough, though, she began to understand that the eyes watching her were de Graham eyes. She was followed everywhere, or green-tartaned soldiers were stationed outside the kitchen's door or in the forward yard whenever she was inside the keep. And not only one or two young men, as Peigi and subsequently, Raina, had noticed, but half a dozen at any given time were never more than twenty yards from her.

Raina supposed she had Torsten to thank for this, and though she remained alert, the fear did gradually begin to ebb, knowing she was well-guarded.

Today, three days after the event, Rain and Peigi walked across the vast heath toward the village. The wildflowers, once a riot of color, had taken on the mellow hues of late August. The clustered bellflower still held onto a few deep violet blooms, though their numbers had dwindled. The vivid red maiden pinks were fewer, their delicate petals starting to dry and curl at the edges. The knapweed's pale purple blossoms had mostly given way to fuzzy seed heads, swaying gently in the breeze. The once lush and vibrant landscape was now dotted with the subtle signs of the approaching autumn, with the grasses turning golden and the air carrying the first hints of a cooler season.

They intended to visit the house of the weaver, Judith, meaning to commission new blankets for the soldiers' barracks and cloths to cover the head table in the great hall. Those previously used for the long board were moth-eaten and discolored. Peigi had suggested another market trip to procure these things, but Raina had recommended they give the work, and thus coin, to the villagers.

"They brought the lad in this morning," Peigi said.

"The lad? Geoffrey?" She'd heard of his previous escape, and though she disliked his part in the scheme to apprehend her, he was only a child in her mind, and she'd been saddened by the possibility that he'd drowned in the sea, as had been presumed.

"Aye, and he's squawkin'," Peigi informed her. "That's what Aonghas imparted, anyway, though little sense was made of it."

"What has he said? Was his father involved? Or did he know?"

Peigi flapped her hand several times toward the ground, asking for patience, or mayhap only one query at a time. "Squawked a bit, but nae any of it useful. Said he dinna tell his father until after it had been done, and then aye, the bailiff hid his son—canna blame 'im there, I'd've done the same."

"But who put him up to it? And how did they coerce him? Did they threaten him? Or—"

"Coin, they offered," Peigi replied, "and plenty of it—mysteriously disappeared from where he'd hidden it, it comes out. Mysterious, my arse. His nae guid father has it and dinna ken he does nae. But nae, the lad had little to offer, dinna recognize the men who approached 'im, couldna say he'd ever seen 'em before."

Raina pushed out a frustrated breath. What little hope had been caused to rise at the mention of the lad was now doused, and she knew no more now than three days ago who had seized her.

"But ye're better now," Peigi guessed, slanting a sideways glance at Raina. "Seem less likely to jump out yer skin today and yesterday."

Nodding, Raina turned a glance over her shoulder. "A week ago I was followed by only one or two, and now there are half a dozen soldiers behind us. It's...not ideal, but much less unsettling than being inundated with fear."

"And do ye wonder how ye might have overcome fear if nae for yer husband's soldiers, his care for ye?"

Raina didn't respond to the last part of Peigi's query, believing it was less Torsten's care for her than it was his fierce possessive pride. *No one takes what belongs to me,* she was reminded once again.

"I wonder," Raina said evenly, "if any attempt would have been made at all if not for the coming of the de Grahams."

Peigi turned a quick scowl onto Raina, pulling the hood of her cloak more tightly around her head, to ward off the sharpening wind. "Ye ken one of the de Graham men—?"

"No," Raina was swift to disabuse the housekeeper of that thought. "Not at all. I only submit that mayhap someone, other than me, doesn't want Torsten de Graham to have Lochlan."

They walked on in silence for several moments before Peigi spoke again. "Ye really wish he were nae here? That he'd never come?"

Raina stared at Peigi with incredulity, wondering how she could even ask that. Her thoughts swirled with memories and emotions, the complexity of her feelings toward Torsten weighing heavily on her mind, a distinct hopelessness outweighing almost every other emotion. But then she hadn't told Peigi about either her humiliating, failed attempt at seduction or Torsten's decree, that he still had no intention of consummating their marriage.

She hesitated before responding, her voice measured and tinged with uncertainty.

"It's not that simple, Peigi. Torsten's presence here—and that of his army—has changed everything, for better or worse." While she couldn't argue that thus far, he seemed to have administered effectively, that a thriving Lochlan seemed his goal, there was no way that she couldn't contemplate what his coming had meant to her. "Consequences abound and not all of them are fine or fair. Lochlan needed change, aye, but at what cost?"

THE NEXT FEW DAYS UNFOLDED in such a way as to wrinkle Raina's brow more often than not.

On Monday, when Raina went to collect the table and chair that she would bring with her down to the beach to pay the fisherfolk, she found Torsten waiting outside the storeroom with a de Graham soldier she hadn't yet met.

"I have the lads busy with other jobs right now," he said, possibly referring to the two who'd accompanied her last week. "I'll escort ye myself, me and Samuel."

Carrying the basket that contained the ledger, the coins, and the ink and quill, Raina hoisted that further up her shoulder and hid her dissatisfaction. She nodded briefly and without a word turned and marched down to the beach.

Having been trained over the last couple of weeks to come when Raina arrived, the folks on the beach began to line up even before Raina had set up her supplies, and thus the trek, the disbursement, and recording took no more than an hour. Little opportunity was afforded for conversation between Raina and Torsten, for which she was glad, but she was not unaware of his imposing figure, standing as a sentry at her side, watchful of each mark made in the journal and each coin set into the hands of the workers. She knew some dismay that she couldn't possibly enjoy this occasion at the beach since all glorious sights and sounds were overshadowed by Torsten de Graham and his unnerving presence.

And when all was said and done and Samuel lifted the small table over his head and started the climb upward, Torsten paused, his hands on the chair, and stared at Raina as she packed up the basket. Aware of his regard, she turned a quizzical glance toward him. His eyes matched the sea, she noted, dark blue, and with a restless intensity swirling beneath the surface.

"Let's walk," he suggested. "Aye, a bit windy, but I would imagine ye'd never deny a stroll along the shore."

Bewildered by his...whatever this sudden interest in her was, Raina did deny him. "No, um, I really cannot." She frowned and thought to add, "But thank you." And then she pivoted and retraced her steps up the cliff path.

Tuesday came, and before he'd exited their chamber in the morning, Torsten politely offered to drive Raina, and Peigi and the lasses if she liked, to the market in Montrose.

Once more puzzled by what seemed a polite overture, Raina had been quick to make up her mind but slower to answer.

"That's very kind of you," she said after a moment, "but no. I haven't a need nor frankly, the time."

Appearing neither aggrieved nor relieved, Torsten offered a courteous bow of his head and left their chamber.

That evening found both Torsten and Raina seated at the high table for supper, a rare sight indeed. The kitchen staff, still grappling with the challenges of feeding such a vast number of souls, often required Raina's aid with late preparations or the delivery of platters to the hall. As for Torsten, he had seldom made it a priority to arrive on time for the evening meal. Tonight, however, was different.

Raina was already seated in her mother's chair when Torsten arrived, coming from the courtyard, smiling at something Gilles was saying.

Smiling, he was, she realized, her gaze fixed on him as he crossed the hall. It was the first time she had seen him truly smile, and despite herself, she considered the sight striking. His smile did beautiful things to his already handsome face, softening the intensity that usually roiled beneath the surface of his dark blue eyes. She felt a pang of something—admiration, perhaps, or an unsettling warmth—that she quickly tried to dismiss. She had resolved to maintain a distance from him, to ignore all that was potentially magnetic, but the unexpected charm of his smile made that resolve waver, if only for a moment.

"Och, ye'll sit tonight and feast with us?" Gilles asked good-naturedly as he took the chair to her right. "And nae be serving us, as that dinna sit well with me."

"Needs must and all that," she said with a shrug to Torsten's captain, in reference to her, the mistress, having served. "But no, Rory politely informed me yesterday that more than a third of the army would be gone this evening, on what he called maneuvers." Rory had explained that *maneuvers* were akin to training exercises, a term previously unfamiliar to her, but now clear. Frankly, she sat here now, having expected that Torsten would be absent, engaged in the drilling and discipline of his men. "Of course, so many less mouths to feed offered great ease to the kitchen staff."

"And yerself," Torsten remarked, sitting down in her father's chair at her left.

"Yes, for tonight," she allowed, stiffening when Torsten very casually reached across her to fetch the pitcher of ale, with which he filled his pewter goblet.

Raina was compelled to lean far back in her chair when Torsten next lifted the pitcher at Gilles in question and then proceeded to fill his captain's cup, stretching his upper body and arm across her front. "Pardon, lass," he said nonchalantly, as if he hadn't a clue about the instant tumult provoked in her for his disturbing nearness.

Swallowing, Raina sat unmoving, and then was further befuddled by Torsten continuing the conversation, this after he'd switched pitchers, taking up the ceramic flagon from which he poured wine into Raina's cup.

"All the officers, save Gilles and I, take part in the training," he explained. "'Tis needed, to determine how the lads act, react, and behave, without their commanders present."

"Guid practice for the lieutenants as well," Gilles said, his eyes widening with zeal as the kitchen servers arrived, bearing platters of smoked salmon, roasted beef medallions, beans smothered in garlic and onions, and baskets of bread, cheese, and fruit, "relying on each other and nae us, to implement plans, instruct the units, and create their own strategies."

Raina was relieved that she had insisted on having a pewter trencher at each place on the high table, ensuring she did not have to share a plate with Torsten, as custom dictated. Unlike those seated at the lower tables who ate directly from communal platters or placed their portions directly on the table, Raina had learned from her aunt's household that there were cleaner, less distasteful, ways to dine. Having years ago endured the unappetizing experience of sharing a trencher with either Seòras or one of her father's officers at Lochlan, Raina had often been repulsed by their eating habits. Determined to adopt her aunt's practice of individual dining, she was grateful for the arrangement she had insisted upon.

Currently, this arrangement suited her well even as Raina observed that while Torsten and Gilles ate heartily, serving themselves generously from the platters, neither displayed unseemly eating habits. They avoided letting grease drip down their fingers or chins and were kind enough to use their eating knives for serving rather than relying on fingers they had just licked.

In truth, though she contributed little to the conversation, Raina was not displeased to have spent the dinner hour with the two men, enjoying their easy banter and learning quite a bit about the architecture of Lochlan Hall and the strategic considerations of defending such a fortress, which they discussed at length as Torsten had recommended building watch towers made of stone and not wood.

But what seemed a sudden series of occasions initiated by Torsten to reduce the distance he himself had instigated between them continued the next day, as Raina discovered Torsten to be among the oft-silent, creeping-in-her-shadow guard that followed her everywhere. However, unlike his men, Torsten did not keep his distance from her as she walked again to the village. Judith, the weaver, had sent word requesting that Raina make a decision about the color of the dyed thread.

He walked beside her, his imposing figure shadowing her smaller stature. The path from the keep to the village, winding through a meadow of flowers, was narrow—ideal for two people to walk abreast as Raina often did with Peigi. Despite Torsten's large frame not easily fitting the path, they managed to walk side by side. He occasionally stepped onto the path's fringe, brushing through wind-swept golden grass that reached his knees.

Since he'd inquired about her destination, she explained briefly about Judith making cloth for the hall and the barracks. And then she couldn't help herself, and she stopped walking and faced him, using her hand to shield her eyes from the sun as she glanced up at him.

"What is it you're doing, Torsten?" she asked, her tone tart. "Why are you here, playing at lowly grunt assigned to so dull a duty?"

"'Tis nae dull, to keep the lady of the keep safe from harm," he answered promptly, a hint of chastisement evident, seemingly in reaction to her minimizing the role.

"If you fear for my safety," she persisted, "why not put the previous detail of guards on me, as you did in the beginning? Why are you part of this detail? Why did you accompany me to the beach?"

Torsten paused, meeting her eyes with an intensity that made her breath catch. "I dinna trust anyone so well as I trust myself to keep ye safe."

Raina blinked, taken aback by his statement. She searched his face for any hint of a deeper meaning but refused to let herself hope. "If that is true, I might suggest ye surround yourself with a better army, sir," she replied, her tone laced with irony, before she began walking again.

Torsten chuckled, a rare sound that made Raina snap her gaze back to him, noting how wide was his smile and how alluring were the crinkling corners of his eyes.

"Nae, wife," he said after a moment, his voice low. "There are some tasks too vital to entrust to lads."

"You trust them to fight," she reminded him, unwilling to assume anything. "You trust them in war. You trusted them previously with me."

"Aye, but it's different now, with the most reliable men away from the keep or busy with other business." He shrugged, the motion detected in her periphery as she was watching the pathway now. "Besides, I have the time at the moment."

It didn't stop there; his sudden, seemingly intentional desire to engage with her continued throughout the day, manifesting in small gestures—briefly appearing at the kitchen's garden as she'd gathered marjoram leaves; there he'd stepped inside the short fence and had proceeded to pull weeds that had proven to be too firmly entrenched for her small hands—and frequent, lingering gazes, which she was sure were meant to either bewitch or befuddle her more, at which they succeeded.

Where before their sleep schedules had rarely aligned, Torsten now arrived in their bedchamber curiously just as Raina was climbing into bed. He did not arrive and only murmur a spare and meaningless good night to her, but rather engaged her in conversation.

One night, after remarking about the soothing sound of the sea's roar, he spoke of Glenbarra Brae, his home.

"A place full of rolling hills and deep forests," he said, "remarkable, for how formidable the keep is, surrounded by a curtain wall three stories high, but nae as striking as Lochlan Hall, perched upon the cliff at the edge of the sea."

"What...what of your family?" She asked, unable to resist.

As if he were a man who engaged regularly in small talk, he answered promptly. "William is my brother and Moira my sister, both much younger than I, nearer to yer age. Moira wed almost two years ago, is a MacRae now, and William took up the cloth, having nae drive to fight."

"And your parents?"

"Gone, my father at Stirling, felled verra close to where William Wallace fought, and my màthair when she delivered another babe nearly five years after Moira," he disclosed. "Too auld by then to be bringing bairns into the world."

Raina sensed a hint of resentment in his tone, and she wondered if he blamed his father for having put his mother in that condition. "Were you...close with your kin? Or rather, are you close now with your brother and sister?"

He shook his head slowly on the pillow and paused to thrust his fingers through his short hair. "Nae, and truth be told, we never were. Aye, I loved my màthair, 'twas she who ran the keep. She was strong, capable, managed everything in my father's absence," he said reflectively, his voice a soothing murmur in the darkness. "I ken she was the heart of Glenbarra Brae for many years. My father was nae cruel, he was simply...indifferent and too often gone. And then, as ye might imagine, I was sent off to foster, spent seven years with the Mathesons of Kintail, first as a page and then a squire, until I earned my knighthood. Was gone when my sister was born, and when my màthair and the babe went. Later, as an adult, war had me gone from home, when Moira wed, and Alistair was ordained."

"Does that bother you?"

He hesitated, but Raina thought only with some intent to put into words his thoughts on the matter.

"If it does or did, I dinna dwell on it," he answered. "I've always felt a bit disconnected from them, certainly from my siblings. It's strange, really, to be bound by blood yet feel like a stranger in your own home."

More than only a wee bit surprised at how open he was with her, Raina boldly pressed on. "Do you wish...um, that it was or that you felt otherwise?"

He chuckled a bit at this, the sound infusing Raina with a pleasant warmth.

"Mayhap I would, but in truth, Moira was a hellion, mayhap still is. Little to recommend her—speaks more of people rather than ideas, does more shrieking than speaking, and where she goes, trouble and drama soon follow."

"And your brother?"

He sighed. "Frankly, I never understood Alistair. He's...soft, weak. Pleasant, he is, but we have little in common."

Knowing Torsten's personality as she did—authoritative, controlling, strong, and proud—she wasn't surprised that he didn't sound too keen with his siblings' personalities. His demeanor suggested he valued order and discipline, traits likely at odds with Moira's spirited nature and Alistair's perceived softness.

She thought she might have just glimpsed her own future, supposing she might now have some idea what all this meant for them and their fractured, impersonal marriage. She could easily guess that one day he would ride away from Lochlan Hall without *dwelling* on her too much either.

She told herself, *the sooner the better*, but in her heart she knew she didn't really believe that.

Admittedly, after a few nights where she either stared blindly at the ceiling or asked but a few questions of the conversation he made, she found herself growing more comfortable engaging with him—even as she was still confused about why he was suddenly behaving so agreeably, why he seemed so eager to devote so much attention to her of late.

Less than a week after her kidnapping, Torsten came to the bedchamber wearing a bandage around his arm, the linen soaked with blood, though not gruesomely so.

Having yet to snuff the taper at her side, Raina gasped at the sight, sitting up in bed. "Torsten? What have you done?"

"'Tis naught," he dismissed carelessly. "We're reroofing the cattle barns and I scraped against one of the beams ere I kent an iron spike protruded from it."

Raina grimaced in response. "But was it cleaned properly?"

"Aye, Uilleam fetched salve from Peigi." He held up a spare linen cloth and a wee ceramic crock in his other hand. "But help me change this, will ye? I dinna want to ooze bluid all over the bed."

Raina flipped back the blankets and got to her feet, following Torsten across the chamber, where he sat down on the stool in front of the small cupboard where she'd just finished brushing out her hair.

The chamber was dimly lit by only a pair of tapers, casting flickering shadows across the stone walls and over Torsten as she approached.

Torsten peeled off his sleeveless tunic and presented his arm to Raina as she knelt at his side.

With careful and deliberate movements, she peeled away and unwound the bandage covering the wound, revealing a ragged tear and a shallow cut on the back of his muscular arm. She used one of the few bloodless spots on the used linen and gently dabbed at the wound, inspecting it closely. The cut was clean, seemingly without infection at the moment, and very close to that other jagged, ropey scar that was much, much longer.

His skin was warm and smooth over finely sculpted muscles. Touching him in such a way, ministering so tenderly, to her great annoyance, caused her to flush and be flustered. Everything about him, from the sheer width of his bare shoulders and chest, the powerful muscles in his arms and back, and even his scent all radiated an undeniable, primal masculinity.

"How did you come by this other scar?" She asked, meaning to distract herself, opening the small crock and applying a layer of salve to the new wound, her touch light.

He glanced down and around at the back of his arm, as if needing reminding because he owned so many scars.

"Ah, that auld one," he said, his voice flat. "Happened at Stirling. I had gone to my father's side when he was felled. Moments after I'd dropped to my knees at this side, an Englishman swung at me." He glanced at Raina, meeting her eyes. "The horse of the assailant stumbled at the last moment, causing the blade to veer off its intended path." He shrugged. "Instead of taking off my head, it ripped down my arm."

"You were lucky," she murmured softly, beginning to wrap the clean linen around the fresh wound. She stole glances at his face, so close now, admiring the jut of high cheekbones in his square-jawed face.

"There is nae luck in battle," Torsten said. "There is fortune and misfortune."

Raina smiled briefly. "You were fortunate, then."

"I was."

They stared for a moment, Raina kneeling at his side, suddenly and acutely aware of her own state of undress.

Torsten's eyes were deep and solemn but his expression unreadable. Then he lifted his hand and traced his finger over the mark on her cheek, his touch warm. "And how did ye acquire this?"

So then she regretted engaging, asking about his scars, as it seemed to serve as an invitation for him to ask his own questions.

"Ye dinna have to tell me if ye dinna want to," he allowed generously after a moment.

"My father gave me this," she said. Coming to her feet, she capped the crock and laid the soiled linen on the cupboard. "With the back of his hand and his signet ring." Assuming he had no further need of her, Raina returned to bed, ducking under the blankets. "But that was long ago," she added dismissively.

Chapter Fifteen

In consideration of Torsten's confounding about-face, how, seemingly overnight, he'd gone from a cold and autocratic stranger to a sometimes engaging man who appeared to desire her company and conversation, Raina remained puzzled and wary. She began to wonder if she'd only been so damnably pathetic after the kidnapping attempt that his behavior now was simply rooted in pity. This idea was discarded nearly as soon as it was imagined; she hadn't remained abed for days and days, wallowing in fright, inciting sympathy. She'd gotten right back to work, had shown herself in the kitchens the next morning, returned to her new duties. And the notion was more easily rejected by her conviction that Torsten de Graham was incapable of either pity or sympathy.

With no explanation for his behavior, Raina simply waited for his mood to shift once more, as she knew it could.

She didn't have long to wait.

Though the door to Lochlan had always been closed, in fair weather and foul, since the arrival of the de Grahams it was mostly kept open, so that as she crossed the great hall one day she became aware of a disturbance in the courtyard, voices raised in anger.

She quickened her pace and stepped out onto the cobblestone bailey, her eyes scanning the crowded scene. The courtyard inside the nearly-completed wooden palisade was filled with dozens of de Graham soldiers, a few of them mounted, uniformly wearing fierce expressions, more than one having drawn his sword. A few peasants milled about at the edges, observing the commotion with apprehension.

Torsten stood at the center of the courtyard, his formidable figure and wide-legged stance commanding authority. Raina saw only the back of his head as he confronted a man atop a horse who was gesticulating wildly as he hollered. Raina gasped, recognizing Lochlan's bailiff, Ronald.

"Ye put my boy—a bairn!—in the dungeon! What kind of man—"

"The lad was part of a scheme to kidnap my wife," Torsten interjected, his tone sharp and commanding. "Nae quite a bairn, old enough to engage in treachery, and thus auld enough to be punished for it."

Raina's heart skipped a beat, her hand flying to her chest. Without thinking she rushed forward, pushing through the throng of soldiers while Ronald continued to argue for his son.

"And what? How long will he rot down there?" Ronald wanted to know. "Or are ye a monster as I've heard? Nae mercy, and ye'll hang my lad?"

Raina reached Torsten's side, tugging at his arm. He glanced down at her, his mien ferocious, unyielding.

"Torsten—"

"Yer lad," Torsten said, ignoring the fingers dug into his arm and the pleading of Raina's expression as he faced Ronald atop the steed, "was thrown into the dungeon to provoke yer return. Where was this concern when ye abandoned him, departing Lochlan to—"

"Torsten!" Raina tried again to gain his attention. "Please tell me this is false. You didn't really put a child—"

He turned on her, his scowl vicious now. "Cease!" He ordered harshly. "Dinna insert yerself into matters that do nae—"

"This does concern me!" She argued heatedly, appalled by what he'd done to a boy so young.

Pivoting toward her, Torsten snarled as he peeled her fingers away from his forearm. "Enough, woman," he gritted through his teeth. "Take her inside," he ordered and two de Graham soldiers appeared at her side, taking hold of her arms.

"You are a monster," she breathed, so stunned by this truth that she allowed herself to be dragged away. When she was turned around and made to walk toward the keep, she shook off her captors, showing the one on her left her own savage snarl, before stomping into the keep.

She paused just inside, standing in the long rectangle of light made by the open door, the shadows on the floor in front of her advising that the two de Graham soldiers remained in the doorway. Straightening her spine, she walked stiffly, regally toward the far door, stepping into the passageway that led to the kitchens. But rather than retreat to the kitchens, Raina took the narrow corridor off to the side, where the air grew cooler and the light dimmer with each step.

The stone walls closed in around her, their surfaces damp and rough beneath her fingertips. Torches mounted at intervals in the main passageway flickered weakly here, casting a feeble glow that barely pushed back the encroaching darkness. The smell of earth and mustiness grew stronger, mingling with the faint, acrid scent of old fires and the tang of iron from the metal sconces and chains.

Raina briefly retraced her steps, confiscating one of the torches from its wall ring before treading further.

Her footsteps echoed hollowly as she descended the spiral staircase, the stone steps worn smooth by centuries of use. The further down she went, the more the temperature dropped, the air becoming thicker, almost oppressive. The faint drip of water somewhere in the distance added to the sense of foreboding.

As she reached the bottom, she stepped into a low-ceilinged corridor lined with heavy wooden doors. The smell here was more pungent, foul but unrecognizable.

Her heart pounded in her chest, but she pressed on, her expression grim. Though the damp stone ceiling was not particularly low, she hunched her shoulders as she moved, hoping to avoid the eerie veil of cobwebs. She walked past the cellar doors, where the smell of aging wine and stored provisions briefly masked the more unpleasant odors. The crypts lay further ahead, their shadows deep and impenetrable, but she steered clear of those, moving forward.

Finally, she arrived at the dungeon, its heavy iron-bound door looming before her. Taking a deep breath to steady herself, she pulled the door open and stepped inside. The dim light from her torch revealed the rows of cells, each one a dark, forbidding space behind iron bars. Dread engulfed her, imagining the small boy trapped down here in this vile darkness.

"Geoffrey?" she called softly.

Silence answered her. She peered into each cell, expecting to find the young lad huddled in one of the dark corners, but every cell was empty. Confusion warred with dubious relief in her chest as she moved from one barred cage to the next, confirming that the dungeon was indeed unoccupied.

Sighing and lowering the torch a bit, Raina spun around, her brow crinkling. She paused only a moment with her puzzlement before exiting the dungeon, eager to escape the dank bleakness. She scurried now, the torchlight casting swiftly dancing shadows along her path. She squeaked as a critter crossed her path, her fingers clutching at the fabric covering her chest, and scooted to the right as what she hoped was only a mouse ran along the edge of the wall to her left. This brought her into contact with a drapery of cobwebs. Startled, she frantically brushed her hands over her hair and face, shivering at the sensation of the fine, sticky threads clinging to her skin.

She moaned aloud, shuddering with revulsion, and marched on, but was again startled when she realized a presence looming ahead in her path, standing just inside the archway that separated the crypts from the storage area.

Though cast in black shadow, Torsten's form was instantly recognizable.

"Where is Geoffrey?" She demanded at once, as he stepped forward into the light.

His eyes blazed yet with fury, glinting like shards of ice in the shadowy cellar.

"Dinna ever challenge my authority in so public a manner," he began, his voice dripping with annoyance. "I will nae tolerate—"

"I *will* challenge you," she claimed, fisting her hand at her side, "when you behave so shamefully as to...to—" she couldn't go on; obviously, he had not imprisoned the boy in the dungeon. "Where is Geoffrey?"

"Did ye come to release him?"

"Yes, I did," she hollered at him, "and why won't you answer me? What have you done to the child?"

"He's in the gaol inside the barracks," Torsten answered tightly. "Nae alone and shivering, but warmed by blankets, surrounded by soldiers, given the same meal as what comes to the hall."

Reduced by shame, and embarrassingly so, Raina's body went soft. "But why did Ronald think—?"

"Because that was the rumor I wanted spread. If I'd sent the lad home with a slap on the wrist, the bailiff might nae have shown himself. I dinna ken what kind of man he is, but I was assured a father would nae allow his son to reside inside a dungeon for too long."

"You...you let it be known—believed—that Geoffrey was imprisoned most awfully to provoke Ronald to surrender himself?" When he nodded, she felt most particularly foolish, and more than only a little poorly for having accused him of grander evil, for having called him a monster. "I am... I apologize for having imagined the worst." *—of you*, she added silently. Lifting her chin, she said, "In my defense, however, I was not made aware of your scheme."

"Even had it been true, Raina," he said, his tone less menacing though still tense, "ye canna dispute my decisions in front of others. Raise yer concerns privately, by all means, but dinna undermine my leadership. I apologize for my harshness in the courtyard, but it could nae be allowed to stand, yer defiance."

The entire episode only baffled her more.

She *had* assumed him capable of such ruthlessness, and for that she was remorseful.

But he...this now: Torsten de Graham had just apologized to her.

Nearly warm and engaging of late and today returned to his ruthless demeanor, and now inviting her to voice concerns to him, and... apologizing?

Staggered by his variability, she murmured, "I...I don't even know who you are anymore." Not that she ever had.

"I am your husband," he reminded her.

AN INTERROGATION OF Ronald took place but Raina was not allowed to attend. Torsten told her quietly that night at supper that it yielded scarcely more than what they already knew or surmised.

"The lad was alone when approached by the brigands," Torsten informed her. "His father dinna ken of his son's part in it until after the fact. He did try to hide his son and then himself, he admitted, but claims 'twas nae a large sum paid for the boy's part, and already spent, first bribing others to say they dinna ken where either the boy or his father had gone, and then used to secure a room at the inn in Montrose, where Ronald concealed himself for two nights."

The lad was released to his father, Ronald relieved of his duties as bailiff, and Torsten was forced to confess he still had no idea who the perpetrators might have been or what lay comprised their motive.

The days continued in much the same manner as they had before the disruption of Ronald's return. Raina was pleased that the kitchen had finally met the challenge of feeding so large a populace. Admittedly, they had help from the de Grahams themselves. Twice weekly a unit of soldiers went hunting, often returning with two or more red deer, and less frequently a boar and smaller game, grouse and quail included. And to her surprise, another twenty men of the de Graham army had begun to construct their own currach, or something similar to it. Torsten explained he didn't want to subtract from Lochlan's fishing revenue, but having his men fish as well would mean they could contribute to the feeding of so many.

More pertinently, and though Raina had assured Torsten that the ground was not suitable for crops—as her father had always claimed— Torsten instructed that the area just beyond the army's camp of tents was ploughed for planting. "Ye say it's nae arable, but ye admit it's nae been attempted in more than a decade. 'Twill cost little but the labor of my men and seeds from the market to try."

Torsten intended to plant winter barley in another month or so, allowing the seeds to establish roots before the onset of winter. "Lochlan is rich in many ways," Torsten had argued effectively, "but she can and should be more self-sustaining."

Torsten's courtesy toward Raina, and what she deemed an attempt to reconcile their marriage to one of polite civility, continued.

He accompanied her to the beach on the following Monday as he had the week before. Once he'd set the table firmly into the sand, he leaned over it and announced to Raina, "Ye canna continue this indefinitely. Come the winter, or sooner, ye'll manage this inside the hall."

There was no reason to argue with him since she'd essentially thought the same thing. She adored the beach and the sea but wasn't willing to brave lashing winds and ice to sit here miserably.

Giving a noncommittal shrug, she smiled at Samuel, thanking him for carrying down the chair she used. While she set up her supplies, little concerned by today's uncommonly light breeze, she watched as Torsten strode toward the water, speaking with some of the fishermen. He stood casually, hands on his hips and his weight on his left hip, seemingly unconcerned that the small waves lapped over the foot and ankle of his boots. He pointed toward the sea at one point, his finger skimming along the horizon where the water met the sky and then turned his hand over, as if asking a question. Artair, one of the oldest fisherman, chuckled, the sound carrying up onto the beach, and replied to Torsten, who nodded affably.

Torsten turned several times, once seemingly without purpose, and another time pointing in her direction, rousing a frown from Raina, while he continued his discussion with a handful of men, which presumably included her for whatever reason. She tried not to look very often, but again and again her gaze wandered back to Torsten, who stood taller and broader than any man in the small grouping at the edge of the sea, and who appeared, uncharacteristically, to be without his perpetual scowl. Although, she did have to admit that his scowl had been less and less discernable since her kidnapping, much to her confused chagrin.

Deciding she much preferred his inattention, so that she was not made anxious by his close proximity or his oft-studious scrutiny, Raina set to work, counting out coins and recording names and figures in the journal while Samuel ushered the queue forward.

Nell eventually stood in front of Raina, looking more worn and unkempt than normal. Her face, which was neither bonny nor precisely unattractive and was usually set in a stern expression, now betrayed hints of exhaustion and perhaps a touch of resignation. Her two bairns clung to her silently, their gazes doleful, one of them barefoot.

"Good day, Nell," Raina greeted, her voice polite despite their strained history. "You seem... tired. Is everything alright?"

Nell shifted uneasily, as if uncomfortable with the unexpected display of concern, before she bit out, "Nae concern of yers."

Raina hesitated, choosing her words carefully. "The offer still stands, to work inside Lochlan if you would prefer."

Nell's brow furrowed, her expression hardening once more. "I dinna prefer."

Matching her coolness, Raina nodded in acceptance of this and dropped coins into Nell's waiting hand. "Good day."

Torsten returned when only two more people stood in line and waited without speaking until Raina had completed her task and began packing up the basket.

Again, he plunked his hands down on the table, drawing Raina's attention.

"Shall we join them?" He asked mysteriously.

"Join who?"

He chuckled and waved his arm toward the currach. "Them, on the boat," Torsten said.

Entranced as she was by his rare smile, Raina had to wrench her gaze away from him, to follow the direction in which he'd pointed. Edane, one of the fisherman, stood in knee-high water, waving in her direction.

Perplexed, she returned her regard to Torsten. "You want to go out on a fishing expedition?"

"Should we nae see what they're about?" he challenged, his scowl amazingly still missing in action. "Those we're paying to haul in the fish? Might be we find they're under or overpaid."

"I don't know anything about...I've never been on a boat."

"As I have nae for nearly a decade," he admitted.

"I-I cannot," she stammered, lifting the heavy basket onto her shoulder. "I have to return this to—"

"Samuel can see the coins get back to the steward's office," Torsten said, stepping closer, taking the straps off her shoulders. Before she could argue, he said, "I forget already who is who, but the elderly fellow invited me and then ye. And truth be kent, lass, I daresay they were pleased by the privilege of taking the laird and lady out to sea."

"Yes, and I'm quite sure they will be happier still to leave us out there," Raina supposed.

Torsten found this amusing and laughed again.

Raina stared at him, briefly captivated by how laughter so quickly and effortlessly softened the sharp edges of the man. He had very nice teeth, gleaming white against the backdrop of his sun-colored complexion.

She hadn't fully relinquished the basket, had instead covered the handle with her free hand. Torsten took her hand in his, threading his fingers with hers, while he used his other hand to take possession of the basket.

"C'mon, lass," he cajoled. "It'll do ye guid. And we canna disappoint them."

Raina stared at their connected hands, fascinated by the way they fit together, palm to palm, even as her hands were so much smaller than his. Fancifully, she imagined that their hands formed a bridge between them, built on the foundation of

Torsten's inexplicable kindness to her in the past week. The notion was as titillating as it was unnerving.

Raina glanced up at Torsten, meeting his eyes briefly, finding a softness in his gaze that she hadn't expected.

"I'll nae let anything happen to ye, Raina," he said solemnly.

Feeling as if she had little choice, lest she be labeled a killjoy—she absolutely did not need or desire another nickname!—Raina acquiesced, though she couldn't quite manage a smile or rouse any excitement, save for what Torsten's touch had already awakened.

His smiled widened and Torsten handed the basket to Gavin. "Get that to the steward's office first thing, lad."

He gave no instruction about the table or chair, but turned their joined hands around and strode toward the water's edge, pulling a nervous Raina along with him.

She was slightly mollified by the small cheer that rose from those men waiting at the boat, even as she was quite certain they were satisfied with their new laird's company and much less the prospect of hers.

At the water's edge, and without warning, Torsten pivoted and scooped up Raina in his arms. Reflexively, her hands reached up and clung to his shoulders, trying to ignore the quickening of her pulse, hoping the instant flush of her cheeks was not noticeable.

"Ye dinna want yer skirts to get wet," Torsten said by way of explanation.

His mood was such—relaxed, lighthearted, enticing even—that Raina wondered, not for the first time, who this man was, and what had become of the one she married.

He carefully set her down in the currach, making sure she was steady before releasing her. Raina settled herself on the closest wooden bench, trying to find her balance in the unsteady boat.

She knew their names, these fishermen, but little else about them. Jasper, a burly fellow with a thick beard, pulled in the small anchor, and a moment later, Torsten and the fisher, Edane, a tall and lean man with sharp features, pushed off from the thigh-high water before climbing into the boat. The currach wobbled fitfully until the two men took their seats, Torsten plopping down next to her.

Artair, the oldest, with deep-set wrinkles and silver hair, and Peile, a very young man with a mop of unruly straw-colored hair, sat in front of her, sharing a bench seat. Artair eyed her cautiously.

Torsten tapped Raina's leg and pointed at the bottom of the boat. Her feet were sitting on a pair of oars, and she lifted her legs so that Torsten could retrieve them.

"Aye, I dinna tell ye," he confessed, grinning once more as he handed one of the oars to her, "we have to earn our seat."

"Oh, good heavens," Raina declared, gingerly handling the heavy oar. "I don't know anything about rowing."

"Nor I," said Torsten, "save I do ken this upright peg is the thole pin," he said, fitting his oar to the boat.

Raina inspected her oar, discovering a notch that rested against the pin, and attached hers in a similar manner. She needed no further instruction, but simply replicated the actions of Artair and Peile. Or tried to. Though the motion looked simple enough, and constantly repetitive, she learned fairly quickly that rowing was not so easy as they made it look.

"Dig the oar deeper into the water," Artair instructed, watching her fumble quite a bit. "Aye, like that. And find the rhythm."

Her strokes improved but were not as smooth as these seasoned fishermen, or even Torsten's strong efforts. And pretty quickly she wished that the rhythm was much slower; her arms soon began to protest the strenuous motion. She wouldn't complain, though, lest they regret allowing her on the excursion. She understood that it likely wasn't expected that she would be able to keep up with them, but she didn't want it said that she'd given in, and so she rowed on.

"Do you not ever sail toward battle?" She asked her husband, needing a distraction. "Isn't it quicker?"

"Aye, it can be," Torsten answered, not quite out of breath as she was. "But we're mainly a cavalry, and a large one at that. It would need a heavy purse and many boats to move my army up or down the coast—and planning and usually waiting on ships' availability." He rowed several more times before adding, "'Tis easier, in the end, simply to start marching."

"And less taxing?" She guessed.

"Much less."

It was another ten minutes, by which time she was sure she'd have blisters if she didn't already, when Artair called for a halt.

"Thank God," Raina mumbled.

All the rowing ceased and yet the currach glided a bit further over the relatively smooth surface of the calm sea.

"Sweet Mother Mary," Raina whispered to Torsten, "but how much more difficult is that rowing when the sea is rough?"

He chuckled lightly and answered in a low voice. "I'll make sure we dinna ever have to find out."

"Yes, please."

A bit of scrambling took place, men moving around the boat. As the others had done, Torsten returned the oars to the bottom of the boat.

Staying put on the wooden bench, clinging to the side of the boat as it wobbled left and right with all the movement, Raina rather envied Torsten's ease, how confidently he acted and involved himself.

"Milady," Artair addressed her, swinging her head around, as she'd been watching the men position themselves at the back of the boat. "Sit here, milady," he said, patting the wooden bench next to him. He hadn't moved, and his wrinkled hands still help two oars. "A better view," he offered, when she hesitated.

Raina stood but remained bent, to hang onto the wooden slats as she stepped over the bench seat between her and Artair. At his side, at what she guessed was the front of the currach, she sat next to the thin man on the narrow seat, now facing the entire boat and the men working at the rear of it.

A better view, indeed. "Thank you, Artair."

"Take the oar," he instructed. "Move as I say, when needed, forward or back."

"All right," she replied, poised, waiting, her gaze returning to where Torsten labored with the fishermen, hauling in the nets.

Just as the others did, he gripped the coarse, wet rope and pulled with a steady rhythm, his muscles straining under the effort, the sinews of his arms and back flexing with each pull. Sweat beaded on his forehead, but he didn't slow down, matching the seasoned fishermen move for move.

Raina watched him, admiration and curiosity in her gaze. His easy manner with the men and his willingness to participate in the hard labor intrigued her. She realized a spark of pride, seeing him so at ease in this environment.

"What are those...things attached to the nets?" Raina asked of a series of elongated sacs affixed at intervals along the top of the net, now clumped in the bottom of the boat.

"Inflated bladders, milady," said Artair, before he instructed, "Forward—nae, milady, the other direction. Aye, once, again."

She understood then it was their job to keep the boat steady, not allowing it to drift from this location.

"Inflated bladders?" She questioned Artair, grimacing.

"Aye. Cow's bladders are best, but pigs will do. A hollow reed is used to blow air into them. They're tied off and secured to the nets."

"Oh, I see. They float and then the nets are easy to find in the sea."

"Aye, that's it, milady."

"Do you ever catch more than you can carry?"

"Sometimes we do," Artair acknowledged with a shrug. "Then we have to throw some back or send out the other boat. Forward again," he directed. "Again."

Raina blindly responded to the old fisherman's command, her eyes glued to the action at the front of the boat.

It seemed they dragged in an awful lot of net before Raina began to see it filled with fish. But soon, the nets revealed a bounty of silvery herring, their scales catching the sunlight as they flopped and wriggled in the mesh. There also, sturdy cod with speckled skins emerged, alongside fat mackerel gleaming with iridescent blues and greens, and the occasional salmon.

Raina's jaw dropped at the same time a smile evolved. "Oh, my," she breathed with awe, impressed with the catch, which seemed to be hundreds of fish.

The net was emptied until all the fish settled into the bottom of the boat. Jasper and Peile used buckets and scooped water, emptying it into the bottom of the boat as well, just enough to keep the fish wet, while Edane and Torsten sat again to row, and Aulay cast the empty net, with its iron weights and inflated bladders into the sea for tomorrow's haul.

They moved on then, all hands rowing for a short time, heading to the next buoy.

"I see them!" Raina exclaimed with excitement, rowing with greater confidence next to Artair. "The bladders," She said, pointing them out.

"Care to lend a hand, milady?" Edane asked, surmising her interest.

"Oh, no, I-I don't want to...ruin anything or break anything. I've never—"

"Ye canna break a net, milady," Edane assured her, laughter in his tone. "Jasper's out here almost every day and has yet to turn the boat. If he can do it, so can ye."

Raina cautiously stepped forward. Torsten turned sideways at the prow and Jasper moved left to allow room for her, which caused the boat to rock, and Raina to lose her footing. She began to tip sideways only to be caught by Torsten.

"Sea legs and quick hands," applauded Peile. "He's a fine fisher already."

Raina blushed, grateful for Torsten's steady grip. "Thank you," she murmured, steadying herself.

Torsten kept a hand on her arm, guiding her toward the prow.

She gripped the net hesitantly, feeling the rough texture against her palms. The weight of it surprised her, and she struggled to find her balance.

"Just follow the rhythm," Edane instructed, demonstrating the motion. "Pull, and then rest a beat, like this."

Raina nodded, trying to mimic his movements. Her first attempts were clumsy and weak. She hadn't the strength of these men. Gritting her teeth, she tried again, giving a good yank on the heavy net. *Pull, rest, pull,* she repeated in her head as she followed their tempo. The task was physically demanding, and her arms soon ached, but she was determined to keep up. The net did not get lighter but heavier, and soon fish begin to appear.

"Pull! Pull!" Peile commanded, increasing the pace.

Pull, rest, pull, but only quicker now. Raina sent a glance to Torsten, who worked directly beside her, sharing a broad smile of accomplishment with him. "This is amazing!" She cried enthusiastically.

She was astonished again at the number of fish and was hardly bothered that her léine and kirtle were nearly completely soaked from the waist down by the time the entire net lay in the bottom of the boat. She also had a newfound respect for the fishers, for the hard work of this, wondering how they managed this back-breaking labor every day.

"Oh, but the smell," she realized a moment later, putting her hand to her nose.

"Nae for the faint of heart," Jasper commented with a chuckle.

"Or nose," she replied with a wry smile.

"Go on then, milady," Edane instructed kindly. "We dinna expect ye to pick fish from the nets."

Raina returned to her seat more cautiously, stepping from bench to bench until she reached the back of the boat.

They rowed slowly again and Peile and Torsten cast the net now into the water.

Jasper paused while slopping water into the boat. "'Tis a fine catch," he said, looking at Raina. "Are ye a witch after all, to have brought up so many fish?"

Though caught off-guard by the question, and noticing how Torsten swung around, his scowl seen for the first time in hours, Raina sensed no animosity in the query.

"If I had such powers," she responded lightly, "we'd need a much bigger boat and lots of them."

To her relief, and apparently Torsten's, a bit of laughter answered her quip.

Shortly thereafter, the seven of them rowed back to shore.

Raina wasn't sure that she wanted to repeat the adventure, but in truth, she'd enjoyed herself tremendously.

She said as much to Torsten as they rowed.

"Same, lass," he readily agreed. "But aye, give me a sword and a battle any day."

Assuming he was jesting at least a wee bit, Raina laughed at this.

Returned to the beach, she refused Torsten's offer to carry her again to the sand, referencing the state of her garb.

"But help me out," she asked, "lest I tumble face first into the water."

He did, taking her by the waist, lifting her up and out of the boat. Raina latched onto his shoulders until she was set on her feet, and then she walked out a ways until she was nearly waist deep in the water, hoping to rid herself of at least some of the stench and offal clinging to her.

The lightness and the joy remained. She was so damn tickled by the experience that when Torsten took her hand, leading her up the cliff walk, as naturally as if he'd done so a thousand times before, Raina did not resist.

Chapter Sixteen

He was forced to relinquish her hand as they neared the top of the cliff in that small stretch where the path was only wide enough to accommodate one person at a time. Raina carefully navigated the trail a step ahead of him, holding up her skirts as she trudged along.

Want and need simmered inside Torsten, awakened by the fantastic liberation glimpsed in Raina over the last few hours. Gone, the guarded, cautious Raina who wore thin-lipped expressions and looked upon him as she had of late with naught but wariness. In her place, this vivid and vibrant woman, who'd embraced so readily, so happily a chore that was not her own, one that was more unpleasant than most, and that was even to him taxing.

At the top of the cliff, Raina turned to Torsten, her eyes shining with an exuberant glow. Her cheeks were flushed with the exertion of the climb and the excitement of the morning's adventure, giving her a healthy, sun-kissed radiance. The sea air had lent a gentle curl to her hair, and the wind now tousled it about her face and neck.

"Oh, but that was exhilarating," she exclaimed, skimming her forefinger along her cheek to pull a strand of hair away from her nose and mouth. "I'll suffer blisters aplenty and likely carry around the stench of fish for days and I don't care. Thank you for suggesting it."

Torsten nodded, his gaze steady and thoughtful. Introduced to this lively and radiant side of Raina, he couldn't help but wonder if he'd have approached their marriage differently from the beginning, setting aside his own reservations—enemy or no—allowing their bond to grow from that first night.

Aye, they reeked like the worst dredges of the sea and aye, his hands were blistered as well, his left palm abraded from the net, and he was parched, his throat dry, but he was possessed of a violent yearning stronger than he'd ever known to kiss her wildly.

Besieged with mad desire, indifferent to the lack of control, which he normally would have spurned, he acted, needing to mark this moment, not in triumph, but to remember.

He stepped forward and framed her face in his hands. Though her smile faltered, and she tensed slightly, she did not pull away or resist his touch. Torsten lowered his mouth to hers.

Her lips trembled under his, forcing him to proceed slowly, but damn, Raina's lush mouth under his and the shy touch of her tongue nearly caused him to forget his name. Melting into his embrace, she parted her lips and clung to him, stroking his tongue with her own, moaning softly. Her arms circled round his waist, her fingers clawed softly at his back.

Though there was a great risk to himself in advancing their union, he somehow knew that not doing so would be a bigger one. Certainly when she met his kiss with so much passion, as though she too had imagined, often, another kiss, as if she wrestled daily with this. *This*—this need, this staggering desire.

Her breath hitched as he deepened the kiss, and he gathered her closer, the swell of her breasts pressing against his chest.

Blood rushed through him, surging toward the lower half of his body.

Recalled to reason well before he might have been, Raina pulled away, shaking her head. She brought her hands around, between them, and pushed at his chest.

"No, I won't let you—I don't understand you, or what you're playing at," she said to his chest, unwilling or unable to meet his eyes. "I begin to believe you do it simply to confound me."

"Kiss you?" Nae, kissing was his need, was selfishly all about him.

Her dark lashes fluttered open and closed several times.

"No—well, yes, that, too. But why do you say one thing and do another? Why are you so contrary? Why do you behave of late as if you had not said that you didn't want...this?"

"Is nae a man allowed a change of heart?"

Her eyes widened and lifted to his. "A man is," she allowed, her brows drawing down, " a...a normal man is. But not you." She pushed herself further away, until they touched not at all. "Not Torsten de Graham, who prides himself on his rigid control, who is as sure and certain as a stone fortress, whose arrogance is as constant as the tide, to whom a change of heart must seem a mortal sin."

He was, of course, at pains to refute any of this as there was so much truth in her assessment.

Save that it was true, the change of heart, wrought by being utterly—indeed, willingly now—captivated by his wife.

"Raina, imagine if ye will—" he began.

"Laird! Milady!"

Torsten and Raina turned at once, to find Uilleam coming round the soft corner of the keep, sprinting toward them.

The lad's gaze was focused on Raina and not Torsten.

"'Tis yer sire, milady," Uilleam said, coming to an abrupt halt five feet away. A wince accompanied his sparse announcement, evidently sorry to deliver this news. "The nurse sent for ye."

Raina clutched her hand to her throat and after only a swift glance at Torsten, lifted her skirts and ran toward the keep.

Uilleam's grimace remained as he said quietly to Torsten, "Too late, she'll be. He's gone already."

Exhaling a large sigh, Torsten followed his wife.

He arrived inside the chamber, which Malcolm MacQueen had not left for more than three months by Torsten's understanding, to find his wife standing at the bedside. He spared only a fleeting glance at the miserable bastard in the bed, having a quick impression of a pale and flaccid expression, the man's eyes closed. The blankets had been neatly arranged around his shoulders so that all that was visible was his lifeless face. The chamber stank of piss and death.

Torsten knew not even a hint of sympathy as he imagined MacQueen meeting his maker, and likely being rejected at heaven's gate for the enormity of his sins upon this earth.

And maybe his hatred might have been pierced by sympathy for a daughter losing her father, save that when he fixed his gaze on her, he perceived no emotion there. Raina stood passively, three feet away from the side of the bed, hugging her arms around herself, her fingers squeezed into the sleeve of her opposite arm, seemingly devoid of any grief.

She simply stared at the figure in the bed, unblinking, neither pain nor sorrow discerned.

After a long moment, she dropped her arms and turned, showing a reaction now, but which he judged as naught but a wee surprise to find Torsten standing just inside the door. She approached him with a purposeful stride and stopped in front of him. Her lips were yet red and slightly puffy from his kiss, the flesh around her mouth pinkened as well from the scratch of his stubble. Her eyes were dry.

"Might I have leave to arrange his funeral?" She asked. "A simple burial—it doesn't need anything grand."

Torsten nodded, a brow raised for her coldness, for the use of *it* rather than *he*.

"Aye, lass. Do what ye must."

She swept out of the room, neither her shoulders nor her head slumped with grief.

FOR WEEKS, SHE HAD thrown herself into tasks and chores as mistress of Lochlan Hall, eager to see improvements, so bloody motivated to finally have been given the chance to contribute *something*. Each completed task had brought a sense of accomplishment, a sense of worth, so that she was more than only the daughter of Malcolm MacQueen or the *Killer of Men*; she felt as if she'd finally become Raina MacQueen.

Raina de Graham, she corrected herself.

She had something to offer, something to contribute. She was not merely a pretty face, useful only to attract suitors, and thereby wealth, or power, or alliances.

And now, as she faced the grim duty of planning her father's funeral, all she felt was a desperate need to see it done. She wanted to put him to rest and out of her mind, his presence a shadow that had loomed over her for far too long. Guilt gnawed at her heart for feeling this way, but she couldn't deny the truth. Her father had been a harsh man, and what truths had come to light in the last few weeks, even supposed ones, had only reduced what meager affection she'd ever felt for him. She didn't even suffer any guilt for how infrequently she'd visited him recently, naught every day as she had dutifully done at one time.

The shame she did feel was owing to the reality that his death stirred more relief than sorrow. This funeral was just another task to be completed, another burden to be lifted from her shoulders. She would bury her father not only in the ground, but in her mind as well.

Raina paused by the hearth in the great hall, the heat from the fire warming her cold hands. She watched the flames dance, her mind drifting back to her childhood, and then over all of her twenty-four years, attempting to cull some memory, some instance, some speck of warmth that she might attribute to her father. When she could not, and being wise enough to understand it was not on her as a bairn or child to have created or inspired love between her father and herself, Raina made peace with the fact that she had no desire to give him a farewell befitting a king as he would have wanted or expected.

In her mind, he hadn't earned it.

And so, the very next day, Raina stood in the courtyard of Lochlan Hall before a plain wooden casket, holding a handful of wildflowers gathered from the fields and forced into her hands by Peigi, while a few muted candles flickered in the breeze. The overcast sky mirrored her mood, casting a somber light over the modest gathering.

Torsten stood at her side though she didn't know why. Certainly, he was not paying tribute to some worthy foe for whom he'd long had great respect. Peigi, as dry-eyed as Raina, stood on her right. They hadn't even bothered to garb themselves in black mourning robes.

Lochlan's priest, Father Walter, his voice softened by years of service, stood ready to deliver the brief eulogy she had requested. No grand processions, no lavish feasts, no lengthy speeches. Just a quiet, unadorned ceremony to mark the end of a life that had left her with more scars than fond memories.

As she watched the handful of attendants mill about, she felt another pang of dull guilt.

When she couldn't force herself to grieve, she focused on practical matters. She and Peigi and the lasses would clean out her father's bedchamber later today, scrubbing and scouring until all traces of illness and death were obliterated. She would suggest to Torsten that he make it his own, for however long he planned to reside at Lochlan; there was no more a reason for him to occupy her bedchamber.

The service proceeded as planned. The priest's words were few, touching briefly on duty and honor, avoiding any mention of warmth or love. The villagers who attended offered their polite but sparse condolences. Raina could see in their eyes that they understood; her father's reputation as a hard man was well-known.

As the ceremony drew to a close, Raina felt a weight lift from her shoulders. This chapter of her life, built on the poorly stacked stones of obligation and duty, and devoid of affection, was finally over. She could now turn her full attention to the future and what she might make of it, unencumbered by the shadow of a man who had never truly been a father to her.

And when she cried that night in her bed, she cried not for her father or what should have been, and neither did she waste tears on the guilt she'd finally thrust aside.

She cried because she had no one, no family left at all.

She went still when Torsten arrived in their bedchamber, clamping her lips to stifle her weeping, keeping her back to him. He seemed to undress leisurely, and it was several minutes before she felt the mattress sink under his weight.

Raina maintained her stillness, waiting for the candle to be snuffed.

Before that happened, Torsten's hand landed on her arm.

Raina didn't move.

He stroked his hand up and down her bare arm. "Raina?"

The tenderness of his gesture and what sounded suspiciously like concern in his low voice wrought a strangled cry from her.

Damn him.

She swatted his hand. "Leave me alone."

He returned his hand to her arm. "I will nae." He applied some pressure, trying to get her to turn over.

Expecting that he would not give up, Raina groaned her displeasure and flopped over onto her back, forcing him to scooch back a wee bit as he'd been so close. Frustrated, she blew the strands of hair off her face, undisturbed that her cheeks, nose, and eyes were no doubt blotchy red.

Torsten was propped up on his elbow at her side. "Ah, lass," he said, using his thumb to wipe at her tears.

She wanted to howl at him to leave off with the pretense of concern.

"I will nae pretend to understand yer grief," he said gently, "nae any lasting affection for a man who—what?"

Her swift scowl had given him pause.

"I do not grieve my father," she informed him, flinging her forearm over her forehead, displacing his hand. A sigh of resignation was breathed through her lips. "To some degree, I guess I'm not so different than you—there's a coldness in me." Lowering her arm, she met his gaze and confessed, "Mine is born of pride and stubbornness. I feel nothing for my father and do not weep for him, but selfishly for myself. I am, for the first time in my life, truly alone. I am an orphan now. I have no kin. I have...no one."

"Ye have a husband," he reminded her, a gruffness to his voice.

"Who cares no more for me than he does for dust on the hearth," she said, cruelly repeating words he'd once uttered to her, which seemed to anger him.

"Christ, Raina," he growled furiously, "have ye held onto yer initial impression of me? From day one? I daresay ye have nae. Though ye tried to hide it well, ye were horrified by me. Does that remain? The horror? Nae, dinna lie to me and say it does." He pressed his fingers against his eyelids, squeezing them shut as he massaged them, exhaling sharply as he did so. And then he dropped his hand again, softly onto her arm, and opened his eyes. "Raina, I ken I've nae much to offer ye. I ken what I am—aloof, exacting, and with a foul temper I dinna even try to control—and nae, I dinna expect or want to wed. And aye, I'm cold, ye say. War will call and I will leave, and I dinna ken what the future holds." He stared at her, his blue eyes glittering with an unfathomable harshness.

Unsure how she was expected to respond, or even if she were, Raina waited, sensing that he was only gathering his thoughts.

"I *am* cold," he continued tersely, "hollow, indifferent. But ye are nae. And I am nae any of those things when I kiss ye." He took her chin in his hand. "At six and thirty, I've determined I'm nae capable of true affection—love or any other tender sentiment. I'm nae saying I am, or that I'm offering anything in that regard. But Raina, ye dinna have to be alone. Ye...ye asked me to give ye a child."

In a thousand years, she would never be able to even begin to describe the magnitude of her shock. Her breath caught sharply in her throat, and her heart pounded as if trying to escape her chest. She felt her face go pale, a cold wave sweeping over her. Her eyes widened, staring at him as if he had spoken in a foreign tongue, while her hand fisted on her chest.

At length, she found her voice. "And ye are offering to do so? Since you assumed I would be riddled with grief, did you also assume that would make me weaker, more amenable?"

"I assumed nothing," he said, still imbued with a wee annoyance it seemed, "but what I ken to be true. Ye stated yer want of a child and I've said to ye, I've changed my mind on the matter." He picked up her hand, easily unfurling her clenched fingers. "What, then, should keep us from making a babe?"

Breathlessly, she asked, "I guess I would want to know *what* has changed your mind?"

"Ye have, naturally." He paused, staring at their fingers, entwined once more. "Ye were the enemy, I canna deny. That's how I saw ye. As a millstone and nae a wife. But my enemy is nae someone who cares for people, who takes on the burdens of Lochlan Hall, defends the verra lad who lured her into danger, who shows kindness to me even though I have acted harshly and have been unyielding."

Her chest rose and fell in a dramatic fashion, stunned by his words and the reaction of her body. She sensed this was a pivotal moment in her life and their marriage. Now was not the time to allow pride to recklessly refuse what he offered. He *would* leave, she was sure of it. Likely, he wouldn't look back, not at the wife he didn't want—dust or no. But she could have this, the child he now offered.

Yet, would achieving her greatest desire demand surrendering her heart? Could she resist, or mend it once he departed? Though she wished it were not true, she was vulnerable; she understood that more lived and breathed inside her than merely a desire for his touch or only a child with him.

He cocked a brow at her, moving his face gradually closer to her. "Dinna say, Raina, that ye dinna want my kiss," he provoked, his breath hot against her lips.

Beginning to understand that surrender was inevitable, Raina didn't bother to lie. "I cannot say that with any certainty."

He brushed his lips briefly over hers, gently moving them side to side. "I should endeavor to remove all doubt," he whispered.

"You cannot undo this, Torsten," she was compelled to bring to his attention.

He paused and met her gaze. "I have every confidence that I will nae want to undo this, Raina, but that I will want it often. I want ye, as a man wants a woman. I offer ye a child."

"But you will still leave one day?" *You won't ever love me.*

"Aye," he admitted, confirming her forlorn suspicion. "Lochlan is nae my home."

A palpable sadness enveloped her, a cold wave washing over her heart.

Take what you can get, take all that he'll give.

Unless and until a child was born, it might be all that she would ever have, her first and only spark of joy in her adult life.

Torsten paused, pulling back to stare down at her. "Ye have nae said aye, ye want this."

And she wouldn't, though she did, very much.

Instead, she lifted her hands and threaded her fingers into the short hair over his ears, drawing him down to her kiss.

His warm lips brushed across her, igniting a flame she hadn't any intention of dousing. Raina's pulse pounded as he traced her lips with his tongue, demanding entry. She opened willingly for him, and a deep groan signaled his satisfaction. While she was nervous, Torsten suffered no similar qualms. His mouth covered hers hungrily and his tongue plunged inside. And though she'd thought he'd have devoured her, abandoning all restraint, there was a softness, a measured deliberateness, as if she and her kiss were something to be savored.

Raina enthusiastically returned his kiss. She moved her hands down from his face and hair, enthralled by the chiseled flesh of his shoulders and arms. Of their own accord, her hands slid between them, onto his chest. She'd dreamed of this, hadn't she? Imagined it, at the very least. She was inundated with sensations: his solid, naked flesh under her curious fingers, his heartbeat thudding against her palm, the feel of gliding her fingers over the crisp hair that covered his chest, the way he stiffened when she encountered a flat nipple.

She was consumed by impressions and reactions she hadn't known existed—a stirring of heat in her belly, some decidedly female pleasure at making him growl against her lips when she continued exploring his nipple, an instinct to arch against him, seeking more. Most significantly, she was imbued with a vast desire to abandon her own inhibitions, to give freely of herself. Though he'd said he suspected he would want more, she felt she had this one chance with Torsten.

A breathless sigh escaped her, knowing heaven of some sort was within her reach.

Torsten again trailed a kiss across her cheek and around her ear and Raina did arch against him.

"There's more," She guessed, unable to open eyelids that seemed ponderously heavy now. "More than only kissing."

"Christ, lass," he seethed, "so much more."

His voice was such, ragged, husky, that she imagined him as lethargic with passion as she was.

A chuckle broke the spell, forcing Raina to open her eyes.

Torsten was close, his lips only inches from hers, his eyes shards of blue crystal in the dim light.

"More, ye surmise. Impatient, are ye?"

"I must be," she said, unable to imagine any clever retort. "I beg you, do not...go slowly under some misconception that I am afraid."

He brushed his fingers and palm over her cheek and forehead, moving strands of hair off her face. He gazed deeply into her eyes before brushing her lips once more with his. "I would nae have ye imbued with fear at this moment, Raina. This is...well, this is simply kissing. There are about forty-three other things I want to do to you, with you."

Raina gasped, hardly able to credit—

Another chuckle—wonders never cease.

"Fine, nae forty-three," he confessed. "Nae all at once, tonight."

"Tell me," she requested.

"Do ye want to be told?" He asked, his gaze piercing as it moved from her eyes and over her nose and lingered on her lips. "Or do ye want to experience? To feel?"

The voice he used—sensual, smoldering—advised what her answer should be.

"I want to feel."

"Ye've never lain with a man?"

Her cheeks pinkened. Raina shook her head.

"Then I am compelled to go slowly," he said, "though it will pain me to do so. I want ye to feel, Raina, everything I do to ye."

Torsten inched backward until he was on his knees and gathered the hem of her shift, sliding it up along her body. He pushed with his palms against her skin, and Raina gasped with heretofore unknown delight when his calloused palms scraped over her breasts. She raised her arms mechanically and he pulled the linen garment over her head, leaving her entirely naked.

Her thoughts shattered as Torsten raked his gaze over her body with excruciating languor.

She might have been embarrassed or felt vulnerable, but it was impossible to know these things when he stared at her with such hunger. Fire burned in his blue-eyed gaze. It was then, her first awareness of the power of her own body, and she likened it to the effect the sight of his masculinity had on her.

Then he dropped over her again and his lips were on hers, his tongue exploring. Raina nearly went out of her skin at the feel of their chests pressed together, soft round globes cushioned in coarse black hair and solid muscle. She returned his kiss with a wildness that stunned her, and which put to shame what she only *thought* was desire prior to this moment.

But then he disappeared again, taking his lips from hers, branding her chin and neck with his lips and tongue before he sat back on his heels again.

"Christ, Raina," he breathed coarsely, "but ye are magnificent."

Casually, as if she would not be made to feel awkward, he studied her at length, examining her with hooded eyes and searching hands. Forcing down the leg she'd lifted and bent over the other with a fresh blush, he ran his hand up her shin and over her knee, mirroring the action with his other hand on her other leg.

Raina's breath caught as he stroked over her thighs and higher, but he did not pursue that tuft of dark curly hair between her legs, where pleasure knotted and pooled. He went further, over her hip bones and abdomen and then, most fantastically, filled his hands with her breasts.

Raina whimpered incoherently, her gaze locked on his face, in awe of the chiseled contours carved by longing, as he grazed his thumbs over the taut peaks of her nipples.

"I will die," she presumed, feeling weakened and awakened all at once.

A wicked grin curled Torsten's beautiful lips. "Ye will nae. Ye will live and ye will feel."

Chapter Seventeen

Here, naked upon the bed, his eyes alight with feverish desire, Torsten had seemingly shed the cold, austere exterior. Raina marveled at this as much as she did at his touch.

He returned to her lips, appeasing that hunger while one hand remained between them, closing over the fullness of her breast. He kneaded gently at first and then more deliberately, stroking and teasing her nipple, until her breast was swollen and aching. His touch was at times light and sensuous and then nearly painfully teasing. His hand roamed intimately over her breasts, her belly, her hip, marking her as his.

"Madness," she remarked, for the wealth of the tumult rising inside her.

"And just the beginning," Torsten whispered before he ducked his head and gently sucked her nipple into his mouth. "Easy, lass," he coaxed when she stiffened, and then returned his attention to her breast and its aching peak.

Pleasure warred with an agony of confusion, for what he was building and how it might end. He laved her breasts with his tongue and grazed her nipples with his teeth. Desire clenched deep inside her. Raina glanced down, fascinated by how the light rippled over her pale, tender flesh and the contrast of his suntanned, roughened hand, capable of rousing so loud and clamorous a desire.

Hot, seeking lips burned a trail over her navel and beyond. Raina squirmed. His hand settled firmly on her thigh, pushing it upward. She cried out when his mouth settled into the patch of hair between her legs, tasting her, stroking his tongue until she writhed beneath him. He spread her legs and caressed her until every inch of her trembled and she clutched at the blankets and furs.

She wrenched her hands free, threading them into his hair, but didn't know if she should push him away or pull him closer. His fingers briefly took the place of his tongue, parting her, sliding between her slick folds and then inside her, rousing a whimpered groan from deep in her chest. And then his tongue returned, swirling against her as he stroked his fingers in and out.

She was mindless at the same time she was attuned to every decadent caress of his tongue and fingers. His tongue toyed with her, teasing her, one moment lapping fully against her, the next flicking only the tip against her sensitive bud. Raina was pulled into a frenzy of pleasure, drowning in its sea. She lifted her hips to meet his mouth and fingers and simultaneously pushed at his shoulders, twisting beneath him as she tried to evade the unrelenting, ruthless pleasure, but he held her firmly until all the waves roared at once and pleasure exploded inside her. A cry sounded inside the bedchamber and Raina realized it had been torn from her lips.

Strands of iridescent delight coursed through her. Her breathing was labored, and her eyes would not open. She pushed Torsten's hands away, her flesh and nerves on fire now. God's bones, but how her body sang and strummed and tingled. She was only vaguely aware of Torsten crawling up her body on his hands and knees.

Awareness returned with new sensations, realizing he was as naked as she now, and his rigid manhood skimmed enticingly along her flesh as he climbed. Raina opened her eyes as he nudged a knee between her legs.

She lifted her hand, her fingertips tingling yet, and lay it against his cheek, wanting to smile her appreciation for what passion and joy he'd wrenched from her.

With infinite care, he brushed his lips against hers. A faint sheen of perspiration glistened on his brow and shoulders. Her heart beat against his.

"And how could I have told ye of that?" He asked, his voice naught but a rasp, as if he, too, were consumed by pleasure.

"You could not," she whispered, breathless. "It's fresh and upon me still, and I cannot describe it."

"So much better to feel," he remarked, settling between her thighs. The hot length of his erection met with her moist entrance.

Her body responded to the unfamiliar but achingly sweet feeling, clenching and prickling with awareness.

"Oh, God, yes." Her voice was not yet her own, was wispy and fragile.

Torsten bent and kissed her, bringing to her a curious scent, the musk of her desire, she guessed, boldly swirling her tongue with his. He deepened the kiss and joined his body with hers, shifting his hips forward as he entered her. It was strange, the way he filled her and stretched her. Nothing was familiar, everything new. Raina embraced it, all the delicious torment.

Torsten eased forward and withdrew, brushing the hair away from her face as he laid heated kisses along her jaw and the column of her neck. Then he met her lips again, devoured her now, and thrust his hips against her, wringing a gasp of pain from her.

His blue-eyes found hers. "Once and nae ever again," he said. "The tearing."

Shivering at the picture painted and grounded from the delights of heaven, Raina was given pause. Now what?

"Feel," he reminded her after a moment, his face buried in her hair, his breath warm on the side of her neck.

His hips moved, his cock retreated and returned with an agonizing deliberateness, tantalizing her with the fullness of him. He rose above her. Raina wasn't sure what he saw when he looked down at her, but her heart ached for how beautiful he was, his expression hard and yet tender at the same time.

Another luxurious stroke and a breathy snort of amazement erupted from her, for how swiftly and expertly he'd unleashed all the wonders of her body. The intimacy of this act, skin against skin, the delicious friction, brought to life what she was sure had nearly killed her a moment ago. She gripped his shoulders, not sure she could survive it this time, even as she rocked her hips instinctively against him. She clamped her lips, craving this, more, him. Sweet torment grew, blistering, spiraling.

"You are fire," she murmured, "and I am burning."

"*Jesu,* lass," he said with a hint of wonder, shifting over her, rocking into her as his hand found her breast and his fingers deliciously tormented her nipple.

He began to move faster, with more urgency. Raina opened her legs wider.

Divine pressure built inside her, tremors of arousal rising again. Aware now of what awaited her, she clutched at him, pulling him deeper, frantic for another release. Once more pleasure engulfed her, in deep, long strokes. Raina felt again as if she were flying, soaring upwards. She arched her body against the stone wall of Torsten's chest and was certain the earth moved. She felt as if her body were turned inside-out.

He gave several more thrusts and then one final shove, and he grunted, rearing up. His broad shoulders shuddered, and he filled her core with warmth, uttering her name through clenched teeth.

Wrapping her arms around his broad shoulders as he collapsed against her, Raina inhaled his deeply male scent and the heat wafting off him. A belated soft moan squeaked past her lips when he next moved, slipping free of her.

Cool air kissed her skin as he rolled onto her side and Raina deflated inside, until he pulled her roughly up against him, wrapping his arm around her waist while she snuggled her back into his chest.

After a moment, she confessed in a sleepy voice, "To be honest, I wasn't much thinking about a babe during any of that."

His chuckle rumbled against her spine. He pressed a kiss to the back of her head. "Nor I, lass."

Raina sighed, filled with a vast contentment. She scratched her short fingernails lightly over the hair-covered forearm around her middle.

She absolutely adored this man who'd finally, properly made her his wife, who wore neither frowns nor scowls, but various expressions of awe and desire, who spoke in that husky sensual tone and had curled her toes with his touch, who exuded so much male virility and made her believe she was utterly beautiful.

Raina fell asleep understanding that she very much liked her husband, the Torsten de Graham who'd allowed himself to lose control with her tonight.

But she was bitten by a small bug of apprehension as well, very much afraid she was bound to lose her heart to her husband.

PERHAPS HE WOULD NOT return to war, after all. Or not so soon, at any rate.

How could he possibly leave her? he wondered several nights later.

The day after he'd made love to her for the first time, he'd told her at last meal that they would not repeat the night before, not yet, not until her body had healed.

His wife had frowned at him and was quite disagreeable for several minutes, refusing to speak to him as she finished her supper.

At length, Torsten cajoled, "Raina? Ye understand why."

"I do not. And I don't understand how *you* can feel what's inside *my* body."

She realized the nuance and innuendo as soon as the words left her mouth.

Neither had any success restraining the intimate grins that brightened their faces.

Though her grin remained, she attempted to maintain her annoyance, exhaling a tart sigh, staring out over the crowded great hall, saying quietly for his ears alone, "And here I was about to tell you that I was feeling unusually fatigued today and would likely be retiring earlier than normal."

So how could he leave?

How could he leave behind pleasure so intense, unlike anything he'd ever known? Raina was…suddenly, she was everything to him. Torsten willingly allowed himself to be drowned in her, her scent, her body, her touch, those charming little noises she made when he rocked deep inside her.

Frankly, he didn't recognize himself, the man who allowed every barrier, every wall, every inhibition to be so easily swept away and kicked aside by a wife he didn't want but whom he couldn't get enough of.

She was a wonder in how at ease she was, even speaking about what they did in the bedchamber each night, making light of it one morning, saying, "I'm not complaining at all, mind you, but this does create an awful lot of laundry."

He had noticed that fresh sheets were fitted on the mattress each night. The furs had been folded and tucked away in the kist at the end of the bed, no longer needed. They slept in each other's arms, sharing body heat, sometimes waking in the wee hours and disturbing the bedsheets yet more.

Her curiosity and her own lack of reticence was another constant matter of wonder to him. She was eager to be initiated, asking how to please him, her eyes widening with wicked expectation when he'd sat naked in the unbroken chair before the hearth, guiding her, naked as well, to straddle his legs.

He hadn't slipped immediately inside her, though it took quite a bit of effort to resist the temptation. He allowed his erection to linger there between them, wanting her to feel how hard and hungry he was for her.

"You mean to tease me," she'd said, her breaths coming quickly.

Torsten had cupped her breasts in his hands, teasing her nipples to stiff peaks. Raina had latched onto his shoulders, squirming in reaction. And then, having discovered that small movement moved the soft, sensitive flesh between her legs against his iron-hard staff, her gorgeous mouth had formed a small *o* and she'd done it again.

"And now who teases whom?" He growled at her, eliciting a smile from her that seemed to him a siren's beckoning.

He let her go on grinding herself delicately against him, until he could suffer the torment no more, and he might have wept for the beauty of sinking into her slick, warm heat on that occasion. In that moment as her body melted against him, his world was filled with her. He knew nothing else. And he let it be.

Granted, on another night she talked through what should have been a delightful instance when he took her hand and closed her fingers around his cock for the first time. She had questions ("where do you put this when you're atop your destrier?"), was eminently curious about the appearance ("it looks rather red with anger"), and wondered what she might call it ("I once heard a maid—I won't say who—refer to it as a sword; she said she'd liked to be speared by a certain gentleman, but I cannot imagine myself speaking so... cheekily"), but damn if he didn't grow and surge just as swiftly under her artless handling and in spite of her chatter as easily as when he hardened with arousal watching pleasure enfold her.

Still, he rejected any notion that he regularly joined his soul to hers and not only his body, even as it felt like that at the time. 'Twas simply he, a new husband, giving into the delights of the flesh—with Raina they were endless—all in an effort to solidify his position as laird and commander of Lochlan Hall and give her the babe she desired so badly. At night he allowed himself to feel with both body and mind but during the day, he staunchly reminded himself that he had no intention of developing feelings for his wife outside the bedchamber.

That's what he told himself, anyway. And yet, in the ensuing days he'd begun to think that rather than abandoning Lochlan completely and forever when eventually he did return to the king's side, that he might in the future split time between Glenbarra Brae and Lochlan, if God wished that he should survive the war well enough to do so.

Even as he listed numerous reasons in his head why he might do this—Lochlan having a far greater thriving industry, being richer and requiring more than only an absentee laird; being further south and closer to either fighting as needed or perhaps the capital once it was established; the lure of the beach and the sea, which he'd come to appreciate as an appealing setting—he knew, deep down he knew, it was her. She would be what brought him back to Lochlan.

RAINA AND PEIGI SET out from Lochlan Hall, the keep standing tall behind them, its stone walls softened by the warm light of the late summer sun. The sea's briny scent faded as they walked inland, though the cliffs and dunes hardly shielded them from the needling wind. Beyond the newly erected palisade and the even rows of tents belonging to Torsten's army, the path before them was dotted with late-blooming wildflowers, their colors muted but still lovely.

As they strolled toward the village to collect the commissioned linens from Judith the weaver, Peigi huffed and shook her head.

"Nigh on a week, milady," she said, clutching her hood at her throat, "and I'm waiting on ye to tell me aye, he's finally made ye his wife and ye have nae more need of plots and schemes to entice him." She hooted a bit with ribald laughter. "And dinna demur, milady. I dinna ken ye're trying to hide it but I'm saying ye canna. Och, but it's written all over yer face."

Raina rolled her lips inward. In truth, she thought she might burst for wanting to tell *someone* what had transpired—many times, over many nights by now. She watched the treads of her feet, not quite sure how one went about sharing such intimate news.

"So, he's made ye his, made ye a woman and naught but a blind man winna have kent. And I'm guessing by the grins ye wear all morning, and all the extra washing ye're throwing at the lasses, he's nae only willing but..." she glanced sideways at Raina, her smirk broad, "but he makes like a great luver, dinna he?"

Raina clapped her hands over her mouth to curtail the burst of laughter that came. While her cheeks flamed bright red despite the nip in the air, Raina heard herself confess, "If I'd known then what I...I, well, saints be praised, Peigi, I'd have lobbied right from the start for a real marriage."

Peigi chuckled. "I kent he'd be guid between the sheets, he has that look about him."

Raina laughed softly, her cheeks flushing. "Yes, he does. I understand what that means now." She felt a pang of regret for speaking so personally, so bawdily, with the housekeeper.

Sensing her remorse, Peigi wagged her finger at Raina and said, "Ye dinna have a mother, nae sisters nor friends. Yer still Lady Raina, but it'll do nae harm to have a friend, aye? And ye ken, I've got big ears but I dinna have flapping lips."

"Thank you, Peigi."

"Aye, and am I nae looking forward to bairns? Fill the keep with them, milady. Please, will ye? Bairns everywhere!"

Raina laughed more freely even as she blushed again. She laid her hand over her cheek and one over her stomach, thrilled by the very idea.

"Winna be long," Peigi predicted. "So long as ye keep showing those dark but happy circles under yer eyes, tired but happily so for how he manages to keep ye awake at night, it winna be long."

Raina blushed even more, but her heart swelled with hope.

Of course, repeatedly she told herself it was all about that, making a baby. 'Twas lies, all of it. Yes, she would dearly love to hold a child of her own, to cradle a tiny life and feel the warmth of a family. But what she truly wanted was Torsten. She yearned for his love, for a connection that went beyond the mere act of creation. She wanted his affection to be rooted in his heart and not simply be a physical desire for her body. Though she was enslaved by his touch and wanted it desperately, it wasn't enough for him to seek her out in the quiet moments of the night, driven by passion and need. She craved the tenderness in his gaze, the whispered words of love that spoke of a deeper bond.

Wishful dreams and naught but that. Though Torsten satisfied every desire inside their bedchamber, he did not often seek her out during the day, did not seek her counsel or her company. During the day, he remained mostly absent, immersed in his duties, training, and the business of administering to Lochlan and its people. She feared that, despite their intimate moments, his heart was still shielded by walls she could not breach. It was clear to her that he still saw her as a temporary companion, one that he would soon leave behind as he marched off to fight.

She knew he would not remain at Lochlan forever, would likely be called to war or go looking for it, leaving her behind with only memories. The prospect of him leaving gnawed at her, a painful reminder that she was not indispensable to him. She told herself repeatedly that she must not fall deeper, that she must not hope for more than what he was willing to give. Despite the tenderness they shared under the cloak of darkness, daylight revealed the stark reality: Torsten's heart was still out of reach, and his inevitable departure loomed over her like a dark cloud.

Many times she had to remind herself of the objective. It was a child she wanted originally, not Torsten as a devoted spouse who after three and a half decades understood that he was incapable of love. He *had* warned her.

Ah, but a babe.

I won't need Torsten, she told herself, *if I have a child. I won't miss him if he leaves me with a babe.*

These words became her mantra, a shield against the ache in her heart. She convinced herself that the joy and fulfillment of motherhood would be enough, that the love she would pour into her child would fill the void Torsten's absence would create.

Raina immersed herself in the daily routines and duties of Lochlan Hall, her mind constantly returning to the thought of a child. She imagined a small life growing within her, a tangible connection to the future that did not rely on Torsten's presence.

The idea of a child became her anchor, grounding her in the midst of uncertainty and emotional upheaval.

And sometimes she hid herself and cried, her heart breaking a little each day, knowing she lied to herself, and that she was in love with her husband, and that she desperately yearned for him to love her in return.

Chapter Eighteen

"Ye want towers built, and aye, that can be done," Gilles said. "But it'll need ye meeting with the carpenter and his apprentices. And it'd do nae harm to include James—ye ken he can bring to life concepts as vague as *build me a tower*."

Seated at the high table between Gilles and Torsten, while they broke their fast on the first Monday of September, Raina hid a smirk for the captain's seeming frustration over what he supposed was Torsten's ambiguity.

Torsten had mentioned the idea to her a few days ago, musing that neither her father nor any MacQueen before him had never built watch towers. Conceit might have been a reason, was Raina's suspicion though she did not say this.

Torsten believed the keep vulnerable—his effortless siege of Lochlan proved this—and desired that eventually Lochlan could defend itself from the west since the east posed no problem, having the sea and the cliff as its defense.

Raina listened to the two men discuss options, including the number of towers needed and whether they would entrust the job to the carpenter, as opposed to contracting masons and having them built of stone.

The morning sun cast a golden glow through the tall windows of the great hall, dappling the floor with patches of light. The air was filled with the comforting aromas of fresh bread, smoked fish, and stewed fruits. Raina picked leisurely at her breakfast, her gaze falling often upon Torsten. She enjoyed tremendously the tentative peace established between them but couldn't yet reconcile the gruff and capable leader, the man who gave ponderous thought to his ideas and sometimes snapped with impatience at the grunts of his army with the man who for many nights in a row now had loved her so tenderly, with infinite patience and a sometimes boyish charm.

"Monday it is and down to the beach with ye?" Gilles asked Raina when he'd concluded his discussion with Torsten.

"Yes," Raina replied, brushing crumbs from her hands and from the table in front of her. "It's Monday, and they'll be expecting their pay. I'll take care of it shortly."

Before Gilles could respond, the shrill blast of the alarm horn echoed through the hall, cutting through the peaceful morning like a knife. The great oak door burst open, and a de Graham soldier rushed in, his face tensed with urgency.

"Laird!" he called, making straight away for the high table. "Fire, laird. In the woodland beyond the cattle barns."

Torsten shot to his feet. "How bad is it?"

"It's nae guid, sir," the young man said. "The flames are spreading quickly, they're saying, threatening the buildings on the east side."

Torsten grumbled an expletive and faced Raina while Gilles and several other soldiers within hearing had stood and made for the door. "Dinna go to the beach with nae escort," he reminded her. "And mayhap stay close to the keep otherwise, until we have this under control."

Raina reached out, touching his hand lightly. "Be careful, Torsten."

He nodded, squeezing her hand briefly before striding out of the hall, barking orders as he went. The courtyard beyond the open door buzzed with activity, soldiers hustling to follow his commands.

Raina watched Torsten leave and the hall empty of almost every person. A frown came to her, and she laid a hand over her stomach as a chill of unease settled over her, a gnawing sense of foreboding that turned her stomach. Refusing to entertain it and before she made her way down to the beach, she marched toward the kitchen, advising Cook of the fire and of her intention to prepare supplies for those fighting the fire.

"Let's ensure that we have available in the hall plenty of food, water, and ale for when the men return," she instructed.

She directed two of the kitchen lasses to set up two barrels in the courtyard, and fill them with water for washing, imagining soldiers' faces and hands coated in layers of ash and soot. "Have plenty of rags available as well as drying towels," she added.

She climbed the stairs next, in search of Peigi, whom she encountered on the second floor, carrying a small hammer in her hand.

"Fixed that bluidy shutter in the solar," Peigi said, explaining the tool's presence. "I was sick of listening to it bang all the live long day. Dinna ken how ye—"

"Peigi," Raina interrupted. "There's a fire in the woods, threatening the cattle barns, a fairly dangerous one it seems."

The hammer was dropped to her side. "Och. Shite."

"Exactly. Torsten took his army—I imagine whoever was near—and hopes to contain it. But I know you'll want to check on your husband and lads."

Peigi shoved the hammer at Raina, who barely caught it before Peigi was off, skirts raised and running down the stairs.

"Be careful!" Raina called after her.

Of course she was very tempted to follow the housekeeper, but she knew her place was here. Torsten would never allow her to be of any use around a fire, she guessed, and knew that one more person when he had so large an army at his disposal would hardly make a difference. She turned and stepped into a rarely used guest chamber that faced the west, going directly to the window.

She pushed back the long and heavy tapestry that covered the window and peered through the narrow opening, spotting immediately a column of smoke rising in the distance. Below, closer to the keep, Peigi was seen sprinting through the open gate of the palisade and directly across rather than around the hundreds of de Graham army tents. The camp seemed deserted, scarcely more than a handful of soldiers milling about. Returning her gaze to the fire, she judged it neither too large nor too awful. The smoke was a thin column rising lazily into the sky, not too widespread. The flames were just a faint flicker, barely discernable from this distance and through the wall of trees at the far perimeter of the army's camp—more a suggestion of fire than a roaring blaze. Yet the sight of it, combined with her earlier unease, made her heart race.

Returning belowstairs, Raina busied herself with the household tasks, trying to keep her mind occupied and her worry at bay. The hours dragged on, each minute feeling like an eternity.

She'd wanted to be inside when Torsten returned, but knew she'd put off long enough getting down to the beach. Deciding to complete that task and hopefully be returned in time to greet him, she searched out two soldiers to escort her. The keep and yard and the camp beyond the palisade, however, were eerily quiet; aside from Cook and a few lasses out front, watching the gray and white smoke waft up to the sky more than half a mile away, it was otherwise empty. Raina wondered if the fishermen were likewise distracted. Maybe they were not even upon the beach today.

They were, she realized, having scouted the beach from the top of the crag at the back of the keep.

Deciding the fire obviously posed little threat to the beach, Raina decided to carry on, but without the table and chair. Sure, it would make the disbursement more challenging—she'd have to sit in the sand and use her lap as a desktop—but she wasn't about to waste an extra half hour today toting the table and chair down there.

Raina collected the basket from the steward's office, which of late she employed more than anyone else. When she arrived outside the back door, she found the de Graham soldier, Samuel, who had accompanied her several times now to the beach.

"Samuel!" She called to him as he was making his way around to the front courtyard.

"Milady," he answered, his eyes lighting a bit as he turned and approached.

Lochlan's own might despise her, but she had to admit, the de Graham soldiers were unfailingly courteous to her.

"Good day, Samuel," she said. "I wonder if you might accompany me to the beach. I'd rather not invoke my husband's ire by marching down there by myself."

"Nae, milady," Samuel answered promptly. "Ye dinna want to do that. Give a minute to collect the table."

Raina waved her hand. "Let's not bother with that today. I want to get back before Torsten returns—and all the men. They'll be hungry no doubt, and I wouldn't be surprised if at least a few injuries or burns need attention."

Samuel glanced toward the western sky though little could be seen with the keep between them and the fire. "Smoke dinna look so bad as it was earlier," he said. "Shouldna be too long now." He very kindly took the straps of the basket off Raina's arm. "If ye're sure ye dinna want the table and chair, I'll carry this."

"Thank you. Yes, let's hurry."

Down upon the beach, Samuel walked along the sand, past the barrels and baskets of fish brought in along the shore, past the drying racks and the storage huts and the salting station, announcing to the folks to come and receive their due.

Raina reached the beach and set herself up as the pay station, sitting down with her legs crossed beneath her, and burying the ink pot up to its neck in the sand at her side. The pouch of coins sat in her lap under the ledger. The fisherfolk gathered around her, accepted their pay with the usual crusty nods and scarcely a murmur of thanks.

Neither currach was moored presently and Raina guessed that Artair, Edane and the rest of their crew, plus a second crew were likely out hauling in the nets. She'd have to seek them out later today perhaps to settle up with them.

Just as she recorded the last entry and cinched the bag of coins, she spied a boat coming in. Assuming it was one of the fishing boats, she waited, pleased that she might have fewer people to chase down later. She frowned, however, as the boat neared, approaching the shore with uncommon speed.

Raina frowned, setting aside the ledger as she came to her feet. Absently, she brushed sand off her bottom and dropped the pouch to the ground. Only briefly was she befuddled by an awareness that the currach looked different before she understood that this boat, longer and broader, was not one of Lochlan's currachs.

Those on the beach, having returned to work, paused once more. Slowly, they began backing away from the shore. Several of them turned and began climbing up the cliff path.

"What is...?" She tried to ask of Duncan as he rushed past her, ignoring her.

From the opposite end of the beach, where he'd been speaking with Nell and her bairns, Samuel turned and sprinted toward Raina, waving his hand wildly, though his shout was lost to the roar of the waves.

She spared one more glance at the boat, which seemed to hold no more than half a dozen men. But before she could fully process what was happening, the boat reached the shore, and what might have been as many as twenty men spilled out, storming the beach with swift and purposeful strides. This was not a friendly party. Raina's heart pounded in her chest as she backed away, the scene eerily reminiscent of many weeks ago when the de Grahams had stormed the beach, albeit from a different direction.

Samuel was closer now, his shout loud and desperate. "Run! Run!"

The last thing she saw before she turned was the coming party running *by*—without engaging—the fishers on the beach.

They'd come for her. She didn't know who they were or why they wanted her, but she knew they'd come for her.

Abandoning the coins and ledger, she scurried up the path, but was made clumsy by her haste. Having failed to lift her skirt, she tripped within a few steps and, losing her balance, skittered downward. She started again, lunging frantically, sparing a glance over her shoulder at the scene below.

One that gave her pause.

Samuel stood as a sentry between her and the raiding hostiles, nearly twenty men.

"Samuel! No!" She pivoted and dashed back down to the beach, stumbling a bit until she crashed into Samuel's back. She tugged desperately at his arm. "No, Samuel. No. 'Tis certain death."

The young man never took his eyes off the assailants, who had just about reached him, and were now slowing, likely waiting to see what the lad would do.

"Dammit, milady," he gritted through his teeth, sounding very much like his commander at the moment. "I said to run."

"Look at me, Samuel," she said, circling round to his front. "Look at me," she commanded harshly. When he did, she said quietly, "Lay down your sword. You will be killed otherwise, and they'll still take me. I need you to tell Torsten to come find me."

"I will nae lay down my sword," he said, the veins in his neck throbbing.

Raina turned and considered the faces of the men meaning to abduct her. She held out her hand to keep them at bay, which miraculously seemed to work.

"You will," she said to Samuel, returning her attention to him. "They won't tell him, these wretched people, and how will he know? You're the only chance I have. Lay down your sword and tell Torsten I promise to stay alive." Tears gathered, her fright nearly overwhelming her good intentions regarding the outnumbered lad. "Tell him I am counting on him to come for me," she whimpered. Laying her hand over his, she pushed his sword downward until the tip of the blade met the sand.

Samuel's face reddened and his mouth twisted brutally, reacting physically to the very idea of surrendering. Angrily, he thrust down his sword and glared at Raina.

She was seized even before she turned around to accept her fate, unfriendly hands clasping her roughly. Two men shoved her forward into the custody of other waiting men. As was the case previously, so now she did not recognize these men; a fleeting glance over the faces showed nothing remarkable or distinguishable. Being kidnapped twice in a matter of weeks left her in a daze of disbelief. She couldn't fathom how or why it was happening again.

Her arms held in vice-like grips, she went along, more bewildered than fearful, too stunned to fight, and not willing to risk that Samuel wouldn't again raise his sword if he thought she'd changed her mind.

Between her and the boat to which she was being taken stood the fisherfolk.

They did nothing to stop the assault, the abduction. In fact, it seemed they had cleared a path, as a large swath of sand lay bare between two groups of Lochlan's own, where they stood untouched and untargeted.

She met the gazes of several people as she was marched past them, Nell, Donal, and Kenneth among others, none of whom spoke up or acted on her behalf. Their expressions varied from shame to dread to scorn.

Some of the men who'd come for her ran ahead, beginning to shove the long boat back into the water. She was walked out into the surf and lifted into the boat. Once inside, she was shoved down onto a wooden seat, facing the vast and endless sea in front of her.

To her horror, she saw that Samuel was being manhandled and brought to the boat as well. Having dropped his sword, his resistance was mostly for show. He climbed up into the boat himself but was seated toward the prow, his back facing Raina.

As the boat pushed off from the shore, Raina cast one last, desperate look back at Lochlan Hall. Several people stood atop the cliff, at the precipice—Duncan and those who'd ran, not anyone who might come to her rescue. The fishers on the beach hadn't moved yet.

Still too stunned to even cry in fright, Raina realized she'd forgotten to scream, recalling Torsten's praise for having done so last time.

She should have screamed before she'd let herself be taken.

THERE HADN'T BEEN ANY storms today that might suggest lightning had sparked the fire in the small forest. And it hadn't been so dry of late that it was possible the fire had started from a mere spark or carelessly discarded ember. The conditions simply didn't add up to a natural cause, leaving an unsettling question hanging in the air: how had the fire begun? And who was behind either a rash carelessness or an intentional act of arson?

Torsten drank thirstily from a horn being passed around and then wiped his forearm and sleeve over his brow to catch the dripping perspiration. The heat from the fire and the strenuous labor of fighting it had taken a toll on him and his men.

The battle against the blaze was a grueling one. Men had formed a line from the nearest water source, the loch the sat several hundred yards away, passing buckets hand to hand to douse the flames. Others used shovels and tools to create firebreaks, cutting down brush and trees to halt the fire's progress. Wagons, hastily repurposed for the task, sped along the makeshift path, carrying barrels of water to the frontline.

Roughly four hours later, the fire was contained. The cattle barns and pastureland had been spared, thanks to the tremendous and exhausting effort put forth by the de Graham army and the herders and those who labored in the barns. The forest, however, bore the scars of the battle, charred and smoldering.

Torsten stood back, surveying the damage and the weary faces of his men. Hundreds of them sat or laid in one huge clump, very close to the barns as they'd been backed up constantly by the flames before they'd finally controlled the blaze. Dozens or more had trekked back to the loch, eager to wash off the lingering smoke and acrid smell.

"Nae accident, that," Gilles commented, putting into words exactly what Torsten had been thinking.

"Nae," he agreed. He was one of the few men standing presently, too much on edge to sit. He passed the horn onto James and set his hands on his hips, casting his gaze back toward the keep, beyond the village and across the vast heath, which remained as undisturbed as when they'd been alerted to the fire hours ago.

"Leave a unit here," Torsten said, pausing to cough out more of the smoke he'd inhaled. "Have them continue to douse that for a while." He bent and picked up his belt and sheathed sword, where it had lain for the last few hours, holding it in his hand rather than attaching it.

They'd sent the horses back hours ago, too many of them spooked by smoke and flames, and now as Torsten began the walk back to the keep, one by one his men picked themselves up and followed, trudging wearily toward the army camp and Lochlan Hall.

They weren't halfway there yet when Torsten noticed a figure dashing straight through the quiet encampment. He squinted, but it was another moment before he recognized the fisherman, Edane, who had invited Torsten and Raina onto the boat last week, as the man racing through the rows of tents.

Immediately and inexplicably Torsten was pricked by apprehension.

"Getting somewhere in a hurry," Gilles remarked, having noticed Edane's approach.

"But why?" Torsten wondered, quickening his own pace until he was jogging toward the fisherman, already fearing the worst, that something had happened to Raina.

"Laird!" The man called when still a great distance separated them.

Though mayhap not imbued with the same sensation of dread, many of the de Graham men ran with him.

"Laird! 'Tis Lady Raina!" Edane shouted when they were closer.

With a fright eerily familiar, Torsten's heart dropped to his stomach.

He and Edane halted abruptly at the same time, only feet apart.

"Taken, laird," said the man, breathless. "A boat came and...men took her." He pointed toward the south. "Went off that way."

"When?"

Edane hesitated, wincing.

"When, goddamn it?"

"More than an hour ago," Edane answered, his voice small.

"Is this a fecking jest?" Gilles shouted, having reached Torsten's side. "An hour ago!"

Torsten saw red, made speechless by the magnitude of his rage.

He clasped his hand around Edane's arm, directing him to walk, striding furiously toward the keep. "Was anyone else taken? Was she harmed?"

"Yer lady and the lad, Samuel, but we've since recovered him. She went willingly, they said. Begged yer man nae to fight—one against so many—and," he shrugged, "she said she'd go if they dinna harm the young lad."

"And nae one else did anything to stop her from being taken, I imagine," James supposed with a venomous irritation.

"We only just returned now with the currach, laird, fished yer lad out of the water—they'd taken him but dumped him out at sea," Edane rushed to explain, having to run, sprinting to keep up with Torsten, who'd broken into a sprint toward the keep. "If we'd been there, I'd have—"

"How many came for her?" Torsten cut him off.

"Nae more than twenty, 'tis said."

"Where is Samuel?"

"On the beach yet, laird," Edane answered swiftly. "Broke his leg, they did, and he's lucky he dinna drown—was floating and treading, carried by the tide, for the last half hour."

"Send a party down there to bring up Samuel," Torsten called out to his men, "I want the keep locked down, everyone out. Get those bastards off the beach, the fishers. Seize their boats. Put crews of ten in the currachs and forty in the knarr." He was quickly out of breath, but continued, his brain sifting through actions needed. "Gilles, Rory, James, on the boats. Aonghas, leave forty at the keep and bring the rest with us—we ride for Montrose."

Though Edane had not kept pace with him, the de Graham men did.

"I want them questioned," he commanded, "Anyone down at the beach who witnessed it. Go at 'em hard until ye get answers."

"Ye want a guard round the village?" Aonghas asked.

"To hell with them, all of them," was Torsten's response. He couldn't care less about their safety. He cared only about Raina and getting her back. They could retake Lochlan Hall itself for all that he cared.

"I'll skin 'em myself," Gilles vowed gruffly, "every one of those bluidy fishers, if a hair on her head is harmed."

He lost precious but necessary moments interviewing Samuel, who was indeed in rough shape, drenched and dripping inside the hall where he'd been brought, his faced wreathed in agony for the damage done to his lower leg.

"She ran but then stopped, laird," he informed Torsten, a wee frantic yet after his ordeal. "She returned for chrissakes! She kent they'd nae kill me if she went willingly." When Torsten put his hand on Samuel's shoulder to calm him, Samuel gripped

Torsten's forearm desperately and held his gaze. "She kent those bastards on the beach wouldna told ye. She said: *Tell him I am counting on him to come for me.*" Samuel shook his head, exhibiting disbelief he'd yet to come to terms with. "Terrified, she was, but she went with them. Ye have to find her, laird."

Samuel knew little more than Edane had already told, though he was able to confirm that the kidnappers had indeed traveled south along the coast with Raina for as long as he'd been with her.

"But ye cannot discount north, laird," the lad insisted. "After they dropped me into the sea, they went east for a long while, as long as I could see them."

Some discussion was had over this.

"To avoid currents?" Gilles wondered.

"To avoid the lad seeing them turn north?" Aonghas posited.

"*Jesu*, crossing the sea?" James introduced.

"Nae," Gilles dismissed this. "Samuel said the boat was nae big enough to cross the sea."

Less than thirty minutes after Edane had first sprinted toward him, Torsten set out with the bulk of his army, riding hard along the cliffs. He was hardly able to imagine that they might reach Montrose before the brigands put into port there, having such a large head start, and more troublesome, Montrose was only a guess; frighteningly, he had no idea who they were or from where they hailed, so that he couldn't rightly say where they'd come ashore again. He sent the knarr and those forty men north along the coast.

He blamed himself. Aye, he'd investigated the previous attempt to kidnap her, as much as he was able, but with so few clues and no one willing or able to identify even one of the dead men, his investigation had stalled fairly quickly. He'd sent James and Uilleam into Montrose to make discreet inquiries, but this, too, had yielded no results.

Today's fire, though, now made sense. But here he blamed himself as well, for not suspecting some treachery, for not commanding that Raina not leave the keep, for not assigning a larger retinue to her. He'd made the mistake of assuming the hefty perimeter guard would have kept her safe—and it had, until they'd come in from their posts, the majority of them, helping to fight the fire.

There was no excuse for his carelessness in this regard. In light of the first attempt to abduct her, Raina's safety should have overridden every other consideration at all times.

Tell him I am counting on him to come for me.

Bluidy hell, and how would he live with himself if...he couldn't?

Nae, failure was not an option.

He would find her.

Chapter Nineteen

They sailed for what seemed like several hours before docking. The rhythmic rocking of the boat had done nothing to soothe Raina's nerves; if anything, it heightened her anxiety. She tried to focus on the coastline, wishing she recognized more of it. Shortly after they'd thrown Samuel into the sea, they'd headed out to open water, the captors rowing hard and fast, and Raina had lost sight of the shoreline altogether.

Her fear for Samuel was desperate, for a long time greater than her own. She could only suppose they'd brought him along to delay word getting back to Torsten, but oh, how they'd discarded him! Upon his initial capture he was not abused so greatly as he was moments before he was tossed over the side. Without warning, without a word, one man had stood and kicked Samuel's leg, bringing his boot down hard against the side of his lower leg. Samuel had howled in pain, squeezing his eyes shut while the skin around his mouth turned white. Raina had screamed as well and rose in protest but was quickly subdued, someone's backhand connecting with her mouth. She was sent flying, bouncing over the wooden bench seat, her skirt and feet in the air. She righted herself just in time to see two men hoist Samuel up under his arms and legs, his leg dangling at an odd angle, and heave him overboard.

Any effort to maintain courage fled in that moment as she watched helplessly as Samuel's arms flailed as he tried to tread water.

Her captors had a good laugh at his efforts, watching for a while as he sank periodically or was submerged by slow-moving waves. Eventually, they resumed their rowing, leaving Samuel to his fate. Raina watched the brave young man until he became just a speck on the horizon, and then until she could no longer see him. She found little comfort in the fact that in the twenty minutes it took for the expanding distance to erase him from sight, he was still afloat. But for how long could he actually keep his head above water with only one good leg to support him?

But her supposition that they might have abducted Samuel simply to prevent him from alerting Torsten of her dire circumstance, only to abuse him, giving him little chance to survive, roused grave questions: how did these kidnappers know that the fisherfolk wouldn't lift a finger to prevent her abduction? How were they so sure that none of those people would have alerted her husband? It reeked of treachery from one of Lochlan's own.

Her captors didn't speak to her, but then they spoke very little at all, even amongst themselves, and all conversations were quiet, intentionally so, Raina thought, not meant for her ears.

Several hours into the trip, a man with a wiry build and what she thought were soulless brown eyes approached her.

"I dinna want to strike ye, but I'll nae lose any sleep over it if ye force me to," he said. He lifted his hand, revealing bits of fabric, what she guessed would gag her.

Knowing these men and what she endured now were but the transport—presumably to whoever was behind the vile plot—Raina understood there was little cause to argue now.

They were minions, paid to follow orders. In all probability, they didn't care what shape she was in when she arrived at her final destination.

But not only was she gagged, but they bound her wrists and ankles, and to her horror, wrapped her tightly in several jute sacks. The rough material scratched against her skin, and the ropes they used to secure the sacks dug into her flesh, making her discomfort almost unbearable. Fear had truly taken hold now. Though the daylight was not completely obliterated—it poked through the tiny holes between the weave of the jute fabric—Raina was unable to see, and she felt utterly helpless.

About a quarter hour later, the rowing ceased, and the boat glided for a short distance before it came to a stop.

Her world became a series of sensations: the musty smell of the sacks, the constriction of the ropes, and the jarring motion as she was hoisted over someone's shoulder. She tried to remain calm, but panic clawed at her insides.

She was carried off the boat and across what seemed to be a dock, the sound of footsteps echoing on the wooden planks beneath her. The distinct scent of saltwater and fish hung in the air, confirming her suspicion that they had arrived at a larger harbor, not just a small coastal dock belonging to a clan or family. A regular and robust clamor of voices, the gentle lapping of water against wooden hulls, the creaking of mooring ropes straining against the tide, and the occasional clank of metal as boats jostled each other suggested a busy port. She would have thought they'd come to Montrose but imagined they had sailed too far, had been too long upon the water to have only arrived at Montrose, naught but forty miles south of Lochlan. Surely, they were much further away from home.

And how would Torsten ever be able to find her?

Raina struggled to make sense of her surroundings, but the darkness and confinement were disorienting. Each step her captor took felt like a countdown, bringing her closer to an unknown fate. The only thing she could do was focus on her breathing, trying to keep her fear from overwhelming her completely. The heat was stifling, her hair curling against the perspiration dotting her forehead.

At length, the creak of a door was heard and the man lugging her as if she were naught but a sack of grain ducked to enter a structure. He mounted a set of stairs, circular, she realized, and brought her to a second floor chamber, where the door was kicked open. Raina was unceremoniously dumped onto a hard surface, the impact jarring her body. She lay still, listening intently to any noise around her, hoping to glean even a tiny bit of information about where she was and what was to come.

But nothing was said and nothing was heard, either before or after the door was closed, leaving her lying on the floor in the darkness, still bound and tightly wrapped in jute sacks and rope.

Though the wait seemed interminable, not more than twenty minutes had passed since she'd been left before the door opened again. It was barely a second after this that a voice grumbled some harsh dissatisfaction.

"Sodding halfwits."

Raina froze, something about the voice tickling her awareness, being...familiar— though it was hard to tell, being muffled by the bag covering her and crowded out by the sound of the pounding of her heart. The ropes were soon sliced away and in one swift motion she was brought to a sitting position, manhandled really, before one of the sacks was lifted off her head.

Her fear was enormous, suspecting whoever had come and stood behind her now was an authority of sorts, with the power to complain about the way she'd been left. and now doing something about it.

She shook her head, trying to throw the hair off her face, having an initial impression of a chamber of timber walls and floor, devoid of furnishings and illuminated by a lone taper in a small holder sitting on the floor. She swung her head around, her eyes landing first on a pair of legs dressed in wool breeches and shoddy leather boots as the man came into view.

Raina lifted her face, her eyes widening as they took in the familiar features of the man standing before her. Her breath caught in her throat as recognition set in.

Exhibiting a limp he'd not owned when last she knew him, the man stepped forward and bent toward her, lowering the gag.

Raina spit out the rag from her mouth.

"Donald?" she whispered, the word croaked as a whisper.

Her brother, whom she had believed dead for more than a year, was here.

Fear for her own circumstance was stymied by confusion.

"You're alive," she said.

Straightening, her brother grinned. "I heard that only recently," he said, his voice lacking any warmth or joy, "that I was presumed dead."

"But how...what is happening? Why are you here?"

He tilted his head at her, raising his brow, waiting for Raina to discern the answer.

"You are behind this?" She gasped, struggling mightily with her bewilderment. "This and the previous attempt?" His expression answered while he did not. Her brother, Donald, stood there—she was still trying valiantly to process the shock of it. He looked older, much older and more haggard, closer in image to their father, the lines on his face deeper. His once thick frame was now leaner, and his lush auburn hair, of which he had always been so proud, hung limply around his long face. And though his eyes were the same intense brown as she remembered, they now held a hardness she did not recall.

"Did you...are you attempting to rescue me from Torsten?" She ventured, unable to conceive any other reason for her own brother to have kidnapped her. She would be happy to disabuse him of his erroneous notion that there was any need for this.

Her heart sank when Donald snorted an unkind chortle.

Sadness engulfed her. She should have been overjoyed at this happy turn of events—her brother lived!—but she sensed immediately in him some dark and twisted delight in her fear and confusion. At the same time, she was imbued with a sense that this had always been in him but she, in her youth and hopefulness, had refused to see it.

He seemed quite pleased to tell her, "Less an effort to rescue you, sister, than Lochlan."

"I don't..." she paused when the truth did dawn on her. "Oh. You mean to take back Lochlan from the de Grahams." She blamed the shock of discovering that her brother actually lived for her inability to understand the cause behind her abduction. "But why abduct me?" The grim set of his mouth and the cold calculation in his eyes advised that he'd hadn't merely removed her from potential harm, if he planned to lay siege to Lochlan.

"To bring your husband to heel," he answered. He narrowed his eyes at her. "It's the damnedest thing, Raina. It took me months to heel from Methven—one day I'll tell you all about the disgusting crone who dragged me to her putrid hovel and labored to save my leg; thought I fought for Robert Bruce, she did—and many more months to track down the MacQueen army, who'd been integrated with Acheson's forces while they, too, believed me dead. Left me for dead, those bastards, and the English king would not return them to me." He waved his hands dismissively, as if to suggest he'd gotten off track. "For more than a year I fought and struggled to get back to Lochlan—if only you knew of the harrowing peril I faced and overcame!—only to arrive exactly two days *after* Torsten de Graham and his army." He held up his forefinger and middle finger. "Two days, Raina. I was two days late."

Raina thought it wise not to point out that without a suitable army or one only composed of *those bastards*, there wouldn't have been anything he could have done to have prevented Torsten from seizing Lochlan.

"But lo, I hear my sister wed the dragon," he sneered. "Put up no fight, 'tis said—and if that alone was not cause for disgust, it seems she developed a taste for the enemy. She bows to his authority, smiles as she breaks bread with him, and warms his bed most willingly, I hear." He waved his hands again. "But I digress. And in truth, your affinity for the usurper works in my favor so I must applaud you for aiding my cause as you have. Or rather, I should say, his affinity for you works in my favor."

Torsten's affinity for her?

"Oh, Donald," she breathed, her tone filled with dread. "You have erred grievously."

He snickered, his face ugly at that moment. "I have not. What I have done is watch carefully. His preoccupation with you is obvious—amazing and incomprehensible, but obvious all the same. You, Raina, are his weakness."

A laugh broke from her, incredulous and untimely, but she could not prevent it. He may have watched, but he hadn't really seen. "Donald, I am thrilled that you are alive but if you do not release me, you will not be for long." She paused to consider if she were overthinking it, if Torsten would really respond so harshly—was his feeling for his wife large enough, did it exist outside the bedroom, that he would kill whoever dared to kidnap her? "Who are your spies?" She wanted to know.

"Lochlan belongs to the MacQueens, Raina. There are many inside who have not turned traitor." He stared down at her. "You don't believe he'll come for you."

"He will," she assured her brother. "He most certainly will." Not for her, but for justice, for having dared to take what belonged to him, for his pride. "He will not simply retrieve his wife. He will eradicate the threat entirely. He will kill you." She thought to appeal to him from a different angle. "Donald, come back to Lochlan *with* me," she suggested with some urgency. "As Torsten's ally. Lochlan is thriving under Torsten's stewardship." Under her own as well, she was proud to think, inside the keep anyway. "You could be a part of—"

"Only an idiot could nae turn a profit with Lochlan," was her brother's response. "Father had a relationship with Edward I, an understanding. They're gone now, old men turned to dust. Edward, the son, has returned my army to me, has promised me wealth beyond what father could have ever dreamed, and land inside England if I return Lochlan to a subject of his crown."

"Donald, if you think for one minute that Torsten will simply roll up his banners and march his army away from Lochlan, you are sadly mistaken. He'll come after me with an army numbering in the hundreds and how do you intend to fight against that?" The MacQueen army, from what she knew, had never known numbers even half so much.

"Do you have any idea where you are, sister?"

This gave Raina pause. "I don't," she answered after a moment.

Donald smirked. "But your husband will assume Montrose, will he not? A boat took you and looked to be sailing south. That makes Montrose the most likely place from where it came and where it would dock. But no, I am equipped with more sense than most. Of course, I am not simply expecting that your husband will hand over Lochlan, not immediately anyway. I expect it will take some time, which he will use stalling while he has his army searching high and low for me—for you. He won't find me, Raina," he said, enunciating those words. "So aye, eventually, he'll have to surrender Lochlan to me if he expects to recover his wife alive. Once I garrison *my* army in *my* house and"—he smirked again—"make use of the wee palisade recently constructed, he will not so easily retake Lochlan."

"And if he refuses to cede Lochlan?"

"I have no intention of harming you, sister, unless your husband forces me to do so." The expression on his face horrifically suggested he rather hoped Torsten would not come immediately.

"What—what do you mean?"

"I heard the craziest tale from some locals a while back—actually in Montrose, as a matter of fact. 'Bout some captor who demanded a ransom for a soldier. The lad's father argued against it, stalling, and asked if he was expected simply to believe they had his son. So the captor chopped off the lad's finger, the one wearing the family's ring, and sent that to the lad's father. Naturally, he paid up swiftly then."

"You mean to cut off my finger?"

Donald shrugged negligently, as if he'd not just suggested something so dishonorable, so horrid.

"You don't wear a ring, and I'm sure I don't need to prove that you are a captive. But then I imagine any harm done to you—and shown to him by way of a small body part delivered to him—should provoke him to turn over Lochlan to me. Of course, if he doesn't care for you or about you, that might only be a waste of body parts." He winked, a hideous and cruel action, displaying his lack of...everything: honor, shame, integrity. "Here's hoping you charmed de Graham, sister, better than you have any other person in your life."

Appalled by him, by this man who shared blood with her, who at one time had been under the gentle and agreeable influence of their sweet mother, Raina decided she didn't care what became of him. "He will kill you. And I will not stop him."

Donald's brows shot up into his forehead as he feigned a sinister delight. "Someone's found her backbone. Good for you, sister. That was a long time coming, eh?"

She didn't know for sure that he spoke of any particular moment in their history, or of her in general, but she wouldn't let him rebuke her without returning the same. Everything whispered and suggested years ago about him seemed now ridiculously plausible. "It was hard to project confidence," she said tersely, "when being accused of being a witch. More difficult yet to believe that my brother could be capable of heinous, wicked deeds. But Donald, I know what you've done."

He faltered for a moment, almost unnerved by her accusation, but managed to maintain his composure. "Do you divine things, being a witch?"

"I divine things by the power of common sense. I'm ashamed to admit that I suspected, though in truth I scarcely allowed those thoughts to intrude, refused to entertain the very possibility. But I know—I've always known—that it was you. That what you did to Barbara and likely to countless others, you did fatally to Clara, I suspect."

"You know nothing."

"I know that when my husband kills you, you will face your judgment from God."

"If you're worried for my soul—"

Raina scoffed at him, her smirk as ugly as his. "I'm not concerned where you spend eternity. That should be what keeps you awake at night, huddling in fear. You will be brought to justice, and since it wasn't here on earth for the crimes you committed, I am confident that you will pay for your sins in your eternal life."

Coolly, he said, "And that will be my burden to bear but not quite yet. You, of course, have your own burden, here and now. We shall see, I imagine, how well you endure it."

With that, Donald turned and exited the chamber. A key was heard turning the lock, trapping her inside.

"WE'VE SCOURED EVERY dock along the coast," Gilled reminded Torsten, "from here to Dundee and as far north as Aberdeen. Nae one of the harbormasters recall seeing a boat matching the description, and the locals are equally tight-lipped. Shite. It's as if they vanished into thin air."

Aonghas added, "We've checked the nearby keeps and burghs, every lord's holding within a day's ride. I had lads out searching the abandoned ruins near Kinneth and those north of Fordoun. Nothing, Torsten. Nae sign of Raina."

"The Kincaid at Stonehaven put out some men in his own birlinns," Gilles added, speaking of Gregor Kincaid, the laird of Stonehaven, a fellow patriot and ally. "He kens the east coast better than we, said he'd make some inquiries."

Unable to sit, Torsten paced in front of the high table while his officers watched. He was missing something, obviously. For two days and nights, they'd searched relentlessly. He'd scoured Montrose himself, had visited the inns and had spoken with the burgesses who operated the market and just about every merchant and tradesman he encountered.

He was desperate, and for the first time in his life, fearful, nearly broken by what felt like helplessness. But he wasn't about to quit. He only needed to discover what or where he'd missed, what had been overlooked.

Gilles sat in his usual chair behind the table, his countenance pale, while Aonghas sat three removed from him, wearing a frustrated, fierce expression. James leaned an elbow on the front of the table, his gaze following Torsten's footfalls. Uilleam stood, his stance wide, attentive, as confounded as any other by their inability to locate Lady Raina and her abductors.

James MacGilchrist stepped forward, his anxiety evident. "We've sent scouts to the forests and hidden coves. Thomas and two units rode for two days with nae rest, questioning travelers and merchants."

"What of the fisherfolk?" Torsten asked Rory.

The lad shook his head sorrowfully. "Half of them gone since we chased 'em off the beach. Only Artair and Edane and their crews remain. Nae fishing, nae processing now."

Uilleam added, "We chased the trail of a group of them, following the river inland, but laird, they're as ghosts, gone in the wind."

Torsten clenched his fists, his frustration palpable. "They are nae ghosts," he ground out, "and obviously hiding to prevent what they ken from being beaten out of them!" Reining in what felt like an impotent rage, he commanded, "Keep those patrols, track them again. Find them."

Gilles cleared his throat, swinging Torsten's gaze round to him.

"We ah, have to consider, lad," he stated, a graveness softening his gruff voice, "that she—all of them—may have been lost at sea. Samuel said they struck out toward the deep—"

"That is nae an option," Torsten growled. "It is nae possible. She's alive and hidden well, but she's nae gone." He knew that, believed that, with every fiber of his being. If she...*Jesu*, if she were gone, he'd feel it. He would not burn with fury to find her, he'd know deep inside, in some manner or sensation, he'd know if she were gone. Torsten's certainty that Raina was not dead stemmed from an unshakable connection he felt deep within his soul, a newly discovered notion that their bond was so profound that he would intuitively know if she were truly gone forever.

"Raina is alive," he reiterated tersely. "We keep on, retrace all our steps if need be, again and again, until she's recovered."

"Aye laird," Aonghas agreed.

The others murmured their understanding as well.

Torsten took his leave of them but heard James's words ere he exited the hall.

"It needs just one person to give up what they ken or one guid piece of intelligence about these kidnappers."

As it turned out, intelligence would play a role but not before Raina's captors themselves sent word to Lochlan Hall.

The communication came by way of messenger the next morning, who carried no missive but relayed verbally what he'd been paid to say. Having been picked up by Torsten's soldiers patrolling near Catterline, halfway between Lochlan and Stonehaven, the man was delivered to the great hall where Torsten and his officers were huddled over a large map of the area, sent down from Stonehaven by Gregor Kincaid.

"I'm to let ye ken first," the man said, nearly quaking in his shoes in the face of Torsten's dangerous scowl, "that yer lady lives for now but nae for long." He uttered these words with a shrinking stance and voice, likely expecting to be harmed for having to utter so menacing a message. When he was not struck down, he continued. "Yer lady will be exchanged only for Lochlan Hall. If agreeable to the terms, you should raise a plain white flag on the sea side of the keep and await further instructions."

He was questioned extensively, and aye, with a wee bit of violence, before the de Grahams were satisfied that he was indeed only a messenger, was not part of the plot itself, and that possibly the instruction for ransom, such as it was, had been forwarded by at least three other messengers, its source unknown.

Knowing now for certain that Raina was only bait, and possession of Lochlan Hall the goal, they were left with hardly any choice but to imagine that a considerable force and not only a small faction were behind the abduction, leading to the conjecture that a MacQueen might be responsible.

"Raina told me once her brother was only presumed dead," Torsten recalled to his men. "She dinna ken where the MacQueen army was. She never mentioned and I have nae idea if there are other kin, cousins, uncles...."

In short, they knew little more now than they had a few days ago.

After another day of fruitless searching, there came a missive from Gregor Kincaid.

Torsten scanned the written message before reading it aloud. "Strange happenings in Peterugie, at Deer Abbey," the note read in part. "The community of monks has numbered fifteen for decades, but reports suggest others have come recently, making use of some structures on their grounds. Might be worth investigating, my friend." He lifted his gaze to his men. "He says he'd investigate himself if his wife was nae due to give birth at any moment. His army is at our disposal, he offers."

"We have enough men and arms, itching to find and fight whoever this bastard is, but aye, we should nae dismiss the Kincaid's offer," Gilles reminded him. "Twas only this we lacked, some seemingly insignificant report to say something was nae right somewhere."

Nodding, Torsten instructed, "Ready the army to depart in thirty minutes."

Chapter Twenty

By dawn on the morning of the fourth day, Raina struggled to maintain hope, harassed by a diminishing certainty that Torsten would come for her.

Her brother was truly wretched. Though she was provided with sustenance once a day, no other care had been shown to her. She was forced to sleep on the hard timber floor, was not offered a blanket to chase away the icy chill of the night. Though a chamber pot had been provided she was not afforded either a cloth or water to wash her face or scrub her teeth. The door opened but once a day. Then, under the watchful gaze of one of Donald's minions, a timid lad who had yet to make eye contact with Raina entered to deliver food and a cup half filled with warm ale. He retrieved the plate and cup from the day before and emptied the chamber pot and that was all. Raina saw no one else.

Her brother had not returned, and any residual familial connection or love born of duty was quickly eroded.

Inside an empty chamber whose lone window was covered with planks and boards nailed to the wall, in creeping darkness every minute save for when the door was open, Raina struggled with many emotions. Fear had not completely left her, but it was often overshadowed by a deep sorrow. In those moments when she allowed herself to think that it wasn't that Torsten *couldn't* find her, but that he had chosen *not* to, the sadness became overwhelming. Mayhap he'd received Donald's demands—the return of his wife for the return of Lochlan Hall—and had simply decided he would not risk losing Lochlan Hall. Perhaps what she had considered genuine tenderness inside their bedchamber had been only a subconscious hope of hers, painting him with broad and wishful strokes.

Her fingers were raw, having spent hours and days scratching and pulling at planks, the wall, the floor, the boards covering the window, all to no avail.

Despite having little else to do but listen for hours on end, Raina had only gleaned a few scraps of information, and even those were mostly conjecture. She surmised that she was kept in a two-story structure or dwelling, likely not very large. When the door to her prison chamber was opened, she could see only the opposite timber wall, but not the stairs, other doorways, or windows. She had begun to recognize the sound of the lower, perhaps outer, door creaking and groaning as it was opened. The proximity of that door's sound to her own door, along with the echo of footsteps on wooden stairs—less muffled than they would be on stone steps—suggested a rather primitive structure, not a fortress or keep. In the ceiling of this chamber there was one sliver of space between two planks, which allowed for the thinnest slice of sunlight to creep along the floor throughout the day, by which Raina approximated the hour.

Several times she'd heard what had sounded like a number of mounted horses galloping nearby, suggesting her brother's army was close. Occasionally, she heard the distant murmur of voices, muffled by the walls but unmistakably male, often punctuated by harsh laughter or abrupt shouts. The clinking of metal suggested soldiers' armor or weapons being handled. Once or twice, she caught the faint smell of smoke and roasting meat, indicating a nearby campfire.

That was the extent of her knowledge about her own circumstance.

And while she didn't wholly believe her brother would actually kill her, she realized that the Donald who stunned her with his presence four days ago was a different animal entirely from the brother she'd known in her youth. At least far different from what her mother had allowed her to see, and later, from what she'd allowed herself to believe.

Late in the morning on the fourth day, mayhap an hour before her meal would arrive, she heard again the pulsing of hooves against the earth, but today the thudding was different.

The tremendous sound that suddenly erupted was unlike anything she'd heard or experienced. It was deafening, a cacophony of earth-shattering noise. Her heart raced, a wild mixture of hope and fear surging through her veins.

A call to arms echoed through the air, a primal roar, unmistakable and urgent. Her breath caught in her throat.

Torsten had come for her.

Raina crumbled with relief, tears springing to her eyes. But scarcely did she revel in her own joy before she was overcome with worry. She dropped to her knees and prayed for Torsten and for every de Graham man who'd just marched into battle. She startled at the first clang of metal against metal, imagining that to be Torsten's blade, and was forced to abandon prayer as the noise outside enlarged to a flurry of screeching, strident sounds as the battle was met in full. Men bellowed and screamed, horses whinnied, and the clash of metal continued, the sounds drawing closer as if the de Grahams pushed back on the MacQueens.

After what felt like an eternity but was possibly not yet a quarter hour of listening to the tumult outside, the door below her slammed open and footsteps bounded up the steps.

Raina faced the door, her hands fisted in anticipation, expecting Torsten to crash into the chamber in triumph.

But a key turned in the lock and it was her brother, Donald, who burst into the room.

His face was nearly unrecognizable, contorted into a mask of frenzied panic and seething anger. His eyes were wild with desperation. Wearing an ugly snarl, he seized Raina roughly and dragged her from the chamber and down the stairs and outside.

The scene that met her eyes was one of utter chaos as the de Graham army clashed ferociously with her brother's men. Bodies littered the ground, and the air was thick with the bitter stench of blood and sweat.

The blood drained from her face, never having witnessed such intensity or carnage. As her brother dragged her along, moving swiftly, swords flashed in the sunlight, while axes and maces swung with deadly precision. Horses, wild-eyed and frothing at the mouth, reared and kicked, their riders struggling to control them amidst the fray. The cries of the wounded and dying could be heard with the clang of weapons and the shouts of commanders. Raina saw the silhouette of what looked like an abbey in the distance, a watchful spectator to the violence unfolding before it. Her brother's army was in disarray, falling back under the relentless assault of the de Graham forces, who pushed forward with a disciplined ferocity, hacking and slashing to cut through the chaos.

She searched desperately for Torsten amid the fight, imagining his imposing silhouette would be easy to recognize but she could not find him.

Watching the fight rather than where she was going—where Donald was dragging her—Raina stumbled and fell, her arm jerked from her brother's grasp. Donald paused and yanked at her, first wildly at her hair until he clasped his hand around her arm again.

"Look!" He growled in her ear as he bent over her. "Look! See what your precious husband has done! This is his doing!" –As if he, himself, and his unsound mind had not perpetrated this carnage!

Raina resisted his desperate efforts to lift her to her feet, making herself limp as her gaze swept again, still, over the battlefield, searching for Torsten among the mounted green-tartan-ed de Grahams. But she and her brother and the building in which she'd been held were behind the scrambling MacQueen army, and a veil of dust had risen, enveloping the fight, obscuring much of her view. While Donald cursed and tugged at her, for a moment dragging her through the short grass, Raina's heart pounded, waiting, wishing fervently to see Torsten emerge from the swirling dust.

Her brother bellowed another expletive and heaved her upward at the same time he laid a dagger against her throat. Donald's desperation was palpable, surely having realized that the battle was lost. When she was on her feet again, he held her in front of him and shoved her forward toward the line of MacQueen horses, skittish and dancing where they were roped between many trees.

Just then, a thunderous roar rose above the deafening din of warfare. Raina's heart leapt at the sound of Torsten's voice, and she turned to find him, but the cold press of the blade against her skin stymied her desire. Donald's grip tightened, his movements growing more frantic as he dragged her toward the horses, likely meaning to make his escape. Raina struggled against him, trying to stall him, glancing backward all the while.

At the exact moment the blade cut into her neck, Torsten emerged from the churning dust like a ruthless specter, his eyes locking onto Raina with an intensity that sent a shiver down her spine. He bellowed again at the sight of her, this time a wordless war cry that resonated with raw power. Several de Graham warriors surged forward in his wake.

Donald was given pause, pulling Raina closer, using her as a shield.

Torsten's approach was relentless, his gaze never leaving Raina, his eyes filled with blazing fury—he, too, nearly unrecognizable for the ferocity of his expression.

The de Grahams closed in, forming an arc around Donald and Raina.

"Halt!" Donald called urgently. "Halt! Don't make me do something I might one day regret." He gripped a portion of Raina's hair at the back of her head, forcing her chin up, and pressed the knife closer to her neck.

Torsten brought his steed to a halt, seemingly calm to one who didn't know him.

"'Tis your end, man," Torsten vowed in a low voice.

"'Tis *her* end, wrought by you," Donald countered with a high-pitched nervousness, "if you do not back away." He moved again, striding slowly backwards, taking Raina with him. "Lay down your swords now!" He commanded, as if the idea had just come to him. "I'll release her when I'm far enough away."

Agreeably, and without hesitation, Torsten lifted his sword, bright red with the blood of MacQueens, and tossed it aside. He held up both hands then to demonstrate he had no other weapons. Aonghas, James, Rory, and several others she recognized did the same, relinquishing their arms.

Raina whimpered at their easy capitulation.

Her gaze returned to Torsten, her fear not relieved but mounting.

The raging fury behind her husband's blue eyes was tempered by a brief, gentle flicker, what she understood as a silent vow that he would not let any harm come to her.

TORSTEN'S RECENTLY born suspicion that Raina's own brother was behind her abduction and commander of the army they'd just decimated was supported by the obvious resemblance between Raina and her captor—the man was almost exactly her height, was of a slim build, and owned eyes shaped and colored as were Raina's.

For Raina's sake, he was sorry that her brother would be killed. For the senseless carnage behind him and the loss of his own men today, Torsten knew he would lose little sleep over the man's death—he would be naught but one less traitor breathing the same air as him.

He was sorrier that the man's final retreat was made so haltingly, and that Raina continued to know fear. He tried to let her know with a fleeting but intense look of reassurance, that he was in control, that it would be over soon.

He and his army, their numbers inflated by Gregor Kincaid's men, had not ridden hastily into battle. They'd scouted ahead and had set up a perimeter, and for the last two hours, De Graham and Kincaid archers flanked the entire scene. When came the battle, those archers had in truth done much of the work, having neutralized a quarter of the MacQueen force before Torsten and the charging armies had first drawn blood of their own. At this moment, at least four nearby archers, yet concealed, had Raina's brother in their sights, and were only waiting an opening.

Having realized her brother's intent—to get to the horses and ride off with Raina—Torsten knew their best opportunity for a clean shot was nearly upon them; Raina and her brother could not mount at the same time.

Though it pained him greatly, he did not move to pursue the coward fleeing with Raina but held his destrier still as his wife was dragged further away from him. The sight of the harm already done to her made Torsten want to murder the man with his own hands—she was more greatly disheveled than he had ever seen her, pale and wan, and with blood creased around her neck—but he would not risk any injury to Raina by engaging her brother himself.

Torsten knew of bit of unease as Raina's brother did not merely pick the closest horse to him but ducked under the rope and went several rows into the crowded throng of chargers, making the chances of an easy shot less likely. However, though the man was watchful, sending anxious glances at Torsten and his motionless men, he did not extend his gaze beyond what he believed to be the most immediate and discernable threat, and thus he was not aware of one of Torsten's own, Frederick, stealthily moving closer with his bow and arrow to have a better sightline.

Frederick crept on foot between James and Rory's horses, holding steady now while Rory angled his horse just a hair to block him from view. At the same time, a Kincaid archer positioned himself at the edge of the brush near where he'd been concealed.

And then Raina's brother made it almost absurdly easy. He pushed her up into the saddle ahead of him, jabbing impatiently at her bottom as she placed her foot into the stirrup. Once Raina was seated, and just as Donald MacQueen hoisted himself up, two arrows flew through the air with a familiar swoosh, striking their mark in Donald's back. He staggered, his grip on the pommel failing, and he tumbled to the ground, clutching at the dirt as he landed.

Raina screamed, her mouth wide with horror. The horse beneath her and those nearby reacted violently, rearing and snorting in fear and confusion.

Torsten and his men sprang into action, leaping from their destriers. Aonghas, having retrieved his sword, hacked at the rope penning in dozens of horses, causing them to burst forth in a frenzy of whinnies and pounding hooves. Spooked and agitated, a few chargers reared and bucked, their eyes wide with fear and their manes flying wildly.

The presence of Torsten and his men slowed the small stampede somewhat. Torsten ran toward Raina, able to latch his hand on the harness before the horse beneath her might have bolted. While his men shouted and waved their arms, directing the stampede away from Raina, Torsten swiftly pulled her from the saddle and into his arms. He held her tight against his chest until the last of the horses had raced by him and then bore her away from the ghastly sight of her fallen brother, whose body had been mercilessly trampled underfoot.

In front of the building in which she'd been held prisoner—an abandoned and decrepit outlying farmstead, was his guess—Torsten went down on one knee and set Raina down. She clung to his arms even as she was released from his embrace. Before he met her gaze, he gently took her face in his hands and lifted it, bending to inspect the blood at her neck, judging it an incidental scrape of the blade by a desperate man.

Satisfied that the wound was not grave or in need of immediate attention, he met her watery eyes. The torment of the past five days was evident in the dark circles beneath them. Her once bright gaze was haunted, staring back at him with a hollowness that tortured him. Her hair, tangled and matted from neglect, framed her pale, dirt-smudged face. Her soiled and torn léine, a purple bruise on her cheek, and the general air of exhaustion he noted spoke volumes about her ordeal.

Torsten's heart ached for her. He brushed a thumb across her unmarred cheek, wiping away a tear. "You're safe now, Raina. 'Tis done."

She breathed shakily, and tried to nod, but it was wobbly.

Torsten turned to his hovering men, stretching out his hand. "Water," he requested. Rory jumped forward, setting his horn into Torsten's hand. Uncapping it, Torsten handed it to Raina, who drank thirstily.

When she was done, she returned the flask to Torsten and sat wearily, drained, her shoulders curved inward.

She lifted her brown eyes to him.

"I...I didn't know if you would come," she said, her voice weak.

Torsten froze, a riot of thoughts and emotions responding to her statement, words that cut him deeply.

Aye, they had never spoken of love or of any affection, and their connection, though warm in moments of intimacy, was built on shaky ground, but how could she have doubted him? And Christ, what torture must she have endured, captive and waiting, unsure if her own husband would even bother to save her?

More stung by her words than he cared to admit, he replied tightly, "Ye are mine to protect."

HE LEFT ALMOST HALF of his army behind to clean up the aftermath of the battle. The men set about their grim tasks: tending to the wounded, burying the dead, and scouring the field for any remnants of the conflict. They gathered weapons and armor, sorted through the scattered supplies, and ensured that the fallen de Graham and Kincaids received proper rites.

As ever, Torsten was sorry for any loss of life, but knew some gratefulness that his own losses, including de Grahams and Kincaids, were not larger. Conversely, the MacQueen army had been decimated, its number reduced by more than half. The surviving MacQueens would be offered the chance to swear fealty to him and Robert Bruce. If accepted, his own army would be bolstered by the additional numbers, and pardons would be granted after each man had proven himself loyal to the de Graham name and Scotland. If they refused, and depending upon the vehemence of their refusal, they would either be banished from Lochlan Hall or imprisoned.

With Raina in his arms upon his destrier and surrounded by half his army, Torsten returned to Lochlan Hall. She'd asked almost immediately after Samuel, and after assuring her the lad would be fine once his leg healed, Torsten gave her a wee bit of grief for having disregarded Samuel's command to run and save herself initially when her abductors had stormed the beach.

"'Twould have meant Samuel's death," she countered woodenly, "and I could not have lived with myself."

He did not have the heart to tell her that the lives lost today might have been spared had she managed to escape then. Given her understandable lack of experience with conflict, strategy, and decision-making, he recognized that she was unlikely to comprehend necessary sacrifices and the consequence of actions made in the heat of the moment.

While Raina slept most of the ride, Torsten wrestled with thoughts he'd ignored over the past few days. His dogged focus on finding Raina had precluded any consideration of a background truth, which he was compelled to deliberate now.

The recent ordeal of her kidnapping had shaken him in ways battles never had. Torsten clenched his fists around the reins, feeling the weight of the truth press upon him. As laird and commander, he was expected to be resolute, unwavering in his decisions, yet he knew now that his actions to rescue Raina had been driven not just by duty, but by desperation, by a fear that had clawed at him like some unseen beast.

Tender emotion was to blame, was a vulnerability, he'd come to understand. It clouded his judgment, turned his fierce determination into a desperate frenzy to protect her at any cost.

His men had looked to him for guidance, and he had led them, but each decision felt heavier, laden with the knowledge that his heart was now exposed, that decisions and actions had felt more frantically reactive than intuitively sound.

Could he afford such weakness in times of war? Torsten closed his eyes and felt the wind whip through his hair, struggling to reconcile the role he'd single-mindedly cultivated for more than a decade, an efficient, detached, unyielding leader with the man who had felt a soul-deep agony when Raina was torn from him. He had not spoken of love to her, nor had she to him, yet in the depths of his heart, he knew.

And yet...love, he feared, had already begun to weaken him.

MANY HOURS LATER, RAINA welcomed Torsten's fierce thrust as he drove deep inside her. He withdrew and plunged again. He rolled his hips and rubbed himself against her until she cooed in surrender.

"Oh, God," she moaned, her neck arched to his kiss, "that feels good."

In truth, he'd resisted at first, had said she was weak and fatigued, and needed to recover. Raina had pursued him, had brazenly run her hand over his naked chest and beneath his braies.

"Raina," he'd warned, his body stiffening.

"Torsten, I need this. I need you."

He'd relented at her plea, his touch tender and careful, but Raina craved more than gentleness. She yearned for him, needing to feel his power, his energy—to be enveloped by his strength and desire. She sought a return to wholeness, normalcy, and vitality once more. She wanted to forget.

After his initial reluctance, he'd complied willingly, soon as hungry as she it seemed so that their coupling was frantic and quick, both of them possessed.

"*Jesu*, how I feared for ye," he'd admitted a moment after his release, when, spent and perspiring, he dropped his head to her chest.

Raina likened so fierce a statement to an admission of feelings. She entertained a fleeting thought, scarcely gladdened that their marriage had needed a tragedy to bring them closer.

Or so she imagined in that moment, and sadly, only for a moment. She waited, hoping more distinct words would come, but they did not.

In the ensuing days, he began to distance himself. At first, she didn't recognize it, brushing off his late returns to their bedchamber and the absence of his usual kiss and caress as residual effects of their recent calamity—the tragic loss of lives in Peterugie. She, too, struggled with haunting memories and fears from her captivity, often besieged by intrusive thoughts that started with "What if...?"

But as his touch grew more sporadic and his aloofness extended to the supper hour, Raina's unease deepened. Soon, his withdrawal permeated every hour of the day, and his habit of slipping into bed late and rising before she woke became a regular thing. With each passing day, Raina's fragile hope waned. They weren't making progress, they were regressing.

The distance between them felt insurmountable, the void widening with every day.

And how could she question him? He'd warned her, had he not, that he had little to give, that he wouldn't allow emotion.

And then one day, a fortnight after her rescue, Torsten announced his intent to depart Lochlan Hall. By this time, having resigned herself to their loveless and now cool union, Raina was not surprised but the pang of sorrow sliced deep.

"You and your army?" She questioned. A wee bit of hope might be retained if he left without his army, meaning he had every intention of returning.

"Aye," he answered, avoiding her gaze. "The king has sent a messenger. He intends to expand his warfare against houses loyal to England, against Comyn's followers. We're to meet him anon upon Carrick lands."

Raina had some suspicion that even if the king had not called him to duty, Torsten would have left eventually. Soon.

Boldly, she questioned, "And will you return to Lochlan Hall?"

"We'll see what the king demands of me," he hedged. "I imagine when next the king grants me leave, my time should be spent at Glenbarra Brae, where I have nae stepped foot in—"

"Will you return *ever* to Lochlan Hall?" She persisted rigidly.

Torsten clamped his lips and met her gaze, his blue eyes unfathomable.

"I dinna ken."

Tears pricked at the corners of her eyes, but she held them back, unwilling to let him see her pain. She nodded.

"I wish you Godspeed, Torsten," she said, her voice steady despite the weight of sorrow crushing her.

Chapter Twenty-One

As the days grew shorter and the chill of autumn settled over Lochlan Hall, Raina threw herself into her duties as chatelaine with renewed vigor. Having no other choice, lest she go mad for mourning something that had never stood a chance, she found solace and purpose in the responsibilities that came with administering to Lochlan Hall.

Each morning, Raina rose before dawn, her breath visible in the crisp air as she donned her woolen shawl and made her way to the great hall. There, she met with Peigi as she was coming in, discussing the day's tasks and addressing any issues that had arisen. She took pride in ensuring that every detail was attended to, from the maintenance of the castle grounds to the well-being of the servants, whose numbers were steadily growing.

Aonghas and Uilleam had remained behind with another forty soldiers, but Raina didn't know whether Torsten intended to ensure her safety or merely to secure Lochlan Hall as a de Graham stronghold. The construction of the watchtowers and the ongoing fortification of the palisade, which grew taller and more impenetrable by the day, suggested a strategic defense. Raina reassured herself that with forty men, supplemented by the locals if necessary, they could hold off a siege for a considerable time.

The MacQueen men from her brother's army—Lochlan's army now, she reminded herself—had joined the king's forces with Torsten. Aonghas had hinted that Torsten didn't fully trust them yet and wanted to safeguard against them causing trouble at Lochlan Hall if they'd remained.

"They'll nae challenge him out there in the field," Aonghas had remarked. "They'll learn to look to him, to depend on him for their safety, for their very lives."

Though Raina still looked to Peigi for advice on household matters, she now freely turned to Aonghas and Uilleam for support in other areas, such as estate management, security, and strategic planning. The de Graham men had become dear to her, with Aonghas and Uilleam specifically emerging as her champions and cohorts. She found herself consulting with them on matters beyond Peigi's expertise, such as overseeing the construction of new defenses, managing disputes among the tenants, and ensuring the overall security of Lochlan Hall.

She valued their intelligence and their opinions, seeking their counsel on everything from the best locations for the new watchtowers to the most efficient methods for storing and rationing provisions for the winter. Their insights were invaluable, and their unwavering support gave her the confidence to make decisions that would benefit the estate and its people.

In every meaningful way, Raina was laird of Lochlan Hall. She felt that way, and she reveled in both the challenge of it and the reward of it.

As often as time allowed, Raina took time to visit the tenants on the estate. She listened to their concerns, offered assistance where needed, and made sure that their needs were met. She liked to think that her relationship with the peasants was improving, and she found that she had grown considerably in her ability to manage these interactions with confidence and grace.

Despite the many improvements in and around Lochlan Hall, and her own personal growth, there had been little reconciliation between Raina and the fisherfolk, not all of them. Those who'd fled after her abduction, including Duncan, Kenneth, and several others, had not returned, and she suspected some or all of them had been her brother's spies. Over time, she had adopted an aspect of Torsten's leadership style, ruling the fishermen with a disconnected, authoritative approach. She established the rules and ensured they were followed, understanding that their respect or approval was secondary to maintaining order and efficiency. Aside from Artair and Edane and their crew, the fishers' disdain for her lingered, but Raina was gradually learning not to let it affect her. Her focus remained steadfast on her duties and the well-being of Lochlan, rather than seeking validation from those unwilling to offer it and unworthy to give it.

She no longer visited the beach on Mondays. At the insistence of both Aonghas and Peigi, those seeking payment were now required to come to her in the hall. After the incident of her kidnapping, where the fisherfolk had stood by, seemingly pleased with her suffering and relieved they were not targeted, she refused to go out of her way to accommodate them. They were now compelled to come to Lochlan Hall, and sometimes, out of sheer defiance, Raina would make them wait for up to thirty minutes before attending her duties.

There was another reason, however, that prevented her from making the trek to the beach. Though she had always considered the trail down the cliff face more challenging than treacherous, Peigi and Aonghas had repeatedly urged her to consider the danger it now posed, to respect her condition.

Her condition, they called it.

Aye, she was pregnant with Torsten's child.

Her child, truly, she thought with prideful vehemence, allowing herself to embrace the joy of impending motherhood. Though she mourned what she believed to be true, that Torsten would never return to Lochlan, in this new life growing within her she found such great solace. Each flutter of movement filled her with joy and hope, painting a future ripe with the promise of love.

As the weeks passed, Raina found herself immersed in a quiet, wonderfully uneventful life at Lochlan Hall. The winter that followed was blessedly mild, the chill softened by occasional days of unexpected warmth. The castle walls, fortified against the elements, stood steadfast against the gentle winds that swept in from the coast. Inside, the hearths crackled with warmth and Raina's belly grew, stirring with life.

Raina came to realize that she thought of Torsten less and less as time went on. While she freely acknowledged that she loved him, she found solace in cherishing the small piece of him she had—the child growing within her. Yet, she deliberately pushed aside memories of him, knowing that dwelling on his absence would only bring unnecessary pain. To again pursue any idea of love would be to abandon reason altogether.

With the passage of time, Raina found herself less plagued by the grief over what might have been. She looked back on their time together with a sense of clarity, recognizing it as her first experience of a broken heart—and silently praying it would be her last. Aye, she ached at times to see him, to hear his voice, to be warm and safe in his strong arms, to know his kiss, but she knew that yearning for Torsten's presence would only reopen wounds that time had begun to heal.

If Torsten ever did return, he would discover what Raina had: she was self-sufficient. She was capable and powerful. She didn't need him or anyone to carve out this most rewarding life for herself. After only months she considered herself older and wiser, certainly beyond an age and mentality that would allow her to attach any hope to his return. He might one day come—anything was possible—and she might even allow him to plant his seed again, desiring another child, but she would stand steadfast and detached as she waved him goodbye when he inevitably left again.

Sweet heavens, but I've become as cold as Torsten, she thought.

No matter, though. All her love and joy would be reserved for her child or children.

She didn't need Torsten. And she certainly wasn't foolish enough to give her heart twice.

NOT A DAY PASSED THAT he didn't think about her. Hell, there was scarcely an hour that he did not entertain some thought of Raina. And this, despite the dreary and worrying five months passed entrenched with Robert Bruce's royal army.

Securing Lochlan Hall, as Torsten had been directed, was part of Robert Bruce's strategic plan. After the death of Edward I, Bruce aimed to capitalize on Edward II's apparent reluctance to continue his father's aggressive policies against Scotland. Bruce pursued daring campaigns to rally support and reclaim territories held by English forces.

However, Bruce's participation was minimal due to a severe illness, confining him to his tent and often necessitating transport by litter. His brother, Edward Bruce, frequently commanded the army in his stead, while the troops, a defiant eight hundred, prayed for the king's recovery.

Torsten and his seasoned warriors played a crucial role in Bruce's raiding tactics and strikes against English strongholds, disrupting supply lines and communications between places like Carlisle and Ayr. Throughout the autumn and mild winter, they engaged in battles at locations such as Strathbogie and Slioch. Despite being outnumbered, these engagements highlighted Bruce's tactical brilliance and the faithful spirit of his followers. Although Bruce's illness often prevented him from leading in action, he remained decisive in his directives, with his brother, Torsten, and loyal knights, Robert Boyd and Alexander de Lindsey, maintaining their faith in him.

Still, winter campaigns were long and grueling, exacerbated by relentless cold and dwindling resources. As late winter approached, the challenges once again raised doubts about the pursuit of Scottish independence—not in terms of their dedication, but in light of the king's ongoing illness. Although, Torsten admitted, albeit reluctantly, that perhaps there was a slight faltering in his commitment as well. Aye, he was deeply troubled by the inexplicable shift within himself; his heart no longer burned with the same ferocity for the fight as it once had.

On a quiet night at the end of February, Torsten and Gilles and a few others sat round their campfire, hidden deep in the fastnesses of Ayr, keeping their own council. It was during these moments of enforced idleness that thoughts of Raina intruded most persistently.

Leaning his back against the trunk of a birch tree, he sat, using part of his plaid as a cushion between himself and the icy ground. He stared into the flickering flames of the small fire and pictured Raina's smile. More often than not, this was the image he brought to mind. True, he often imagined her in the throes of passion, but even then she was smiling.

"Night after night, ye make nae sound," Gilles said, interrupting Torsten's pleasant reverie. "Ye just stare into the flames and...what? I've nae ever see ye so pensive, nae in all the years I've ken ye."

Torsten shrugged and frowned, admitting only, "Everything is... I dinna ken, it's different now." Nearly worrisome.

Gilles gaped in response before he harrumphed loudly. "Of course it's different now," he stated heatedly. "Ye have someone waiting for ye—though I dinna blame her if she's nae, nae after the way ye closed her out. And what was that? Aye, nae for me to meddle in, but damnation, she could nae have made herself any more transparent, what she felt for ye. Christ, but ye trampled all over that, did ye nae? Ye with yer cold demeanor. That farewell ye gave her at the gate dripped with ice colder than any we've seen this winter. And I'm left to wonder if ye're more fond of battle than of a woman, able to resist those brown eyes of hers and the way she sets 'em on ye, all earnest and hopeful."

Stunned by the vehemence of Gilles's argument, it took a minute for Torsten to figure out how the conversation had taken such a drastic turn.

"I *meant* it's different now, with the king unwell. It raises regrettable questions of *what if* and *what next.*"

Across the fire, huddled deep in his plaid, Gilles shrank a bit. "Och," he said, his tone mild now, as sheepish as Torsten had ever heard his captain. "I kent ye meant it's different for another reason."

"Aye, ye made that verra clear," Torsten said crossly.

A long moment of silence passed before Gilles scowled and directed his gaze at Torsten. "But why *did* ye do that? Why were ye so cool to her after we recovered her from the fiend, her brother? *Jesu*, that was awful, watching her shrivel up a wee bit each day. I ken it was nae heading in that direction before she was abducted. I kent ye was falling in love with her and why nae? There's nae one damn thing about her that would scare ye off. In fact, I—"

"*Jesu*, Gilles, cease," Torsten growled.

""Aye, I will. Nae my matter to mind anyhow. I just wonder what changed yer—"

"I canna be in love with her," Torsten snapped, in part with some hope simply to shut him up. "Christ, Gilles, she was used as a pawn. It made me weak. I have an army to command, and canna afford to rule by my heart and nae my head. Love dinna have any place in...Shite, the men need a leader they can depend on, not one distracted by his emotions."

Another pause before Gilles persisted. "So...ye *were* in love with her?" He asked, treading carefully.

Were? Torsten thought. *Am. Will always be.*

"Leave it alone, Gilles," Torsten said.

"By the saints, but you two are entertaining," said a voice from the shadows. "And this conversation is fascinating."

Simultaneously, Torsten and Gilles—and the others nearby who were no doubt equally engrossed in the vexing conversation—swiveled their heads to find the king encroaching upon their camp.

The king's presence commanded immediate attention. Despite his frailty, his regal bearing was evident. Aye, his once robust frame had thinned, and his face was lined with pain and fatigue, but his eyes burned with his invincible spirit.

Torsten and his men rose swiftly to their feet, briefly bowing their heads.

Robert Bruce waved his hand to dismiss the formality and stepped closer to the fire. Having endured months of winter campaigning and the unfortunate illness, the king appeared in weather-beaten attire, a sturdy woolen cloak, now faded and patched, draped over a simple yet durable tunic and breeches of rough-spun fabric. His boots, once polished and fine, were now caked with mud and scuffed from the harsh terrain. A weathered belt was cinched at his waist, adorned only with the essentials of survival—a dagger and a pouch for provisions. His hair, once neatly trimmed, now fell unkempt, windswept and graying at the temples. He was, despite all this, a remarkable figure, with eyes that glistened with intelligence and a devotion to his cause.

"You've served us well, Torsten," the king began, his voice weakened but resolute, carrying over a loud pop in the crackling fire. "It's time you return to Lochlan Hall and see to your new wife, loved or not."

As Torsten frowned with surprise, pondering the king's unexpected command—and ready to do bodily harm to Gilles for his interference!—Robert Bruce stood by the fire, his gaze entrapped by the glowing flames.

"I, myself, was given cause to wonder," the king said after a thoughtful pause, "what had brought about the transformation in you. I recalled Torsten de Graham as a stalwart and commanding presence, resolute in every decision and unyielding in adversity. Yet now, there is a discernible shift—a depth of introspection and hesitation that I had not seen before. Turmoil lives within and now I understand its source."

Gilles's harrumph did not go unnoticed. Torsten seriously intended to throttle him.

"Aye, I should have guessed it might be a woman—even better, a wife," said the king. "And now you think that caring, that loving someone, makes you weak. That it exposes a chink in your armor for your enemies to exploit."

Torsten's jaw clenched, but he said nothing, though he supposed his silence served as an acknowledgment. Instead he imagined himself skinning Gilles alive.

"May I?" The king requested, indicating an empty seat, a short and standing log.

"Please do, sire," Gilles invited.

The king sat and drew his cloak about him. "When they captured my wife, my sister, my daughter... I felt the same. I raged against the vulnerability, the pain of it. I blamed my love for them, thinking it was my undoing."

He paused, letting the words sink in. Torsten finally looked up, meeting Bruce's steady gaze across the fire.

"But I learned something, de Graham," Bruce said, his voice softer now. "Love doesn't weaken us. It makes us stronger. Stronger than any armor or sword. Fighting for glory, conquest, duty, or honor—all have their limits. But fighting for those you love, for what awaits you at home, gives you boundless strength." Surrounded by the de Grahams, apt pupils in the moment, the king lifted his hand from inside his cloak, using it to highlight his speech. "Loving deeply isn't a weakness; it's your greatest strength. You distance yourself now to protect her—and yourself, you believe—but true protection comes from letting love fortify you. Let it guide your sword, steady your hand, and ignite your heart. Only then will you be truly invincible. And I need you invincible, de Graham. Go home. Go to Lochlan, where apparently a lovely young wife waits eagerly. Let yourself love her," he said, and grinned, "or as Gilles says, *if* she'll allow it. Love is not the enemy. Fear is." He paused before adding, "And then come back to me. By then I shall be of sound body and ready to harry Buchan as I've been meaning to do."

While Torsten digested this—and aye, suffered a wee bit of shame to be schooled in so basic a human function by a man, king or no, who was several years younger than him—Gilles suffered no qualms about his meddling, but daringly persisted with it, now directed at the king.

"Why do ye nae pursue the freedom of yer own wife?" He asked.

King Robert smiled grimly. "I expect I'll hear about it from her, brave lass that she is. But nae, and you understand why. 'Tis exactly what Edward—the son now, and all of England—wants, hopes. I haven't the resources presently. Aye, we can take these castles and harass this region, having these hundreds of men, can keep on with this irregular warfare. But a march to England would require ten times that." He frowned a bit and became reflective. "I cannot risk that it wouldn't lead to harsher treatment or even execution. I've resolved that I need to be cautious and consider the potential repercussions. My best efforts at the moment are employing diplomatic channels and political pressure to negotiate the release of my kin."

Not yet willing to give up his position with the king, knowing the royal army, such as it was at the moment, would be drastically reduced without the de Grahams, Torsten attempted to put off his leave-taking. "I can abide here for now, sire, and return to Lochlan when you are returned to robust health."

Robert Bruce shook his head. "Nae, sir. By then I'll want to move and fight again. Go now, as we idle. Spring will break soon; this bothersome ailment shall depart as the snows melt, I trow." He turned and fixed his steady brown-eyed gaze on Torsten. "I do not ever doubt your physical courage, but I need you to address the mental aspect of it. Go home and discover the heart of it in your wife."

Torsten had learned over the last year that best practice when disagreeing with the king was to challenge once and then accept his king's decision, and so he pressed no more.

Robert Bruce, renowned for his perseverance and ambition but not generally his wit, rose from the log and clapped his hands, announcing, "And that will be all tonight for lessons in gentle humanity. Good evening, sirs."

Torsten and his men rose to their feet once more and did not resume their seats until the king had disappeared into the shadows whence he'd come.

When Torsten sat, he glared at Gilles, who smirked irreverently at him.

"Aye, and ye're welcome," Gilles said, his impudence unmatched. "Least now, we can spend what remains of the winter nice and warm at Lochlan. And mayhap ye winna mess it up this time."

"I'm going to take you out to sea when we get home," Torsten vowed, his voice a low growl, "and leave you there—and in worse shape than Samuel was left."

Gilles chuckled in response. "Aye, I imagine ye will. And home, is it now?"

Torsten was given pause. *Home.*

Aye, Lochlan was home.

Because Raina was there.

As the camp settled into quiet and the night's chill deepened, Torsten found himself grappling with this stunning realization and more thoughts of Raina. The prospect of returning to her brought a slow, unexpected pleasure, a warmth that fought against the winter's cold. He couldn't deny the way his heart quickened at the thought of seeing her again, of hearing her voice, of simply being near her.

But alongside this excitement was a persistent doubt. Was he truly capable of love? Could a warrior, hardened by years of battle, truly open his heart to another?

Whenever he thought of her, a soft, tender ache spread through him. It was more than mere attraction or duty. It was a longing—one he'd steadfastly tried to ignore—a deep-seated desire to be with her, to protect her, to share his life with her. Could it be that this was love? The way she lingered in his thoughts, the way her smile brightened even his darkest days, the way he yearned to hold her close and know her kiss again.

He remembered the way she looked at him, her eyes full of hope and affection, even after all the pain she had endured, plenty of it wrought by him. She had touched something inside him, something he had thought long buried under the weight of his responsibilities and the brutality of war. She made him feel alive in a way he hadn't felt in years.

This yearning, this passion, this untiring need to be with her, to cherish her, to make her smile—if this was not love, what else could it be?

Any resolve to embrace these feelings did not happen immediately, did not in a moment displace his long-standing determination to ignore what he felt. But over the next few days as he guided his army toward Lochlan—winter marches were always slower than any other time of year owing to the shorter days and harsher conditions—Torsten decided he would go home to Raina not merely as a soldier returning from war, but as a man willing to open his heart.

For the first time in a long while, the future seemed bright, filled with possibilities.

He would see her soon. He would make things right.

Chapter Twenty-Two

"Who knows, Aonghas," Raina asked, "when next we'll have an opportunity to visit the beach? It might be months again before the weather gives us such a fine day."

Looking decidedly uncomfortable, Aonghas shook his head. "I have to put my foot down, milady," he said, though he sounded more apologetic than confident. "Aye, ye said ye'll use the far path, where the decline is gentler, but I dinna ken ye should be traipsing through the woods and the dunes, which may verra well be covered in ice."

Raina winced, sorry to inform him, "I appreciate your concern but I'm going, and since I don't suspect you will use force to prevent me, I suggest you retrieve your heavier cloak to stand against the wind."

Aonghas sighed, defeated. "Fine. But wait here, will ye? I'll nae ever speak to ye again if ye set off without me."

Raina smiled but only a little bit. "As I would not risk such a thing, I will await your return."

Aonghas exited the hall and Raina turned at the sound of chuckling behind her.

Peigi approached, wiping her hands on her apron. "Sure and ye keep him on his toes."

Raina shrugged, donning the cloak she'd brought down with her. "I didn't ask him to be my keeper." But then, she was still a wee bit hesitant about going anywhere outside the keep by herself.

"Dinna need to," Peigi replied. "He and Uilleam have made ye their life's work."

The housekeeper stopped a few feet in front of Raina and plopped her hands on her hips, which informed Raina a grousing was forthcoming.

"Milady, I dinna ken how much more I can take," Peigi began. "I dinna ken Nell will work out in the kitchen—or anywhere near me for that matter. Christ, and her bairns, with their brooding gazes, always lurking underfoot, never speaking—it ain't right, something's wrong with those two."

Raina bit back a smile. While she hadn't expected that Nell's transition from fisher to house servant would progress seamlessly, she still believed this was a better circumstance for her. To Nell's credit, she'd swallowed her pride and had approached Raina—with a mended though still limping Samuel by her side—to request a position inside the hall, as Raina had once offered. Citing the winter weather, much harsher upon the beach itself and her lads' threadbare garb, and wearing a grim expression, as if she expected to be denied, Nell had asked if the offer still stood. Raina had been happy to comply.

"Her lads are shy," Raina said now to Peigi. "Nell's husband was heavy-handed, if you recall. They simply need time to understand that there is no danger and that not every man will speak with his fists."

"Aye, and to that, Cook's barking is nae helping. The weans jump and cry every time Cook opens his mouth."

"Hm. I didn't think of that," Raina admitted. "Let me give it some thought. I'm sure we can find a different position and circumstance for Nell that better suits her...special needs."

"What would suit, milady, is if she'd close her trap for at least five minutes every hour. Saints in heaven, but she dinna shut up. All day long with her blathering. I canna take it, find myself avoiding the kitchen and my own duties."

"All right. I'll think of something today and we'll move her out of the kitchen." She retrieved her basket from where it sat on one of the trestle tables, having some idea that she might collect seaweed for either the apothecary or the kitchen, and mayhap some nettles if she found them.

"I ken same as ye, she had nae business down there on the beach, nae with her bairns hanging on her skirts—nae place for them so small—but she dinna fit in the kitchen, milady. Too disruptive."

"Understood," said Raina, supposing Nell might be better suited to house maid than kitchen chores.

Aonghas returned then and Peigi waved her away. "Go on with ye then, though I dinna ken what fancy strikes ye, wanting to be down on the beach yerself."

"There's beauty and glory and peace down there, Peigi," Raina called over her shoulder as she followed Aonghas to the door. "You should try it sometime."

Peigi's response chased Raina from the keep. "As if I've got time for that!"

"Prickly one, innit she?" Aonghas commented.

Raina chuckled, drawing her hood close; though the sky was clear, and the sun was fine, the wind was a wee bit dastardly. "*Nell* is prickly," Raina corrected. "Peigi is...she's simply bossy."

"Should've been an army commander," Aonghas supposed.

"Imagine coming up against Peigi MacGregor and her army on the field."

"I'd run the other way, milady."

Raina chuckled. "Me, too."

Raina's cloak billowed about her as they walked, turning right beyond the gate to pursue the northern trail. Before they entered the trees she gladly tipped her face up to the sun, her cheeks warmed despite the wild breeze.

Raina felt the familiar surge of tranquility as the sound of waves crashing against the shore filled the air. At the top of the slope, just above the dunes, she paused to take in the scene, the sea's vast expanse meeting the horizon, the crisp air invigorating her.

"There's something restorative about the sea," she mused aloud.

"But nae quiet," he called loudly as they descended, to be heard above the sea's roar.

Upon the beach eventually, Raina strolled just above the mark of the furthest-reaching wave, bending and collecting the kelp, which lay in abundance along the shore. The strands were slick and cold to the touch, and bending was not so easy these days, making the process slow.

Aonghas idled about, occasionally picking up a stone and tossing it into the waves or poking at interesting shells with his boot. It had taken weeks and weeks, but she'd finally gotten through to him that she was expecting a child, but was not an invalid, which she supposed accounted for his ability today to leave her to her own devices, not jumping to help with every little task.

Her eyes lit up when she spotted a patch of sea fennel. "Fortune favors us today, Aonghas," she called out, holding up the bunch of green, waxy leaves.

He glanced back at her. "Ye've an eye for treasures, milady." The wind tugged at his cloak, but he seemed content to let it play its mischief.

Before Raina removed her gaze from him, she saw his smile fade, replaced by a gaping mouth as he stared beyond her, higher, beyond the dunes by which they'd come.

Raina whirled around, her cloak blown all in front of her.

And her breath caught in her throat at the sight.

Torsten had returned, and stood now, a solitary figure upon the low cliff, bathed in winter's bright sunlight. His silhouette was striking against the clear blue sky, his broad shoulders and tall frame commanding attention. The wind tugged at his dark cloak, revealing the glint of his armor beneath. His hair, longer than when he'd left, was tousled by the breeze, and his eyes seemed to be fixed directly upon her.

For a moment, he seemed almost otherworldly, like a hero from the old legends, returned from battle to claim his place once more. Raina felt a surge of emotion, a mix of relief, joy, and something deeper, something she'd adamantly refused to acknowledge during his absence.

He began his descent, jogging easily down the winding path, and Raina briefly lunged, overwhelmed by a desire, an instinctive want, to run into his arms. She caught herself before she'd taken more than one step and stood still, her pulse pounding, swallowing a sudden dryness in her throat.

Torsten was home, her heart screamed.

Torsten was here, she amended, *but this was not his home*, she reminded herself.

I am not his home, came to her as a mournful dirge.

He didn't slow upon the level beach but continued to jog toward her, giving Raina pause as it seemed he was...happy to see her?

Oh, but his face was so beloved, she thrilled, leaner and paler than she recalled but handsome all the same. His blue eyes pierced her across the lessening distance. Though no grand and delighted smile creased his face, there was an ease about him. His lips parted, teasing a small smile, anyway.

Her cloak was the first thing he met, fluttering forward at the wind's insistence, and he didn't stop but took her face in his hands and kissed her with an inexplicable wild urgency.

Against all her better judgement and while tears of gladness formed behind her closed eyes, and though her response was tepid at best, wary, Raina melted against him as he pulled her closer.

He stopped abruptly, pulling back, wearing a startled expression as he glanced down between them, his eyes lighting on what her billowing cloak had concealed, her rounded belly.

Torsten's entire broad and imposing frame seemed to soften as he gazed at Raina's expanding middle, his usual brooding expression replaced by one of awe and wonder. His brows, typically furrowed with the weight of command or his infamous impatience, now lifted slightly in surprise. The lines around his eyes softened, and his lips, which often wore a serious or stern demeanor, parted slightly in amazement.

Raina was startled and then somewhat gratified by the emotions displayed, shock and disbelief overcome by what seemed a slow-dawning joy.

Torsten met her gaze. "Raina?"

She nodded and hadn't the power to refuse the smile that came. "Yes. Mayhap in the beginning of June the babe will come."

And Torsten smiled and kissed her again, conscious now of the bump between them, his kiss gentler by far than the hungry one that had greeted her.

Frankly, though, she didn't understand what was happening, why he was being so...warm, so loving.

Why he was smiling when he'd shown them so rarely, when he'd never not once expressed any desire for a child, but only in the making of it all those months ago.

Aonghas, having allowed them a moment of privacy for their reunion, showed himself now.

"Christ and are ye nae a sight!" He exclaimed. "Brought the whole troop with ye?"

Torsten disconnected himself from Raina, his smile intact as he greeted Aonghas, the two men clasping forearms and bumping shoulders.

"Aye, all of us home," Torsten said, sadly having to qualify his response with, "save those few lost over the winter."

He mentioned a few names, men and lads that Raina did not know well, and she felt poorly for being thankful that Gilles, Rory, James, and others she knew better were not among those listed.

"Go on then, will ye?" Torsten asked politely. "And give me a moment with my wife. I'll talk to ye later, as I mean to give ye grief for allowing her down here in her—"

"Don't you dare reprimand Aonghas," she interjected with no small amount of censure. "He's been my loyal friend and guard for more than five months. He's been relentless, almost annoyingly so—and Uilleam as well—scarcely letting me feed myself, hoping to avoid the danger of a spoon and God-knows-what misfortune." She lowered her voice, compelled to disclose, sheepishly, "And today, he was rather coerced against his will, I have to admit."

"Fair enough," Torsten allowed, his grin returned. He patted Aonghas on the shoulder. "Spared the reprimand, my friend."

Aonghas chuckled and meandered away.

Torsten returned his attention to Raina, reaching for her hand.

She stiffened and held her ground while he tried to draw her forward.

"Kiss me, Raina," said Torsten. "Kiss me like ye once did, with hope in yer heart."

Bewildered, unsure who this man was and what he'd done with her real husband, Raina gawked without an ounce of cleverness at him.

"Nae arrested in surprise at my return," he cajoled, "or with some small gladness that I live. Kiss me as if ye love me."

Her eyes widened in furious alarm.

Ooh, she was angry. Why was he doing this to her!

Slowly, she began to shake her head. She tugged to have her hand returned.

No! He was not allowed to do this. She would not let him.

"I should—" she began breathlessly, her words nearly lost in the wind.

"Ye should kiss me again. Unless ye mean to tell me everything I need to ken about the babe, the pregnancy. Are ye well? Ye look radiant, but I ken a sickness sometimes—"

"I'm fine," she stated starkly, her brows drawing together. Her pregnancy was, by Peigi's assessment, relatively easy. The upset morning stomach hadn't visited her in several months, she knew no pain or cramping, and aside from just recently beginning to struggle to get comfortable in bed, she couldn't honestly say she had any complaints. She didn't tell Torsten this, though. "It's been uneventful...normal, according to Peigi. There's nothing to tell."

"I want to be a part of this, Raina," he said. "'Tis our child ye carry. I want to go through this with ye. Why do ye shut me out?"

Raina stared at him, the blazing pain in her eyes asking him without words how he could dare to ask her that, after he'd done the same.

"I am in love with ye, Raina," he confessed, as easily as if he'd only announced the sky was cloudless today. "Surely... surely that must count for something."

And the surprises continued relentlessly! Raina was sure she appeared as a fish caught in the net, gaping and gasping.

"I-It would," she stammered before indignation hardened her voice, "but only if I believed it would remain true on the morrow, or next week or next month." She snapped her lips closed then.

Shock aside, she was imbued with sadness, for having to rebuff a seemingly earnest Torsten, for being too afraid to even pretend that he meant it, that he might love her.

Oh, but if he did...!

"Raina—" he began again.

"You say this today," she cut in, lifting her chin, "and what of tomorrow? How will you feel then?"

"A fair question, considering my behavior. And aye, I freely admit, I was an eejit. Gilles and the king confirmed it. But Raina, hear me, see me, listen to yer own heart. Forget even that ye want it to be true, just ken that it is."

Her eyes grew even larger. "My God..." she began, but had no words, stuck on that part that seemed to suggest that he'd discussed their personal affairs with—never mind Gilles, but the king!

She was quiet for a moment, her mind churning with both joyous possibilities and tremendous doubt. "My mother used to say that dreams never die natural deaths. I did have hope, Torsten, hope that you crafted, but which you also shattered." He nodded, apparently willing to accept his culpability. "I...in truth, I want to seize on this, to believe you...but I'm afraid to trust you again, Torsten."

"Aye, I imagine ye are." He ignored her protest and her rigidity and stepped forward to claim her lips again. His kiss mirrored those of her dreams, tender and ardent at the same time. "But love me, Raina," he said against her lips, "and let me love ye. I vow from this day forward, ye will nae ever again have cause to doubt."

A war raged within, between her heart and mind, and Raina refused to respond.

Torsten sighed and distanced himself by several feet.

"I'm going about it all wrong, I ken," he said with apparent dissatisfaction in himself. "What do ye want me to say, Raina? I dinna ken the...right words. I'm nae guid with tender sentiment.

I only ken what I feel—what frightened me, aye, but what I now am ready to embrace. But what do ye need to hear?" He asked, lifting his hands in a helpless gesture. "That I want ye with me all the time? Aye, I do, spring and summer, and in the dead of winter. That I need ye? Aye, same as roses need rain, as much as tides need the moon. That I dreamed of ye, of holding ye, loving ye? That, too. Raina, ye are the beat of my pulse, the—"

"You broke my heart, Torsten," she finally acknowledged, even though she hated the vulnerability of saying those words.

He nodded, scrunching up his nose and baring his teeth, as if he was shamed to be reminded of it. "And I canna promise I'll nae ever hurt ye again." He paused and sighed, searching for words to express himself. "Raina, I ken war. I understand how to train men and lead men, how to raise fine war horses, how to command. I ken strategy and odds and ugly politics and a ferocious want of freedom. That's all I ken. That's all I've ever kent. But I'd give every bit of knowledge, all of it, simply to ken how to convince ye of what's in my heart now."

She drank in the sight of him, still amazed that he stood before her, beautiful, beloved, so vital and vibrant even as he was vulnerable in a way she had never seen him.

Her heart warred with her head. She had every reason to doubt him, to shield herself from the pain he had caused. But as she looked into his eyes, she saw the raw honesty, the plea for forgiveness, and the deep longing that mirrored her own. Her breath hitched. Could she risk it? Could she open herself up to the possibility of being hurt again?

Yet, in the stillness of that moment, a realization began to take root. She had longed for this, dreamed of a love that was real and true. Here he was, offering it to her with all the uncertainty and messiness that came with it.

Raina's eyes softened as she felt the fragile buds of hope stirring once again within her. She had been so afraid, so guarded, but she knew—she'd known for some time—Torsten was her heart's desire. To reject him now, after he had bared his soul, would be to deny herself the very thing she yearned for.

"If you...if you are lying, if you start again with that coldness, that insufferable indifference, I vow to you, Torsten I'll take a blade to your—"

"I'll lend ye my sword and expose my neck if I do, lass." His voice was steady, and his eyes held hers with a promise she was beginning to feel deep in her soul.

There was one final obstacle. "I won't come to you. I—I just can't. I can't close the distance and simply...give in."

Torsten did though, closed the distance between them, his movements deliberate and filled with purpose. "Then I'll come to ye, love." His hands gently cradled her face, his touch warm and reassuring. "I will come to ye every day, every hour if need be. I'll prove myself to ye. I'll be there for ye, always."

The wind whipped around them, but in that moment, it felt as if they were in their own world, isolated from everything but each other. The sincerity in his voice, the earnestness in his eyes, and the gentle touch of his hands made her believe, for the first time, that maybe, just maybe, love might prevail.

Her lips trembled as her heart soared with hope.

"Ye want to say it," he guessed.

She nodded, fighting larger, happier tears. She was thrilled to lose the fight. "I am so in love with you."

Torsten pulled her closer, his strong arms circling her. He kissed the top of her hair. "That's all I need, love. That's everything."

Epilogue

Summer 1318
Lochlan Hall

THE DE GRAHAM BAIRNS, no one could deny, were a handful. For all his command of his men—the dragon's dedicated and disciplined fire-breathing army—the laird was no match against four bairns. They came one after another, and Peigi was sure the laird still didn't know what had hit him.

Ah, but had not the laird embraced it? Peigi didn't know a more dedicated, attentive father. He made the most of every hour at home, making up for long stretches gone to the king's side.

Sure, and hadn't he said, naught but a few days ago, "They have but one childhood, Peigi. I aim to let them be bairns while they can."

"Could've knocked me over with a feather," Peigi had said, repeating the shocking statement to Cook and the kitchen staff later that day.

Likewise, Lady Raina had embraced the role of motherhood with even more gusto than she had the title and responsibilities of chatelaine to Lochlan—Christ, she'd horrified the staff years ago with her intent to nurse the babes herself. Och, the shame of it, as if she were naught but a peasant and not the lady of the manor. Peigi still remembered the first time she saw Lady Raina nursing the first bairn; she'd clutched her chest as if struck by lightning, sputtering, "Blessed Mother bawling!"

But aye, the bairns were wild, the three lads mostly. The boys, with their boundless energy and mischievous natures, seemed to find trouble wherever they looked—and did they not look far and wide for it? They scaled walls, waded through streams, and swam in the sea as if they'd been born as fish.

"Ye'd ken they were raised by wolves, nae by a laird and lady," Peigi had said, more than once.

The wee lass, though, that raven-haired doll with startling blue eyes—well, she was an angel, was she not?

Peigi's favorite, and it was no secret. Let Gilles and Aonghas and the soldiers fuss over the lads as they did, fashioning swords that'd likely take out someone's eyes soon enough and riding to Aberdeen to purchase ponies upon which the laird's sons learned to ride, but Peigi liked wee Lili right here in the keep, safe and doted upon by either her mother or Peigi herself.

The lass was the image of her father with the heart and mind—and expressions—of her mother. Peigi marveled over it almost daily. She had her father's striking blue eyes and strong features, yet the softness of her mother's smile and the fire of her spirit. "Best of both, ye have, and are ye nae blessed?" Peigi would say, ruffling the lass's dark curls.

"And here we go, luv," Peigi said now to five-year-old Lili, as the lass sat eagerly upon her knees atop the long work table in the middle of the kitchen, helping Peigi make custard.

Lili watched with wide, attentive eyes, as Peigi whisked the eggs in a separate bowl.

"I'll dump in the eggs and ye stir, lass," Peigi directed, adding the whisked eggs to the larger bowl.

She then held the bowl firmly while Lili lifted her bottom off her heels and began to stir, a wee bit clumsily for the weight of the milk, eggs, honey, and sugar in so large a batch.

The long spoon and the batter got away from her, the spoon flicking up and out of the bowl, sending a spray of half-mixed batter across the kitchen. Lili's face twisted into a grimace as she looked at Peigi before both of them turned their heads toward the door, where the batter had been flung.

There stood the dragon of Lochlan Hall, wearing a stripe of batter that cut across his front, from his right shoulder to his left hip and hand.

Peigi contained her chuckle while Lili's eyes widened, her cherubic face otherwise arrested.

The laird glanced down at his now-soiled tunic and plaid and then glanced up at a wide-eyed Lili, his expression seemingly fierce.

Even before her father grinned in response, Lili began giggling.

"'Tis a guid catch, laird," Peigi said, allowing her chuckle to come.

"'Twas a fine pitch," he replied. He swiped his forefinger over the dripping batter and brought it to his mouth, quickly making a face to suggest something wasn't quite right as he approached the counter. There, he picked up a squat porcelain crock and offered it to his daughter. "More honey, I ken." And he kissed her bonny black hair. Of Peigi, he asked, "Any idea where I might find my wife?"

With one hand on the big bowl and now holding the honey jar steady while Lili carefully spooned way too much into the batter, Peigi inclined her head toward the back door. "In the garden, she was, a few moments ago."

Torsten dipped his finger into the bowl and grinned when his daughter playfully swatted at his hand, as she'd seen her mother and Peigi do countless times before. "Nae, da'. Ye hae to wait."

Torsten winked at her as he backed away, putting his finger again into his mouth. "Ah, perfect, lass."

While Lili stirred again, her tongue sticking out from the corner of her mouth, as it did when she was focused and determined, Peigi smiled lovingly at her before glancing out the kitchen door, the yard and sea and sky offering an inspiring view.

In the bright sunshine of the yard, the laird and lady stood together, Raina's forearm raised to her forehead as she looked up at her husband. Two of their lads—Lord only knew where they'd come from!—were seen through the open door. The oldest, Robert, tapped a long branch at his mother's foot, none too gently, while Aindreas, one year younger, tugged at his father's hand for attention, calling repeatedly, "Da! Da! Da!"—before hollering, "Father!"

Uilleam walked by, with the youngest lad, Christian, attached to his hand. The laird and lady ignored the ruckus all around them. The dragon bent and said something quietly to his wife, wearing a grin that made him look twenty years younger. Lady Raina dropped her forearm and showed her husband a broad smile before she responded, shaking her finger at him with what seemed a playful admonition.

The laird's responding laughter rang out over the yard and wafted into the kitchen at the same time he scooped up the persistent Aindreas and twirled him fully around in mid-air, plopping him on his shoulder. He kissed his wife and then, at Aindreas's insistence, turned his shoulder so that the lad could do the same, taking his mother's face in his hands and smacking his lips against hers.

Peigi watched, a wee bit envious, a wee bit wistful. The years of war and peace had not always been easy. There'd been kind and cruel years, battles fought, and peace hard-won, so much change and so much growth, but aye, life was good at Lochlan Hall.

Rich in love and laughter, Peigi often thought.

Lili couldn't be bothered with what went on outside, busy with her task. "Look, Peigi," she said. "All gold now."

Indeed, the batter was thoroughly blended, a velvety pale yellow mixture. "Aye, luv. As it should be."

She stared at her sweet face, her perfect porcelain skin, and blue eyes that would one day break hearts, Peigi was certain. Smiling softly, she tucked a wayward curl behind the lass's ear.

"Ye have nae idea how lucky ye are, luv."

The End

Highlander: The Legends

The Beast of Lismore Abbey
The Lion of Blacklaw Tower
The Scoundrel of Beauly Glen
The Wolf of Carnoch Cross
The Blackguard of Windless Woods
The Devil of Helburn by the Sea
The Rebel of Lochaber Forest
The Avenger of Castle Wick
The Dragon of Lochlan Hall

Heart of a Highlander Series

Heart of Shadows
Heart of Stone
Heart of Fire
Heart of Iron
Heart of Winter
Heart of Ice

Far From Home: A Scottish Time-Travel Romance

And Be My Love
Eternal Summer
Crazy In Love
Beyond Dreams

Only The Brave
When & Where
Beloved Enemy
Winter Longing
Stand in the Fire
Here in Your Arms

The Highlander Heroes Series
The Touch of Her Hand
The Memory of Her Kiss
The Shadow of Her Smile
The Depths of Her Soul
The Truth of Her Heart
The Love of Her Life

Sign-Up for My Newsletter and hear about all the upcoming books.
Stay Up To Date!
www.rebeccaruger.com

Printed in Great Britain
by Amazon

49605532R00199

Peter Edward White
HIDDEN
IN
PLAIN
SIGHT
1952
Part One

STOP!

Not so fast!! 1952 is the second book of a series. Please read...

Hidden in Plain sight: The Blackstones, before reading this.

ACKNOWLEDGEMENTS

This book is for anyone who dares to question things and has an appetite for the truth.

Christopher Crawford: For all your amazing artwork and encouragement.

Alice Underwood: You will always get to read things first.

Beth Navaro: For believing in this from the start.

Madeleine Hutt: A great editor and even better friend.

Lee Caswell, A lighthouse for many, including me.

My brother in arms, Dunk Mclaughlan – I'm lucky to have you in my life.

My wife Jocelyn, for your belief in me.

Contents

1. Epilogue 1
2. The Collision of Past and Present 2
3. London : 1952 4
4. Living for the Weekend 11
5. Council of thirteen - The Shadows 21
6. Down and Out 31
7. The Bookshop 42
8. Mind Over Matter 54
9. One Way or Another 58
10. Park life 72
11. Washer, Washer, Washer 78
12. The Invisible Line 88
13. Monday Morning 93
14. The Bookkeepers Apprentice 96

15. School's Out Forever 111

16. The Things We Leave Behind 114

17. Would Wood Still Be Wood, Even If It Could Be Metal? 122

18. Crossing the T's and Dotting the I's 129

19. The Green, Green Grass of Others 135

20. Going Underground 141

21. Xavier the Savior 147

22. The 7 P's 149

23. Moving Pieces 156

24. Disclosure 170

25. Under the Radar 178

26. Like a Spider to a Fly 191

27. Preparing for the Worst 197

28. Redundant 207

29. A Catch of Breath 216

30. Q&A 225

31. Between the Lines 235

32. Building Bridges 237

33. Mean Time 249

34. Shaky foundations 259
35. Revenge isn't a Four-Letter Word 268
36. The Garden of the Abbey 275
37. Train Hard, Fight Easy 292
38. Setting The Stage 295
39. The Definition of Courage 302
40. Emmanuel's Demise 312
41. Building Blocks 317
42. Predator vs Prey 321
43. South of the River 335
44. First of Many 349
45. Stay Down 360
46. Moving On Up 368
47. From the Crow's Nest 375
48. The Hard Sell 391
49. The Savoy 399
50. Market Research 406
51. Head On 428
52. Run Rabbit, Run 439
53. Race for Life 449

1

EPILOGUE

UCJAMKC – ZYAI

RFGQ - QRMPW – GQ – JGIC – Y – QMSRF – YKCPGAYL – KMLICW – RPYN.

BM – LMR – ZCAMKC – RPYNNCB.

FMJB – RFC – NPGXC – DMP – Y – UFGJC
ZSR – ZC – UGQC – CLMSEF – RM – JCR
GR – EM – YLB – ZC – DPCC.

2

The Collision of Past and Present

1952

The dream always started in the same way. Andrew and his friend Ed are back in the Georgian house on that fateful day when they were ten. Ed, cuts his hand, forcing the cellar door open, only in the dream there is more blood. It's everywhere, dripping down the walls and forming into pools on the floor. They get down into that damp and dusty cellar and find the little black statue of the fawn with the dish, only this time Ed drips blood on to the dish with a smile, and doesn't seem surprised at all when the door to the tunnel rumbles open.

The dream then switches to the keyhole and all those people with black stone jewellery eating body parts, laughing, and joking. The eyes of the man who spots Andrew looking, glow red and lock onto his gaze like magnets. He finds it hard to look away. He's rushing to leave, but Ed is routed to the spot like he’s in a daze. Andrew can't work out why he can't move him. It jumps again.

The nightmare always finishes in the same way. They are in the second, cleaner basement, just in front of the jet-black tunnel. The huge arm comes out to grab Ed, but moves past him and grabs Andrew instead. It's the same gurgling noise every time, ringing in his ears, but now it's him that's making it. Ed just smiles at him while he’s taken backwards in slow motion into the darkness.

Andrew woke up suddenly in shock, breathing deeply and in a cold sweat and a damp bed.

Not again, he thought.

It had been five years after all.

3

LONDON : 1952

Earlier that year, King George VI had died overnight. His eldest daughter, Elizabeth, was in Kenya with her husband at the time, and had to hurry back to Britain to take up her role as Queen Regnant. She was only twenty-seven. In an era of post-war restoration, some saw the opportunity for a fresh start, instead of trying to reinstate things to how they used to be. Some older state figures had imperialistic views and longed for a return of the 'good old days.' Queen Elizabeth II, had to be strong enough to keep the peace between the two factions. The only way to achieve this was by establishing her authority and gaining the respect of the men. That was easier said than done.

Women's roles in society were shifting again. Many women had taken up work while their husbands were away at war, but as a result of the men returning, they were now blocked from doing their jobs. This in turn reduced them to roles of a more 'suitable nature'. Some women were not happy about this. To top it all off, they became a lost generation of women who were mostly alone. Too many men had died in the war, and that had affected the ratio of men to women. The chances of a woman finding a husband were at an all-time low. Instead, they had to find work to get by.

Andrew and his mother now lived with his grandparents in Kentish Town. His father had died in the war, and his mother had been struggling to afford the rent on her own. So, by his grandmother's orders, they moved in with them. His grandparents lived upstairs, and he and his mother had the two rooms on the ground floor.

His grandfather was a quiet man. He had fought in WWI and according to Andrew's grandmother, when he finally came home, he was the shell of the man he used to be. He was never the same again, and just sat in his study either looking out of the window or at the sagging shelves of books.

Growing up, Andrew didn't really understand why he was that way, but later he felt secretly thankful that his own father had died, rather than returning home to them like that. A distant observer; ex participant of life. His grandmother, however, was larger than life and her volume compensated for his silence. She was quite strict, but with young Andrew in the house, she had to be.

Once, when he was twelve, she caught him swearing at one of the boys in the street. She was furious and marched him home to be punished. He could still taste the soap now, and even washing his hands made him feel a bit nauseous. It must have done the trick though, as he no longer felt the need to swear.

Where they lived in Kentish Town, there were many private and grammar schools close by in London. These schools taught some of the finest minds in the country, and students progressed to achieve great things. High Birch Secondary Modern in Camden, however, wasn't one of those schools. The student body consisted mostly of underachievers, rejects and thugs. It's only claim-to-fame was that a local lord with a temporarily flatulent mind, decided to send one of his sons there. He only lasted a term, but his sun-faded picture with a yellowing black eye, still beamed from the barren trophy cabinet outside the staff room.

Andrew, never had much enthusiasm for school. High Birch had at least forty students per class, so it was very crowded and difficult to concentrate. Even when they could hear what the teacher was saying, he got bored quickly. He couldn't help feeling that they had decorated lies and sewn together coincidental facts to conceal what was really going on in the world. As the years progressed, he realised that if he really wanted to find things out, he would have to go digging for answers himself.

Nobody could tell him anything about what he saw in that tunnel with Ed. Even after countless hours of searching the books at home or in the library, he still couldn't find a single thing. By the time he had reached his final year, he had just turned fifteen. He had a few friends but only two he felt he could really trust: George Langley and Lee Beaks. They were thick as thieves. They were the only ones that knew what happened all those years ago in the tunnel, and they shared his enthusiasm for discovery and exploration. It was such a weight off his mind to be able to talk about what had happened, as keeping it to himself all those years had been difficult.

George was quite tall and skinny with an insatiable appetite. Lee suspected that George had hollow legs, as he was constantly eating. George had lost his dad in the war too, and he had a younger sister called Lucy who was ten. Their mother owned and ran a newsagent near chalk farm, and they lived above. This gave him an unlimited supply of sweets.

Lee was a bit shorter than both of them, but he was broad, and as strong as an ox. He was the youngest of four children, all boys. Growing up, his brothers took turns to tease him and beat him relentlessly to toughen him up, and it had worked, a bit too well. Years of this conditioning had taken the shine off his humour, but he had built up an incredible armour.

The triangle they forged was strong, and they spent most weekends finding places they shouldn't be. They sat at the back of Mr Wilson's English class as usual, and whispered to each other while Mr Wilson had his back to the class whilst he wrote. The eight-foot high, dusty chalkboard wobbled back and forth as he did so, like a sail in a light breeze. Two tables over to their left was Tom Adler, a nasty piece of work. He was busy intimidating the person next to him when the wooden blackboard eraser hit him right in the ear with a clack.

"QUIET ADLER," screamed Mr Wilson from the front of the class, hand still outstretched from throwing the eraser, like a dagger throwing performer at the circus.

"OWWW," shouted Adler, rubbing his ear while most of the class giggled cautiously. They soon stopped when he glared.

CLICK CLICK, snapped Mr Wilson's fingers, which meant Tom Adler had to pick up the eraser, walk down to the front and place it back his desk. He did so begrudgingly, whilst still rubbing his red ear. Mr Wilson returned to his board and continued to write out some poetry and talk as he did so. They began to whisper to each other again.

“So, what’s the plan for this weekend?” asked George, looking at Andrew as he slipped a boiled sweet into his mouth discreetly.

Most of the bomb sites had been cleared out by then and were slowly being replaced with modern houses or high-rise, blocks of flats. The local authorities had tightened up security too, boarding up windows and fitting heavy locks and chains on the unused buildings of interest.

But Andrew had found something interesting last week around the back of Russell Square tube.

“There’s an empty workshop around the back of Russell square that has a set of stairs... they go down,” Andrew whispered.

“Down into the service area of the tube, maybe?” said Lee.

“We’ve tried tubes before,” said George, whilst opening a packet of salt and shake crisps, slowly and carefully trying to muffle the crinkles.

“I know that, but this one is different,” Andrew said. “I spotted a few men with black rings, go in there, and they disappeared for about an hour. It must lead to a chamber.”

George's eyes lit up. “We better be careful.”

Just then, Mr Wilson threw another eraser directly at George’s head. He was too preoccupied adding salt to his crisps to notice the projectile. Lee’s hand shot out and caught the eraser with a snap, placing it down quickly on his desk in front of him. George looked up in dismay.

"BEAKS!" shouted an enraged Mr Wilson at Lee.

Lee smiled, as he knew what was coming.

"Get out of my class, NOW! and report to headmaster Donahue."

"With pleasure," Lee said, while standing up and putting his books into his bag. He picked up the caught eraser, holding it aloft like a prize cricket ball. "See you two later," he said, as he walked down towards Mr Wilson, and put it on his desk. "Caught out, Sir. Never mind."

"OUT!!"

The class laughed.

Once things calmed down, another teacher arrived at the class door and asked Mr Wilson for a brief chat outside; Probably about Lee.

"Lee's going to see Donahue again," George said, eating a biscuit.

"Mm yeah, I wonder how it goes this time," said Andrew.

Lee, being sent to the headmaster's office was a regular thing. It was only the end of April, and Lee had already broken (or had broken on him) four rulers, three canes, and he even put a crack in the paddle. It must be quite amusing to watch Donahue try and inflict some pain on Lee, only to get nothing back except broken punishment paraphernalia. Towards the end of last year, Donahue had his arm in a sling.

'Tennis elbow' they said. They knew better. So did Lee... and the paddle.

"Saturday, 10am, out the front of Russell Square, ok?" said Andrew.

"Looking forward to it. I'll tell Lee when I see him in French," said George.

"If Donahue has finished with Lee by then that is," said Andrew.

Andrew had always struggled with different languages, especially French. He found it hard to get his head around the concept that a book is masculine, but a table is feminine.

Why couldn't things just be things?

4

Living for the Weekend

Andrew and his friends were in their last year of school, and as they had no plans for further education, this meant that they had to have awkward conversations about 'the future' with careers advisers. From what Andrew could see, his options were somewhat limited. Lee planned to do exactly what his father did, and three of his brothers did too, which was working in the Whitechapel bell foundry. It was hard work, but that didn't put Lee off.

Nerdy fact:

The White Chapel foundry began trading in 1570, in Whitechapel, but moved in 1739 to an old pub called the Artichoke, where it has been ever since. The bell foundry still had lots of work replacing the bells that were damaged from the London bombing raids of WWII. As well as many cathedral bells, they also cast some truly historic and important pieces. In 1858 they cast 'Big Ben' which is the name of the main bell in the clocktower of Westminster. At over 13.5 tonnes, it was the largest bell they ever cast. Another notable bell is the Liberty Bell in America. This was cast as a symbol of their independence from the British, but It was damaged in transit and cracked on the first strike.

The bell cracking must have been such a disappointment for the Americans and their newly found freedom. It was a bit like when Andrew was seven and his mum let him make his own toast for the first time. He'd burnt it so badly that it was black. He still ate it though, every last bite. After all, it was a taste of independence.

George had taken up his mum on the offer of working at her newsagents. He'd learn the business inside out and would take over when she retired. "Think of all the sweets," he had said, like someone who was destined to inherit a gold mine.

As for Andrew, he had no idea. He had no family business to get involved in, or trade skills that he wanted to learn. His mum worked at a bakery. She said it was 'fine' a lot, but he could tell she hated it. Up and out of the house at 5am most days and she looked constantly tired. He wanted something else, but he wasn't sure what just yet.

Back at home, Saturday morning started off with a bang, literally. The kitchen window must have been left open again, which caused the front door to slam as Andrew's mother left at 5am for work. He was now awake thinking of the day ahead, and what may lie waiting for them beneath Russell Square. He got up and wandered into the breezy kitchen to close the window. There was still another hour before sunrise, so he put a fresh kettle on the hob for some tea.

Walking into the lounge, the curtains that separated off his mother's bedroom area were open, and her bed was unmade. Very unusual. She must have got up late and had to leave in a hurry. Next to her bed was a silver framed picture of his dad in his military uniform, and a fan spread book about Europe, pages down on her bedside table.

He sometimes wondered if she was lonely. As to go from looking after a house of her own with a husband and child, to her husband dying in a field somewhere in France, and struggling to pay the rent. Then having to move back in with her parents, working at a place she hated just to put food on the table for a child she barely saw.

It just didn't seem fair.

'Life isn't fair, Andrew. Get used to it,' his grandmother said, routinely.

But I'd love to make it a bit fairer on her... he thought.

The kettle began to whine as it boiled. Back in the kitchen, he took a mug from the cupboard with a picture of a man smoking a cigar. It was his dad's old mug. 'Manikin cigars - Make it a Manikin weekend'

"I think not," said Andrew to himself, as he put the mug back and picked another. He remembered the smell of those cigars well, as his dad used to smoke them occasionally, and constantly the day before he left for the war. It wasn't rational to blame a cigar brand for his dad's death, but for some reason he did.

He made his tea and sat down in the lounge. As he sipped his tea in silence, the house groaned and tapped as it prepared to wake up. It gave him time to think. He thought of the house they lived in when he was five, on Hardwicke Road. It was near Bounds Green tube. A really nice house, and he liked it there. It had a big red front door, a great garden and the neighbours were friendly with kids around his age.

But it all changed one day with a knock on the door.

It was a rainy Saturday morning, and Andrew was busy in the kitchen, sketching in his book.

"This one's for Daddy when he gets back," Andrew had said, as he held it up for his mother to inspect.

"That's lovely Andrew, I'm sure he will love it," said his mother, as she went to answer the door.

The sound of the rain ricocheted off of the tiled floor of the entrance hall and Andrew could just about hear the conversation between his mother and someone else. He couldn't quite make out the words they said, just the '*sorry*' at the end.

He got up and walked into the entrance hall, just as his mother turned sideways and slid down the wall. She sat down on the floor, exposing the silhouette of the boy at the door. The letter had slipped onto the floor next to her. As Andrew's eyes adjusted, he could see the soaked telegram boy in his navy-blue uniform, turning ever-darker from the rain. He looked down at Andrew's mother and then at Andrew. "I'm sorry," he said, like it was his fault.

The telegram boy walked back out towards his bicycle that was leant against the front gate and pushed it up the street as the rain hammered down, bouncing off the pavement. Andrew walked up to his mother with crayons in his hand, and she was just staring at the wall opposite her, blankly.

"What's wrong, Mummy?" he asked.

“It’s Daddy,” she said, “He’s not coming home.”

“Why, Mummy? Did we do something wrong?”

“No no, sweetheart, we didn't do anything wrong. He’s gone to heaven... to be with Buster.”

Buster was their rabbit that died the previous year.

“Was Daddy eaten by a fox, too?” he cried.

His mother pulled him down to her and cuddled him tightly. They sat crying in that doorway for what felt like forever, while stray raindrops occasionally bounced in. A few neighbours opened their front doors opposite and just looked on, wanting to come over but were held back by the downpour. They cried so much that Andrew could no longer tell the difference between the tears and the rain.

Andrew shook the memory off. He finished his tea with a final gulp and got up to make some breakfast. The bird song was building, and the sun was starting to rise. After two rounds of toast, he made his mother’s bed, and tidied the kitchen in the hope that she would be able to come home and relax for a change. He even popped out to the corner shop to get the Saturday paper for his grandmother and left it on the Welsh dresser outside her bedroom door.

By the time he got back and changed into his boots, he could hear his grandparents beginning to stir.

It was time to leave.

He closed the front door slowly until the latch clicked, holding back the brass lion's head knocker as he did so. It was a forty-minute walk to Russell Square from where they lived in Kentish town. He couldn't even afford the bus fare, let alone the tube, but still... he had legs.

He walked past Camden Road, over the canal and down towards Somers Town, then passed St Pancras hospital. There were so many interesting buildings in London, and it was a miracle that so many had survived the war. He made it down to Russell Square with a few minutes to spare, so he bought a lemonade from the nearest shop. The sun was up and shining, but it still had a chill in the air. It had rained for most of the month so far, so he doubted the sun's sincerity.

Andrew walked around to the front of Russell Square station to find George leant up against one of the burgundy tiled pillars, having an argument with his little sister, Lucy.

"YOU said we were going to the park!" she said.

"Well, I LIED!'' George, flared back at her.

"Hello, Lucy," said Andrew. That seemed to calm her anger briefly, as she turned to him.

She was only ten but was a right little madam. Right from the age of five, she had her mother wrapped tightly around her little finger and could get pretty much anything she wanted.

"Hello, Andrew. Mummy told George that he had to take me to the park, but he's brought me here to this station. It's all a pack of lies. There's NO ice cream, and something smells of -"

"We... should keep an eye out for Lee," Andrew interrupted, nodding. George nodded too.

Just then, Lee appeared from inside the station after getting the tube. He was holding a railway-style signalling lamp.

"All right, Lee, money to burn?" asked Andrew.

"Found it last week in my dad's shed, actually," he replied, as he looked down at the lamp, turning it on and off.

"No, I meant that you got the tube," explained Andrew.

"Oh, yeah. I hate walking, especially before a run," he said, as he winked awkwardly.

The butterflies in Andrew's stomach fluttered. He hoped the toast he ate was enough.

"Hi Lucy, why are you here?" asked Lee.

Lucy was looking more and more angry by the minute, so just pointed at a sheepish George and stamped her foot.

"Sorry, guys. I'll have to be your lookout, I guess," George said, pathetically.

"Look out for what George?!" demanded Lucy, who was turning more crimson by the second.

"Lucy, listen," said George, in a kind tone and kneeling down to her level. "This won't take long, I promise. Here, have a sweet." George produced a boiled sweet from his pocket that held about a hundred. "And when we are done, we will find an ice cream cart, and you can have whatever you want, ok?"

"Whatever I want?" she repeated.

"Anything," said George.

"Ok, but if this is another lie, I'm telling Mum."

They walked down the side road and into Colonnade, past the cut corner of the horse hospital and the Friend at Hand Pub. About a hundred yards down the cobbled street on the left was the entrance to the workshop that Andrew had found. As they approached the door, a large removal van was coming up the Mews and parked up near them where the road was wider. A couple of men in white overalls then walked fifty yards down the road and through a back gate.

"This is it. This is where the men went in and were gone for ages," said Andrew.

It was a large wooden door that was painted dark green. Most of the paint had faded and flaked off to expose a lighter green underneath, but the legacy of it remained around the edges.

"Look in there," said Andrew.

Lee and George took turns to look through one of the cracks and into the dusty garage. Sure enough, you could clearly see the handrail of a staircase that went down.

"Oh yeah," said Lee. "I think you're right; They go down."

The small pedestrian door set into the large panel had a hasp and staple, with a chunky grey padlock bolted shut.

"Well, that's the end of that idea then," said George, momentarily lifting the lock.

"We've opened harder ones," said Lee. Lee put his free hand into the back pocket of his trousers and produced a paperclip. "I'll have this open in no time."

The others watched carefully for onlookers as Lee went to work on the lock. He unfolded the paperclip and started to bend it back into the shape he wanted. He just managed to slide the metal into the lock when George jumped.

"Watch out, car coming down."

A car had pulled into the mews at the pub end. Lee removed the paperclip and instinctively turned to sit down against the garage while they pretended to be preoccupied in conversion.

The car moved past slowly and carried on up to the top of the road, before turning right and out of sight.

"Phew!" said George. "That was close."

"Good spot," said Lee, as he re-inserted the paperclip back into the lock and started to twist it back and forth. Lucy was bored already. The sugar from the sweet must have worn off already, as she began to complain about ice cream again.

CLUNK.

The padlock was now open and Lee dropped it on the floor outside of the garage. Lee had a smirk on his face, which was rare to see.

"George, take Lucy over to that removal van. If things turn sour, find a way to sound the horn, OK?" asked Andrew.

"Good luck," said George, as he led Lucy over to the van.

Lee opened the door just enough for them both to enter. "Ready?" he asked while picking up his lamp and testing it again, out of habit.

Andrew took a deep breath, “Yeah, let’s go.”

5

Council of Thirteen - The Shadows

Meanwhile, elsewhere in London...

On the highest floor of the Hotel Russell in London, exists a large meeting room with blacked out windows. This suite is not on any of the hotel lists, and no keys for it are held at reception.

Henry Malone, a young man of twenty-two, was dressed in a Saville Row suit and was running late. Of all the things he could do wrong right now, being late would be the worst. He stepped out of the jet-black chauffeur driven car and moved quickly towards the main entrance of the hotel.

Doors were opened and shut behind him, but he didn't acknowledge any of the staff, as usual. This was the correct etiquette for someone that was too busy to talk.

He walked straight up the steps and saw the zodiac mosaic on the floor but had no time to look. Every inch of this hotel ached to be observed and admired, but not today. He turned left to head towards the reception and headed straight for the elevator on the far left.

It had to be that one.

Once inside the lift car, he let the doors shut firmly in front of him. The button panel was highly polished brass, and at the very bottom was a small keyhole, barely noticeable. Henry reached into his jacket pocket and produced a small brass key. The red, tassel keyring danced and swayed as he gently inserted the key into the lock. The moment he did so, the lights went out, and a single blood-red light illuminated the elevator car. He turned the key to the right in one full revolution.

His father had warned him over and over again. "Turn clockwise by a full rotation...just one, Henry," Mr Malone senior had said. "Anything else, and you will end up in the basement feeding the rats."

As he completed the key turn, the light came back on in the lift car and he felt the elevator start to move upwards. He breathed a temporary sigh of relief and removed the key before placing it back in his pocket. The elevator then slowed and stopped. Henry could feel his heart in his mouth when the doors opened into a candlelit hallway. As he walked towards the only door at the end, he noticed all the paintings on the walls either side of him. The portraits were of men. Members that came from the thirteen families stared back at him intently. Their black eyes seemed come alive and sparkle in the half light. He moved up to the door and could hear the loose chat from the other side, which was a relief. The meeting had not yet started.

The brass door handle was in the shape of a dragon's head with dark green eyes. As he stepped through the threshold, none of the men took notice of him, but the older lady already seated at the back did. She was the Grand Matriarch, and the weight of her stare was unbearable. It seemed to burn into him, making him sweat even more.

This suite is one of three that the council of thirteen uses in London, and has done for over fifty years since the Hotel Russell opened in 1900. In the centre of the room, the large semi-circle shaped table seated thirteen in a crescent comfortably and was handmade from the boughs of the Mary Celeste. In the middle of the table is a large ornate depiction of a pyramid with thirteen tiers of bricks, crowned with a single eye at its summit: the all-seeing eye. From this eye, thirteen intersected arrows pointed out to each seating position. The room is dimly lit by some black candles on the table, and more on the mantelpiece. A large, open fire crackled and popped in a black ornate fireplace on the other side of the room, filling the space with winter smells and warm air.

The heads of each of the thirteen families were there for the bi-annual meeting to discuss the state of the world, and in turn, their interests. Set back from the table, on her own black and gold, throne-like chair, the Grand Matriarch who presided over the meetings caressed the brass snake's head handle of her black walking stick. Its red eyes glowed. A young, pale boy around eight years old was dressed all in black and stood obediently to the left of her.

Boom... Boom... Boom...

The Grand Matriarch thumped her stick on the wooden floor, and the chat came to a halt by the time the third strike came down.

“Gentlemen, it is time,” said the Grand Matriarch. “I see you are all present and correct, except for Mr Malone senior. Where is he, Henry?”

The young man took a deep breath to answer.

“Please forgive his absence, Grand Matriarch. My father sends his regards and me again, as his bearer,” said Henry, as he bowed his head cautiously. “He has urgent business in Australia.”

“I see. Things have progressed sooner than we planned,” she braised. “But I digress.” She unsheathed a silver knife with a black glass handle from her jacket sleeve and pointed it at Henry. This knife was very old with a black obsidian handle and had been handed down through many generations.

“Your father knows the rules, as we all do, Henry. Please remind him that one more absence from this meeting will force him to make a choice, and from what I can see, the only one he can spare at the moment is you. For your own sake...don’t end up on my altar.”

He nodded respectfully and looked down at the table nervously.

The Grand Matriarch took a deep breath, “Onto the matters at hand. We must start the meeting.”

“Place the knife please, Jacob,” she said, while passing the dagger handle-first to the young boy stood by her.

“You will spin first, Henry,” she proclaimed.

Henry stood up, walked around to the table, and waited for the knife. Jacob, stepped towards the table centre and placed the silver knife with both hands on the eye, its point aimed in the middle, and moved back to be by the Grand Matriarch's side.

Henry hesitated, but then gently spun the dagger with a flick of his wrist. The dagger slowed, reflecting the candlelight onto the ceiling, creating a swirling pattern above them on the white plaster. It slowed further and finally came to a stop with its point towards a man dressed in a dark suit with a thin black tie.

“House of Temperspawn, if you will,” the Grand Matriarch said. “Old business first.”

The man with heavily defined features and black eyes spoke delicately yet precisely for all to hear.

“As we all know, World War II, albeit messy, was overall a success. Adolf did what he was bred to do. He and his family have now been granted new identities and will now reside in Argentina, as planned.”

"The Freemasons are very unhappy with the Nazi's conduct towards the order," said Mr Ashton,

"That may be so, but it was essential for us to show that even they are not beyond our reach," said Mr Temperspawn,

"Besides, we now have the ancient documents that we needed to confiscate, and..."

“New business,” interjected the Grand Matriarch,

Mr Temperspawn shot a hard look, which instantly softened at the Grand Matriarch, and carried on in his calm, collected manner.

"The Hague tribunal has come to a head, and west Germany has faltered. By August there will be no backing out. The IMF and World Bank will welcome them as new members and lend them the money they need for the reparations." Mr Temperspawn bared a rare smile.

"Be cautious of who makes the bandages, as they own the blades too. Utter fools."

This news came of great surprise and relish to the other twelve families, and they tapped their whisky glasses with their black stoned rings in support and praise.

"Mm, you have been busy," said the Grand Matriarch. "House of Temperspawn, spin the knife please."

"Certainly," said the man. He stood up and walked around to the lower part of the table, placing his hand over the knife that was flat on the table. He spun the knife into a blur.

As the knife spun and reflected, the Grand Matriarch looked at the seated twelve to gauge their reactions. The blade slowed and finally came to rest with its point focused on her nephew, James.

"House of Wordsworth, if you please. Old business first."

Mr Wordsworth nodded and stood up. "Over the past five years, this council has invested significant sums of money into the development of HAARP for our own ends. This technology, with the ability to control the weather, is most secret, but I have been assured that we can easily sell it to the

Americans, when we have found its limitations. We managed to test the technology in the Swiss alps in January last year. They had never seen such avalanches. I trust all your families received the messages to avoid the area. Plus, southern Italy in October was beyond our expectations."

Glasses clinked once more.

"New business," prompted the Grand Matriarch.

A small smile began at the edges of Mr Wordsworth mouth as he had been preparing for what was to come next for some considerable time.

"We mourn the loss of our King, King George VI. As we are well aware, he was a Grand Master Mason, but he stepped away from masonic duties to be king. He was not for turning. This year marks the ascension of his daughter, Elizabeth, to the throne, but it is also the year we await a very rare planetary alignment: Planet nine. This alignment provides us with a favourable opportunity to strengthen our ranks. This particular incantation has never been attempted before. It is simply known as 'Extensio Vitae'."

The other twelve heads of houses looked on intently.

Mr Wordsworth continued...

"The inscription in the Necronomicon clearly states that the ceremony must be conducted at noon, but at 'the beginning of time.' This made little sense and had eluded even the brightest of minds under our control. Finally, it has been deduced that the ceremony must take place on the Greenwich meridian at zero degrees. The very start of time itself. We plan to use the grounds around the Greenwich observatory."

"The inscription is quite specific," he explained.

"The blood from the Vampyre must be taken by force, and the incantation begins. This is to rid the blood of its infectious qualities, leaving only some of the prolonged life and healing effects, amongst others. Once this is complete, it is to be fed to a pure child. The child then must be petrified before their blood is drawn. The combination of Vampyre anti-oxidants and the adrenochrome is beyond compare, and this blood will be the most valuable liquid on the planet. There should be more than enough left to sell or trade. It will provide a prolonged life, enhanced healing and a brief insight into the fourth dimension to anyone who consumes it. Wars have been waged and fought for less."

A very rare round of applause started around the table, so rare that most heads of house had not seen one in their lifetime. The Grand Matriarch, however, did not clap, and instead stared at Mr Wordsworth with her dark inquisitive eyes, waiting for the silence to resume.

"I admire your ambition, Mr Wordsworth," she said. "Your father and I had heard whispers of this incantation, and often wondered whether we would live to ever see it performed, but you seem to have forgotten one thing. The blood of the Vampyre must be taken by force! Have you not considered the consequences for that kind of action, with the blood treaty in place?"

Her watery, pitted eyes fixed on the council as she continued.

"We, as the weaker species, have invested heavily for peace, and avoided a war with the Vampyres at... all... cost. This could set us back a hundred years and re-light a fire that has almost gone out." Her stick slammed into the floor with a boom.

Nobody, except for young Jacob, flinched.

Mr Wordsworth considered his words carefully. "With the greatest respect, Grand Matriarch," he bowed his head, "the Vampyre will not die from this, and regardless, they live a very different life now, especially here in London. Most of them no longer hunt for blood, as you know. It is provided through a subscription agreement with the blood banks that we own and control, and very specialised and authorised wine dealers. I doubt they have the numbers or resources to organise an uprising in the city, let alone in Europe."

"A tiger in a cage is still a tiger, Mr Wordsworth...and this could open the gate." A hint of fear danced within the voice of the Grand Matriarch. Under her left sleeve, the scar that ran down her forearm tingled slightly, as if the nerves had suddenly woken up. She and her brother were very young when the Vampyre had pursued them through the woods in Switzerland. The very thought of it woke her in a cold sweat, occasionally, even at seventy years old. It was like being chased by death itself.

"And this must be done in Broad daylight? she quizzed. "How can we conduct a ceremony involving a child and a raging Vampyre, in full view of the public?"

"I have a plan for a cover," said James, "We shall use the HAARP machine to create a fog over London like never seen before. No one will see a thing. It will be so dense they will be stuck inside their homes."

"When?" she asked, like it was a terminal prognosis.

"When the alignment will be at its peak. December, Grand Matriarch. We are making preparations as we speak."

"Very well. I want the full plan submitted with every detail before I approve it. Is that clear?" she demanded.

Mr Wordsworth nodded.

"I hope you know what you are doing, for all of our sakes," she said. The Grand Matriarch snapped out of her worried state and back into business with a nod.

"Spin the knife, Mr Wordsworth."

"Certainly."

6

Down and Out

Russell Square

Lee stepped into the damp and dusty workshop first; Andrew followed and shut the door shut behind them. Some interrupted mice ran along the dusty shelves, hopping over the abandoned rusty tools that had been disguarded, never to earn their keep again.

"I wonder how long this place has been empty for?" asked Andrew.

"Was probably a cover all along. Why would it have these stairs otherwise?" said Lee, pointing to the ironwork that protruded out from the floor for the handrails.

"True...still a bit creepy though, right?" said Andrew.

He walked over to the top of the stairs and looked down at the worn, concrete steps that stacked down into the darkness underground. Flashes of the tunnel where he lost Ed all those years ago popped into his mind, but he batted it away, as he always did. Lee walked behind him at the top of the stairs and handed him the lamp.

"You first this time, Andrew."

Andrew took the lamp and found the switch to turn it on. As he did so, a circle of yellow light penetrated the darkness of the void, teasing the shadows with its flare. They could see another landing at the bottom, then another set of stairs returning, heading even deeper into the ground. They stepped down in tandem onto the concrete stairs, trying to make as little noise as possible. Before long, they were already at the first landing making the turn. As Andrew moved round, the lamp flickered a couple of times but stayed on. "Don't you dare go out," he whispered to the lamp.

Meanwhile up top:

Lucy's temper was beginning to boil over and she was now screaming at George behind the van for 'ruining her day.' George didn't even hear the van pull up outside the workshop until it screeched its tyres to halt. Six big men dressed in suits with Blackstone rings, piled out of the van. They took one look at the padlock that was now on the floor and opened the workshop in a hurry. George had just seen this unfold and was now in a panic.

"Lucy, hide. NOW!"

There must have been the look on his face as she stopped whining instantly, and now looked scared as she moved out of sight. George rushed around to the driver's side of the removal van that they had been hiding behind. The door was ajar where it hadn't been shut properly. He swung it open and hopped up and into the driver's seat, looking for the horn. The large, heavily used button bulged in the centre of the steering wheel.

Back underground:

Lee took the lamp, "My turn," he said.

Just then, they could hear a horn. It was distant but they could hear it.

BEEP. BEEP. BEEEEEEEP. BEEEP.

Back up top:

After beeping the horn aggressively, George now had the attention of two of the men in suits who had turned around, and some removal men too. The men in white overalls had opened the gate at the bottom of the road and moved quickly towards their van. Luckily this seemed to deter the men in suits and they headed back into the workshop.

"Oi!!, What do you think you are doing? Get out of there!" said the lead removal man with a large moustache and big arms, covered in tattoos. They were picking up pace and were almost upon them.

George jumped out of the van and ran around the back to collect Lucy who was hiding near one of the wheel arches. "Come on Lucy, we have to run."

Lucy joined George and they ran down the cobbled street and turned the corner at the end, by the pub. "Slow down." said Lucy, "I'm not as fast as you."

They crossed the road in front of the station making a few cars stop and honk. Not slowing for anything, they ran into

Brunswick Square gardens, finding an empty bench while they caught their breath.

“I’m... so... telling... mum,” Lucy wheezed, in between breaths.

“Made it... to... a park... didn't we?” George huffed back, with a small smile. The smile didn't last long, as he suddenly became very worried about his friends.

Back underground:

After hearing the horn, Lee and Andrew made it halfway up the first flight of stairs before they heard the voices in the workshop above. Just then, a large man appeared at the top of the stairs.

“They're down here!” the man shouted.

Lee and Andrew turned around on the stairs and ran down both sets as quickly as possible, hearing the scuffing of shoes and grunts from the large men now chasing them into the dark depths. At the foot of the second set of stairs, was a long corridor that stretched further and further away from the workshop above. Glancing back, the minimal light of the workshop gleamed down over the men moving down the stairs and open bannisters, and it seemed to shine brighter the deeper they went into the blackness. The corridor turned sharply right, and they sped up as much as the space and lamp light would allow them to. After a hundred yards or so there was a problem, a familiar one to Andrew.

“Hold on,” said Lee from the front, “It’s just a wall. A dead end.”

“Are you sure?” asked Andrew, desperately, the sound of footsteps getting louder and closer behind them.

“Yeah, but... oh wait... there's a little dish here.”

“Put some blood on it,” Andrew said quickly.

The sound of steps coming from the big men rattled off the walls.

“How? I don't even have a knife,” Lee said.

“Do it.”

Running out of options, Lee then elbowed Andrew in the nose with a crunch.

“Ahhhh!” Andrew's eyes filled with tears, his nose running, and he could taste blood in his mouth. His head now hung in his hands. He felt a couple of sausage-like fingers reach into the gap between his hands and wipe themselves over his nose, which then seared with pain. The door rumbled and he felt the rush of air move over him before being pulled over the threshold by Lee. The men were now running towards them shouting "stop" as the door rumbled shut, silencing their voices.

“We have to move,” Lee said, leading Andrew into a large chamber on the other side of some huge stone arches that supported the earth above.

They were decorated in what looked like dried blood. Characters, symbols, were everywhere. The combination of his tears and the dimming lamp light meant that Andrew struggled to see all the details in the artwork, but it was enough to know they were somewhere they shouldn't be.

"What is all this stuff?" Lee asked.

"Something to do with devil worship, I think. No one I've asked seems to know," said Andrew.

As they moved deeper into the chamber, Andrew managed to wipe his eyes on his sleeves and could now see a bit more, but his nose was throbbing in time to his heartbeat, and his headache was the kick drum.

"There should be other tunnels that will get us out," said Andrew.

They rushed through the chamber which opened out into an even bigger space with black and white checked floor tiles. They ran over to the far side when they heard the door rumble. The men were coming.

This room was huge and had a stone altar in the centre. Silver candelabras holding unlit black candles and a single, bone handled dagger, laid straight on top. Andrew grabbed the dagger from the altar. With nowhere else to hide, they crawled behind the altar and Lee turned off his lamp, causing them to be in almost complete darkness. The men walked out of the corridor and into the chamber at the far end. Two of them had lit torches, and were looking around for any sign of movement.

"They must have run straight through," said one of the torch bearers.

"WE KNOW YOU'RE IN HERE," boomed the voice of the large man who had spotted them on the stairs. Both Lee and Andrew flinched but managed to stifle themselves behind the altar, forcing their eyes shut.

"Maybe they're not here after all. Let's take the fourth tunnel and head to Warren Street. They're bound to show up."

Their footsteps could be heard heading out of the chamber and into one of the tunnels opposite, becoming fainter and quieter with every step. Lee and Andrew waited for the sounds to disappear completely before they looked around the side of the altar. They were gone.

"That was close!" whispered Andrew, as they both stood back up. Lee turned his lamp back on.

"Imagine what would have happened if we-"

"GOTCHA!" said the large man as he stepped out of the shadows behind an arch,

"Oldest trick in the book. THEY ARE HERE!"

Footsteps could now be heard running back. They panicked. Andrew and Lee picked a different tunnel and ran down it with no idea of where it would lead. The lamp was flickering occasionally, and they were pounding the flagstones beneath their feet as a rumble of a tube train could be heard passing through the tunnel above their heads, behind the stone.Fully charged on adrenaline, they ran as fast as they could before they hit the wall at the end of it, at full pelt. Andrew smashed into Lee's back, but it was like bouncing off a bear. He dropped the dagger he had picked up and it clattered onto the stone. Andrew's nose splattered fresh blood all down his front, and if it wasn't broken before, it definitely was now. His headache returned with a vengeance. Knowing that they didn't have much time, Andrew got to his feet and smeared some of the blood from his nose onto his fingers looking around at the dark wall for a dish. Lee stood up with half of the lamp in his hand, crunching the glass underfoot and the dimly lit bulb was dangling from the broken lamp. Lee picked up the dagger.

“Where's the dish, Lee? I can't see the dish?”

The light behind them in the tunnel was growing and creeping around the bend from the torch bearing men. They were getting closer.

Just then, the light from the broken lamp reflected off of the dagger, and onto the edge of a black dish in the top right-hand corner of the door.

“There!” Lee shouted and angled the knife like a mirror.

Andrew reached up and smeared his blood onto the dish just as the men came around the bend towards them. The door rumbled and opened inwards with a rush of air. They stepped out into a well-lit basement with stairs directly in front of them. The fastest man of the group had reached the door and managed to get an arm around Lee’s neck and pulled him into a headlock.

This can’t happen again. Not again, thought Andrew, in despair.

But this was Lee after all, not Ed, and Lee didn't take kindly to being man-handled. In the grip of the man, Lee turned around and picked the guy straight off his feet. The man’s eyes bulged with fear, as he had probably never been picked up like since he was a child. Lee then threw him right back into the tunnel like a rag doll. The other men who were still catching up fell over him creating a bundle of arms and legs, knitting together in the tight, darkened space. Wasting no time, Lee and Andrew turned and climbed four flights of stairs before reaching an emergency exit door, which burst outwards onto the street. They couldn't believe it, but they were now opposite King's Cross station.

"How did we get here?" asked Andrew in disbelief. The door shut behind them and it looked like the entrance to a maisonette above a shop.

"Crafty buggers," said Lee, looking back at the door as they moved on.

"I wonder how many doors in London don't go where you think they go?" Lee contemplated. He cautiously slid the silver dagger into the inside pocket of his jacket. They walked quickly, even though Andrews legs still burned.

"We need to hide," said Andrew.

"Yeah, and you need to wipe that blood off your face," said Lee.

They crossed the road and went into King's Cross Station to use the toilet. Andrew washed his face the best he could, but he still looked awful. His nose was crooked, and the black eyes were already beginning to appear, making the bright green tint of his eyes even more profound.

"Sorry about your nose, Andrew... I wasn't sure what else to do," Lee said, apologetically.

"Look at the state of it? my grandmother is going to kill me ." said Andrew.

"This exploring lark is getting quite dangerous, Andrew." said Lee,

"Was just a bit of fun at first, but now there seems to be a lot of blood involved."

"Well, I'm sorry about that, but I never said it would be easy," Andrew defended.

"Nothing worth doing ever is, is it?" Lee said, enthusiastically.

They walked out of the toilets at the station and headed back out onto the main road.

"We'd better split up," said Lee, "harder to spot that way."

"Ok, stay safe and we'll catch up on Monday." said Andrew,

Lee wandered off in the direction of Hoxton with an occasional glance over his shoulder, and Andrew decided to head north, towards home. Just as he walked past the St Pancras hospital, he heard the screech of tyres in the road.

Really? Don't these guys ever give up?

Four of the large men scrambled out of the van towards him. Across the road was an alleyway, so he bolted for it. He wasn't quite sure where it went, but anything was better than being dragged into that van. It was an alleyway, connected to multiple others with little break-out points into residential estates. Kids were playing in the street with abundant energy. The sound of their games made Andrew question his use of time. At the end of the last alleyway, he emerged behind a small parade of shops and walked around the front of them, trying to keep his head down.

A butcher's, a green grocers', and a newsagent's were on one side with lots of people waiting, keen to be served and going about their daily business. There was nowhere to hide, but opposite the parade two separate buildings.

A smart old wine shop called Bluvines and next to it, a dilapidated one that had a badly faded sign.

XAVIER'S BOOKS

"Perfect," he said to himself. "I like books."

7

The Bookshop

Xavier's Books was established in 1922 by none other than Richard Xavier himself. Back then, his parents were so proud that their twenty-five-year-old son, had managed to save enough money to move to London. He opened his own shop selling exactly what he loved most: Books, books, books, and more books. That was thirty years ago now. His mother had always called him Richard, but since she died over ten years ago, he didn't like it anymore. He now only answered to the name Xavier.

Sure, the early days had been tough, like it probably is for most new businesses. Sometimes a week would go by without him selling much at all. But with no wife to complain or family to feed, it didn't seem to matter that much really. He could survive on very little when he had to. Occasionally, someone would come in looking for a very special kind of book that only a few dealers could get hold of, and Xavier was one of those dealers.

He was resourceful, but they came at a hefty price. Over the years, that shop gained a reputation, and Andrew was about to find out why.

'Ding' sang the tarnished, brass doorbell as he opened the door into the shop. As it shut behind him quickly with a ker-plunk, he peered back out through the dusty glass for any sign of the men that were chasing him. The smell of old books hit him straightaway. It's such an amazing smell. Some people detested it, but not Andrew, quite the opposite.

The closed door muffled the sounds from the street, and all that could be heard was the sound of a ticking clock, from the back of the shop by the till. Around the perimeter of the shop were some glass cabinets; some with books inside and others with scrolls of some sort. The dusty, freestanding shelves that stood in the middle were groaning under the weight of the books they held. Some very large volumes low down, and some no bigger than a ration book higher up. Reds, greens, blues, pinks, and yellows. Gold leaf titles and some with no titles at all.

Andrew stepped towards one of the freestanding units and saw the title of a green book that caught his attention. "Great British Tunnels and their exploration." he said under his breath, whilst his hand was outstretched for it.

"Looking for a book about tunnels, eh?" said a deep, gruff voice from behind him.

It startled Andrew, but then again after the day he'd had so far, it was hardly surprising. He turned around to face the voice.

"Just browsing, really," said Andrew, insincerely.

“Who are you hiding from?” asked the man, his inquisitive brown eyes bared down on Andrew. “You look like you have had a right kick-in.”

“No one,” said Andrew, but his eyes were drawn back out through the windows to the other side of the street. The four men were now searching for him in the shops opposite. He couldn't leave now, even if he wanted to.

Xavier followed his gaze untill he saw them.

“Bloody Blackstones. Satanic scum! They know better than to come round here. Did they do this to you?” he asked.

Andrew was shocked. This man is the first person that knew anything about them.

“Come on, I’ll introduce you to Berty if you like?” he said, as he walked to the back of the shop.

“Berty? Who’s Berty?” asked Andrew, awkwardly as he shuffled with him towards the till and feeling quite scared that he was about to be fed to his dog.

The man went behind the counter and pulled out a massive double-barrelled shotgun and broke it over his arm. Andrew froze. He then clumsily tossed a box of cartridges onto the counter and grabbed a couple.

“This is Berty,” he said, whilst inserting a cartridge in each barrel, and stuffing more into his dirty, trench coat pocket.

“Not many people ask him twice.”

CLUNK. He snapped the gun straight while walking quickly towards the shop door.

This man is NUTS, thought Andrew.

He opened the door with a ding, and Andrew watched him from the safety of the shop. He walked over towards the men and pointed his gun into the sky to let off a shot.

BAAAAAANG went Berty. Some kids screamed and the world seemed to come to a shuddering stop. He then proceeded to point the gun at the largest of the men, who was now standing on the pavement before him.

"What have I told you lot about coming around here?" hissed Xavier.

The man held out his big hands, "Xavier, we are just looking for a boy that stole something from-"

BAAAANG went Berty.

The shot hit the man in the leg, and he fell to the ground hollering in agony. Xavier seemed completely unfazed. He broke Berty over his arm again, letting the shells fly out and into the gutter with a dual clink, reaching into his jacket pocket for more cartridges.

"Anybody else going to tell me why you are here?" Xavier asked sarcastically, like a primary school teacher, "Or... shall I just let you take him and leave?" he said, turning deadly serious to the other three men. Nobody moved.

"Oh well, have it your way," he said as he started to calmly load the fresh cartridges into the barrels.

The others ran over to the man on the floor and dragged him towards the rear of the shops leaving a dark trail of blood, just as a black van pulled in. With the men now onboard, the van wheel-spun out from behind the parade of shops with the side door still open and onto the road towards Euston, almost crashing head-on with a car coming down. Xavier looked at the customers and shopkeepers opposite who had their mouths open.

“Show’s over folks, come on now...shop shop,” he said, as he walked back towards his bookshop and stepped back through the door.

“Bloody Blackstones.”

Xavier walked sat down on a stool near the door, blocking Andrew’s exit. Berty's barrels were now broken but still loaded, smoke still drifting from the barrels.

“Who are you?” asked Xavier.

“I’m... well, I’m...”

“WHAT IS YOUR NAME, BOY?” forced Xavier.

“Andrew, Andrew Fairchild,” he said, a little scared.

“Andrew, Andrew Fairchild”? asked Xavier. “What sort of shit name is that, eh? They called you Andrew and couldn't be bothered to come up with a new middle name, so just repeated Andrew again? That’s just lazy.”

“No, no, sorry,” Andrew said. “Just Andrew Fairchild”

“Just? as in the cousin of justice?” asked Xavier, becoming quite animated. “Or... you are just, like a morally superior, positive plausible and justifiable action? Sir robin- the brave!” He held the shotgun aloft and shook it in salute.

"No." Andrew took a deep breath to try again and avoid further confusion. "My name is Andrew, please, just call me Andrew."

"Well, Andrew, I'm Xavier, and you were moments away from being in a lot of trouble, if Berty and I hadn't stepped in. You have no idea what those men do or who they serve, do you?"

"I know what they do," Andrew said.

"How so?" asked Xavier.

"It's a long story," said Andrew.

Xavier reached around and turned the shop sign from open to closed. "I'm all ears."

Andrew took a breath.

"You're not going to believe me," said Andrew.

"Try me," said Xavier, kicking over an upturned box for Andrew to sit on.

Andrew sat down and tried to gather himself.

"When I was ten, I used to explore bombsites with a friend of mine called Ed. We found this posh house in Mornington Crescent that had a basement, but the door to the basement was stuck shut. Ed cut his hand as we prised the door open. Once down there, we didn't find anything unusual at first, but Ed spotted a black glass figurine of a creature supporting a dish. It was fixed to the wall with a penknife next to it. Ed, accidently smeared some of his blood onto the dish."

"A blood door," said Xavier. "It opened, right?"

“Yes, yes it did,” said Andrew, feeling quite shocked that this thing had a name.

“What happened next, Andrew?”

“We lit some candles and walked into the dark tunnel which led onto a larger chamber. There was a door there that was quite heavily reinforced with metal, but we could see through the keyhole.”

“What did you see?” asked Xavier.

“It was like a dinner party, with wine and food. Only the food turned out to be...”

“What? What were they eating, Andrew?” asked Xavier.

“Body parts.” said Andrew.

"Body parts?" enquired Xavier.

"Yes; Body parts... body parts...of.."

"Body parts of?" asked Xavier, encouraging him to continue.

"Babies.” said Andrew, feeling a sense of shame.

“Sounds to me like you saw a post ritual feast, Andrew. One of the Blackstone's favourite things." said Xavier

“Blackstones? Is that what they are called?” asked Andrew.

“That’s what we all call them,” said Xavier. “But it’s a shortened version of their name.

Their official name is the Blackstone Society, or even just the Society, in some circles.

Anyway, what happened after that, Andrew?"

"Oh, well, one of the men at the dinner table saw me looking, Ed and I rushed to leave but didn't realise there were so many tunnels. I had forgotten which one we had come in by."

"Mornington Crescent. Let me see...," said Xavier. "That would be the Dominion Chamber. It's quite large and has at least a dozen ways in and out."

"How do you know all of this?" asked Andrew, feeling quite unnerved.

"Let's just say that I have had my dealings with these people over the years and know some of their secrets. Where did you end up?"

"We panicked and just chose a tunnel, ending up in a basement much further away. As we opened the door our candles blew out, leaving us in the dark. I re-lit mine and tossed the matches to Ed. He tried to light his candle whilst he was still by the door, and a huge arm draped in black cloth grabbed him around the neck and pulled him into the tunnel. The look on his face haunts me. "

"Scum," said Xavier, looking angry.

"I managed to make it out, but only just," said Andrew.

"Incredible," said Xavier.

"I still have nightmares where I'm back down in that tunnel with Ed," said Andrew.

"I'm not surprised, and that's quite a tale," said Xavier.

“I know you probably don’t feel like it, but you are lucky, Andrew. Most people don’t make it out.”

“You’re right, I don’t feel lucky,” said Andrew, “You’re the first person I’ve met that can tell me anything about them.”

“Why were they chasing you today?” asked Xavier, “Exploring with friends again?”

“Yeah," said Andrew.

"We were around the back of Russell Square, and there's a workshop with stairs that go down.”

“Faded green door, right? ” Xavier said, knowingly. Andrew was surprised. “Carry on.”

“We broke in and headed down the steps, but our lookout warned us of trouble.”

“Let me guess, the guys I just scared off?” asked Xavier.

“Yes, but there was no other way out. We had to head down deeper to try and get away, but there was a dead end.”

“Little dish?” said Xavier, rolling his hand over and over.

“Yes, but no knife this time, so my friend elbowed me in the nose for some blood.”

“Resourceful, although, ouch,” Xavier said, kindly.

“We almost got caught, but we made it through somehow and got out by King’s Cross. After splitting up, I was headed home but then they started chasing me...thats why I ended up here.”

“Well, well...that explains a lot,” said Xavier, “Missed a bit out though, didn’t you? What did you steal?” Xavier asked.

“We didn't steal anything!" said Andrew, but then he remembered what Lee still had in his pocket.

"Well...only a dagger,” said Andrew.

“What kind of dagger?” pried Xavier.

“Erm, bone handle, silver blade with some etching on it. It was sat on top of this black, marble table thing, under Russell Square. Lee took it home.”

“Now that is a *very* dangerous dagger,” Xavier said, looking worried.

“Don't worry, my friend Lee has loads of knives, he'll be fine.”

Xavier’s tone darkened,

“They call that chamber under Russell Square the Vetus Sacrum, and it is over four hundred years old, and there has been a working infernal cult there since its creation. Every year, a single cult group will sacrifice a minimum of fourteen people on the high altar. You do the maths, that's over five thousand people that have died in that place to satisfy their needs for change. They have only ever had ONE altar there, and only ONE dagger. That dagger holds more dark energy than you can possibly imagine. It has to stay on the altar, as it’s the only place that it doesn’t start to affect people.”

“Affect people?” said Andrew, now feeling worried for Lee.

“It has taken too many lives, shed too much blood,” said Xavier, “It brings out the worst side of people, makes them angry, spiteful, and aggressive. Where is it now?”

“Lee lives in Hoxton,” said Andrew.

“Right, I have a car outback. Can you navigate?” asked Xavier.

“Really? Andrew said, feeling confused. “Do we really need to go now?”

“If you want to see your friend alive again then, yes. Come on Berty, we are going out again!”

Xavier stood up and bolted the shop door. They headed towards the back of the shop and Xavier collected the rest of the cartridges that were sprawled out on the countertop, stuffing them into his pocket. Before Andrew knew it, they were out the back of the shop, but his legs were not working properly.

“What's the matter with you, boy?” asked Xavier.

“I haven't eaten since breakfast,” said Andrew, feeling quite embarrassed.

“Get in the car,” said Xavier, as he walked over to a black and rusty rover 75.

Andrew opened the door and sat down. The leather seats were heavily worn, but very comfortable. The over-powering stench of stale cigar smoke clung to the interior.

Xavier got in and reached over to the glovebox and pulled out a map of London and threw some chocolate on Andrew's lap,

"Here, this will help until we can get you something better."

Andrew ate it as fast as he could while they pulled away in the car.

"End of the road, Andrew. Left or right?" prompted Xavier.

"Erm," still chewing, "Left. I mean, hang on...," as he struggled with the folded map and all its creases. "Right!" gasped Andrew.

"Right, you are."

8

Mind Over Matter

Earlier that day...

After spending half an hour in the park and all the money he had on some ice cream for his sister Lucy, George was now very worried about Andrew and Lee. Lucy didn't seem to care, as she finally had what she had wanted all day. She sat on the bench eating an ice cream sundae as big as her head.

The uneasy frustration bubbled up in George. "Stay right here Lucy, I'll be back in five minutes, OK? Don't speak to anyone or move." She was too busy eating to verbally acknowledge his request.

George left the park the same way they came in, crossed the road, walked around the back to Colonnade and walked down the cobbled street once more. He hung back, watching for any movement. The removals van and men had now gone, and there was no sign of the suited men either. He walked with caution towards the green workshop door and saw that it was shut. It had a new lock to replace the one Lee had picked and had two more fitted to it, one down low and one high up. “They didn't waste any time,” he said.

Neither did George. He ran back across the road and into the park to collect Lucy, only to find she was no longer on the bench where he had left her. Panic grew in his chest, and he was spinning around to try and catch a glimpse of his sister amongst the kids that were playing in the park, laughing, and shouting at each other in a swirling of rhythms. Just as he was beginning to think the worst, he heard her voice from behind him.

“There he is. That's my brother George, right there.” He turned around to see Lucy standing with a smartly dressed couple who looked very out of place. The younger lady was in her late twenties, wearing a fur coat, and the gentleman wore a black, leather jacket.

“George, is it?” the lady asked.

“Yes Ma'am,” George said, politely.

“Your sister was just telling us all about you and your friends? Where are they now, George?” She had a feline quality to her. George knew that something wasn't right about these two. They didn't dress like regular people and seemed to be asking a lot of questions.

“My name is Pandora, and this is my fiance, Archie,” she said. As she twisted to introduce the man, George got a good look at her pendant necklace. It had a large Blackstone. Archie raised his hand to offer a handshake with a Blackstone ring. George knew they had to get moving. He shook Archie's hand, and he had a very powerful grip. He finally let go and George seized his chance.

“I really need to get my sister home; Lucy, we need to go. Mum wants you back home by four, remember?” he said to Lucy.

“No, she...,” Lucy started.

“Don’t argue with me Lucy, or I’ll never take you out again,” said George, his temper brewing.

“Where is ‘home’, George?” asked Pandora, seductively.

“Not too far,” George said, “closer with every step.”

He grabbed Lucy by the arm and left the two strangers standing still in the middle of the park whilst the kids played around them, completely unaware of the pure evil that was in their presence.

“What did I tell you about talking to strangers, Lucy? Huh?”

“They were nice!” she said, “They saw I was on my own and offered to give me a lift home.

I was just about to say yes, but you turned up and ruined everything. Now we have to walk, and my legs hurt. Just for that you can give me a piggyback.”

“I'm sorry I left you, but I had to check something. They may have seemed nice, Lucy, but they were bad people. God only knows what would have happened to you if I hadn't turned up when I did.” He stopped in front of Lucy and crouched a tad. “Hop on, LuLu.”

She did so and laughed as George ran around with her on his back like they used to. The last person that gave George a piggyback was his dad, but he didn't make it back from the war either and that distant memory seemed like a lifetime ago. He walked north towards Euston with a very sleepy little sister on his back. As he walked, he decided that the best plan of attack would be to take Lucy home to Chalk Farm. From there it was only ten minutes from Andrew's house in Kentish town. He knew that if they had made it out, they would probably be there.

We better get a move on, he thought, *Camden is a bit of a hike.*

9

ONE WAY OR ANOTHER

"Are you sure it was left?" asked Xavier whilst skidding to a stop at the top of the road. They had just gone past Angel, so it felt too early to turn off the main road. Hoxton, by Xavier's memory, was a left, but only once you were past Shoreditch police station. He'd been there occasionally in the past, sometimes overnight, but not so much these days. That was one of the few benefits of getting older. People dismissed you a bit, and automatically assumed you were a law-abiding citizen.

Yet here he was in a battered old car without any paperwork, a black and blue teenager riding shotgun, and a loaded one lying on the back seat. Good old Berty.

He remembers when he found Berty. Well, vaguely, as he was quite drunk at the time. Berty had come from an antiques auction that Xavier had stumbled upon about a decade ago. He knew lots about books, but very little about antiques. Following the funeral of his mother in a village in the Cotswolds, he went for a drink at the local pub. A week later, he still hadn't stopped. Being drunk numbed him from it all, so the idea of sobering up just so he could feel everything again was too much to bear. For some reason all the pubs shut between 2 and 4pm, so Xavier had to find something to occupy himself for a couple of hours.

On this particular Friday, he stumbled down into the village and looked longingly through the windows of the other pubs that also did the 'shitty-shut' thing, as he called it. Across the road there was a sign; 'Auction today.'

"Yay! hic," mumbled drunk Xavier, the taste of cheap whiskey blossoming in his mouth. He stumbled towards the auction house. Once inside, he looked around at all the furniture that was piled high inside the hall. Loads of brick-a-brack, and old games. Lots and lots of books, but nothing worth having. Even the first and second edition classics cabinet was a bit lack-lustre. He had multiple copies at the shop of pretty much everything in there.

Seeing the books on display had made him think, and he could feel his frozen mind starting to thaw out a bit. That wasn't a good thing. He still had at least an hour before the pubs re-opened, and that seemed like an eternity. He looked around the hall desperately for something boring, just as the auction was starting up.

Bang, bang, bang, as the auctioneer slammed down his gavel. Xavier winced from the noise.

"Shh, shooshy shoosh," drunk Xavier said, holding his grubby hands over his ears and closing his eyes.

Some of the old people there gave him a concerned look, while most people ignored him. He'd become used to that look in the last week. He just didn't care anymore, and he knew he couldn't carry on like this, but at that moment he couldn't see any other alternative. Drink or pain. Trouble was, drinking was becoming painful now too, in the form of loud noises.

Bang, Bang, Bang, came down the auctioneer's gavel again.

"Aghh."

"Lot number 001. The complete works of Joseph Conrad. Eight leatherbound books."

"Ahh, I've got two sets of those, collecting dust under the stairs," mumbled Xavier to himself, trying to keep his balance after an acidic burp.

"I will start the bidding at £20."

Xavier scoffed quite loudly. He thought these people were having a joke. Those books were only worth £5 at most. But hands started to raise.

"£20... £22... £24 with the lady in the purple jacket. £28... £30 I have with the gentleman in the orange wellies at the back. Anymore? No? Lot 001 at £30 going once, going twice...SOLD to the man in the orange wellies for £30."

"Unbelievable!" Xavier exclaimed.

£30!!? That's six times the price of what it's worth, Xavier thought, but the old salesman mantra crept into his head, leaving a cold shiver in its wake: *'Things are only worth, what people are willing to pay for them.'*

Just a fluke, he thought.

“Lot 002. First edition copy of Sense and Sensibility by Jane Austen,

Illustrated by Hugh Thomson.”

Xavier yawned....“Such a boring book,” Xavier said to himself.

“I will start the bidding at £15.”

“£15 for that overrated drivel?” Xavier snorted.

“£15 I have, with the man with an Eskimo hat. £17... £19 I have with the lady in red. £21... £23... as he pointed back and forth between the two interested parties.

£25 with the lady in red, going once, going twice. SOLD for £25 to the lady in red.”

This was unbelievable; it had to be a joke. His complete underestimation of the value of these books had started to make him paranoid. Maybe he was out of touch? Had he been selling his books too cheaply at the shop? Is this why he rarely had any money? Was the whole of London laughing at the shop in his absence saying things like, ‘Oh, that cheap bookshop? The one where the guy has NO IDEA what things are really worth?’

These thoughts, coupled with the death of his mother and slowly sobering-up, were too much.

“Lot 003. W.W. Greener oversized 12-gauge, double barrel shotgun in average condition. Circa 1850, heavily worn walnut stock and some light corrosion on the barrels. An inscription on the body states ‘Happy hunting, Berty.’ No reserve. I shall start the bidding at £10. Who will give me £10?"

The room felt quiet. It seemed that the village folk had more interest in crap literature than self-defence.

"OK then," said the auctioneer, "£8, anybody? No?" He was just about to hit the gavel down to write the gun off as unsold when Xavier's hand went up.

"£6! I'll give you six for it," said Xavier, as clear as he could manage.

The auctioneer looked around the room for someone else to steal the gun away from the drunk man who could barely stand, but no one was interested.

Auction houses are greedy. The commission to them was only about 7 shillings, but money is money after all.

"SOLD to the, erm, man in the middle." Bang went the gavel.

"Ouch" said Xavier, holding his ears once more. He stumbled over and found the counter to pay for the gun and collect his paperwork. Luckily the shotgun came with a leather holster, so he could carry it back through the village without scaring people.

A plan was formulating in his head. He'd had enough right now, and when the gun came up at the auction it was a sign. He was going to get some ammunition from the farm shop on the way back to his mother's old house, then sit in the garden and finish a whole bottle of whisky. And when he built up enough courage, he'd blow his own head off with both barrels. A smile crept out of his mouth for the first time in a month.

"The end," he said. "Well, no more of THIS, anyway," gesturing to his surroundings.

He did as he planned and stumbled back to the old house with the gun, a bottle of whisky and a box of cartridges. The garden was nice in the spring, albeit a little unkempt. So much wildlife and new plants opened out to show their colours. He sat at the rusty iron table on the patio, sipping his whisky with the loaded gun laid out in front of him. Three quarters of the way down the bottle, he realised that he was so drunk that he might not be able to do this. It had to be now.

Putting the butt of the gun on the floor, he placed his forehead on the front of the large barrels, but his balance was awful due to the whisky. He decided to try something else. He opened his mouth and just about managed to fit the figure of eight shaped barrels in with a tight squeeze. He felt kind of silly, but this just made him angrier. He thought of all the mistakes he'd made; moving to London for a dream that turned out to be a nightmare. His poor mum dying her on her own as one of the many consequences.

The pain of being alone with no partner, as it would be frowned upon. He was queer, he couldn't help that, but he'd never allowed himself to be happy either. None of that mattered anymore. The gun barrels were starting to hurt his mouth. He reached down, barely able to focus on his hands. The edge of his index finger found the triggers side by side. He placed his finger across them allowing them to cradle it briefly. *The End*, he thought and pushed down as hard as he could.

Click, click. fizzzzzzzzzzz

Nothing happened. He opened his eyes and moved the gun over so he could just about see his finger across the triggers. They were all the way down; the gun had failed to go off. Just then his jaw cramped up hard, squeezing the barrels in his mouth.

"Aww doh," he said, mouth still stretched around the barrels, "Imd stuuck."

Realising now this whole thing was a terrible idea, he had to find a way to get his mouth off this gun. First of all, he really needed to unload. Standing up, he placed the butt of the gun onto the table and moved the underlever that broke the barrels. The gun collapsed in half, releasing the damp, whisky-sodden cartridges out onto the tabletop and causing his mouth to slip down the barrels even further. "Aaaghhgh," he said, as he gurgled and wretched.

"I dink I deed elp," he said trying to find the energy and balance to head out of the garden gate. With the barrels still broken and holding up the gun that was still in his mouth, he stumbled to the side gate and opened it. He stepped out onto the road as the sun was setting over the Cotswolds hills.

He wasn't sure if it was the fact that he tried to take his own life had given him a refreshed perspective, or if it was just simply that beautiful. Either way he was still in awe as the car hit him, knocking him flying into the ditch.

"Stay awake, mate. The ambulance is on its way, OK?" said the driver that had hit him.

Xavier must have blacked out as the next thing he knew he was in the back of a travelling ambulance. The gun was still stuck in his mouth, being held by a kind lady.

"Hi, I'm Angela," said the nurse, "Looks like you were hit by a car, and you must have slipped onto your gun in the ditch, silly billy."

Xavier had groaned and held out his hands to signal for her to try and remove the gun, but she thought he was pointing towards the inscription.

"Oh, sorry," she said. "Berty, is it? It's a bit stuck at the moment. Not a happy hunting day after all, is it Berty?"

By that point, he was too drunk to argue anymore.

A strange memory, that. Snapping back into reality, Xavier massaged his jaw.

"Right!" said Andrew. Xavier gave him a sideways glance as if to say, 'we are lost, aren't we?'

They wiggled through the backstreets like a snake in a maze and finally drove into Hoxton, crossing over the main road and into New North Road. Lee lived with his parents and two of his older brothers halfway down in the townhouses. The eldest had got himself circled last year, and now lived with his wife in Shoreditch. Andrew had always liked the look of Lee's house. It had a lovely big front door with a swirl carved out at the centre, and large curved windows on the ground floor.

"Just here, on the right," said Andrew. As they pulled into park up, a typewriter came crashing through one of those beautifully curved windows and onto the bonnet of the car, spraying glass onto the pavement and road. Andrew looked at Xavier in shock. Xavier just opened his door and said, "Just in time, I see."

Walking round to the bonnet, he picked up the typewriter by the X and Y and held it away from himself like a very heavy dead rat. Walking up the steps to the front door of the house with a gaping hole for a window, you could hear the shouting coming from within. Horrible, vindictive words followed by screaming and threats of violence.

KNOCK, KNOCK.

The shouting didn't stop, and nobody opened the door.

KNOCK, KNOCK.

Just then, the door was violently opened by a very large man in his fifties. "What the bloody hell do you want, eh?" said Lee's dad.

"Is this yours?" Xavier asked, holding up the typewriter at his eye level briefly before lowering it again.

"Well, it was, but I threw it away. And as a taxpayer, that's my right to do that! What gives you the audacity to bring it back to me when I clearly don't want it?"

"It landed on my car," Xavier said, realising there wasn't anything he could say to calm him down.

Lee's dad looked over his shoulder down to the rusty Rover, with a few new scratches and dents on the bonnet. "Oh, it's money you want, eh?! Just like everybody else, you are. Come here, dangling my things in front of me, and demanding money. I have a good mind to make you eat that thing."

Andrew decided to step in and try to calm the situation. "Is Lee home, Mr Beaks?" he said, hoping he didn't bite his head off too.

"Of course, he is. He's in his room, as per-bloody-usual. Reading more crap about exploring, no doubt."

Xavier put the typewriter down gently on the top step. Mr Beak's rant continued.

"I can't wait for him to get to work and start paying some rent, instead of wasting his time and energy with the likes of you.

Lee!! come down here now! Your useless friend is here with a strange bloke trying to extort me for money!

'Oo, you hit my car," he said, mocking Xavier,

"it's a shit car anyway, mate."

Lee came to the door and seemed quite calm about everything, "Alright, Andrew, what's up?"

Lee's dad was now bored and went back inside to reheat the argument he was having with his wife before he was rudely interrupted. Lee came out front and closed the door to for a little privacy.

"Lee, this is Xavier. Xavier, this is Lee. He owns a bookshop near Somers town, and he saved me from four of the big men earlier. He even shot one in the leg," said Andrew, "He knows all about them and knows something even worse about that dagger we took today."

"What about it?" asked Lee.

"That dagger needs to be returned. It's already tearing your family apart," said Xavier.

"It's not even here. I'm not that bloody stupid," said Lee.

"Where is it, then?" asked Andrew.

"I buried it in a box in Aske Gardens, down the road."

Xavier and Andrew looked at each other in confusion.

"But what about your dad, the window, and you know... the nastiness?" asked Xavier.

"Don't worry about that," said Lee, "He's always like that, especially on a Saturday. You get used to it."

Andrew had only met Mr Beaks once before, but that was at school when he was younger. He must have been on his best behaviour.

"We need to get that dagger, Lee. Can you come and show us where it is?" asked Xavier.

"Yeh, of course. Let me grab my coat." Lee opened the door, allowing some of the shouting onto the street once more. He swung his coat on and shouted, "I'm going out, back soon!" Either nobody heard him, or they just didn't care, as they continued to argue. He shut the door and walked with them down to the pavement by Xavier's car.

"Dad's been throwing stuff through the window again, I see. Was an iron last week. Landed on a little convertible sports car. Luckily the roof was up."

"That could have been a lot worse," said Andrew.

"Well, the iron was still burning hot so the man who owned it wasn't best pleased. The trouble is people come to complain and then see how big and angry my dad is and have second thoughts. He gets away with murder. It's a complete nightmare."

"Where is Aske Gardens?" Xavier asked.

"Only five minutes walk down the road," said Lee.

"Hop in the car then," said Xavier.

Andrew let Lee sit in the front as he had to hide Berty in the rear footwell. Xavier turned the car around and drove down the road following Lee's directions. Just as they got a hundred yards down the road, the boys saw a tall and skinny chap with a familiar walk, walking towards them on the pavement. It was George.

"Stop. Stop here, Xavier. It's George," said Andrew.

"Oh, more the merrier," said Xavier, sarcastically.

"George!" Andrew shouted through the crack of the open window. He looked very surprised to see them both alive and in a car with a strange bloke.

"You made it!" said George, "Did you hear the horn? I got chased by some very angry removal men and Lucy almost got pinched from the park by a couple wearing Blackstones.

Only left her for five minutes. The bastards are everywhere. I went to your place first, Andrew, but you weren't in."

"George, this is Xavier. Xavier, this is George."

"Get in, George... I don't have all day," Xavier said, as politely as he could. Andrew moved over and George climbed in the back. They moved off again down the road in search of Aske Gardens.

"Ooh, your nose is a bit bent, Andrew, and you have a couple of shiners. What happened there?" George asked, "Oh, and why is there a massive gun in the footwell?"

"That's Berty!" said Andrew, and without the context of seeing Berty in action earlier, he realised how ridiculous that sounded.

"So, what happened guys? I had a horrible feeling you got caught," asked George.

"We nearly did, mate," said Lee, from the front, "Had to smash Andrew in the nose so we could open a door or two, because needing blood to open doors is a normal thing, right? Bloody weirdos, these Satanists."

"Blackstones," said Xavier.

"Blackstones?" asked George.

"Short for the Blackstone Society," said Andrew. Andrew tried to explain where they were with things.

"We ran off with an old dagger from the chamber under Russell Square, but according to Xavier here, it's very old and has killed too many people. It's infected with dark energy and must be returned to the altar we stole it from."

"Sounds bad, but you can't return it," George argued. "Not there anyway, they've added more locks and everything."

"Ha," said Xavier, dryly. "You honestly think that's the only way into that chamber? One of many, boys, on that you can be certain."

"So, where is this dagger now?" George asked. Just then the car came to a screeching halt; they were there. To their left was Aske gardens.

10

Park life

Aske gardens was a green space for the community where the old Aske Hospital used to be. Its name came from an Alderman and Haberdasher in the City of London, called Robert Aske. The old trees were tall and cast long shadows in the late afternoon light. It was a nice park and surrounded by some beautiful buildings including a bold, white stone manor with high pillars.

They stepped out of the car and before they could even get into the garden, they could hear the cacophony of animals fighting. Yes, the sun was beginning to show signs of setting, but this tension was not light related. It was more than that.

As they walked through the gate, they could already see multiple bird fights going on in the neglected grass and hedges. Squirrels were chasing each other around the park at breakneck speed. Cats were hissing in the bushes and even the snails seemed defiant and angry.

"See what I mean?" said Xavier.

It was the strangest sight to watch all these animals raring up and tearing into each other.

"Where is it, Lee? Where did you bury it?" Andrew asked.

"Over there, by that tree," he said, walking over towards the area.

Some shadows in front of them moved slightly in and out of focus. It became apparent suddenly that they were not alone. One of the men stepped out of the shadows and into the light. The animals were still going crazy trying to kill each other around them.

"Xavier, we did na spect to see you 'ere," said Marlon.

Marlon was an Obeah man and the Leader of the Yardies in London. Obeah was a Jamaican form of Voodoo.

"We felt diss ting from tree miles away, yah knaw."

"Felt what, Marlon?" asked Xavier.

"Don't play dumb wid me maan," said Marlon. "I figured, sumting datt strong must be worth 'aving."

"You figured wrong," said Xavier. "This thing is so dark; it will destroy you and all you care about, Marlon."

"Didn't come all de way out here for nutting blud," He hissed. "Man be takin what me came fa."

Then, eight other Yardies stepped out of the bushes holding machetes and clubs.

"Here, it's here, just take it," said Lee, trying to calm everyone down. The silver dagger shone, even in the half light. They could see the inscriptions on the blade, and the stresses in the bone handle.

Marlon held up his arm in a fist, which stopped the others from advancing. His eyes fixed on the shimmering blade. He walked over to Lee who was holding the knife flat in two hands and took it slowly from his palms.

"So diss is the ting that woke me up. Time for us ta get acquainted. He, he." He held the blade up to look at it properly, before putting it into his inside pocket and began to walk away.

"Much respect, Xavier, see ya soon yeh?" The other Yardies all followed Marlon slowly out of the park.

Once they had gone it was like someone who had control of the angry switch had gone home for the evening, and the volume slowly turned down. The birds stopped fighting on the grass and flew their separate ways, and the squirrels stretched out on the flower beds exhausted from the chase. The snails, well they just seemed very snail-like, which was a relief.

"That was weird; Who was that man?" asked Andrew

"Marlon is an obeah man, a very powerful voodoo high priest. He also happens to be the leader of the yardies, a Jamaican gang. A couple of years ago, he came to the shop for a book and left with a few more bits than he planned to."

"Great," said Andrew, frustrated. "So, what now? These yardies, who happened to be armed to the teeth, now have this dagger that turns people close enough into maniacs. How many people will die, do you think?"

“I don't know, but I think an anonymous tip off to the Blackstones wouldn't go amiss,” said Xavier, as he made his way out of the park and towards his car.

“How on earth do you do that?” asked Lee, following him but looking confused.

“Some shops, but the best bet is a launderette,” said Xavier. “There's a cult one on Upper Street in Islington. He climbed back into the driving seat.

“That's just for clothes, isn’t it?” asked George, getting in the back of the car.

“Clothes, money, and information. They all need cleaning, you know,” said Xavier.

“How do you know they are connected to the Blackstones?” asked Andrew.

“A star... they nearly always use a star in either the name or as a symbol. Although recently I've seen a 666 dressed up in a circle, and even devil horns. Most people don't bat an eyelid at any of it. If it wasn't bad enough to be worshiping the devil and sacrificing people. They get a kick out of being able to advertise the fact they do these things, and still, nobody knows or wants to know. Hidden... it's always hidden in plain sight. There for all see, if only they knew what to look for.”

“Need me to map read?” asked Lee, who was back in the passenger seat.

“I’m all good thanks, Lee. I've been there once or twice.” Xavier drove off in the direction of Islington while they tried to make sense of what had happened today.

“That chamber under Russell Square was huge. You could have got a thousand people in there easily,” said Lee.

“That’s only one of many, boys,” said Xavier.

“How do you know so much about them, Xavier?” asked Andrew.

Xavier looked straight ahead at the road but talked anyway.

“When you are at the lowest point in your life, you will be presented with choices. Some internal, some external. Some bad and some very bad. A Blackstone found me when I was ready to call it quits, and he convinced me that their way of life would provide some solutions.”

“So, you joined them?” asked George.

“Not quite,” Xavier said. “They invited me to a secret gathering in Shoreditch that I was told would be my initiation. I overheard a couple of them call it the ‘Volens sacrificium’, but they underestimated me. Being of an inquisitive nature, I looked it up. ‘Volens sacrificium’ translates as ‘willing sacrifice’ in Latin. They needed me to turn up willingly, only to be slaughtered in front of their people for their own gains. I was quite upset, but those feelings quickly crystallised into anger. So, I made a plan to get back at them. I blocked all the exits to that chamber where they waited for me. I remember It was a cold November evening. There must have been at least two hundred of them waiting down there when I pumped the petrol down. The fuel tanker was only half empty when I lit the match. Some made it out, most didn't. Every time I see them now, I either try to run them over or shoot them with Berty.”

“Jesus, Xavier, that is dark!” said George.

They all sat there in silence for an awkward moment. Andrew couldn’t help but picture someone in a black robe, on fire and trapped behind a gate.

“Don't offer them any sympathy, boys, because I'm telling you now, if any one of you end up on their altar you will receive none whatsoever. Trust me,” said Xavier.

Xavier was right. Andrew was confused why he still had sympathy for bad people. Maybe somewhere in the back of his mind he feared that letting go of that would also mean losing a part of himself. As if by doing so it would make him just as bad as the Blackstones.

“The Blackstones are not going to be happy when they find out their dagger is now in the hands of a Jamaican gang of loonies,” said Andrew.

“Well, they are probably the only ones who stand a chance of getting it back before it's too late. They need to know, it’s as simple as that,” said Xavier.

They had just turned right at Angel and were now heading north into Islington. Driving past the shops, the transition between day and night trade hung in the balance. The grocers and butchers were clearing down for the day and bringing their produce in, whilst some bars and off-licences were just getting set up for their busy night ahead. Xavier pulled in and parked twenty yards down from the Eastern Star Launderette. One of the few businesses that was always open day or night.

“Wait here.” said Xavier. “The less they see, the better.”

11

Washer, Washer, Washer

Xavier left the boys in the car and walked down the pavement towards the launderette. There were about ten shops in between him and his destination, and four of them were using a star either in their logo or name.

“It's getting worse here,” he said to himself as he avoided a drunk guy that almost walked into him.

Once outside the launderette he could see the windows were heavily steamed up from all the washing going on inside. As he reached the door, he saw a familiar sign was hand-etched into the glass. It was highlighted by the condensation behind. Three sixes, all joined at the holes to resemble a circular blade. He pushed on the door and entered the launderette.

“Thirty-five, ready!” said the little old Chinese lady, behind the counter.

A man in his forties stood up from the small seating area to the side and went to collect his laundry. He paid and left, leaving the laundrette empty, except for the two other staff who were loading and unloading the oversized machines. Xavier walked up to the counter to catch the attention of the little old lady.

“Ticket, please,” she said, politely.

“I don’t have one, sorry,” said Xavier. She looked confused, as he wasn't carrying any bags of clothes either.

“I have important information to trade.”

Her eyes sharpened. “This is launderette, we wash clothes here, dummy.”

“I can see that, but what I know is quite valuable and the people you serve will want to know this as soon as possible.” said Xavier.

She waited for the two other staff to move away from the machines and into the staff area, out the back.

“Know what?” she asked.

“Money first, then information,” said Xavier

“No, no, you lie,” she said, crossing her arms in distrust.

Xavier did not budge or remove his gaze from hers.

“Oh well,” teased Xavier. “I’ll head two doors down to the restaurant. They open in twenty minutes, I think.” Xavier checked the wrist where a watch would be if he had one. “They will be so surprised when I tell them that you passed this up and delayed things for the Society."

"Sayonara!” he said, feeling smug.

That feeling didn't last long when he remembered that Sayonara was Japanese, not Chinese. *Smooth Xavier, real smooth.* He turned on his heels and counted down silently as he walked towards the door, but he never even made it to three.

“STOP!” she said and swore under her breath in Chinese.

Xavier turned back around and played the fool. “Yes?” he said, walking back towards the lady with a big cheesy smile.

“How much?” she said, bluntly.

“Oh, well this information I have is hugely important. They will thank you endlessly for it...”

He was like a car salesman. She rolled her eyes as he continued.

“Well, they probably won't because they are a very ungrateful bunch generally, I find.

But you will probably get back double whatever you pay me, or at the very least get your money back if you fill in the expen-,”

“STOP TALKING WEIRD MAN!” she screamed. “£10!” she shouted and slapped the money on the counter.

“More,” said Xavier with an even cheesier smile.

“AGGHHHH, BLOODY WEIRD MAN!” She slapped another £10 note on the counter and said, “No more. Take or leave.”

“Take, take,” said Xavier, softly raising his hands to feign defeat having had his fun, winding the poor little satanic lady up. She may have not been satanic herself, but she did her bit for them. He folded the money up and placed it in his top breast pocket. The Blackstones used these types of businesses to launder their money for them, no pun intended, as it was very hard to actually prove how much money was actually taken in. There was a lot of money in drugs, prostitution and people trafficking, but as it was illegally obtained, you couldn't use it easily. Not everyone accepted cash, especially when you purchased bigger things like property. The Blackstones would take over the accounts and syphon as much dirty money through the business as it could take, rack up huge debts to suppliers and then shut it down, avoiding all taxes, only to start a new, albeit very similar business elsewhere.

"Ok. Information, now," she said, a bit calmer, unfolding her arms and placing both hands on the countertop.

Meanwhile in the car...

The boys were talking in the car when they noticed two large men walk out of the star hair salon and waved farewell to the owner.

"Blackstones! Heads down," said Lee, as they all tried to lean out of sight and not move until they passed. The two men walked up the pavement towards the launderette and stopped outside, looking in. They seemed surprised by what or who they saw inside, and decided to go in.

"Uh oh," said Lee. "Xavier is in trouble... they've gone in."

"We've got to do something!" said Andrew.

"Like what? Offer to hold their coats while they give him a kick in?" asked George.

"Well, we do have *that,*" said Lee, looking around into the footwell.

"Berty? Are you mad?" said Andrew.

Back inside...

Xavier had stopped toying with her. She was starting to become agitated again.

"The High Altar at Russell Square lost its companion today."

She nodded all too quickly. This told him that the word must have already gotten around.

"It is in the hands of Marlon, the head of the yardies."

Her eyes lit up and a small smile crept in. The two giant Blackstones that were outside walked into the launderette slowly and quietly through the steam towards the counter. Xavier could not hear them because of the washing machines, and he was too fixated on the lady's reaction to care.

"Money back now," she said, coldly.

"What?" said Xavier. "Why is that?"

But she didn't answer, just looked over his head at something behind him. He felt both of his arms being seized by two large hands before being picked up off his feet, like a chip ready to be dipped. He was turned around to face the front of the shop and placed down again into the gaze of a huge Blackstone.

"We've been looking for you everywhere. You shot Darren in the leg earlier, and now we've got to bring you in."

"Can't you see I'm a bit busy?" said Xavier.

"He stole money, he stole money!" screamed the little Chinese lady to the Blackstones. "£50!"

"No, it wasn't!" said Xavier, as he turned to face her. "It was £20, you lying little-"

BONK.

Xavier felt a crunch in his neck and his vision slowly turned black. One of the Blackstones had used one of his oversized fists as a mallet and knocked Xavier out cold onto the floor with a crumpled thump. The Chinese lady wasted no time in coming around and retrieving her cash from his top pocket before the Blackstone dragged him on his back by his collar towards the front of the shop. They stopped two feet short of the door. The other Blackstone said, "Stay here, I'll get the car." before leaving the launderette and walking up the high street, while the boys walked towards the launderette with Berty concealed vertically in Lee's jacket.

They looked at the steamed up windows and couldn't see much at all, but they could hear the vibration of a finger on wet glass. Looking down, they saw a single fingertip writing something in the condensation at the very bottom pane of the door.

It was 'Help', only the 'p' was the wrong way round.

"He's right there," said Andrew.

"I've got this," said Lee, removing Berty from his coat and straightening the barrels to load him. He kicked open the launderette door straight into the face of Xavier who was lying on the floor just inside.

"AHHHHH," hollered Xavier, as the door bounced off his head with a juddering sound and shut again leaving Lee outside.

"We closed, we closed," shouted the little old lady from the back of the steamy shop, muffled by the door.

Lee opened the door slowly this time and stepped inside. He saw the large dark figure of the remaining Blackstone move towards him through the steam.

"WE... ARE... CLOSED." Lee stood still with the raised shotgun and waited for the Blackstone to be close enough for him to feel the barrels press against his chest. The Blackstone did and froze, realising his mistake.

"I've come for him," said Lee, looking down briefly at Xavier on the floor, who was still writhing in pain. "Not clothes."

George opened the door behind them enough for Xavier to be pulled out onto the pavement by Andrew.

"Are you sure you know what you are doing?" asked the Blackstone. "People have been killed for less, boy."

"Tell me about it," Lee retorted. "People have been killed for no reason at all by you horrible lot. Innocent people, with families and friends."

The Blackstone just laughed gently to himself, becoming less intimidated by the shotgun that was still pressed into his chest.

“You don't know the half of it,” said the Blackstone. “But I promise you this, it won't be long before we get to know who YOU are, and where YOU live.” A flash of worry must have registered on Lee’s face.

“Yeah, we’ll get to know all about you, your family, and who you care about.”

Lee took a deep breath as a small ray of hope dawned on him.

“But you're the only one who has seen me,” Lee said.

The Blackstone considered it, “True, but that won't-”

BA-BAAAAAAAAANG, went Berty.

Lee’s ears rang instantly from both barrels exploding into the Blackstone’s chest at point blank range, sending the large man back into the shop and onto the floor. As Lee’s hearing adjusted, he could now hear the little old lady screaming from the back, while the washing machines still turned and splashed. The recoil from the gunshot had pushed Lee back into the door, causing one of the windows to crack. Blood was everywhere. It was all over the near walls and ceiling like a mist coat, and it hung in the air combining with the spent gunpowder and steam to create a pink hue.

Is this really what it felt like to kill someone? Because he didn't feel sorry at all. He felt relieved. This guy was threatening to hurt people he cared for and he couldn't let that happen. This was the only way. Concealing the still smoking gun in his jacket as best he could, he stepped out of the launderette. Quite a few of the shoppers and a few shopkeepers opposite were looking over. They must have heard the blasts, but nobody said a word.

George and Andrew had just about got Xavier to his feet and were walking him back to the car when they had heard the shots. The noise seemed to give Xavier a new lease of life as he shouted "Berty!" before turning around to see Lee walk out with the gun held down in his coat, barrels smoking down low like inverted ship vents in the wind. He was looking a bit dazed.

"Come on, we've got to go," said Andrew. Lee caught them up as they walked towards the car.

"Can you drive?" said George to Xavier, who was beginning to look a bit sleepy again.

"He's not bloody driving!" exclaimed Lee, fishing into Xavier's pocket looking for his keys.

"Can you drive?" Andrew asked Lee.

"Of course, I can," he said, shaking the recovered keys. "My dad taught us all when we were very young."

"You are full of surprises," George said, getting Xavier into the back seat and joining him. Lee jumped in the driving seat and started the engine while Andrew shut the passenger door.

"Where to?" asked Lee.

"Anywhere but here; Just go," said Andrew.

As they drove off, a car pulled up and the other Blackstone got out. They could see him walking over to the door of the launderette, completely oblivious to what was waiting for him on the other side.

12

The Invisible Line

Lee had driven them north up the Holloway Road towards Highgate and stopped at a fish and chip shop on the way. Andrew got some money from Xavier's pocket and went in to order, just in case people were on the lookout. This also gave Andrew the opportunity to eat a few handfuls of chips secretly before taking them to the car. He was starving after all, surviving on toast, some chocolate and a few of George's sweets. It had been the strangest day. They found a quiet backstreet where they could park up and get themselves together a bit. Xavier woke up enough to eat some chips and complained about his banging headache.

"They must have really whacked you," said Lee with a straight grin, hoping Xavier had forgotten about the door incident.

"I've had worse," said Xavier, massaging his own temples. He finished his chips and seemed much more lucid.

"What happened with Berty, Lee?" asked Xavier. George and Andrew stopped eating suddenly.

Lee looked down at his hands that were resting in his lap, either side of his chips in the newspaper.

“I didn’t have a choice really. That Blackstone threatened to hurt my family, Xavier, and then he laughed at me. Didn't see any other way out to be honest,” said Lee.

“How do you feel now?” asked Xavier.

“A bit sick, but I think I ate too fast. These are small portions from that place?” said Lee.

Andrew avoided eye contact whilst still eating his chips.

“But I'm not sorry,” Lee continued. “I thought about what you said, Xavier, and the lack of mercy stuff. These people are horrible, and one less Blackstone around can only be a good thing, right?”

“That’s right,” said Xavier.

Andrew was still in two minds. One part was worried for Lee and wondered how he could be so calm when he just killed a man in cold blood less than an hour ago; the other part of his mind felt a sting of jealousy that he didn't expect. Killing a Blackstone to protect your family took courage, and although he would like to think he could have done the same thing, he still wasn't sure if he could. Even after all he had seen, and Ed’s abduction by these people, he still couldn't guarantee that if he was faced with the same ultimatum, he would pull that trigger and that worried him.

“Will it be safe for you back at the shop, Xavier?” asked Andrew.

"Not tonight, that's for sure," said Xavier. "Good job I don't actually live there, eh?"

"Where do you live then?" asked George.

"Now that would be telling, wouldn't it?" said Xavier. "It's not that I don't trust you lot, especially after tonight's performance, but the stakes are too high right now. They could threaten you to talk, but if you don't know you can't say, right? No offence."

"None taken," said George.

"All change, please," said Xavier, doing the impression from the railway while opening the door and stepping out of the car. He swapped positions with Lee and jumped into the driver's seat, feeling ready to drive again. They turned around and headed back down the Holloway Road and drove past the Eastern Star launderette, expecting to see the worst. But there was nothing. No police, ambulance, or road closures. Customers were going in and out like nothing had even happened. So weird. Further down, they turned off towards Hoxton.

"I'm going to have a quiet day tomorrow," said Lee.

"Yeah, me too," said George with Andrew nodding in agreement in the front seat.

The eventful day had knocked the life right out of them. They pulled up outside Lee's house at 10pm. Lee got out. "Thanks, Xavier, nice to meet you." He shut the door and walked up to his front door while Xavier drove off towards Camden. Andrew directed Xavier to George's house through the back streets and they dropped him off.

“See you on Monday, Andrew. Thanks, Xavier,” said George.

George shut the door, and it was just Xavier and Andrew again.

“I still can’t believe that Lee shot a Blackstone. He really does amaze me sometimes,” said Andrew.

“Everyone has an invisible line, Andrew, without exception.”

“What's that?” asked Andrew.

Xavier explained.

“It's the point where someone will find the inner strength to do terrible things in order to protect what they care about the most. That Blackstone underestimated Lee and crossed his line without knowing, and he paid the ultimate price.”

“I hope I can find my inner strength, if it’s needed,” said Andrew.

“What do you mean?” asked Xavier. “You're still alive, aren't you?

And from what you've told me about your time in the tunnels and close scrapes with them so far, I’d say you have a lot of strength. More than you know. It’s one thing to land a few blows, but it takes real grit to take a hit and keep coming.”

“I don't feel very strong,” said Andrew.

“That will come in time... you’ll see,” said Xavier. “So, where do you live, Andrew?”

"Now that would be telling," he said, opening the door and stepping out. It was only a ten-minute walk for Andrew from George's, but Xavier didn't need to know that.

"Because if you don't know, you can't say, right?" said Andrew, with a wink.

"Clever boy," said Xavier, smiling. "Fancy a Saturday job? I could use a hand sorting the shop out."

"Yeah, why not," said Andrew.

"Great, we open at 9am. See you next week."

Andrew shut the car door. Xavier lit a cigar and drove off with smoke billowing out of the gap of in the window. Andrew started the walk home with a bit of a spring in his step and a fizz of excitement. He had a job! In a cool bookshop with a wacky guy and a gun called Berty. What could possibly go wrong?

13

Monday Morning

Monday felt like a very normal day considering all that had happened at the weekend. After getting back late on Saturday night, with what looked to be a broken nose and two black eyes, Andrew's Mum wasn't best pleased. She was convinced that he had gotten into a fight with someone. He just said that he had run into Lee in the park playing football with some kids and they had clashed heads, but he could tell that she didn't believe him. Even telling her about his Saturday job did little to cheer her up. He had spent most of Sunday making up for being late by cooking and tidying, wishing he was somewhere else, like the bookshop.

The walk to school on Monday seemed to take forever. He had already sat down at the back in his usual place in English when Lee and George arrived. Mr Wilson wasn't there yet, so he knew he was early.

"Alright, boys, have a good weekend, did we?" asked Lee.

"Walking on eggshells for most of Sunday because of this," said Andrew, pointing to the bruises around his eyes.

"Mine was pretty bad too, Andrew," said George. "Lucy snitched on me about the park, and I had to spend the whole of Sunday as 'her slave'."

"George, are you wearing makeup? asked Lee, noticing some blue eyeliner still present on one side of George's face. George rubbed his eyes rapidly before opening his first bag of sweets.

"What about you, Lee?" asked Andrew.

"My Dad was quite drunk by the time I got back, so he wasn't that bad really. Had weird dreams though, about the launderette, and... you know... Berty," said Lee, quietly.

"Yeah, that's been playing on my mind too," said Andrew. "I know why you did it, but it must feel very strange. I just hope you're ok, that's all."

Lee, not being used to anyone caring about him, just shrugged and let out an awkward "Thanks."

"What about you Andrew? Did your grandmother catch up with you?" he asked.

"My nose is straight now, isn't it? well, she saw to that," said Andrew.

"There isn't enough soap in the world for what we did yesterday," teased George, eating an apple.

"Enough to get that makeup off, George," smirked Andrew.

"Oh, guess what? Xavier offered me a Saturday job in the bookshop," said Andrew, proudly.

"Wow, now that will be interesting. How long before the place is burnt to the ground do you think? If it hasn't been already, that is," said George, sarcastically.

"No idea. I'll find out this weekend, I guess. We may have to swap our exploration day to Sundays now, if that's ok guys?" Andrew asked under his breath, as Mr Wilson walked into class.

"On the day of rest?" Lee teased, sticking his tongue out.

"After the last one, you must be bloody mad! Where are we going this week?" George said with a smile.

"I think we need to wait for a while, just until things calm down a bit," said Andrew.

Andrew honestly felt blessed to have such funny and courageous friends. The rest of the week dragged on relentlessly as they were revising heavily for their O levels the following month. By the time Friday came about, Andrew felt like his mind was ready for the scrap heap. They walked together down to the school gates and as they neared their parting point George said, "Hope your first day goes well, book slave."

"Ha ha, very funny. Tell Lucy to go easy on the blusher," said Andrew. George went a bit red.

"Say hi to Berty," said Lee as he walked away, shouting 'PULL' and pretending to clay pigeons from the sky.

All joking aside, Andrew did wonder what his first day would entail.

14

The Bookkeepers Apprentice

Three weeks later…

"All this...off," said Xavier, handing Andrew the sponge and razor blade.

"Ahh really?" whined Andrew.

The shop windows had been vandalised with black paint, again. Usual rubbish. A pentagram How original. *'Die Zavear Die!*

If you are going to threaten someone, at least spell their name correctly. It's even written on the sign above for gods' sake.

'Curs-ed be who enters here.'

What are you, a pirate?

Andrew was halfway through his O level exams at school and his head was spinning. This was the second Saturday in a row that he was stuck outside the front, cleaning the graffiti off the glass while the people shopping on the other side of the street looked on. He could see them in the reflection, pointing and talking about the shop. Still looking at the reflection in the window, he could see that he looked a state. His clothes were wet from the sponge work, and he was covered head to toe in little black dots from scraping the paint. At least his blackeyes were pretty much gone now.

Stepping back to inspect the whole window, he bumped into a pale man in an old suit that seemed to have come out of nowhere. He had knocked his newspaper out from his hand, so he bent down to pick it up.

"So sorry, Sir. I didn't see you," Andrew said, handing back his paper.

"That's quite alright," the man said, nervously. "Accidents happen."

Just then he realised something that confused him. He looked at the window in front of them but could only see himself, even though the man was right there. He had no reflection.

"Good day to you," said the man politely, before quickly walking into the wine shop next door.

Andrew finished cleaning and brought the bucket and sponge inside to empty into the sink out back. Once he had done so, he dried his hands and found Xavier reading a book about Freemasonry. It was a red book with a golden square and compass intertwined on its spine.

"What's that about then?" asked Andrew, as he sat down on a pile of books nearby.

“Do you know what the Freemasons are?” asked Xavier.

“Not really, but I've seen them at some charity events in Camden. Something to do with lodges, isn't it?”

“Yes, there are many lodges in England, but the headquarters are right here in London, near Covent Garden. The United Grand Lodge of England, or Freemasons’ Hall. A very sinister looking building, I might add.”

“Oh, I think I've walked past that,” Andrew added.

Xavier continued. "It's a meeting place for a few unsavoury groups.

Legend has it that the Golden Dawn met there weekly.

Aleister Crowley was a member before he became obsessed with Thelema, that is."

"Who's Aleister Crowley?" asked Andrew.

"A certifiable, lunatic, that's who." said Xavier,

"But a very well educated and knowledgeable one, with a twisted-kink for sex magik."

"Yuk" said Andrew, "There are some weird people out there."

Xavier continued...

"As for the Freemasons, it's a men only organisation. They have been around for hundreds of years. In the early days, stone mason's work was in high demand, as it was a very skilled profession and took a long time to perfect. But like anything, where there is money you will find tricksters, frauds, and fakes. In this instance, imposters who claimed they were timed-served masons. They tried to steal the work from the worthy.

The Stonemasons guild, or Freemasons were later known, set up a system that allowed a way for other foremen to recognise fully fledged, travelling masons and to quickly identify one another. A series of handshakes and phrases with required responses. As the numbers grew, deeper levels of secrecy were required, and ranks were formed. Your place within those ranks depended on your length of service, ability, and status. By the time the Freemasons were three hundred years old, it was no longer just stonemasons in their membership. They had everyone from solicitors to plumbers, accountants to fence erectors. They are not a secret society, as they will talk about the organisation willingly with anyone, but they are a society with secrets. What they really want is high level individuals with influence to join them. Knowing that having such power in the lower ranks granted them power by proxy, most Freemasons are the pillars of society and they do so much for the communities they live in, providing much needed funds via charitable work and support for the needy.

They are good men, and the social opportunities and events are amazing. The majority of people that join the Freemasons will never see what they secretly fund with their membership fees, as It is only at the pinnacle, the 3rd and 33rd degree - Scottish rite freemasons, and members of certain bloodlines, that will ever get to witness the true power of what they support. Only 1% of the Masons secretly considered themselves to be satanic, but pretty much all the Blackstone men in London are Freemasons, so go figure."

"Well, they sound like a hoot," Andrew said.

"Just be careful, they are not as innocent as they appear," said Xavier.

He closed that book and flopped it on a pile that was already eight high. A hand scrawled label sat beside the pile. 'Andrew's summer reading.'

"Great," said Andrew with a sigh as he noticed the sign. "Anything else you want me to do while I'm here?" he said. "As I'm doing everything else already."

The exam pressure was starting to get to him, and the idea of having to read all these books too, was a little overwhelming.

"I could sweep the floor for you as well, if you like? Just stick a broom up my-"

"Arsenic, and other Medi-evil poisons," interrupted Xavier, pondering over books to add to the pile. "Nope, not ready for that one. Antique mirrors and their uses, ah now that *is* fun."

That reminded Andrew about the man he had bumped into out front.

"Xavier, there was a man out front that I bumped into. He went into the wine shop next door."

"And?" said Xavier. "Or is that it?"

"He didn't have a reflection." Andrew expected Xavier to call him a liar, or that he was making it up.

"Oh, I see. That was probably Mr Allen, he normally pops in for his wine about this time on a Saturday. He's a Vampyre, you know," said Xavier calmly, as he continued to search through a box of books.

"Myths and Legends, now that is a very good book!" He placed it on Andrew's ever-growing, teetering pile.

"What do you mean he's a Vampyre?" asked Andrew. "Like the ones in the films? You know, turns to dust in sunlight, hates silver, allergic to garlic, killed by a stake through the heart, fang-wielding, blood-sucking, cape-wearing Vampyre?"

Andrew now realised he had fallen for it and waited for Xavier to point at him and laugh. But he didn't, he just stared back waiting for him to finish.

"Films exaggerate these things, Andrew. Sunlight thing? Sort of. They sometimes have to wear something to shield their skin a bit and avoid going out when the sun is really bearing down. That's why they like England so much; not only is there a lot of history, and Vampyres LOVE history, but there's not too much sun. Silver, that's an interesting one. It seems it makes them quite angry – not sure why though. Garlic, now that's a myth. Mr Allen loves it, especially with roast chicken. I had him over for dinner once.

"You are lucky he didn't have you for dinner... do they even eat normal food?" asked Andrew, looking confused.

"Yes, of course they do, but they do need fresh blood too, once in a while, otherwise they become quite aggressive. Not every day though."

"Bit like George when he runs out of sweets. That's an experience, I can tell you," Andrew said.

"Quite," Xavier paused. "Capes? – films. Stakes through the heart? – possibly, but I'd like to see you try. They move too fast, especially when they are angry."

"So do they hunt people for blood?" Andrew asked, feeling a bit nervous working next door to where one regularly shopped.

"Not since the blood treaty," said Xavier.

"What on earth is that?" Andrew asked.

"In 1920, a treaty was drawn up between men and Vampyres that prohibited them from feeding on humans, which in turn prohibits us from trying to harm them. In exchange for this they would be given a blood prescription from the blood banks.

It took some time, and there was some resistance on both sides for some years, but in the end that treaty finally put the brakes on hundreds of years of turmoil and fighting, allowing us as two species to live in England in relative peace."

"Just in England?" Andrew asked.

"England, Wales, Germany, France, Spain, and most of eastern Europe. Scotland, Ireland, Russia, and America are still thrashing it out, but it takes patience and time," Xavier explained.

"So, they only have blood from the blood banks?"

"Well," said Xavier. "Every now and then they fancy something a bit special. They go to a very particular wine shops, like the one next door, and pick up a little bottle of single source blood that they normally can't get access to. It may be someone of a certain age or a particular type of person they have a craving for. Sometimes they even sell blood from celebrities, but even small vials of those go for astronomical prices. You see, to them, it's not just food. It's more of an experience. They see visions, memories, and feel the emotions swimming in the blood from the donor. The blood banks just sort the donations into blood type then mix them all together. This makes for a very jumbled up experience."

"What happens if someone breaks the blood treaty?" Andrew asked.

"This is where it gets darker," said Xavier.

"Because it took so long for the peace agreement to take hold, anyone that breaks the treaty in England will be given the same punishment as someone who commits high treason.

And because the fact that Vampyres even exist is a closely guarded secret, a secret punishment exists for breaking the treaty too: being hung, drawn, and quartered.

If you are human, there's a twist. They feed you Vampyre's blood before they start just so you live longer and suffer more before being torn apart, but not in public of course."

"Note to self, don't kill any Vampyres," Andrew said, jokingly.

"At all costs," said Xavier, while searching for more books.

"But what if you had to kill one?" asked Andrew. "How would you?"

“Well, there’s a few flowers that grow in Scotland that can take care of them. You have to juice them and add a few other things first, then they would have to drink it, of course. Mr Bluvine always keeps some in stock just in case. It's for Vampyres that... you know, want to call it a day."

"They poison themselves?" asked Andrew.

"They call it Dignity,” said Xavier.

“Why would he stock that?” asked Andrew.

“But that itself is a question, Andrew, and I can assure you for that tonic, the policy is no questions asked,” said Xavier.

“Speaking of things coming to an end,” said Andrew. “It’s my last couple of weeks at school, Xavier, then I’m finally free.”

“That's good,” Xavier said. “So, what the hell are you going to do with yourself then?”

“Not sure, to be honest. My results won't be good enough for anything further, like the new A levels coming in, and I feel like I’m done with school now, anyway. I love to learn new things, but I want the truth... the real truth.”

“The truth isn't always pretty, Andrew, and sometimes you’ll wish you hadn't found out what's really going on. Ignorance really can be bliss, you know.”

Xavier started to put all the books he picked out for Andrew to read into a box. “I can't have you wandering the streets. Who knows what kind of trouble you’ll end up in! I suggest you come and work here full time, until you figure out what you want to do with your bloody life."

"Er, ok," said Andrew.

"Tuesday to Saturday, 9am to 5pm. Sunday and Monday off," said Xavier.

"Deal! How much are you going to pay me?" asked Andrew.

"Just enough to keep you out of trouble," said Xavier. "Speaking of which, pop over the road and get a paper please, would you?"

"Sure, which one?"

"The Guardian, please," he said, handing over some change from the till.

Andrew left the shop and crossed the road to the newsagents. A few people were leaving the shop just as he approached the paper stand. They were looking at him strangely. Andrew thought they must be wondering why he was working at the weird bookshop with the eccentric owner, but it was just his paranoia kicking in again. When he saw his reflection in the window, he realised why they had looked at him so oddly. He still had millions of black paint scrapings all over his face from the cleaning.

"Ahh great, Xavier, why didn't you say?" he muttered to himself, whilst trying to remove some flecks that were not budging. Realising he was just going to have to go with it, he picked up a copy of the Guardian and opened the door to the shop to go and pay. Inside the shop the owner was weighing out some sweets in the bowl of a polished chrome set of scales. He put the lid back on the sherbet lemons, the zesty flavour hanging in the air wonderfully as Andrew walked in. He placed the giant jar back into the gap on the shelf where all the brightly coloured sweets were kept in full view, just at the right height for temptation.

“There we go, quarter pound of sherbert lemons. Anything else, Mrs Greene?” said the friendly shopkeeper.

“No, no, that will be all, Mr Jeffries, thank you. That’s cleaned me out, I think. Five kids will do that to you.”

“Oh yes, hungry ones at that,” said Mr Jefferies. “Something for the journey home.” He placed a small bar of chocolate into her bag with a wink.

“Four pence please, my love.”

She handed the money over with an awkward smile. He pulled the handle on the huge iron till that opened with a ‘ching’. “Goodbye Mrs Greene, have a good day.” He was still smiling as she walked out of the door.

“Next please,” he said, as she shut the till again.

Andrew walked forward and placed the paper on the counter. “Just that please, sir.”

“Sir?” Mr Jefferies exclaimed. “Haven't been called that in a very long time. Tell me young man, have you been painting or something?” He rang up the till for the paper.

“Quite the opposite, really. I had to remove the paint from the bookshop, again,” said Andrew.

“Ah, you are the boy that works for that lunatic. Haven't seen him in a while. Shot anyone else lately?”

"He's fine, just keeping his head down, if you know what I mean," said Andrew.

"Probably a wise thing. Those people don't forgive, and they never forget," said Mr Jefferies.

Just then, Andrew realised that there was something odd about Mr Jefferies left hand. His little finger was missing.

"Thruppence, please," said Mr Jefferies.

Andrew handed over the money and folded the broadsheet newspaper over his arm. "I better get back," he said awkwardly.

"You take care now," said Mr Jefferies.

Andrew left the shop into the light of a day that was trying to brighten up. He crossed the road and entered the bookshop with the paper for Xavier.

'Ding-ding' rang the shop bell as he re-entered. Xavier was now sitting down behind the counter asleep with a book in his hand. He made it all the way up to the till before he stirred.

"Ah ha, you took your time," said a sleepy Xavier, rubbing one eye.

"Sorry, the newsagent was quite chatty," said Andrew, handing over the newspaper. "I noticed he had a finger missing."

"Oh yes. Let's just say that Mr Jefferies has always had a keen eye for the ladies. He loved to play card games too and would often lose a lot of money. One day his wife found out."

Xavier spread the paper out onto the counter and examined it.

"His wife cut off his finger?" asked Andrew.

"Not quite. His wife's older brother was deeply involved with the Blackstones and did not take kindly to the rumours he kept hearing about Mr Jeffries' behaviour. One night whilst walking home he was knocked out cold and put into a van. He woke up handcuffed to a card table with a small meat cleaver in front of him. Everything in the room, including him, was soaked in petrol, but there was no winning this game. He had a choice: cut his own finger off there and then, or they would burn him alive. No prizes for guessing which option he chose."

"Nasty," said Andrew.

"Ah ha," said Xavier, looking deeply at the newspaper. "Now here's something."

YARDIE GANGWAR: BRIXTON IN TROUBLE

Fights involving the Jamaican Yardie group, and an unidentified but organised group of individuals, broke out at an address in Brixton on Friday. Four people were pronounced dead at the scene and two were fatally wounded and died later in hospital. One local, Mrs Caine of Rushcroft Road, commented, "They were fighting over something in a box. Drugs probably, but it's anyone's guess. We don't know what has been going on around here lately, but people have been very angry. It's so unlike them, shouting and yelling all day. Like the devil awoke in them. Whatever it was, it seems to

have calmed down now. Maybe I can finally get some sleep."

A black van was seen fleeing the scene at high speed. Police are appealing for any information.

"That's the dagger!" said Xavier. "I hope Marlon survived."

"Looks like they finally got it back," Andrew said.

"Or did they? Let's keep an eye on things to see if another neighbourhood becomes heated, shall we?" said Xavier, shuffling the paper in his hands. "I will make enquiries about Marlon this week. Despite what you saw of him in that park, he's actually a very respectful man."

Towards the end of the day, it started to rain heavily and no one had come into the shop for at least an hour.

"Let's call it a day, Andrew, shall we?" said Xavier.

Andrew looked out of the window at the rain hammering down.

"Come on, I'll give you a lift home," said Xavier.

"But I'm not supposed to tell you where I live, am I?" said Andrew.

"Indeed, but that doesn't stop me from finding out, does it?" said Xavier. "19 Lawford Road, Kentish Town? Blue door, brass lion's head knocker?" He studied Andrew's face for a reaction and must have found what he wanted, as he smiled. "And if I can, then so can others. Be aware of that, Andrew."

Andrew picked up the box of books for him to read and dashed to the car outback. Xavier drove to drop him home with the windscreen wipers struggling against the torrent. Andrew felt quite thankful for the lift, as the rain was relentless. It pooled in the roads and formed mini rivers that cascaded down the edges of the streets in search of a drain, only to be met with storm drains that were already overflowing. London and rain, a match made in hell.

15

School's Out Forever

They saved the worst exam until last for Andrew. It was maths and he pleaded for it to end.

He knew that he had already failed, as he could only answer four questions of the ten that had been set, but Andrew consoled himself knowing that he didn't really need maths for his current job and never planned to have a job where he would. After the exam and out on the quad, he saw George talking to Lee by the steps.

"How did it go?" asked George.

"How do you think it went?" Andrew's disappointed tone said everything.

"Don't worry about it, Andrew. You don't need maths to sell a book," said Lee. "George will though, to count all of those sweets he eats."

Lee had a point. Andrew was just glad it was over and the idea of never having to sit through hours and hours of utter waffle again made him feel relieved.

"So... we are free! Where will we be exploring this Sunday, Andrew?" asked George.

Andrew hadn't found anywhere new in quite a while. With all the studying and working at Xavier's on Saturdays, he hadn't really had the chance.

"I think I've found somewhere," said Lee. "The little park in Soho square has a hut in the centre of it."

"The little black and white Tudor building?" asked George. "That's just a gardener's shed."

"There's more to it than that," Lee continued. "It has a chamber underneath it that was big enough to shelter two hundred people during the blitz, but it goes down even further than they knew then. I was in the Soho Square very late when I saw at least ten Blackstones come out from there. Out of sight, I overheard what they were talking about as they left. The 21st of June is the summer solstice this year, and they are planning a ritual under Soho Square. I say we sneak in beforehand and make their lives difficult."

"Really? Are you mad?" said George. "Knowing our luck, we'll get caught and end up being carved up by these lunatics."

Andrew had his doubts too but wanted to hear the argument playout before he decided which side to rest on.

"If we get in early, no one will know. It's the summer solstice so there will be a sacrifice, I'm sure," said Lee.

"And what if there is, Lee? How will we put a stop to it? When there's hundreds of them and just three of us? Huh?" George fired back.

"We will be long gone by the time that happens." said Lee,

“HOW?!” George was becoming quite heated.

Lee explained, “My dad bought a job lot of bits from his dodgy mate down the pub. Some military gear, ammo cases and some boots too. He sold quite a bit of it, but some was left in the shed. At the bottom of a box of rags was something I didn't expect to find. A couple of unused landmines.”

“Landmines? Are you nuts?” said George.

Lee continued, “I say, we get there early and dig the landmines in right by the head of the altar. If it’s a human sacrifice it must be on the altar, right? Kaboom! ‘Ahh my leg!’ and so on.” Lee trying out weird voices always made Andrew chuckle.

George and Andrew just stared at Lee, partially in awe, but also worried about what he was becoming.

“Now that’s a plan, Lee,” Andrew said. “That sound ok, George?”

“Yeh, yeh. I love a landmine, my favourite kind of mine,” George said, sarcastically.

“So, 21st June; We plant the mines and leg it.”

16

THE THINGS WE LEAVE BEHIND

Even though Andrew had to wait until August to find out his O level results, he already felt like he was leaving that chapter of his life behind. The only worthwhile thing about school was the friendships he had made. It wasn't too much of a shock to the system for him to enter full time work either. Xavier was a very laid-back boss and did not mind if he was late occasionally, as long as he made the tea and didn't talk too much.

Andrew was happy that he finally had some money coming in. He didn't exactly earn a fortune, but it was enough for him to get the bus every day and buy himself lunch. He even managed to leave some money for his mum by her bedside each week.

"Oh Andrew, there's no need for this?" she'd say, with a smile.

He secretly hoped that it would mean she could cut back on her hours at the bakery, but it didn't seem to have the desired effect. They hardly saw each other at all these days. She was up and out the door before he even woke up. In the evenings they would have dinner together, but by the time she had finished eating she'd already be yawning. Andrew would try to tell her about his day, and what Xavier thought about things, but she always seemed too tired to really engage in a proper conversation. By 8.30pm she'd either be asleep in her chair or heading to bed. Not much of a life for either of them.

One day at the bookshop, Andrew was busy removing all the books from a cabinet so he could dust it. Xavier walked past and picked up a book from the pile next to him about Soho.

"Now there's a great place; Soho. One of the many reasons I chose to move to London, you know," said Xavier.

Xavier casts his mind back to the time when he came to London in 1920 to open his bookshop. He had to get out of the village he lived in with his parents. He was different. He knew that, and so did his parents, but they had collectively and subconsciously developed a fool-proof system that avoided any disappointment on either side. They never asked, and he certainly never told.

When he first arrived in London, he couldn't believe how busy it was compared to what he was used to. Everyone seemed to be moving at a hundred miles an hour and nobody had any time for anything, especially newcomers who were struggling to navigate the intermingled city streets. Asking for directions was seen as a form of begging. Even finding the shop he had come to see was a test of his patience and nerve.

"So, this is it?" Xavier, had asked the estate agent who was dangling the keys in front of him with a big nicotine-stained smile, dripping with insincerity.

He stood before a very tired shop with a very faded old sign.

Harding's Hardware

Everyday maintenance, made easy.

Xavier had opened the front door to the shop with a scrape, collecting a rake of junk mail and bills behind the door. It had been vacant for a long time by the looks of it, as the dust was an inch thick in some places. Even with all the neglect and work required, there was something about the space that made Xavier feel hopeful. He took the plunge and signed the lease.

He then spent two weeks solid just cleaning, removing junk, and making small improvements to the place. The nearest hardware store was over a mile away now, ironically.

And as he had spent every penny he had on the shop; he couldn't afford a cart. For him, a bicycle was the only way to travel until that was stolen a week later, and the second-hand replacement bike a week after that.

"Bastards!"

He decided to walk instead.

After a month of gruelling hard graft, painting and putting up shelves and cabinets, Xavier decided that he needed a break. He got cleaned up, dressed into something without holes in for the first time since starting the work, and felt the buzz of excitement as he left the shop, mid-renovation for the evening.

Back in his home village, he had read stories about Soho in the papers. All the negative words and comments had passed him by, and he picked out the words of hope like a poor man panning for gold. He walked south out of Somers Town and towards Soho with a spring in his step and a wild curiosity.

Night-time in London is so different to the day. The city comes to life with a completely different set of people. Some that are just looking for a party, some a good time, at a price, and some that just seem to want to go home, wherever home maybe. The saddest part were the people that didn't have a home at all, seeking comfort in the nooks and cracks across the city. That was a rough sight.

Xavier had nothing to lose. As he got closer to Soho, he could see the bright pink lights and red neon reflecting off of the windows of nearby cars and shops, shimmering as he passed. He walked further into Soho with wide eyes and turned into Old Compton Street. His heart fluttered with anticipation. Halfway down the street, was a cute little bar with a jazz pianist playing softly by himself in the corner. He wandered up to the bar and sat down on a tool stool. There were a couple of guys sitting over by the piano, holding hands and in deep conversation. He had never actually seen a public display of affection between two men, and he was fascinated.

The barman walked over and smiled.

"Ello duckie, you have a dolly eek," he said, in a European accent.

Xavier had felt completely out of his depth and wasn't quite sure what to say.

"Ah... You're new, I can tell," said barman encouragingly.

“I may be new here, but I'm where I belong, finally,” said Xavier.

“Indeed. What can I get you?”

“Oh, I'll have a whiskey sour.... and one for yourself, perhaps?” Xavier’s heartbeat rose from the suggestion.

The barman laughed as his eyes twinkled.

Snapping back into reality....

Xavier was smiling but realised he had drifted off. Books always had a way of taking him off somewhere.

“You can be whoever you want to be in Soho. Ever been?” asked Xavier, as he placed the Soho book back down on the pile stroking its cover.

“No, but the boys and I are planning a mission under Soho Square on the 21st,” said Andrew, wiping into the corners of the deep shelves with a polishing rag. “So, I’ll need the day off.”

“What?” Xavier said, looking quite shocked.

“The boys and I...”

“Yes, I got that bit. Day off??” said Xavier. “And a mission? What do you mean by a mission?”

“Lee found a chamber under Soho Square, the little gardener's hut. He saw a load of Blackstones come out the other week and they were talking about a ceremony on the 21st of June. That's the summer solstice.”

“I’m well aware of that, Andrew, but that's a very dangerous time to be knocking about Blackstone chambers. I know the Soho chamber well; It delves very deep. There are two exits; one out of the little gardener’s hut in Soho square, and the other is two-hundred yards north and brings you out onto Oxford Street.”

“Lee is convinced they will be making a sacrifice that night,” said Andrew. “we plan to put a stop to it."

“And how do three teenagers, albeit very brave ones, plan to deal with more than a hundred Blackstones in an underground chamber with only two exits?”

“Lee has a couple of landmines. We are going to get there early and dig them in by the head of the altar and get out before anyone turns up. That should do the trick, right? Ka-boom!”

“You three are mad. Ingenious and resourceful, but utterly bonkers.

Do you realise the kind of damage a landmine will cause in a confined space like that?” Xavier sat down on the floor against the next bookshelf with a sigh.

“A lot, probably,” said Andrew, sounding excited.

"And say if someone does turn up early? then what?" asked Xavier,

"Well.. I'm not sure, really." said Andrew,

"When doing somthing like this, you need to think about all the possibilities, Andrew."

"We should be able to outrun them," said Andrew, optimistically.

"And what if they block both exits?" asked Xavier,

"We'll manage."

"Listen Andrew, these people are really nasty, and wouldnt think twice about killing anyone they find snooping about one of thier chambers; Believe me, I know...I've seen it." said Xavier,

"We will be careful...in and out in a flash." said Andrew,

Xavier took a long breath and sighed.

“I can see you’ve already made up your mind, so there’s no point in trying to talk you out of it.”

Andrew nodded.

“We better get you ready then, I suppose,” said Xavier.

“What do you mean?” asked Andrew, as he started to replace the books.

"You'll need an exit strategy."said Xavier,

"What do you suggest?"

Xavier pondered and idea.

"Berty has a little sister, you know...and I think you may need her," said Xavier, as got up with a groan as most people over forty seem to. They don't even know they do it. He wandered out back and Andrew carried on cleaning. He had finished putting all the books back on the shelves when Xavier walked down to Andrew with a leather satchel.

"Come on then, Andrew. We are going out."

"Ok, but where?"

"We need to get out of London for a couple of hours. I know the perfect place. Lock the shop door, turn the sign, and meet me in the car."

Andrew had no idea what was going on, but he wasn't about to turn down a road trip, that's for sure. He locked the door, twisted the hanging sign to 'closed' and turned all the lights out. By the time he had made it out the back door, Xavier was already sitting in his car with the engine running.

"Where are we going?" asked Andrew, as he hopped into the passenger seat.

"North. There are some woods out of town on the other side of Watford that will do."

"Do for what? And where the bloody hell is Watford?" Andrew asked.

"You'll see."

17

Would Wood Still Be Wood, Even If It Could Be Metal?

They had driven north and reached Archway; Andrew had had enough of the music that was blaring from the distorted speakers on the dash.

"HERE IN MY HEART!"

Xavier had taken it upon himself to sing along badly to an awful song on the radio by Al Martino.

"Argh! Nope, nope, no more," Andrew shouted, as he turned the radio off suddenly, creating a brief, social vacuum in the car.

"You can't turn a radio off mid song. It's bad luck!" said Xavier.

"Who told you that? Al Martino?... How much further is this place anyway?" Andrew asked.

“Another twenty miles, give or take. What’s really bugging you, Andrew? You haven't been right all day.”

“Nothing, really, just been thinking a lot,” he said.

“About what?”

“George and Lee have everything mapped out and seem to know what they want to do. Me? I don’t have a clue. Just feel a bit lost,” said Andrew,

“Lost? You’ll be fine, Andrew, mark my words,” said Xavier.

“It’s not that I don’t like working for you, Xavier, because I do, but I need to find my own thing, I guess.”

“Look at me,” said Xavier. “When I was your age, I thought I knew exactly what I wanted from life. I thought I’d like to have a bookshop, make lots of money and friends, and be... happy. Did all of that happen? No. Would I change it for all the world? Absolutely, yes, in a heartbeat.”

“And the moral to that story is?” Andrew asked, feeling confused.

“Never buy a bookshop or follow your dreams, Andrew. It will make you angry, bitter, and twisted like me.”

“Ever thought about going into career advice, Xavier? You’d be great,” said Andrew, rolling his eyes.

“Ok... ok,” said Xavier, trying to salvage some hope from the wreckage of his comments.

“What I meant was, yes, some of us have an idea, a dream, or a predetermined destination, but sometimes the aims and parameters of that dream, can make us inflexible to other opportunities that may come along. I met a friend once, a really special friend, right here in London. they were from Italy, and one day they decided to head back home. they invited me to go with them and see what I thought of the place."

"So, how was it?" Andrew asked.

"I don't know. I didn't go," said Xavier,

Andrew looked confused.

"How could I? When my only means of scraping a living was sitting on those shelves, waiting to be bought. They wrote to me for a while, asking for me to reconsider, but the bookshop had me right where it wanted me."

Xavier seemed quite sad.

"I have a handful of big regrets in life, but that's a big spikey one. Be mindful about the things you own in life, Andrew, because if you are not careful, they can end up owning you."

"Well, I certainly don't want that," said Andrew.

They continued north through a place called Stanmore and onto Watford, a strange town with quite a large high street. As they left Watford the buildings seemed to disappear and become less frequent. The smell of the air was far cleaner than Andrew had ever smelt before, except for the occasional stench from the farmers' fields they passed. They pulled off the main road and into some back lanes. The tree cover became dense as the little lanes narrowed.

"Almost there now," said Xavier.

They finally slowed and turned into an old, abandoned farm with a large five-bar gate that had fallen off some time ago and was now face down on the floor being strangled by weeds.

"What are we doing here?" asked Andrew, as they stepped out of the car.

"If you are going to wield this thing." He held the leather satchel up. "You'll need to learn how to use it."

"Erm, ok, but what is it?"

"Say hello to Edna, but I warn you, she is quite a handful," said Xavier.

Xavier took out a large handgun from the satchel. It was a Webley mark VI top break revolver that fired massive .445 cartridges. A very scary looking gun.

"Where did you get that?" asked Andrew.

"It was a few years ago now. I kept getting some unwanted customers in the shop, suggesting that I should be paying them money for protection. I didn't want to go down that road, as you become an easy target for these people. I already had Berty, but he is far too big to be used inside. So, I had a word with Marlon."

"The Jamaican guy who took that dagger from us?"

"Yes, that's the chap. He knew a guy, that knew a guy... and hey presto. When the nasty lot came in for money again, they left rather quickly with Edna pointed at them."

"Why Edna?" Andrew asked.

“That was my mother’s name,” said Xavier. “She certainly didn't take any crap from anybody. Here, take her.”

He thrust the gun into Andrew’s hands. It was so solid and heavy for something of its size that he had to hold it with two hands outstretched.

“Ready to have a go?” asked Xavier.

Andrew thought he was. He had seen war films before, where the soldier is shooting multiple enemies with a large revolver, only holding it with one hand, making it look easy. Yet again an example of popular culture making light of how difficult things are in real life. Xavier set up a line of old, mudstained bottles on a log, ten yards away. The backdrop was the old, abandoned farmhouse that backed onto an unkempt field. He walked back and took the revolver back briefly to load it, showing Andrew the process as he did so. “Never leave it loaded!” Handing back the pistol, he began his instructions.

“Hold the grip firmly, but not too tight. You have to allow for a little movement as it's a large calibre. Not too loose either, though, as it will fly out of your hands and hit you. Don’t pull or yank the trigger, just squeeze it, and don't forget to breathe.”

“How am I supposed to remember all of that?!” Andrew exclaimed, feeling quite worried now. The gun was outstretched and already felt too heavy. He looked down the gap of the sight and to the point where a bottle stood.

“Ready?” said Xavier. “Go.”

Andrew breathed out and maintained focus on the dark bottle in the middle while squeezing the trigger. Nothing seemed to be happening.

BAAAAANG!

He heard shattering glass and felt a huge jolt. The next thing he knew he was on his back looking up at the treetops swaying gently in the breeze. Xavier's head came into view, blocking out the sunlight.

"Are you having fun down there, or would you like another go?" He asked, before offering his hand and pulling Andrew back up onto his feet.

"Packs a punch, eh?" said Xavier.

"Yeh, it really does... did I hit a bottle?"

"Nearly... just grazed it enough to make it fall over. Or it might have been the wind."

Now Andrew knew what to expect, he took a more stable stance while holding the gun with a bit more purpose. He took a deep breath and slowly exhaled while squeezing the trigger.

BANG!

The sound echoed amongst the trees, and some birds flew out of the canopy above. The green bottle had smashed to smithereens before him, and he was still on his feet.

"That's more like it!" said Xavier.

They heard the noise of a distant engine in front of them and could just about see in the distance that there was a dark green land rover 4x4 driving across the undulating field towards them with two people on the back of it. They both had large shotguns.

POP... POP. They heard the distant gunshots, and some of the shot scattered into the canopy above them, sending more birds flapping.

"Time to go!" said Xavier. "Quickly, quickly."

They packed up fast and put the gun back into the leather satchel, both running to the car to jump in. Xavier reversed out into the lane, and they headed off back in the direction of London as fast as they could.

"Who were they, Xavier?" Andrew asked.

"Don't know, don't really care," he said. "They had guns, and that was enough for me."

The journey seemed a lot quicker heading back into London, perhaps because it felt more familiar, like a retracing of steps. Firing that gun was quite an experience for Andrew, but he wondered if he could actually use it like Lee had in the launderette. Deep down he knew Lee was built differently. By the time they got back to London, it was time to put the shop to bed.

18

Crossing the T's and Dotting the I's

Rules: Covent Garden.

Getting a table at Rules restaurant in Covent Garden for some people is and always will be impossible. Its fine interiors and firm grasp on tradition make it the place to be, if you can afford it. Because of its long history and discretion, it is a firm favourite of the London elite. The Grand Matriarch was already halfway through her first cup of afternoon tea when James Wordsworth arrived. There was a light but distinct knock on the door of her private dining room situated on the third floor. This dining area was reserved permanently for the council of thirteen members.

"Enter," said the Matriarch.

"Mr Wordsworth, ma'am," said the Rules waiter, holding the door waiting for the *ok* to let him through.

"Proceed," said the Grand Matriarch, coldly.

The waiter entered the sunlit room briefly to hold the door for Mr Wordsworth and closed it behind him quietly as he left. James took a deep breath before he walked across the highly polished wooden floor, past the large windows overlooking Maiden Lane. His aunt was early and was now waiting for him. He knew that he would need all the answers to her questions before she would even consider letting him continue with his plan for December.

"Grand Matriarch," said James, he bowed slightly before being prompted to take a seat.

"Tea?" she asked.

"Yes please," he said, as he sat down, running things over and over in his head. The Grand Matriarch picked up a small, black crystal bell and rang it quietly just once, letting the sound ring out into the room. The waiter who was still standing right outside of the door walked in and over to the table to serve tea. He poured the tea into the fine bone china cup in front of James and made sure he had everything he needed before being dismissed by the Grand Matriarch with a nod. He sipped his tea and placed it back on the saucer. Every noise seemed too loud given his heightened senses. The adrenaline flowed through his veins in anticipation.

"Tell me, James, have you finalised all of the details for the proposed action?"

"Yes, Grand Matriarch. Everything is ready to move, upon your approval, of course."

"What is the name of the Vampyre you plan to use, and how will they be captured?" she asked.

"We have consulted the Vampyre high council, and they have agreed to let us capture someone who has been causing them problems for some time. His name is Verne Daniels. This particular Vampyre didn't sign the 1920 blood treaty and has been at large ever since he killed one of our placements in Westminster. He has continued to hunt humans viciously throughout, and the Vampyre council feel he would be a suitable candidate. Our sources say that he is currently in Ireland."

"Impressive, James. The Vampyre council's complicity is paramount," said the Grand matriarch. "And when you catch him, what about security?"

"Obsidian restraints are being made as we speak," said James.

The Grand Matriarch remembers being very young when her father sat on the end of her bed and told her about the mysterious black glass they called Obsidian. She used to always play with his Blackstone ring, polishing it on her cotton skirt and looking deeply into the reflection, sometimes catching a glimpse of things that didn't seem to exist anywhere else. She asked her father why he and his friends wore the same rings.

"It's a club, my darling, and all the members wear one. Besides, the Vampyres... they fear it." he had said, but he could never tell her why. Nobody could.

"Are the Vampyre council aware that he must remain incarcerated?" she asked.

"Yes, that happens to be *one* of their conditions," said James.

"They have other conditions?" she countered.

“They have requested twenty lives, ma'am. Twenty people they can hunt before the ceremony with immunity. The Vampyre council will issue the coins to their chosen few, and the bodies will be marked with roman numerals I to XX for accountability.”

“Just twenty? I expected more,” said the Matriarch, picking up a small cucumber sandwich.

“And one final demand,” James swallowed hard. “They want half of the blood.”

“Half? The greedy blood sucking parasites!” The Grand Matriarch’s words echoed off the hard surfaces of the room and hung in the air leaving silence in their wake. She was furious. Her eyes seemed to dance with flame.

“They have no idea how much that blood will be worth. Sultans, kings, and emperors will bow down for a mere taste of this elixir, this gift of long life, healing and insight. Knowing the Vampyre’s weakness for blood, they would sooner consume it themselves and neutralise the effects without even knowing. Without a care. All they would probably gain from it would be a brief respite from their ever-present thirst.”

James started calmly, “Grand Matriarch, I agree that this arrangement is less than ideal, but half of something is far better than all of nothing. I trust you agree. If we jeopardize the blood treaty and proceed without the Vampyre council’s consent, it could mean war.”

The Grand Matriarch considered her thoughts. She knew he was right, but the thought of having to lose half of the blood tormented her. She kneaded her napkin. "If this is the only way, but I cannot help but feel that it is such a waste."

"Quite," nodded James.

"Can we not negotiate?...Offer them a thousand lives for all I care," said the Grand Matriarch.

"Their terms are final, I'm afraid."

Just then, the Grand Matriarch had an epiphany.

"But... there is nothing to say we can't use multiple children, is there? A passage says the incantation must be spoken 'twice, for each child'."

"Mm, interesting. It would certainly capitalise on the opportunity," said James.

"Which brings me to my next point; how is the search for children progressing?" she asked.

"Pandora has been scouting around London for quite a while now. She has a few possibilities lined up."

James' sister always delivered what they required without fail.

"I want seven, James," she said, plainly.

"Seven children? That will require more resources," he sighed.

"Whatever it takes, James."

"Understood."

"And what about the HAARP?" she asked.

"The machine is working well and has passed all its tests so far. We should be able to bring a dense fog to London, when required."

She hesitated. He persisted.

"If you give me the green light of approval, Grand Matriarch, I will send a bulletin to every Darkheart Sect in southern England. We have over ten thousand here in London alone, ready and willing to serve the Council."

She paused and looked out of the window deep in thought before turning to him. He reminded her so much of her brother, who had died a few years ago when James was only twenty. James, her nephew, was now the youngest member of the Committee, but he had guts and an insatiable desire to prove his worth.

"OK, you may proceed. I will inform the council of my decision. Don't let me down."

She rang the bell for more tea.

19

THE GREEN, GREEN GRASS OF OTHERS

Andrew loved having Mondays off as he got to sleep in and then wander around London while everyone else was either at school or work. It always felt naughty, like he was truanting, but he had a job now and this was a part of his weekend, effectively, just at a different time to most people. George had already started working at his Mother's Newsagents in Chalk farm, so Andrew decided to head to Camden to see him in action.

It was now mid-June and London was basking in sunlight for a change. The walk to Camden was hot, but really nice. Overpriced ice cream was being sold by the bucket-load to clueless tourists who stood out like sore thumbs. The pavement shimmered in front of him as the wave of heat was moved sideways by a passing van. Andrew had made it to Camden by noon and he walked down to the newsagents in Chalk farm, stepping inside Langley's News. He was one of three customers in the shop; the others were just there to buy a cold drink.

Andrew could hear George from the till side before he could even see him.

"Yes, the fridge is BRO-KEN... BROKEN as in it doesn't make things cold at the moment," George was saying to a tourist, very loudly.

Andrew walked down the aisle past the magazines and towards the till and could see George. He was all dressed up in his shopkeeper's apron, still struggling to convey why the lemonade was warm. The customer had given up and just left the warm lemonade on the counter and walked out.

"Sir... Sir! Put this back please, Sir."

When it was just George and Andrew left in the shop, he turned the corner to surprise him.

"Sir... Sir, do you have any cold drinks, Sir?" teased Andrew.

"Ah don't you start, Andrew. The chiller has decided to pack up on the hottest day of the year. Bloody typical. Mum has called the repair man, but he's fully booked for a week. I've got a cabinet full of warm drinks that no one wants to buy. It's not good, not good at all."

"All going ok, apart from that?" Andrew asked.

"Well, since we left school all I've been doing is either babysitting Lucy or looking after this shop. There's so much to learn about; The ordering, the pricing, and margins."

Another tourist had entered the shop and was moving all the drinks in the fridge to try and find a cold one.

"IT'S BROKEN, SIR," George hollered at the tourist, who didn't really seem to understand but gave up and left anyway. He turned back to Andrew.

"There's stock rotation, vetting the personal adverts to make sure there's nothing *dodgy.* Not to mention the paper rounds to organise for everyone. It's chaos, utter chaos."

"Yeh, it sounds like it. Not much time for eating sweets then?" Andrew asked, with as much sympathy as he could stomach.

"That's the weird thing, I've sort of gone off them!" George spoke like someone who had given up on a lifelong passion.

"I now seem to associate them with feeling stressed for some reason, and the worst bit is that for my birthday last week, all my Mum got me was some business cards for this place with my name on them. five-hundred of the bloody things. What am I supposed to do with them?"

"You could use them to impress all the girls," Andrew said sarcastically as he picked up one of the cards George had discarded from his stack on the counter.

"They will love a 'trainee manager', I'm sure."

George, who sensed that Andrew was now just teasing him for fun, decided to change the subject.

"Anyway, how's the life of a bookseller, Andrew? Sold many books?" George asked.

"It's going ok, so far. Xavier is an interesting character, as you know. It's mostly cleaning at the moment, but there is lots to learn, and I have a stack of books to read. I get Mondays off too, hence why I'm here now."

"That's good then. Yes, Xavier, he is a very odd bloke, isn't he?! But he does seem to know a lot about the Blackstones," said George.

"He knows a lot about everything, trust me," said Andrew. "I told him about our mission this Saturday and Lee's idea for the landmines. He thinks we are crazy."

"Maybe we are!?" contemplated George.

Andrew nodded in agreement.

"Either way, he told me there is a second exit that runs two hundred yards north and comes out onto Oxford Street."

"That will come in handy if anyone arrives early, I guess." George said, worriedly.

"Xavier is lending us a gun!" Andrew proclaimed quietly but proudly.

"Not that huge bloody shotgun! How will you run with that?" whispered George.

"No, not Berty. We are taking Edna!"

George looked at Andrew like he was going mad, and he had to admit perhaps he was, but he liked Xavier's habit of giving things names.

"It's a big handgun... with lots of power," said Andrew under his breath.

"Well, that should buy us some time if it all goes south," George said.

"What time are we meeting at Soho Gardens on Saturday morning, then?" asked Andrew.

"Lee popped in here on Saturday to tease me about my apron and the business cards, funnily enough. He thinks we should meet there at 5am when there's no one else about."

"Sounds sensible," agreed Andrew.

"Well, it's the only part of the plan that is," said George, turning his attention to the door.

Another tourist walked in and wanted to buy some cigarettes, so Andrew said goodbye to George and made his way out of the shop. The sun was high in the sky and there wasn't a cloud in sight. Andrew really fancied some ice cream and because he had been working, he could afford it. He walked over to the cart at the corner of the street and ordered a cone with two scoops. He felt something unfamiliar in the back pocket of his trousers. It was one of George's trainee manager cards. He didn't have anything else in his little brown wallet at that time except a little cash, so he put it in there for safe keeping - just so he could tease George with it another time.

Moving slowly down towards Camden town eating his ice cream as he went, he felt quite good about everything really. Some young children were laughing at a street performer, who was a one-man band, while the parents chatted happily amongst themselves in the sun. One of those rare moments where you are happy to just be.

Andrew was excited but nervous about Saturday, but the week leading up to an adventure was always a bit tense. With all the doubts at the back of his mind, he knew that they were doing the right thing. But he had to dig deep to find the courage from somewhere. Right now, the ice cream and sunny weather was all he needed.

20

GOING UNDERGROUND

SATURDAY 21ST JUNE

Andrew, woke startled, like he was already running late. The clock in his bedroom said half past three, which was far too early for anyone to be getting up in his opinion. He got dressed slowly and sneaked into the bathroom, outback to brush his teeth. At the end of his bed was a bag that he had packed the night before and fastened around one of the straps was his dad's old watch. It was a silver watch with a bright red leather strap. He had found it a few weeks back when he was looking through some old bits in a case.

They had to get rid of so much stuff when they had moved in, but there were some things his mum couldn't part with. In that case was a load of old photos of Andrew's mum and dad looking quite young on holidays and smiling at parties. He was wearing that watch in most of the pictures, so when Andrew found the watch at the bottom of the case it was a strange feeling. He didn't feel ready to try it on, so it had sat in his bedside drawer since.

He took the watch off the bag and placed it on his wrist, hesitating before doing the strap up. The strap had to bend in a place where it wasn't used to, as his wrist was one hole smaller than his dad's. Picking up the bag, he could really feel the weight of the handgun. He wasn't sure why Xavier had given him so many bullets. There was a box of about thirty. What did he think they were going to do, rob a bank? Even banks had more sense than to be open this early.

He crept slowly out into the lounge and towards the front door. His mum was still in bed with her curtain mostly drawn, which was a rare sight for Andrew. She would be up in an hour, so he really didn't want to wake her. He got out of the front without any disasters and closed it quietly with a slow click. Sticking to the back streets, he weaved his way down through the empty roads and into Somers Town. The sun was already starting to rise, and the bird song faded in like a familiar record. He had emerged back out onto the main roads near Mornington Crescent, but acutely aware that he was carrying a gun and enough bullets to start a war. That would be difficult to explain to any patrolling police who would probably stop him just out of curiosity for being out so early.

Making it past Euston and into the streets of Fitzrovia was a relief; So many alley ways and passages that he knew quite well. If he was chased here, Andrew was quite confident that he could escape.

Brief nerdy Fact:

Fitzrovia was derived from the name Fitzroy, which in French, means 'son of the king'. This surname was inherited by the 1st duke of Grafton, who happened to be the bastard son of King Charles II. The area was well known for bohemian lifestyles and attracted actors, painters, and writers such as Virginia Woolf, Quentin Crisp and Dylan Thomas, to name but a few.

• • • • • • • • • • •

Soho was just beyond Fitzrovia, and Andrew knew some back streets and alleys that led him to the west side of Soho Square Garden. As he got nearer to the gates, he could feel his heart rate starting to rise. Soho Square was empty, and the birds were busy tweeting in the bushes nearby. Andrew walked into the gardens and headed for the gardener's hut in the centre, keeping an eye out for anyone looking on. But there was no one around, including Lee or George. He found the door to the gardener's hut, and it was locked from the outside.

"That will be an old FB key then, I bet," said Lee's voice from behind him.

Andrew turned around to see he had quite a large bag on his back.

"You'll have that open in no time, Lee," said George standing next to him.

"I wondered where you two were," said Andrew.

Lee took off his rucksack and placed it gently on the ground. Andrew realised that the landmines must be in there.

Rummaging in the front pocket of the bag, he removed a large ring of keys varying in shapes and sizes. Examining them, he isolated three into his hand before walking up to the door as Andrew moved away.

"Yeh, sorry," said George. "It was a bit of a nightmare to get here without being seen."

"Tell me about it," said Andrew. "It's nice when it's quiet, but you feel like you're making too much noise."

"We're in," said Lee, as he stepped back to pick his rucksack off the floor.

Andrew walked back over to the door that was now open and stepped inside. The small hut smelled of stale, cut grass and fresh flowers, and the early morning light trickling through the small, leaded windows made it harder to see. Dirt, grass, and leaves were all over the floor.

Gardening equipment hung from rusty metal hooks on the walls and a tipped wheelbarrow was leant up against the back wall to one side. George and Lee walked in behind him.

"See...it's just a bloody gardening shed," said George. "I can't believe we got up so early on a Saturday, just for this."

"I'm telling you; they came out of here," said Lee, looking around. "There must be a hidden entrance somewhere."

There didn't appear to be one and they looked around for anything unusual. Andrew tugged at one the forks hanging from the hooks when George drew their attention to something.

"Hang on a minute, this wheelbarrow doesn't move," he said. "It's fixed somehow, and there's a latch bolted to the back. Sort of thing you'd use to hold a door back or something."

"Trapdoor!" Both Lee and Andrew said it at the same time. Lee opened his bag and pulled out a military grade folding shovel.

"Had these exact ones in the trenches," he said, proudly. He used the shovel to scrape back all the leaves, soil and debris from the floor and moved it to one side. They hunted around the floor for some kind of handle, swiping their hands across the floor to shift the remaining grass and dirt until they found it. There was a recessed ring that rose from the floor. Pulling on the handle, the trapdoor opened, revealing some brick steps. Once all the way open, they found the ring nested perfectly on the latch fixed to the wheelbarrow.

"Right, this is us. Lee, lock the door," said Andrew.

Lee walked over and locked the door from the inside, placing the ring of keys back into his bag along with the shovel. He then pulled out a torch and handed it to George.

"Your turn now, lookout boy," said Lee.

George took the torch reluctantly and walked towards the steps.

"Here we go then," he said, as he walked down into the unknown darkness.

Lee grabbed an armful of leaves and grass then dumped them behind the open trapdoor to disguise the entrance once the trap door was shut.

"Ready, Andrew?"

"Ready as I'll ever be, I guess."

They unhitched the trap door and walked down the steps, shutting themselves in and hearing the leaves scatter over the lid above.

21

Xavier the Savior

Xavier had woken up at 5am in a cold sweat. His first thought was of Andrew and the boys being set upon by hundreds of Blackstones. "Ergh. WHY DO I CARE??!!" He was so frustrated with himself, swinging his achy legs out of bed and jammed his feet into a pair of coffee-stained, tartan slippers.

"See... SEE! This is what bloody happens when you let people in. 'Ooo, fancy a job?

Fancy letting me get quite attached to you and not wanting you to DIE!?'"

He fidgeted down the stairs, avoiding the piles of books at his house in an undisclosed location. Walking towards the kitchen and tripped on the same step he always did, causing him to curse the floor. The floor in that area was almost completely brown with the coffee stains.

In the kitchen, he filled up the kettle and placed it onto the gas hob. He ignited the hob with a long, cooks' match, then used the same match to light a half-smoked cigar he had previously discarded on the windowsill opposite, puffing on it heavily. The smoke filled the kitchen and the early morning light combined to make a light mist. He coughed, whilst in deep thought.

"No shop today I'm afraid; Books will have to wait. I'll be needed in Soho."

22

THE 7 P'S

SOHO.

George led the way, holding the torch out front as they headed deep into the depths below. They passed many bunkbeds left over from when it was used as an air raid shelter, and even stinky toilets as they kept moving down. After walking for a few minutes, they realised that the air was starting to become warmer and damp. At the end of the passage was a wall. Lee and Andrew knew exactly what this was, but they wanted to see George's reaction.

"Dead end, guys," said George with a sigh, turning towards the others. "What are you two smirking at?"

Andrew had already spotted the black dish to the left of the wall.

"You need some blood, George," said Lee, knowing all too well how this worked.

"Is this one of those bloody doors?" asked George.

Their eyes fixed on the black dish. He followed their gaze and saw it.

"So, what do I do? Just a bit of blood on the dish, yeh?" said George, handing the torch to Lee and removing a small lock knife from his pocket.

"Yes, just a drop should do," said Andrew.

George pricked his finger with the tip of his blade, causing him to wince. He stretched his left hand out and dripped some blood onto the dish. The door started to rumble and opened inwards slowly, to reveal a further corridor.

"Quickly through," Andrew said. "They don't stay open for very long."

As Lee was now holding the torch, he took the lead into the new tunnel. They stayed close to him as it was darker than before, trying to match the speed of their steps. They felt the chamber open into a much larger space and heard the door rumble shut further back behind them. Lee walked to the side and lit a match. There was a wall hung torch on the left and Lee used his match to light it. Soon, the light from it spread across the large chamber to reveal a figure of eight or infinity type arrangement on the floor. On one side was a circle with a plain floor. The remains of an old fire were in the centre, and chalk marks around the outer edges. The low ceiling had holes that the smoke from the lit torch drifted up and over to escape.

A sheet of ply wood was leant up against the far wall and had firewood stacked in front of it, creating a triangle of darkness behind it.

In the centre of the second section stood an altar. This wasn't marble like the one in Russell Square; it was a solid stone altar on a bed of earth. Andrew had a feeling this chamber was even older than what they had seen so far.

On the altar was a slate dagger with a cloth-bound handle. Andrew picked it up and it was remarkably light. Feeling the blade, it was still so sharp he almost cut himself. He placed the slate dagger back on the altar, but he had failed notice the marks on one side of the blade and not the other.

"Xavier was right," he said to the other two. "This altar has an old dagger as well."

They set about preparing the landmines. Lee proposed to split their resources and bury one landmine by the head of the altar, as planned, and the other on the passage out towards Oxford Street, just in case the Blackstones made a run for it.

They planned to leave the chamber the same way they came in.

They got to work. Lee dug a hole by the head of the altar and carefully set the landmine in place, double checking the height compared to the surrounding earth. It was a British B, type C mine, and the detonator had to be inserted separately when everything was in place. Without the lid on, it looked like a green biscuit tin with a hole in the top. Lee unwrapped the detonator gently and inserted it into the hole very slowly.

"I had to read one of my uncle's manuals to figure out how these work," Lee said, reaching over for the lid. "The trick is not to over-compact the soil when putting it back."

The mine now had its plate fitted and the detonator primed. Lee carefully reinstated the soil around and on top of the mine, being careful to not pat down too hard at any point.

“One down, one to go,” he said.

As there was only one other way out from the chamber, they decided to take a torch and walk the passage to see where it went. They had time after all. The passage funnelled down the further they got away from the chamber, and before long they were in single file.

They carried on walking for a couple of hundred yards, at least until George at the front said, “It's another one of them bloody doors again. I’m not doing it this time; my finger still hurts from earlier. Why can't they just use keys like everyone else?”

Lee stepped forward and pulled out a knife he had on his belt. He made a small cut on his hand and let the blood drip on the dish.

The door rumbled to expose its outline and started to open. Once opened, they could see the set of stairs on the other side. They walked through and up the stairs to a fire exit door. From what Andrew could hear, London was starting to wake up. Finding a gap in the door, he looked through to try and gauge where they were, but he couldn’t see anything that was familiar, just an optician’s on the other side of the road.

“They wont use this entrance as its too exposed." said Andrew.

"It's probably just an emergency exit."

Retracing their steps, they walked back down into the depths and along towards Soho Square. Once the path widened enough, they found a suitable spot for the landmine. They helped Lee dig up the soil and he placed the landmine like he had done with the one by the altar. He pushed the shovel into the ground gently, just behind it. “Just so we know it's there.”

"Right, all done then?" asked George, "Can we go now?"

"Whats the rush?" said Lee,

"We didnt get up this early just to dump and run, did we, Andrew?"

Andrew didn't even respond. He was too fixated on the markings all over the walls in the chamber trying to use the lamp to see the details. He had seen them a few times now. That time with Ed of course, and the recent times in Russell Square, but he never really had the chance to look at the markings properly.

Some of them were almost like Egyptian hieroglyphs, and other more generic shapes like pentagrams and hexes. All of them had the same brown, dried blood look about them. As he moved further down the chamber, he found one that caught his eye because it looked newer and had bold colours. It was a series of large pictures, like an ancient comic strip.

In the first picture there was what looked to be a Vampyre, shackled on one side, and on the other was a young girl, who was also tied up. Up high in the centre is the sun with its rays spreading out finely. In the second picture a dark robed character looked to be taking blood from the Vampyre. The third picture showed them to be focusing on the blood and conducting a ceremony. The fourth picture showed the dark robed character making the young girl drink the blood. In the fifth picture, the Vampyre and the girl are brought close together in the centre of the circle, but there's something else that didn't make sense. The girl looks to be having her throat cut by the dark robed character and her blood collected into a pot. The sixth and final picture showed the dark, robed character holding the pot with the blood from the girl above their head in both hands, a whole circle of people bowing down around them.

"What on earth is this about?" he said to himself.

"Come and look at this" Andrew said to the boys. George and Lee were now arguing about who had to get up earlier, but they stopped and came over to look at the drawings.

"Looks like a strange ritual, and that guy doesn't look human," said Lee.

"It's a Vampyre," said Andrew.

"You've been reading too many books, Andrew," laughed George.

Lee pulled the collar on his jacket up and stretched out his arms. "I vant to suck your bloooood."

"They exist!" said Andrew. "I bumped into one outside the bookshop as he didn't have a reflection. I asked Xavier about it, and he said that there are thousands of them in London, but most of them have signed an agreement not to attack humans."

"Poppycock," said Lee. "So, what do they do instead, hunt pigeons and rats?"

“They get blood from the blood transfusion service,” said Andrew.

“Blood banks? No way!” said George. “So, you’re telling me that Vampyres actually exist, but are bound from attacking us because of some poxy agreement?!”

“Yes, but not everywhere,” Andrew relayed. “Some countries still haven't signed up yet.”

“Sounds like a wind-up to me,” said Lee.

“Speaking of wind ups,” said George, looking at the painting on the wall. “The first picture isn't square, it's round. Oh... it's a clock face.”

“Oh yeah,” said Andrew.

“Both of the faint hands are right at the top, see,” said George, pointing at the faint lines above. “Midnight or noon? Hard to tell.”

“This lot are fond of a midnight ritual, I'm sure. But look at that there.” Andrew pointed to the top centre.

“It's not the moon, it's the sun,” he said. “Which means it must be noon.”

“You know, I've had to get up at 5:45 every day this week to sort the paper rounds.” whined George,

"Cry me a river, George." said Lee, rolling his eyes as he began to re-pack his bag.

23

Moving Pieces

Xavier had finally left his house at 7am and drove towards the west end. He found somewhere to park in a side road just off Oxford Street and walked over to Soho Square. The weather was nice and the little garden in Soho Square always attracted lots of people who liked to meet up, and lay on the grass with a blanket. Sometimes with a picnic, chatting about their nights out, or some people who still hadn't quite made it to bed yet from the night before.

Xavier had sat in this garden quite a few times with Franco, on a warm, hungover Sunday morning and he missed those days. He decided that it wasn't the time for sentiment. The boys could be in big trouble if he didn't focus.

It had just turned 8am when Xavier walked into the square and spied the little gardeners hut from a distance. There were too many people sitting around the park now and anyone trying to enter the chamber here would attract too much attention. He decided to walk up the road to the entrance on Oxford Street.

There's a small cafe on Oxford Street, on the first floor above the opticians. Xavier had been there many times before and always sat in the same place by the window overlooking Oxford Street. The food was awful, and the tea always had a funny aftertaste, but he wasn't there for refreshment. It was for the view.

Bang opposite his window, in between the barbers and a shoe shop, was a grey, ventilated door with no handle.

So dull that you wouldn't even give it a second look unless you knew where it led, like Xavier did. He sipped his tea, recoiling from the taste and watched the door opposite tentatively. He looked through the food menu desperately trying to find something he could keep down.

"Toast please... just toast," he said to the eager waitress.

Half an hour later and on his second cup of disgusting tea, he was almost relieved when he saw a group of four Blackstones come around the corner from Soho Square, and head towards the grey ventilated door. When they reached it, three of them turned around to shield the fourth man's actions but Xavier, being high up, could still see him.

The keystone or centre brick of the small arch of the doorway must have had a hole in it for a button, as the man pointed up to push it. The grey ventilated door popped open by two inches, which was enough for one of the men to grab it quickly and open it wide enough so all four men could slip inside. The door shut firmly behind them

"Well, that's new... Sneaky," said Xavier. "Xavier see, Xavier do."

Xavier stood up to leave and left the money for his disgusting breakfast scattered and spinning on the table. Heading down the stairs he really hoped the boys had managed to get out intact. He walked around the corner to collect Berty from the boot of his car.

Meanwhile, back inside the chamber...

The wall-hung torch had burned down to embers now and the boys decided that they needed to leave while they still could.

Andrew was still inspecting the many drawings and symbols on the walls. He couldnt get over the fact that they were in a place where hundreds, if not thousands of people had been sacrificed down in this chamber, and on the very altar that stood before them, just a few yards away. It was then they heard it; the rumble of a door coming from the Oxford Street tunnel end and distant voices.

“Hide!!!,” Andrew whispered, and he took down the torch from the wall and burried it in the dirt.

He panicked as there didn't seem to be anywhere to go.

"Over here!" whispered Lee, as he led them over to the sheet of ply where the firewood was stacked against.

"I'm not crawling in there!" whispered George, "There could be spiders and all sorts."

They were running out of time.

Andrew crawled in first and George reluctantly joined him, followed by Lee.

They squeezed behind the wood, and were out of sight when they heard a voice.

"Oh look, a trench shovel," said one of the Blackstones, removing it from the soil. "I killed a Nazi with one of these, you know. Took his head clean off with it." They all laughed.

Andrew and the boys held their breath and covered their ears expecting one of the men to stand on the landmine that was right next to them.

"But why is it here?" said another Blackstone.

"Probably left here by one of the society pledges. I sent five of them here last week to tidy up from the last offering and reset for today," said the first.

They walked towards the altar, missing the landmine by shear luck.

"Who do we have for the offering tonight, Greg?"

"Just some homeless bum who turned left when he should have turned right," said Greg. "That's not even the best bit, as you may have heard."

The boys were now listening intently.

"Yeh, so what is the big announcement then, Greg? Why all the secrecy?" asked one of the men.

"Yeh Greg, come on... it's us," said a new voice.

"Ok, ok," said Greg. "I'll tell you now before the others start to arrive, but you must keep this quiet until tonight. This comes down from the very top, right from the Shadows themselves."

The chamber fell silent.

“The first week of December, there will be a fog over London, like never seen before,” said Greg.

“For what?” asked one man.

Greg continued. “To hide what will take place up at the Greenwich observatory. You know the new artwork we had painted on the wall over there?”

“Oh, the thing involving blood from a Vampyre?” asked another.

“Yeh, well, it's for that. It’s an incantation that must be conducted at noon on Sunday the 7th of December, and it involves the Shadows. It's called Extensio Vitae, and they have ordered every Darkheart in London to provide protection while the ceremony is going on. In reward, they have promised the head of each sect special privileges. These will trickle down to benefit everyone, including us, of course.”

“What does it do? The Extensio whatsitcalled?” asked a voice.

“Vitae.... Extensio Vitae, it’s in the Necronomicon,” said Greg. “What it means in Latin is ‘long life’, but what it *actually does*, only the Shadows will really know.”

“But what about the blood treaty?” asked one of the men.

“That’s all in hand,” said Greg. “The Vampyre council have agreed to let the Shadows use a Vampyre who has caused them a lot of trouble. They have just captured him in Dublin, and he is being transported to London as we speak.”

The boys had listened carefully from behind the board and could not believe what they had just heard.

Back out on Oxford Street,

Xavier had collected Berty in his leather case and crossed the road towards the unremarkable grey ventilated door. Looking up at the keystone he saw a small hole about an inch in diameter. He looked around to see if anybody was watching. Looking up opposite at his normal place by the window in the first-floor café there was a man sipping a cup of tea and pulling a strange face. Xavier winced in sympathy.

He pretended to yawn and raised both arms for effect. His right index finger found the hole and pushed the black sprung loaded button, but nothing happened. The door didn't open. A little confused, he looked around and raised just his right arm this time and hit the button again.

This time he looked down and happened to notice that a small stone button appeared out of the pavement for only a second, before disappearing back down to be flush with the floor once more.

"Really? You have got to be joking," said Xavier to himself.

A little old lady with a stick was walking up the high street passing him, and her kind eyes locked with his. "Having a bit of a stretch, dear?" she asked, tittering. He didn't quite know what to say, but just felt embarrassed. So, he looked around to prepare for another go.

"Right." He moved his arm up and his finger found the button again. He then looked straight down for the pebble sized button. He stepped on it the moment it popped up, and the door popped open with a gap of two inches.

“Ah ha!” said Xavier, feeling quite proud of himself for a change. That was short lived though, as two seconds later the door shut again with a snap.

“No, no, no, no, bastard door!” Xavier said under his breath.

He was drawing too much attention to himself, so he decided to walk down the street, cursing with each step. He then doubled back on himself before preparing to try again, determined to get in. Standing in front of the door, he took a deep breath. His hand went up and index finger pushed straight on the button. His right foot stepped straight onto the floor button and the door popped open. His hand shot out and he grabbed the door with his right hand with his fingers in the gap, but it wouldn't budge. Before he knew it, the door was now trying to shut on his fingers in a vice-like grip.

“Argh.”

He definitely had everyone's attention now.

“Hello again, dear,” said the same little old lady to Xavier who was wriggling around like a fly on tar paper. “You look a bit stuck...do you need help?” she said, waving her stick at his hand in the door.

The extreme pain in his fingers meant he found it hard to talk.

“Yes please,” Xavier whimpered.

“What can I do?” asked the kind old lady.

Xavier composed himself. “Right, I'm going to push a button on the ceiling, and a little button will pop out of the floor right by your foot. When it does, can you step on it?” said Xavier, wincing from the pain of the door on his fingers.

“I will try my best to,” said the little old lady.

Trying to breathe through the pain, Xavier composed himself.

“Ready, steady, go.” Xavier pushed the high button and the floor one popped up. The lady didn't even move before it sank back down, and she finally stepped lightly where it had been.

“Oh dear,” she said. “I’m not very good at this. am I? My reactions are not what they used to be, I'm afraid.”

The door closed even tighter on Xavier’s fingers, making him reel in pain. He realised that he would have to try and do it himself.

“Can I borrow your stick please?” asked Xavier, but he could feel his patience being squished just like his fingers. She handed it over. He took the stick and prepared himself.

He reached up, pushed the keystone button, and slapped his outstretched foot onto the floor button as it popped up, causing the door to release his fingers. He then jammed the stick into the gap and used it to open the door wide enough to get his legs in, holding the door firmly open.

“Thank you,” he said, as he handed back the stick to the lady.

“You are welcome, dear. Never a good thing being locked out, but you might want to get some normal locks fitted when you can, love. You won't be able to push and stamp like that forever, you know," she said as shuffled off.

Xavier massaged his throbbing hand trying to get some blood back into it, while letting the door shut with a snap behind him. He walked down the stairs towards the chamber with a new determination.

Back inside the chamber...

The Blackstone men were chatting about what privileges may be granted to them after December, when Greg shouted "Look at the dagger! It's upside down! I am going to kick some pledge's arse when I find out who left the dagger on its wrong side." He walked over to the head of the altar.

CLICK.

BOOOOOOOOOOOOOOOM.

No one could breathe. It was like the air in the room had been replaced with salt and smoke.

The shockwave had scattered the firewood from the front of the ply sheet and caused it to fall forward, exposing the boys from their hiding place.

Greg, the Blackstone, had stood directly on top of the landmine they had buried by the altar, and it had detonated upwards, compressing his leg so much that half of it tore off and threw the rest of him upwards into the low, solid ceiling, killing him instantly. The other three Blackstones were thrown back by the blast, and one of them was now near the boys as he stirred.

The blast had not gone unnoticed, and the persistant ringing of their ears couldn't shield the sound of a rumbling door and multiple footsteps coming from the Soho Square entrance. The dust was starting to settle, and Andrew wasn't sure what to do.

They stood up and Lee pulled the nearest Blackstone to his feet in a rear choke hold and put Edna to his temple. "What are you doing Lee?" said Andrew.

"We can't shoot them all," he said.

He had a point, and they needed a way out. As the dust had settled enough, they saw that there were now fifteen Blackstones in full robes, standing in the chamber and helping the other two up off the floor. They saw the boys standing there, and then noticed the gun to one of their members' heads.

A large Blackstone stepped forward to speak. "Don't even think for a minute that you will be leaving here alive," he said angrily.

"Well, that's debatable," said Lee. "All depends on if you want to keep him, I suppose." Lee pressed the gun on the Blackstones temple, hard enough to make him grunt.

"Kill him if you must. Either way, you three are finished."

Lee pushed the Blackstone forward and he collapsed on the floor between the two groups. He then turned the gun to the large Blackstone who was making all the threats.

"So, what about you? Huh? Shall I just kill you then?" Lee snarled.

“I'd like to see you try, boy,” he cursed back.

Lee didn't say a word but pulled the hammer of the revolver back. He stared at the robed man with intent, waiting for him to make a move.

“I dare you,” said the Blackstone.

CLICK.

Lee had pulled the trigger, but the gun hadn't gone off.

CLICK. CLICK. CLICK.

“Looks like someone forgot to load the gun,” said the large man, taking a slow step forward.

“Good job I didn't,” said Xavier, walking through into the chamber with Berty pointed straight at the Blackstones.

“Xavier, this is not your business,” said the lead Blackstone. He knew Xavier was a loose cannon.

“Of course, it is,” Xavier said. “These boys are here on my orders, you philistine.”

“You will pay for this dearly, Xavier. Mark my words.”

“Ahh, you bore me. Come on boys, up. Time to go,” said Xavier.

“Enjoy your walk in the sun, Xavier, as it will be your last. Your shop will be ash by nightfall; all your precious books, gone.”

Xavier, who was dusting off the boys, had heard quite enough of this. He never appreciated being threatened, not by anyone. He turned and walked towards the large Blackstone and pushed Berty into his chest. Xavier knew him, his name was Derek, and had had a few encounters with him before.

"Say it again, Derek. Come on, I double-dare you!" A hint of regret registered on Derek's face.

Xavier continued..."You satanic scum do not scare me. I've been to hell; I've lived there in my own mind, plagued by my own thoughts for most of my life. Killing me would be doing me a favour."

"What about these boys, Xavier? They will die for what they have done today '*on your orders,*'" said Derek.

Xavier slowed his mind. The realisation had neutralised some of his anger, leaving only the idea of preservation. Meanwhile, Lee was now loading Edna.

"Kill me instead," said Xavier. "Do it however you want to, just let them go."

Derek tilted his head to one side in feigned pity. "Has the ruthless Xavier finally found a way of martyring himself? That's so sweet."

The sound of a rumbling door from the Oxford Street tunnel could be heard, and even more steps and voices bounced down the passage. They were being surrounded, and time was running out. Ten more Blackstones walked into the chamber, and Andrew hit the deck with his hands over his ears. George and Lee did the same. Xavier, not knowing about the other landmine, just looked down at them in confusion.

“Boys...”

CLICK.

BOOOOOOOOM.

The landmine exploded, sending several of the Blackstones flying into the walls and ceiling, filling the chamber once more with dust and unbreathable air. Xavier sat up with a face full of dust.

“NOW! GO NOW!” he screamed at the boys as they were getting back up in the smoke and mist.

They moved towards the Oxford Street tunnel as fast as their vision would allow them to, dragging their bags behind them. As they walked past some of the Blackstones on the floor, the damage from the landmine was quite clear, and blood was everywhere. They hurried down the single file tunnel with Xavier leading the way.

Xavier had swiped his finger on some Blackstones’ blood from the walls and he wiped it on the dish for the exit, but something unexpected happened. The door didnt budge and there were popping and crackling noises coming from the dish whilst the blood burnt up in smoke.

“Ah, dead blood,” he said, wiping the excess on his trouser leg with a “yuk.” He handed Berty to Lee then took out a small knife and cut his hand for the dish. The door rumbled open, and they moved through and up the stairs to street level, but George tripped on the stairs with a yelp and was now limping badly. Feeling a bit shell shocked, they paused, ears ringing and eyes stinging. Xavier took Berty and put him back in his sleeve and around his shoulder. Lee forced Edna into his pocket.

“Ready?” said Xavier, about to open the door that had crushed his hand earlier.

They pushed the bar and opened the door, spilling out onto Oxford Street looking like they had just got back from a festival in the desert. It was a bit busier than before. Some people looked at them strangely but soon walked past in the direction of food. George could no longer stand properly let alone walk, so Andrew supported him as they crossed the street following Xavier. They walked around the corner and saw Xavier’s old Rover parked under a tree. It was now covered in spots of bird poo.

“Ah, that's why there was a space there!” said Xavier, as he got in.

Andrew helped a badly limping George into the backseat while Lee sat in the front. They drove away with a smeared windscreen, ears still ringing, and dust blocking their noses.

24

Disclosure

Xavier drove for miles without saying a word. They drove all the way to Archway before any of them even spoke.

"Where are we going?" asked Andrew.

"A safe house," Xavier said. "My god do we need it."

They headed up past Archway and towards Highgate, turning off the main road and ending up in the back streets of old houses. Parking up on a dead-end road, they got out of the car.

Andrew helped George out with great difficulty, as he couldn't weightbare.

They shuffled through the back gate and into the garden of a rundown house.

It was a nice house, but the paint was peeling from the woodwork and a few tiles were missing from the roof. Xavier walked towards the backdoor passing some flowerpots on the patio with long-dead plants in them. On the back porch was a growth of mistletoe. He traced the root back towards the house and as it met the house there was a high-level shelf with a rusty backdoor key. He took the key and opened the door, beckoning them in.

"Quickly," he said.

As they stepped in, he locked the door behind them and pulled the curtain across the door, blocking out the morning sun. They walked into the lounge, which was a very plain room that smelled of damp. It had high ceilings and shutters over the windows. He got them seated on the mismatched furniture, elevating George's leg.

"You boys must be hungry?" Xavier asked.

They all nodded, still struggling to speak easily. Xavier disappeared into the kitchen for a while.

Andrew went to the bathroom to clean his face that was covered in dust.

He brushed himself off as best as he could, found some rags and filled a bowl with cold water.

"So, what happened to your foot, George?" asked Andrew, as he walked back into the lounge with the bowl.

"I slipped on the stairs in the rush, but I heard a pop too, which is a bit worrying."

Andrew helped him take his shoe off as carefully as he could, but it was still causing him a lot of pain.

"Well, that's not good, is it," George said, looking down at his swollen foot.

"Looks broken to me," said Lee, as he was unloading Edna. He then put everything back into the leather satchel.

Andrew pulled out a couple of the rags and rinsed them in the cold water then placed them gently and slowly over George's foot. He winced a bit but settled.

"Well... our mission didn't exactly go to plan, did it," said Andrew.

"You could say that," said Lee. "And all because that bloody dagger was upside down."

"I didn't realise, the markings were so faint. I just didn't think it mattered," Andrew said.

"The devil is in the detail," said Xavier as he re-entered the lounge with a huge tray. He placed it down on the coffee table. It was a large saucepan full of tomato soup and huge offcuts of stale bread.

They each took a bowl and spoon and finished off the whole lot in less than five minutes flat.

Nobody said a word. Fighting the evil in the world really works up an appetite. Even after the food, Andrew still felt a bit on edge after what had happened today. Xavier did not force them to talk and let them doze off for a while.

Later, around 6pm, he walked back into the lounge with a bottle of brandy and four smudged glasses. He placed them on the coffee table unceremoniously and poured four large measures, handing one to each of them. Andrew wasn't sure what to say. He had a few drinks before, but mostly beer, and two at the most. This seemed different and the smell of the brandy made him shiver slightly, re-awakening the aches in his legs.

“Don't think, just drink,” said Xavier, as he downed his brandy in one.

They all followed his lead. Andrew managed to swallow his in one large gulp, but the heated sensation in his throat and mouth made him gasp. The heat kept building but tapered off slowly, just in time before it became too much for him to bare. Lee managed his glass without any issue at all, whereas George was coughing and spluttering like he had inhaled it by mistake. His involuntary movement made his foot hurt even more.

Just as they were recovering from that experience, Xavier was already pouring another.

“Really?” said Andrew.

“Don't think!” said Xavier.

“Just drink!” the rest of them chimed in.

They all managed their second glass without any coughing. The warmth of the brandy started to surround them and softened the hard edges of the room. Even the waning light peeking in from behind the window shutters and into the lounge seemed softer and more forgiving. Xavier had put the bottle down, and took a seat on the coffee table, so he could be near them.

“What happened in that chamber? Tell me everything,” said Xavier.

They explained about how they got into the chamber through Soho Square, and how they had buried the landmines, once they had decided the best location for them.

But just as they were about to leave they heard voices, so they had to hide.

"It would have all been fine if it wasn't for the dagger being upside down." said George, as he shot a dirty look at Andrew.

“The markings must be face up,” said Xavier. “Otherwise, the spell doesn't work, you see. Every time someone sees the spell, whether they consciously read it or not, they reinforce its intent. The spell on that dagger is to keep it bound to that altar, so it doesn't infect the Blackstones with its malice. So, what happened then?”

“One of the Blackstones, a man they called Greg, saw the dagger was upside down, and walked over to the head of the altar.” said Andrew,

Andrew made an explosion with his hands, as he did so his dads watch fell off. one side of the strap had come away from the body.

“Oh no, my dad’s watch,” said Andrew, picking it up off the floor.

“It's only the strap, show it to me?” asked Xavier.

Andrew handed it to him, and he looked it over.

“Red strap? Very unusual for a man’s watch. There's a watch shop in Camden I know well.

They could fix this in a jiffy," said Xavier, handing it back.

Andrew took the watch and put it in his pocket before continuing.

"Anyway... before we knew it, we were slowly being surrounded by more and more Blackstones and it wasn't looking like we were going to make it out. That was until you showed up."

"Tell Xavier about the thing in December," said Lee.

"December?" asked Xavier.

"Oh, that...We overheard them talking about the first week of December," said Andrew.

"The 7th" said George.

"There will be a lot of fog to hide the thing they are going to do."

"What thing?" Xavier asked, with side eyes.

"It's an incantation that a group called the Shadows will be conducting; The Blackstones will just be the security," said Andrew.

"Mmm...I see." said Xavier, making several intense mental notes.

"The Shadows, now that is a controversial subject," said Xavier.

"Who knows who, or what they are? Anybody?"

Their silence indicated their ignorance.

“This is where the tunnel gets deeper,” said Xavier.

“The Shadows are a group of thirteen families that allegedly control the world and have done so for hundreds of years. Rumour has it that they are behind every world war, pandemic, famine, arms race, and some say even natural disasters. They own most of the banks and control the movement of money, natural resources, and food. They can crash economies at will, and buy up all the assets that are sold off, only to wait for the recovery before selling them again for healthy profits. Their primary mission above all else is for a single world government: a new world order. If you consider the current government of this country to be like wallpaper hanging to cover what is really there, the colour may change occasionally, but the wall remains the same. The same bricks, the same mortar. The Shadows are the wall.”

“And thirteen families have been in control all along?” asked Lee.

“Apparently so,” said Xavier. “What did they say the Shadows were doing?”

“It's a spell from a book called the necro... something,” said Andrew.

“Not the Necronomicon, was it?” Xavier asked, looking concerned.

“That's the one!” Andrew said. “Something called... hang on a minute... erm. Extensio...Vitae?”

“Mm, I’ll have to look that up I’m afraid,” said Xavier. “But there's only one person I know who has a copy of the Necronomicon, and he was stabbed a few weeks back.”

“Marlon?” Andrew asked.

Xavier nodded.

“Did he die?”

“No, he survived. But the cursed dagger experience has made him re-evaluate his life choices somewhat. I visited him briefly a couple of weeks ago when he had just been discharged from hospital. He was recovering at home in Brixton when I popped by.”

“You found out where he lives?” said Lee.

“Everyone knows Marlon,” said Xavier.

“Looks like I need to pay him another little visit.”

25

Under the Radar

Xavier left soon after to head back to the bookshop. He took Lee with him to help load up the most valuable books and things into his car. "The rest can burn," said Xavier, looking at the stacks of books in the rear seats and shutting the over-filled boot.

"Oh, Lee, do me a favour, will you. Have you used a camera before?"

"Once or twice," said Lee.

Xavier handed over a camera in a black leather pouch. Lee took it out and got it ready, screwing in the flashbulb. "You might want to cross the street to get the whole shop in," said Xavier, as he walked forward to stand in front of the bookshop.

"Are you ready?" asked Lee.

"Go." Xavier raised one eyebrow as the flash went off.

“One more,” said Lee, winding the film and changing the flashbulb.

Xavier smiled and held his arm out pointing his finger to the sign. The shop lit up again.

Realising that this could be the last time he saw the shop as it was, Xavier wanted to be able to look back and remember it. He dropped Lee home in Hoxton, then headed back to the safehouse for the others.

“Right chaps, I've only got room for one, I'm afraid, as the rest of the space is taken up with books. Judging by the fact you can’t actually walk, George, I think it should be you.”

Andrew agreed and helped George out of the back of the house and into the car waiting behind. Xavier locked the backdoor and took the key with him.

“Thanks, Andrew, but what about you?” asked George.

“Don't worry, I’ll get the bus,” he said.

“I’ll drop George off and come straight back.” said Xavier

“Honestly, the bus will be fine." said Andrew,

They turned around in the road and pulled away, leaving Andrew to walk towards the main road by himself. He wondered how much the bus would be from Highgate and it was then he realised that he no longer had his wallet. He must have dropped it somewhere.

Meanwhile, back in the Soho Square chamber

A number of Blackstones had just finished cleaning up the mess after today's events. This chamber had to be ready for the ceremony tonight, regardless of what had happened. These ceremonies are not exercised by choice, they are an essential part of Satanism. One of the workers was inspecting a small brown wallet he had just found in the dust and inside was just some cash and a single business card.

Langley News

George Langley: Trainee Manager

Chalk Farm

Camden.

"Well, well, well, Mr Langley. Have I got news for you, bad news." He handed the card to another Blackstone. "Deliver this to Derek Matthews, immediately."

Back in Highgate

Without his wallet, and no way of getting back into the safehouse, Andrew sat down on the curb and decided to wait for Xavier to get back. If he had known that Xavier was going to Brixton after dropping George off, he would have probably just walked.

•••••••••••

In Chalk Farm, Xavier helped George out of the car and supported him while he hopped to his front door. He quickly retreated to the safety of the car and drove off just as the door opened. It was George's sister Lucy who opened the door.

“Mum! George is back and he’s hurt his foot!

You really will do ANYTHING to get out of taking me to the park, won't you?” Lucy huffed.

Xavier drove down past Holborn and towards the Thames. Having crossed over on the Waterloo bridge, he then headed south towards Brixton. He always disliked being south of the river, as it never felt right. Pulling into Mervan Road in Brixton, he parked up behind an old flatbed truck.

Marlon’s house had a Jamaican flag in the top window, as usual. It’s green, yellow, and black cloth brought some much-needed life to the plain and rundown houses. He stepped out of the car and crossed the road to Marlon’s gate and opened it with a creak. The wrought iron gate had rusted through the black paint and hung on for dear life to its hinges. He stepped up to the door and knocked twice. Nothing happened. After thirty seconds, he knocked again.

“Who dis?” asked Marlon, from behind the door.

“Marlon, it’s Xavier.”

“Back so soon? Why dat?”

"Something has happened. I need some advice," said Xavier.

Multiple chains and locks could be heard unbolting and sliding out from their keeps. The door opened slowly, and a pale looking Marlon stood in the doorway.

"Well, ya betta come in den, blud," Marlon said, looking over Xavier's shoulders for anyone else.

Xavier stepped over the threshold and into the hallway. He noticed Marlon had a pistol. Marlon shut the door and re-applied all the locks with clicks and pops.

"Still worried about the Blackstones?" asked Xavier, and he followed Marlon slowly into his lounge and placed the pistol down onto a small table by the door. All the curtains were drawn, and a single standing lamp in the corner struggled to light its local area, let alone the room. Its red shade glowed for its own amusement. There was a small wooden table and two chairs at the side of the room lit by a single candle. A knife lay on its side and reflected the light onto the ceiling.

"Nah, more bout me own mandem," Marlon said, as he sat down slowly at the table with a wince.

"How's the wound?" asked Xavier, while taking a seat opposite.

"I'll live. I av ad worse, ya naw. Dat dagger me took from ya, turned everybody crazy. Dem Blackstone crew didn't av to do a ting. Just rock up and take da box from a dead man's ands."

Xavier sighed. "I've never been one to say I told you so Marlon, so I won't start now. Affected things like that have to stay where they belong."

“Nail on de head, bro. But you here for my advice, huh?” asked Marlon, reminding Xavier of why he was there.

Xavier sat forward and placed his hands in front of him.

“The boys that were with me on that day in Aske Gardens; they are good boys. My god are they brave. They took it upon themselves to head into the Soho Square chamber and bury a couple of landmines to try and stop a ritual."

“Wow,” said Marlon, and he clapped quietly.

“Great idea, but it all went a bit pear shaped,” said Xavier. Xavier held up his hand to show three heavily bruised fingernails.

“Dat bloody Oxford Street door? I feel ya,” said Marlon.

“But before it all went wrong, they managed to hear some very confidential information.”

Marlon leant in.

“It's the Shadows. They plan to perform a ceremony at the Greenwich observatory. It will be at noon on the 7th of December, and they plan to use all the Darkheart cults to protect it.”

“At noon? Dem crazy. All de world could see.”

“Well, according to what the boys overheard, they have that covered too,” said Xavier. “They must have access to a weather machine or something as they are planning to bring in a really heavy fog.”

“Dat will be da HAARP,” said Marlon. “Word on de ground says dey have been testin it.”

“Harp?” asked Xavier.

“It’s big! da biggest, baddest wedda machine eva made,” said Marlon,

“I’d heard rumours too, but I didn’t realise it was already operational,” said Xavier.

“The incantation they plan to use is called Extensio Vitae, and it's written in the Necronomicon. And you, Marlon, are the only person I know with a copy, hence why I am here.”

“Now dat is a very special book. You know that, Xavier, as you sold it ta me for a lot of money, blud."

"It's very rare." defended Xavier,

"If I let you see dis spell, what you gonna give me in return, eh?” asked Marlon.

“What do you want?” said Xavier.

Marlon sighed and collected himself. “I need ta disappear, Xavier. Outa London, outa everyting.”

“I can make some enquiries, Marlon. I’m owed a few favours,” said Xavier.

Marlon looked at Xavier sincerely for a moment before regaining his composure and front. “You are lucky, doh, as I only just bring it back to me yard from storage. Keepin me treasures close to me chest.”

Marlon stood up from his chair with a groan, holding his side. Once the pain subsided, he walked out of the lounge. Moments later, he re-appeared with something wrapped in a dark cloth and a large brown onion. He walked in and placed it down gently on the table in between them and unwrapped the cloth to reveal a pale, leather-bound book with faint markings. The room suddenly felt a bit colder.

"Talk bout tings dat are affected, 'ere's one for ya."

A couple of years ago Xavier had collected the Necronomicon from a guy who knew a guy.

It had sat on his passenger seat wrapped in a broadsheet newspaper while he drove it to Spital Fields where he met Marlon to trade. That was a very good week. Rare books are expensive, and they don't get much rarer than this.

The Necronomicon, or the *book of the dead* as it is sometimes known, is reportedly bound in human leather, stretched back, and secured to it by large dark metal rivets. Its dull brass latch held the covers tightly shut. The human skin has had the same treatment as cow hide, but the moles and freckles still stood out. The pages are Egyptian papyrus, and it is written entirely in blood.

Xavier had only seen the Necronomicon once, and for twenty minutes or so. He never dared to even open the catch. This Grimoire, a collection of incantations and spells, was written around 720-730AD by the "mad arab" Abdul Alhazred. He called it 'Kitab al-azif', but it was generally known as 'Al-azif'. It was written while he was living in Damascus towards the end of his colourful life. He drew on inspiration from his adventures in far flung places such as Babylon and the subterraneous city in Memphis, Egypt. It was finally translated into Greek in 950AD and given the name the Necronomicon, which translates loosely into English as the 'book of the dead'.

Over the centuries this book in all its forms has been banned, burned, and even disguised. Some people believe that the witch trials were a massive cover to try and find copies of this book. Being accused of being a witch meant your house and possessions were searched. Now, as of 1952, only five copies are said to officially exist.

They are allegedly held in...

- The British Museum, London

- Bibliotheque Nationale de France

- Widner Library in Harvard University

- The University of Buenos Aires

- The Vatican vault library

Considering that the book has been condemned by the Pope for being truly evil, the fact they might have a copy is quite ironic. But there are a handful more, like the one that sits in front of Marlon, and unless you use the right protection, even the study of it is said to cause madness and a premature end.

Marlon grabbed the onion and picked up the knife that was on the table. He cut the onion in half and places the two halves cut side up, wobbling in the middle of the table, and he cleared space around the book.

"Praise to John Dee!" said Marlon. "Or we'd be strugglin to read dis ting in Latin."

"It's dangerous to even look at this, Marlon," Xavier said, worriedly.

"Dats what the onion is dere for, man. When da onion turns black... time is up."

"Is there an index? Or will you have to hunt for this spell?" asked Xavier.

"Bit more advanced dan dat, Xavier. What dis spell called again?"

"Extensio vitae," Xavier said clearly.

"Watch diss," said Marlon, a grin appearing on his face in the low candlelight.

"Fructum - Extensio vitae."

Nothing happened for a few seconds. Xavier went to say something, but Marlon stopped him with a blunt hand.

"Shhhhh." Marlon pointed to one of the onion halves that was starting to peel at the edges and discolour.

The book started to glow slightly, before the latch opened with a click. It then opened itself gently and fanned out, creating a movement of air above it. The dust of Marlon's neglected lounge could be seen moving through the candlelight. The pages stopped moving and drifted down, fully open on a section.

Xavier could see the heading that was upside down to him; 'Extensio vitae' written in very ostentatious dark brown calligraphy. This was it.

The onion started to brown even further and shrink slightly. Marlon turned the book around for Xavier to read the page.

Planet nine must be in alignment with Saturn and earth.

The incantation Extensio Vitae must be conducted at the start of time but at noon.

Blood must be taken by force from the covered Vampyre before the following inscription is read.

The inscription must be repeated twice for each pure child host.

The blood must be placed at the centre of a sacred circle.

The inscription,

Mundetinfectio,

ex hac vita vi.

rationemvitae accipiat.

tenebrisfidelis servitui,

qui tibiin perpetuum.

The drawing showed a captive Vampyre covered partially in cloth on one side of a sacred circle, and a young girl dressed in white on the other. Xavier thought he was hallucinating, as he thought he could see the picture move slightly.

“Did you see that?” he said to Marlon, but he didn't answer as he was too transfixed on the drawing.

The picture suddenly burst into life, like an animation. The covered Vampyre struggled in his restraints on one side of the circle. A robed man walked up to the Vampyre and unsheathed a dagger. The Vampyre grew angry and was hissing at the man.

This did not deter the robed man, and he made an incision in the Vampyre's arm causing it to let out a deep predatory sound. The dark blood dripped down to his elbow where a chalice was now waiting for it. Once there was enough blood, the robed man turned and walked towards the centre of the circle and placed the chalice of blood in the middle, before stepping back out of the circle.

They were now chanting what was written in the inscription. As they were doing so, the chalk markings that formed the sacred circle glowed bright white. Once they had finished, the white marks dimmed down somewhat, and the simmering dark blood glowed with a purple half-light. The robed man re-entered the circle and picked up the chalice.

He then walked over to the child and forced them to drink the blood. A large silver platter was placed on the floor in front of the Vampyre by others in robes. The silver platter and the child being brought over causes the Vampyre to enter a rage like state. They remove the covers. Being this close to a raging Vampyre is enough to petrify her. The child's throat is then slit, and they are held upside down by the robed men to collect every last drop of their blood onto the silver platter before them. The animation darkens and morphs to hundreds of robed and unrobed figures circled around a single man on a pedestal in the centre.

In his hands aloft is a clear vessel of glowing blood, its purple light reflecting off the green eyes that surround it. The

Vampyre is now seen locked up in a cell and a figure of eight, infinity sign is being traced above him. In the air above the glass vessel looks to be a vision of stars and planets, rotating in motion and some numbers: 1:100.

The onion on the table in Marlon's lounge was now almost entirely black and started to smoulder. "What's that bit Marlon?" Xavier asked pointing towards the numbers, but Marlon slammed the book shut and fastened the latch. Light smoke could be seen coming from the book edges, and the onion on the table had almost completely gone.

"Time's up. Dat was close, Xavier...bit too close," said Marlon.

26

Like a Spider to a Fly

Highgate

Andrew had become bored of waiting for Xavier and was starting to become restless sitting there on a cold curb. A car pulled up opposite and a middle-aged man and a young boy got out. They then helped a younger brother, who looked quite pale and sickly, into the house. The wife got out of the car and was struggling with some shopping bags and a large box of things. Andrew being Andrew felt sorry for her struggling with it all. He jumped up off the curb and headed over to help.

"Are you ok?" he asked, reaching out to take the weight of the box.

She looked reluctant to be helped at first, but soon changed her mind when he took the strain of the weight away.

"Where is this going?" he asked.

"That's very kind of you...er,"

"Andrew," he said, picking up on the awkwardness of her not knowing who he was.

"Straight into the hall please, Andrew." she said, gathering up the other loose groceries.

Andrew walked the box into the house and into the hallway. The house was beautiful, with black and white checked mosaic tiles on the entrance hall floor just like the ones his family had at their old house when his dad was still alive. This brought back some memories that felt too painful, yet seemed to calm him.

Lots of family pictures hung perfectly straight on the walls, showing the family on various holidays and adventures. The smell of freshly baked bread hung in the air, and it made him feel quite hungry even though he had eaten only a few hours before.

After Andrew placed the box down, the husband appeared in the hallway. He seemed to be a nice man with bright eyes.

"Ah, my wife has found herself a younger man, I see," he said. "I'm Julian," he said, holding his hand out to shake.

"Oh, I'm Andrew," he said, accepting his hand. "Sorry for the intrusion, Sir. I was just waiting for a lift to arrive and saw your wife struggling with a box."

"That's very charitable of you. You're not from around here, are you lad? I can tell," said Julian.

"No, Sir, I live in Kentish Town."

"I know Kentish town well. That was my old stomping ground, *before I got married,*" he whispered.

"Fancy some tea while you wait? The sun's going down now, and it will start to get cold out."

Andrew's gut reaction was to say no, but looking at him and his family he didn't seem like a bad man at all. No rings, except for his wedding band. And more importantly, no black stones.

"Or a sandwich perhaps?" said Julian.

"Thank you, Sir, but I must be going," he said.

"Please, call me Julian. It's no trouble at all. Oh, and you must have dropped this out front?" He took Andrew's dad's watch out of his pocket and handed it over. It only had one strap on it now and the other was missing.

"Oh yes, that's mine," said Andrew, feeling too embarrassed to ask where the other strap was.

"Now, please, please take a seat in here," said Julian, pointing him towards a lounge at the front of the property. "You'll be able to see the road for when your lift arrives."

Andrew stopped for a moment but decided to take a look in the lounge. As he peered in, he could see a large marble fireplace dominating the space with a prepared fire. There were a few large leather armchairs in the middle of the rug and a coffee table in the centre.

"Take a seat," said Julian. "Far more comfortable than a curb, that I promise you."

Andrew felt rude to not take him up on his hospitality, and after the day he had had, a comfortable chair was most welcome. He took a seat opposite the door with the fireplace to his left and sure enough, he could see the road and Xavier's safe house out of the window to his right. Very comfortable.

The wife walked into the lounge with a large tea tray with a sandwich, biscuits, and a pot of tea, and she placed it down gently onto the table in front of him.

"Thanks for your help with the box, Andrew," she said.

Andrew could sense some nervousness in her voice, but he wasn't sure why. "You are welcome, thanks for the refreshments," he said. "I won't be here long; my lift should arrive any minute, really."

"Stay as long as you need to," she said, but she never made eye contact.

That's odd, he thought. But then again, having a grubby teenager in her immaculate house probably wasn't ideal for her on a Saturday night.

Her husband Julian walked in behind her and started to pour the tea.

"What brings you to Highgate then, Andrew?" Julian asked.

"Just visiting a friend, but he left to drop someone else home. I just realised that I've lost my wallet somewhere and now I can't get the bus home."

"Oh dear, that's highly unfortunate," he said kindly, as he poured the tea. "Buses this time of night can be so unreliable. Help yourself to these bits and wait for your friend. I shall leave you in peace."

Julian turned around and knelt by the fireplace, lighting a long match before placing it in the fire. The paper in the fire started to catch and spread to the neighbouring kindling. Smoke slowly rolled up and out into the chimney as Andrew sipped his tea. It had a strange taste to it, but he put that down to the brandy he had earlier. He had only drunk half of it when he could feel his eyes becoming very heavy. It must have been the heat of the fire and the busy day that caused him to feel so tired. He felt so embarrassed to fall asleep but felt helpless against the warmth of the fire and leather chair that cradled him like a child.

Julian walked into the kitchen where his wife was cleaning white powder off the sides left over from the crushed sleeping tablets, whilst their dog snored from his basket in the corner.

"He will be asleep in five minutes. Is the basement ready for the ritual?" asked Julian.

"Of course it is; It's been ready all week," she said.

As a family, they had been in and out searching all day for a suitable offering. The homeless around Euston had grown wise to their charms. They had almost given up and were contemplating the sacrifice of their dog as a last resort, even though the children would be very upset. When human sacrifice is required, the sacrifice of an animal will not bring about any change you wish for, but it will stop the nightmares and visions that will plague you for not fulfilling your oath. They were not Blackstones, but Darkhearts none the less. A small sect of Satanists called Polaris, and they had their own ways.

Just then, they heard the teacup hit the floor and rattle in the lounge, knowing what that meant. Andrew had let go of everything including the cup and was now out cold.

27

PREPARING FOR THE WORST

Xavier had left Marlon's around 8pm with the thoughts of seeing the incantation spinning in his mind. He promised Marlon that he would make some enquiries about getting him out of London to somewhere west, like Bath. Right now, the most important thing was to find Andrew and tell him what he had found out about this Extensio Vitae, and how dangerous this could actually be.

"He must be home by now," said Xavier, as he drove through Camden towards Kentish town. He pulled into Lawford Road and found a space near number 19, the blue door of Andrew's house.

Xavier stepped out of the car and walked through the gate, and up to the door. The ground floor lights were off, but the ones upstairs were on. He used the lion's head knocker and tapped gently, twice. Nothing happened, but then a door could be heard shutting upstairs and footsteps came down the stairs towards the door. It opened slowly to reveal a silver security chain and the stern face of an older woman.

“Yes?” she said, curtly.

“Good evening, Ma'am. My name is-”

“I know who you are, Mr Xavier. You own that tired and dysfunctional bookshop that my grandson works at, don't you?”

Some people have a way of including negative opinions along with statements of facts. Yes, he owns the bookshop, and yes, Andrew works for him, but simply saying yes would mean admitting that the bookshop was tired and dysfunctional also. Not that he had the chance

“Well, no...” Xavier started.

“He was working for you today, wasn't he?” she interrupted.

“Oh yes, he was.” said Xavier, figuring out that he must have lied to his family about what he was up to.

“Well, Andrew hasn’t come home yet, leading me to believe he has gone out with his troublesome friends." she said,

"He will make it home I'm sure, as he always does. I just hope that he doesn't wake his mother as she has work early. I’ll be having words with him in the morning. Close the gate on your way out, Mr Xavier.” With that, she shut the door and walked up the stairs.

Xavier stood there a bit punch-drunk from the verbal onslaught.

“Where the hell is Andrew, then?” he said to himself as he got back into his car.

He couldn't have gone back to George's, as his broken foot was probably causing some tension. As for Lee's, not a chance. His dad is a lunatic.

Xavier decided to drive the same route the bus took from Camden to Highgate, watching the pavements for any sign of Andrew, but it being Saturday night, that was easier said than done.

"This is hopeless," he said, and decided to head back to the safehouse in Highgate and drop off all the books. He pulled into the dead-end road again and parked up in the same spot he had earlier. He got out of the car and opened the boot which caused a pile of books to fall out onto the road.

"Ahh shit."

One of the older books had some loose pages and one got away from the pile and drifted on a low breeze over to the other side of the road. Xavier made sure the books were safe before crossing the road to retrieve the pages that were now stuck on the garden gate.

"Come back here, naughty pages."

As he peeled them free from the gate, he noticed something that made the hairs on his neck stand up. It was the house opposite the safe house. Just the other side of the garden gate laying on the path was half a watch strap. It was red. He looked up at the house and the lights were now on. The stained glass above the door illuminated from the entrance hall light.

Moons of blues, greens, and reds in different phases and a single white star in the centre.

“Oh Andrew... you silly boy,” Xavier said.

Julian and his wife had carried and dragged Andrew down the narrow steps and into the basement. He was now tied to the altar. The wife had cleaned the lounge and was scrubbing the tea stains from the floor when she found the watch. It only had one red strap. She wasn't quite sure what to do with it, and when she could hear her husband calling for her in the basement, she placed it on the dresser in the entrance hall with the intention of moving it later. She then headed back down to prepare for the ritual.

The family, including the two children were now all wearing their dress robes. They had finished lighting the black candles and placed them around the sacred circle. Julian lifted down a wooden box that was on a nearby shelf and opened it to reveal a silver dagger. His wife took the dagger slowly, and Julian shut the box and placed it back on the shelf.

The snap of the box lid caused Andrew to stir, and he woke up on a very cold and hard surface, being looked down on by a pair of dark eyes glowing from a hood in the candlelight.

“What's going on?” he asked wearily and tried to move but couldn't. The ropes burned tightly on his wrists.

“Nothing personal,” said Julian, coldly.

“Are you ready, Annabel?" looking at his wife who was holding the dagger.

She nodded and moved over to the head of the altar.

“You don't need to do this.” Andrew said, as he tried to wiggle free but exhausted himself. There was no hope, as the restraints were too tight. Julian walked over to him and tied a rolled cloth around his head, covering his mouth tightly and making it harder to breath.

He then began.

“Hail Satan. Please accept this offering of flesh and blood to honour our requests. Remove the sickness from our child and take this life laid out before you as payment.” He looked at his wife and nodded. Annabel raised the dagger in both hands over her head.

Andrew closed his eyes, realising there was nothing he could do to stop this. He thought of his tired mother and imagined her crying in the dark.

“Hold the intention everyone. Hold it. Annabel... NOW!”

KNOCK, KNOCK, KNOCK.

The knocks echoed down the hallway from the front door. Everything stopped, and their dog started to bark upstairs in the kitchen. The family waited in silence.

KNOCK, KNOCK, KNOCK, came the same noise from above.

Whoever it was, they were not going away, and the dog continued to bark.

“Stay here,” whispered Julian. “I'll get rid of them and be back in a minute.” He removed his black robe over his head and hung it up on a peg before climbing the stairs out of the basement.

KNOCK, KNOCK, KNOCK.

"I'M COMING," shouted Julian, checking his hair in the mirror in the hall and telling the dog to be quiet. He walked to the front door and opened it wide.

"Excuse me, Sir, I'm looking for a lad called Andrew. He's fifteen, 5ft 11, light brown hair, very green eyes, have you seen him?" asked Xavier.

Xavier's gaze was drawn to something on the dresser in the hall. It was Andrew's watch. He now knew for sure there was something going on.

"No, I'm afraid not," said Julian, in a concerned tone. "But I can keep an eye out for him,

What did you say his name was again?"

"Andrew," said Xavier. "That's his watch on your dresser."

Julian turned around to look at the dresser, and sure enough it was there. Julian started to sweat. He had to think of an excuse quickly as to why it was. "Oh that, I found that..."

He turned back to face the scruffy man in his doorway only to find a large revolver pressed into his chest. The game was up.

"Where... is.... he?" asked Xavier, precisely.

"I can assure you; I don't know what you are implying," said Julian, in a last attempt to deceive.

Xavier pulled back the massive hammer of Edna with a click and started to count down.

"Three, two, one..."

"Ok, ok, he's in the basement, but my family are down there too," Julian said, nervously.

"Move," said Xavier, pressing the gun hard.

Julian walked slowly down the hall and opened the door to the basement.

"Who was it, dear?" asked Annabel from the basement.

But Julian didn't answer, he just walked down the steps slowly with his hands raised with the gun pressed firmly into his back.

"Untie him, now," said Xavier. "The rest of you, over there."

"Ok, ok, just don't hurt them," said Julian

The family, still dressed in robes, stepped back deeper into the basement.

"What's going on, Julian?" asked Annabel.

"It's fairly obvious, isn't it dear?" he said, whilst he loosened Andrew's ropes. "He is here for the boy, and he has a bloody gun."

"DO NOT swear in front of the children," shouted Annabel.

"Don't swear?" Xavier snorted. "You were just about to let them watch you kill this poor lad, and you are worrying about a swear word? Beggars belief."

"Sacrifice is necessary, swearing is not," retorted Annabel.

"Says who?" hissed Xavier. "There is another way. It is possible to walk away from the darkness. Believe me, I know."

"Not for us... not anymore," said Annabel, with a hint of sadness.

Julian had finished untying Andrew and he got to his feet as soon as he was free enough. He moved towards the exit, behind Xavier. He felt awful.

"If it wasn't for the children, I would have killed you both. You know that, right?" said Xavier.

They stood there at the back of the basement and watched Xavier and Andrew leave up the steps.

"How did you know I was here?" Andrew asked, still feeling a bit groggy as they walked towards the front door.

"Because of this," Xavier said, while picking up his dad's watch from the dresser and handing it over.

"And that," as he pointed towards the stained glass above the door. "Polaris."

The star shone with the moonlight behind it. "They had until midnight to kill you.

Open your eyes Andrew, it's all about the details."

Outside, they got into Xavier's car and drove back down into London towards Kentish town. On the way back they talked about his visit to Marlon's and the Necronomicon.

“The incantation involves taking blood from a Vampyre and giving it to a pure child, petrifying that child, and then slitting their throat for the blood,” said Xavier.

“What is the matter with these sick, twisted people?!” asked Andrew. “And what the bloody hell is a pure child, Xavier?”

“A child dressed in white; It means a child that hasn't been abused. Pretty much all the kids in satanic families have been abused from a very young age as a part of their mind partitioning.”

“Mind partitioning?” asked Andrew

“They figured out years ago that if you put children through extreme trauma, they can create split personalities that have no idea that each other exists. This allows them to see and do terrible things on one day, but then carry on the next day like nothing had happened.” said Xavier

“That’s awful,” said Andrew. “Is there no limit to what these people will do?”

“If there is, no one has found it yet,” said Xavier, lighting his cigar.

Xavier pulled into Lawford Road and parked up a few doors down from Andrew’s house. Andrew thanked his lucky stars to be back home. He almost died tonight; it was close... too close.

“What will this blood actually do?” asked Andrew.

“Extensio Vitae is Latin for long life. So, we can presume it uses some of the qualities that Vampyre blood has to prolong your life and probably has some healing abilities too. Rich and powerful people will be cueing up for it."

"And the Shadows; all of this effort, just for money?" Andrew said.

"People have done far worse for much less, Andrew, believe me. Speaking of which, I have a promise to keep. I need to get out of London for a bit," said Xavier. "I have some business in Bath and a few other places. I've shut the shop, so you'll need to have some time off. But don't worry, I'm still going to pay you."

He dug deep into one of his trench coat pockets. "Here, take this." He handed Andrew some crumpled pound notes. Andrew looked confused.

"When will you be back?" asked Andrew.

"Two, maybe three, weeks, I expect. Try and stay out of trouble please, OK?

No exploring or blowing things up.

Read those books, especially Openov. I'll keep in touch by mail. Look out for postcards."

Andrew got out of the car and Xavier drove away, heading west.

28

Redundant

Once at home in bed, Andrew fell asleep quite quickly and had vivid dreams of lying on that altar in Highgate. He could still feel the cold hard stone pressing into his shoulder blades. That family had seemed so normal. He had no idea they were satanists. Because of how easy the Blackstones were to spot, he was oblivious to the danger his was in. He slept on and off all day on Sunday, only getting up for something to eat and heading back to bed to avoid any conversation.

He just couldn't face it. Andrew dreamt of Xavier and all the books he had left him to read, and the bookshop, burning in the dark with its orange and yellow flames illuminating the dark sky.

He woke up to the sound of a radio that was on in the kitchen, it was Monday. "Why's that still on?" he said to himself, as he swung his bruised legs out of bed. He got up and walked out the back for a wash. The dust and grime from the Soho chamber was everywhere, but he had been too tired to clean himself up properly. His poor bed sheets really needed changing.

He got dressed and wandered into the lounge where the radio was playing some jazz in the corner, and he saw his mum was sitting at the table with a cup of tea. Looking over at the clock on the mantelpiece it was 10.30am.

“Hi Mum, you're home? No work today?”

“Yeh, weird, eh?” she said. “Tea?” she said, and started to get up before he stopped her.

“Don't worry, I’ll do it. You sit down for a change,” said Andrew, sensing something wasn’t right with her.

He brewed a fresh pot and brought it over to the table, sitting opposite her. She didn't seem to want to make eye contact.

“Sorry I was back late again on Saturday, Mum; I was with George and Lee. We-”

“I... I've been made redundant, Andrew,” she interjected, her hands fidgeting and fighting with the handkerchief in her grips while she just stared down at the table.

“What? I mean... why? You work harder than all of them put together!” he said, feeling a bit shocked. “Is the shop not busy enough?”

“Busier than ever,” she said, in an exasperated tone, looking down at her hands once more.

“So why now, then?” Andrew asked, confused.

“Mr Brown has always been happy with my work, and I thought he liked me. Trouble was, I think he liked me a bit too much. His wife came in a few times and noticed him acting very strangely, like he had been caught out or something. I had always batted off his advances and played down his remarks as 'just the way he is'. Turns out that it wasn't. He wasn't like that with anyone, including his wife. He couldn't even look me in the eye when he told me I had to go. Nine years I've been there, NINE, and all he gave me was two months wages."

"Does Grandma know yet?" Andrew asked.

"Does Grandma know what?" said Andrew's grandmother, who was now standing in the doorway of the lounge.

They froze.

"Would you like some tea mother?" said Grace, ushering her to sit down.

Andrew stood up to let his grandmother her take his place opposite his mum. She sat down slowly, never taking her eyes off her daughter's face.

"What's going on, Grace? Why are you looking so worried?"

Andrew's grandmother was a stern woman, but she really did care for his mum.

"I've been made redundant," she said with a small tear rolling down her cheek.

"REDUNDANT?! YOU?" his grandmother hollered. "YOU work harder than all of them. This is quite simply an injustice."

"I know, mother, but Mr Brown, he..."

"Oh, I know all about that old sleaze," she interrupted, bitterly. "He's been unhappily married to that old bat for years and years. I'm not having you lose your livelihood and have your reputation tarnished just because he can't keep his eyes off you. Andrew, get dressed; We are going out," she barked.

"No, mother, no, don't." Grace knew she wouldn't be able to stop her but tried anyway.

Following orders, Andrew got dressed and put his shoes on and waited out the front of the house for his grandmother to appear. She came out of the door in a long brown coat, black shoes, and a wooden stick with a silver handle. She looked a lot younger when she was angry. She stepped through the gate and onto the pavement and lit a small cigarillo. The blue smoke lingered in the air around them.

"Come on, Andrew. Let's go and see Mr Brown, shall we?" She marched remarkably quickly considering she was almost seventy. It was usually a ten-minute walk from where they lived to Camden Road where the bakers was. They made it there in seven, and his grandmother didn't even seem out of breath. Andrew on the other hand still ached all over from Saturday's antics. They stood outside of Brown's bakery by the tube and looked through the window.

Brown by name, and brown by nature. Everything was brown, except for the staff who were all painfully white, allowing very little contrast against their white uniforms. Their tired eyes peeked out from their pale faces. Probably even more tired today due to the absence of a key staff member; Andrew's mum.

"Stay here, Andrew," said his grandmother.

She opened the door and stepped into the busy bakers, allowing the smell of fresh bread to escape and dance down the street in the wind, and causing a few pedestrians to change course and walk towards the shop, in search of something nice to eat.

Andrew watched his grandmother asking one of the tired girls for something. They looked worried but turned to go into the office that was out the back of the shop, behind the bread cutter that jiggled and jostled as it sliced a granary loaf. A sweaty, overweight chap in his late fifties came out of the office, took one look at Andrew's grandmother and panicked.

"MR BROWN, I WANT A WORD WITH YOU," she hollered. Andrew could hear it quite clearly from the street.

She walked behind the counter and forced Mr Brown into his office with her stick and shut the door. Andrew took the opportunity to enter the shop so he could listen to the shouting, and maybe get a cake or two. All the staff and the customers were wincing in unison at his grandmother's caustic words.

"Next," said the young woman behind the counter. Andrew stepped closer and said,

"Have you got any-"

"YOU FAT, SLEAZY, PIECE OF-"

"Cake?" Andrew finished, trying to talk over the barrage of abuse erupting from the office.

"Yes, we do, but it all depends on how much is left in your ration book?" said the lady.

"Er, she has it," said Andrew, gesturing to the office and pretending to box the air, comically.

"Well let's play it safe then, yeh? How about a couple of bits of pineapple upside-down cake?" she asked.

"That will do nicely." he said.

"HOW DARE YOU GET RID OF MY DAUGHTER, JUST BECAUSE YOU CAN'T CONTROL YOURSELF! YOU UTTER COWARD."

You could cut the tension in the shop with a knife, and the cake was efficiently bagged up and ready almost instantly.

"I'M GOING TO GIVE YOU A CHOICE, MR BROWN. REINSTATE HER, AND GO MANAGE YOUR OTHER SHOP IN ARCHWAY, OR I WILL MAKE YOUR LIFE A LIVING HELL."

"But I'm already married," whimpered Mr Brown.

"YOU SPINELESS PHILANDERER!"

"Fourpence, please," said the lady, holding back a smile. The staff were obviously enjoying the deconstruction of Mr Brown, as they all seemed a bit happier and brighter suddenly. Andrew handed over the money and received his change.

"MY DAUGHTER IS TAKING THE REST OF THIS WEEK OFF TO SPEND WITH HER SON. I EXPECT A LETTER OF APOLOGY AND A NEW OFFER ON THE MAT BY THE END OF THE WEEK. DO YOU UNDERSTAND?

...DO YOU?"

"OK, OK," whimpered Mr Brown, knowing he was beaten.

Just then, she opened the office door and walked out from the back to the shopfront. "Come on, Andrew, we are leaving."

"Er, can I have the ration book please, grandma? I've bought some cake for you and Mum."

"I don't have it with me I'm afraid. Your mother will have to sort that out when she returns in a week's time."

For the sake of their ears alone, the staff didn't dare to disagree.

They left the shop and stepped out onto the pavement to start the walk home.

"Well... that was impressive," said Andrew. "He looked terrified."

"So, he should be," she said. "I know enough about him to ruin him, and he knows it."

"Would be great if Mum gets her job back," said Andrew.

"More than just that," she demanded. "I think a promotion is in order."

When they were halfway back home, she changed the subject.

"Why were you out so late on Saturday night, Andrew? Your activities are starting to concern me."

"George and I were at Lee's house; I went there after work," he said, as calmly as he could manage.

"Oh right, is that before or after George broke his foot?"

How did she know about that? he wondered. *Who had she been talking to?*

"Before," he said. "We went to the park for a late kick around and someone tackled George a bit hard."

"Was your boss there too, then?" she asked.

"No, why?"

"Well, he dropped George off at his door and drove off, you see," she explained.

"We called him for help, as he has a car," Andrew said, clutching at straws.

"From the park?" she said, her tone staying very flat.

"Lee used a phone box."

"LISTEN, Andrew. Sometimes when you find yourself in a hole the best thing to do is stop digging. You are not telling me the truth about whatever you are mixed up in, and I don't expect you to. Just be careful, OK? Your poor mother couldn't handle another loss like that.

Not after your father."

"OK, OK, I will," Andrew said. "But we're not the bad guys, we are trying to help people."

"The road to ruin is paved with good intentions, Andrew. Remember that,"

29

A Catch of Breath

Back in Kentish town, Andrew's family all had lunch together for the first time in months. Andrew told his mother about their march to the bakers, making her squirm a bit, but she was a bit happier knowing that Mr Brown cowered. Andrew's grandfather ate his food in silence as usual, and when he was finished, he walked back upstairs without saying a word to anyone. Andrew knew It wasn't unusual for him to just leave like that and didn't think he ever meant any offence by doing so.

"Grace, it seems that you have a rare opportunity to spend some time with Andrew."

"Oh, he probably doesn't want to hang out with his old mum anyway, do you Andrew?"

"It would be nice, actually," he said. "We could go out somewhere for the day tomorrow, if you like?"

"Well, yes. That would be lovely," said his mum, with a smile.

Andrew imagined that just the idea of her getting up when it's not still dark and not having to be at work was enough. Everything else seemed like a bonus.

"Anywhere you have in mind?" she asked.

"I'd like to go to Greenwich. They have a lovely market there, and we could even visit the observatory? It will be quiet too, as it's mid-week."

"Sounds like a wonderful day," said his grandmother, smiling.

"Would you like to come too, mother?" asked Grace.

"No, no, dear, just you two. It's important."

After lunch, Andrew found himself at a loose end. He decided to head to his room and look through the box of books that Xavier had given him to read. He lifted the box of books onto the bed and looked through the various brown, grey faded covers.

'Tactical warfare of the 1900's'

Not sure how good this will be to me, he thought, as he skimmed through. They were not exactly a battalion, and a third of his company already had a broken foot.

'Freemasonry in England'

This would take a lot of concentration, as there was so much to it.

'Morals and ethics'

"No."

'Myths and legends'

"Mm, maybe," he said, as he put that to one side.

At the bottom of the box there was a light blue book that seemed to be covered in little marks. Upon closer inspection, they were little drawings of keys and locks of various types.

'Codes and Cyphers' by Boris Openov.

"Now this is interesting." He started to flick through the pages, but instantly felt out of his depth. Too many numbers and letters in random orders. Struggling to concentrate, he realised that today wasn't the best day to read after all, and he put all the books back into the box and slid it back under his bed. He had left out the Myths and Legends book and thought George might like to read it while his foot heals. He needed to catch up with George and Lee anyway and see how they were doing after the disastrous day they had. Andrew knew George would be home because of his foot, so he planned to head there first and take the book. He kept the money Xavier gave him in his bedside drawer, and as he had lost his wallet somewhere, he had to put the loose cash in his back pocket.

Andrew said goodbye to his mum, who was now attacking a crossword at the table.

"Don't be back late, and stay out of trouble please." she said, not taking her eyes off her paper.

Andrew headed out towards Chalk Farm. When he got closer to the newsagents, he passed a florist and decided to get a small bunch of flowers for George's mum in the way of an apology. He even picked up two scoops of vanilla from a street cart for Lucy, who would be furious that her 'slave' was now housebound.

The white painted door to the left of the shop led up to the maisonette above where George's family lived. Andrew rang the bell and waited for the sound of small, impatient footsteps which arrived in a flurry. The door was opened by Lucy, as expected.

"What did you do to my brother, Andrew?" she said, in an accusing tone. He didn't say a word but produced the ice cream in front of her. That seemed to do the trick, as she smiled.

"Mum... Andrew is here, and he's ever so sorry." she stepped out the front and sat down on an upturned milkcrate to eat her ice cream in the sun.

George's mum walked down the stairs to see Andrew. She was quite a tall woman, and her hair was in tight curlers. It was Monday and her only day off. George usually looked after the shop on Mondays, but because of his injury she had to call on help from a friend instead.

"Hello, Andrew," she said, in a kind but tired tone.

"Hello Mrs Langley, these are for you," he said, as he handed over the flowers to her.

"What on earth are these for?" she asked.

"George's foot," said Andrew.

"It's not your fault that my idiot son decided to play football in the dark, is it?"

"Well, it was my idea," he said, going along with the story.

"He has his own mind, and if you told him to jump off a cliff, would he?" she said, while inspecting the flowers.

"I hope not," he said.

"Well, thank you all the same, they are lovely. I haven't had any flowers for a while."

Being a war widow like Andrew's mum, he knew exactly what she meant.

"George is in his room. GEORGE?" she hollered.

"Yeh?" said a distant voice.

"ANDREW IS HERE. Go up, love," she said.

Andrew climbed the stairs up to the flat and heard the clamour coming from George's bedroom. He walked out into the hallway on wooden crutches, his foot and ankle in plaster.

"Wow, definitely broken then, George."

"Yes," he said, whilst swinging himself like a pendulum between his crutches towards the kitchen. "I woke up very early and my foot was twice the size. Mum took me to the hospital this morning. Fractured in two places. Getting back up those bloody stairs took me an hour."

"Was your mum angry?" he asked.

"My mum doesn't really do angry, Andrew, but she does do 'disappointed' very well," George said, as he angled himself in front of a tall kitchen stool and sat down with a groan.

“How long will you be out of action?” Andrew asked.

“Six weeks, they said. Six bloody weeks of listening to Lucy go on and on about how I'm the worst brother in the world, just because I can't take her to the park.”

“She’ll get over it; I guess I'll just keep bringing her ice cream," said Andrew.

"Oh, I've brought you this book to read,” he said, as he handed it over.

“Myths and Legends,” said George, as he inspected its cover. “Thanks for that; One of Xavier’s?” he asked.

Andrew nodded.

“Xavier’s shut the shop and gone to Bath for something. Couldn't tell me what for though,” said Andrew.

“I've been there!” said George. “It's a very old Roman settlement, you know. Massive buildings and lots of history.”

“Said he’ll keep in touch by post, whatever that means. But either way he’s given me a month off, on full pay,” Andrew said.

“Wow, he really is a nice bloke, Xavier. A bit odd, but good,” said George.

Andrew told George what happened about his mother being made redundant and the march to war with his grandmother. He winced just hearing the story. “She is one tough old boot,” George said.

“So now, my mum and I are having a day out tomorrow... and guess where we are going?” said Andrew.

“Erm, the west end?” guessed George.

“No... think about December,” said Andrew.

He did so for a while.

“Not Greenwich?”

“YES! We are going to the observatory. Little does she know that I will be scouting out the place, so when December comes around, we’ll stand a better chance.”

George looked down the stairs to make sure the coast was clear and could hear his mother talking to a neighbour.

“Stand a better chance of what, Andrew? Staying alive?” George whispered but snapped back. “Do you really think that we have a hope in hell of stopping these Blackstones and these “Shadows”, whatever the hell *they* are?”

“We have to try,” Andrew said, calmly.

“Do we though, Andrew? Why is it always us? Look at the state of me! Our last outing has put me in a cast for six weeks, and I think I got off lightly. If it wasn't for Xavier, we’d be dead. Not just in a cast like me, but DEAD.”

“It was a close one, for sure,” said Andrew.

“Close? Close doesn't even cut it, Andrew. Don't get me wrong, I'm not blaming you for all of this. We made the decision to do what we did, together. What I am saying is that maybe it was the wrong decision, that's all. And we were lucky to escape.”

“Talk about lucky, that's not the only scrape I had yesterday,” said Andrew.

“Why, what else bloody happened?” asked George.

“Well, after you and Xavier had driven off, I realised that I had lost my wallet so didn't have any money for the bus. I decided to wait for Xavier to get back and ask for a lift. A family turned up at their house opposite and the wife was struggling with a box. So, I helped carry it in for her.

The husband offered me some tea and somewhere warm to wait for Xavier and I accepted.

They only drugged my tea, and I woke up on an altar in their basement."

"You are having me on?" said George.

"The whole family was in on it.”

“NO WAY! Blackstones?” asked George.

“No, not Blackstones; members of Polaris, apparently.”

“Polaris?”

“It’s a different sect, but still satanists,” Andrew explained.

“What happened?”

“Well, I was seconds away from being stabbed when there was a bang on the door. Luckily, Xavier had spotted my watch on the dresser in the hall and noticed a star in the stained-glass window above the front door. Remember what he said about stars? He came in and rescued me.”

“Whoah, you see... this... this is getting way out of hand,” said George, starting to lose his nerve.

“Yes, it is,” Andrew said. “And nobody else seems to be doing anything about it. So, it's our duty to try. We both know how it feels when one of our family doesn't come home, don't we?”

“Yeh, it's sad,” George mumbled. “I still catch my mum crying sometimes. And I know it’s weird, but I can’t remember the sound of my dad’s voice anymore."

“Me neither,” said Andrew, realising how alike they were in that respect. “Well, these people are destroying families all over, killing whoever they fancy just for their own greed, and they need to be stopped.”

“I agree, but we are going to need help,” said George.

“Yes, we will. Just not quite sure who to ask yet.”

30

Q&A

Andrew left George's around 2pm and decided to walk down to Somers Town and see if the bookshop was still standing. He followed the same path he had when he first found the bookshop all those months ago whilst being chased by the Blackstones, walking the little alleyways that threaded through the estate. Once at the end of the passage he could see the back of the familiar parade of shops and as he walked around the corner, there it was; still there, but covered in even more graffiti than ever before and it had a couple of small windows smashed in on the first floor.

"Not burned down yet," he said to himself.

Andrew crossed the road and walked up to the shopfront. The 'Xavier's Books' sign was practically unreadable now, due to the black paint. Cupping his hands to look through the dirty windows, he could see all the books that had been abandoned, still on their shelves.

Xavier had already taken the valuable ones, but Andrew was surprised at how much he had left to be stolen, or worse still, burnt.

He felt like someone opposite might be watching, so he walked on. Andrew passed the wine shop, but as he did so something caught his eye on the edge of the pavement, reflecting the sun's rays into his eyes. He picked it up and wiped it clean on his trousers. It was a heavy coin; a gold one the shape of a thruppenny bit, only twice the size. But upon closer inspection it didn't have a king's or queen's head on it, just the words 'Blood Treaty 1920 - Exemption' and on the other side was a V.

"Exemption?" he said. "Exemption from what?"

He really needed Xavier back so he could ask him what this was. Even if he didn't know, he would find out. It suddenly dawned on him. "I could find out, couldn't I? Just do some research, Andrew."

Looking back at the wine shop and then down at the gold coin, he decided to take a punt and go talk to the owner. He put the heavy coin in his pocket and walked towards the door. Andrew needed an excuse to walk in there, as he was obviously too young to buy wine. He decided to ask about the damage to Xavier's shop, and if they had seen anything.

The door was incredibly heavy to start with but finally gave way and swung inwards causing the shop bell to ding. There was a man being served at the till as he entered, and the door shut behind him. The shop had the same layout as Xavier's next door, only a lot tidier. It had dark wooden cabinets and shelves on either side. The lower shelves held the bottles upright, but the higher the shelves went, the more tilted the bottles became. Andrew couldn't see any prices on anything either, which meant only one thing: that everything was very expensive.

Some people must really love their wine.

The two men at the counter realised that they were no longer alone and decided to cut their conversation short.

"Will that be everything, Mr Constantine?" said the shopkeeper.

"Yes, thank you, Mr Bluvine. Good day."

The pale gentleman walked towards the door carrying his purchases in a canvas bag. He opened the door with one hand and walked out into the street. When the door closed again, it was just Andrew and the shopkeeper. He took a deep breath and walked up to the counter.

"Hello young sir, what brings you in here?" asked the shop keeper. He was a tall and thin gentleman in a sharp, pinstriped suit, with black hair that was greying at the temples.

"Hello, Mr Bluvine, My name is Andrew. I work for Xavier next door, in the bookshop."

"Oh, right... yes," he said. "I was beginning to wonder where he had gone."

"He had to go away on business and as you can see, the shop has been vandalised again. I just wanted to see if you had seen or heard anything?"

"Well, that's the strange thing," he said. "The bookshop was fine when I locked up on Saturday night, and I didn't notice anything different when I walked past yesterday either. But the mess was very obvious when I opened up this morning."

"So, they must have done it overnight," concluded Andrew.

"Precisely, he really seems to have really upset someone," said Mr Bluvine, with an inquisitive tone.

"Blackstones," said Andrew. He wasn't sure why he said it, but he wanted to test how much he knew. Mr Bluvine's expression warped slightly, before returning to his professional standard.

"A troublesome lot, I find," said Mr Bluvine. "Thugs and thieves who fancy themselves as lords of darkness, but the reality is that they destroy far more than they ever really gain."

He looked intently at Andrew. "I wonder what other secrets Xavier may have trusted you with?"

"I know what you sell here," said Andrew.

"And to whom?" Mr Bluvine asked quickly.

Andrew nodded. "He also told me about the blood treaty."

"Interesting," Mr Bluvine said, as he stepped out sideways from behind the counter. He walked up to the front door and peered through the glass for any approaching customers before sliding the bolt shut, locking the door.

"Don't worry," he said, as the fear on Andrew's face must have given him away. "This conversation must stay private."

He walked back behind the counter and took a perch. “So... what do you know about the blood treaty, Andrew?”

“Xavier told me that it was drafted in 1920 to stop the fighting between Vampyres and humans. They have access to as much free blood as they want in exchange for leaving humans alone, and anyone on either side that breaks the treaty suffers a very horrible death. Must take a lot of willpower, though.”

“Très bien,” said Mr Bluvine. “Except for a couple of things, you see, the blood...it isn't free.”

“Really? Well, that doesn't seem fair,” Andrew said.

Mr Bluvine continued.

“The Vampyre’s pay a subscription every month, which can fluctuate depending on supply. During the war, blood was at an all-time low in supply and therefore the most expensive it had ever been. There had been an outrage in the Vampyre community about the fluctuating prices, considering it was supposed to be free. But like all contracts, the devil is in the detail. They stated in the treaty that a nominal fee would be charged purely for the administration, but like any tax it's based on a percentage of the value of the goods. That has steadily risen over the years, meaning at the peak, some Vampyres needed to sell everything they owned just to quench their thirst, while the one thing they needed was flowing freely in the veins of their neighbours, their friends and pedestrians that walked by, just feet away. And for any Vampyre that ran out of options and broke the treaty?”

Mr Bluvine pretended to cut his own throat with his index finger and made a weird choking noise.

"Now that, Andrew, is the definition of discipline."

"But they still come to you?" Andrew asked.

"Yes, but I'm not as busy as I used to be. I have had to diversify somewhat, and now I concentrate on the higher end of the market. Some of my small vials go for hundreds of pounds," he said.

"Small vials? As in the blood of famous people?" Andrew asked.

"Bravo. Xavier really does tell you everything, doesn't he?" said Mr Bluvine,

"How do you even get the blood from celebrities?" asked Andrew.

Mr Bluvine seemed quite enthusiastic to explain. "Right from the start of the blood banks, or blood transfusion service as it is officially known, there have been celebrity endorsements to try and encourage the general public to donate blood, especially during and post war. 'Do your part- give blood.'

"The blood taken from VIP's is kept separate, processed, and sold off for considerable sums. The other way is if a VIP goes in for an operation. They have doctors that will extract blood and pass it to a runner."

"They steal the blood?" asked Andrew, in shock. "Unbelievable... then what?"

"There are a few specialist auction rooms in the City of London that can handle commodities and lots of a 'sensitive nature.' My contact deals with that side of things and sets the price."

"Wow... I never knew blood would be so sought after," said Andrew, looking around at all the bottles. "Is this all blood?"

"No, no, of course not," said Mr Bluvine. "Everything your side of the counter is wine. Some are very expensive and rare, but just wine. Everything this side, however, is." he raised his arms like a conductor of an orchestra.

Behind the counter were four glass fronted fridges concealed with a black curtain. Mr Bluvine slid the curtain to one side to expose them. Smaller, darker bottles were tilted back on their shelves and had little handwritten labels. He started from the left and started to point.

"It's quite simple, really. Men, Women, Boys, Girls. Higher up the shelves mean higher status, and therefore a higher cost."

"So, what is the most expensive one you have right now?" asked Andrew, honestly intrigued.

"Let me see... in the men's fridge I have... Oh, here we are... Frank Sinatra. £30 per fluid ounce."

"Woah, that bottle probably costs more than I could earn in a year!" Andrew exclaimed.

"Yes, but I often sell it in quarter and half measures. If you were a Vampyre and happened to be a massive fan of Sinatra, you would jump at the chance to experience this, to experience... 'him'.

Maybe music isn't your thing?" he said, looking through the top shelf bottles. "You like books. How about Earnest Hemingway, perhaps? Or maybe you prefer art.

How about half a fluid ounce of Jackson Pollack?"

"Like all art, it will probably be worth more when he dies," Andrew said.

"Sadly not," said Mr Bluvine, shutting the fridge and drawing the curtain. "You see, the blood dies with them, almost like it's tied to their lifeforce somehow. Only last year, I had thirty fluid ounces of Ivor Novello! Such a talented man; he could sing, dance, act and write. Massive heart attack at 58, and dead. Thirty fluid ounces right down the drain, but that's the risk you take, I guess."

"Hang on a minute, so if blood is tied to the donor's lifeforce, how does it react when it's put in somebody else's body, like a transfusion?" Andrew asked.

"All depends, I suppose," said Mr Bluvine. "On which blood has the stronger force. Some people reject donor blood and have bad reactions to it. Must mean the original blood just simply refused to comply."

"That's interesting" said Andrew,

"But there's something I dont really understand."

"Whats that?" asked Mr Bluvine.

"How do you know if the person is dead and the blood isn't ok to sell anymore?" asked Andrew,

"Very good question, Andrew, you don't miss a trick, do you." Mr Bluvine pointed towards the counter in between them. To the right of Andrew was a small, round wooden board with a darker groove around its perimeter. Sat in the groove was what looked to be a large marble, but not the sort that Andrew could ever remember seeing before.

Dark green, with a speckle of red spots.

"I use this little thing, here." he said.

"How does that tell you?" asked Andrew, looking confused.

"The ball is made from Ematille or Bloodstone, as it is commonly known.

Like Obsidian, it reacts to blood." said Mr Bluvine.

He opened the curtain and took out a small vile from one of the lower shelves of the fridges, and examined it in the light above the counter.

"Good colour is crucial." he said.

"Blood tends to look a little darker once the donor has passed."

He opened the bottle, and carefully dripped a tiny drop of the blood onto the top of the ball.

The Ball suddenly came to life and began to roll away in it's groove, around and around like a stone-age trainset.

Andrew was suprised to see the ball move on its own, but then thought of the blood doors.

After a few steady revolutions the ball slowly came to a stop.

"You see, living blood." proclaimed Mr Bluvine.

The Ball then started to glow slightly.

Just then, there was a knock on the door. Mr Bluvine thought quickly and wrapped a cigar in a paper bag and passed it to Andrew. He then ushered him out towards the door, just as the person was banging on the door again.

“Come and see me again soon, and we can finish our chat,” he said, as he unlocked the door.

A very skinny and pale man in a heavily creased, brown suit and a pork pie hat, that must have been a Vampyre, burst in shouting. “I've lost it Mr Bluvine... it's GONE! It must have slipped out of my pocket. It’s not in here, is it?” he said, looking around the floor frantically.

“Goodbye, Andrew. Send my regards to your boss, won’t you?”

Andrew left them in the shop as the door shut. He could hear the pale man becoming more desperate in his tone.

“The coin! It must be here. I've already done it you see, and they will know it's me as I've marked the body with the V just like they said to. Without that coin I'm a dead man. THEY WILL RIP ME APART!”

Andrew felt the heavy coin in his pocket through the fabric of his trousers and knew exactly what he had to do.

31

Between the Lines

George was now reading the book that Andrew had left for him. So many weird tales of pixies in woodland and nymphs that can steal your soul. Nothing about Satanism yet, but he persevered. He heard the bell go on the door again and heard Lucy huff when she had to go down to answer it. She opened the door.

“Yes,” she could be heard saying. “Yes, George is my brother. He has stupidly broken his foot though, so can't come down. I’ll give it to him. Thank you.”

“Who’s that, Lucy?” George said. but she didn't answer. She could be heard running up the stairs and walking towards his bedroom where he sat reading. She appeared in the doorway with a small brown wallet in her hand.

“Is this yours?” she said, throwing the wallet onto the bed. “Well, the boy thinks it is, as it has your card in it.”

“What did he look like, Lucy?”

"Like every other sweaty boy, I guess, but a bit different. About your age, dark hair with a silver streak in the middle, dressed all in black."

George recognised the wallet. "This is Andrew's."

But the last time George had seen it was in the chamber under Soho Square. He opened up the wallet, but it was empty. In the section where notes were kept was a single strip of paper, with a handwritten note.

RETRIBUTION AWAITS YOU FOR SOHO.

WE ARE WATCHING YOU.

A chill ran down George's spine.

"Oh, boys. What have we done."

32

Building Bridges

Andrew, hesitated for a moment before knocking on the glass of the shop door. Mr Bluvine stopped the distressed man from speaking while he came over to the door. He mouthed the words, 'This is not a good time', as he opened the door.

"I think I can help," Andrew said, looking over Mr Bluvine's shoulder towards the man behind him that was currently tying himself in knots by the counter. Mr Bluvine let Andrew in, out of sheer curiosity, locking the door again behind him.

"Frank, this is Andrew. Andrew, this is Frank," said Mr Bluvine. "Andrew seems to think he can help you."

Frank uttered an empty 'hello' but his mind seemed elsewhere, like he was planning his own funeral.

"Is this yours?" Andrew asked, pulling the gold coin from his pocket, and displaying it on his palm.

Upon seeing the gold coin, both Frank and Mr Bluvine gasped audibly.

“YES. YES, IT IS!” said Frank. “Where did you find it?”

“It was outside of the shop when I walked by earlier. You must have dropped it,” he said, holding it out to him.

“You have no idea what this means to me, Andrew!” said Frank, as he took the coin gently and spun around in a circle right in the middle of the shop holding it aloft.

“Well, I overheard your conversation about a lost coin when I was outside, and it sounded tense,” said Andrew. “Oh, and don’t worry, I know about you... as in, your people, and the blood treaty.”

Frank looked at Mr Bluvine, as if to check that it was ok to talk freely. Mr Bluvine nodded.

“He knows more than most, Frank, he works for Xavier.”

“Oh, why didn't you say so?!” said Frank. “Any friend of Xavier, is a friend of mine.”

Andrew saw his opportunity to find out some more. “What is this coin for?” he asked.

Frank was busy inspecting the coin but spoke anyway. “It's a coin that provides exemption from punishment when breaking the blood treaty. You can only use it once, and the body has to be marked with the same number as the coin that was issued to you.”

“What did you do to earn this, Frank?” Mr Bluvine enquired.

"You have to volunteer for various duties before they will even consider you."

"Like what?" asked Andrew

"Like helping the police to catch people," he said, holding the coin as if it were a long-lost family heirloom. "Or interrogation of suspects, as Vampyres can spot a lie a mile off. I had been on the waiting list for an exemption coin for over fifteen years. They don't come around very often, you see, and I was so excited when I got the letter."

"Who did you decide on?" asked Mr Bluvine.

Frank suddenly became quite bashful, and the embarrassment almost brought a hint of colour to the pale cheeks of his.

"I carried the coin in my pocket for a couple of days like a child," he smiled to himself. "Kind of like knowing I had the money to buy any sweet thing I wanted, but only one, just one. I loved that feeling so much, I didn't want it to end. As much as I craved the taste and the experience that was waiting for me, I also knew all too well the depression and muted feelings the next day would bring. Like a world briefly seen in vivid colour, only having to watch it slowly and inevitably fade back into shades of grey, and I would return to a state where I'm no longer living, just simply surviving."

"Who was it then?" asked Andrew.

"It was a tourist," said Frank, almost shamefully. "Francois Cloutier, was his name; even the sound of it makes me thirsty. I have always had a 'thing' for French guys. I don't know what it is, but they intrigue me.

Just after nightfall, I carefully tracked him through the back streets of Leicester Square until he walked down a dead end. It was glorious and amongst other things, I saw that he had been cheating on his wife for quite some time. He won't be doing that anymore, or anything else for that matter. Afterwards, the city came alive for me like never before; the lights shone vibrantly in colours I hadn't seen in years. I danced in the streets in a bubble of my own happiness all the way up to Regents Park. I didn't want the feeling to end, so I got together as much money as I could find and came here earlier to buy half a fluid ounce of someone French, just to prolong the feeling. That's when I must have dropped the coin."

"Well, at least you have it back now," said Mr Bluvine.

"Yes, only thanks to you, Andrew," he said, smiling to expose some very long and sharp teeth. "I am indebted to you, and if you ever need any anything, you let me know. I must be going. The authorities will probably be on their way to find me, but that doesn't matter now, as I have this." He smiled and tapped his pocket twice.

Mr Bluvine unlocked the door, and Frank left with a sincere bow.

"Goodbye, Frank," said Mr Bluvine, before shutting the door and locking it once more.

"Well, you have made a very powerful friend there, Andrew. That was a very noble thing you did."

"It was the right thing to do," said Andrew, plainly.

"That it was," said Mr Bluvine. "But it doesn't always mean it's the easiest thing. That coin is very rare and struck from eighteen carat gold. You could have sold that for a lot of money."

"At the cost of his life, though?"

"Yes... his life, in trade for a more enriched version of your own," said Mr Bluvine.

"What about the guilt?" asked Andrew. "If I found out that I was the reason that he died, that would make me feel awful."

Mr Bluvine took his perch once again.

"When it comes to money and power, some people have no guilt, Andrew. For instance, you can have someone that loves animals and even keep pets. Yet you will find them happily eating meat when they can afford it with no guilt. It is the primal side of our brains that allows us to switch off that guilt and eat what we need to, in order to survive. Some people have developed the same switch when it comes to money and power. It's all about them, and it doesn't really matter how it may affect others."

"I've never really thought about it like that," said Andrew.

"It is Frank's bad luck that he lost that coin," said Mr Bluvive, "And also his good luck that you found it. So many others wouldn't have lingered to overhear that conversation, and would be walking out of a jewellery shop in Hatton Garden right about now with quite a lot of money. The dichotomy of loss and gain. For every up there is a down, for every give there is a take. What you did, Andrew, makes you truly noble. You could certainly never be a Darkheart."

Mr Bluvine pretended to tip his imaginary hat.

"Darkheart?" Andrew asked.

"Yes, a Satanist, like the Blackstones. But there are other sects too, you know, like tobacco products. The Blackstones are like cigars: they have more members of the elite than any other sect, but there are many cigarette-like brands, lesser-known sects that still honour their demons in their own way."

"I encountered a different sect the other night," said Andrew. "The lack of Blackstone jewellery made them hard to spot."

"They all have their give-aways, Andrew. You just need to know what to watch for. Xavier knows a lot about all of this."

While Andrew had Mr Bluvine's attention, he decided to dig a little deeper.

"There's been something I've wanted to ask Xavier for a while, but I think you may well be better qualified to answer it, given your trade," asked Andrew.

"Ask away," he said. "I'll answer if I can."

"How does a drop of blood open a stone door?"

"Now that is a very, very important question." said Mr Bluvine. "Le coeur du problème', some would say. Satanists have it ingrained in them that the devil is to be praised or feared for any change they bring about by sacrifice. Even a drop of blood on the dish to them is a small offering to the powers that be, and it is the devil that opens the door.

They do not realise the magical qualities that ‘living’ blood possesses. See my little ball there?" he said, pointing to the board on the counter.

"As I said before, It's made from Ematille, Vampyres do not fear it as it has no effect on them, but it informs me when a Vampyre is close by glowing."

Mr Bluvine picked up the small ball and examined it fondly.

"I saw it glow when Frank was at the door." said Andrew,

"I did wonder if you had noticed that, Andrew." said Mr Bluvine,

"My Vampyre customers always comment on how they like the way the ball glows and ask where they can buy one.

Yet my regular wine customers pay it very little attention to it at all. When it comes into contact with blood, it absorbs most of the magic but as it does so, it moves, round and around, like you saw earlier. But when blood is applied to obsidian,however, the magic is magnified, so much magic in fact, that a single drop of living blood can open a door that weighs well over a ton."

"Must be very strong." said Andrew, "Is that why the Blackstones use Obsidian?"

"I dont think they know of it's true power, and they definitely dont know about the power of living blood." said Mr Bluvine,

"You see, when the Darkhearts conduct a sacrifice, they hold an intent in their collective minds of what they want to achieve. They then slit the throat of someone and watch them bleed out. The magic given off by the released blood is quite powerful, but then the heart stops. Game over - dead blood - no more magic. If they were not so blinded by their faith, they would have worked this out by now, and we would be living in an even darker, twisted place than we do now."

This was a true revelation for Andrew. It was all starting to make sense. That time in the Soho chamber when Xavier tried to open the door with some blood he got from a wall, and it just fizzed and smoked. "Dead blood. Yuk." Xavier had said. Xavier knows. Mr Bluvine had entrusted Andrew with this, so he felt like he could trust him in turn.

"What do you know about a long-life spell involving the blood of a Vampyre?"

"Sounds interesting, and devastating in equal measures," said Mr Bluvine. "Tell me more."

Andrew explained all he had learned about Extensio Vitae, and what was involved.

"And this incantation will be conducted in public you say?" asked Mr Bluvine.

"Yes, according to the Necronomicon," said Andrew.

"And this Necronomicon book is centuries old and has details about all manner of magic and spells?"

"That's right, but it is a very dangerous book; even just to read, apparently," said Andrew.

"But if what you have told me about the dead blood theory is correct, then this spell won't really work for them, because when they kill the child to take the blood, the magic will die with them, surely?"

Mr Bluvine sat and looked on.

"Well, it's rather more complicated than that I'm afraid," he said. "What I told you about blood applies to the magic in human blood, but Vampyre blood reacts very differently. From what I can tell, they will be using a spell to rid the Vampyre blood of its infectious attributes but preserve some of the long-life and healing effects."

"If that's true, then why do they need the child?" asked Andrew.

"Seasoning," said Mr Bluvine, sadly.

"When a child is scared, and by that, I mean petrified, they secrete a lot of adrenaline into their bloodstream. The combination of the blood and adrenaline is called adrenochrome. This has been a delicacy of the Darkhearts for centuries and they add it to their rituals just like we add spice to our food. In this occasion the dominant magic lies within the Vampyre blood and supersedes any magical effects the child's blood may have."

"Right, I see, and why does it have to be a 'pure' child?" asked Andrew.

"The Shadows are formed from the highest society: the elite. They don't mind sacrificing people from any walk of life or class, as an offering is an offering in their minds. But blood that will actually be consumed? They prefer that to be as clean as possible."

"Let me get this straight," said Andrew. "As long as the Vampyre is kept alive then the incantation will stay with the blood?"

"Precisely, Andrew, but heavily protected also. If they die, the magic in that blood dies with them, but this is just a legend, of course. They wouldn't actually attempt this incantation. I mean, would they?" snorted Mr Bluvine.

Andrew's silence said more than he ever could.

"Really?! Utter madness. When?"

"7th of December, at the Greenwich observatory. My friends and I want to stop it, but we don't know how to yet."

"Well, if you need help, I heard through the grapevine that a group of mercenaries attacked and killed a few Blackstones last Saturday. They managed to get into an underground chamber under Soho Square and planted landmines. Maybe you should look them up, as they sound rather useful." said Mr Bluvine.

"That was us, and Xavier, of course." said Andrew.

"You really are full of surprises, aren't you?" said Mr Bluvine, wide eyed.

"Well...there are *some Vampyres* that might help you, for a price," he said.

"How many Vampyres are in London, do you think?" asked Andrew.

"Oh, around thousand legal ones. As in, those who have signed the treaty, but they won't dare help for fear of prosecution. But there's probably a similar number who shunned the treaty. Maybe more," contemplated Mr Bluvine.

"I wonder if some of the illegal ones would help put a stop to this? asked Andrew.

The shop became slightly darker due to a presence at the shop door.

Andrew looked at the ball to see if it was glowing, but it stayed dormant.

Mr Bluvine looked towards the front. "Ah, like clockwork. You will have to excuse me Andrew, a customer who likes to spend a lot of money is waiting to get in. Keep me informed and I will help where I can, OK? And be careful who you talk with about this with, Andrew. Spies are everywhere," said Mr Bluvine.

Andrew nodded and held up the cigar in the bag that Mr Bluvine had passed him earlier as they walked towards the door. He unbolted the door and opened it for him. "Send my regards to your boss," he said.

"Ah, Mr Brubacher. What a pleasure it is to see you. Please, please come in." Mr Bluvine ushered a very big man with a menacing hat into his shop and shut the door behind them.

It was now almost four, so Andrew decided to call it a day and walk home. He had dinner with his mum that night and they talked about their trip to Greenwich the following day.

"It takes about an hour and twenty by bus from Russell Square," his mum said. "If we get up at nine and leave by ten, we should be there by noon."

"Sounds like a good plan to me," said Andrew, finishing off his apple crumble, but the thought of returning to Russell square, worried him.

That night in bed, he read for as long as he could about mirrors. His eyes gave up at the bit about them using molten silver poured onto glass into a very shallow mould and being left to cure. *Is that why Vampyre's hate silver?* he wondered. With heavy eyes, the room faded to black as he drifted off.

33

Mean Time

Andrew woke up at 8am in a cold sweat, again. The recurring nightmare about Ed always left him feeling sick. His mum was already in the lounge, so he sat down to have breakfast with her. It was so nice to have her at home and not at the bakers, like she always was. The light in her eyes was starting to return after catching up on some well needed rest. He had heard the letter box go, so walked into the hall to retrieve the mail. There were a handful of bits. Three of the letters were addressed to his grandmother. He nipped up the stairs and placed them on her dresser on the landing, as usual. Walking down, he looked at the few he had left.

One was a letter to his Mum, and there was a postcard from Bath of all places; There was a picture of a Roman Bath at night. It was beautifully lit by wall mounted torches, mounted on the ten tall stone pillars that surrounded the pool in the centre. The sheltered areas glowed in a warm yellow light. On the picture, someone had drawn a 'I' on the first pilar, an 'L' on another, and finally an 'X' on the last. Andrew turned over the postcard only to find a load of jumbled up letters that made no sense whatsoever.

"Well, this means nothing to me, Xavier. Nothing at all."

The final envelope had a few grubby fingerprints on one corner that smelled like vanilla ice cream. It wasn't stamped but it had Andrew's name on it. Andrew noticed that it looked like George's writing. He walked back into the lounge where his Mum was doing her crossword and put her letter down in front of her.

"Post for you, Mum."

"Thanks love, I'll open that later," she said, trying to work out ten down.

He took his seat again and placed the postcard face down in front of him. It didn't make any sense.

KRSH – BRX – ILJXUH – WKLV – RXW

VXFFHVVIXO – WULS – LQ – EDWK

KHDGLQJ – ZHVW – WR – FRDVW

IROORZLQJ – QHZ – OHDG

EH – LQ – WRXFK – VRRK

ADYLHU

Giving up on the postcard, he opened the other letter.

Andrew,

We need a meeting.

Something has happened but I don't want to write it down.

Meet at mine on Wednesday evening, around 7?

G

Andrew's mind began to race. *What on earth could have happened?* he thought.

After breakfast, they got ready to go, and managed to leave the house by 10am as planned. The walk to Russell Square felt faster than normal, as they talked most of the way. They chatted about Andrew's friends, his job at the bookshop and what he wanted to do next. It was so nice for him to be able to talk to her in depth for a change, instead of her being so tired that she couldn't really engage properly.

"Why didn't you open that letter, Mum?" he asked. "It might have been from Mr Brown, asking for you to come back."

"Maybe so, but then again, maybe not," she said. "I didn't want to take the chance as I really want us to have a nice day. Therefore, I'm pretending that the letter says that they want me back and that I'll work less hours, but for more money. That way, I can have a good day with you and not worry. Sounds silly, eh?" she smiled and touched his arm.

"No, not at all," he said. "Sometimes that's what we need, isn't it? A little bit of hope and each other, right?"

She had the biggest grin and linked arms with him as they crossed the street towards Russell Square. Andrew felt very uncomfortable waiting for the bus near the station. The day they broke into the chamber beneath it and took that dagger was still fresh in his mind, but he didn't see a sign of any Blackstones.

They caught the 188 to Greenwich at 11.05, which meant that they should be in Greenwich in time for lunch. They sat on the top deck right at the front so they could get a good view. The roads were relatively quiet as it was a Tuesday, and the bus swerved in and out of lanes with ease as they headed down to cross the Thames. The river sparkled in the morning sun, and they looked up to see the Tower Bridge in the distance rising to let a ship pass. Once across, the bus then headed east through Elephant and Castle, then Deptford and onwards to north Greenwich.

They got off the bus at the Maritime Museum. Greenwich really is a beautiful place, with its stunning white-stone architecture that glowed in the sun. They walked down towards the Thames to get a drink and took a seat near the Greenwich foot tunnel and watched a group of tourists being led by a small man with an incredibly loud, yet husky voice.

The loud man cleared his throat.

“Greenwich has had many names since 918AD. How ever you choose to spell it or say it, it means Green Wic.

‘Green’, as in the amount of luscious green space we have here compared to the other parts of London, and ‘Wic’ being an old English term for an emporium: A trading settlement normally found on the banks of rivers.

At the time of its peak, huge sailing ships and tea clippers would travel up the Thames and dock at this section of the river to sell and trade goods from all over the world.

Wonderful smells and bright colours would entice you deeper into the crowded markets, where exotic people would be displaying bright fabrics or preparing interesting foods with flavours you had never tasted before.

If we were here in the 1500s, you would see voyagers fighting over the prices of their cargo with local merchants.

Some would return injured or with damaged vessels, due to storms or piracy."

"Ooh," said the tourists.

"And if you look down the river and see the large set of white buildings on the right, that is the original site of the Palace of Placentia, which was a royal residence in the 15th century."

"Ahh," said the tourists.

"It was the birthplace of Henry VIII and many years later, Elizabeth I, too. This later became the site of the Royal Naval Hospital for Sailors, which was credited to Sir Christopher Wren and his assistant, Nicholas Hawksmoor. It's now a naval college. Let's go and take a closer look."

The gaggle of tourists followed the loud man down towards the college, oohing and aahing as they were tossed another nugget of information.

Andrew and his mum finished their drinks and decided to head up towards Greenwich Park. On the way there was a market in the square, so they had a quick look around. His mum bought a nice scarf, and Andrew found a red leather-bound book for writing in. He paid for it and put that in the front pocket of his bag, knowing it would come in handy when trying to decipher those coded messages from Xavier. They left the market and walked up King William Walk and into the base of Greenwich Park. Such a lovely calm space with a gentle hill ascending towards the observatory. Well, it looked gentle, but both he and his mum were quite short of breath by the time they got there.

So, this is it? Andrew thought. He wished he could tell his mum why they were there, but he suspected that she wouldn't believe him. More to the point, even if she did, she would only worry, but Andrew had to see where they planned to conduct the incantation.

When his mum went to use the public toilet around the back, he took the opportunity to look around. At the side of the observatory was a flat section of ground surrounded by high-level, wrought iron fencing. It was rare to see fences like that, as most had been melted down for use in the war.

"It will be in there; it has to be, either that or right out the front," said Andrew, talking to himself.

"What's out front?" said his Mum, who was now standing beside him.

He panicked and said the first thing that came to mind. "Oh, just wondering exactly where the zero-degree line starts."

"Zero degree? What's that then?" she asked.

Andrew had covered this in geography last year and he remembered thinking how strange it was that London marked the beginning of time. There is a line called the Greenwich meridian where the sun is at its highest point at noon every day. This line is considered to be the 00.00-degree mark for the rest of the world. This time does vary a bit, due to the shape of the earth and rotational axis shifts, but as an average (mean) this still stands true today. At the time, Britain was a naval superpower and had an empire that stretched around the world. So, it is hardly surprising that Britain decided to base the start of time here in Greenwich. In one of the greatest shipping ports that ever existed, in what they considered to be the most important city on earth: London.

“The start of time, Mum.”

After looking around the observatory, they decided to sit underneath one of the many trees in the park, taking refuge in the shade from the summer sun. Even the grass was starting to fade and scorch a bit from the recent hot weather.

“Fancy some lunch, mum?” he said. “My treat.”

“You don't need to do that, Andrew. I know you are earning money now, but don't squander it.”

“How often do I get to take my mum out for lunch?” he said with a smile.

She stood up with a grin, stretching her legs. “Race you,” she said, and before he could even get up, she was running off down the hill and laughing towards the river.

He ran after her, but there was no chance of catching up. She was too fast. As she ran through the gate, she looked back at Andrew to see if he was still there. She didn't see the car that changed lanes at the last minute and swerved onto the paved area. Andrew watched in horror as it hit her head on, rolling her over the bonnet and slamming her down onto the hot slabs with a crunch. The car didn't even stop, just sped up and disappeared into the distance.

"Mum... Mum," he said, feeling the tears well up in his eyes, looking up the road for the car that was now speeding away. She was unconscious and bleeding heavily from her leg and a cut on the side of her head. Andrew knelt beside her feeling helpless and angry.

People just stood and watched as he sat helpless on the ground. The publican from the inn opposite brought a blanket out and stayed with them until the ambulance arrived. Andrew sat in the back of that ambulance holding the blood-stained scarf his mum had bought only a couple of hours before, blaming himself and that driver that didn't stop, so angry at the world.

His mum was a good person, she didn't deserve this.

They drove to St Alfege's hospital near Greenwich, and his mum was rushed in and taken into surgery soon after. A young nurse came over to where Andrew was sitting.

"Is there anybody you need to call?"

"My grandmother, but I'm not sure I..."

"Don't worry, we can tell her what's happened. Just write her name and number down here, please." She handed Andrew a pad and a pencil, and he wrote the details down.

A doctor came and found him a few hours later asleep on a chair in the waiting room.

"Andrew Fairchild?"

"Yes," he said, wiping the sleep out of his eyes.

"Come with me, please."

He followed him into a separate room with blinds that shielded the windows.

"Is my mum ok?"

"She has suffered quite significant internal injuries. We managed to stop the bleeding, thankfully, but she is in a coma, and we won't know the extent of her head injuries until she comes round."

"How long will that take?" he asked.

"We don't know. She is stable though, so if you want to go and see her, that will be fine. OK?" He took Andrew through a maze of corridors and into the recovery ward where his mum was. They stopped at a cubicle with closed curtains.

"Take as long as you need," said the doctor, before placing their hand on his shoulder in support.

Andrew took a deep breath. He was scared of what was on the other side of the curtain, but he opened it up a few inches so he could see inside. And there she was. She looked awfully pale, covered up and asleep. Her head was bandaged, and her right leg was in a cast just like George's. Taking a seat that was by her side, he didn't quite know what to do or say.

"Hi mum. I'm here," he said, feeling quite silly but sad at the same time. "You were hit by a car, but you're going to be ok. Aren't you?" he felt the tears rising again but he shook them off. The sudden prospect of losing his mum made him feel very alone. He contemplated the idea that if she did die, that at least she would be reunited with his dad. These thoughts circled his mind for what felt like an age. He had already developed quite a lot of worry over the years for his mum, probably due to losing his dad so young. All those memories came flooding back.

He thought of his dad's funeral, with all the people dressed in black. The countless flowers piled up in the hall for weeks afterwards, wilting and turning darker shades of brown and giving off a pungent smell. Followed by his mother, crying in the dark of her bedroom, minutes turned to hours, and hours rolled onto days.

Andrew couldn't stop the tears anymore. Reaching out, he took his mum's hand and held it to his cheek for some kind of connection, while the tears ran down his face and burned his throat.

He felt a soft arm wrap around his chest from behind. A gentle touch, a warm embrace. He wept.

"Come on, Andrew," said his grandmother, softly. "Let's get you home."

34

SHAKY FOUNDATIONS

Andrew made another cup of tea and sat down at the kitchen table. His mum's unfinished crossword was still folded up on the tablecloth, and the cryptic postcard from Bath was still quietly taunting him. He decided that he was going to visit his Mum later and take her some flowers for when she woke up, but right now he needed something to occupy his mind. A distraction. He thought the best thing to do was to have a proper go at cracking this message from Xavier.

Andrew went back to his room and found one of the books Xavier had left him: 'Codes and cyphers' by Boris Openov. The keys on the cover shimmered. He also picked up the red leather-bound notebook that he had bought the day before in Greenwich market. He took them both back to the table in the lounge and placed them down, side by side. Picking up the codes and cyphers book, he tried to stay open minded.

How will I know what code to use? There's too many. Let's try and be logical about this.

Bath… what is significant about Bath? Well, it's Roman. Right, let's see what I can find.

The Alberti's disk? No.

The Vigenere square? He hoped not, as it looked far too complicated.

Next: The Caesar shift. Now, this looks interesting, and Caesar was the name for the emperor of Rome. Roman baths? It's a start.

It's a basic principle of shifting the Alphabet to a number of defined places to encrypt a message. For example:

A R2 shift would be as follows.

A	B	C	D	E	F	G	H	I	J	K	L	M	N	O	P	Q	R	S	T	U	V	W	X	Y	Z
Y	Z	A	B	C	D	E	F	G	H	I	J	K	L	M	N	O	P	Q	R	S	T	U	V	W	X

In an R2 encoded message, HIDE AND SEEK would become

FGBC – YLB – QCCI.

"Now this seems more like it! But how do I know what the movement is?" he wondered.

He turned the card over to show the Roman baths with the pillars around it. He looked at the pillars again. The first with an I and last with an X.

"Roman numerals!"

There were ten columns in the photo, and on the third column was an L. Could it be? An L3 shift?

He wrote out the lines of text in his book. He shifted the bottom row left by three places, and stuck what was now overhanging back on at the end.

A	B	C	D	E	F	G	H	I	J	K	L	M	N	O	P	Q	R	S	T	U	V	W	X	Y	Z
D	E	F	G	H	I	J	K	L	M	N	O	P	Q	R	S	T	U	V	W	X	Y	Z	A	B	C

He plotted out each letter and converted it using the L3 shift.

KRSH – BRX – ILJXUH – WKLV – RXW

VXFFHVVIXO – WULS – LQ – EDWK

KHDGLQJ – ZHVW – WR – FRDVW

IROORZLQJ – QHZ – OHDG

EH – LQ – WRXFK – VRRK

ADYLHU

Became...

HOPE YOU FIGURE THIS OUT

SUCCESSFUL TRIP IN BATH

HEADING WEST TO COAST

FOLLOWING NEW LEAD

BE IN TOUCH SOON

XAVIER

“Wow.” He couldn't believe it. He had just decyphered something.

He travelled back to the hospital that afternoon and every day after. They had moved his mum into her own room now, and Andrew appreciated the privacy. He had run out of small talk after the first week, so he decided to tell her about what he had been getting up to with the boys. He started right at the beginning with Ed, and the first encounter with the Blackstones, right up to the present day, even their mission in December. He found that saying all of it out loud was quite cathartic, but it made him sound like an absolute lunatic.

Blackstones, Satanists, blood doors, underground chambers, Vampyres, enchanted daggers, landmines, and guns with names, but the weirdest bit was spells involving blood.

There was a little bit of him that secretly hoped that she would be so outraged with the risks he had been taking, that she would wake up, just to tell him off, but she didn't, she just slept.

With visiting hours over again, he collected his things and prepared himself for the over-familiar journey home. At least he had his meeting with the boys. He was looking forward to seeing George and Lee, as he had so much to tell them.

“Bye, Mum,” he said, as he kissed her on her forehead before leaving.

It was almost July now and London was in full summer swing. Looking out of the window of the bus on the way home, he could see dozens of teddy boys in their smart grey suits drinking and smoking outside of the pubs. Some were cueing outside the pictures to watch the midweek film with pretty girls in their long, new-look skirts and stockings. Huddled under umbrellas as it began to spit with rain after a hot summer’s day, laughing and joking without a care in the world. He envied their carefree ignorance of what was really going on. If only they knew, but then again, maybe they didn't want to know and maybe they were the smart ones after all. As Xavier said once, ‘ignorance is bliss’, and sometimes Andrew questioned his insatiable appetite for the truth. After all, it hadn’t done him any favours so far.

Andrew’s return bus from the hospital pulled into Russell Square around 6pm, and he started the well-trodden walk back towards George’s in Camden for the meeting. He could see a black plume of smoke in the distance on the left before he even passed St Pancras hospital and could smell the ash that hung in the air. He crossed the road and walked down the set of alleyways that led to Xavier’s bookshop. He could hear the kids from the estate shouting at each other and the sound of marbles being thrown at the fence.

“Wow, it's like bonfire night,” one said.

He walked faster in a hope of seeing a large fire in one of the gardens, but his disappointment grew along with the smoke that filled the air, catching in the back of his throat and making it harder to breathe. He jogged out of the alleyway and could instantly see the flames creeping over the top of the first parade of shops and reflecting off the shop windows. Mr Bluvine was standing out front of his wine shop, looking towards the bookshop as he rounded the corner, and Andrew could see the reflection of the fire in his eyes. Xavier's shop was an inferno. Flames were belching out of the broken windows. Their bright yellow tails whipped the air, lighting up the evening sky and reflecting in the eyes of those who stood outside of the parade opposite, looking on. The firemen were already hosing down the shop, but were struggling to calm the blaze that threatened to collapse the whole building.

"My God, what will Xavier do now?" Andrew said to himself. After all, it wasn't just a shop up in smoke, but his job too.

Mr Bluvine saw him standing there and walked over.

"Started about half an hour ago, Andrew," he said. "Blackstones, for sure. Pulled up in a van and threw a load of petrol bombs through the windows and drove off."

The only relief Andrew had was knowing that Xavier was far away from this mess. Just then he noticed some graffiti on one of the unbroken panes of glass on the shopfront. 'Justice for Soho.' Andrew's mind suddenly shot to George and Lee. "Must go, Mr Bluvine," he said, picking up the pace towards the alley.

"You two better be ok."

Andrew ran north towards Somers Town, only stopping when he could literally run no further.

As soon as he felt able to again, he ran towards Chalk Farm where the newsagents stood. He could see the white Langley News sign in the distance, and the fact that it wasn't on fire made him stop, breathe, and walk for a bit, but he was still 50 yards away. His lungs burned from running so hard and his legs hurt. That's when he saw the black van on the opposite side of the street.

“Oh no.”

A large, bald man with a heavily tattooed neck and head, got out and crossed the street to ring the doorbell for George's maisonette. Meanwhile, three others were getting something out of the back of the van. Lucy had opened the door with a petulant “Yes?“ and the large man picked her up. Her little arms and legs were kicking out in a frenzy as he walked her slowly towards the van. Andrew started to run again, as fast as he could towards them screaming, “STOP!!”

As the man put Lucy into the van, the other three men walked towards the shopfront each with a lit petrol bomb in their grasp. They threw them, crashing through the glass while the shop became a fireball in seconds and shattered glass spilled out into the road. The three men, their Blackstone rings now obvious, got back into the van and drove off. Lee came out of George's doorway and ran off up the road, chasing the van. Andrew go to the shop just as they had pulled away in a screech of tires and burning rubber. He had to get George and his mum out, fast. The door to the maisonette was still open so he ran up the stairs.

“GEORGE! GEORGE!”

George was at the top of the stairs, standing there with his mum in her dressing gown.

"What the hell is going on?" George asked.

"Blackstones! They just grabbed Lucy and the shop is on fire. We've got to go... NOW!"

"Blackwhat?? Where is Lucy?" George's mum screamed. "WHERE IS SHE?...LUCY?!"

"She's been kidnapped!" George said.

George tried to calm her down whilst the smell of the fire and light smoke was starting to come up through the floorboards.

"COME ON!" Andrew screamed.

George's mum ran into her bedroom and appeared thirty seconds later in an old fur coat and was holding a small wooden jewellery box. Andrew escorted her down the smoky stairs and out onto the street, where the extent of the fire could be seen.

"LUCY!!?" she screamed, over and over until she couldn't speak anymore. Her sorrow was uncontrollable.

Andrew saw Lee return. He was out of breath but he stood with George's mum, freeing up Andrew to return for George. He ran up the stairs once more and saw George just sat at the top of the stairs in his cast, looking defeated. The smoke was beginning to fill the landing.

"I had one job, Andrew. One job," George coughed. "Just to keep them safe, and I couldn't even manage that."

"This isn't your fault, George. And we will find her, I promise, but we've got to go." said Andrew.

Andrew held his arm out as a bar for George to take, and he did so. They descended the stairs one step at a time, and out onto the street to be with Lee and George's mum. Some of the neighbours who had seen the fire, rallied to support. The fire engine arrived soon after in a hail of sirens and boots, and began to extinguish the flames that were still raging inside the shop. George stood there in his cast, holding his mum while she sobbed still whispering his sister's name in a broken tone.

Andrew took Lee to one side.

"My mum got hit by a car when we went to Greenwich, she's still in hospital there." said Andrew,

"Jesus, Andrew..." said Lee,

"Is she going to be ok, or what?"

"She's still asleep," said Andrew,

George was now trapped in a bubble of his own anger and looked deeply into the fire whilst holding onto to his broken mother.

He had two more weeks in a cast, just two.

After that, that was his green light for revenge.

They were going to pay for this.

35

Revenge isn't a Four-Letter Word

George and his mum were taken in by a neighbour, Mary. She had been a loyal and daily customer of Langley News forever and was the first to offer help, just as the fire was dying down. George had nothing. No clean clothes, no sense of humour and certainly no patience.

He took to walking up and down outside of the burned-out shop in his soot covered cast without his crutches, as if he was in training for a fight. His mother slept in Mary's spare bedroom, waking up in tears when she realised that Lucy was still missing. The police had been and had asked all their questions. They even came to see Andrew at home in Kentish Town the next day. He had told them all he could about what he saw but didn't hold much hope of them finding her, knowing in the back of his mind that getting Lucy back was his job.

Andrew walked over that morning and took George some spare clothes of his, but explained that he couldn't stay long as he was running late to see his mum. They agreed to meet as soon as possible.

“Xavier’s shop was torched last night too, George. We need to regroup and figure things out. Just don’t do anything stupid,” said Andrew.

Andrew was running late to catch the bus to the hospital. It was now mid-afternoon, and as he got nearer the station, he saw that a section of the park nearby was sealed off with police tape. Half a dozen policemen were now guarding the entrance into the park, and a few people outside were asking questions. Andrew popped into the florist opposite and picked up some flowers for his mum. Whilst waiting to pay, he overheard them talking outside.

“The man, he was lying in the bush. Dead as a doornail. He had some scratches on his head... three I’s or something,” said a tearful woman to a police officer that was busy writing down every word on his notepad.

Andrew remembered his conversation with Frank at Mr Bluvine’s.

That sounded like a blood treaty exemption mark, he thought.

He left the florist with his bunch and headed to the station, stepping onto the bus to Greenwich with seconds to spare. Staring out of the window, he realised he was no longer fascinated by the journey over the Thames. It's funny that you can become so numb to things that used to leave you reeling in awe. Familiarity really can breed contempt.

He arrived at the hospital for 3pm, which would give him a couple of hours to spend with his mum. Climbing the stairs to her floor, he opened the large doors and carried on down towards her room.

Traipsing down the poorly lit corridor and thinking about what to tell her today, he clutched the small bunch of flowers. He turned the corner to see a young doctor coming out of her room.

“Hello, is everything ok?” asked Andrew.

The doctor looked a bit shocked and said, “I’ll be right back...Don’t go in,” and then he ran off down the corridor, disappearing at the end.

Andrew was begining to panic and wondered what on earth was going on. Moments later, half a dozen doctors and nurses came galloping down the corridor and went into his mum’s room. They were talking to his mum, very slowly and loudly.

“Mrs Fairchild. Hello, Mrs Fairchild, can you hear me?” said a young nurse while the rest were taking measurements and pressures.

Andrew walked in slowly behind them, flowers in a low clubbed hand. The blinds were doing a poor job holding the light back as the sun poured through the windows. His mum was still in bed, but her eyes were open, squinting a lot but actually open. She was awake. She didn't talk, just looked straight at the nurse who was asking all the questions and nodded. There must have been some weight in her stare, as the young nurse stopped talking.

Andrew's mum turned her gaze towards him at the foot of her bed.

"Hello mum," he said, feeling shocked to see her awake. "You're back."

She took her time for her eyes to adjust, and her hands seemed rather stiff to begin with. The nurse beside her filled a glass with water and held it for her while she sipped. It made her cough initially, but she persevered.

She slowly began speaking. Small answers at first. "Yes" and "No" whether she could feel this sensation or that, squeezing the doctor's hands. Once the medical staff were satisfied, they started to leave in dribs and drabs. One of the nurses asked Andrew if she should inform his grandmother.

"Yes please, if you could," he said.

She left, leaving Andrew sat beside her.

"I was really worried about you," he said.

"What happened?" she asked, looking at her hands and the cast on her leg.

"We were running down the hill in Greenwich, towards the market. You had beaten me to the gate and ran onto the pavement, when a car swerved out of nowhere and hit you."

"I remember the park," she said, closing her eyes. "But that's about it. What am I going to do about work? I can't work with this thing on." she said, looking at her cast.

“Don't worry about that, mum. They’ve waited three weeks, waiting another month isn't going to make a difference. Grandma will see to that.”

“THREE WEEKS? What do you mean three weeks?” she asked, looking confused.

“That’s how long you’ve been asleep for, Mum. Doctors said it was rare, but does happen sometimes. You are lucky to be alive.”

Andrew took her hand as she struggled with the idea that she was out for that long. She looked quite tired already, and all of this was too much.

“It's all going to be ok, you know that right? Look...these are for you,” he said, holding up the flowers. “I’ll get the nurse to put them in a vase at the end of your bed.”

“Thanks Andrew, that's very sweet of you,” she said, seeming troubled.

“I had the weirdest dreams about you, you know. You were being chased by these awful people in tunnels, wearing black robes and daggers. Something about blood, not quite sure what now."

"It's just weird dreams, mum." said Andrew, regreting he had told her so much while she slept.

"I hope you are staying out of trouble?”she asked.

“Yes mum, I’m fine, please don't worry,” he said.

His mum was struggling to stay awake, so he decided to head off with a promise of coming back the next day with his grandmother. This seemed to relax her. He kissed her on the forehead as usual, leaving her to rest.

Andrew now felt absolutely drained. He had underestimated how pent up with worry he had become. It was almost like his mum waking up was permission for him to relax a bit. The bus ride home felt so long, and he was dreading the walk home. As the bus pulled into Russell Square, he got off and began to walk when he heard a whistle so loud that it startled him. He turned around to see who it was, and it was none other than a very scruffy man, sitting on the bonnet of his beaten-up Rover 75.

"Where the bloody hell have you been?" Andrew asked.

"Looking for answers!" said Xavier.

"Well, I hope you found some, because since you left, things have been falling apart. Have you seen what's left of the shop?" asked Andrew.

"I drove past it earlier," Xavier said, sounding unfazed. "You look exhausted. Get in."

The familiar worn leather and cigar smoke welcomed Andrew like an old friend.

"I heard about your mum, how is she doing?" he asked.

"She woke up today, at last." said Andrew.

Andrew lasted untill the third set of traffic lights before passing out. Xavier woke him up when they were outside of his house.

"Andrew, Andrew... you're home."

Andrew woke up and felt so bad for sleeping the whole way.

"Sorry for falling asleep, I couldnt keep my eyes open," yawned Andrew,

"What are we going to do about the shop?"

“Shh, shh, all in good time. Right now, you need sleep. Meet me at Covent Garden market tomorrow at midday, by the fruit and veg. OK?”

“OK, will do,” said Andrew.

Andrew climbed out of the car and walked towards the house. Once through the door, he didn't even make it into bed. He collapsed in a heap on the lounge floor near the coffee table, feeling the familiar tasselled edge of the rug tickling against his face as he fell deeply, and soundly asleep.

36

The Garden of the Abbey

“Andrew? Andrew! Why are you asleep there, of all places! What's the matter with you, are you drunk?” said Andrew’s grandmother.

Raising his head off the rug with one eye open, he looked towards his grandmother who was standing in the doorway, again.

“No, grandma, just really tired from yesterday.”

She nodded.

“Mum woke up,” said Andrew, while stifling a yawn.

“Yes, so I hear.” she said. “A nurse called me yesterday to say that she had. Then your scruffy boss came around, looking for you again. Told him you were probably on your way back from the hospital.”

“Oh Xavier, yeh... he met me at the station and gave me a lift home, which was lucky as I was too tired to walk,”

"Yes, I can see that... and too tired to make it to bed, it seems."

Andrew flapped his arm as if to say, 'it is what it is' and noticed the clock in the hallway behind her. It was 9am.

"I'm going to visit your mother at the hospital at three, to enquire when we can get her home. Would you like to join me?"

"I have a few things to do first, but I can meet you there," he said, getting up off the floor and feeling the aches from sleeping on the hard floor. His grandmother looked at him stretching in pain and just tutted.

"Fine, just don't be late." she said, as she walked back upstairs to her room.

Andrew walked out back to have a wash and brush his teeth as they felt truly horrible. Looking into the small round mirror on the wall by the sink, he saw the state of his face. Having fallen asleep on the rug tassels, they had left red imprint marks all down one side of his face, like a birthmark the shape of a tree. "Great, just great."

He finished cleaning himself up and headed back into the kitchen for some tea. It was at least an hours walk to Covent Garden market. Because of that, he decided to get a bus most of the way. He packed a bag and made sure he brought his red leather book, finally leaving the house at 11am. Andrew got off the bus at Holborn and walked across towards Covent Garden, crossing Drury Lane. Getting the bus had saved him a lot of time, and he was fifteen minutes early for his meeting. The market was at full-bore and the bellowing voices of the fruit and veg stall holders could be heard from hundreds of feet away.

Nerdy fact alert:

Covent Garden got its name from the convent (place for nuns) that used to reside in the Abbey of St Peter, which is now called Westminster Abbey. The Abbey, was a catholic establishment, which meant that most of the money collected there either stayed in the Abbey or went back to the Vatican in Rome. Henry VIII's insatiable desire for an heir, prompted the formation of the church of England. This allowed him to divorce and re-marry multiple times and in the end, led to the dissolution of the monasteries. Some saw it as nothing more than a land grab. This genius move also meant that all of the land that was previously owned by the catholic church, now belonged to the crown, as in, him. It was shrewd.

The land where the market now stands used to be in the Garden of the Abbey, where the convent stood, hence the name. Over the years Convent, became Covent, as it's easier to say in a hurry, I guess. From what Andrew could see, people here were always in a hurry.

"BUTTON MUSHROOMS, TUPPENCE A BASKET, COME ON NOW."

People were milling in and out of the market like worker ants, moving fresh produce in and empty wooden boxes and crates out. A steady stream of water trickled out from the cobbled entrance, as market traders refilled the water butts for the ever-thirsty flowers on display and the smell of fresh veg and ripe soil hung in the air.

Andrew decided to buy his mum some grapes and headed into the crowded market. So much to choose from, with bright fruit and veg being illuminated by gas lamps under the covered market. It was far too busy for him, so he found the first trader that had some white grapes and bought a large bunch. Twisting them into a large brown paper bag, the trader wrapped them in a loop-de-loop and handed them over. Andrew paid and walked out.

Moving out of the bustling market, he instantly felt a bit calmer, and he had no idea how people dealt with that every day.

Once he was in the clear, he opened his bag to put the grapes away, and saw Xavier walking up the road towards the market with a load of newspapers under his arm. Perfect timing.

"You made it!" said Xavier. "Feel better after a good sleep? Err, what's that on your face?"

"Oh, this," said Andrew, rubbing his face where the tassels had marked his skin. "I fell asleep on the rug. What are we going to do about the shop?"

"Never mind about that now, Andrew. Let's go and get a cup of tea, shall we? We have much to discuss."

He followed Xavier around the side of the market to a busy cafe called Albert's. They entered and were soon given a cup of freshly brewed tea in a cup with a saucer, then ushered through to the back to sit down.

"Any food?" said the owner.

"Two bacon sandwiches please, Albert," said Xavier, as they passed.

Andrew was still full from his breakfast, but the smell of the bacon on the busy grill made the prospect too good to pass up. They took a seat right at the back opposite each other and the room was full of people on their break. Some were porters who were waiting to port and a few delivery drivers sharing a paper, probably dreading the drive home up north, or east to Kent. The level of chat in the room meant they could speak and be heard by each other, but busy enough for the others in the room to not pick out the details.

"First things first," said Xavier. "Did you get my message?" He placed the wad of newspapers to one side.

"Caesar shift, L3. Glad Bath went well; did you have fun in the west?" said Andrew with a smile as he took his red book and pencil out from his bag.

"Excellent!" said Xavier. "Keeping notes? remember...if you write it down, it might be found." He lowered his voice.

"I found a place for Marlon. He wants to get out of London, and Bath is a great place for a man with his abilities."

"What made you head west after that, then?" asked Andrew.

“A man I met in Bath knew something about ‘*you know what*’ in December. The ‘V’ they plan to use for December has been brought to the west coast of England from Ireland. As it turns out, we are not the only ones who want to stop this.”

“Who else?” said Andrew, but his gaze was diverted to Albert who just arrived with the bacon sandwiches. He placed them down on the table between them. The smell was divine.

“Thanks Albert,” said Xavier, while slipping him a banknote and holding his hand up as if to say, ‘keep the change.’

“Grazie mille,” said Albert as he disappeared back through the busy cafe.

Xavier took a huge bite from his sandwich and gestured Andrew to come closer so he could keep his voice down.

“The Shadows have been testing a weather machine called HAARP, and it has caused quite a lot of upset in the North Sea.”

“HAARP?” asked Andrew.

"Shhhh" said Xavier.

“High frequency – Active – Auroral – Research – Program,” said Xavier, looking surprised that he managed to remember what it stood for. He continued. “High winds, ocean swells and unexpected thunderstorms caused a ship to be hit by lightning and sink. Out of a crew of over fifty only twenty survived. Captain went down with the ship.”

“That's terrible.” Andrew said.

"Normally, that wouldn't be an issue, right? Just one of those things?" mused Xavier, whilst taking another bite.

"Ships sink every day, but it was the Shadows; it was HAARP, and word got out. Trouble for them is, the late captain of that ship has a younger brother, and that younger brother is arguably the most powerful Mage in the whole of England. His name is Curtis."

"Mage? What's that?" Andrew asked.

"Err... like a male witch, generally erratic, but very powerful," said Xavier. "He currently lives in a small fishing village called Boscastle in Cornwall, but he will be coming to London, and when he does, it will begin. He is angry and has now turned his attention to the Shadows activities."

"Wow, really? That's good news... when?"

"He will be here by September, but we have quite a lot to get ready beforehand."

Xavier pulled the first newspaper off the top of the pile and began scouring it for some information. Andrew ate his sandwich and drank his tea, waiting for him to find something.

"Ah ha," he said, tearing a strip out of the paper.

HAMPSTEAD MOURNS THE LOSS OF FAMILY MEN AND BROTHERS.

Gregory Peters 41, Alan Prichard 40 and Luke Gifford 39.

All three men were involved in a rock-climbing incident on 21st of June.

The emergency services were called to the area in Wales, but all three men died at the scene.

A local service for the men will take place in due course.

"See? this is how they cover themselves. Remember Greg from the Soho Square chamber?" said Xavier.

"No way?! They really can manipulate anything, can't they?" said Andrew.

"Look at the words, Andrew, 'Family men and brothers'. These men were not related. This always refers to the fact they were either Masons or Blackstones. Probably both. Oh, and more importantly," said Xavier, frantically flicking through the paper for something else he had found.

GIRL ABDUCTED

Mary Ellen, aged 10, from Holborn.

Police Appeal for Information.

Looking through the next paper in a frenzy, he found another.

- **CHILD ABDUCTED -**

Lorna Greene, of Archway, aged 9.

Last seen being driven off in a black van.

Police Appeal for Information.

The list went on. Before too long, there were seven articles ripped out and on the table that basically said the same thing. All happened last week, all abductions, all young girls, black vehicles. The last one was Lucy. Andrew's heart sank as Xavier held up the article in front of him and placed it down.

"George's sister, right?" he asked.

"Yeh, I was there... but I wasn't fast enough. They torched the newsagents on the same night they burnt the bookshop."

"We'll do everything we can to get her back, I promise. All these girls are for the collection, the pure children for the incantation. The Shadow's greed knows no bounds. Trust them not to be satisfied with the blood of one child, they want seven."

"Why seven?" he asked.

"More blood, more money. And seven, it's a sacred number, for starters. Linked to Ancient Egyptian magic. The ceremony will happen on Sunday 7th of December at 12 noon. See the pattern here? 7th on the 7th day, at 12 on the 12th month? 7 chakras, 7 planets, 7 days of the week, 7 metals of alchemy, 7 deadly sins and 7 virtues, and 7 sections of a hexagram. The most powerful occult symbol of them all."

"I thought the pentagram was their favourite?" asked Andrew, looking confused.

"The Darkhearts only like a pentagram as it looks neater with a body on top of it, but the Hexagram combines all four elements in a different way."

"Can I borrow your notebook?" asked Xavier. Andrew handed it over to him.

He drew some shapes. "These are alchemical symbols," said Xavier.

"And watch what happens when you combine them," said Xavier.

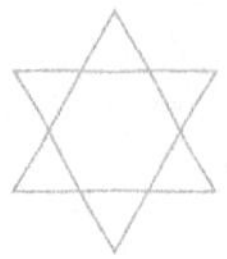

"All 4 elements... in one!" proclaimed Xavier.

"But that looks just like the star of David?" said Andrew. "Does that mean Jewish people are involved?"

"Don't be so quick to jump to such conclusions, Andrew. Symbols are used in different ways.

Look at the Swastika, used by the Nazi's. Do you think they came up with that themselves? No. They borrowed it from a Hindu peace symbol and turned it diagonally. The irony that a symbol taken from one of the most peaceful religious movements on earth, could be used to strike fear into the hearts of men, isn't lost on me. Like all these things it boils down to one thing: intention.

"As for the hexagon being the star of David, or the seal of Solomon, it is similar in shape, but this symbol has been an occult symbol for many thousands of years. Jewish people didn't use it at all, until 1008, on the Leningrad codex, I believe, which is a very old manuscript. But they have adopted it, and even included it recently on the flag of Israel.

Ever been to the countryside, and seen a 5-bar gate? Look close enough at the centre intersections and you will see this symbol. It is everywhere." He closed the book and slid it back over to Andrew.

"What are we going to do about getting Lucy back?" asked Andrew. "And the others, of course."

"That's where things get a bit... sticky," said Xavier. "When I got back to London last night, I saw the black, smouldering mess that used to be my bookshop and decided I needed some answers. After dropping you off, I popped home to grab something from my medical cabinet and a smart coat, then went on the hunt for a Blackstone."

“Medical cabinet? For what?” asked Andrew.

“Oh, nothing really... just a syringe,” he said,

Andrew was intrigued.

“Hunting for a Blackstone that knows enough can be difficult. But there are a few places in London where you can find them, if you know what to look for. I tried the Old Bell in Fleet Street first, but I drew a blank. Then I ventured down the alley to Ye Olde Cheshire cheese pub. This pub is very old, if not one of the oldest in London, and has many discrete rooms and areas that provide privacy for guests. I slipped through a few of these areas, paying attention to the clientele along the way. Everyone appeared to be quite drunk which gave me an advantage. I saw a barmaid deliver drinks to an obscured booth of men, and the hand that paid her was covered in tattoos and had a rather large Blackstone ring. I sat in a place where I could observe the men without being seen and waited for the tattooed man to get up. I must admit it took longer than expected, and quite a few pints, but then suddenly, he stood up. He was a rather large, bald man that had tattoos on his head and neck.”

“That's the guy! That's the guy that grabbed Lucy,” said Andrew.

“I know...but I didn't know that, then.” said Xavier.

“What happened next? Did you interrogate him?” asked Andrew.

“Not exactly,” said Xavier. “I followed him down the basement steps and into the toilet, and he was relieving himself in the urinal. But because he was a very big guy, he had to duck his head to avoid the low ceiling. I wasn't quite sure what to do, so I stood by the sink awkwardly and ran the tap as if I was washing my hands. I took out the syringe and screwed on the needle. I walked up behind him, and he didn't seem to notice me at first. His head was looking down as he pee'd. Suddenly, his head turned to the side as he must have sensed me.

I panicked. I saw the tattoo on his neck of a snake and the head finished around his temple. Unsure of what else to do, I jumped onto his back and stuck the syringe deep into his crooked neck. He didn't even wince, just pushed his giant hands into the wall in front of him, which in turn slammed us both back into the wall behind us, right next to a steel section that was protruding from the brickwork.

My back hit the tiled wall with a crunch. He had knocked all the breath out of me, but I held on for dear life. It was stay on or die. He moved forward again briefly and then back again, pinning me against the wall. This freed my hands up to extract some blood from his neck with the syringe as I gasped for air. He moved forward towards the urinal, constricted himself into a bench press position, and threw himself backwards again, only this time I yanked the syringed out of his neck and fell off his back just before he crashed into the wall, knocking himself out on the steel section. He lay there, face down on the piss-covered tiles with blood weeping from the pinhole in his neck, while I gasped for breath with the syringe of his blood in my hand."

"Wow, that's crazy! What happened next?" asked Andrew.

"I checked that he was still breathing and left the pub quickly through a back door, found my car and drove back to Somers town."

“Nobody chased you?”

“Rule number one, Andrew. Always know your exits. I hurried back as quickly as I could, and luckily Mr Bluvine was still in his wine shop checking stock.”

“I forgot to say, I had a really interesting chat with Mr Bluvine,” said Andrew.

“Yes, he told me. He really likes you, Andrew. He also said what you did for Frank.”

“Oh that, yeh... seemed like the right thing to do,” said Andrew bashfully.

“Very noble, Andrew. It really was, but I have a small confession to make. I took the liberty and used your favour.”

“That's ok, not quite sure what I would have used it for anyway,” said Andrew. “What did you ask for?”

“After our talk, Mr Bluvine called Frank and asked him to come down to the shop. I showed him the syringe, and I asked him to taste the Blackstones blood for answers. He was very reluctant at first, but once I reminded him of your good deed, he was much more compliant. Mr Bluvine also offered him half a fluid ounce of Jean Marais, which probably sealed the deal. After tasting the blood, he told me everything. Who they had taken, including Lucy, and where they were being held. Even the name of the ‘V’ they were using for the incantation."

"Who is it?" Andrew whispered.

"Verne Daniels,” whispered Xavier.

“That's a strange name for a Vam... I mean... V,” Andrew said, looking around for eavesdroppers.

Xavier continued.

“Frank also told me something that he saw which made him very angry. The restraints used for the ‘V’ were made of obsidian, as in Blackstone. I asked Frank why this was so bad, and he explained V’s fear of obsidian. Apparently, it makes them physically exhausted and lose their power to read minds.”

“So, is that why the Blackstones wear them?” Andrew asked.

“Possibly... maybe the reason is twofold. It’s a great way of recognising each other too,” said Xavier.

"Mr Bluvine explained to me about the magic of living blood" said Andrew,

"Really? he should know better than that." scorned Xavier,

"It's a dark world that awaits us, if that sort of information gets into the wrong hands."

Andrew sat there in quiet disbelief. The world is full of wonder and magic, sacrifice, and blood. Most people, including the men sitting around them in the café, were completely oblivious to it.

“The strangest bit about all of this,” said Xavier. “Is that all 7 girls and the ‘V’ are less than 5 minutes’ walk from where we are sitting.”

“Well, what are we waiting for?! Let's go!” said Andrew, trying to keep calm.

Xavier could see that Andrew was getting agitated. He pulled a small, folded leaflet out of his jacket, the kind a tourist would be seen with trying to navigate the twists and turns of London's streets. He opened it up on the table, and it was a local street map of Covent Garden.

“Look...we are here,” he said, hovering his finger next to the market.

His finger slid up the map and stopped. “And this happens to be the headquarters of the ‘V’ council.” His finger pointed to a building further up on Longacre. “The ‘V’ in question, is being held here. No chance of doing anything there, especially with that angry lot guarding him. The girls, however, are being held here.” His finger slid up the road a bit more and stopped at the junction of Great Queen Street and Wild Street. It was none other than the Freemason's Grand Lodge.

“No way,” said Andrew. “That evil looking building?”

“I’m afraid so, deep down in the vaults,” Xavier said. “It is fortified and heavily protected.”

“We have to get them out.” Andrew said, feeling his temper starting to rise again.

Xavier stared at him. “I have thought about this long and hard, Andrew. The way I see it, the only way we can get the girls back will be when they transport them to Greenwich. Or worst case, at the incantation itself.”

“But that’s in December.” said Andrew. “George is already on the war path.”

“We are all going to have to hold our nerves, Andrew. Curtis the mage will be with us in September, and we need to gather as much information as possible and come up with a plan of attack. We will need maps, drawings, journey timelines; all possible transport routes that they may take, which may include tunnels, as there are many. Believe me, I know. We will only get one chance at this, one shot, and we have to make it count.”

37

Train Hard, Fight Easy

Andrew left Xavier in Covent Garden just after lunch. Xavier had come up with a plan moving forward regarding Andrew's mum. Once she was back at home and settled, Andrew would say that an opportunity had come up at work and he was invited to travel north to help buy and transport books. But really, he would be moving in temporarily with Xavier, *wherever that was.*

This would get him out of the house and meant that he could concentrate on the tasks at hand. Andrew made his way to the hospital by 2.30pm, which was good, as it gave him a little bit of time alone with his mum before his grandmother arrived. He handed over the large bunch of grapes that he had bought from the market, which she accepted with a smile. His mum seemed much brighter today and seemed to have better control of her hands, which was encouraging. He told his mum about the fire at the bookshop, and Xavier's plan moving forward.

"Xavier wants me to travel with him up north to buy lots of books, and help bring them back."

“Oh really, that’s good,” she said, softly. “How long will that take?”

“Well, there is a lot of stock to find and replace, so it could take a while.”

“The trip away would probably do you some good anyway, Andrew. It’s all been a bit full on for you lately. You know, with me in here, Lucy being kidnapped and now the fire at the shop.”

“As long as you will be OK, Mum? That's all.”

“Yes, of course I will Andrew, my doctor came in to see me today and said that if I keep recovering as quickly as I am, I should be home in a couple of weeks, which is good..." she lowered her voice.

"As the food here isn’t great.”

“Good job I brought you something from home, then,” said Andrew’s grandmother from the doorway.

What was it with her and doorways?

“Hello mother.” said Grace. She walked into the room and took a seat by her daughter’s side, placing her bags down at her feet with a sigh.

“You gave us all quite a scare, Grace. Andrew has been worried sick.”

“I know, mother, it hasn't been easy on anyone I bet. I am sorry, though. I should have been more careful. Andrew and I were having such a wonderful day in Greenwich, too.”

“Can you remember what happened?”

"I remember being up in the park by the observatory, looking down on river, then running. Next thing I knew, I woke up here."

"Well at least you did wake up, Grace, and for that we have to be thankful."

"Yeah, we are," said Andrew, holding his mum's hand.

38

Setting The Stage

The next two weeks flashed by in a blur. Andrew had seen Lee, briefly and arranged a meeting at George's to talk over what was next. Andrew and his grandmother visited his mum every day and she applied pressure to the medical staff when needed. They just wanted her home. In the end their wish was finally granted.

His mum walked slowly out of the hospital on the hottest day in August so far, and straight into the outstretched arms of a bustling city. London was heaving. His grandmother paid for a taxi, as she wasn't sure they could have coped with the bus. It all seemed a bit much for his mum, and by the time they got home she was ready for bed. As she slept, Andrew sat at the table. Another of Xavier's postcards was on the mat when they got back, but he lacked the energy required to decode it.

His mum woke early the next day with much more energy. She was still slow on her feet, but seemed a lot more confident now she was home. Andrew made breakfast for them both and they sat listening to the radio while they ate. He left her reading and had a go at deciphering the postcard in his bedroom. By mid-morning he had managed to decipher the message. He got dressed and told his mum that he was going to see how George was getting on.

"Send my regards to Mrs Langley, won't you?" she said, as he kissed her goodbye.

"Will do." said Andrew; he hated lying to his mum.

He shut the front door and headed towards the tube. Xavier's encrypted postcard had given him an address to meet him that morning at 11.30am. The next stage had begun.

Andrew got out of the tube at Holborn and walked down to an address on Drury Lane, which took him a while to find, as the numbers were badly faded from the sun. Through process of elimination, he found himself outside an old, boarded-up shop premises. Looking through a gap in the boards and dusty glass, he could see the shop was mostly empty except for a few abandoned boxes within. The cars and trucks rushed past behind him. "Why on earth did he ask to meet here?" he said, under his breath.

"Because this is the perfect place!" said Xavier from behind him, jangling a set of keys in his hand and a large, beaten-up leather bag in the other.

"You made me jump," said Andrew, catching his breath. "Perfect place for what? A new bookshop?"

"Well, that's what the current owner thinks, anyway." said Xavier. "He's out of town and has entrusted me with the keys to 'inspect the place' in a view to possibly leasing it." He tried one of the rusty keys in the door, but it wouldn't turn. He cursed as more trucks screamed by and up the road.

"It's a bit rough," said Andrew.

Xavier looked at him as if to say, *do you think I'm stupid?*

"Ah ha," he said, as the latest key he was trying, turned. The lock opened. He ushered Andrew in and shut the door behind them, drowning out the sound of the traffic.

"Don't worry, I have no intention of leasing this dusty relic, but we have the use of it for a while. The owner isn't back until next spring, which gives us time. Besides, its location is perfect."

He set his bag down into the dust and walked to the back of the shop and through a door that led to a stairwell. Andrew followed him up multiple flights of creaky stairs, before long they were both spent and gasping for air as they neared the top. The grey door before them had a rusty push bar. Xavier walked up and burst the door open out onto a flat roof area.

"Come and see this," he said. Andrew followed him out onto the roof terrace and towards the far edge, looking down at the road that ran parallel was the Grand Lodge Masonic Temple.

They could see everything, all the exits on the south and east side and even into parts of the compound.

"Wow...It's perfect," said Andrew.

They could see that there were three large men in black suits patrolling the walls, looking out for something.

"They're keeping watch," said Andrew, looking over at the lodge.

"On the day they move, there will be plenty of them to deal with. We can count on that," said Xavier.

They walked back to the stairwell and shut the door. Back down in the shop, they cleared some space and arranged some boxes in the middle as support, then pulled a big sheet of timber from the wall and placed it down flat to form a large, albeit slightly unstable drawing board.

"This is where we work things out," said Xavier, as he looked intently at the board. "Hand me that bag, will you?"

Andrew picked up Xavier's leather bag and shook off the dust before handing it over. Xavier unbuckled the straps and pulled out a gigantic, folded map. They unfolded it from its broken concertina shape onto the board, pinning it tight at the corners with some drawing pins that he found behind the counter. Xavier found an old table lamp, removed the shade, and hung it from a bit of wire in the ceiling, and plugged it in with a crackle. Under the brighter light they could now see things clearly.

The map was a few years old, but very detailed. It was big enough to show all the roads and train lines from as far up as Islington and all the way down to Lewisham. All the routes above ground from Drury Lane to Greenwich. Xavier pulled out a pack of coloured pencils, and a few leather-bound journals from his bag. He held the journals up in a fan-arch.

"I began compiling these when I was planning my revenge on the Blackstones all those years ago. Even after I watched that chamber in Shoreditch burn, I kept adding my findings to these books. It became a bit of an obsession, I suppose. Every tunnel I found, blood door, chamber and underground crypt is right here... in these books. I'm just glad I kept them at home, and not at the shop."

Using the coloured pencils, he started to transpose the information in the journals onto the map in front of them.

Blue = Secret doors, circled in black for exit only

Orange = Tunnels.

Red = Blood doors.

Purple =Chambers.

Green = Stairwells.

Yellow = Basements.

Andrew watched the map as Xavier slowly and meticulously evolved it into a mass of colourful spaghetti. It took hours and furious hunting through his journals, but Andrew was truly fascinated. He saw the chambers in Soho and Russell Square that he had visited with the boys grow in front of his eyes. The basement, tunnel, and blood door in the old Georgian house in Mornington Crescent, where he lost Ed. There were so many he couldn't quite believe it. After many hours work, Xavier finally put his journals down.

"That's it," said Xavier, with a sigh of relief. "That's all of the ones I know about."

It was too much to take in. If people knew what went on beneath their feet in London they would never sleep again.

“That’s enough for one day, Andrew,” he said. “Only a fool attempts to hold a line with a tired mind.”

“Who said that?” asked Andrew.

“I did,” he said. “Come on, let’s go.”

They shook off an old dust sheet and covered the colourful map and placed a few paint cans on top for good measure. They walked out of the shop. Xavier locked the door with difficulty, but the road was quieter now as it was early evening. Xavier’s car was parked in a side road, and he offered Andrew a lift home.

On the way out, they drove past the Freemason's Lodge and sure enough, they could see more very large men standing guard, their masonic pins shining from their black suits in the twilight.

They got back to Kentish town quite quickly. Xavier pulled up outside Andrew’s house and he got out.

“What now?” asked Andrew.

“You’ll come and stay with me,” said Xavier.

“But I need a bit more time to get things ready. Here, you must be running out of money by now?” Xavier handed him a load of crumpled banknotes from his jacket pocket.

It did occur to Andrew how suspicious this would look if anybody saw them. Andrew suspected that Xavier had a sixth sense, as Andrew was down to his last twenty shillings.

“Thanks,” he said awkwardly. “It was all the buses to Greenwich and flowers, I think."

"Let's meet back at the new shop next Wednesday, say 6pm?" asked Xavier.

"Can I bring George and Lee?" asked Andrew.

"Well, they are with you, right?"

"Yes... all the way," Andrew declared.

"Then bring them."

"I'm meeting with them in the morning, so I'll let them know," said Andrew.

Xavier nodded then drove away, almost hitting a preoccupied pedestrian who was crossing the road in front of him. "Watch it," said Xavier, with cigar smoke billowing out of his open window.

39

The Definition of Courage

Saturday morning began with Andrew looking for his shoes. He had a meeting with Lee and George at 9am, which he was already running late for. Leaving the house and walking towards Chalk Farm, he wondered how they both were doing after all that had happened. It had been so long since they had talked, and he had so much to tell them.

Andrew turned a corner and walked towards the newsagents. One of the lampposts that lined the street ahead of him had a white notice of some sort attached. It was only when he was close enough, he saw a face he recognised all too well and it stopped him in his tracks. Lucy. It was a missing poster that had been crudely fixed to the lamppost with twine. Even though it was on an angle, her smiling face stared out at him from the picture. "We are going to get you back, just hold on," said Andrew under his breath as he continued on his way.

As he approached the side of the newsagents he saw Lee, sat on the step outside George's maisonette, reading a book about tanks. "Bit early for warfare, isn't it?" Andrew asked.

“No time like the present,” said Lee, placing the book down next to him.

Andrew, sat down next to Lee on the step. The street was quieter than usual other than the occasional person realising the newsagents was closed, pushing what was left of the door to check and wandering off in frustration again.

Andrew looked straight ahead, feeling guilty for all of what had happened. “George is really angry, isn’t he?”

“Of course, he is.” scowled Lee. “Wouldn't you be? We had no idea what we were getting ourselves into.”

“It seemed like the right thing to do at the time though, didn’t it?” defended Andrew.

“I’m not saying it wasn't the right thing to do, Andrew, but at what cost? How much are we prepared to lose? If we don't get Lucy back, George will never be the same. And right now, the odds, well, they are not in our favour.”

Andrew didn't know what to say. He knew Lee was right, of course. All this had gotten out of hand. Andrew tried to salvage some hope without giving everything away. “Xavier has a plan.”

“Xavier, is a crackpot with a gun, Andrew,” said Lee, bitterly.

“He has help arriving from the west. A very powerful man that will help us stop this,” said Andrew.

“And you believe him?” spat Lee.

“We don't have a choice, Lee, we are out of options.

So, what? Shall we just give up now then? Huh? Just let them do whatever they want with Lucy? Who cares?"

"I'm not saying that, am I?" said Lee, lowering his tone and putting his head in his hands.

"So, what are you saying then?" said Andrew, softening his.

"I'm just.... I'm scared, Andrew. For the first time in my life, I am truly scared of what could happen if we get this wrong, and I'm not sure what to do," Lee said, sadly.

"Well, that's an understatement," said George dryly, from the front corner of the shop.

"George!" said Andrew. "You look... well... awful."

"What did you expect?" asked George, coldly. George had huge bags under his eyes, was wearing an ill-fitting floral shirt, and the cast on his leg was covered in engrained soot and ash from the fire. You could barely see Lucy's graffiti anymore beneath the smudges. He was carrying a bundle of paper that looked dog eared and wet, its bindings stressed and sheets bulging.

"Let's talk inside." said George, taking out his door key for the maisonette.

Andrew and Lee followed George into the stairwell and up the stairs. George refused any assistance up the steps, determined to do it alone. Once on the landing, the damage to the flat was evident. Black dust was everywhere, and the smell of mould was so overpowering that it was hard to breathe easily. George slapped the bundle of wet paper on a small table on the landing, then went from room to room, opening as many windows as he could to try and air the place.

While he did so, Andrew looked at some of the photos on the wall in the hallway. In a small, gilded frame was one of little lucy in her school uniform. A handwritten label beneath the glass said *First day at school.* Andrew's heart sank as he brushed off the soot from her innocent face.

Lee collected three stools from the kitchen and set them down on the landing. Andrew and Lee took a seat, but George didn't move.

"Take a seat," said Lee.

"I'll stand, thanks," said George, looking down at them, angrier than ever.

"Suit yourself," said Lee.

"Yes, I will. I-"

"STOP IT," shouted Andrew. The others jolted into silence.

"We have got to sort this mess out," said Andrew.

"And how do you propose we do that then, Andrew?" asked George.

"Because of us sticking our noses in where they don't belong, Lucy has been taken away. My mum is in bits. She barely eats, cries all the time, and just sleeps. And it's my fault. No, no, that's not exactly true is it. It's OUR fault."

"No use in just pointing fingers George," said Lee. "We knew that what we were doing was risky."

"RISKY?" reeled George. "Risky... is being caught smoking behind the bike sheds, Lee. Risky... is stealing a bar of chocolate or falling over and breaking something." He pointed to his own leg.

"This is beyond 'risky'. How would you feel if you lost one of your family?"

"I almost did, didn't I," said Andrew. "Mum got hit by that car in Greenwich, and I wasn't sure she was going to make it." This seemed to defuse George's anger slightly.

"How is she now?" asked Lee.

"It was touch and go for a while, but she's home." Andrew said,

"That's a relief. Is she going to be OK?" asked Lee.

"Early days. She's still weak, but the doctors say she will get better. She had a cast just like yours, George, only less sooty."

"Who do you recon it was that hit her?" asked George.

"It all happened so fast; I couldn't see. Just a large dark red car. Didn't stop, just carried on," said Andrew,

But I can't help but think it must be the Blackstones."

"Blackstones? really?" asked George. "I mean, how could they? They wouldn't even have known who she was or that you were even there."

"I don't know why, just a gut feeling," said Andrew.

"Accidents happen every day, Andrew," said Lee. "Maybe it just one of those wrong place, wrong time things?"

"Well, you know something that wasn't an accident? That horrible lot taking my sister." said George, as his anger was bubbling up again. "What are we going to do about it?"

"Anything back from the police?" asked Andrew.

"Nothing. The police don't care, Andrew," said George. "Look at those." He pointed to the bundle of wet paper on the table.

Lee picked up the wad of bound paper and snapped the bindings to release what was inside. It was hundreds of missing posters. Missing posters of Lucy.

"I saw one of those on my way here," said Andrew.

"Yeh, there's one or two around," said George. "But I found hundreds under a bush, down by the canal. It's like the police want to be seen like they are doing their job, but really, they know they don't have a chance of finding her. Either that, or they are in on it."

"Remember when I told you about Ed?" said Andrew. "The policemen that came to see me that day had Blackstones on. Doesn't mean they are all bad, but who knows."

"We have to do something, because I can't go on like this," said George. "With Lucy gone, I'm now alone with my shell-shocked mum and I don't have a clue what to do, or where to begin."

"You're not alone though, George," said Lee. "You have us."

Andrew took a nervous breath, as he knew what he was about to reveal would not go down well.

"I know where Lucy is."

"What do you mean? How?" George spat through clenched teeth. "TELL ME NOW!!"

Andrew stood up, which made Lee do the same, sensing that something was about to go wrong. Andrew explained.

"After Xavier's shop was set on fire, Xavier went on a hunt for a Blackstone. He managed to steal some blood from a guy with a syringe; It was the one who took Lucy."

"That massive guy covered in tattoos?" asked Lee.

"Yes, that's him," said Andrew.

"What did Xavier want the blood for?" asked George.

"He took it to Mr Bluvine's, which is the wineshop next to Xavier's bookshop. Mr Bluvine asked a Vampyre to taste the blood and see the memories."

"Blood has memories?" asked Lee.

"Apparently so," said Andrew. "They have collected seven girls for this incantation in December, and Lucy is one of them," said Andrew.

"Seven? But the drawings only showed one," said Lee.

"Greedy, I guess. Xavier managed to find out where they had been taken to," said Andrew.

"WHERE ARE THEY?!" demanded George.

"The Freemason's Hall at the top of Long Acre, near Covent Garden, deep in the underground vaults."

“What are we waiting for then?” said George, heading for the stairs. Lee blocked his path.

“I’m warning you, Lee, if you don’t get out of my way, I’m going to thump you.” Lee didn’t move.

“George, just calm down,” said Andrew. “The Freemason's Hall is heavily guarded, but we have a plan.”

George took a swing at Lee, which bounced off his head causing no damage whatsoever. Lee swung back and punched him in the stomach, causing George to be bent in two and collapse in a heap on the landing, gasping for breath like a freshly caught salmon in a carrier bag.

Andrew stood between them. “Was that really necessary, Lee?”

“He started it.” said Lee.

Andrew pointed to the nearest stool and Lee took a seat like a reprimanded boxer would after a low blow.

“We have got to stick together. No point in fighting amongst ourselves,” said Andrew, as he pulled George up to his knees.

“But we know... where she... is,” panted George, struggling for air on the floor.

“Yes, we do George, but Xavier thinks the only way we will get them back is when they are being moved from the Masonic Lodge to Greenwich. There are so many different routes they could take. We have to map out all of the possibilities.”

"But that's months away," said George. "Who knows what horrible things they could be doing to her?"

"They won't be George. The girls will be untouchable until the incantation. The girls have to be pure," said Andrew.

"And how can you be so sure?" asked George.

"Xavier told me. He also told me about a Mage called Curtis that is coming from Cornwall to help us," said Andrew.

"What the bloody hell is a Mage?" Lee asked, standing back up.

"A male witch, and a very powerful one," said Andrew.

"What the hell is he going to do, turn them all into frogs?" said Lee.

"Let's hope it's more than just that," said Andrew.

"I hate frogs," said George, recovering slightly. "Slimy, horrible things."

Lee came over to George and put his hand out for him to pull him up off the floor. George took it reluctantly and dusted himself off when he was back on his feet.

"Sorry for punching you, but you were being an idiot," said Lee, with a slight smile.

"Apology accepted, you sweaty arsehole," said George, trying and failing to hide the smile of his own. "What now then?" asked George.

"I will be moving in with Xavier so we can concentrate on the plan of attack," said Andrew. "My mum thinks that I will be travelling up north, buying books. Xavier has found a new base for us on Drury Lane, and he wants us to go there for a meeting on Wednesday at 6pm."

"I finish work at 4.30pm so should be OK," said Lee. "And George is still an invalid, so he's free too, I imagine?" he said, looking at George with a smirk.

"Cast comes off on Monday, boys, and not a minute too soon," said a tired George.

"Great, so I'll see you there," said Andrew. "It's the boarded-up shop near the Italian restaurant on Drury Lane. Can't miss it. Xavier has the most amazing map of London. I've never seen anything quite like it."

"Maps are dull," said George.

"This one isn't, I promise you." said Andrew.

40

EMMANUEL'S DEMISE

THE VAMPYRE COUNCIL, LONG ACRE

The bald and heavily tattooed Blackstone, had his ring removed by thin Vampyres in foil suits, and it was placed in a lead lined box for their protection. The giant man was shackled wrist to wrist, ankle to ankle, and being dragged face down with the tips of his boots scraping against the uneven flagstones beneath him. He had been found unconscious, face down in the toilet at Ye Olde Cheshire cheese pub in Fleet Street and had been heavily sedated by the Blackstones ever since. They needed to make sure he hadn't been compromised.

Once inside the chamber, they lifted him up and onto a wide, dark stone slab. His shackles were taken off and replaced by larger ones attached to rusty chains that drooped diagonally out from ports in the stonework around him. This was no Blackstone chamber.

As he woke, he found himself in the execution dock at the Vampyre Council. He couldn't focus and still felt weak from the blow to his head, but what was becoming clearer in his sight were some words painted delicately onto the ceiling of the chamber above him, inscribed there for anyone who found themselves at the mercy of the Vampyre council.

'The insatiable thirst for everything which lies beyond, and which life reveals, is the most living proof of our mortality.' C.B.

"Emmanuel," said Vladimir, who was the head of the Vampyre Council. His deep voice resonated in the chamber. "Do you know where you are?" Vladimir was the oldest vampyre in London. To the layman he probably only looked fifty at most, but his eyes gave it all away. They were black but flickered with bright yellow flame occasionally.

Emmanuel nodded his head, trying to clear his vision. "I'm in the vaults at the Vampyre Council."

"Yes indeed," said Vladimir. "But do you know why you are here?" he asked.

"Not really. I remember taking a piss in the Cheshire Cheese," said Emmanuel, still trying to clear his eyes.

"Yes... that is where they found you. Do you remember anyone else there?" asked Vladimir.

"Not really. Sorry... I just feel... really, really, tired." Emmanuel had been kept asleep by a variety of sleeping aids, some of which were starting to wear off.

"We need to see what happened, Emmanuel. We must take a small sample of your blood," said Vladimir. Emmanuel nodded and closed his eyes to rest.

A painfully thin Vampyre stepped forward with a syringe and stabbed it into Emmanuel's thigh. He drew some blood. Once he had finished, he walked over to Vladimir and handed the syringe over to him gently. Vladimir cradled the syringe.

"OUT!" Vladimir boomed.

Moments later, it was just the two of them, bonded by what the Vampyre held in his hands. Vladimir slowly squirted the blood from the syringe out onto the palm of his hand. He watched as it pooled and stuck to the lines and folds of his 500-year-old skin. So mesmerising, so elegant... just perfect. He caught himself before he got carried away and took a deep breath. He slurped the blood from his cupped palm and shut his eyes.

Vladimir saw a list of names and the kidnapping of the girls for the ceremony. Verne Daniels in obsidian shackles. He saw the wild nights out and the parties in London. Emmanuel removing his Blackstone ring and a raunchy night spent with a redhead Vampyre that Vladimir recognised.

"Lucky boy," he said, with his eyes still shut. "But a Vampyre? And a rebel one at that. Now, that is forbidden."

Then he saw Ye Old Cheshire Cheese pub. The countless beers, the toilet, then it all became harder to see what was going on. Someone had jumped on his back, but it was impossible to see who. He felt the syringe go into his neck and then a massive bang to the back of the head. He snapped out of his vision.

"Were you drugged?!" said Vladimir.

“I have no idea,” said Emmanuel, still struggling to keep his eyes open.

“And what of the red head?” asked Vladimir.

Emmanuel’s eyes opened quickly. “Oh, she is just someone I met on a night out.”

“She is a key member of the Vampyre resistance, Emmanuel,” said Vladimir.

“Really?” said Emmanuel. “I didn't know that she was even a Vampyre.”

“I don't believe you. What have you told her about our plans?”

“Nothing... I swear. She had no idea I was a Blackstone.”

“Really? I saw the night you spent together. Get a bit nibbly, did she?”

“A little, but not like that. I swear.”

“There is too much riding on this deal with the Shadows for all of us. YOU are not a risk that WE are willing to take.”

“What do you mean?”

“I have spoken with Derek, your elder, and he has granted me permission to do whatever I see fit, under these circumstances.”

“And what is that?” said Emmanuel. “Are you going to lock me up?”

"You are a liability. Time to discard the weak," hissed Vladimir.

Vladimir walked out of the chamber and whispered to a guard that was waiting in the hall. The door shut on Emmanuel, leaving him alone in the chamber. For the first time in years, Emmanuel thought of his mother and where he grew up in Suffolk. The green fields and the animals they kept, the amazing sunsets and the friends he had when he was young, before the fights, the tattoos, and long before he lost his way in the darkness.

He heard a whirring noise start up and felt the heavy chains that were attached to his shackles move slightly. He knew what was to come, as he had seen it before as a spectator.

All four chains suddenly rose and tightened at once and stretched him out, lifting him off the slab by a foot. He resisted for as long as he could in silence, holding his breath before letting out an almighty roar as the chains pulled so hard that his body started to pop at all the joints as the chains ripped him in half and then into quarters. His blood was splattered all over the slab and chamber floor, innards trailing, leaving just his heavily tattooed arms and legs hanging from the walls from their chains in the four corners of the chamber.

41

Building Blocks

Derek Matthews

The matt black desk reflected no light, even from the large windows in his tenth-floor office. A silver frame to one side had a picture of his family from when they went skiing last year. Derek had been a Blackstone for over twenty-five years now. By day, he worked in the City of London as a hedge fund manager and on the surface of it, lived a well-adjusted and balanced life. He had a wife, two young children, and an old house in Hampstead. Money was never too much of an issue; The children were privately educated, and their social circle was made up of high achievers and go-getters.

This wasn't always the case for Derek though, as he was from a poorer background. He and his sister had become orphans when they were very young due to a train crash that killed both of their parents. Derek and his sister Claudia ended up moving to London to live with their uncle who was a bank manager in town. Although their uncle seemed unable to provide any emotional support or affection, he did, however, provide financial support for their education. They both ended up going to university and graduating, thanks to him.

Post Graduation, his sister went travelling but was tragically killed whilst climbing in Australia.

Whilst Derek had met the girl that later became his wife whilst at university in Cambridge. Amanda.

Her family were very traditional and quite wealthy. The first Christmas that she took him home changed everything. Her father was a powerful but endearing man, but he saw something in Derek that he didn't quite expect. He was practically un-shockable. They stayed up late into the night, drinking single-malt whiskey, sharing stories and truths. The following night was different.

Amanda had woken him up with a shake at 3am. She didn't say much, just handed him a black robe to wear. "It's a family tradition," she had said. She led him down the stairs all the way into the large cellar where the rest of the family were standing by an old marble altar, they were all dressed in black robes; nobody said a word.

That night he watched a young girl of about twelve be brought down by others and laid out onto the altar. He even helped tie her down while Amanda took the honours of sacrifice that night. He remembered the absence of emotion on Amanda's face. No remorse, no regret. A simple and stout reaction as the blood ran down and pooled into the altar. The chanting carried on for at least twenty minutes after that. He went to bed that night and tried to sleep. It wasn't guilt that kept him awake, more his curiosity of what he had just witnessed.

Amanda's father knew people that worked in the City of London and had offered to provide opportunities for Derek as long as he had serious intentions with his daughter.

Knowing this, he proposed within a month, but she wasn't the only one to get a ring. Amanda's father gave him a signet ring with a small black stone in it, but it also had a small emerald in the opposite corner.

"This, young man, will open doors that were previously closed," he had said. Derek attended the interview in the city wearing his ring as he was told to, and found that the three men interviewing him for the internship all had Blackstone rings, although a lot bigger than his. They didn't mention the ring at all, but the job was his.

Within a year, he had finished his initial training program and was well on his way to becoming a stockbroker. He had also risen in the ranks elsewhere, too. The other Blackstones in the company had taken him under their wing and invited him to all manner of social gatherings. After a couple of months, they finally invited him to a ceremony in a secret chamber, deep in the heart of the city. He had proven his worth and was now given the honour of his first sacrifice.

He thought he would be nervous, but he wasn't. All he remembers was the immense feeling of power when he was holding the dagger above the boy that lay on the table. When his knife came down, all his doubt disappeared. He finally felt like he belonged and was given a larger Blackstone ring to prove it.

Fast forward twenty years and his climb had continued at work and in the Blackstones. The Society had grown significantly in numbers, and naturally the cream rose to the top. Here he was at forty-five, still working towards a better future for all Blackstones.

KNOCK, KNOCK.

"Come in," said Derek, sorting through some ledgers.

His secretary walked in with a note. "Sorry to disturb you Mr Matthews, I have a delivery for you." she said as she handed a small but heavy box to Derek, before she left. He opened the lead lined box to see a note.

IT IS DONE.

V

"Ah, Vladimir, about time," said Derek. Under the note was a large Blackstone ring.

Dealing with Vampyres was notoriously difficult, but they were very useful, as long as you had something on them; Some leverage. This recent temporary coalition with the Vampyre Council meant that he could use the head, Vladimir, to do some of their dirty work. The tattooed thug, Emmanuel, could have jeopardised the whole operation. This wasn't the first time that his partying and conspicuous body image had caused some issues. The situation also served as a good test of obedience for the Vampyre council, which they passed with flying body parts. Vladimir had done what he requested and now Emmanuel's large Blackstone ring sat on Derek's desk. He placed it into his drawer for safe keeping with the others and carried on with his day.

42

PREDATOR VS PREY

After leaving George's, Andrew said goodbye to Lee as he walked off, but he didn't feel ready to go home just yet. The smell of damp from the maisonette was still in his nose and the air was still stuffy from the hot day. He decided to take a walk down towards Camden Lock, in search of a breeze. Halfway down the main road he could hear footsteps behind him, fifty yards back. He didn't think anything of it really, as this was a main route down into Camden. The trouble was, the footsteps were becoming synchronized with his own, making them very difficult to hear. Yet they were getting louder, which obviously meant closer. He stopped and turned around to look at who was walking, but no one was there.

That's odd, he thought, before starting to walk again.

Twenty steps on, he could hear the footsteps following again, almost perfectly instep with his own but even closer this time. Andrew now realised that he was being followed. His heart rate started to rise.

He crossed the road looking behind him but there was no one there. *Was it his mind playing tricks on him? Or was he just being paranoid? Was it Blackstones?* Either way, he felt uneasy. He crossed the road and sped up a bit. On the right there was a short cut through an alleyway that he knew would get him out amongst the shops and around people faster. He took it and sprinted down the fenced alley like there was a fire behind him.

As it turned out, the alleyway was the worst idea as whoever was chasing him broke step and caught up with him before he was even halfway down. Before he knew it, he was slammed into the fence and lifted off his feet, pinned by one small, cold hand around his throat. The black eyes of the Vampyre before him glowed slightly red as she anticipated the taste of his blood.

Andrew, struggling to breathe, didn't know what to do. His arms and legs were flailing around like a slack chain on the back of a door. Andrew's windpipe was almost shut completely, making his throat burn as he tried to swallow. The red headed girl opened her mouth exposing many long sharp teeth. Andrew had just about enough breath left in him for one word. He panicked and said the only word he could manage.

"Trea-ty," he gurgled.

Her eyes dulled slightly, and her mouth slowly closed as she let him go. He slid down the fence to the floor with a thump. He was now sitting on the floor up against the fence, trying to catch his breath while massaging his throat back into shape.

"Talk," she demanded, coldly. "What do you know about the treaty?"

He tried to stand but was instantly slapped down to the floor again with extreme force. He peeled himself off the floor. "Well... I know your people got a bad deal," he said, sitting up slowly, still struggling for air. "A subscription with prices that go up and down like a yo-yo," he coughed.

"Mostly up, actually," she said. "Some of my people have lost everything because of the government's greed."

"So... what number am I?" Andrew asked, but she looked confused.

"Number? What do you mean 'number'?" she asked.

"The number on your treaty exemption coin," said Andrew.

"I have no idea what you are talking about," she said.

"But you were about to kill me, weren't you? That would mean breaking the treaty, wouldn't it?"

"I have never signed that bloody thing, and never will." The anger flashed in her face. She was quite a feisty young woman. She looked about eighteen to Andrew, but she could be far older for all he knew.

"I don't blame you; I wouldn't have either. Mr Bluvine told me there were Vampyres in London that didn't sign it," said Andrew, desperately searching for some common ground.

"You know Mr Bluvine? As in the wine merchant?" she asked, looking surprised.

"Yes, that's the one. I worked in the bookshop next door, that was until it burnt down of course," he said.

"Xavier's books? I've heard stories about that guy," she said, holding out her hand to help Andrew onto his feet. "Sorry about the *almost killing you,* thing. I haven't fed for a while and I'm starting to feel the burn."

"No problem, I understand...It must be tough," said Andrew, dusting himself off. "Why don't we go and see Mr Bluvine now and get you something; My treat?"

"Really? Why on earth would you do that? You don't even know me!"

"True, but everyone has to eat, right? And I just got paid," said Andrew. "What's your name?"

"Fiamma," she said, quietly.

"That's an unusual name?" Andrew asked, as they walked slowly back out of the alley.

"It means Flame, in Italian," she said, flicking her red hair.

"Are you from Italy, then?"

"No, but that's where I was turned, so to speak. Most Vampyres take on a new name when they start out. Just easier that way."

"When were you turned, Fiamma?"

"Oh, it was the summer of... 1846, if I remember correctly," she said.

"Wow! So, you're over a hundred years old? You look incredible, if you don't mind me saying."

She blushed slightly, but the rouge soon faded from her pale cheeks. She then looked into his eyes intensely. "And what's your name, I wonder?"

He went to answer, but she placed a cold finger on his top lip to silence him. "Actually... don't tell me." she placed her hand on his forehead and closed her eyes.

"Andrew," she said. "That's a nice name, too."

He was shocked. "You can read minds?"

"Not always, but with you I can. Well, some bits anyway."

He instantly felt a bit embarrassed thinking that she could tell that he had a bit of a crush on her. She linked arms with him, and they walked in the direction of Mr Bluvine's wine shop in Somers Town. They talked all the way there about lots of things, like who she used to be in her previous life. Her name was Matilda, but it never suited her anyway. She was abroad with her family in Florence in Italy at the time, and in the process of being married off to a man she barely knew. The evening meal had not gone well, and her new fiancé was an arrogant, selfish pig who didn't speak a word of English. He even mocked her when she tried to converse in Italian. She decided that she needed to take a walk and clear her head.

She had walked to the Ponte Vecchio bridge when the Vampyre found her. Before she could run or even scream for help, she was bitten by him. Luckily, some of the locals had seen what had happened and managed to scare the Vampyre off. She was taken back to the hotel to recover but was never the same again. Over the next week, she gradually changed into what she is now. She knew had to leave her family and friends behind, or risk being imprisoned in a mental asylum. She decided to fake her own death by jumping from the train in France into a cold, dark river whilst on the way back to England. As the years went on, she missed her family. She had snuck back to the family estate a few times, just to watch them fondly through the windows. She watched them at Christmas sometimes and longed to be inside so she could hug her mother once more. But she knew it could never be so. Her family were all dead and buried now. Well, anyone that would still remember her anyway.

"Such a strange thing to watch everyone you love grow old and die, Andrew. While, apparently, I don't seem to age. Then again, I haven't seen myself in years, as mirrors don't work for our kind, you know."

"That must be quite tricky, not being able to see yourself," said Andrew, as they got to the first parade in front of the wine shop.

"Yes, putting on makeup is a test, that's for sure."

"I'm sure you're pretty enough without it," said Andrew, bashfully.

"You know, Andrew, you are quite the sweetheart for a human. I'm actually quite glad I didn't kill you."

"Me too," he said.

Fiamma pushed on the heavy door of Mr Bluvine's and opened it with ease. They stepped inside the shop and Mr

Bluvine was busy checking his stock with his back to them until he turned around.

The small ball glowed in Fiamma's presence.

"Ahh, the lovely Fiamma," said Mr Bluvine, "And Andrew, I see?" he said, looking surprised.

"Do you two know each other?"

"We met over dinner," she said, with a smirk.

"Pleasure to see you both. What brings you here on this fine summer's evening?" he asked, gently.

"Andrew here, insisted on buying me a drink, and who am I to refuse? You know me... always thirsty," said Fiamma.

Mr Bluvine drummed on the counter with enthusiasm.

"What will it be?" he said. "I don't have much teenage boy in at the moment, I'm afraid, unless you want to go up a shelf?"

Andrew knew exactly what that meant; this was going to be expensive. She looked at Andrew to make a decision. He took a deep breath.

"How much are we talking for half a fluid ounce of something that Fiamma would like?"

"Well, mid-shelf is a lower rated celebrity and some aristocracy. I've just procured a 16-year-old count of Naples?"

"Namby-pamby old-world blood," said Fiamma. "I want something new and exciting."

“Ok then,” said Mr Bluvine, looking through the middle shelf and stopping on a bottle. “Ah ha... how about this? 17-year-old, Argentinian presidential aide?”

“Now we are talking,” she said.

“How much for that, Mr Bluvine?” Andrew asked, wincing.

“Seeing that it is you, and what you did for Frank, I’m willing to give it to you at cost price. That will be £1.”

Andrew reeled inside at the cost, but figured it was a fair trade for not being eaten. “Make it a whole ounce, then.”

Andrew handed the money over and Mr Bluvine rang up the till. He then walked to the front door and slid the bolt, locking them in. He took the bottle out of the fridge and uncorked the stopper with a dull pop.

He checked the colour and then dripped the smallest drop onto the Ball on the counter, which came alive and rolled around its groove.

"Excellent" he said.

He then placed a small shot glass on the counter, along with a thin measuring flask, the kind you would find in a chemistry set, only smaller. Using a clear glass funnel, he poured the blood into the flask and stopped at the one fluid ounce mark precisely. You could tell he had done that many times before. He then took out a small paraffin blowtorch and pumped the handle.

“Nobody should be made to drink cold blood,” he said, as he lit the torch. He warmed it gently and let it rest before transferring it to another cool glass to drink from. Fiamma looked visibly excited by the blood in front of her and she giggled on the spot before settling down. Her hands were shaking slightly as she picked up the glass. She turned to Andrew.

"To Andrew, the best dinner I never had."

She slowly drank the blood from the glass in one go, not wasting a single drop. It was truly a strange experience to observe. Her eyes were closed, and she moved like she had just gotten into a warm bath. Her skin blushed with colour, and her long red hair seemed more vibrant than before. As it all calmed down, she opened her eyes and looked straight ahead, glowing brighter than ever. It was verging on erotic, and Andrew looked visibly nervous.

"Now that... was something else," she said, licking her red lips.

"Did you see anything?" asked Andrew.

"Death. A very sick woman. Eva... Eva something, and a few naughty moments with a young chambermaid. Just so young...so fresh."

"Glad you liked it," said Mr Bluvine.

"I really did. Thank you, Andrew, and you of course, Mr Bluvine."

"Much obliged, Miss Fiamma."

Watching this reminded Andrew of what Frank had done for Xavier.

"So, how is Frank after drinking that Blackstone's blood?" The mood in the room suddenly changed.

"BLACKSTONES? BLOODY BLACKSTONES?" Fiamma was enraged.

"Whoah, whoah, Xavier and I fight them; we are against them. OK?!" said Andrew. That seemed to calm her down a bit, but her temper was still simmering under the surface.

"He's telling the truth, Fiamma. They have been up against it lately, too." said Mr Bluvine in support.

"Why, what's going on with them now? What have they done?" she demanded.

"It's a long story," said Andrew, not knowing quite where to start.

"Andrew... there *is* an easier way," said Mr Bluvine, quietly. "Just a couple of drops would suffice."

Andrew wasn't sure. *What if she couldn't be trusted with all of this? What if it jeopardized the mission?*

"You are going to need all the help you can find, Andrew. That I know...Here is your chance," said Mr Bluvine.

Andrew took a deep breath. "OK. How do we do this?"

Fiamma produced a small but beautifully made silver knife, the size of a finger. "I will be gentle, I promise. OK?"

Andrew nodded and closed his eyes. He felt a light scratch just behind his left ear. He opened his eyes to see the knife had a line of bright red blood on it, his blood, and it was dripping down towards the handle. She balanced the blade, so she didn't lose any of it.

She licked the blood off the knife and stood there with her eyes closed, only this time she didn't seem to be enjoying the experience at all. She twisted and buckled as the memories and secrets flooded into her mind. All of Andrew's loss, all of his pain, everything he had done and seen over the last ten years. She stood there with her eyes shut, yet a single tear managed to escape and run down her cheek. By the time she had opened her eyes, it had gone. She didn't say a word.

"What... what did you see?" asked Andrew.

She didn't say a word, but just pulled him in and hugged him. He could smell her sweet perfume and felt her body on his. Even in the heat of the night she was cold. She let him go and stepped back leaving him more confused than ever.

"Everything. I saw everything," she said, sadly. "You have been through the mill, haven't you?"

"Still here though, and not finished yet," he said. "They have seven young girls, and one of them is my best friend's sister. They plan to kill them in December."

"Yes, I saw that," she said. "They are getting very brave, taking a spell from that book. I don't think you realise what you are up against, Andrew. There are thousands of Darkhearts in London, literally thousands. You'll need a bloody army."

"We have a Mage, and a few friends," he said.

"That's not an army!" she countered, sounding frustrated.

“But it's a start,” he defended.

“And the Vampyre they are holding, it’s Verne,” she said, Mr Bluvine looked shocked.

“Verne Daniels?” Mr Bluvine said, in awe.

“Yes, apparently. Who is he?” asked Andrew.

“He was our leader, the head of our order,” she explained. “That was until the Vampyres were split in two by this sham of a treaty. He saw through it all and the government’s greed instantly,” said Fiamma. “But there were some of us that were tired of fighting. Tired of running from them. We were significantly outnumbered. London’s population had exploded since he got here and humans were becoming more and more demanding, imposing all sorts of restrictions. He knew it was only a matter of time before some of us gave in and bowed down to the demands, in exchange for a quieter life. But they were lied to. Crooked Vampyres took all the bribes. They were the ones who gathered the support for the treaty, only to sell their own kind down the river. They are now known as the Vampyre Council.

Vladimir, he may be the oldest Vampyre in London, but he is the worst.

Now their own people are stuck in this situation where they are no longer allowed to hunt but can't afford the extortionate subscription price either. It's a form of genocide. Using Verne will be the final nail in the coffin for the resistance.” she said.

“How many of you are there?” Andrew asked.

"About a thousand of us left in London. That's all, and less every month," she said.

"Do you think they would help us stop this? "Andrew asked.

"I don't know, but I can try. Verne's brother, Sebastian, is now head of my order. I will have to talk to him, but he is not as wise or as kind as Verne and has little time for humans, or 'cattle' as he calls you," she said.

"It may be our only chance," said Andrew.

"What about all of the Blackstones, though?!" she exclaimed. "The obsidian black stones render us practically useless, and there will be thousands of them there in that park."

Andrew racked his brain for some solution. "There must be a way around it, there simply must be."

•••••••••••••

They left Mr Bluvine's and Fiamma walked with Andrew arm in arm all the way back to his home in Kentish Town. It was now 10pm, and the heat of the summer evening felt oppressive. She was so easy to talk to and they seemed to finish each other's sentences a lot. A few drops of Andrew's blood meant that she knew pretty much everything about him now, which in normal circumstances could have made Andrew feel insecure. The truth was he felt the complete opposite. Nobody else knew everything that had happened to him so far, and for some reason, her knowing everything made him feel a bit lighter.

“So this is where you live, Andrew,”

“Yes, me and my mum downstairs, and my grandparents up top.”

“Cozy,” she said and grinned a little.

“How will I get hold of you?” he asked.

“You won't have to; I'll be in touch,” she said. “Oh, look at that!” she pointed at something behind him.

He turned around but couldn’t see anything of interest; Turning back, he said, “Look at what?”

But she had already gone. Vanished.

“Great.” He went in the house quietly, but his mum was already asleep with her curtain drawn.

That night in bed, he lay there thinking about the day. The colourful map Xavier had drawn in the new shop, and almost being killed by a cute Vampyre. If Fiamma can get the Vampyre resistance on side, they might just stand a chance. It's amazing how she could just vanish like that.

"One way of getting out of goodnight kiss, I suppose."

43

South of the River

Whilst most of London slept, others were busy cleaning the streets. The Vampyres were always careful not to be spotted by anyone. Ruthless, yes, but greedy? No. They would take the occasional homeless person or drug addict that had picked the wrong alleyway to take their drugs. They tried to pick people that would not be missed, and they never left the bodies on show. They would always be dropped in the Thames with all the rest. One day, in many years to come, they would find a way to dam and drain the river Thames. If they did that, they would expose thousands upon thousands of remains, forever resting in their dark, watery graves.

After a few other errands, Fiamma had crossed over the Thames and was now walking along the Southbank. There were many Vampyre safe houses around London, if you knew where to look, often mistaken for basement bars.

At ground level, the security could tell quite quickly that you didn't belong there and deny you entry. Be thankful they did, otherwise your evening would be cut short, along with your life, and you would join the rest in the river.

Fiamma could hear the drunk Americans from fifty yards away, even their heartbeats were loud and cumbersome. There were three of them trying to get in, convinced that the basement was some kind of VIP club. Their military money was no good there. This place was for the damned and the only way in, was to join them.

"Come on man, let us in," said the first intoxicated G.I to the bouncer.

"Do yourself a favour, mate," said Rufus, the bouncer. "Go home while you still can, eh?!"

"Make me," slurred the drunk American. "Come on."

Realising that they were not gaining entry, they decided to do the next best thing on their list: Fight.

The three Americans were quite big, as they usually were, but Rufus was truly enormous. He stood up from his perch and towered over the three drunks, who couldn't even stand still. Rufus didn't even have to speak; he just bared his teeth for a second, so fast that if you blinked you would have missed it. It was enough to turn the Americans white with fear. They scrambled trying to get their feet beneath them and fled past Fiamma screaming as she walked up to the entrance.

"Having fun are we, Rufus? Did the horrible, loud Americans make the big scarwy wampyre flash his gwin?" She teased him in a funny voice and tickled him as she always did, like a huge rottweiler receiving a belly rub.

"No, not really Fiamma, just a few drunks. They have no idea what this place is," said Rufus.

"You used to be fun, you know. You used to let them in occasionally," said Fiamma.

"Yeh, in the past," said Rufus. "But I got tired of having to clean up the mess afterwards.

The guts I can deal with, but the piss?" shuddered Rufus. "YUK!"

"Sebastian in?" she asked.

"Yeh, he went down about an hour ago. After dinner, of course." Rufus unlinked the rope barrier and waved her through.

"Thanks, Rufus, I'll catch you in a bit, OK?" she said, as she tapped him playfully on the arm.

She walked down the stairs and into the first sub level which was effectively a lounge bar with soft furnishings and polished brass. The low-level lighting was easy on the eyes and highlighted the incandescent glow of the other Vampyre's stares as they followed her into the room. The walls were adorned with Hollywood depictions of vampires. Huge cloaks, bats, wolves, white faces, and thin teeth. So theatrical. As with all these things, the reality of what it actually meant to be a Vampyre doesn't live up to the expectations of man. They put the posters up for amusement, but also as a reminder that mankind has an addiction to fantasy, and that they too were insatiable.

Fiamma took a stall at the bar and ordered a drink from the smartly dressed barman. "Dry Martini please, Marco."

"Coming right up," he said.

Fiamma caught a familiar scent encircle her and the man behind her sat down.

"Thought it was you," the man said, in a neutral tone.

"Hi Oscar," she said, like she had been caught out for something.

Oscar, was very persistent. He had pursued Fiamma for over twenty years, offering dinner, bringing her flowers. Fiamma had made the biggest mistake one night after a rough day. That night, she had a little too much to drink, and went home with him. Only once, but she had regretted it ever since. That was over ten years ago now, but that was enough for him to think he still had a chance with her.

There was nothing wrong with him. He was clean, smart, well-travelled and he was rich, but there was no fizz, no buzz, no... tension. Well, not that kind of tension anyway. And there needed to be, right? She preferred men that had a bit of an edge, maybe with tattoos or piercings.

"I haven't seen you in months, where have you been hiding?" said Oscar, as smoothly as he could.

"Oh here and there," she said, trying to give away as little as possible. "I'm here to see Sebastian."

"What, you two are... are you?!" said Oscar, looking crestfallen.

"No, no, not like that, Oscar. I need to talk with him urgently."

"Oh, I see," he said, looking relieved.

“But even if we were, you know, like that, it wouldn't be any of your business!” she defended.

“Of course,” said Oscar, taking his handkerchief out of his pocket and waving it above his head in surrender, before pretending to dab the sweat from his brow. “He’s a bit old for you anyway, isn’t he?”

“And you... are a bit young,” she fired back. She stood up, downed the rest of her drink in one and headed towards the stairs for the lower levels.

“One day, Fiamma, one day,” Oscar muttered to himself, as he sat alone at the bar.

She started down the stairs and could feel the air becoming cooler the lower she went. The next floor down was private rooms that could be rented out by the hour. One of the doors was open. There was a man tied up in the centre of the rug, a young, fledgling Vampyre was being cheered on by her friends into making her first kill. Fiamma remembered that milestone well.

Back in 1846, she was making her way back to England. She had pulled herself out of the river and had walked all the way to Annecy in France before the thirst started to come on strong. It was like all the water from her body was evaporating and she was desperate. No amount of water helped. Every single molecule in her body cried out for something. She sat in a park at dusk and watched the teenagers sitting around a campfire near the trees, laughing and drinking. The sound was starting to get drowned out by the sound of their heartbeats. Deep throbbing drums in her ears. She knew what she had to do.

She waited in agony until she saw one of the boys get up and stumble into the woods for a toilet break. That was her chance. She tip-toed around to the wooded area and could see him up against the tree. He was so drunk he could barely stand.

She walked up silently behind him and listened to him singing a slurred, French song. She had no idea what she was doing.

Should she just jump on him and bite him?

But she knew that he would probably cry out and then his friends would come.

Or should she try and knock him out?

She decided that the latter was the safest option and looked around the floor for something substantial to hit him with, until she found a thick branch. But then it happened. He had finished peeing, had turned around and caught sight of her.

"Coucou, demoiselle. Veuillez-vous prendre un verre?"

Fiamma had no idea what he was saying, but he seemed friendly enough.

"Venez avec moi et mes amis. Ne vous inquiétez pas, on ne mord pas..."

She was holding the branch behind her back and just nodded in agreement. He turned his back on her and started to walk back to his friends while still chatting away. She smashed him over the head with the branch and stopped him talking. While he lay there unconscious, she moved in towards his neck. It felt so wrong, but the pain in her chest was becoming unbearable. Some primal instinct must have taken over, because she bit him hard. The blood tasted sweeter than anything she had ever tasted before in her life, and the pain started to wash away like snowflakes in a summer rain, only to be replaced with pure contentment and joy. She could feel herself coming back to life. The boy was now dead and completely drained. She got out of the woods as fast as she could and listened to his friends calling for him. Poor boy.

By the time she had reached the lowest floor the of the facility the memory had faded somewhat. This facility was eight levels deep, and the lowest entrance hall was protected by two more guards: Eric and Schneider. Fiamma knew and liked Eric, but Schneider had always been resistant to her charms.

"Hi Eric," she said, in her kindest tone. "Is Sebastian in? Really need a word."

"He is busy," interjected Schneider, coldly.

"I wasn't talking to you, Schneider," Fiamma said, sharply.

"I'll go and see if he is free," said Eric. "Play nicely, you two." He walked over to a massive, ornately carved wooden door. The carving showed a snake eating its tail, symbolising the perpetual nature of creation and destruction.

Fiamma was now stuck with Schneider until Eric got back. He was a large Vampyre with blonde hair and bright white eyes. His ill-fitting suit did little to detract from the coldness of his stare.

“So,” said Fiamma, filling the awkward silence. “Had much fun lately, Schneider?”

“Life is not all about ‘fun’, Fiamma. Some of us have commitments, and cant sit around all day, sketching and writing poetry.” he said, with conviction, his European accent added nuance to his coldness.

“Commitment to what? Being miserable?” she teased.

"I get paid to write, you know."

"Do you get paid to be an arse?"

"I have everything I need," said Schneider,

“Don't you ever feel the need to let your hair down? and go a bit wild?” she asked,

“Discipline is not a concept I expect the likes of you to understand.” he shot.

“Oh, I understand it, Schneider. I really do. I just don't agree with it. That's the difference.”

Luckily, Eric came out of the door and walked over. The conversation would only have gone one way with Schneider. Last time it took six guards to separate them as they tried to kill each other.

“He will see you now,” said Eric.

“Thank you, Eric. You are a delight as always. Your friend, however, needs to lighten up.” she walked towards the big door and stopped just outside. She took a deep breath to steady herself and opened the door.

The large room had a huge, oval meeting table set for twenty on one side and an ornate mahogany desk on the other. Every inch of the carved wooden desk was polished to a high shine, and it reflected the candlelight that sat on top, casting long shadows.

Sebastian was Verne's younger brother, but he looked older due to being a recluse. He was calculating and smart but lacked compassion. He would rather stay away from others in the order and rarely socialised with anyone. Too busy ensuring that the order remained out of reach from the Vampyre Council's grasp. Sebastian was sitting behind the desk, as he often was, looking over some old papers. He didn't not look up as she walked over to him.

"Fiamma. Twice in a year? What have you done now?" Sebastian asked, in a tired tone.

"Nothing, Sebastian, not this time at least," she said.

He was referring to their last encounter when she needed some assistance in disposing of some bodies. The night in question had not gone to plan, and a couple of drunks had tried to take advantage of her. She repaid them for their unwanted attention with death.

The trouble was, one of them was huge. Luckily, Sebastian granted her the use of Rufus, the doorman, to help carry them. Even he had struggled a bit with the dead weight, but they managed in the end. What a splash he made!

Sebastian looked up from his papers and locked eyes with her, searching for the lie.

“Then why are you here?” he asked, suspiciously. He was a thin man, but incredibly powerful. His long talon-like fingernails gripped the parchment. His deep-set black eyes were reminiscent of a shark, only conveying less sympathy. It was like staring into the depths of hell itself.

“I have some troubling news and a call for action,” she said, maintaining his gaze.

“Let us start with the news first and I will decide on the action, if any is to be taken,” he snarled.

“Of course, forgive me,” she said, bowing down, forgetting her place. “It's the Shadows. They are planning a ceremony with an untested incantation in December.”

“And?... What they do doesn't really have anything to do with us, Fiamma, you know that. It's best that we stay out of their way.” He went back to reading his papers.

“It involves Verne, Sebastian,” she said.

He looked up.

“They have him locked up at the Council headquarters on Longacre.”

“What the hell has my brother got to do with it? He is supposed to be in Ireland!” Sebastian said.

“Well, we never got to the bottom of why he left in the first place, did we? Either way, they captured him and plan to use him.” she said.

“What on earth would they want with him?” said Sebastian, beside himself. “That could be seen as breaking the treaty.

That will not go down well with the subscription suckers, will it?"

"The Vampyre Council are assisting them, along with the Freemasons," said Fiamma.

"BLOODY TRAITORS!" he scorched. His skin flashed red before slowly settling down and back to his normal green pallor. "As for the Freemasons, bloody mortals with ideas above their station. Someone in their infinite wisdom had the hare-brained idea that they could trust men, mortal men, with Egyptian magic and secrets of old. It didn't take long for them to alienate themselves from the rest of society, did it? And now, for them to take sides with the Vampyre Council to facilitate the Shadows is beyond me." He stared at his shaking hands.

"Fiamma," he said, standing up slowly. "I must know what you know. I must know everything."

She instantly thought of her recent one-night stand, and then Andrew. She feared the raw judgement Sebastian would make on their entanglement , but it was a risk worth taking because of what was at stake. She consented with a small nod and bunched up her long red hair to one side exposing her neck to him. She shut her eyes.

He moved closer to her, and she felt the temperature in the room drop. He used the long nail on his index finger to make a small cut on her neck. The dark red blood lingered on his nail, and he watched it trickle down his finger with fascination. The cut on Fiamma's neck was all but healed up by the time he had tasted the blood.

Sebastian stood there in silence with his eyes shut. He opened his eyes suddenly, glowing slightly red, and he instantly grabbed Fiamma by the throat and lifted her off the floor.

“Why are you playing with your food, Fiamma?” he demanded.

“He’s different,” she gurgled, struggling to breathe.

He left her go, and her feet slapped on the flagstones.

She massaged her burning throat.

"He's experienced pain, loss and much sadness, but is still kind." she explained.

“Well, that's good then because the way he is going, there will be a lot more of that to come,” said Sebastian. “And what of the tattoo'd reprobate?”

“Oh, him? Just a guy I met in a bar, a one-time thing. Meant nothing.” she said,

“Along with the rest of them, I suppose?”

Sebastian’s attempt to shame Fiamma had little effect. Realising that, he moved on.

“I can't believe that this boy, Andrew, and his merry band of idiots have managed to uncover something this big and survive. Extensio Vitae is an incantation that is well known to me as it involves Vampyres too, but from what I can see there is little we can do to stop it.”

"But we must," said Fiamma. "One of the boy's sisters is an offering and your brother is an ingredient. That should be enough."

"But it's not," said Sebastian, coldly. "Please remember who we are dealing with here. This is not some petty gang who fancy themselves as the next big troublemakers in London. All those gangs come and go, all of them. But the Shadows? No. They are ETERNAL. If you dare to kill one, another takes their place just before adding you to the list of who's next to destroy."

Fiamma, fought back. "They are NOT eternal, they are mortals. Just very organised ones."

"We have been hiding from them, and the Vampyre Council for years, Sebastian.

It's only a matter of time before they figure out where we are, and then what? Run again?" Fiamma could feel her temper rising.

"If that will ensure the survival of this order, then SO BE IT!" he screamed.

"I don't just want to survive, Sebastian; I want to LIVE! REALLY LIVE! They tricked some of our kind into signing a bad treaty, remember? Now they can charge what they like for blood and keep everyone on a very short lead. That isn't a life. You and your brother saw the limitations of that treaty from the start. You knew this would happen. They are using Verne as an example, aren't they? The one-time leader of the resistance. Comply or end up like him. Our very own Guy Fawkes. We are losing numbers every week. Many have either given up and signed the treaty or have fled. Some have even ended themselves. This is our chance, and probably our only chance we will ever get to fight back."

"Fight back?!" exclaimed Sebastian, his words dripping with sarcasm. "There will be thousands of Blackstones in Greenwich park on that day. That means more refined obsidian in that one spot than probably anywhere else on earth. All...right... there.

Do I have to remind you what it does to our kind?"

"We are working on that," said Fiamma.

"Who is 'we'? Your veal toyboy and his haphazard friends?"

"His name is Andrew, and he has found the courage to try. We just need you to do the same.

Your brother Verne saved my life more than once, you know, and he saved yours too, if I remember your words correctly."

Sebastian didn't argue, just sat down with a sigh.

"Sebastian... for Verne. Come on. For all of us," she pleaded.

He visibly wrestled with his own thoughts. "OK, Fiamma, OK."

She jumped happily on the spot.

"But I want to hear every detail of the plan."

"Deal!" Fiamma said, happily.

"Set up a meeting here, Fiamma, but I am warning you; I am NOT taking any orders from the cattle."

44

First of Many

Andrew woke up on Monday with the sun pouring through a slit in the curtain, heating up one side of his face. His encounter with Fiamma at the weekend had left him feeling very confused, so he spent most of Sunday eating toast, drinking tea, and trying to not think too much. He got up and went into the bathroom, which was even brighter, making his eyes sting. Looking in the mirror, all he could see was a very tired person staring back.

"She's a Vampyre, Andrew, you can't have a crush on a Vampyre," he said to himself in the mirror. He could pretend otherwise, but he knew it was hopeless.

He had a wash and brushed his teeth, trying to clear his head. Moving into the kitchen, his mum was already sitting at the table reading her paper. "Morning, love," she said, smiling at Andrew briefly.

"How are you feeling today, Mum?"

"Oh, I'm still a bit tired, but getting a little bit better every day," she said, putting her newspaper down onto the table.

"When are you off up north then?" she asked, while pouring a cup of tea for them both.

"Soon, I think. Just waiting for Xavier to finalise the travel arrangements," said Andrew.

"That reminds me, one of those weird postcards came for you today." She placed it in front of him. "All gobble-de-gook again. Why can't you and your friends just write properly? I mean, look at it! It's like a doctor's note."

"Just a bit of fun, Mum. We like coded messages."

After breakfast, he took it back to his room to study. Xavier had used an L3 shift as usual and he managed to decipher it fairly quickly.

REMINDER

MEETING AT NEW SHOP TODAY

ALL THREE

6PM

XAVIER.

Andrew arrived at the shop just before 5.30pm in time to see Xavier fighting with the door lock again.

"BLOODY THING!" he screamed, making the people coming out of the shops opposite look over and tut. He finally managed to open the door and they walked into the dusty shop. It was just how they had left it. They turned the hanging lamp on and removed the dust sheet from the colourful map with all its twisted lines and secrets of subterranean London.

“Oh, before the others get here,” said Xavier. “Things are now ready, so you can come stay with me on Friday, OK?”

“Where is that, exactly?” asked Andrew.

“All will be revealed. I’ll pick you up on Friday morning at ten-ish. Pack plenty of clothes.”

Finally, Andrew could concentrate on the problems at hand. His mum was getting much better now and leaving was the safest thing for her while they prepared.

“Oh, and I saw Mr Bluvine last night,” said Xavier.

“I was going to talk to you about that,” Andrew said, getting in there first. “I bumped into a Vampyre called Fiamma and I took her there for a drink.”

“Yes, the name did ring a bell... how did you meet?” asked Xavier

“She tried to kill me,” said Andrew, still finding the experience quite amusing and terrifying in equal measures.

“Mmm... being friends with a Vampyre isn't easy, Andrew. Believe me, I know,” he said.

“She knows everything, Xavier. The incantation, George's sister, the lot.”

“You told her everything? Are you mad?” said Xavier.

“You said it yourself that we will need all the help we can get.

She is going to ask the head of her order,” said Andrew.

“Yes, Sebastian. He is the younger brother of Verne Daniels, the captive vampyre.”

“Is he nice?” asked Andrew, expecting the truth as usual.

“Let’s just say he is more head than heart. We will need to choose our words carefully if we get the chance.”

BANG, BANG, BANG.

Someone was at the door.

“This isn't a conversion for now,” said Xavier, looking at the door.

Andrew knew it was George and Lee straight away as he could make out Lee’s voice in between the rush of cars.

“This place is a shi- VROOOOOOM hole.” The truck whipped up the dust and junk mail as it passed by the door. He walked over and opened the door to let them in.

“Is this it?” asked Lee, verging on disgust.

“Yes, great isn't it!” Andrew said, refusing to have his spirits dampened by Lee’s negativity. They both walked in and over to where Xavier was studying the map. He locked the door behind them. "Just wait until you see the view from the roof!"

“Ah, boys,” said Xavier. “It’s been a while. Cast has gone I see, George?"

"Yeh, at long last," said George.

"I heard about what happened with your sister, hope your mum is OK?” asked Xavier.

“She’s not too good, really. Lucy getting pinched has pretty much broken her.” said George

“We are going to do everything we can to get her back, George. You know that, right?” said Xavier, placing a firm hand on his shoulder.

“So, what's all this then?” asked Lee, looking intently at the map in front of them.

“This, Lee, is everything I know about subterranean London. There may be more, but it's a bloody good start,” said Xavier.

“Wow,” said Lee. “There is so much more than I ever thought. Look, Andrew, there's the chamber under Soho, right there, and look there's the one near Russell Square. And St Paul’s. See that? There's a bloody massive chamber underneath it!”

Seeing it all laid out like this was fascinating. Xavier pulled out a tin of map pins with different colour bobbles and placed them out of the way on the Thames.

“So, come on then boys, what do we know?” asked Xavier, gathering their attention. “There are seven girls being prepared for the incantation on the...” He paused for their participation, and waved his hand.

“7th,” they all chimed in.

“of December...good!” he said.

It was like a crash course in espionage.

“The incantation must take place at noon, so they will want to get there early to set up. We need to be ready to move before dawn. They won't risk transporting them separately, just in case something happens and they get separated. There will be at least two guards for the girls and a driver. That's a minimum of ten people, which means they will need to use a minibus or a large van, which is more likely.”

He picked up a green map pin and pressed it in on the Freemason's Hall at the end of Great Queens Street and then another all the way east onto the observatory in Greenwich.

“They need to get from here all the way over to Greenwich without stopping. Let’s rule out any vehicle tunnels or bridges with height restrictions.” He took out a pencil and lightly crossed out a few tunnels and areas along the way.

“They will not want to leave the Freemason's Hall in the van, as it might attract too much attention and would be easier to hijack. So, they will probably get them out of the lodge on foot, via a tunnel. It is likely they will be chained together in a line. And because of that, it kind of rules out blood doors, doesn’t it?

They are usually a bit tight and don’t stay open very long, as we know, but they will use a tunnel to get away from the lodge and to a suitable location. There are only three tunnels out of the Freemason's Hall, as you can see. The one that heads east is a main conduit that is heavily protected by blood doors. They won't use that."

He crossed that out.

"Another one heads north towards St Pancras, and the other one goes south to Charing Cross. They will head south." He crossed out the north tunnel.

"Once at Charing Cross, the tunnel's secret exit comes out in the underpass for the station.

They will have a vehicle waiting for them somewhere around here, on the Strand." He placed an orange pin.

"This area is always quite busy, so a large van or bus will go unnoticed. Once in the vehicle, the nearest bridge across the Thames is the Waterloo bridge. This will take them over to the Southbank. From there they would head south-east down to the main roads that head east to Newcross and over towards Greenwich. If they make it to the main roads, we are sunk. We need to stop them before they get there."

He placed a red pin right on the Southbank side of the Waterloo bridge.

"How do you know what they will do?" asked George.

"I don't, but it's an educated guess," defended Xavier.

"But what if they do decide to just leave the Freemason's Hall in the van? What route would they take?" asked Lee.

"Well, if they were that bold and decided to drive the whole way, they would be coming right past this shopfront and down towards Temple, Waterloo bridge and so on, and so forth."

"We will need to prepare for both possibilities, then," said Andrew. "We'll need a way of blocking the road, something strong enough to stop a van."

"Another van?" suggested Lee.

"Or we could barricade the side roads with roadworks?" said George,

"I like it, George," said Xavier. "We could force their hand and make them use the tunnel; Control the outcome."

"We'll need people in each location, just in case," Andrew said

Andrew took some bright blue pins and placed them on the map. One by the shop front. One on the shop roof. One hidden in the south tunnel, halfway between the lodge and Charing Cross tube. One on the Strand by the underpass. One on the Waterloo bridge, and finally, one on the Southbank.

"If we cover these locations, we stand a chance," said Xavier.

"But where are we going to find these people?" asked George.

"I think we have some help coming, but we don't want to jinx it," said Andrew.

"But even with help we'll need a way to communicate with each other."

“Leave that to me,” said Lee. “I know a guy on Spitalfields that sells ex-army radios.”

“How much?” asked Xavier.

“I don't know, but I’m sure he’ll do us a deal, if we are buying half a dozen,” said Lee.

“Good,” said Xavier.

“So, what's so good about the roof?” asked George.

“Come and see for yourself,” Andrew said, leading them up the stairs.

By the time they reached the top floor they were all puffing for air. Andrew opened the door out onto the roof and staggered out. They followed him and took it all in.

“Wow...now this is a good view,” said George.

“I take it all back, Andrew, this is the perfect spot,” said Lee, looking over the edge at the Freemason's Hall compound.

“This could actually work, Andrew,” said George. “Feels so weird to know my sister is right there, somewhere deep in that creepy building.”

“I know, but we have to be patient,” said Andrew. “They have no idea that we are here, or that we are on to them.

But one wrong move and they could move them somewhere else, and that could be anywhere.”

“This is great, Xavier,” said Lee, looking dumbfounded. “I’m sorry I doubted you, and called you a crackpot.”

“I wasn't aware of that?” Xavier said, looking at Andrew with some questionable malice, but he played it off.

“These are unprecedented times, boys. The Shadows think they can do whatever they want, whenever they want.

It's a long shot, but IF we get this right, they will think twice before they try again, I assure you.”

“So, not trying to bring the mood down, but what if we fail. What's plan B?” asked George.

Xavier breathed deeply in thought.

“If… we fail to stop them and they slip through the net, then we will need to get to Greenwich as fast as we can,” said Xavier.

“And do what? Be carved up by thousands of Blackstones?” said Lee.

“I’m still working on plan B,” Xavier said. “We’ll know more when Curtis the Mage gets here. Which reminds me, I received a letter from him yesterday. He has moved things forward and is now planning to get here next Friday.

So, I suggest we all meet back here next Saturday at 10am, OK?”

“That's good,” said Lee. “He can finally see what the bloody hell a Sage actually does.”

“Mage, Lee, it’s Mage. Sage is a herb,” said Xavier, rolling his eyes.

Andrew was excited to meet the man of mystery. Ever since Xavier told him about Curtis in Covent Garden, he had been wondering what kind of man he was. They left the shop in the late afternoon feeling quite nervous but positive about what they were attempting. Andrew thought of Lucy, chained up in a dark room. His biggest concern was that he and George needed to toughen up if they were going to go up against the huge Freemasons in their suits, and even worse, the Blackstones. Lee would be fine, but Andrew knew that he and George needed some work. They agreed to meet twice a week at Lee's, as he had quite a big garden and a heavy leather punch bag. The idea of being punched by Lee was not appealing, but he knew in the back of his mind that there was no other way.

45

Stay Down

WHACK. The third blow hit Andrew square on the nose and the next thing he knew he was on his back staring upwards. Lee had hit him so hard that he could see stars swimming around the bright blue August sky. Lee's head came into view.

"You ok Andrew? I told you to keep your guard up!"

They had spent most of the afternoon being shown a few self-defence moves by Lee. He made it look easy due to his strength and high pain threshold, but he was actually quite a good teacher. Andrew learnt how to block a few attacks, and how to disarm someone. Although the only weapon they had for training with was a grubby carrot that they nicked from the veg patch. At least it was more forgiving than a blade. They had just spent the last thirty minutes taking turns to box Lee, toe to toe. Lee extended a gloved hand and pulled Andrew back onto his feet. He still felt quite giddy, so sat down on the step nearby.

“George, you're up,” said Lee, slamming his crumpled, brown leather boxing gloves together with a heavy thump.

“Again?” complained George. “My head still hurts from the last one.” George reluctantly pulled on his gloves and cautiously moved closer to Lee.

“Not so hard this time, Lee, please.”

“Keep your guard up, then,” said Lee, with a smile.

Within thirty seconds, George was knocked down onto his back again, cursing a lot.

“I think we’ll call it a day,” said Lee, like a bored P.E. teacher.

“Thank god for that,” said Andrew. “I was beginning to think that you were enjoying this.”

“Well, maybe a little bit,” said Lee. “But the most important thing is to build up some resistance and get used to people hitting you. That way when it happens, you won't find it too much of a shock.”

“I'm not sure I'll ever get used to this,” said George, still holding his head like it was going to fall off.

“I still remember the first time I got knocked out in this garden,” said Lee. “I was twelve, I think, and Jerry, my brother who was eighteen at the time, had had a rough day at work. He decided the best thing to do was to take it out on me.”

“That seems a little unfair, doesn't it?” Andrew said. “You were only twelve?”

"Yeh, well, I had been 'winding him up' I suppose," said Lee. "Oh yeah, that reminds me. They all got the conscription letter this week. Dad is furious, he's trying to get them out of it."

"They're going into the army?" asked George.

"Yep, all three of them, along with a few other lads at work. Could be away for as long as two years," said Lee with a sigh. "We are short staffed at work already."

"That's really bad, Lee, but at least the war is over now," said Andrew, thinking about Lee's family.

"I wish ours was, but I think it's only just begun," said George.

They sat in silence.

"Tomorrow's the big day then, Andrew?" said Lee, trying to change the subject. "Finally moving in with your nutty boss?"

"Yeh, at last," said Andrew. "At least my mum will be a bit safer, and less worried about what I'm up to."

Andrew had told his mum yesterday when he got back from the meeting at the new shop. She seemed genuinely pleased for him, which for some reason made the lie about heading north even harder to swallow.

"But that means that you will be away for your sixteenth birthday?" she had said, with a sad tone.

"I know, but we can do something to celebrate when I get back, OK? I will be home in time for Christmas." He really hated lying to his mum, but deep down he knew it was the right thing. Curtis the Mage was arriving in London soon, and they had to be ready. Andrew shook off the memory, and the guilt.

"Remember that Xavier wants us to all meet at the new shop on Saturday at 10am. Curtis will be there too, OK?" Andrew asked.

"Of course," said George. "I wouldn't miss this opportunity of meeting a magician. Will he have his own rabbits, or shall I bring some?" They both giggled.

"I'm not sure either, guys, you know," said Andrew, trying to appear conservative with his enthusiasm.

"We'll be there," said Lee. "Guess what, I think there are some cold beers in the fridge, fancy one?"

On a day like this, it was the perfect way to unwind. They sipped beer in the garden, looking out over the veg patches and sheds of neighbouring gardens. They laughed until the sun started to set on London. It made him realise that yes, there are some bad people in this world; Horrible, truly selfish and evil people, but the light that shines from love and friendships will always shine brighter. He had read wartime stories of people bonding with their fellow soldiers. Brothers in arms. But had never really understood how you could become so attached to people that were not family.

But after what we had gone through and seen over the past six months, the pain, the loss, the horrific violence, he finally got it. You celebrate the good, and you hold each other up during the bad. Andrew realised that it didn't get much better than this. Being in the company of people that you truly trusted and to know that they had your back too, no matter what. For the first time in his life he felt like he belonged to something.

Andrew and George left Lee's around 10.30pm and walked to the tube, chatting along the way. George still had a bit of a limp, but it was improving day by day. They talked about the newsagent's refurb, the contractors and the decisions he had to make.

George's mum was not in a good place, so he had to step in and decide on everything.

"There are so many different shades of white, Andrew. You have no idea! I have finally decided on apple green and a white called arctic blossom. They don't even have any plants in the arctic, do they? It's all very confusing."

Due to an issue with the tube, they both got out at Camden town, said goodbye, and walked in their separate homebound directions. By the time Andrew had walked to his road he felt ready for bed. Being punched repeatedly by Lee probably helped. As he approached his door, he could see that someone was sat on his doorstep, her long red hair looked almost brown in the yellow streetlight.

"Where have you been, you dirty stop-out?" asked Fiamma. "On a date, I hope?"

"Boxing. My friend Lee is trying to get us in shape."

"What is it with men and fighting?" she contemplated to herself.

"We are not all blessed with your strength, Fiamma."

"Excuses, excuses," she giggled. "Can we talk? Somewhere private?" she asked, standing up.

Andrew felt his pulse quicken; just being around her made him feel on edge.

"My mum will be asleep, so we have to be really quiet, OK?"

She zipped her mouth shut with an imaginary zip. He took out his keys and opened the door expecting her to follow, but she didn't. Andrew stepped back into the hallway to see her standing on the threshold of the door looking sheepish.

"You have to invite me in," she whispered, rolling her eyes in boredom.

He had never heard of this rule for Vampyres.

"You are welcome in," he whispered back.

She tiptoed into the house and closed the door quietly. They walked through the lounge while Andrew's mum slept with her curtain closed, completely oblivious to the fact that a Vampyre was now in her house. They got to his bedroom and shut the door behind them.

Fiamma sat on his bed and looked at the suitcase that was packed and ready to go.

"Off somewhere?" she asked.

"Only Xavier's. I'm moving in with him in the morning. My mum thinks I'm going up north to buy books."

"I see," she said. "Does that mean that when I come and see you, we can talk properly instead of sounding like we are avoiding tuts at the theatre?" Her smile was cute.

"Should be fine," he said, trying to play it cool.

"Anyway, I have some news," she said, putting on a very regal accent. "The head of our order, Sebastian, requests a formal meeting to discuss the potential participation in the operation."

"Err, what does that mean, exactly? In English?" he asked.

"He wants to know the plan before we get involved," she said.

"Oh... I see. When does he want to meet?"

"Saturday night at 11pm, in Southbank. Xavier will know where," she said.

"OK, I will talk it over with Xavier tomorrow and-"

KNOCK, KNOCK.

Andrew looked at Fiamma with despair. She stood up quietly and opened the window. From there she seemed to jump headfirst out of the window and disappear without a sound. Andrew picked up a book. His mum opened the door to see him lying on the bed reading.

"Are you OK, Andrew? I thought I heard voices."

"No, just me, Mum," he said. "Just reading and talking to myself, as usual."

"I see you are all packed. Are you excited about your trip?" she asked.

"Yeh, I am. Be nice to see some other parts of the country for a change."

“OK then Andrew, we’ll have breakfast before you go, yeah? Oh, and love, you might want to... change your cologne?”

He realised that Fiamma’s perfume hung in the air. Such a wonderful smell.

“It's a bit, you know, sweet,” she said. She wished him a goodnight and shut the door.

Fiamma had gone too. He looked out of the window hoping she would still be there, but she wasn't. Andrew shut the window halfway and read the book about the Freemasonry until his eyes were heavy enough to sleep, which didn't take as long at all.

46

Moving On Up

Andrew stirred at 9am the next morning to the sound of someone cutting the grass nearby. He had left the window open as it was quite hot overnight, and on the fixed part of the window was some lipstick. Fiamma, had kissed the glass as a goodnight to him and left the imprint. He walked over to the window to look at it before reaching out and wiping it off. Knowing that he couldn't deal with all the questions it would provoke from his mum, he headed into the lounge. His mum was just coming out of the bathroom behind him.

"Kettle's on, love. Be a dear and make the tea while I get dressed, will you?"

"OK, Mum," he said, realising this would be the last time that they talked for a while. He made the tea and grilled a stack of toast too.

"What time is Xavier coming?" she asked as she sat down to eat.

"Around 10," he said, noticing the clock on the mantelpiece. It was 9.30 already.

"Have you packed everything you need?" she probed.

"Yes, Mum."

"Pants, socks?"

"YES, Mum. I'm not five, you know," he said.

"Shirts, French letters?"

Andrew didn't know what to say. He just went a bit red and sat there, like an awkward tomato.

"Err, it's not that kind of trip, Mum."

"I realise that, love, but life doesn't always work that way. You might meet someone who you really like. I just want you to be safe, that's all. Just promise me you will be careful."

"OK Mum, I promise," he said, feeling the redness recede slightly.

He didn't realise it at the time, but that conversation was a defining moment for him and his Mum. It was the first time she seemed to accept that he was growing up. Although, judging by his embarrassment of even the mention of anything to do with sex, he knew he had a little more growing up to do yet.

"Oh. Guess what?" she said excitedly.

"What?" he asked, praying it wouldn't be some revelation about her own anatomy, like they had crossed the bridge of sharing and all subjects were fair game now.

"I'm going back to work at the bakers on Monday," she said, beaming.

"But what about Mr Brown? Will he still be there, leching over you?"

"That's the best bit. He's only gone and put me in charge. He's now running the other bakers in Archway. I'm only going back three days a week to begin with, but it's a start, right?"

Andrew knew that his grandmother had had a large part to play in that. She had really scared Mr Brown. Either way, his mum had her job back and on better terms too.

"That's amazing, Mum. Well done." He was so happy for her. After all she had gone through, she deserved it.

"You better go up now and say goodbye to your grandmother, Andrew. You know what she's like."

He finished his toast and walked up the stairs to the first floor. Andrew could hear the radio quietly playing some classical music, so he knew that she was probably reading. He knocked on her door and waited.

"Come in," he heard her say. He opened the door to find her reading in her chair, as usual, and his grandfather sitting quietly by the window, staring out vacantly.

"Andrew," she said, suspiciously. "Today is the big day, so I hear?"

"Yes, grandma. Xavier is collecting me soon."

"Where is your first stop along the way?" she enquired, not even taking her eyes from her book. He had to think fast.

"Birmingham, I think," he said, trying to stay as relaxed as possible.

"I see, and how far north will you go?" she asked, only this time looking him straight in the eyes, willing him to make a mistake.

"Only as far as Carlyle," he said. *Thank God he had memorised the place names.*

"Carlyle is a wonderful place. Be sure to send me a postcard, won't you?"

"Of course, grandma," he said, trying to think of a way of sourcing a postcard from there.

"I have something for your trip. Wait here," she said, getting up and leaving him alone in the study with his grandfather.

The room was a pale green and had many pictures hanging from the dark picture rails. Various portraits of long passed relatives, a few family pets, and a single landscape. From a distance it looked like a field full of red flowers, like poppies, but as Andrew moved closer to it, the bodies started to be distinguishable. What he had mistaken to be red flowers was blood, and lots of it. Thousands of men lying in a field, their blood staining the crop as they fell. The initials at the bottom were G.F. Andrew recognised it as his grandfather's. He had painted this quite a few years ago by the looks of it. It wasn't the best painting in the world, but like all good art it made you feel something. Whatever it was, Andrew felt it. He really did.

Looking over at his grandfather who looked silently out of the window, he wondered about what horrors he had seen to make him so withdrawn. Judging by this painting Andrew concluded that he had seen too much.

Andrew started to think about his own journey and what he would have to endure. Was he destined to end up like him? Would he see too much blood and death and not be able to cope? He decided to say goodbye to him too. He wasn't sure whether he would respond or not, but it felt like the right thing to do.

"I'm going away for a while, grandpa, travelling up north for work."

He didn't acknowledge what he had said.

"Mum is better now and is going back to work, so you don't have to worry about her."

He still didn't move a muscle or say anything.

Seeing no response, he decided to walk back over to the door and wait for his grandmother to return when his grandfather grabbed his arm firmly. Not to hurt him, just to stop him.

"Beware... the Shadows," his grandfather whispered. His eyes looked out into the room intensely.

He slowly loosened his grasp on Andrew's arm and turned back to the window and continued with his vacant staring. Andrew was shocked. *Did he know? Was he aware of what they were up against? He never left the house, and they never saw him read. He must be recalling a memory. Did he once have dealings with the elite?*

Just then, his grandmother returned to the room with a small, wooden box.

“Now, this is very special,” she said, handing him the box. “This was your grandfather’s from when he was in the war. He wore it every day to keep him safe.”

Andrew opened the box to reveal a simple but heavy chain and a round silver pendant with the embossed shape of a single lit candle.

“Thank you,” he said. “I shall wear it, too.”

“Good,” she said. “Because light will always overcome the darkness, you know. You just make sure you shield the flame from the wind of doubt.”

“I will,” said Andrew, knowing she knew far more than she was letting on.

“And don't worry about your mother, Andrew, she will be fine.”

It was quite clear to Andrew that if she had kept asking him questions about where they were travelling to, she would have smelled his ‘wind of doubt’ for sure. He said goodbye and headed back downstairs to kiss his mum goodbye. There was a part of him that felt guilty for leaving her, but he had to remember why he was going. To try and keep them safe...all of them. Their little group was about to attempt something never seen before by the Shadows, a true resistance.

Andrew was back downstairs when there was a knock on the front door.

“That will be Xavier,” said Andrew.

"Oh love," his mother said sweetly, holding back her emotions as much as she could. "Have a good trip, won't you, and stay safe. Remember to send postcards when you can."

"I will, I promise," kissing her goodbye on the cheek.

He picked up his over-filled leather suitcase and limped it towards the front door. The silhouette of a very scruffy man could be seen on the other side of the glass, so he opened it wide.

"Are you ready, Andrew?" asked Xavier. "We have to hit the road."

His mum watched them put all the bits in the rusty car and waved them off. Must be so hard to watch your only child leave the house, not quite knowing when you will see them again.

"Where are we going Xavier?" asked Andrew.

"You'll see," he said, re-lighting his cigar and taking a deep puff, and then filling the car with smoke. Andrew had become used to the smoke by then. It's amazing what you can learn to like over time.

47

From the Crow's Nest

Xavier drove south, past St Pancras and onwards towards Covent Garden. London was busy and the traffic was becoming more congested the nearer they got to the market. Around the back of the market there were a number of workshops in a mews that were often used for storage of goods, or repair shops for the local traders. They stopped halfway down the row in front of some badly faded, brown double doors.

"Here we are," said Xavier, getting out of the car.

"A workshop? We are staying in a workshop?" asked Andrew, getting out of the car, feeling confused.

"Not just any old workshop, this place is fit for purpose," said Xavier, proudly. "Besides, it was cheap."

He opened the padlock and slid the large doors open to reveal a large freshly painted and clean area with enough space for three cars on the ground floor, a first floor mezzanine area that had a bathroom, two other rooms, plus a lounge area with cooking facilities at the rear.

“This looks great, Xavier. We should be able to manage here.”

Andrew got his heavy case out of the boot and waddled in with it, giving up for a rest at the foot of the wrought iron staircase. Xavier looked at him in dismay at how heavy the case was.

“What?! You said, ‘bring plenty of clothes’, didn’t you?” He struggled with it up the stairs and once on the landing saw the doors to two rooms, one either side. “Which one is my room?” he shouted down.

“The one on the left!” shouted Xavier, getting back into the car to reverse it inside the workshop.

Andrew opened the door to see a single bed with a side table, a wardrobe, and a small bookshelf full of books. He opened the wardrobe and unpacked his clothes as best he could and placed the silver candle necklace in the bedside drawer. By the time he had finished, the doors were slid closed on the workshop again with the car inside and Xavier was already upstairs, brewing the kettle for some tea.

A large round table stood in the middle of the space with a stack of short, bar stools to one side.

The light wood looked out of place under the harsh industrial lighting. They sat and had tea together, and Andrew felt relieved to finally have some freedom. Not that he found his mum to be restrictive, but he was always worried about her either finding out what they were doing or her getting hurt again. At least this way they could finally get on with what they needed to do.

“We have a busy weekend ahead, Andrew. Curtis will be here in the morning, and we need to get to the shop for 10am to meet the boys.”

“Not just that,” said Andrew, sipping his tea. “Fiamma was on my doorstep last night, needed to talk privately.”

“You didn't invite her in, did you?” asked Xavier, looking a bit worried.

“I had to. She couldn't come in otherwise,” said Andrew. “Besides, I trust her.”

“You know that she can go in any time she likes now, don't you?” said Xavier, taking a gulp of his tea.

“Well, that doesn't bother me. She’s cute,” smirked Andrew.

Xavier spat his tea all over the table and choked on what was left for a while. “DO NOT FALL IN LOVE WITH A VAMPYRE!” Xavier shouted, even though his throat was burning.

“I’m not. I'm not. She is quite interesting, that's all,” he said.

“She may look sweet and innocent, Andrew, but believe me, she is a cold and efficient killer.”

“Oh, you don't have to tell me that. She pinned me to a fence with one hand on the night we met,” he said.

“Anyway,” said Xavier, calming down. “What did Fiamma want?”

"Sebastian wants a meeting at 11pm on Saturday night, said that you would know where."

"The facility at Southbank," said Xavier.

"I think they want to help," said Andrew.

Xavier didn't say a word. He looked up into the air and breathed an audible sigh.

"Meetings with Vampyres rarely end well, Andrew. We'll be lucky if we don't end up in the Thames."

"But we must try. We need help. Otherwise, we won't stand a chance of getting Lucy back," said Andrew.

Xavier considered the prospect carefully.

"Let's talk it over with Curtis in the morning and see what he thinks. Right now, we need to go shopping for supplies."

With Covent Garden on their doorstep, they didn't have to go very far to find what they needed. Fresh fruit, vegetables, and even some cured meat, bread that was still warm from the oven, and some amazing cheese.

They even managed to borrow a trolly to cart it all back with.

"Can you cook, Andrew?" asked Xavier, while stocking the cupboards.

"Not really...but I'm good at toast," he said.

"I was taught to cook a few dishes by my friend, quite a few years ago now. I can show you if you like?" said Xavier.

"Yeah, that would be great."

Andrew laid the table using a massive tablecloth and they spent the next couple of hours cooking.

Xavier showed Andrew how to make a ragu which was pork mince in tomato sauce, and how to cook perfect spaghetti. He even showed him how to add garlic and herbs to butter and spread it onto toasted bread, which was now Andrew's new favourite food. After dinner, they sat quietly up on the mezzanine, listening to the workshop roof pop and groan as it cooled down from the blistering, August day. Xavier was reading a book about Italy, as if the food had put him in the mood. He noticed that Andrew had become a bit restless, and they still had a couple of hours before bed.

"Fancy a game of chess?" said Xavier, putting his book down.

"Yes, but I don't know how to play," said Andrew.

Andrew had seen a few people play at school, but mostly the type of people that got bullied a lot. He had put two and two together and decided to avoid the beatings.

"Don't worry, I'll show you," said Xavier excitedly, heading to his room to grab his chess set

He set a green velvet bag of pieces down gently onto the table and placed the board in between them. The large round table made it difficult, but they managed. The chess set was very old, but in good condition. Ivory and ebony squares framed in an orange mango wood.

"I won this in a card game many years ago," he said, tipping the pieces out of the bag onto the tablecloth and setting the black ones out on his side.

“Copy me,” he said.

Andrew laid out the white pieces just as Xavier had. Xavier swapped a couple around, but then they were set and ready to go. He explained the movements of the pieces and what they could and couldn't do. Once Andrew had the gist of it, they began.

“Oh, wait. You can't play chess without brandy, it's the law.” said Xavier

“Really? I doubt that,” said Andrew in mistrust.

“Well, it is in my book,” he said, grabbing a fresh bottle and two glasses from the cupboard.

“Which one? You have hundreds,” Andrew said with a laugh.

“Ah... funny boy you are. You won't be laughing when I take your king in six moves.”

They played three games that night and drank quite a lot of brandy. Andrew lost them all but felt like he learnt a lot. By the time he went to bed his head was spinning and he dreamt of shadow-like figures on a giant chess board. The deep laughter echoed in the atmosphere, and it didn't stop until he woke with a jolt. This also coincided with the banging on the workshop door.

BANG, BANG, BANG.

BANG, BANG, BANG.

Andrew heard Xavier stumble out of his room and stub his toe on something, cursing to himself as he flopped down the iron stairs to the lower level. It was 8am.

BANG, BANG, BANG.

"ALRIGHT," rasped Xavier, as he unbolted the door to the workshop.

Andrew heard the small door squeak open.

"Ahh, hello Curtis, welcome."

Curtis didn't say a word, but Andrew heard Xavier open the larger sliding doors with a screech. A vehicle started up and pulled into the workshop. Someone got out, but he heard two doors shut out of time on a hollow sounding vehicle. He had someone with him. After sliding the doors shut again, Andrew heard all their footsteps come up the iron stairs and onto the mezzanine.

"Tea?" he heard Xavier say.

"Yes please," said a sweet, female voice. "Coffee for me," said a gruff one.

Andrew decided to get himself dressed and ready to meet them. He walked out into the space and saw an older man, about sixty, with long salt and pepper hair and electric blue eyes staring back at him. He was wearing a black trench coat, with a heavily wrinkled checked shirt underneath. Andrew noticed that Curtis and Xavier had the same sense of fashion, as in none.

The other voice belonged to the girl that was sat by his side. She was a little older than Andrew, very pretty, and had beautiful long auburn hair that was plaited.

“Ah, this is Andrew, my apprentice if you like,” said Xavier. “Andrew, this is Curtis and... sorry, I didn't catch your name?” he gestured to the young lady.

“Emma,” she said.

“Andrew, Emma. Emma, Andrew,” said Xavier, waving his arms back and forth crudely. He scurried back to making the refreshments.

“Nice to meet you both,” said Andrew. “How was your journey?”

“In that bloody thing?” said Curtis, pointing down to the workshop floor. “It's an old ambulance, not designed for long distances. More suitable for sleeping in than driving now.”

His west country twang made the phrase far more entertaining than it should have been. Andrew looked over the balcony down onto the workshop floor. There was a faded yellow Bedford CA ambulance that looked like it had undergone some modification. It had a red and white, rolled-up awning bolted to the side, and a couple of bicycles strapped to it too.

“We stopped halfway, just this side of Exeter, refuelled and slept in the van overnight. Bed is comfortable enough,” said Curtis.

“Slept? In the van?” said Andrew. “Didn't know that was a thing to do.”

“Oh yeah, you watch,” said Curtis. “Camping vans are the way forward, Andrew. You mark my words.”

Andrew found that hard to believe. *Sleeping in a van? Why on earth would you want to do that?*

Like all trends, that would die out...

“We set off again from Exeter at 3am and made it here in good time. Sorry we are so early,” said Curtis.

“That's alright,” said Xavier. “We have a busy schedule after all.”

“Have you come up with a plan then?” said Curtis, as he rolled himself a cigarette.

“Yes, but it’s not set in stone yet,” said Xavier.

“Nothing ever is, Xavier, you know that,” Curtis said, lighting his roll up. Xavier took a deep breath and steadied himself. He wasn't sure why he was so nervous.

“There are seven girls being held at the Freemason's Hall, just up the road. We have premises nearby that overlook the site and plan to intercept the vehicle when they transport them.”

“Right,” said Curtis. “So, you’re going to try and stop a crucial ingredient of the incantation from even getting there?”

Andrew felt a flare of anger in his chest. “One of those ‘crucial ingredients' is my friend's sister, I'll have you know,” he said, in the most measured tone he could muster.

“I see,” said Curtis, standing up to take the space in. His parade made Andrew feel uncomfortable as he walked around.

“Have you been here long?” he asked, taking the air in on the mezzanine. “As I don't feel the loss here.”

They looked on in confusion.

“You know... the vibes, the verve. All I can smell here is Italian food and wet paint.”

“We only got here last night,” said Xavier.

Curtis took his seat again and stared deeply into Andrew’s eyes.

“Xavier has kept me up to speed with the incantation. The time, the date, and the place, but if we stop the delivery of the girls there's a high chance that the Shadows won't even show up.”

“What's so bad about that?” asked Andrew, trying to understand.

“Listen...the only important thing to me is getting close to the Shadows. They will pay for what they did to my brother,” said Curtis.

Andrew remembered the story that Xavier told him about Curtis. A ship of that size to be lost is a terrible thing. All those people dead and his brother was the captain.

Andrew tried to reason with him. “I totally understand why you are angry with them,” he said.

"YOU HAVE NO IDEA!" cursed Curtis, as he banged the table.

Emma seemed unfazed by this outburst, which led Andrew to believe this was a regular thing.

Curtis explained.

"I haven't had the easiest existence, you know. I was always... different. My mother and father couldn't deal with me, and people in the village avoided me. The only one who understood me and gave me the space to grow was David, my older brother. He wasn't even magical himself, but he protected me. But every time the locals blamed me for something that had happened, he was the first to stand by my side. The blood, sweat, and tears he invested into my safety meant everything to me. I hadn't seen him for two years when his ship went down. He was a good man, you know. When I found out it was them, it was enough to awaken something in me I didn't even know existed."

His eyes flashed brightly, only for a brief second, but they all saw it.

"Well, someone's sister, in fact seven sisters, will be sacrificed that day if we let this go ahead," countered Andrew,

"Ahh, Andrew. Do you really believe I would ever let it get that far?" said Curtis. "I have something in mind that will upset the applecart, trust me."

"Andrew here, might have some help from a few Vampyres, here in London," said Xavier.

"Vampyres, eh?" said Curtis. "Very tricky characters, I find. I had a few run-in's with them myself, over the years.

But I can see why they want in, 'cause that blood treaty was a sham from the very start."

"There are around a thousand left in London who never signed it," said Andrew. "We are meeting with the head of the resistance this evening to talk about them helping us."

"Verne Daniels," said Curtis. "He used to be the head, now he's caught up in this incantation.

He is one of the good ones, but some of them, including his weasel of a brother, Sebastian, cannot be trusted."

"Well, that's a shame, as that's who we have a meeting with," said Andrew. "What makes you think he can't be trusted?"

"He is the reason that Verne had to run, you see," said Curtis. "Sebastian took the life of a high-ranking official at Westminster, and Verne took the blame for it. Verne knew that they wouldn't stop until they found the person responsible, so he took the blame and ran."

"So, Sebastian is a bit tetchy," said Xavier.

"And yes, he can be a bit creepy sometimes, but limp in moral fibre. His brother was only looking out for him, really. Surely, Curtis, you of all people can see that?"

"I get it," said Curtis. "But there comes a time where you must put your hands up when you make a mistake. My brother only ever protected me from injustices, and I never lied to him... NEVER."

"When is this meeting?" asked Emma.

"Tonight, at Southbank, 11pm," said Xavier.

“Going to need a nap this afternoon then, Emma, we’ve been up since three,” said Curtis.

“Well, I have,” Emma said. “You fell asleep quite a few times on the way here, which made navigating quite hard.”

“But you like driving!” said Curtis.

“So, how did you two meet?” asked Andrew, trying to defuse the argument that was just starting to boil.

“Oh, well, we're not together, not like that. That wouldn't be proper,” said Curtis.

“She was born in a village close to mine and grew up in a normal family. That was until she hit puberty and odd things started to happen around her. The locals from the village had heard about me and my old ways, so they brought her to me.”

“Dumped me off, more like,” said Emma.

“They couldn't wait to get me out of the house, but then again, I had caused quite a lot of damage to be honest.”

“And you just took her in?” asked Xavier.

“Well, yes,” said Curtis. “I had a big enough house and I guess I saw a bit of myself in her really; Thought I could help. I saw how scared her parents were of her, and I remembered that feeling well. It was upsetting. I never had a wife or children due to being, you know, how I am. So...I saw this as an opportunity to maybe pass on all the things I had learnt along the way. When she first turned up, she was so angry and scared of everything, but that slowly changed when I taught her how to control herself.

“And for that I'll always be grateful,” said Emma, sweetly, whilst holding his hand. Her long-plaited hair was draped around her shoulder. Such a beautiful shade. She seemed to have forgotten the travelling tension. His relationship with her wasn't paternal, more like a wayward uncle. It seemed to work well for them.

“We also have a meeting at the shop with the other boys in an hour,” said Xavier.

“Who are we meeting with?” asked Curtis.

“My friends, George and Lee. They have been in this from the start,” said Andrew.

“From the start?!” scowled Curtis. “I've been following the Shadows since I was eighteen years old, and they have been in place for hundreds of years.

From the start? Pah,” Curtis scoffed, and could be quite intimidating when he wanted to be.

“Well, everyone has to start somewhere,” defended Andrew.

Curtis explained.

“Thirteen families. The oldest male of each family is a lifelong member of the committee. They play the world like it is a game of chess, and it is... when you think about it. The committee is presided over by the oldest female of all the families. They call her the Grand Matriarch. Right now, it is Regina Wordsworth. The coldest woman alive. She lives in Surrey, not too far from here actually, although she has estates all around the world.

She has been the longest reigning Grand Matriarch so far, and has been in place for over twenty years, which gives you an idea of her perseverance. She is very powerful, and the blinding spell I cast on her a month ago is already starting to wear thin. Just hope it holds long enough for me to reinforce it."

"I've had an idea for that," said Xavier. "I have an Obeah man that now lives in Bath who can reinforce it. I will send him a letter."

"So, when one member dies, they are just replaced by the next in line?" asked Andrew.

"Exactly," said Curtis. "Their wealth and power have no limits. If you knew some of the things they have done over the years, you would never sleep again."

"Well, we have the chance to upset something quite dear to them," said Xavier.

"But they must not know that it was. That is fundamental. As they will spare no expense to discover who you are, so you must be careful." said Curtis

"We will need balaclavas," said Xavier.

Andrew picked up on the fact that Curtis had said 'you' and not 'we'.

"What about you, Curtis?" asked Andrew. "Don't you want to be hidden too?"

"No, no. My life is limited anyway. I found out I have cancer a couple of months back."

He didn't really seem that upset by it. Emma did though.

“That's awful,” said Xavier. not knowing what else to say. “Are you going to get treatment?”

“It's beyond that, to be honest,” he said. “Besides, I want them to see the face of the man that helped destroy their plans. Their greed is out of control.”

This man had cancer and is still willing to drive across the country to fight. He rolled himself another cigarette and tapped it on the table. He lit it with his silver lighter and blew the smoke upwards.

"Where is this bloody shop then?”

48

THE HARD SELL

They left the workshop and walked out of Covent Garden, towards Drury Lane. Andrew noticed that Curtis was slow on his feet and had the occasional sharp pain in his side, which he shrugged off. When they got to the shop, Andrew could see Lee and George were already waiting outside, tugging at the boards that covered the windows impatiently. They crossed the street to meet them. As they did so, George seemed quite bashful and didn't seem to be acting naturally. Emma had sparked something in him he didn't expect. To Andrew, Emma was lovely, and pretty, but all he could think of was Fiamma. Andrew knew that Fiamma would never be interested in him. After all, he was too young and a mortal, but then again, even if he was thirty, she would still be seventy years older. Plus, a relationship with a Vampyre? How on earth would that work? Far too complicated.

Xavier fought with the door lock as usual, and they finally got off the street and into the dusty shop. They walked over to the board and Xavier tore off the sheet that covered the map.

"Now this is a work of dedication," said Curtis, as he looked down at the map. "How long did it take you to find all of these?"

"Ten years or so," said Xavier. "It became an obsession for a while."

"Anything with this level of detail has to be," Curtis said.

"George, Lee, this is Curtis, and this is Emma," Andrew said, realising the awkwardness of the situation.

"Nice to meet you," said George, going a bit red.

"So, you're the magician?" asked Lee.

"I wouldn't necessarily describe myself as that," said Curtis. "More of a disciple of the old ways."

"Old ways?" said Lee. "We need more than that for what we are about to do."

Curtis seemed on edge but spoke clearly. "We collectively need to use all our skills to overcome this darkness. There are certain things I can do that will help."

Curtis looked at Lee and his eyes glowed slightly. The light level in the room seemed to dim down. Lee grabbed his own throat with both hands and dropped to his knees, gasping for breath. Curtis had let go quickly, and Lee was now recovering. Lee stood up again, but he wasn't angry, just straightened himself out and dusted his knees off.

Lee needed to see some demonstration of power before he trusted him. Curtis walked over to him and placed his hand on his shoulder. They both joined the others around the map.

“Right, there’s no easy way to say this,” said Xavier. “So, I’m going to just say it.”

George and Lee looked confused.

“Curtis doesn't want us to stop the girls from getting to Greenwich.”

“WHAT?” screamed George, his temper instantly boiling over. “How else are we going to get Lucy back?!”

“George, please understand,” said Curtis. “I’m here for the Shadows, I must make sure they turn up. If we stop the girls getting there, then the whole thing is blown.”

“Who cares!” said George. “At least I will have my sister back where she belongs.”

“Yes, true, you will,” said Curtis. “But for how long? And what about my revenge?

they killed my brother."

George went a bit red and fell silent.

Curtis continued.

“If we foil this too early, they will try again, as It's worth too much to them.

It may not be your sister next time, but it will be someone else's.

If we can get close enough to the Shadows, I think I can change things."

"How?" asked George. "There will be thousands of Blackstones to deal with."

"There are ways and means," said Curtis.

"We have a meeting at 11pm tonight with the Vampyre resistance," said Andrew. "They want to help."

"But what about the Blackstones, Andrew?" asked Lee. "You told us what the Obsidian does to them, makes them as useful as chocolate teapots."

"Lucky that I brought some toys with me then," said Curtis. They all looked at him feeling more confused than ever.

Curtis left the shop and walked up the high street. "Where's he gone now?" Andrew asked.

"One of his mad ideas, no doubt," said Emma, laughing to herself.

He returned a few minutes later with two small wine glasses and a bottle of wine. He placed them on the table.

"From the Italian a few doors down," he said.

"Bit early for a drink, isn't it? but if you insist" said Xavier,

Curtis had no intention of opening the wine until later. Out of his pocket, he took out a small vial of thin oil.

"Every bit of glass, gem and crystal has a resonant frequency, you see," said Curtis. "It's partly why they look the way they do."

He dabbed some of the oil onto his index finger, held on to the base of the glass and proceeded to trace it around the rim of one of the glasses. As he did so, the glass started to sing in a high pitch tone. He sped up.

“Everyone... close your eyes,” he said, as the glass started to get louder and louder. They all heard the second glass join in and they rang out together. More strange noises could be heard from the front of the shop too.

“All you have to do, is find the right frequency.”

Andrew wasn't sure what was going to happen, so he closed his eyes tightly just before he heard a glass smash on the table, and more breaking at the front of the shop. A few shards of glass landed on Andrew’s hands in front of him.

“You can open up now,” said Curtis, already starting to clean the broken glass from the map.

“What happened there?” asked Xavier.

“Find the right frequency, and you can shatter pretty much anything,” he said. “Sorry about the windows.”

“Wow,” said Andrew, reading in between the lines. “So, you can shatter obsidian too?” he asked.

“Yes, you can,” said Curtis. “But you it would have to be a hell of a lot louder than that, that's for sure”.

Looking towards the shopfront, Andrew could now see all the glass panes were shattered. Luckily the boards were still in place. Andrew’s mind was racing.

"What will you use? A giant wine glass or something?" asked Lee.

"I have a modified glass armonica, back in the van," said Curtis.

"What on earth is that?" asked Xavier.

"It's a bloody monstrosity, that's what it is," said Emma. "I'm sick and tired of stubbing my toes on it."

Every time Emma spoke it seemed to captivate George.

Nerdy fact:

The glass armonica is a musical instrument like no other. One of the earliest versions of the mechanical glass armonica was perfected by none other than Benjamin Franklin in 1761, one of the founding fathers of America.

Coloured glass bowls on their sides are fixed to a horizontal shaft that rotates, and water is pumped or dabbed over them. Then the players fingers are placed to generate the harmonic tones as they spin. The smaller the wheel, the higher the frequency.

These instruments are remarkably rare due to the delicate nature of the glass. They fell out of trend around 1830 due to the difficulty of amplifying the sound for larger auditoriums. Due to the ethereal quality of the tones, there were also many reports of people going quite mad from either listening to or playing the instrument too frequently. It seemed to awaken a great depression in some people, from which they never recovered.

Curtis continued. “I have had a large obsidian disc made and fitted to that thing especially. Cost me an arm and a leg, it did. The only thing we need to sort out is a way to make it louder, which is easier said than done.”

“We’ll need a pretty big speaker system and a microphone,” said George. “But I can look into that.”

After a lot of talking and deliberation they all decided to go along with Curtis’s plan. The logic made sense. They needed to try and get to the root of the problem, not just create a setback for the Shadows, or they would obviously try again. Having a thousand or so Vampyres to help tackle the Darkhearts meant that they stood a chance. They would be outnumbered ten to one, but Andrew knew that if they were anything like Fiamma then their strength would be a distinct advantage. The next step would be to get the Vampyres on side. As much as Andrew was secretly looking forward to seeing Fiamma again, he was nervous about the meeting. What Xavier had said had really made him think. He really didn't want to end up dead in the Thames.

When they were finishing up and getting ready to leave the shop, Xavier looked at the map that he had painstakingly put together.

“All that time wasted... and for what, eh?” said Xavier.

“It's amazing, and it will be useful too, I bet,” said Andrew.

Xavier removed the coloured pins from the map and began to fold it up in long thin strips. Then in half, and in half again. Before long it was only 5” by 8” but quite thick.

"I suggest we have dinner at the workshop at 8pm as we need to be in Southbank on time. Let's not do anything to arouse the anger of this lot," said Xavier.

"Where is the workshop?" asked George.

"Andrew will explain," said Xavier.

He put the tightly folded map into his inside coat pocket, and they left the shop. They all headed their separate ways. Xavier had some errands to run, Curtis and Emma went off to get some lunch, and then back to the workshop for a nap, while Andrew, Lee and George decided to head to the market to see what they could find.

49

The Savoy

The Grand Matriarch had arrived at the Savoy suite with Jacob an hour earlier than she needed to. She needed time by herself to think things over. The Savoy was the first hotel in London to provide a private space for their meetings. The Mains Cachés Suite, like the other carefully selected places, was for the council of thirteen only. And just like the others, it was decorated and furnished to the highest possible standard. From the unique antique brass handles to the crystal chandeliers and silver candle stick holders.

Due to the sensitive nature of their business, the tapestries and the paintings had to be hung by people of their order. They employed only the best tradesmen to work on the renovations and paid huge sums to have the work completed, but when it was finished, the tradesmen and their families were killed and disposed of. They had to ensure the complete secrecy and security of their investment. This all came at a hefty price, but the cost wasn't important.

In the silence of the room, she knew that something wasn't right, but she still couldn't put her finger on what it was.

She had been doing everything in her considerable power to see into the future. Scrying, water pools, and even a ritual sacrifice followed by a meditation. She had even tried the most sacred of crystal balls, a gift from the sultan of Brunei - still nothing. Almost like there was something or someone stopping her from seeing what was to come. It had never been that difficult before. She worried that she might be losing her power.

She poured herself a large brandy from the crystal decanter on the dresser and sipped it whilst looking at the oil painting of her father on the wall. It was one of the many gilded frames that decorated the candle-lit room. Each told a story, a tale to remember, if you knew how to see them. He deserved to be there amongst the others, as he too was a great man. She looked over at her grandson, Jacob, who was now reading a book, quietly in the corner. He looked so much like her brother had done at his age, and it reminded her of him.

She would never forget the day her father had saved her and her brother from the Vampyre in the woods. He and his friends fought with strength and bravery. That Vampyre was beheaded before he was taken deep into the woods and buried. The only thing left of that experience was the scar on her arm, but it still burned and tingled sometimes. She had already finished her drink but was still on edge, so she poured another. She overheard her guards in the foyer talking to someone who had just stepped out of the elevator. It was time.

Knock, knock.

"Enter," she said.

A tall, dark man of about sixty entered the room and shut the door behind him. He had pitch-black eyes and a pronounced forehead with deep lines.

"Ah, Mr Malone," she said. "So good of you to attend, *finally.*"

"I am sorry for my absence, Grand Matriarch," he said, bowing slightly. "Australia proved to be a long but worthwhile trip. It is all prepared for the 3rd of October," he said respectfully.

"I was more concerned for Henry, to be honest," she said. "I even brought my family dagger just in case."

He began to defend himself, "The rules-"

"Are there for a good reason and must be adhered to," she hissed at him.

"I am truly sorry, Grand Matriarch, I am here now," he said, bowing apologetically.

"Yes, you are, but where are the others?"

"They are on their way up. There was an issue with the elevator, but it is working again now."

Knock, knock.

"Enter," she said, her tone still quite sharp from the altercation with Mr Malone. The other men filed into the room and took their places at the table in front of her.

"Please be seated," she said. They obeyed.

This table was different from the one in the Hotel Russell. It was made from a darker wood, and it still had the same symbols and arrows, but in this table, they were inlaid with a white ivory-like material. The all-seeing eye shone brighter than ever because of it. She knew whose bones they had used for the inlays. They were of Madhatma Ghandi. The elite can't resist flaunting their wealth and power. One of the Grand Matriarch's favourite pairs of shoes in her vast collection were cobbled using the skin of someone she truly hated. They had been sacrificed by them first, of course. Human leather is very expensive but worth every penny. Just to know that you are wearing a part of your enemy was the ultimate win. Native Americans knew this all too well when they collected scalps from the cowboys who dared to cross paths and strayed into their territory.

Boom, boom, boom, went her stick, signalling the start of the meeting. She unsheathed her silver dagger and held it aloft for a moment before bringing down and pointing it to the tall dark man.

"Mr Malone, as you have returned, you will spin first."

"As you wish, Grand Matriarch," he said, and stood up from his place at the table. He walked around to her to collect the knife, but as he put out his hand for the knife she scratched his hand with it, drawing a bit of blood. He let out a short wince. This wasn't the first time she had done this to a member of the council. The Wordsworths were the most powerful family of the thirteen, when dealing with occult matters. This made them revered, but slightly temperamental. There was a drop of blood still on the blade. She touched her fingertip onto it and smeared it across the knife and began looking into crimson silver. She inhaled deeply like she had seen a ghost and dropped the knife onto the floor with a clatter. The men looked on without concern, just interest. She had seen something, but whether she would tell them what it was, was another matter.

Mr Malone bent down and retrieved the knife from the floor begrudgingly. He wiped his own blood off the blade with his handkerchief and turned around to place it on the eye on the table.

The Grand Matriarch calmed herself and her breathing slowed. She couldn't believe the vision she had seen. Bright blue eyes, a long piercing noise followed an explosion, like a thousand windows shattering all at once. Was it something to do with Australia? Or was it finally an insight of something to come for her?

The knife was already spinning but slowed and stopped at Mr Wordsworth.

"Mr Wordsworth," she said, recovering her breath and authority. "Old business."

"Yes, Grand Matriarch," said Mr Wordsworth, as prepared himself with a cough.

"The Extensio Vitae incantation will take place on the 7th of December, as planned. We have all the necessary components ready and will now be using seven pure girls to maximise our yield of blood. The Blackstones along with other Darkhearts have been charged to protect the event, and the HAARP machine will start bringing in the fog on Thursday the 4th of December."

"Who will be conducting the ceremony?" she asked.

"I was hoping that you, Grand Matriarch, would honour us with your strength in this area," said Mr Wordsworth. "I have some high ranking Blackstones that will assist in the preparation and blood related tasks if you wish, but the incantation must be carried out to the letter."

This incantation still made the Grand Matriarch nervous, but she wasn't sure why. "Of course," she said, knowing that she was the leading Occultist in the council and there wasn't really any way out of it.

"Are the Vampyre Council aware that we are using seven girls?" she asked.

"They only know of one, Grand Matriarch, as requested," said Mr Wordsworth. "And the Freemasons have agreed to transport the Vampyre too. The Vampyre Council have him locked up in their vault, but it's the obsidian shackles. They can't stand to be around them."

"How will they transport them to Greenwich?" she asked.

"By boat, Grand Matriarch, it will be the safest way in the dense fog," said Mr Wordsworth.

"Excellent," she said. "We stand to reap a very healthy profit from this, gentlemen."

"Yes indeed," started Mr Wordsworth, smugly.

"New business," she said, cutting him off before he could gloat anymore.

"This leads me well onto my next point," Mr Wordsworth said, playfully. "We have had considerable interest in this blood from leaders and occult powers all over the world. We are in the midst of a bidding war, and we are already up to half a million sterling, per fluid ounce. Who knows what sum it will reach by the time we hold it in our grasp?"

"Take no chances, Mr Wordsworth. Remember, we need thirty fluid ounces for our own prosperity."

"Of course, Grand Matriarch, not a drop less," he said smoothly, spoken like a true salesman.

"Spin the knife, Mr Wordsworth." She couldn't concentrate properly. Her nephew was beginning to irritate her. All she could picture was those piercing blue eyes, staring right into her soul.

50

Market Research

Covent Garden

Covent Garden market, as big as it was, only really sold food and flowers. Andrew and the boys needed to branch out and find somewhere that sold useful things for their mission in December. They decided to jump on a tube and head west. Using the Hammersmith and City Line, they got out at Ladbroke Grove tube and walked across to Portobello Road Market.

"Now this is more like it," said Andrew, as they broke out into the bustling crowds walking in and out of the street market. There was so much to see, from second hand clothes to motorcycle parts, kitchen appliances to gardening tools. Lee found a military stall quite quickly and started to try on some ex-army helmets, but none of them fitted his oversized head. They had some balaclavas for sale though, so they made note of the price and carried on down the market.

Further down, they found a stall where a guy was selling vintage speakers. They set their eyes on what appeared to be a Magnavox system from the 1920s. It had a horn-type speaker that looked like the type you would get on a gramophone record player, only much smaller.

"The secret is in the horn," said the elderly gentleman who owned the stall. "I designed the speaker that sits in the base myself," he added, looking very proud of himself, playing with the left tip of his heavily waxed moustache.

He had a silver grilled microphone, the type that American movie stars used when they sang. It was fixed to a short tabletop stand. He placed a record onto a standalone record player with its own small speaker. The classical music coming from the speaker was barely audible amongst the shouts and general noise of the thriving market.

"Now... watch this," he said. He flicked the switch on the microphone to on and leant it over to the small, tiny speaker on the record player. Suddenly, the whole market was filled with the sound of violins playing at a furious rate. People passing by were baffled by the music emanating from the stall. It was incredibly loud. The old chap moved the microphone away from the speaker and things calmed down again. The passers-by took their hands away from their ears as he turned the switch off. The other stall holders didn't seem as shocked, just irritated, like he had done this too many times today already.

"As I always say, the punch is from the horn, but a good speaker works wonders."

"What's the biggest speaker you've ever made?" asked Lee.

"For a horn resonator?"

Lee nodded.

“About three inches in diameter, I suppose,” said the kind man. “Any bigger than that and the horn would have to be very large to make the most of it, and my back isn't what it used to be.”

“Can we commission you to build us a twelve-inch speaker with a big enough amplifier and a microphone?” said Lee, looking him straight in the eyes.

“Oh, and portable. It needs to be battery powered,” interjected George.

“Twelve inches?!” said the man. “That's far too big!”

“So, you can't do it then?” teased Lee.

“Of course, I can. I mean, it would take me sometime. I'd have to place an order for all manner of things... but it could be done. You would need a horn resonator in the region of...”

He made some quick calculations in his head. “Forty inches or so to project that kind of sound effectively.”

“Don't worry about the horn,” said Lee with a smile. “Just the speaker, the amplifier, the battery, and the mic. How much?”

“Oh, well, the materials I'd have to acquire are very costly, then there's the labour involved.

It takes ages to...”

Lee stopped him short. “Have a think about it and come up with a price. We'll come back next week to talk about it, OK?”

"Yes indeed," said the now very troubled old man, playing anxiously with his moustache.

They left, thinking about the sounds they had just heard coming from the small horn on that table.

"But what about the horn, Lee?" asked Andrew, as they neared the entrance to Ladbroke Grove tube. "Where on earth will we find a horn resonator that's forty inches?"

"I was thinking about using a bell," said Lee, smiling to himself.

"A bell? Would that work?" asked George. "It's the right shape, I guess."

"We make a forty-four-inch bell at the foundry," said Lee. "Only trouble is that it weighs about 1500 pounds."

"You must be joking. That's as much as seven or eight men!" exclaimed Andrew. "How are we supposed to lift that?"

"The same way we do at work," Lee said. "Bars, ropes and winches."

They headed east and got off the tube at Euston Square and decided to find something to eat. There was a small workers café along the parade, so they sat down and ordered. They were the only ones in there and sat right at the back away from the kitchen. While they were waiting for their food, the conversation returned to the bell.

"But how will we transport such a massive thing, Lee?" asked Andrew.

"I'll have to borrow a flatbed truck from work, too," said Lee.

"Will be tricky, but I know where all the keys are kept. The incantation is on a Sunday, right?"

"Sunday the 7th of December," said Andrew drearily, like a bored pupil.

"Right, so as long as I get the truck and the bell back to Whitechapel by Sunday night, then they won't have a clue."

George seemed a bit quiet, like he had something on his mind.

"Are you ok George?" asked Andrew.

"Yeh, just thinking about Lucy," said George.

Andrew and Lee didn't know what to say. She had been playing on their minds too.

"We are going to get her back, George," said Andrew.

This didn't seem to change George's sombre mood.

"But even if we do get her back, will she ever get over this?" he said.

"We'll cross that bridge when we come to it, I guess," said Lee.

"What about the other girls? You know, the other six," said George. "They must have families too. Shouldn't we try and contact them?"

"There would be too much for them to take in I think, George," said Andrew. He was in a sarcastic mood, probably because he was hungry.

"Oh hi, Mr and Mrs so-and-so. My name is Andrew and I know where your daughter is! She's been kidnapped by a Blackstone satanic cult that regularly sacrifices people in their underground chambers, right here in London. Oh no, don't worry, she won't be sacrificed by them. The Shadows will do it. Who are they? Well, they are only the most rich and powerful people on the planet who decide on everything that happens in this world. Rest assured your daughter won't be sacrificed to please the devil. It's worse than that, it's all for money as her blood will become magical when she drinks the blood of a Vampyre and has her throat slit. Oh yeah... they exist too. Did I forget to say?"

Both Lee and George looked at him in silence.

"You're right, Andrew," said George. "I wouldn't believe us either."

They ate their lunch quietly and didn't really know what to say to one another. The reality of the ludicrous situation they were in was starting to dawn on them. After lunch they decided to head their separate ways. George had more decisions to make regarding the shop renovations, and Lee had some work to do in the garden at home. Andrew invited them both to dinner at the workshop. He explained where it was, and they both agreed to get there at around 8pm.

"Dinner, at a workshop?" Lee had said.

"Don't worry. It's better than it sounds," said Andrew.

Andrew headed back to the workshop and heard Curtis snoring heavily from his van while Emma was sitting at the table on the mezzanine, reading.

"Didn't fancy a nap then?" he said, as he reached the top of the stairs.

"With that racket?" she said, glancing at the van. "No chance."

"Where's Xavier? Is he still out?" asked Andrew.

"Yep, haven't seen him since we left the shop," she said. "Just gave us a key and told us to make ourselves at home."

"Mind if I join you?" he said.

"Sure, take a seat," she said, as she closed her book.

"Le Petit Albert?" he asked, reading the spine of her book.

"Nicely pronounced, Andrew, a very old but great book for natural spells. It's translated from French, so it can be a little hard to follow sometimes."

"Natural spells?"

Emma didn't seem interested in explaining much about it, so he quickly changed the subject.

"So, how is he doing?" asked Andrew, nodding down towards the snoring van. "It's hard to know what to say when someone has cancer, isn't it?"

"Oh... well he has his moments," she said. "Sometimes he comes across as being a bit short changed. He gets quite angry over little things. Problems with the van, with me... with the world really. Other times he seems like he wants to just give up."

"Must be horrible to have that hanging over your head all of the time," said Andrew.

"At least this business with the Shadows has given him a focus and something to live for, I guess. Revenge is a strong emotion," she said.

"George knows all about that!" said Andrew.

"Ah, George? The one that goes a bit red around me?" she teased.

"Yeh, I think he likes you."

"Really? Do you think so?" she said, dripping with sarcasm. "I may be from the west, but I'm not bloody stupid, Andrew."

"He's sixteen, you know," Andrew said, rushing to his defence.

"Yeah, he seems it," her disappointment disarmed him.

"Well, George is determined to get them back for taking his sister Lucy, and for burning his shop."

"I can appreciate his anger, Andrew. It really can be a driving force, but it seems like some people ricochet wildly from one drama to the next. As if life isn't hard enough on its own, without being obsessed with settling some score or another."

"He's not normally like this," Andrew said. "Just this year has been tough on all of us with the Blackstones, finding out about the incantation, and then Lucy."

"Mmm... the truth is, Andrew, if you are not careful the emotions can blind you from reality. One of the first things

Curtis ever told me is that I need to be able to centre myself and calm my emotions, when I need to."

"How is that working out for you?" he asked.

"I'm still struggling with it, to be honest, but it's a life's work."

"I just hope we can all stay calm tonight at the meeting," said Andrew.

"Ever had any dealings with Vampyres, Emma?"

"Only once, a few years ago. He came to see Curtis at the house. Curtis wouldn't let me in the meeting as I was only like fourteen at the time, but a few weeks later he had that obsidian bowl made for his Armonica."

"That was a few years ago?" Andrew asked. "Why did he have that made then?"

"Who knows, but he kept going on and on about how much it had cost him. The Vampyre said that he would return and cover the costs, but he never came back."

"So, that's why he doesn't trust them," said Andrew.

"It's starting to make sense now, but it seems a shame to write a whole race off just because of a few bad apples."

"Vampyres have a very chequered history, Andrew. I think there's more than just a few bad ones."

"There are some good ones, too," said Andrew. "Well, I know two that are."

Emma caught Andrew's blush.

"Oh really, like that is it?" she said, inquisitively. "What's her name then?" smiling at him, like they were on a girl's sleepover and telling each other secrets about boys. He tried to ignore her patronising tone.

"Fiamma. Her name is Fiamma," he said, dryly.

"What is she like?" she pried. "I mean apart from the cold-blooded killer instinct, mind tricks, manipulations; and not forgetting the complete lack of compassion for anything with a heartbeat?"

Having it spelled out for him like that had put him out of step.

"Er... she... is very sweet."

"Very sweet?! You MUST do better than that," she snapped.

"OK. She has long, red hair. Cute, smart, funny, and intuitive. Oh, and she's also over 100 years old."

"Oh, like an older lady then, Andrew? That's good to know," she winked, playfully. "Not very practical though is it. Her being undead and you being, well...a mortal."

"Yeah, not great. I'd be lying if I said I hadn't thought about it a lot."

"Of course, you have, Andrew. Boys your age do 'think' a lot."

Dammed blush! His face felt the size of a pumpkin. He stood up to find a window. "Far too hot in here," he said.

Emma laughed briefly and went back to reading her book.

Andrew walked over into the kitchen area and opened the louvered vents on the rear window, praying for some air. There was hardly any breeze at all, but it was a slight improvement. He sat back down at the table with Emma, and she put her book down again to sip her water.

"So, you can do magic?" he asked.

"No, I don't 'do' magic, Andrew," she said, curtly. "But I can focus my intentions and allow the energy to move through me."

"Right, so the energy isn't in you, it's elsewhere?" he asked.

"Not elsewhere... everywhere."

"Can you show me something then?"

"Ah, I'd rather not. I don't work well under pressure."

"Oh, go on, please? Nothing big. Go on... anything?"

"OK, OK," she said, looking nervous. She brought her beautiful auburn hair plait around her shoulder, so it was now in front of her. She closed her eyes and held onto her hair with both hands like it was a rope. Andrew could hear her muttering something under her breath and could feel the table starting to vibrate softly underneath his elbows. The water in the glass in front of her turned cloudy and was starting to bubble, almost like it had turned to acid and was trying to dissolve itself. Her hair started to change colour, slowly at first, but soon it spread all the way up to her head. It was now a light shade of light purple. She opened her eyes and took a deep breath.

"Wow!" said Andrew. "Your hair, it looks really... different."

"What colour is it?" she said, squinting and holding the tail up to the light.

"It's purple-ish!" he said, trying to sound positive. Andrew had never seen anyone with purple hair before, and now he knew why. It drains the colour from your skin making you look a bit ill.

"Ahh, dammit. I was aiming for red."

The thought of red hair made him think of Fiamma. She was trying to tease him, he thought, so he was quite glad she had missed her mark.

"I still can't land on the colour I want every time."

"What was going on with the water?" asked Andrew. The water had dissolved completely leaving only a thin film of white dust in the bottom of the glass.

"The energy has to come from somewhere, Andrew. I created a pathway to take the energy from there, and use it here," she said, holding up her hair.

"Oh, I get it, so you channelled the energy!"

"Exactly."

"So how much energy is in blood, then?" he asked.

She stopped dead and her smile disappeared.

"Too much," her tone darkened. "It's very powerful, but it's a dark path, Andrew.

It never ends well for magical folk who work with blood."

"Why is that?"

"It's very potent, so the power it provides can become addictive."

"Just like the stone doors the Blackstones use?" asked Andrew.

"I've read about those" she said. "These satanists think they are so smart. Why would the devil be hanging around every stone door in the world, just for a small offering before opening it? It's pathetic. The truth is obsidian is quite a mysterious crystal. It can be imprinted with an intent, which it will repeat over and over again. The blood just provides the energy. Well, when I say 'just' I mean, it's quite a lot."

"Mr Bluvine runs a wineshop that sells blood too. He says the magic in blood dies with the person," said Andrew.

"Well, that is true, to a degree," she said. "It does die, but not instantly. I'm just glad these satanists don't realise the full potential of blood."

Just then, Andrew noticed that her hair was starting to change back to her original colour, one strand at a time.

"Look, it's starting to go back," he said.

"It does that, I'm afraid. Not much nerth in water."

"Nerth?" he asked, looking confused.

"Yeh, nerth. You know, oomph...power."

The snoring stopped and Curtis sneezed. He cursed to himself a bit before the van could be heard moving about on its springs. He opened the door with a clatter and sat down on the bumper with his socks in hand, wrestling to reach down and put them on.

“Finally,” said Emma, getting up from the table and closing her book with a snap. “My turn for a nap. See you later, Andrew.” She walked down the steps to the van where Curtis was struggling to get his shoes on. She helped him out, hugged him, and climbed into the van shutting the door behind her.

“Have a good kip,” said a tired Curtis as he walked across the workshop floor. He struggled with the stairs and was quite out of breath by the time he reached the top where Andrew was sitting.

“Sleep well?” Andrew asked.

“Not really; Never do, Andrew, but something is better than nothing I suppose.” He took a seat where Emma had been sitting and looked down at the dusty glass.

“Ahh... Emma’s been showing you her parlour tricks, I see?”

Andrew wasn't sure whether to confirm or deny, but the evidence was right there. “Yeah, she changed the colour of her hair,” Andrew said. “I made her. Sorry.”

“Made her?!” bellowed Curtis. “Codswallop. She is a force of nature, that girl. You couldn’t make her do a single thing if she didn't want to, believe me. Even getting her to tidy her room when she was growing up was almost impossible. ‘Made her’... ha.”

Andrew had worked out that she was very headstrong, but he hadn't realised she was so stubborn.

"The colour swap, she loves that one. Was one of the first things I ever managed to teach her. Still can't control the colour though, can she?"

"Purple," Andrew said. "But she was aiming for red."

"I see," Curtis scoffed. "She still hasn't got her head around the different types of energy, then."

"There are different types?"

"Of course there are, Andrew. Just like if you had to make something. You wouldn't try to make a knife out of chocolate, now, would you?"

"I guess not," Andrew said. "Unless the main reason for making it, was to eat it?"

"Because that is what it's good for, you see," said Curtis.

"So, the reason she can't control the colour is because of what type of energy she is using?" he asked.

"That's right, boy. You are smarter than you look. If she wants red, she needs lithium. If she wants green, she needs barium. Blue is copper, and so on, and so forth. I haven't told her any of this because I want her to figure it out for herself. Some of the best lessons are the ones you teach yourself. When it comes to colours, fire is the biggest taddler there is."

"Taddler?" Andrew asked.

"Yeah, tell-tale, grass, snitch, or whatever words you kids use these days. I can't keep up. But if you ever want to see what colour something is, shave some small bits off into a fire. Will tell you everything you need to know."

"That's brilliant," said Andrew,

"Anyway, what's going on with you then, Andrew?" he said, taking out his tobacco tin and rolling himself a cigarette. "Xavier has told me about all your efforts with the Blackstones. From what i've heard, you and your friends are very brave."

"Very stupid, more like," Andrew said. "I mean, why did we think that using landmines in a chamber was a good idea?"

"Xavier mentioned that too." Curtis began to cough on his smoke a bit.

"If it wasn't for Xavier and Berty, we would be dead," he said.

"Berty? Who the bloody hell is Berty?"

Realising how stupid he sounded, Andrew explained himself. "Berty, is Xavier's gun."

"Strange name for a gun?" said Curtis, putting out his cigarette.

"Strange gun for a man like him," said Andrew.

"Touché," said Curtis.

"What does that mean?"

"It means you give as good as you get, Andrew. I can see why Xavier likes you." Curtis' bright blue eyes sparkled. "Got anything to eat?" he asked.

"Oh, I can make you spaghetti Bolognese if you like?"

Curtis must have sensed Andrew's nervousness when being asked to cook.

"It's a bit early, but some toast would get me by?"

"Now that I can do," Andrew said, feeling quite relieved.

Xavier got back around 6pm carrying a large box full of stuff. Emma was awake by then and they all sat around the table when he plonked the box down onto it and began dumping bits onto the table.

"Right," said Xavier. "I have masks, balaclava's and hats. It will be very cold in December. These will help."

Emma and Andrew tried a few things on, making weird faces at each other and laughing. Curtis just continued to smoke and pass the occasional comment. Xavier and Andrew were still cooking when there was a knock on the door. Lee and George had arrived at the workshop at 8pm for dinner, as planned. Andrew gave them a tour of the place and they were quite impressed. After that, they sat at the table with Curtis and Emma while Xavier and Andrew dished up. He had shown him how to make a beef stew, which was quite simple to make, but very tasty.

"This is a quick one, but the best stews are the ones that cook all day at a really low temperature." Xavier said, as they were eating. They had some of Curtis's red wine, which was a first for Andrew. With the food going down, the conversation turned to the meeting with the Vampyres later. Xavier had had some dealings with them and Sebastian in the past, so offered some guidance.

"Where we are going is a Vampyre only establishment. It is an underground facility that delves very deep. Don't worry, there are no blood doors to worry about – they wouldn't dare. Vampyres have used it in London for many years, and the resistance have now taken it for themselves as their unofficial headquarters."

"An underground facility," said Curtis. "Great...limits our escape options if it all goes pear shaped, doesn't it?!"

"That's why we all need to be on our best behaviour," said Xavier. "The guards will be aware of our meeting and will issue us a red ribbon to wear around our necks. Don't take it off. There could be over a hundred Vampyres on the premises, and without that red ribbon around your neck you are as good as dead. Is that clear?" said Xavier, concentrating his direction towards the younger members present.

"Crystal," said Curtis, unfazed.

George and Emma looked a bit worried. Lee just looked a bit bored.

Xavier, held court. "We need to go over the plan to ensure we are all on the same page. Help me clear the table."

They all stood up and took everything off the large round table and into the kitchen. Emma wiped the table down and George dried it. Having more people around really made life easier. Xavier took out his tightly folded map and they all helped to unfold it on the tabletop. They pinned the corners with jars of condiments and stared down at the colourful map. On the far-right hand side of the map was Greenwich Park. near the top of the park was the observatory. Andrew remembered it well from his day out with his Mum before she got hit by that car. The view down to the river Thames was amazing.

"Here," said Xavier, as he circled the observatory grounds with his finger. "This is where they will conduct the incantation. The Greenwich meridian line cuts straight through this open patch of ground. It's perfect for them."

"We need to get the armonica as close as we can to that site," said Curtis. "The Avenue, brings you right up alongside the observatory, but there are heavy wrought iron gates at the bottom."

"Nothing a torch or grinder won't open, if need be," said Lee. "I can get what we need from work."

Emma looked worried. "Even if we get the armonica there, how do we know it will be loud enough? It doesn't exactly pack much of a punch," she said.

"We have a plan for that too," said Andrew. "The boys and I went to Portobello Road Market today and met a very interesting old man that makes horn speaker systems."

"Oh, right?" asked Curtis. "Does he have something we can use?"

"He's going to make it for us," said George. "A twelve-inch speaker, microphone, and a battery powered amplifier." He looked at Emma to see if she was impressed or not. She wasn't, but the others were.

"How much is all that going to cost?" asked Xavier.

"Not sure yet," said Andrew. "But we'll find out next week. The only trouble we have, is sourcing the horn. According to the speaker man, it needs to be at least 40 inches in diameter."

Curtis whistled, as if to say, 'good luck.'

"I'm going to borrow a bell from work," said Lee.

"Erm, excuse me, lad," said Curtis.

"It's Lee, not lad," Lee said, asserting himself.

"Sorry, Lee... First torches and grinders, now a sodding great big bell. Where the bloody hell do you work?"

"The Whitechapel bell foundry," said Lee.

"I see, and this bell, what will that weigh? 1000lbs?" asked Curtis.

Andrew could see where this conversation was heading.

"1500lb's, actually," said Lee. "But it will be fixed to a bracket on the back of a flatbed truck. We move them all the time at work. This one is a baby."

"And how loud will it be?" asked Emma.

"Well, put it this way," said George, doing his best to flirt with Emma while going a bit red from all the attention. "If the one-inch speaker and the horn the size of a saucer was enough to almost deafen a hundred people at the market, a twelve-inch speaker and forty-four-inch horn should do the trick."

Xavier took stock of what they had so far. "So, if this works, then all the Blackstones gems will be smashed, which means the Vampyres can actually help us, but they will need to be close by."

They all looked at the map and spotted a large open section of ground just south of Greenwich Park, towards Lewisham.

"Blackheath," said Xavier, "It's perfect."

"How will we they know when it's safe?" Andrew asked.

"If it's as loud as you reckon it will be, they should bloody hear the speaker. But we can always pop a flare up, if need be," said Curtis.

With the conversation slowing down, Andrew decided to address the elephant in the room.

"What do you plan to do to the Shadows, Curtis?" he asked.

Curtis didn't look at him straight away. He finished rolling another cigarette and lit it. The others had become interested in what he might say now too, and were waiting.

"Something they would never expect, Andrew," he said, grinning to himself as the smoke trickled from his nose.

"Just remember who's inside the circle already."

Andrew wasn't sure what he meant.

"Right, so, to summarise," said Xavier. "George and Andrew - you are in charge of getting the speaker system. Let me know how much it will cost, and I will get the money. Lee - you are organising a flatbed vehicle, bracket and forty-four-inch bell from work, as well as cutting equipment for the gate, if needed. Curtis and Emma - you are in charge of the Armonica."

They had a plan; Albiet a risky one. Next step was to get the Vampyres onside.

51

Head On

It was now 9.45pm and the group decided to get moving and walked towards Waterloo Bridge. The bridge wasn't too far from the workshop in Covent Garden, but they had to ensure they were on time. As it was Saturday night, there were quite a lot of people still out. A small group of soldiers that were on leave, were just getting thrown out of a pub at the end of the street as they walked past. The soldiers were now shouting and banging on the doors. Half a dozen ladies walked past them admiring their uniforms. This seemed to ease the tension somewhat and they followed the girls up the street, asking their names and if they fancied finding some place to dance.

Was it the uniform? Was that the attraction? And is that why some men liked to have a uniform, just to make themselves more attractive? Andrew thought of the Freemasons with their attire and suits. Even the Blackstones were some kind of exclusive club, he gathered. The secrecy around them creates a mystery. They moved out of Covent Garden, past the Savoy theatre and onto the bridge, crossing the bridge in the light of a setting sun that was quickly moving quickly beyond the horizon. Looking right, Andrew spotted something he hadn't paid much attention to before, a giant stone spike on Victoria Embankment by the Thames.

"What on earth is that?" he asked Xavier.

"What?... Oh, that," said Xavier, "That's Cleopatra's needle."

Xavier caught the confused look on his face, and that he didn't have a clue. "It was gifted to Britain by the ruler of Egypt many years ago. They are more dangerous than they look, and the location is no accident, but that's a conversation for another time." Xavier turned his attention to the path ahead.

The streetlights were now starting to come on and the last rays of the sun were hiding behind the hills in the distance. That's when something caught Andrew's eye.

Long red hair; She was waiting for them at the end of the bridge. His heart started to race slightly, so he took a few deep breaths to calm himself. They reached the Southbank side with Xavier in front.

"You must be Fiamma," he said. "I have heard a lot about you. I am Xavier."

"And I you, Xavier. Your reputation precedes you," she said, bowing her head slightly.

Andrew stepped around the others to say hello.

"Andrew," she said, cutely with a side smile. He thought he saw her blush slightly. Her eyes shone brightly. She then went on to introduce herself to the others. Andrew's heart flipped a bit. *Oh god. I'm actually in love with a Vampyre...*

"Hello, I'm Fiamma. I will be your guide for this evening."

Andrew decided to hang at the back of the small group as they walked down towards Southbank and the buildings on the riverfront. As they walked east along the banks, they could see a very large man in a suit standing by a red, roped barrier, like the type that most Gentleman's clubs have. They walked up.

"Hi Rufus," said Fiamma. "This is the meeting party I told you about."

"I see," he said. "A bit early though, aren't you?"

"Better early than late," she said, winking at him.

Rufus cleared his massive throat but still whispered. "Right, ladies and gents. Please listen up as I will not say this again. Given the nature of your visit to this establishment, and our clientele, you will be given a red ribbon to wear around your neck. Do not remove the ribbon at any time and please stay with Fiamma, your guide."

He reached around the back of a stone pillar and brought out some bright red ribbons already tied into large loops, like oversized necklaces. He placed them over their heads one by one. Taking his time with Emma, making George a little jealous. It seemed that her attractive qualities were not restricted to teenage boys. George's stomach rumbled a bit, but he put it down to the nerves.

Once they were all ready, he unhooked the rope from the barrier and ushered them down the steps into the basement bar, with Fiamma leading the way. Her red ribbon was tied around her wrist. At the bottom of the stairs, they walked through a heavily curtained corridor and into the bar itself. It was cold and dimly lit. All they could see were over fifty pairs of illuminated eyes looking back at them intensely as they shuffled in and up to the bar.

"Don't speak to anyone," said Fiamma, as she turned her attention to the bartender. Jazz played in the background from the speakers in the corner, whilst all the Vampyres just stood still in silence and looked on in disbelief, almost like their buffet had just arrived. They had fifteen minutes to wait before the meeting, so Fiamma ordered them some drinks. The room began to come back to life slowly, and conversation resumed quietly amongst the brass and piano of the jazz. Some of their whispers were obviously about them. 'Why are they here?' 'Who are they here to see?' but the most common comment of all, 'If it wasn't for that red ribbon, I'd...'

They sipped their drinks at the bar and looked around a bit. Most of the people in there didn't even look like Vampyres, except for the eyes. You'd walk past them in the west end without any clue of what they really are, or what they did. They were dressed in sharp suits and evening gowns, and looked like they had money. Bottles of champagne sat in ice buckets and some of the men were drinking whisky out of fine, lead crystal cut glasses. The only give away were their dead, callous stares in the half light.

A few minutes later, a tall, blonde security guard arrived. "Sebastian will see you now."

"Oh, hello Schneider," said Fiamma, pretending to have missed him. "Come on, use your happy words, Schneider. Say hello,"

Schneider looked very bored of her already but knowing Fiamma, she wouldn't let this go, so he decided to participate.

"Hello," he said to the rest of the group, blandly.

"Thanks, Schneider. See, that wasn't hard, was it?" said Fiamma.

He said nothing, just scowled at her as she led us past him towards the stairwell. They followed her down the stairs into the lower levels, each one darker than the last. The wall colours grew darker, and fewer pictures hung from the walls. Andrew lost count of the flights they walked down as he was too interested in the history of this place. The black iron balustrades and dark mahogany handrails grew ever colder with every floor they descended. The last step down was onto some flagstones, and the lobby area was lit by a single red candle on a tall black table, with the legs descending into a fig tree twist. The walls were almost black, and they could barely see a thing.

Fiamma seemed to move without any hesitation, which either meant she had been here many times before, or the fact she was a Vampyre meant that she could see perfectly well in the dark. Andrew suspected a bit of both.

As his eyes started to adjust to the lower light level, he started to make out a large circular door in front of them with some ornate carving. A giant snake with ruby eyes that glistened in the candlelight encircled the door, eating its own tail. Where the tail and head met, a thin brass door handle protruded and there were some dark words engraved into the wood.Some of the letters looked more like symbols.

A Moment In Red

Forever In Death

A large security guard was standing to one side of the door waiting for them.

"Hello, Eric. How are you?" asked Fiamma.

"Fine thanks, Fiamma. Nothing to report really."

"No news is good news, I guess. Is he ready?" she asked, fidgeting on the spot.

"Well, he is free. Doesn't mean he's ready, but good luck." He looked into Fiamma's eyes and meant it. Eric knocked twice on the door.

"Enter," said a quiet but harsh voice from inside.

Andrew tried to put a face to the voice, but the anticipation wouldn't let him. Eric opened the large door by the handle and swung it inwards into the main chamber just enough for Eric to slip through.

"Fiamma's group are here for your 11pm."

"Very well...Let them through," said the voice.

Eric opened the large, round door wide, exposing the stone walls and high ornate ceiling of the deep underground chamber. It had curved ceilings like an underground crypt and was lit by a few naked candles on the table and the ornate mantle, that framed an disused fireplace, that probably hadnt been lit in decades. Deep shadows hung around the chamber which made Andrew feel uneasy. Fiamma, led the way inside and they walked through, trying to watch their step on the flagstone floor. A figure stood up from his desk on the right alcove. He was tall and thin, dressed in all black. His skin was so white that it almost looked green in places, but his black eyes took them in, one blink at a time.

"Welcome, I am Sebastian. I trust you have been treated respectfully upon entry?" He could see that they were all still wearing their red ribbons around their necks. "Everyone still has a ribbon I see. Well done."

"Yes, thank you Sebastian," said Xavier.

"Ah... Xavier. It has been some time since we last met. I trust you are well?"

"Things could always be worse," said Xavier, playfully.

Sebastian had heard about the arson at his shop. Word gets around, especially if you had as many connections as Sebastian did.

"Your friction with the Blackstones has finally caused a few sparks to fly, I hear. That's the dangerous thing about having roots, isn't it, Xavier? People know where to dig."

"It's been coming along time, Sebastian. It was always a matter of when, not if." said Xavier.

"Where are my manners?" said Sebastian, forcing himself to appear outgoing to the others.

He did not ask their names as he didn't need to. He closed his eyes for a moment and saw what he needed to see.

"Lee! Very nice to meet you, Lee." Sebastian's long fingers were interlocked on his chest in front of him and tapped playfully liked pinned spiders. Lee looked a bit uncomfortable with him knowing his name.

"You are strong and very loyal, I see." Lee nodded in acknowledgment and seemed to relax a bit.

"And George! Hello, George. A warm welcome to you also." George looked a bit sheepish.

"A word to the wise, George. Don't let revenge consume you. Otherwise, there will come a time when there is little else left."

George was fascinated but mostly embarrassed. His stomach turned over again, but he still put it down to the nerves.

He then turned towards Andrew.

"Andrew. So, YOU are the Andrew I have heard so much about."

He felt his heart in his throat. Andrew wondered if he could feel him searching through his thoughts like an antique dealer in a junk shop.

"Now, you have an interesting mind for someone who has experienced so much pain. Let that be your trustworthy guide when your heart tries to derail you. Ignore me at your peril."

Sebastian's black eyes paused on Fiamma, then danced in the candlelight over to Curtis and Emma.

"Now, you two. I think we need to do this in a different way as I'm struggling to see anything here."

"And you never will, unless we want you too," said Curtis, brashly. "My name is Curtis, and this is Emma."

"Oh, the accent - It's glorious. Let me guess, Cornwall?" asked Sebastian.

"Yes, and proud of it," said Emma, confidently.

"It is a pleasure to meet you all. Please, please take a seat so we can get this meeting started. Fiamma, that will be all. I will send Eric up when we are finished."

"But..." stalled Fiamma, trying to fight his decision.

"THAT WILL BE ALL."

She paused for a moment, then stormed out of the room leaving the door open behind her with a huff.

"That girl... She's 100 going on 300, that one," said Sebastian, rolling his dark eyes.

Then a girl arrived with a large oval tray with a couple of water jugs and glasses for the table. She placed the tray down in the centre.

"Thank you, Rene," said Sebastian, as she turned to leave the room.

George was now starting to feel quite unwell. He reached forward to get a glass and fill it up. He noticed his hands were shaking. He drank some water, but it did little to calm his stomach and a low dull ache started to build in his guts. He could feel the sweaty nausea coming on fast.

"So, who would like to start?" said Sebastian.

George couldn't concentrate properly, and the walls were beginning to close in.

"I will," said Xavier as he prepared himself.

"Erm," said George.

"What is it, George?" asked Xavier, impatiently.

"I really need to use the toilet," he said, visibly perspiring now.

"Can't it wait!?"

"Erm, no, not really." George could feel his guts starting to squirm and he knew he didn't have long before his dinner would end up on the floor in-front of their host.

"Out of the door, walk straight ahead," said Sebastian. "There is my private bathroom; use that one only.

And try not to make a mess."

"OK," George said, as he hurried to the door. He pulled on the handle and opened the heavy door towards him and into the dim lobby. The guard had gone, and he was alone. He shut the chamber door behind him and walked straight ahead until he saw the other door with no handle, just a brass plate. Reaching out, he pushed on the door, but it didn't move. He pushed it with all his weight, but it wouldn't budge. Time was running out; he could feel it. He decided there was nothing else to do except find another bathroom somewhere, and quickly.

52

Run Rabbit, Run

Walking up the stairs, George reached the top and noticed that a roped barrier had been put in place to stop anybody from coming down. He gently swooped under the barrier, but in his sickly state failed to notice that his red ribbon was no longer around his neck and had fallen off and onto the top step behind him. There wasn't a toilet on that floor either, so he had to climb the stairs to the next floor with his gut ache gaining in strength. Once at the top of the next flight of stairs he saw the glimmer of hope in the form of a W.C. sign hanging from the door opposite him.

He walked through as fast as he could, into the toilet, and found a cubicle.

He had the toilet to himself, thankfully. Being sick with an audience was never ideal. After ten minutes or so, he felt much better, but because of the noise he had been making he failed to notice that someone else had walked in, who was now using the cubical on the end of the row. George came out of his cubicle and wandered over to the sink to wash up. There were no mirrors for obvious reasons, but he splashed some water on his face anyway. He heard a latch move on the end cubicle and the door opened. A middle-aged man walked out and was startled by George.

George put his hand around his neck, desperately searching for his red ribbon but it wasn't there. It was gone. The man's demeanour changed and shifted quickly into a predator. He pounced at George, but luckily he stepped sideways, just at the right time, causing the man to crash into the sinks behind him. George ran for the door and burst out into the lobby. There was a young couple walking down the stairs towards the toilet. They saw George and instinctively started to hunt him.

"Oh shit," said George. He heard the toilet door open behind him too and he panicked. He had to make it back down to the meeting room. Running to the stairs so fast that he almost fell down them, he could feel the footsteps of the Vampyres chasing him. He turned the corner at the bottom and ran for the next set of stairs with the roped barrier. That's when he saw it. His red ribbon: it was right there on the top step. As he turned the corner, he felt one of the Vampyres jump on his back and hold his head off to one side to bite his neck. Another one grabbed hold of his arm. There was only one way out of this.

He threw himself headfirst down the stairs onto the ribbon and grabbed it. He held onto that ribbon all the way down with every bang, scrape, and bounce as they fell down the whole flight of stairs, separating at the bottom into three separate heaps on the flagstones. George then heard one of the Vampyres crawling over to him, so he quickly put the ribbon around his neck again.

"Oh, that's not fair!" said the lady. "Look, Reg, he's got a bloody ribbon on!" She stood up and dusted herself off before helping her companion up off the floor.

"Well, he didn't a minute ago," said Reg in frustration as he straightened himself out. They both looked down at the ribbon and then at him in pure disgust.

"Come along, darling. I guess what they say really is true. There is no such thing as a free lunch." They walked back up the stairs like they had just lost the last of their money at a crooked carnival game.

George stood up slowly with a sigh and felt a twinge in his bad foot. He hoped he hadn't broken it again, as it hurt alot. Behind him he heard a toilet flush and some whistling. Eric, the security guard, came out of Sebastian's toilet with a newspaper under his arm. He took one look at George limping towards the round chamber door and George was shaking his head at him in disappointment.

"What?" said Eric. "When you have to go, you have to go, right?"

George let himself back into the chamber and heard that the conversation had progressed somewhat. Xavier's large colourful map was now unfolded on the table.

"Why are you so sweaty?" Andrew whispered, as he took a seat next to him.

"I lost my ribbon and got chased by some Vampyres."

"Oh."

"12 noon on the 7th of December. Well, at least it won't be too bright. Besides, there will be fog you say?" asked Sebastian.

"Yes, the densest London has ever seen apparently. The Shadows are counting on it," said Xavier.

"And there will be thousands of Darkhearts present, including at least two thousand Blackstones. We know that obsidian is an issue for Vampyres, but Curtis has a plan for that. Something that will turn those stones to dust."

"So, just to be clear," said Sebastian. "You are telling me that you actually have a way of destroying obsidian?"

"That's right," said Curtis. "The armonica will shatter them all, but we have to get close enough."

"Interesting, and this armonica, what does it do, exactly?" asked Sebastian,

"All about resonant frequencies and harmonics: find the right frequency and you can shatter just about anything with a crystalline structure," explained Curtis.

"I see... how clever," said Sebastian.

The trouble with Sebastian is that you could never quite tell if he was being sarcastic or not.

"So, where will this Armonica be?"

Curtis showed him on the map, at the top of the Avenue that leads up to Greenwich Observatory.

"Right about there, we'll get through the gate and move up. Once close enough, I will get round the back to the circle where the incantation will take place. Then Emma will operate it," Curtis said.

"And you want us to wait up on Blackheath Common, until we get all-clear?" asked Sebastian.

"A red flare, that will be your signal when all the Blackstones are smashed," said Emma.

"Mm... it all sounds like a very good plan, ingenious, some might say," said Sebastian, letting the 'but' build naturally as he spoke.

"You destroy the stones, and we help dispatch as many of the Darkhearts as possible. We all stop the shadows and the incantation, and you free my brother. And if all goes to plan, George gets his sister back!"

"That's right," said Xavier.

"So," said Sebastian.

"Oh... here it comes," moaned Curtis, running his fingers through his long, greying hair in frustration.

Sebastian continued. "Say... we do all of this, and everyone is back together, yes?

yay! huzzah...such merriment, etcetera," Sebastian pretended to have fun for a moment, before switching back to his normal dry self.

"What is in it for us?"

"Well, you get Verne back, for a start," said Curtis.

“And maybe you can convince some of the Vampyres bound by the treaty to stand up and fight,” said Andrew. “This could change everything for them, and for you.”

“Viva la liberation,” smirked Sebastian, staring at the table deeply in thought before choosing his next words carefully.

“Yes, I’ll admit that having Verne back would be a good thing,” he played with a pencil in front of him relentlessly.

“But it would mean that I would be taking a step back in my duties. He is the oldest, and the rightful leader of this order, after all.”

“And so,” said Xavier, trying to get to the bottom of what Sebastian is suggesting.

“What else do you want?”

“Compensation,” said Sebastian.

“Like what?” asked Xavier.

“I'd like a copy of this map, Xavier" he said,

"Done," said Xavier, feeling like they had gotten off lightly.

"And" said Sebastian,

The others looked on, waiting for him to finish.

"How about this armonica of yours, Curtis?” Sebastian asked gently.

“Not a bloody chance,” snapped Curtis as he stood up, making his chair fall over behind him.

“Greedy blood suckers. All the same, you are,” he slammed his fists down onto the table.

“CURTIS,” said Xavier, forcefully. “A word.”

Xavier stood up and wandered towards the chamber door, waiting for Curtis to join him. He did so reluctantly, and they went into the lobby to chat privately. Emma seemed unfazed, but saw no point in talking until they returned. She took her book out again and started to read. Lee and George hadn't really said anything during the meeting so far, so they took the opportunity to ask some questions.

“So, Sebastian, how old are you, then?” asked Lee.

Sebastian seemed too distracted by the absence of the others to grant his full attention, especially to these young cattle, who only seemed to ask questions he had been asked hundreds of times before. “471 this year,” he said, watching the door.

George tried his luck. “How many people do you think you’ve killed?”

Sebastian sighed. “Not enough... obviously. Your kind seem to have trebled in numbers ever since I arrived.”

Andrew thought he'd throw a curveball and see how he reacted. “So, why does obsidian weaken Vampyres?”

“Andrew! Finally, a question worth answering!” said Sebastian.

“Well, obsidian is volcanic, It comes from the very heart of the earth itself, right from the centre. It is an extremely hard material, but it absorbs intention like nothing else can. The satanists use it for all sorts of talismans and tasks, but they are a bit too dim to know of its true nature."

"Tasks, like opening the stone doors?" Andrew asked.

"Exactly. Gold star!"

"We knew that, too," said George to Lee, feeling a bit excluded.

Sebastian continued. "You see, a Vampyre's life force is basically 8/10th's intention and the other two, is blood magic. The obsidian absorbs all our intentions and will keep going until we have nothing left to give, rendering us practically powerless. Like pulling a plug in a sink and watching the water simply drain away."

"Does it kill you?" asked Andrew.

"Sadly not," said Sebastian. "Would be kinder if it did. It just wipes us out."

Xavier and a slightly calmer Curtis re-entered the chamber and sat back down. Sebastian waited for them to speak with bated breath.

"Gentlemen, what is the verdict?" asked Sebastian. "When this is over, will I get the armonica?"

"Yes, you will," said Curtis, locking his bright blue gaze onto the Vampyre's dead eyes. "But on one condition."

"Which is?" asked Sebastian.

"We get all the girls back, safe and sound." said Curtis, "If any of the girl get as much as a scratch, then the deal is off. You hear me?"

"Deal!" said Sebastian, raising his hands and looking truly delighted for once. His happiness was not a nice thing to see.

"I will make the arrangements and ensure we have all I can muster for the attack. We have some time between now and then, but it will be upon us before we know it. I suggest we meet periodically to discuss any new findings and times for our rendezvous."

"Agreed," said Xavier, standing up. "Thank you for your time, Sebastian."

They all filed out into the chamber and headed for the door. Emma dropped her book, and it was instantly picked up by George, who handed it back and went red again.

"Ah, George, that is better," said Sebastian. "More of that, and less of the hate."

Sebastian told Eric that they were leaving so he went upstairs to fetch Fiamma to escort them out, but he came back empty handed. "I couldn't find her, Sebastian; I think she left."

"THAT BLASTED GIRL," scorched Sebastian. "Eric, please ensure their safe egress, would you?"

"Of course," said Eric. "Follow me."

They followed Eric up the numerous flights of stairs. Each floor became slightly lighter and busier than the one before. They made sure their red ribbons were on show for all to see. George winced a bit when he saw the young couple that tried to attack him. They were sitting at the bar as they were leaving. He pretended to tip his imaginary hat to them. They did not look impressed. The Vampyres in the bar watched them leave intently with their candle lit eyes following their every move. Once outside, they all breathed deeply. It was quite an experience. It was like walking through the lion's cage wearing a meat vest at the London Zoo.

Andrew went to take his ribbon off, but the large bouncer, Rufus, stopped him. "Ah ah... not until you get home," he said. "Some of the clientele get wound up seeing you here and may decide to follow you. Especially if they haven't fed for a while."

"Thanks, Rufus," said Andrew. "Did you happen to see where Fiamma went?"

"She left about an hour ago in a right huff and walked towards the bridge. Didn't say where she was going though. She really is a handful, that one."

53

Race for Life

Fiamma had stormed out of Sebastian's chamber and made her way up and out of the headquarters without a word to anyone. She was furious. On her way up, a few acquaintances tried to say hello as they usually did only to be ignored. She had a face like thunder and walked out onto the Southbank, saying a curt goodnight to Rufus.

By the time she could even see straight again, she was already halfway across Waterloo bridge. *HOW DARE HE,* she thought to herself as she reached the other side of the Thames and headed east towards Temple tube station.

After everything I did to set the meeting up... he dismissed me like I was a servant.

"I am NOT a bloody servant," she hissed to herself.

A few people turned to look at her but knew better than to ask her anything, as her eyes were incandescent with rage. She walked north, up Surrey Street towards the Strand with

Sebastian's words echoing in her ears over and over again. '*That will be all.*'

“Will it? YOU POMPOUS ARSE!”

Her anger had blinded her senses and she had failed to notice the four Vampyres that were now following her. It was only when she levelled out up onto the Strand that she caught the scent of them, thanks to the wind behind her. They were not from her order. She ran straight across the road, causing a few cars and a bus full of late-night passengers to come to a screeching halt in a tribute of horns. She looked around as she got to the other side of the road, trying to see who was chasing her. Dressed in all black, clearly too fast to be anything other than Vampyres, and they each had a golden pin on their left breast that twinkled in the oncoming headlights. She had seen this emblem many times before: it was the seal of mercy. A giant wolf sitting next to a young deer laying in the grass. They were mercenaries instructed by the Vampyre Council.

“Why tonight?... Of all nights!” she said, as she picked up the pace. She ran as fast as she could and ended up down an alleyway heading towards Holborn. Realising that she was running out of steam already, she knew she had to come up with a better plan. They were still right behind her and closing in fast. As she turned into Chancery Lane, she spotted a building attendant of a large block of apartments, holding open a door for a resident that was leaving. She took the opportunity and ran straight into the building, heading straight for the elevator at the very back of the lobby. The building attendant hollered at her whilst she was pressing the up button with urgency.

“Hello? Excuse me, young lady, you are not a resident here. I’m going to have to...”

The attendant was suddenly shoved by one of her pursuers into the wall with such force that the plaster cracked and dusted his bloodied body that now lay underneath it. All four men walked into the lobby just as the elevator door opened. Fiamma rushed into the elevator and hit the button for the top floor repeatedly until the doors started to close. The Vampyres ran for the doors to stop them, but the doors shut, and the elevator started to rise. One of them punched through the lift door and was now prising the doors apart causing the lift to come to an abrupt stop. One set of hands kept trying to prise open the outer doors, while a whole arm entered the lift car at low level. It's long, dark fingernails were slicing the lower air of the lift car for a feel of her flesh.

Fiamma didn’t know what to do. She slammed her right shoulder into the corner of the elevator next to the control panel and watched the arm flailing around, feeling for her through the rough, peeled back metal edges. She knew she had to close the doors, or she was as good as dead. Just then, she had an idea. These large residential blocks had basements too, which meant the elevator went down as well as up.

She used the wooden, mid rail in the elevator as a leg-up and lifted the loose ceiling tile that gained her access into the elevator shaft above, then pulled herself up onto the top of the elevator itself. She saw that the large, braided wire that suspended the elevator was covered in grease, so there was no way of climbing that. Looking down through the open hatch into the elevator, she could see a second hand starting to come through the gap of the door. She was running out of time.

On one of the deep ledges in the lift shaft was a dusty chair, some empty drinks bottles, and a few scattered tools. Probably a sneaky place for the maintenance people to hide. That's when she saw the old rusty hacksaw. She grabbed the hacksaw and started to cut into the braided cable. The wire was under such tension that the individual braids severed relatively easily with a 'ping', and she was almost through the whole cable when she heard a scream. A lady resident had walked into the lobby and caught sight of the dead attendant. One of the Vampyres took care of her and locked the front door.

There was only a dozen of the thin strands left when Fiamma stepped off the lift car and onto the ledge. She stamped on the top of the elevator car with one foot trying to get it to break, but it didn't want to let go. Then she heard the elevator doors being crumpled open and decided it was now or never. She jumped up as high as she could and straight down onto the top of the elevator, just as she could see some long fingernails appear through the hatch. The remaining strands of the wire finally broke and she jumped back up, managing to hold onto the greasy cable just in time before the lift dropped and stopped with a jerk. One of the men hollered in pain, then the elevator fell at speed, three floors down into the lowest basement level with a crash, causing dust to rise through the dark elevator shaft.

Fiamma wriggled her body to get herself over to the ledge, swinging on the giant frayed cable. She landed on the ledge with a groan. She sat quietly to process what had just happened. Her hands were now covered in grease, and she had to work out how to get down, and out into the lobby below her. As she looked down to the open doors through the dust, she could now see something dark on the floor of the lobby below. It was the torso of one of the Vampyres that had been ripped apart by the elevator as it fell. The open mouth of the lift must have cut him in half. She heard some movement from the elevator that had crashed down in the basement below, and knew she had to move.

There was a silver metal rail above the door below that the doors hung from, so she wiped her hands off on her dress as best as she could and took a deep breath. She jumped down to grasp it like a circus performer on a highwire. She then swung straight out of the opening and landed into the lobby right next to the halved Vampyre on the tiled floor. She heard the crash of opening doors from the stairwell which meant the other Vampyre's were coming back up, and she was running out of time. She went to rush for the front door but was suddenly held back by her ankle. The halved Vampyre on the floor was still very much alive, and now had a syringe in his other hand. He plunged it deeply into her calf, and she winced from the sharp sting. This was no drug; he was taking blood. She panicked but managed to kick herself free of him and over to the front door, struggling with the thumb lock. The door opened and she stepped out to the street just as two of the other Vampyres rushed out onto the lobby before being joined by a third. She looked through the highly polished, glazed door at the Vampyre on the floor. They looked down at him and then at her. He was holding a syringe with her blood, as the others looked on and grinned.

That's all they needed, she thought.

"Time is up...I know too much."

To be continued...

Hidden In Plain Sight: 1952 – Part Two

Printed in Great Britain
by Amazon

48970031R00255